JOHN K. REED

MYSTERY OF
LAWLESSNESS

BOOK III of LOST
WORLDS

MYSTERY OF LAWLESSNESS

This is a work of fiction. Though based on people and events recorded in the book of Genesis, many characters, as well as the places and details of the incidents of this book are products of the author's imagination, are used fictitiously, and not to be construed as real. The reader is invited to carefully compare them to the contents of Genesis and decide which are historical and which are not.

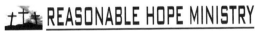 **REASONABLE HOPE MINISTRY**

P.O. Box 26
Summerton, SC 29148

ISBN 978-0-982-74190-0

Cover modified from photographs:
      "Eyes" © Inya Kurhan and
      "Talmud Page" © Benjamin Badach
      www.istockphoto.com

For more information, visit
www.reasonablehope.com

Acknowledgements

Many thanks to those friends who helped develop, edit, and publish this book. Among them are Chris, Jill, Billy, Anne, Beth, Elsie, and Karen. My patient, encouraging, and loving family kept me going during many long months of writing. I am grateful to my good friend Rod for encouragement by word and example. Special thanks to my unnamed illustrator and friend; you and I know who you are. This project would not have been possible without the support of the board of Reasonable Hope Ministry and its director and (more importantly) my dad, Dr. Gordon Reed. Once again, kudos to John Woodmorappe, whose book *Noah's Ark: A Feasibility Study* was the trigger to the Lost Worlds project. Any errors or interpretations of literary license remain my responsibility.

...whatever you do, do all to the glory of God.

I Corinthians 10:31

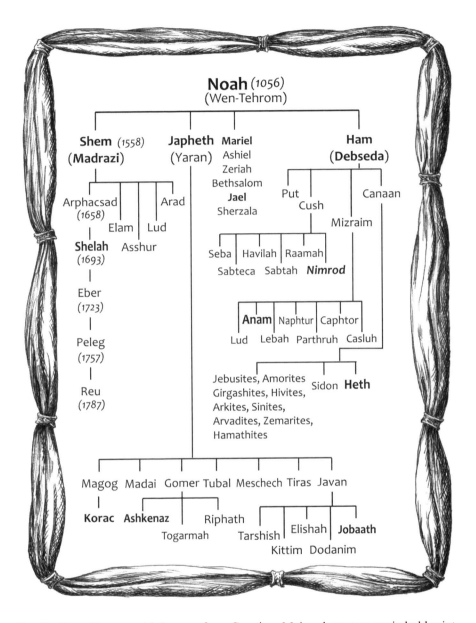

Family Tree. Dates are birth years from Creation. Major characters are in bold print. Wives, in parentheses, are not named in the Bible, and Noah's six daughters are based on legend. Likewise, Jobaath is not found in Genesis, but is found on ancient king lists. Some characters are completely fictional.

Cast

Korac. Nimrod's brother-in-law and right hand; a cold, heartless killer who will do anything for his master.

Shelah. Grandson of Shem and Madrazi, he is the leader of the five friends who oppose Nimrod.

Heth. Strong and fearless son of Canaan, he soon becomes Nimrod's enemy. So he leaves Shinar and befriends Shelah.

Anam. Smaller and weaker than most, Anam is clever and a master of art. But is he clever enough to outwit Nimrod and Debseda?

Ashkenaz. Grandson of Japheth and another of the five friends. Strong, solid, and loyal—he hates the unchecked evil growing in Shinar.

Jobaath. Grandson of Japheth and last of the five friend, he is a clever trickster who is especially close to Ashkenaz.

Togarmah. Grandson of Japheth who settles on the shore of the Black Sea.

Graemea. One of Debseda's maids; daughter of Put, childhood friend of Anam.

Celota. Another maid, one eager to follow Debseda's evil.

Oshetipin. Third maid. Cruel, but foolish.

Zeb. Incomparable rider and wilderness scout, he is the line of communication between Shem, Noah, and Japheth.

Adan. Firstborn son of Mariel and Nimrod.

Lud. Anam's older brother and co-conspirator with Mizraim against Nimrod.

Jalam. Cousin and friend of Korac, he is a man eager for adventure and fame.

Dishon & Dishan. Evil brothers who serve Korac as picked assassins.

Latter Days

Lydia. Madrazi's young servant and steward, she is given the task of taking the Old One's last testament to an heir in Canaan.

Lud. Shem's servant who accompanies Lydia and protects her on her quest.

Abimelech. King of the Philistines in Gerar.

Asak. Ambitious and cruel second-in-command of Abimelech's army.

The Phicol. Commander of Philistine army under Abimelech.

MYSTERY OF LAWLESSNESS

For the mystery of lawlessness is already at work…

II Thessalonians 2:7

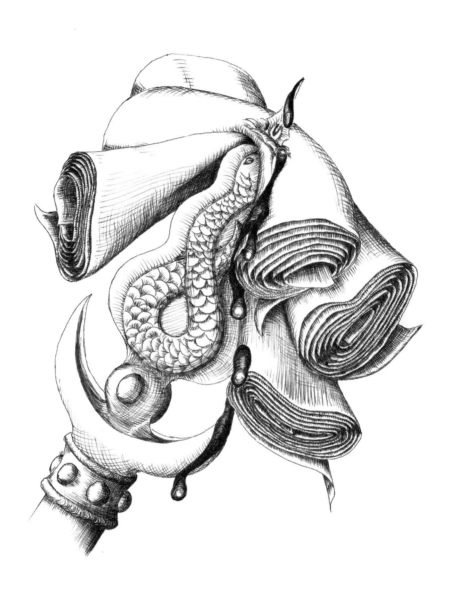

PROLOGUE

5-5-2161 AM[1]

"Call me 'Lydia' on the road."

Lud merely glanced over, his eyes, as always, seeing more than most. That was one reason she respected him. *Yes*, her mind insisted, *respect. That's all*. But did her heart say something else? Uncertainty annoyed her, so she frowned and looked down. No matter. Her feelings were unimportant—her mission was. She must traverse the civilized world and lay three scrolls—heirlooms of ancient knowledge— in the hands of the heir. It was a sacred trust, promised to someone she had most definitely loved.

It would be a perilous journey and would need Lud. Bodyguard and guide, and if he felt that he was more... he would have to wait. Part of her wanted that "more," but that desire remained a selfish luxury until her trust was fulfilled. *Afterward...* He was a good man and she could do worse.

As long as she had known him, he had been a shepherd. What he had been before was as opaque as her own past. As rough as the wilderness he wandered, he was nothing like the smooth, polished, sophisticates who had once courted her. In years, he was little older than she was, but he was old before his time—a grizzled dog who had seen too many hard winters. They also shared the kinship of having served the Elders. Both had come to them wounded, and both had been healed. Maybe that was the source of their friendship... or... attraction?

Stop it! You can't afford this now.

She needed him on the long road south and the last Elder had asked him to take care of her. At first, Lydia had been angry—she had not been told. But the Old One had always been inscrutable. She knew Lydia would respect her wish; love and a debt would ensure it. Tears gathered in her eyes. Even facing death, the Old One had been thinking of her, providing one last time for her needs.

The scrolls would go south. Lydia owed her too much not to honor that debt.

Holding the reins of her horse, she looked around one last time. Lud sat silent, the ropes of the two pack horses tied to his saddle. North, the mountain filled their vision, its constant crown of clouds and ice extending to its base. A few dark lines showed where its roots had recently broken free. There was a story up there and Lydia was privileged to carry it. The scrolls were beyond value—the last link to a forgotten world. For a moment she wanted to keep them, but could not. They were

---

[1] Dates in this book are in years *Anno Mundi*, or from the Creation (cf. Ussher 1658). Months and days follow the Gregorian calendar to avoid confusion for the reader.

meant for another. She would never be worthy to be the heir; she was just a messenger.

From the mountain's foot, a tree-littered meadow rose to the south, merging with abandoned fields and pastures that stretched east and west. Overgrown orchards, just starting to blossom, bordered those fields. A quiet decay hung over the old house, the ramshackle outbuildings, and the fallow fields. For five centuries they had been a home; now it was all slipping away.

Lydia and Lud were the last living souls within a day's walk, and the few who knew of the graveyard on the knoll would never dream of disturbing the rest of the seven elders. Even that hallowed ground would be reclaimed by the wilderness, and men would forget everything. Lud met her eyes. He understood. An age had ended and the world was poorer. But there was still a remnant of the old wisdom in the scrolls, and Lydia swore once more that gift would be delivered.

Uncharacteristically, she decided to explain. "I had another name in Nineveh." She looked down, unwilling to let him see those memories in her eyes. Only the Old One knew the name of her birth city.

Tightening her lips, she continued. "That name might create problems we don't need. Canaan is a long trek and the road to Nineveh is the first step. I don't need to draw attention to my... my... past." Exiled in shame, those memories still had power to draw an angry flush to her face.

"And after that?" Lud interrupted dryly, trying to show no curiosity... sensitive enough to understand the pain memory could inflict. She looked over sharply. Most, she could read, but he was different. She drew a breath and composed her face, forcing a reply in the same dry manner.

"After that we travel east, to Haran, Carchemish, and then south. But our first stop is Tushpa, on the Lake. We won't have any trouble with the Bianili authorities. They'll respect our mission because of the Old One. The Hittites...."

"With the Hatti, you never know," concluded Lud grimly. "We might encounter one of these young fools from Nesa, who worships Teshuba and Hebut, and has no respect for the memory of the elders. One of them could cause trouble."

Lydia nodded. "That's why we'll seek a small caravan in Tushpa. They'll have news from the south too."

She saw the question on Lud's face and shook her head. "We can't join one of the big companies. We must blend in... settlers moving south." Her face hardened in decision. "We're farmers moving to Canaan or Egypt. A caravan where your bow and a piece of silver will make us welcome."

Lud grimaced. Such a caravan would invite the raiders haunting the King's Highway. There were always poor and desperate fools, looking for anything of value. And a weak headman would only invite attack. A moment's inattention and they would be just two more bodies for the jackals. Lydia clearly favored secrecy over safety. He was responsible for her safety, but she was the one commissioned by the Old One. For a moment he thought of them going alone, avoiding the caravans and their troubles, but she was a woman and if something happened to him, she would be dead... or worse.

Lydia read his thoughts. "To all appearances, we'll be a couple moving south, maybe joining family in southern Canaan. We can avoid the King's Highway by taking the coastal road through Byblos and Sidon." She had thought it through.

"The Sea Peoples," concluded Lud glumly.

"The lesser of many evils." She ticked off her fingers. "They've been relatively peaceful for many years. They're safer than the wild nomads. And we may need their help." She sighed. "If we come to Ekron or Gath in the company of a friendly caravan, we might find information about the prince."

"Or our throats cut and our goods taken," he grumbled. "We are not of them and they'll know it. Your face screams 'Akkadian,' and mine, 'Hittite.'"

She failed to stay a sharp glance. It was the first hint he had ever let slip about his past. She had suspected, of course, but respected the sanctity of secrets. But she was female, she was curious, and her mind would dwell on his past on the long hours of the road.

She stifled a smile. At the best of times, it was a long journey. Were his words a subtle gift, something to keep her occupied on that road? He tried to look innocent, but failed, and the hint of a grateful smile on her face had him shaking his head.

She sat up straight. There were many dangers, but no immediate problems. All she wanted was to fulfill her vow—to hand the scrolls to this prince in Canaan. It was simple... yet now it seemed impossible.

But it certainly wouldn't happen sitting here on her horse. With a kick of her heels she turned the animal south toward the Lake of the Islands. There were farms and settlements along the way, people who knew and respected her.

As they trotted up the road, she wondered what it was like, so many years ago, when there was nothing but the bare land. No farms. No settlements. No cities. Just a vast wilderness stretching down to the plains and greater mysteries beyond those borders.

A world full of promise, but one rapidly turning to darkness thanks to the evil of one man and one woman.

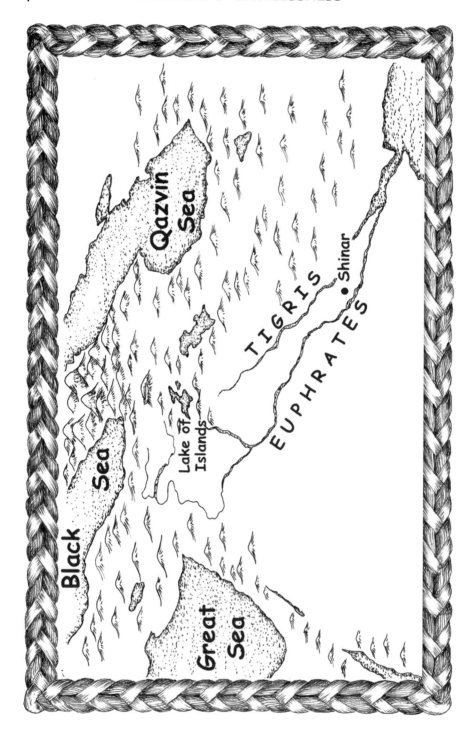

Chapter 1
HEIR & HEIRLOOM

3-14-1754

"Do you feel it yet?" Her soft sensuous voice floated on the air along with a hint of the evening's coolness on his damp forehead.

Nimrod shook his head in frustration, his thick dark hair playing around his shoulders. *What was this it?* He couldn't ask. Being angry, his sharp words would only provoke her towering wrath. Anyone else would have received a snarled curse in reply… but had it been anyone else, he would not be here. But it wasn't *anyone else*; it was *her*—the object of his awe and lust… his grandmother.

But right now, he was just getting angry. He didn't know what he was supposed to feel. He didn't know where they were going. And he didn't know why he had to endure the tortoise-like pace of the women. He usually loved wandering the wilderness—hunting, climbing, swimming, and running all came easily, and he loved pitting his prowess against the land. Like a lion in its prime, he loved his strength and speed. But it was no place for women. They couldn't walk quietly or stop talking or quit complaining. He was ready to explode.

Controlling himself, he surveyed the valley. Like many others near the borders of the northern lands, it wound between mountains of naked rock, following a stream toward its source. They were four days from the Tigris, having followed one of its larger tributaries into the eastern mountains. He grimaced. This was no adventure—just an irritating walk in another featureless valley, its craggy rock faces rearing high above the gathering darkness.

He turned and sneered as four of the women collapsed to the ground. He could have run through the night. Taller and leaner than his grandfather Ham, Nimrod had inherited much of his impressive strength. Years of hunting and training had developed his body to the point of perfection. He smiled, recalling the day he had bested his vaunted cousin Heth, then the best warrior in Shinar. Nimrod had known then that he would be greatest man of his time.

That had been fifteen years ago, and those since had added strength. He could defeat any man—any three men—with any weapon or with none. Fearless and cunning, his reputation as a hunter preceded him everywhere… he had killed every kind of wild beast.

He disdained the weakness of the women huddled at his feet. It would have been easier without them, but Debseda wanted them here. She had said it would be improper for the two of them to travel alone—and she had always been one for appearances.

Though young and attractive, none of younger women looked it now. He frowned at the sight of the recent addition—Tabriz—to the group. A few months ago she had been his favorite lover. Now she was off limits, and for good reason. With a single word from their mistress, any of them would seduce a man and then slit his throat as he slept. That was the kind of power Nimrod wanted. And Tabriz was nothing compared to his grandmother. No other woman could ever satisfy him. It angered him every day that she could not be his wife. Even Shinar would never accept that. His yearning for her was a constant ache.

He looked up at her. One hundred and forty years older than any of them, she looked ready to hike all night. Some inner power, possessed by the elders, lent her a man's endurance. Her bright blue eyes were appraising him in turn, and the stirrings they caused reminded him why he had agreed to this insane trek. Anything to be near her. She had always been a fire in his mind—an unapproachable goddess. As he grew into manhood, she had become the ultimate forbidden fruit.

And then one day… no longer forbidden. He shivered as he remembered. That night had ignited a flame in him no other could quench, though many had tried. His chiseled features, bright blue eyes, and thick dark hair made him the talk of the women, just as his strong arm and quick leap earned him the admiration of the men. Even married women found their way to his rooms.

But his grandmother was different. *She* had taken him, and never let him forget it. Some indefinable force within her shackled his will. Perhaps it was habit; she demanded obedience from everyone (and got it). But he felt something greater than the authority she had embedded in three generations of her descendents. Even something more than her native ability—she was more clever and ruthless than any of her children. No, there was some other power that made her a force to be reckoned with.

He sighed. Here he was, a week from nowhere, wandering up some river valley, and wondering why. When she had decided to accompany the flocks north two months ago, he had seized the opportunity to be near her. After all, he had boasted, a great hunter was needed to protect the stock. Predators still roamed the northern grasslands, though men were beginning to thin them back. He did not begrudge the sluggish progress of the herds or even the nights spent alone. It was worth it to just be near her. But that proximity had also been driving him insane with lust.

A few nights before, she had summoned him to her tent. "It is time," she had said, then broke into laughter as the open passion flared in his eyes. "Not for that… not now. We have a detour to make, you and I."

"Why?" he had asked.

"It is time." That was all she had said. It did not strike him until the next day that he had just entered his thirty-third year.

Thirty-three years. A man now, according to the traditions of the elders, though in his own mind he had been a man from the day he had defeated Heth. The best man in Shinar; as acknowledged grudgingly by the fathers but enthusiastically by their children. Nimrod was the living hope that they could attain adult privileges at an early age.

He shook himself and followed her gaze up the mountainside. The setting sun lit the eastern face, revealing what he suddenly knew was their goal—a dark spot maybe five or six hundred cubits up the slope. A cave. A large one, judging by the entrance. His eyes narrowed. How did he know? Something *was* stirring within. Something dark and terrible, yet enticing. In a flash the tedium of the past days was gone; adventure lay before him. Blood coursed through his limbs, and in his strength, he was ready for any challenge.

"Come," she commanded, and the women rose quickly, shouldering their packs. Most of their load was wood, gathered as they hiked upstream. Nimrod had refrained from asking why. Debseda revealed her plans in her own time and pointless questions irritated her.

The women struggled up the rocky slope, but Nimrod found it easy going, instinctively choosing the easiest path with a practiced flair. He tried to stay ahead of the evening shadow chasing them up out of the valley. The four women labored behind but Debseda kept up with surprising ease.

As they neared the cave he felt something stirring around him, growing stronger. It was delicious yet dangerous, like the lush curves of Debseda. But this sensation was not of pleasure, it was power! His blood raced. The feeling, and a corresponding lust for more, grew with every step. It was raw, wild, strong—like sinking his blade into the throat of a kill. He wanted to sprint forward, but some instinct warned him back.

"You feel it now, don't you?" she laughed. "Enjoy it. Drink it in. This is your birthright!" Her voice held an undertone he had never heard before, and for the first time the power he had always sensed in her was unveiled. Could he share it? He wanted it even more than he wanted her.

The day's last light was fading as they mounted the final ledge. A black hole loomed before them. Huge and daunting, it was at least fifty cubits wide and fifteen high—a gaping maw leading to a place of mysteries hidden from man. Nimrod felt the call of power from its dark depths. Trembling, he tensed to spring forward, but a cool hand stayed him.

"Calm yourself, my son," she murmured. "All in good time. This must be done properly."

His throat was too taut for words, but he nodded. Her grip turned into a caress and his heart raced at the sensation of conflicting passions.

"Stay here until I call," she commanded. He nodded again, not trusting his voice. Then he unslung his spear and planted it before him, gripping it with white knuckles as an anchor against the overwhelming urge to rush forward.

Within moments, the other women were stumbling past him, passing wordlessly into the darkness. Standing rigid like some guardian of the cave's dark secrets, Nimrod felt their heat and smelled their sweat; each pant audible in the now silent evening. Though darkness obscured his vision, he could hear them moving inside, preparing, like priestesses, some ritual of power.

Behind him the sky went black and in that instant he felt suddenly alone, transported into the vast chaos beyond Creation. A feeling of smallness pressed down on him, but he beat it back and suddenly he was back on the ledge, trembling under the spell of the alluring chant within. His spear could no longer hold him. He *needed* to be inside. It took all of his will to resist… to obey his grandmother. Only the habit of obedience kept him there.

Sweat dripped in his eyes from the effort. Wood grated on wood… they were laying a fire. The rasp of a flint caused him to flinch. A spark pierced the blackness and rapidly grew into flame. Suddenly the vast interior was lit, but the fire was a sickly green. He shook his head and looked away. Where was the sacred meal? The sacrifice?

As the flames leapt higher he saw a tangled knot of women, hands busy in the dim light. Then three of them stepped back and knelt, revealing their handiwork. Tabriz was bound to a nearby pillar of rock, her clothing scattered on the floor. She appeared drunk, lolling against her bonds, her head down.

Debseda was nowhere to be seen, but with heightened sense, he felt her presence further back in the cave. Strange words echoed out into the night. The hair on his arms stood up. She was near the source, and she seemed but a pale shade next to its pulsing darkness. He felt her hands grasp it, felt its hard chill as if he were carrying it himself. Now she was returning, coming slowly into the firelight. The three women echoed her chant and Tabriz moaned softly.

Debseda looked across to him, the blue fire of her eyes shining in the black cave. "Now!" she cried.

His feet barely felt the floor as he leaped towards her and his hands lost all feeling as his spear clattered down near the fire. He could not stop, but his pace slowed, as if running through water; each step brought increasing pain. Something was pounding at the doors of his mind with strength far greater than his. In the span of a few paces, he fought across time and eternity. For a brief moment, a faint part of his heart tried to warn him, but he crushed it and fought forward again, against the pain. The world was his, if he could win this battle.

Suddenly he was back in the cave. His eyes cleared and he saw it—a long black spearhead. It was majestic; he had never seen one like it. Yet it was more than a weapon. Its pure ebony surface swallowed light, as if the spear was a gateway to the eternal void. He desired it, but knelt instinctively to its power, aware that he would not claim it. It would claim him.

Or it would not.

It took all of his will to wait, straining to open his mind.

After an interminable moment, he felt… approval. Then more. It desired him too! His heart soared. Ecstatic, he felt the first tinges of that dark power settle inside him. Debseda sensed it too. She raised a hand and the women were silent.

"This is your inheritance from the lost world," she intoned. "It is the symbol of a lost race of superior men—a totem given into my keeping by the greatest of my kind. *Our* kind…." She was staring at him intently, her eyes holding his.

Nimrod felt his head swim. *Her* kind? Superior men? The answer to the riddle of the power seemed within his reach, but he was too dizzy to comprehend. He wanted power, not mysteries.

Debseda continued, as if reading his thoughts. "This is the spear of Sechiall, greatest warrior of the Nephilim, light of the morning, victorious in battle, enemy of the Almighty, and bane of Noah and his kind. Through the chaos of the Creator's anger, I brought it into this world for its true heir."

Nimrod thrilled as scenes of past battles flickered through his head. Debseda pointed it at him. "You are that heir. You are destined to rule over lesser men, bend them to your will, and use them to rebuild that which was lost… to restore our past glory with an empire springing from the ruins of the last world."

She held out the spear and its blackness seduced his mind. "Bathe it in its first blood of this world." She pointed at Tabriz. "It thirsts."

In a trance, Nimrod felt his every desire coalesce around the object. It *must* be his. He reached hesitantly forward, caressed it, and then wrapped his hand around its base.

Its hunger was now his own. Lunging up, he crowded his body into Tabriz. With practiced quickness and strength he rammed the point through her white throat. She jerked, quivered, and slumped forward. Blood spurted over the blade, washing its length and running down across Nimrod's hands. He could feel her life force ebb and he forced his body closer, letting her blood flow down his legs. Time slowed, as Tabriz shuddered once and hung still.

Nimrod trembled. He felt, rather than heard, the next command. Withdrawing the blade, he plunged it into the green fire, ignoring the tendrils of flame licking his fingers. He felt no heat, just the cool nothingness of the metal. Though his hands remained cool, the blood smoked and sizzled, sealing him to the blade at a level far deeper than flesh or metal.

He pulled back, still gripping his prize. Leaning down, he retrieved his own spear and laughed as the new head effortlessly sheared through the iron of the old. Smearing the top of the raw wooden shaft with fresh blood, he fitted the new head over it, feeling the metal bind itself to the wood. He tugged, but could not move it. As he watched, its darkness crept down the shaft until the wood matched the ebony color of the blade.

Nimrod hefted it, a corner of his mind noting that the shaft was now straight and smooth beyond his craft. Its balance was perfect, in spite of being a span shorter from the loss of the original blade. It felt… right. But the darkness was not done. Covering the shaft, it slid onto his hands and disappeared. As it did, he felt new strength and saw the cave with new eyes.

Visions that had danced at the edge of consciousness now flared into vivid detail. Strong cities, powerful armies of yellow-haired giants, blood, destruction. A mighty warrior ascending a throne. Men bowing before him. The face grew clearer… it was his. Conquest and rule were his destiny. With this spear he would be invincible.

Now he knew why his place was at the forefront of mankind. Not because he was stronger or faster than other men. In fact, he was no man. He was inherently superior to even Noah and his sons. The great and powerful elders were lambs to his wolf. A new word formed in his mind. *Nephil.* He was Nephil. He was the reborn son of a glorious race that had prevailed over all mortal foes.

The rumors out of the north were twisted. Noah was no hero. He had not saved mankind. He had been fleeing the wrath of his betters, only to be delivered by the twist of fate that was the great flood.

The snarl became a grim smile as Nimrod recalled those stories. There was one grain of truth. In it, he knew the Almighty had erred! He had promised never to destroy the earth again. By His very word, He was constrained to sit back and watch mankind create their destiny. Where Sechiall had failed, Nimrod would succeed. There would be no flood to stop him! He laughed at the irony. The same ark that had condemned his ancestors had carried their seed and heirloom into this new world. Final victory would be theirs. Noah and his brood would submit or die.

As his eyes cleared and his mind returned to the cave, he saw a dying fire, a woman's body hanging limp against its ropes, and the darkness of night which hid him from the unsuspecting world of men.

This cave was now a hallowed place, secret, yet sacred. Here, his legacy had been revealed. It would always be a place of worship for a select few. All that, he saw in a flash, but his attention was distracted.

His grandmother—the woman he had worshiped—was now kneeling before him. Her blue eyes flashed fire; a rapt smile lit her face. She knew. She had given all this to him! It was a double gift: the power he envied and an eager acceptance of his rule. He was no longer hers; she belonged to him.

He reached down and pulled her up, and she was in his arms, her hands more eager than his. The three other women knelt, looked down, and began a new chant to their new master.

Madrazi was choking; terror gripped her mind and her arms were immobile against her body, held by some unseen force. She struggled until she realized it was the tight grip of her husband. His face swam into focus; his relief evident in the pale moonlight as he felt her body relax.

"You were screaming," he apologized, "and thrashing around. I've never seen it this bad." He had the sense to hold his questions, comforting her with quiet murmurs and the soft stroking of her hair. She clung to him with all her strength, wanting him to squeeze away the memory.

But the dream remained fresh in her mind, and she shuddered. He wrapped a blanket around her shivering form. Her night clothes were hanging in pieces on her shoulders, evidence of the strength of her earlier struggle. She pulled the blanket close, but it did not dispel the chill inside.

Finally she drew a deep breath. "I can't sleep any more. I need something hot to drink."

He simply nodded as he slipped over to the closet to bring her a robe and sandals. The night was cool, so after she dressed in fresh clothing, he lifted the blanket and hung it again around her shoulders, and then led her through the dark hallway into the kitchen.

He lit a candle and kindled a fire. Once it was crackling, he heated spiced cider. She sat and watched, letting these simple tasks pull her back into the world, away from the terror. Shem finally spoke. "Tell me everything. It was bad—very bad—and you need to share the burden. I'm surprised you didn't wake the sheep in the far fields."

Madrazi blushed, then sighed. She knew him well. His weak humor hid his concern and was a subtle hint that she had awakened the entire house. All would be huddled in their rooms, afraid to intrude, but wondering what new thing their mistress had seen. She blushed, but her good sense overcame her embarrassment and she laughed. Shem seemed to relax and chuckled with her.

She wanted to sit and sip the hot drink, but she couldn't put it off—time would not make it go away. And Shem was obstinate; she would speak of it sooner or later. Taking one last sip, she set the cup down and opened her heart.

"I saw the dark king again. He was like Sechiall, but he was another... a son or a brother. He carried Sechiall's spear like the vision I saw on the ark, but it was more... real. The weapon was alive—it had eyes—and it shared its master's delight in evil. I was trapped in a corner and it was playing with me, stabbing here and there, seeking to torment, not to kill. Wherever I dodged, it remained before my eyes. I felt it taunting me." She stopped, frustrated. "It doesn't make sense, but that's what I saw."

Shem sighed. "Prayer will bring clarity. It always does."

"But I'm afraid we may have no time. Something evil is happening, and all I can think of are the boys getting ready to leave next month. Does some disaster await them? Perhaps they should stay or push west, not north."

Shem looked troubled. "We must seek answers from the Almighty. Is there a connection? If not, we need to find a way into the wider world, and stopping the boys will only compound the evil. We are shut off. We are not welcome in the south; even our traders are barely tolerated. To the east there are only mountains and the Qazvin Sea... to the west, rugged wilderness. We must find a way out for our children's children. In a few generations there will be tens of thousands. We cannot let them fall into the dark clutch of Shinar. Our best hope is north and the boys must find a passage through the mountains between the seas. We know the earth is large. Its lands are wide and probably fruitful. Had our grandchildren obeyed the Creator, we would be spreading far and wide even now. But men love the easy life of the plains and few have the stomach to explore for new homes. If Shelah and the boys don't do it, no one will. We've avoided open war to this point. We can't do it forever. We know Nimrod will strike soon. We just don't know where."

Madrazi just nodded. They had discussed this for years and she had no new words to ease the lines of strain that she saw wearing into her husband's grim face.

Chapter 2
SEDUCTION

3-30-1754

Nimrod breathed the morning air with a smile on his face. Last night's chill had not retreated before the rising sun, but he barely noticed. The thrill of the hunt kept his blood up. And what a hunt this was! Hidden in the rocks overlooking the vale of Noah's farm, he focused on his prey. He almost laughed at the irony; there would be no spears or arrows here, only gentle words, soft touches, and softer kisses—his quarry was a woman.

Sunlight glistened off the dew. Noah had settled in a valley west of the Lake of the Islands, with rugged hills to the south, gentle slopes to the north, and a river bringing verdant life to the land between. Nimrod granted a grudging respect; the fields were regular and well-tended, interspersed with orchards and vineyards. Pastures occupied the grassy slopes of the foothills, but the farm had been built in a vale bordering hard against the southern hills, and so Nimrod could see down to the house, the barns, and the fields that ran to the edge of the hills, within a spear cast of his hiding place. It was pretty, but still a farm… not a fortress.

A fierce smile touched his lips. This was the first roll in the grand game his grandmother had set in play two weeks ago. Its end would see him enthroned in Shinar, reigning over all from the southern sea to the northern hills. There were no laws, just his superior mind and body against the fading power of the elders. What a game! Eventually he would slay them, but as Debseda counseled, that must wait. He must first gain a kingdom and establish a dynasty. That required a wife, and as much as they both desired it, she could not be Debseda. His queen must enhance his reputation… make people sit up and take notice. A daughter of Noah would do so.

The lingering mist lent an aura of unreality to the scene; imparting a ghostly appearance to those below, milling around the house and barns preparing for the day's work. He smiled. One of those figures was Mariel—Noah's oldest daughter. Ancient by anyone's standard; Noah was still able to father children, though in his dotage he could no longer produce sons. Nimrod's smile widened as he recalled the amusement shared with Debseda over the fading strength of the old man.

But what had been a source of amusement was now the root of a powerful strategy. Nimrod saw more clearly—the strange new talisman of the lost world had proven more than a weapon. He now understood the strategic potential of that house full of girls. By taking one, he would both emasculate his greatest enemy and cement the allegiance of the plain; many still feared the old man, even if they refused his commands. Before, Nimrod would have been satisfied to ravage the old man's home—to rape and kill. But now he grasped new subtleties. He saw the years unrolling ahead. Success would give him a line of succession that would perpetuate his rule. The ruler of mankind must inspire fear and awe.

Slaying Noah would only anger most, and possibly reunite his three sons. Even with his new power, Nimrod doubted he could face their combined strength. Worse, many in Shinar who hated Noah and Shem still saw them as almost mythical beings—survivors of the flood and the lost world. Noah's self-imposed isolation had only increased their awe. Those who might secretly wish him dead would be in the forefront of the mob calling for the banishment or blood of his slayer.

Nimrod scowled. Mizraim, for example, would be delighted if Nimrod killed the Old One—he would sanctimoniously mourn the loss, call for the death of the slayer of "the new Adam," and be more than satisfied to be rid of both.

No, Nimrod didn't want Noah's life. He wanted his authority. He wanted to humble the old man, and leave him as a living reminder that a greater power was now active in the world. Men would fear that more.

That night in the cave, he and Debseda had talked all night, planning their future. In spite of her burning hatred for the old man, she had agreed that humiliation was worth more than his death. When Nimrod had outlined his brazen plan, she had laughed long and loud. They would take one of Noah's girls out from under the old man's nose to be Nimrod's wife.

Flaunting the old man's home would raise Nimrod's esteem in the eyes of many, especially the myriads of youth who would form the core of his army in years to come. Showing he could strike at the heart of the enemy would raise his status, and siring sons through Noah's daughter would add dignity to his line that would keep coming generations subservient.

Debseda regretted that she could not be there to gloat, but her presence would ruin the plan. So while Nimrod fulfilled his mission, she would begin hers—devising new gods, commandments, and seers. Noah's supposed connection with the Creator brought a sense of unease to even the wildest young heart. The great Destroyer haunted the dark corners of their dreams. Removing that fear would earn the gratitude of all, even if the substitute was false. Debseda understood men's hearts; she knew how to appeal to their instincts.

In time, her new system would cement enmity between the people of Shinar and those of the northern hills. Men who wouldn't fight over a woman or gold would take up spears to defend the honor of their god.

Future generations would accept her lies as common wisdom, and there would be no return to the Creator. Zeal for false gods would lead the conquest of the lands to the north and west—the illusion of divine sanction would keep an army marching into the unknown, or standing against a powerful foe.

But now was the first battle, and Nimrod must beard the great patriarch in his own den. Noah would never voluntarily give up one of his daughters. Nor could Nimrod seize one by force. It would bring the wrath of her brothers—including his grandfather—down on his head. There was only one path to success; he must seduce one that would leave of her free will. Once gone, there would be no return. True to his nature, Nimrod had chosen the eldest—why not aim for Noah's heart?

Thus far, the battle had gone well. His first move the day before had been a feint. As expected, when he had arrived at Noah's front door asking for the hand of

Mariel, the old man had icily refused. His sputtering anger had been almost amusing. Nimrod was still laughing. "Son of the serpent!" If that was the best Noah could throw, there was little to fear. But amusement was gratuitous. The brief encounter *had* fulfilled its true purpose. Curiosity had lured the girls past their mother into Nimrod's line of sight and he had fixed all of his newfound power on Mariel, his fiery blue eyes burning into her cool grey ones. It was enough. He knew as he walked away that the seed had been planted; disquiet would even now be working in her susceptible heart, with an awakening of desire stirring the first small ripples of rebellion.

But the same memory also sobered him. Exerting of his own power, he had felt the beginnings of an answer deep within Noah. Though banked, that fire could still burn—it was the same power that had defended the ark against Sechiall. But it was slow to rise, perhaps too alien to this world to be effective. And Noah was old. Nimrod shuddered for a moment. He would be testing his theory soon, and wondered if his new strength was enough. Then a reckless thrill shook him—he welcomed the test. Succeeding where Sechiall had failed, he would prove himself a worthy heir.

The rest of it had been easy. Feigning respect, he had left Noah's door, sauntering back to the main road… feeling the old man's eyes following every step. He had turned southeast for an hour, until the clumsy youth Noah had sent to shadow his path turned back.

It was a short trip back to the rough hills above the farm. Nearby, he had found a cave, by the pass where the road cut through the hills. He had set up camp there before clambering down the steep hill to the road. It was the work of a moment to stack three rocks off to one side. Few travelers would notice them, and only one would understand the sign. For him it would be as good as a bonfire.

And so this morning, Nimrod watched, learning the patterns of the farm. It was always the most difficult part of any hunt—watching and waiting. But he was a great hunter and knew patience in the stalk.

His careful reconnaissance over the following days taught him the rhythms of life in the valley; workers toiling in the fields, shepherds leading their herds to grassy pastures away east, and the family working together on the innumerable tasks of running a farm. All the daughters worked, and Nimrod gloated, noting that Mariel's chores took her into the field below his perch, away from the others.

He was prepared to wait months, but fate led him to her in just three days, and three minutes more were all it took to have her in his arms. The poison of desire had settled deep in her heart. As he held her, he spoke words to inflame her imagination. "I could not leave without you," he whispered. "I've found my treasure and nothing can keep me from you. I cannot live on this earth apart from you."

"We mustn't be seen," she protested weakly. "My sisters will find us and Father will be angry. He was agitated all day after you came." She glanced at him under her eyelashes. "Why did you name me? Because I am the eldest?"

Nimrod laughed. "Of course not! Your brother Ham and his wife both told me that you were the fairest, and we in Shinar are not so far away as to be unable to glean the praises of your beauty from traders and travelers."

Mariel looked down, but a small smile curled her lips. Nimrod took her hand in his. "Where can we meet?" he begged. "If I cannot see you, I'll go mad."

She smiled up at him, her own longing clear. "Just on the other side of that hill is a spring," she pointed. "I'll be there tomorrow in the middle afternoon. If not tomorrow, then the day after. Stay out of sight until you're sure I'm alone." She looked down again. "Father will be angry, but…."

Before she could say another word, Nimrod silenced her with a kiss. "I'll wait until the world ends," he promised. He kissed her again, feeling her melt against him. Her lips were bewitching, he noted to himself—there might be ancillary advantages to this scheme. She clung to him and it was Nimrod who broke the embrace, noting with satisfaction that she was panting slightly, her color up.

"You will be my wife," he promised. "Queen of Shinar, with the fruit of the plains at your feet. Your father is wise. He will reconsider and give his blessing. But say nothing now. Let us enjoy these fleeting hours while we wait for him to change his mind. He will come to see the wisdom of our match."

Mariel nodded. At that moment, she would have fled with him; would have done anything…. She found her fingers wandering down to loosen the clasp of her cloak.

It shocked her, but she crushed the voice of conscience. This was a new feeling, and it felt good. Nothing had ever stirred her like this. It could only be love. Here was a man—perfect in form and feature. He wanted her and she wanted him. Her hands were reluctant to release his powerful shoulders. She belonged to him. Regretfully, she must deceive her family for a time. The idea grated, but she was becoming something new, refined by the fire of his kisses. And it was only for a short time… Noah would come to see the advantages of his offer. He had to. She was well past the age to marry. She stood there a moment longer, watching the lithe form of her lover slip back up the path. In her mind, she saw the years to come—the whole family would laugh at their odd courtship, while her children played with her mother and sisters.

A girl had come out into the fields; a woman returned to the farm.

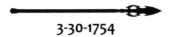

3-30-1754

Madrazi stood on the damp grass, cloak wrapped tightly against the morning air. People huddled with her watching Shem talking to the five men standing loosely around him. There was Shelah—a younger, slimmer image of Shem and Madrazi's favorite. Next to him was the massive Heth, towering over little Anam. Alongside them were the dark haired Jobaath and the fair-skinned Ashkenaz, laughing together at some private jest and paying little attention to Shem's final instructions.

She understood their sacrifice. All of them had farms along the shores of the Lake of the Islands. Lambs would be arriving soon, if not already, and the men would not be present for that crucial and busy time. Hard on the heels of the lambs would come the sowing of their fields. Shelah's wife would manage as best she could. Merab was a competent woman and their neighbors would help, but it would be a hard time. Jobaath's Telah would likewise do her best, but she lacked the iron will of Merab. It would be a thin season for both. Madrazi's lips drew into a tight line. It had taken the direct intervention of Shem to find "volunteers" to watch over the lands of the three single men… she suspected Shem had paid men to care for the flocks of Heth and Anam. Despite their friendship with Shelah and their efforts on behalf of Shem, they were still viewed with suspicion by most of the people. Her own grandson Uz had been at the forefront of discord over Heth's presence. She smiled grimly as she recalled her rebuke and Uz' stuttering apology. Then she sighed. How could men live together amid such easy animosity?

With a snort, she brought her mind back to the present. All five would suffer some loss, but none of them had mentioned it. They were special—what the Creator had intended for this world. She breathed a silent prayer that He would bless their homes while they were gone, and resolved that she would to travel south in a few weeks to make sure the "volunteers" were hard at work. Shem could force obedience, but she could shame them into doing the same, and avoid the hard feelings Shem might engender.

Shelah was waving the men in for a final blessing before they left. It had been just a few short decades since he had bounced on her knee. Those had been happy and exciting times, seeing the potential of so many beautiful lives entering the world. So much happiness shared by Wen-Tehrom and Yaran. But days grew dark, those little boys were now men, and they were staking their lives on her insight and Shem's judgment. She trembled, wondering for a moment if she would cause their death. The mountains to the north were high and harsh. Shem had wandered them briefly. He had never found a way through, though he had not searched hard. At the time, there had been no reason.

But now there was. A desperate need, born from fear of a gathering evil in the south and of the natural barriers around the mountain. The best lands found so far were down on the plains, and men there were forsaking God. Ignoring His command, they congregated together, preferring the easy life of Shinar to obedience to the Creator. "Fill the earth," He had told Noah, but the young just laughed. The northern hills were a rugged wilderness, and would not support a growing population. To the east were more mountains and the Qazvin Sea. To the west was rough wilderness, though Japheth had found some promising lands far to the west. The way north was a logical exit, but blocked by high mountains. Unless the boys could find a pass—a path of escape from the evil flowing through Debseda and her twisted children. It was enough to make Madrazi weep. Then she saw Anam and Heth laughing together. There was always hope. Any man could serve the Creator.

She clutched that hope to her breast as she watched the men shoulder their packs.

Weeks passed as days for Nimrod. Mariel met him regularly. She ran hot and cold as her heart warred with itself, but he continued to cultivate a growing rebellion with desire. He knew the outcome; the question was simply how long. There were many days he could have taken her easily enough, and others when he thought she was slipping away. But he was always patient, allowing her passion to do his work. He was content to whisper promise after promise, allaying fears and inflaming lust. She would be his wife. Her father would come to understand. Her mother would applaud her courage. Her sisters would know a peaceful world because they would unite the fraying strands of mankind. The time drew near; soon she would gather enough courage to leave.

When he wasn't with her or scouting the farm, he spent hours near the cave, running his hands up and down his new spear, attuning himself to its power. It seemed almost alive, and he strained to align his thoughts to see if he could catch a glimmer of the entity within. As he exercised with it, he felt a new speed and skill filter into his limbs. The few men of Shinar who had been close to him in their ability would be in for a rude surprise! No man would be able to face him now.

It was much more than a weapon. It seemed alive, strengthening mind and body. By its power, he knew exactly what to say to Mariel when she was wavering… he read her thoughts as she battled her conscience. He even slept with it in his grip, dreaming of his future rule, with the spear as his scepter. He had left it hidden when he first faced Noah, some instinct warning him to keep it from the old man's presence. But after these weeks of bonding… he could not so easily set it aside. The idea of flaunting it to the old man was attractive. Reckless, yes, but so appealing. But caution now tempered his wrath, and he knew the spear must stay hidden from the old man.

Each day was a fight for patience. There was much to do in Shinar, and new ideas entered his head each day. He must have an army, but would start them as a small force to police the roads, protecting trade. "Nimrod's Legion" he would call them, in preparation for the days when they would be tens of thousands of spearmen winning this whole world. But first, he had a city to tame. Each day, his father and uncles would be scheming to take power, like jackals fighting over a bone. Soon, the lion would return, sending the jackals slinking back to the shadows. So he watched and waited for Korac.

Good old Korac—as certain as the sunrise, as dependable as a fine blade. The man might be as unfeeling as a stone, but even a stone could be chipped into a useful implement. Debseda had promised to send him. If he didn't arrive today, he would come tomorrow or the next day. It mattered little—he would come and then the pieces would be in place. Nimrod would then be ready to gamble his glorious future on the fickle whim of a woman. He laughed at the irony.

Chapter 3
THE KING IS DEAD

4-22-1754

Nimrod woke to the sight of Korac's broad back. He was patiently tending the fire; hands that could snap a man's neck were delicately arranging sticks in the flames. Nimrod laughed aloud with delight. "You did it again," he joked. "The only man that can get that close without waking me. I trained you too well."

"You're awake now," retorted Korac dryly, and for a moment, Nimrod thought he saw the slightest break in the man's iron face. Curious, he tried to read Korac's heart, laying his left hand on his spear beside his blanket and focusing his newfound powers on his friend. He had always possessed an uncanny ability to understand others. But since he had inherited the spear that gift had been amplified, and he was eager to test it on a man who had long been a mystery.

Korac had once been full of life and the two had been closer than brothers. Early on, both had recognized in each other a peculiar competence that demanded instant respect. Hunting together had deepened it to friendship, and Nimrod had rejoiced at Korac's marriage to his sister, Timna. During the following years they had been inseparable; Korac accepting the role of a follower to the only man he felt deserved it. Life had been good until the foolish Timna had grown jealous and had insisted on accompanying them on a hunt. After months of nagging, Korac had given in, hoping that a hard trek in the wilderness would cure her.

It hadn't... it had killed her. Neither spoke of it again. Nimrod frowned; glad that Korac couldn't read him in return... some things were better left buried. It had been a hard time; Korac had been lost in grief. Always a man of strong feelings, he had gone far beyond normal sadness. He had been transformed into something very different. Every emotion had vanished. He became as walking stone—an iron mask where his face had once been—a man of rock-hard fists, and a rock-hard heart. His friends shunned him, but Nimrod had kept him close.

Nimrod sighed. Korac his friend had somehow died with Timna. But Korac his most trusted tool had risen from the ashes of that tragedy. As Nimrod's ambition waxed, his need of someone like Korac grew with it... someone who could be trusted with the quiet, ugly things power demanded. And Korac had done them well, with no remorse. He was feared by all Shinar—a fear that enhanced Nimrod's power.

As Nimrod sat up, he realized this was his opportunity to see within the infamous man of stone. So laying one hand on the black shaft, he absorbed its power and focused his mind. He gasped involuntarily and turned away quickly. The answer struck him like a blow—Korac's heart was not veiled, it simply wasn't there. There was no love or hate, envy or treachery... just a black void. Whatever had once made him a vital soul was gone. He was a husk, but a useful one. Relief followed shock, and his face resumed its sly smile. Korac was just what he needed—a capable man without a conscience.

Smiling more broadly, Nimrod rose and made his way to the fire. Sitting together as the early sun filtered into the cave, the men shared the remains of a chicken that Nimrod had cooked the night before—compliments of Noah's henhouse. It was poor fare, but better than nothing. Korac reached into his pack and pulled out a small wineskin. "Thought you might appreciate a touch of civilization," he said.

Smiling, Nimrod slaked his thirst. "You thought well. Now you must perform equally well."

Wiping his mouth with the back of his hand, Nimrod began to sketch a map of Noah's farm with the charred end of a stick. As he outlined his plan, Korac nodded. He rarely adding anything, but when he did, it was usually right. Nimrod appreciated both his ability to grasp ideas with one explanation and his economy with words.

"I'm meeting her this afternoon," Nimrod concluded. "Start an hour before sundown, and all will be ready. Are the horses prepared?"

Korac nodded. "I rode easy and switched mounts. They're across the road in a small pasture. Good grass and water. They'll be there."

Nimrod rose suddenly and stalked up and down. "Finally!" he exclaimed. "This is my day!" He slammed his fist in his palm. "We have no need of the old ways. A new world needs new leaders. If we succeed today, Shinar will be ours. We will build a city that men will fight and die for. Within a few generations we will have thousands at our command: to fight and obey. Once they are harnessed to our dreams, mankind will rule this world and we will rule mankind!"

Korac sat silent. He was used to Nimrod's fits of nervous energy and boasting. He had no ambition; how could a hollow man desire anything? He was content to feed off of his master's aspirations—to let that fiery soul guide his icy mind. He had nothing better to do. Not now. He might be a puppet, but he was a powerful and useful puppet. A dangerous puppet. Most men would be insulted at the idea. Korac was content.

Early afternoon found Nimrod by the spring. He stiffened and turned as the beautiful woman glided down the rocky path into the hollow. Her face was aflame with desire. Weeks had passed since their first meeting, but today he finally felt what he had been waiting for… Mariel was ready. As he swept her into his arms, he felt the conflict within her dissipate. Her growing passion had finally drowned her loyalty. She did not want to hurt her parents, but Nimrod had offered an excuse. A temporary revolt would bring much greater benefit. They would understand as soon as the deed was done.

Her smoldering gray eyes held his and offered the promise of pleasure. His poison had done its work. Her entire being was now focused on one aim. No thought of repercussions beyond their sheltered valley could fight past that flaming barrier. Her mind was consumed. No longer a daughter of Noah, she was a woman in love. Nothing mattered except her man. Each embrace, each kiss, each whispered assurance from Nimrod further weakened her will and bound her mind. But one excuse remained. "I can't just run away. My sisters watch me day and night," she stammered. "I am hardly able to find these few moments."

Nimrod sprung his trap. "Then come tonight. As my wife. Home… to me." He bored in on another weakness. "In a few weeks you will see the cities, the markets, the squares, and the people. There you will be a queen. Here, you're a farmer's daughter stranded in the wilderness. A beautiful flower deserves richer soil. Meet me tonight and we will be off."

"But my sisters… they will be with me… I cannot…."

"Hush, my darling." Nimrod placed a finger on her soft lips and offered a gentle smile. "I understand and have a plan. Yesterday I met a friend traveling north. He is a trusted comrade—Korac, son of Magog. When I told him of our plight, he generously offered his help. He is a kind-hearted man who wants your happiness. He will come to your father's home near sundown, feigning sickness. Your mother's skills are well known… everyone will rush to help the poor stranger, and you will have your chance to slip away. Korac has even loaned us one of his horses. We will stay out of reach of your father and his men. A night together will make us married in the eyes of all, even if you choose not to make us one in truth."

He softly kissed her. Feeling the rising passion in her questing lips, he was secretly confident that she would eagerly consummate the bargain, but he also knew it important to offer the illusion of choice. Smiling down into her eyes he continued, "We will return to your house tomorrow morning as the repentant couple. You know your parents. They are kind and full of love. How could they not forgive you and grant a belated blessing? Do they not desire your happiness? I will be a good son."

Mariel smiled tentatively. "It must be nice to have friends outside your family."

"He is your friend too, my beloved. And he will be a welcome guest at our table. You will have ample opportunity to repay your debt."

Mariel bowed her head. To deceive her father… her mother. But the fire inside could no longer be denied. It grew with every kiss. If Nimrod left now, she would be miserable for the rest of her days. She could no longer imagine life without him. She was proud to belong to him. It mattered not that he was less than half her age. At thirty-three he was already the leading man of his generation. As she wavered, he traced a gentle finger down the front of her neck, fanning the flames. "I'll meet you here later? Just before sundown?" The scale tilted. Looking down, she nodded shyly and ran back down the path.

Nimrod smiled broadly as he watched her go.

Nearly blind from the pounding in her heart, Mariel rounded a shed at the back of the yard and nearly ran over Jael, one of her younger sisters, sending her stumbling aside. Terrified that Jael could read her passion and guilt, she turned aside. "Where have you been?" the younger girl demanded crossly.

Mariel put her hands on her hips, feeling a sudden strength. "I don't answer to you, little girl," she sneered. Jael couldn't hide the hurt in her face. Mariel instantly regretted her words, but before she could apologize, her sister strode away in anger.

"Why are things so complicated?" whispered Mariel. "Why did I speak like that?" She sighed. "I'll apologize later, when we've both cooled down."

But the opportunity never came. Instead, events unfolded as Nimrod had foretold. As the sun drew low, Mariel saw a figure riding towards the house. He was doubled over in the saddle and clearly in distress. "Father," she called, "someone's here."

Noah came out of the door. He pushed by her and climbed down from the porch. "Get your mother," he urged, and then strode out to help the stranger... this Korac, Nimrod's friend... and now hers. Soon the man was limping across the porch, his arms doubled around his waist, clearly in pain, allowing Noah to help him to a chair. In spite of his pain, he was clearly a powerful man, and his face was hard and bleak.

"Lay him down here," urged Wen-Tehrom. "Get my herbs! Get a blanket! Get some water! Help with his boots!"

Soon the space around the groaning man was a flurry of activity. Mariel saw her chance and ducked back into the house, gliding out the back door. She was committed now. Her heart beat rapidly as she clutched a few precious belongings to her breast and climbed the path to their tryst. Panting at the excitement as much as the exertion, she heard the jingle of a rein before she saw Nimrod holding a horse. Thick blankets were spread across its back.

"Up with you," he whispered, evidently anxious too. It helped calm her and she giggled as he lifted her up and sprang up behind. "I've left a few false trails," he said in her ear. "We should be fine. But there will be no fire tonight."

"I think I'll stay warm," she laughed coyly. Now that the deed was done, her earlier nervousness had evaporated, and she felt sublimely wanted and loved. She could not wait to come home tomorrow to the tender forgiveness of her parents and the envy of her sisters. She was a woman who had found her man, and even on a horse in the hills, she was as proud as any queen.

Nimrod let his arms press against her sides as he walked the horse up the trail, knowing that even that innocuous touch was feeding the fire within her. He smiled too as they rode, but for reasons that would have horrified Mariel.

4-23-1754

The couple rode down the path with the sun in their eyes and the dew sparkling on the leaves of the plants. It was a glorious spring morning, and though Mariel was anxious, it was nothing compared to her pride. She sat erect and regal in front of her beloved. She would be as remorseful as needed to restore unity to the family, and then she would enjoy the new horizons unfolding in her imagination.

Behind her, a small smile curled Nimrod's lip. The blade was set; it needed only the last sure thrust to slay the image that hovered around the old man. He might be the link to the old world, the hero of the ark, the prophet of the Almighty, a giant among men. But as Debseda had explained, he was only a giant among *mere* men... a pygmy compared to Sechiall, to Debseda, and now to Nimrod—the chosen heir of the spear and destined ruler of this new world. As soon as he rode away in victory today, the news would spread like wildfire.

Noah dethroned. Not by Ham. Not by Canaan. But by the fire of the Nephil burning in the chosen heir.

Shading his eyes, he saw the tableaux on the porch. Noah and his wife slumped together, old and knowing—tasting the first bitterness of their diminished place in the world. The other daughters huddled to one side, knowing their lives had taken a terrible turn, but not quite understanding. Korac—dependable Korac—off to the side, standing relaxed yet in perfect position to stop any foolishness before it started. Physical conflict was the last thing Nimrod wanted today. That was the only reason that he had left the spear behind. He would have to wait to rub *that* in Noah's face!

He stopped the horse at the head of the walk. Sliding down, he looped a rein, and helped Mariel down with a possessive embrace. Her face told her story. She had left an anxious young girl. She returned a confident woman. But that confidence faltered when she saw the stony faces of her parents and the anger of her sisters.

"No welcome, Mother?" she asked brightly, starting to feel her heart sink.

"You fool!" It was the first she had ever heard her mother speak in anger. Real anger. "Your lust has destroyed my family. You are no longer mine! Years will ripen your sorrows and give you ample time to regret your stupidity. I leave you to begin!" With that the older woman simply turned and walked back into her house, pausing in front of Korac.

"You think you cannot feel because you lost your soul," she whispered. "But it is not gone. Only hidden. One day it will find you again. When it does, the consequences of your lost years and especially this day will haunt you, and cost you another loved one. When that day comes, only my children will be able to help you, and they will despise your very name. I could almost pity you that misery."

Korac shrugged, the façade of the injured traveler replaced by his normal harsh impassiveness. But Wen-Tehrom nodded to herself before going inside. She had seen a flicker of his eye and knew her words had struck deep. Korac knew it too, but he took a deep breath and sealed them away. He had other business now.

"M-m-mother," called Mariel after Wen-Tehrom's retreating back. She was now thoroughly confused. Nimrod stood back from her, watching her back and Noah's face. He felt her tremble as doubt seeped through her defenses. He would wait— better to let her feel her isolation before rescuing her, cementing his victory.

Jael's anger had been building since Mariel's disappearance. She understood now the guilty start at the shed yesterday… the harsh words. Her sister's heart had been given to evil even then. But the younger girl had not seen it in time, and she had felt a weighty guilt for her blindness all night; first, as Noah and his men had frantically searched the surrounding hills, and later in the hours of tears shared with her sisters and mother. She didn't remember when Noah had returned, but the picture of him slumped in his chair, unseeing and uncaring, would haunt her for years.

All the sorrow and guilt that had been brewing for hours finally erupted in a rage she was ill-prepared to contain. Her last defenses slipped at the sight of Mariel riding down the front path—exhibiting her wantonness with Nimrod—her face telling the story of her night, and looking as if she expected praise for her sin and for the pain she had inflicted on those who loved her. Now *she* feigned hurt, as though ignorant of all the damage she had wrought. The last restraint fell away and Jael felt a white fury take her.

Spitting her rage, she stepped forward. Her voice was as hard as the brilliant sky, as hot as the morning sun in its glory, and she reveled in the way her words flayed the guilty woman.

"You cheap whore! You sold your soul… your family… your father… For what? Him?" It felt good to voice her scorn, yet it was not enough. Stepping around her sisters, she pushed forward to leap down to the path. In her rage she only wanted to strike and rend. But as quick as she was, she was too slow. Her feet were moving, but she was not—stopped by an iron grip around her upper arms. Shock halted her as much as Korac's hands—no man had ever dared touch her like that! Her body went rigid.

Noah finally acted. He did not move but the face he turned on Korac was one Jael had never seen before. She felt Korac quail and heard the deep authority in his words. "Take your hands off my daughter and leave my home." She felt Korac shrink before the power in those deep brown eyes—old eyes… wise eyes… eyes that had witnessed the destruction of a world and had survived—and she was suddenly free as the profaning hands fell limply away. Cautious, Korac slid around her and vaulted down, backing warily towards Nimrod.

Jael felt her spirits rise. Finally, her father had come to his senses. He would curse Nimrod as he had cursed Canaan, and the power of the Almighty would send him slinking away with his tail between his legs. She stared at Korac, memorizing each feature. She would remember his face and name, never forgetting the insult of his rude touch and rough strength. She swore to herself that no man would ever touch her like that again. Perhaps Noah would call down fire on the offenders.

But her hopes were dashed. The expected storm did not break. Instead, Noah seemed to fade. He sighed and spoke softly. "Take your prize, son of the serpent. The power you think you have gained will remain forever beyond your grasp, blown hither and yon by the breath of the Almighty. Take this woman who is no longer my daughter and leave."

Nimrod smirked openly. "She and I will build a new future, old man. Your generation failed, bringing the great flood. But mine will make a new world—one that will know you as the alien, an unwanted relict."

Noah shook his head with a bitter half smile. "In one thing you are right. This land is not my home." He turned away. Nimrod sneered again and then laughed. He boosted the stunned Mariel back on the horse and leaped up behind her. Korac had retrieved his horse and clattered down the path after them.

Jael wanted to scream… to find a blade and flay them all with her own hands… even that whore that used to be her sister. And that man… *especially* the one who dared to lay hands on her. He would die slowly. She would cut them all into pieces and feed them to the swine.

Her heart hesitated. She felt a moment of choice—sorrow or rage. She was a woman… it should be sorrow. But if her father would not be strong, then she must. She let rage take her, not with any outward display, but with an open heart. She felt it purge the silly emotions that sprang from softness; from the core of her femininity. She could not be a son to her father, but she would carry the burden of one from this day forward.

She felt another hand on her arm and jerked it reflexively away, but this was no enemy. It was her father, and in that brief contact, she felt the beginning of healing. She shook it off. She did not want healing. Not now. Not until Mariel was sitting in ashes, and Nimrod and Korac food for the maggots. Let Ashiel and Sherzala comfort their father… she had work to do. She fled through the house, out across the fields to the barns.

In the loft of one was a bow; an old gift from Shem. His patient instruction was a good memory, but she crushed the sentimentality. It was not a toy, it was a tool— one that could slay Korac and Nimrod. She cared nothing for the good times she had enjoyed with Shem; now she strove to recall his lessons. She would find it, restring it, and relearn that skill. She would practice until she was proficient. Then she would learn how to use a knife, a spear—yes, even her hands and feet if necessary. She would learn to survive and fight in a man's world.

But she couldn't do it alone.

She needed help, and as hard as it was to admit, the best teacher would be her own brother… who, of course, would never consent. Unless… unless his refusal carried a price he could not bear. She quailed for a moment at how he would see her if she forced it that far, but the anger within burned away that regret. What did it matter what anyone thought? She had a task to complete. One day she would meet this Korac and she would kill him. Until then she would be satisfied with killing any others who served Nimrod, and would devote her life to thwarting his will, visiting misery on him and his, just as he had brought misery to her and her family. Things would have to change… many things… but she felt her determination rise up, as cold and hard as iron, and she beat back the weak doubts of womanhood.

As she entered the barn, she felt her skirts tangle around her legs. That too must go. She would wear leggings and boots like a man, bind her breasts, and strengthen her arms. Get rid of every impediment and every weakness. She would learn to run, to ride, to hunt, and to kill… with skill and without remorse. If she was the enemy of Korac and Nimrod, she would need to be trained by the best. There was only one option. She saddled Mariel's best mare. It was small consolation that the first step toward making her sister a widow involved stealing her favorite horse. But it would do for now.

Unaware of Jael's silent vows and unconcerned for Mariel's stifled sobs, Nimrod rode proudly back to the road. Korac rode beside him, a silent yet appreciative audience, as Nimrod recounted his triumph over the old prophet. They turned east and stopped a short way from the farm. He left Mariel on the horse, with Korac to watch her, while he climbed up to his cave and retrieved his spear. His hands caressed its smooth blackness as he held it before him in the sunlight. "A great victory," he whispered to it, "the first of many!"

As he climbed back on the horse, he turned to the still weeping woman. "Silence!" His voice was hard and commanding, a far cry from the gentle whispers of the night before. "Your family will understand their debt to you some day. If not for you, I would have visited your house with this," he shook the spear, "instead of kind words. Because you are my wife, their lives are now sacrosanct. No man would dare harm my family.

The old ways are unfit for a new world. Men must move forward and control the earth. But most are weak and need the strength of true leaders to direct their efforts. Your father surrendered his place. Your brothers refuse it. Even Ham is half-hearted." He laughed. "Why not me? Would you prefer Canaan's rule? I'm sure a night with him would convince you of my superior qualities!"

Mariel shuddered. As she began to realize the enormity of what she had done, her heart froze. He didn't love her; he never had. He had used her to destroy the only ones who did. And she had let it happen. Her mother's words kept echoing in her head. *You are no longer mine. Years will ripen your sorrows.* Her father's face haunted her memory. Broken and bowed, with a weight of too many years and too many heartbreaks… of which she was now another. Fearful, she controlled her sobbing, but the tears streamed silently down her cheeks.

4-29-1754

Madrazi was hanging clothes in the late morning sun. The wind was brisk and fresh—the clothes would dry quickly with the aroma of a spring morning. It was a mixture of freshly turned soil and new growth. Spring had a special scent, just at it had its own shade of green, and its own feeling of newness. Down at the barns she saw Shem and Enoch repairing a fence. The eldest son of Tiras, he had left home when Tiras had succumbed to the allure of Shinar. "I'm good with horses," he told Shem when he arrived at the farm. "And cleaning your stalls is better in God's sight than becoming the leading man of Shinar."

He had cleaned stalls for a time, but advanced far. He had a natural talent with horses, understanding their moods and their care. He quickly became headman over their stock. Within a few years, he began breeding fast, enduring steeds that carried them quickly across the wilderness, and larger, more powerful horses that multiplied the yields of their fields. Turning his back on the evil of his own family, Enoch had become a valued member of theirs, treating Madrazi with special esteem. He would do anything for her, and was constantly anticipating and doing many of her tasks, as well as his own. And there was always a long list of chores to be done… as evidenced by his current work with Shem.

The terror of last month's nightmare had faded and the boys had been gone for two weeks. Before summer's end they would return, hopefully with news of a northern pass. After that, they would all return to the Lake of the Islands—the men to salvage what they could of the growing season, and she to teach the children, and care for their hurts and illnesses. She was humming a jaunty tune, when a raven flew overhead. In an instant a black weight pressed down on her heart. Looking up, she saw a man riding down the hills to the southwest; his exhausted horse barely able to stumble onward at a slow trot.

Madrazi dropped the clothes and ran towards the barn. She arrived just before the rider, who would have fallen from the saddle had Shem not caught him. Enoch seized the reins and began to walk the horse up and down. But her concern was for the man. It was Eli, her young grandson through Asshur. He worked for Noah, learning the care of vineyards and orchards. He was exhausted, dirty, and weak, but it was the horror in his eyes that warned her of the coming news.

"Bring him to the house," she said quietly to Shem. Turning, she gathered her skirts and ran back to the kitchen. With the efficiency of her many years, she set water over the fire, prepared a plate of food, and snapped out orders to the girl cleaning the floor to bring blankets to the main room. She followed her out, lit the lamps, and stoked the fire. Water, warmth, food, and rest—these would renew the boy's strength and comfort his mind.

Within a few hours the boy was asleep. Madrazi stared at Shem, his eyes as red as hers, unable to believe what they had heard. Just seven months before, she had been walking with Mariel by the shore of the lake, watching the sun set in the west and talking of the great flood and its aftermath. How could such a lovely young lady have turned to evil? Shem was equally stunned; he just sat shaking his head, looking from Eli to her, as if she might make the hated message go away.

But Shem was too strong to remain incapacitated. He drew a deep breath and set aside his sorrow, turning to the needs of the moment. "We must hurry. Our parents will be devastated and our sisters in turmoil. Many times Noah and Wen-Tehrom have comforted us; now it is our time to return that blessing."

Madrazi forced her mind back to the practicalities of making such a journey. Who would come? How many wagons would they need? Shem, reading her expression, reached out and caught her hand. "You and I will go alone. That is all that is needed. There are still hours of daylight left. Fix food for the journey while I saddle our horses. We'll take one pack horse and travel light.

Madrazi sighed. She knew exactly what to prepare, but having traveled "light" many times before, she considered all the things that she could *not* bring. A woman who had passed one hundred and sixty-seven years should have some comforts! She sighed again. Shem was right. If their parents were in distress, then they must leave comfort aside and ride as fast as they could.

Night found them well down the path into the rough country to the southwest. Madrazi distracted herself from the ride by pondering the words of Eli. Where was Mariel tonight? Where was Jael? And what would they find at the end of their road? The same questions still haunted her hours later as she rolled up in a blanket and watched Shem's sturdy back as he hunched over the small fire, his bow and quiver near at hand. She began to relax. There were fearsome predators ranging the wilds, but with her husband beside her she felt as safe as if she were in her own bed.

Chapter 4
PAIN OF HEALING

5-7-1754

It was a fine spring day. Already halfway up the sky, the sun bathed the land in warmth, enticing new growth from every green thing. Even the rocky hills away to the south showed life as patches of weeds and shrubs fought to populate their thin soil. Madrazi enjoyed life's renewal as much as anyone, but her thoughts were far from such simple joys this morning.

Just across the river were the outlying fields that marked the boundary of Noah's farm, and the only thing more wearing than the fast ride south had been the anguish of anticipating the chaos at their destination. There had been plenty of time for her imagination to unleash its worst, and for the past days, her fear had been augmented by a premonition of evil that grew as they neared the settlement, like the gathering of storm clouds on the mountain.

Her mind kept picking at the little news they knew. Nimrod's assault. Noah's passivity. Mariel's betrayal. Jael's disappearance. She shuddered at the thought of what they would find. Nimrod might think he was subtle, but she understood his plan. He was too young to understand the deeper threads of acquiring and using power. Debseda's hand clearly was in this evil, yet Madrazi could not help but think something else was there. The more she considered the possibilities, the more she became convinced of it. Facets of this were beyond Debseda; full of evil, but showing a malevolent wisdom that her sister-in-law did not possess.

She took a deep breath. The Creator could turn even evil into good…was not her own past sufficient evidence of that truth? He could, but His ways were always full of mystery, and the pain she sensed ahead was real, as were the remnants of evil. She felt its dark presence as they rode.

Shem shared her tension; he had remained preternaturally alert the entire trip, as if an attacker lay in ambush ahead. It was hard for him not to push the pace, but he knew they would need their strength to restore order to a ravaged house. He tried to ease her burden as much as he could, but Madrazi didn't notice; her heart was focused on the challenge. She sought strength, but found only weakness, and she felt singularly unready for the challenge ahead. But the horses' hooves carried her closer, step by step.

When they arrived, there were no pleasant surprises. It was as bad as she had imagined… maybe worse. No one greeted them when they rode up the path. Leading the horses around to the barns, Shem found Noah wandering the grounds in a daze. Madrazi left him to unpack, set her jaw, and entered the house. It was dingy and dark, with no sign of the girls. She strode down the hall and opened a door. She nearly broke at the sight of Wen-Tehrom, weeping alone in her dim room. Her clothes were rent and her hair dirty and unkempt. She had been a rock during the worst days of the flood, but now looked like a lost soul. She seemed not to notice the intrusion, and her sorrow threatened to swamp Madrazi. So she backed slowly out of the room, needing to assess the rest of the damage.

She finally found the four remaining daughters—Ashiel, Zeriah, Bethsalom, and Sherzala. Having lost the security of their father's invincibility—as well as two sisters—and finding no solace or support from parents who had never failed them before, the girls were too shattered to surpass their half-hearted attempts to take care of the day-to-day necessities. Madrazi took in the situation with a glance. Hardening her heart to the necessity of sharp words, she set them all to work. It was better to exhaust their bodies than to let fear fester. When Ashiel protested, Madrazi silenced her with a glance and sent her on her way. The girls had grown up knowing Madrazi's authority—she was the wife of their eldest brother—so Ashiel closed her trembling mouth and did as she was told.

Madrazi kept her face stiff, hiding the desire to reach out and hug away the pain. Comfort must wait until they had set their home in order. They were adults; they needed to accept that responsibility.

Once they were hard at work, Madrazi slipped out the back door and found Shem walking in the vineyard, head bowed in thought. She slipped her hand in his and joined him. For a time they just walked, gathering strength from the Creator and each other. Finally Madrazi ventured to speak. "I've never seen Mother like this. She's drowning. The girls are bereft—like sheep without a shepherd."

Shem bit his lip and nodded. "Father's just as bad. He walks around, uncaring and unknowing. He speaks, but his mind wanders. All I can get from him is that he blames himself."

Madrazi nodded. "Mother is much the same. Not having the strength yet to deal with her hurt, I had the girls start ordering of the house." She sighed. "One step at a time."

Shem stopped and pulled her to him. "Thank you." His smile was genuine for the first time since Eli had brought the news.

"For what?"

"One problem at a time," he answered. "That was the answer I was seeking. We'll address the easy things first. If the household is functioning smoothly, Mother and Father will at least have familiar and comfortable surroundings as they deal with their grief. You take with the house and I'll get the farm going once more. They haven't even finished the planting!"

Invigorated, he walked quickly towards the smaller homes on the north side of the fields. Madrazi felt her heart lighten as she noted his firm step and straight back. She turned back to begin her own work. As the day passed, their plan bore fruit. The laborers had been uncertain and demoralized. Within hours, Shem's firm hand had restored the routine of plowing and planting. No longer rudderless, they turned to their tasks, confident that the master's eldest son would set things right. Many of them were grandchildren of Shem and Madrazi… it was easy for them to accept their authority in lieu of Noah's.

Madrazi spent much of her time helping inside and keeping her younger sisters hard at work. Once the house was cleaned and aired, she turned their hands to other tasks; she set Bethsalom and Sherzala to washing clothes and hanging them to dry in the afternoon sun. She paused to encourage them with a cheerful word, complimenting their efforts. Inside, Ashiel was busy in the kitchen and sounds of Zeriah's labors came from the front room. A savory stew was bubbling over the fire, and dough was rising on the sideboard.

Madrazi smiled as she stepped around the woman. "This looks much better. Do you need any help with the evening meal?"

Ashiel pushed back her thick brown hair, glanced at the table, hesitated, and forced a smile. "How many places…?" She couldn't finish. Madrazi caught her hands and pulled her close.

"Be strong, little sister. You are the eldest now, and need to be a rock for the others. Set for seven; I will serve Mother."

Ashiel shuddered for a moment and pulled back, wiping a tear from her eye. "Do you… can you… will she…?" She shook her head and looked pleadingly at Madrazi.

Madrazi laid a hand on her cheek. "Be of good cheer, Ashiel. The Creator has not abandoned your house, in spite of the evil that has come upon you. It will turn to good… just keep your heart pure and encourage your sisters. Shem and I will stay until all is restored. Do not take burdens on yourself that you cannot bear."

Ashiel looked down. "You know everything, don't you?"

"Of course not," snorted Madrazi. "But I know a little of anxious hearts. I've had a *few* more decades than you to understand them."

"A few?" Ashiel's grin was suddenly genuine and Madrazi's heart went out to her. She was trying so hard. But it faded as a shadow fell across her eyes. "Madrazi? I… I…."

"Shhh." Madrazi pulled her close. "Tell me your grief."

Ashiel shuddered in her arms, sniffling back the tears. "I… Jael was the only one who opposed them. I was older and said nothing. I'm such a coward. How can I be strong for the others?"

Madrazi just held her close for a time. Finally she led her to the table. "Sit." She went to the pantry and brought out a wineskin and poured a cup. Ashiel drained it quickly and Madrazi poured another. Sipping slowly, Ashiel would not look up.

Madrazi sighed. "Look at me, Ashiel!" The younger woman finally met her eyes, tears brimming in their brown softness. "You did nothing wrong! It was not your place to oppose warriors, nor was it Jael's. Don't compound her sin by thinking you should have done the same. Mariel made a choice, as did Father. I do not understand either, but in Noah's case, I bow to his wisdom. If you want to be strong for your family, put your doubts aside and help me restore your home. That will take far more courage than Jael showed. Can you find it?"

"You… you really think…?" The shadow hovered at the back of her eyes, but a new light was growing in them.

"I'm sure." Madrazi held her eyes intently. "That battle was not yours, so it was not a true test of your heart. This is… can you meet your challenge?"

The shadow shrank and Ashiel raised her head, her eyes now clear. "Thank you, Madrazi. I will do my best. Just be mindful of my weakness."

"Hmmmph." Madrazi let her own smile show. "I'll be more mindful of your insinuation of my tender years!"

Ashiel laughed, a pure unsullied sound that seemed to transform the kitchen. Warmth and love rushed into the room, and Madrazi felt her first stirring of relief. "Tender?" Ashiel had a look of innocent mischief now. "Why, I thought you were older than the mountains or the seas."

Madrazi shook her head, showing just enough exasperation. Rising, she looked down at her little sister. "Let's just say I'm old enough to know how to deal with children like you."

Ashiel laughed again, and imitated a young child. "Oh Aunt Madrazi… can I fetch you a walking stick to help you into the other room?" She skipped over to the fire and stirred the stew. "I hope this is soft enough for your gums."

Madrazi stuck out her tongue. "Perhaps I should have Shem cut a switch…."

"Does he still beat you?" The shadow was gone. Life had returned to this one.

Madrazi gathered her courage. It was time to see to Wen-Tehrom. As she reached the door, she turned back to Ashiel. "Why don't you ask him?"

Ashiel giggled. "I might at that!"

Later that evening, Madrazi strengthened herself with the memory of that pure laughter. She needed every resource she could find. For hours Wen-Tehrom barely acknowledged her presence. Finally she began to talk… rambling incoherently. Then as her mind cleared, bitterness poured out, and she castigated herself. Late into the night Madrazi battled those demons of despair and those minions of evil lurking just beyond sight, praying for the angels of the Almighty to banish them from the valley.

It was very late and Madrazi was exhausted before the older woman would converse rationally and her words were tinged with bitterness. But Madrazi was patient, addressing each one with words of wisdom and love. It was hard… as each layer of anguish was stripped away, another was revealed, with a surge of emotion that flared like a new fire. Madrazi beat them back with every resource at her disposal until, at the edge of collapse, she heard the words that revealed the core of the older woman's heart.

"If only I had given him more sons," Wen-Tehrom sobbed. "Oh, why could I not give him a son to take Ham's place? A brother would have protected my poor Mariel." Madrazi cradled her weeping mother, stroking her matted hair until the weeping subsided. Then she brought the ravaged face to her own and kissed each cheek. Then she looked into the red-rimmed eyes and held them in her own, willing strength across that link. "A wise woman once told me to live my own life, not that of the Creator. He gives sons or daughters. Every child is His gift, and there are four beautiful women right here who need you."

Wen-Tehrom started to protest, but Madrazi held her gaze and shook her head. "You know this is true, even if your heart weeps. What if you had a son? If Nimrod slew him and took Mariel, your heartache would be double, and Mariel a murderer as well as a fool." She shook her head. "Come back to me, Mother! You have a husband and four daughters who need you. You have two other sons who want your love. There is purpose at work here. Maybe it will be manifest tomorrow, maybe a thousand years from now. You need not worry about that… you know the love behind it all. Rest in that, and be healed."

"But my Jael… what of my little Jael?" whispered the older woman. Her hand caught Madrazi's wrist with frantic strength.

Madrazi gripped it and replied solemnly. "Shem and I will find her. I swear it. Let it go. Sleep, now! May the peace of our Maker guard you. As He brought us through the deep waters, He will see you safely through this."

Finally Wen-Tehrom drifted into restful sleep, and Madrazi spent the few remaining hours of the night huddled in a chair in the corner of her room, praying peace into the old woman. In the morning, her eyes were clear, but tinged with a sadness that Madrazi suspected would never be entirely absent. It would have to do.

"What do I do?" she asked.

"Let's start with a bath. It always makes me feel better!" With Ashiel's help, she bathed her mother, letting the hot water and fragrant oil leach away the evil of the past days. Ashiel's barely contained joy at seeing her mother responding once more hastened the healing, and many tears mingled with that bathwater.

The sight of four cheerful and hardworking daughters, a clean home, and the occasional sound of Sherzala's sweet music fanned the spark of life. By the end of that day, Wen-Tehrom was walking with Madrazi, hand in hand through the freshly plowed fields, enjoying the scent of fresh earth. Love was beginning to resume its normal flow throughout the house, and mother and daughter fed off that comfort.

"Shem is helping father with the work," Madrazi began.

Wen-Tehrom snorted. "We both know that Shem is doing the work, daughter. My husband is deeply wounded; a dagger of pain and alienation has been plunged into his back—and by his own child. He is old, but wise enough to know what happened…what really happened… as are you.

Madrazi sighed her agreement as her mother continued, "His loss was great. One daughter is no more and another is lost in the wilderness. But worse, he knows now that the honor he held as the father of all—that reservoir of power that could be wielded when the need was most desperate—is gone. He is no longer the patriarch of mankind; he is an impotent symbol of the power of the new evil. Nimrod is his child, but an ungrateful child is a curse on a man in his last years."

"He has lost nothing with those who love him. Nor has he lost the honor of the only One who matters," said Madrazi, more sharply than she intended. "He faced a terrible choice. The temptation to strike must have been terrible, but the Creator stayed his hand. I know not why… I cannot even guess. But as hard as it is to face such a choice, he must rest in wisdom greater than his own."

Wen-Tehrom nodded, but her face was sad. "I know you're right… I just hope he will come to accept it. It is a bitter truth." She sighed heavily. "What of Jael?"

With the workers restored to their tasks, and the planting proceeding, Shem had been searching the surrounding countryside for signs of his little sister. It was a hard task; she had taken a horse and was many days distant. As if in answer to Wen-Tehrom's question, the women saw him ride over the low hill that marked the floodplain of the river. Madrazi tugged on the older woman's robe. "Let's meet him at the barn and see what news he brings."

When he saw them, Shem shook his head. "Inside," he grunted. "I don't want to tell this more than once."

After they had eaten, Shem pushed back his chair and sighed. Everyone was looking at him—they had been the entire meal. Finally he spoke. "I found traces of her trail further out. It's steady to the northeast; I think she's making for our home." Madrazi looked at the others… everyone was equally surprised.

Shem nodded. "I think it best that we return and renew the search with my men. She's probably closer to the mountain by now. I think we'll find her faster if we search from there."

Madrazi had thought they would stay for days, but her oath to Wen-Tehrom drove her to agree with Shem. Jael was in danger. They must leave. A momentary wave of self-pity swamped her; then she thought of the young girl, alone in a wilderness full of savage beasts. She prayed that Mariel would not add her sister's life to her sin.

Madrazi surveyed her saddled horse with a grimace. Another week atop the beast was distinctly unappealing, but necessary. It was still the gray half light before dawn. Shem had driven her up early, and she wondered if he had slept at all. All had risen to see them off, and she had embraced each of them in turn, whispering words of love with her farewell. Ashiel had wrapped herself in a cloak and insisted on accompanying them to the barns. Shem was tightening the ropes on the packhorse.

Ashiel shivered in the morning cool, not saying anything, but clearly wanting to. Madrazi caught her to her breast and kissed her cheeks and forehead. "Be brave, little one. You have a joy that illumines those around you. Now learn wisdom and be a rock for your parents and sisters."

"What of Jael?" she asked.

"If God preserves her life, we will find her and restore her to you."

"Then I'll be praying that it will be sacred in His sight." She leaned forward once more before Madrazi could mount. Shem was busy giving last minute instructions to the foreman. She looked down at the ground, embarrassed. "Thank you for helping me find courage. I needed your assurance. I love you so much!"

Madrazi blinked back her tears. "You're a worthy woman, Ashiel. You will need strength, but your spirit knows where to find it. You have much to give… be free with your sisters." The younger woman nodded and drew herself up. "You can count on me." There was a firmness there that Madrazi had never seen before. Releasing the younger woman, but keeping an arm around her shoulder, she turned to the foreman. "If you have any problems, listen to her."

The man just stared at the two women, but seeing Shem nod slightly, he sighed and smiled. "Change is difficult, my lady. But we must live the days as they come. It will be as you say." Ashiel blushed, but straightened her shoulders. She stood in the yard, waving, until Madrazi could see her no more.

Chapter 5
PATHS TO THE FUTURE

5-10-1754

Mariel sat listless on the horse, trying to ignore the pressure of the arms around her waist. She despised her weakness for enjoying the pleasure, hating her body for its betrayal. *But why not*, she thought to herself? *As the soul, so the body. I'm a traitor and an outcast. So why can't I just embrace my fate with this man? Why do I hate him so... yet want him so?* Those thoughts raced through her mind, exhausting her will. Over the past days, a black despair had begun to creep in. *Why have a will if you can't trust it. I hate myself!*

She looked dully ahead. As usual, Korac was riding a few hundred cubits ahead. She appreciated that small mercy—it limited the universe of her shame. Nimrod's hands began to wander. Two weeks ago, it had thrilled her. Two days ago, it had angered her. Now she didn't care. Let him do what he would with her body... she was better off dead. *How I have fallen! Once the eldest daughter of the new Adam, I'm now the plaything for the new Cain.* She pulled her makeshift veil closer, trying to keep the sun off her face, and giving her at least an illusion of modesty.

They were out of the hills and well out onto the plain, following the Tigris south. Many times in the past three days she had wished for the courage to throw herself into those dark waters and end her misery. For a time, a spark of the old Mariel contemplated killing Nimrod in his sleep, but one of the men was always alert... besides, she had no idea how to do it. She no longer thought about it much. Instead, she thought of ways to end her own life. She wanted to, but lacked the courage. On top of her other sins, she was a coward.

Jael had been right. She was nothing but a cheap whore. From the moment she had realized the extent of her sin, the evil she had wrought hounded her day and night. It was becoming easier to sink into an uncaring apathy, and let her thoughts wander far from her body.

Her long, light brown hair—once a source of pride—was dirty and tangled. Her clothes were tattered and she had none of her possessions—Nimrod had casually discarded them on the road—and her body was dirty. But that was as it should be... she deserved dirt, discomfort, and danger: she deserved nothing from her father's house. Her parents had cast her out. Only in the past weeks did she realize how much she missed the simple habits of home: careless banter with her sisters, household chores with her mother, the quiet comfort of her father's presence. She had never appreciated what kind of man he was... it took the company of an egotistical liar like Nimrod and a soulless killer like Korac to see Noah in his true light. Why had she not understood his depths of wisdom and kindness? She had been the daughter of a stately lion; now she was the plaything of a jackal. She wondered once more why he had not acted in the face of Nimrod's provocation, suspecting that the reason was far beyond her understanding—some insight from the Creator that only Noah or Shem's wife could comprehend.

Guilt compounded despair. Deep in her heart, she knew her first offense to be against the Creator. She missed the quiet morning walks, praying and singing. She would never be able to enjoy those hours of sublime peace again. How could a just God bear to hear any word from the lips of a betrayer of kin, of a fool who had sold her soul for a fleeting passion? She abhorred herself. This body—a source of pride for many years—had become a bitter prison for her soul.

"Cheer up, woman!" came the hated voice. "We can't have you coming to Shinar looking like a bedraggled slave girl. You will be a queen, and must impress the lower sorts. Men will bow to you and women will envy you. A line of superior men will descend from your body. Soon we'll have you looking more presentable."

Mariel let a tear slide down her cheek. Her shame would be public. Others might bow and smile out of fear of her husband, but behind closed doors they would laugh at her… mock her… revile her treachery. And her future companions? Canaan, Cush, Put, Mizraim—enemies of her parents and sisters. She had once enjoyed the gentle grace of Yaran or the serene enchantment of Madrazi; now she would know the wicked spite of Debseda. She had never met her but knew the story of her perfidy aboard the ark… and after. It would be horrible, but what she deserved… shouldn't she embrace a fellow traitor?

A shout from ahead pulled her back to her surroundings. She saw the green line marking a tributary. Large herds speckled the dusty green of pastures on the low hills of its banks. Nimrod slid down from the tired horse and strode ahead, pulling it along. At least she no longer had to endure his touch. Ahead she saw a line of smoke—an encampment… her fate. *Years will ripen your sorrow.*

Her mother was wrong. It had taken only days.

Time slid by as she retreated into herself. She felt the horse stop and looked up. A large tent stood before her, with smaller ones scattered here and there. Three women stood in front of the tent; menace flowed from them, heightened by the facelessness of their veils. Standing in a line, they formed a barrier of matching blue robes—their cleanliness mocking her bedraggled condition.

One stepped forward. For a moment Mariel wondered if it was Debseda… she was short and her skin was olive. But she realized her error when the woman bowed to Nimrod. "We are instructed to make her ready, my Lord."

Mariel shivered at the coldness in the voice, but Nimrod lifted her down. "This is Celota, a friend of my grandmother," he said, and Mariel's ears picked up the odd inflection of 'friend.' "And these are her companions, Graemea and Oshetipin. I'm sure you'll become well acquainted with them in the days to come." He laughed and strode off.

Mariel said nothing, and allowed the three to herd her into the back of the tent. Graemea picked up a neat stack of clothing and led her out a flap in the back. "Hot water we cannot offer, but the river is clean and no man will interrupt." She led Mariel down the bank. Rock steps had been laid into the water and wooden benches held soap and oils. Mariel hesitated. "Come along, girl," snapped Celota. "We're all women here. There's a stone bench in the river bed. Come sit and soak away the dust of the road." She pushed Mariel forward. "Oshetipin, wash her hair!"

Clean and clothed an hour later, Mariel had to admit she felt better. The women were odd. Graemea and Oshetipin were friendly enough, but with an undercurrent of contemptuous curiosity. Oshetipin seemed the simplest of the three, and Celota the most dangerous. But the simple pleasures of being clean, of feminine contact, and of a cup of strong wine eased her tension and allowed her to ignore Celota. She had even managed a smile—her first in days.

Soon, she heard a disturbance at the tent's entrance and the three women scrambled to their feet before bowing low. Mariel tensed; she expected Nimrod and did not want him anywhere near her. But it was not a man who entered. Mariel had only heard descriptions, but the face and figure of Ham's wife were unmistakable. For a moment, she thought to remain seated, but some power in Debseda's bright blue eyes brought her slowly to her feet, though she refrained from joining the others in a bow. A shiver passed up her spine. This woman was no longer her older sister; she was Nimrod's grandmother and thus her new matriarch. That authority seemed to flow from her, suppressing any incipient revolt.

A long silence followed while the sharp gaze probed her soul. She tried to meet Debseda's eyes, but could not. Hot guilt irrationally flared inside, even though her mind tried to tell her that the eyes accusing her now had probably plotted the entire episode. But in a strange place among strangers, that inner voice faltered and a flush rose to her face.

Debseda, sensing the victory, finally broke the silence. "I see my girls have taken care of your needs. It's good to have a home, and it seems that you will be sharing mine for some time." Mariel felt the weight of those words; she had nowhere else to go. Having thrown away an idyllic past, she faced a bleak future. *How could I have been so foolish?* Whatever she faced now was her own fault, and the guilt hurt even more than even the prospect of life under this woman's thumb.

Debseda seemed to ignore her inner turmoil. "We are all thrilled, if somewhat surprised, by Nimrod's choice, but he cannot stop talking about how you won him over, even after your father had turned him away." She saw her arrow drive home and lightened her voice. "A lot of women in Shinar are going to be jealous when we return."

Mariel quailed. It sounded as if she would need an armed guard just to walk to the market.

"Oh, you will be safe enough," laughed the older woman, reading her thoughts. "No one in possession of their senses would dare insult my grandson's chosen." She walked closer and around Mariel, who stood frozen in fear. She flinched as a hand stroked her hair and then slid down her back. "A beautiful trophy for Nimrod. All you need do, my child, is give him sons and your… devotion." The hand traced the top of her hip before sliding away.

Mariel struggled to contain her revulsion at the touch. One moment it felt almost sensuous; the next, like a proud owner admiring a prize cow. Both repelled the girl as she struggled to keep her thoughts to herself and listen to Debseda's words. "But those things are easily granted to hundreds of husbands by hundreds of wives. You should be able to follow their example. Especially since he's all you have."

Mariel felt the moisture in her eyes. Her mind replayed the angry words of her mother. *You are no longer mine!* It was as if Debseda could see her innermost thoughts, using them to hammer any residual courage into the dust. It would be easier to simply withdraw and watch her mother's prophecy come to pass. But she could not. It was her nature to live and to grow. It could not be denied. True, it would bring more pain, but at least she would still be feeling something, and she recoiled from becoming a shell of a woman. She must do something… say something.

Gathering her courage, she spoke. "Your hospitality is welcome after such a harsh journey, and feminine companionship is a welcome change from the silent Korac. Even Nimrod is a bit much when all he can offer is weary days on a horse."

Debseda stopped and looked up into her face, her lips twisting into what could be a smile or a sneer. Mariel re-gathered herself and forged on. "I look forward to establishing my own house, where my husband and my children can find comfort and peace. A haven from the cares of the world."

Debseda laughed out loud. "Very well, little one. You build your home. Just remember that your husband has other commitments," she gave a slow turn, letting one hand slide down her side to an out-thrust hip, daring the younger girl to say anything else. Mariel could not hide the brief look of disgust and amazement, and Debseda smiled again at another victory. She had expected more fire from Noah's daughter. Perhaps Nimrod had taken more from the girl than she had expected. She stepped up to Mariel and laid a hand on her cheek. "I can't wait to help you with your household," she purred. There was no doubt who was in charge. Mariel dropped her eyes and her voice was dull as she replied, "I'm sure your aid will be invaluable."

"Good!" Debseda patted her cheek before letting her hand drop. "You can start by serving your husband and his friend tonight. Celota!" she turned to the shortest of the three. "Make sure our new bride is ready. We'll eat at sundown."

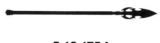

5-10-1754

Though his feet stood on the bare rock of the heights, Shelah could see the dark green of pine forests that mantled the lower elevations. Only the heights were bare rock or ice; much of the country was pleasantly lush and fertile. Beasts and birds abounded; an eagle was circling the valley ahead. And the pass they had crossed the previous week was passable for men or animals. Only winter would close it. Down to their left, the river valley they would follow to the north flowed around the shoulder of the mountain. It was a spectacular view, but best of all, they had found a way through.

He grinned at the others. "We'll look for alternate paths when we return. Right now, I want to see what the lands to the north are like."

"I agree," growled Heth. "Let's get down to the river now. It's cold up here! Why don't you take Ashkenaz and slip over there," he pointed a little east of the direct path to the river. "We could use some fresh meat. Look for our fire."

"Any preferences," asked Shelah with a grin. "We can offer mountain goat, mountain sheep, or maybe a thin hare."

"How about a fat bear," joked Jobaath. "Ash can find one, get it mad, run fast, and lead it to your bow."

"Anam's faster," retorted Ashkenaz.

"But he's too small to be appetizing," returned Jobaath. "Besides, the way you smell right now, any reasonable bear would think you an oversized, two-legged goat."

"As opposed to a fat sloth like yourself." Ashkenaz wasn't ready to let him have the last word. "If a bear stalked you, he'd end up dying from laughter!"

"Children," Shelah aped Shem's 'teaching' voice perfectly, "We'll try for something a little smaller. If you want a bear," he looked at Jobaath, "then just kill one with your knife."

"A knife," Jobaath sputtered. I know Shem has shown you wonders he's withheld from us, but pray tell how one kills a bear with a knife?"

"Easy," grinned Heth. "Just jump down its gullet and stab to the front. The heart's halfway to the stomach!"

The others laughed as Shelah led Ashkenaz away. Heth and Jobaath shouldered the extra packs and Anam led them down toward the river. Smaller and more agile than the others, he was hard pressed to carry the loads of the larger men—Jobaath carefully, but the massive Heth with little effort. Anam longed for Heth's strength—his arm was easily as large as Anam's thigh—and the respect it brought the big man. Being the smallest, weakest, and youngest member of the group led to some rugged humor, though Shelah kept it from getting out of hand.

Nightfall found the five united again, with a steaming haunch twisting back and forth over the fire. Jobaath was enjoying the tale of Shelah's kill. "It was two hundred cubits, downhill, through some brush," Ashkenaz bragged. "I would never have tried the shot, but before I could advise him, Shelah had already loosed his arrow. Right through the spine at the back of the neck—a shot Shem would be proud to claim!"

Shelah laughed. "Shem would have waited for a gust of wind to make it challenging." Everyone laughed with him. All had seen Shem shoot, and all knew they would never approach his uncanny skill.

"What now?" asked Anam.

Everyone looked to Shelah. "The game is plentiful," he mused. Grabbing a burnt stick from the fire, he used the black tip to draw a rough outline on the rock. "The Black Sea is over to the west, the Qazvin Sea to the east. We'll be out of the mountains in two or three days. Heth and I will go east and explore the coast of the Qazvin, and the rest of you can bend west and see what things look like near the Black Sea. A month out and a month back should give us a good picture of the lands between the seas north of the mountains, and perhaps a clue to which way to push on our next trip."

"That's an ambitious plan," remarked Jobaath. "Do we have that much time?"

"If I had my way," answered Shelah, "We'd take a year and follow the lands to far mountains, finding paths that others will follow for hundreds of years. I want to be the first to walk new lands; to see their hills, streams, forests, and vales." His eyes shone in the firelight.

"As much as we might like to join you," responded Anam with a touch of sarcasm, "we have a job to finish. I don't think your grandparents would approve."

"Oh, Shem would understand, but you're right about Grandmother. She can get a mite touchy when you make her worry." The others laughed. "Of course, she also has the sweetest smile while she's telling you what an idiot you are."

"And you would know!" injected Jobaath. Everyone laughed harder.

Shelah joined them. "It's been too many times for you to count... but then, that's just the number of your fingers and toes."

"Nope," Ashkenaz kept a serious face, "Jobaath hasn't made it to toes yet!"

Gradually the banter faded, and large strips of hot meat helped quiet them. Shelah, kept the first watch, hanging the other haunch to cook during the nigh. By morning, they would have an ample supply—one that should last them out onto the plains. The others settled into their blankets, smoothing the thin sand and removing stray rocks to make more comfortable beds. The night closed in on them, but the glittering stars above called to Shelah. He wanted nothing more than to follow them to the ends of the new earth.

He sighed. Perhaps one day....

Chapter 6
FOUND AND LOST

5-16-1754

The seven days home passed as a few hours for Madrazi. Whether it was weariness, worry, or simply grace, the trip was little more than a blur of riding. She slept like the dead at night and dozed on her horse during the day, regaining strength from her ordeal with Wen-Tehrom. "I can't wait to sleep in my own bed," she muttered to Shem as they rode across the outer fields in the late morning sun.

"How would you tell the difference?" he asked innocently, kicking his mount ahead to dodge her pungent answer.

But the moment of humor vanished quickly enough. Though Madrazi would have given anything for a hot bath and soft bed, the search for Jael took precedence, and Shem began making preparations as soon as they dismounted in the yard. While Enoch took the horses into the barn, Shem gathered the men, setting out that afternoon. Madrazi's heart sank down to the dust; as she stood watching the men ride up the west road, she suddenly realized that they had left much of the plowing and planting. Now, the women and children would have to work twice as hard.

She had been so distracted by the past weeks that she had not given a thought to the work that faced her, and it was a crushing blow. After the luxury of a few private tears, she dried her eyes, organized the women and children, and got to work. She understood what was needed, but it had been long decades since she had done the actual work. They could not match the men's strength, and this year's harvest would be small at best. To compensate, she drove herself relentlessly. They worked until dark that day, knowing that they would be back in the fields before the sun tomorrow. Exhausted, sleep skipped out of reach as her mind kept worrying about Shem and Jael, or the plots of Nimrod and Debseda. Finding her distant and tense in the morning, the women whispered among themselves, wondering what new ills waited.

But they had faith in their matriarch, and understood her moods well enough to set worry aside. For twelve days they pushed past the point of exhaustion, Madrazi more than most. But even the pleasant surprise of planting more fields than expected failed to lift her spirits. It was no joke to hold a plow steady behind the oxen—it took two women to do the work of one man, and only long, hard hours held down the difference. Madrazi stayed in the fields from sun to sun, taking the hardest tasks. Despite the effort, she remained fearful for Jael. Was she dead?

On the thirteenth day, she was finishing the last corner of the westernmost wheat field when she looked up and saw the small cavalcade coming down the road. Even in the distance, she could make out the smaller figure beside Shem. It was like the rising of the sun for her heart. Dropping the seed, she sprinted across the fresh soil, scrambled over the fence, and ran down the path to the barn. Others saw her and the excitement flashed from field to field, and soon all were gathered for the return of the men. With the excited cries of joy, Madrazi finally felt the tensions of the past weeks melt away. But a dark corner of her heart warned her that they had not seen the extent of the damage Nimrod had wrought.

She shook it off. Shem was home! She smiled, wanting to give her husband the welcome he deserved. But as the horsemen rode up to the barn, her smile faltered. Shem's face—usually calm and composed—was hard and tight. She recognized the raging anger behind it and her heart sank. The reason sat beside him—the wild-eyed creature was not the Jael she remembered. An untamed thing of the wastelands, her hair was hacked off, her body tense, and her eyes dark with rage.

Madrazi stepped forward, but could not avoid her shock at the girl's appearance. She wore the leggings and tunic of a man… in public. Her face was reddened by the sun and her once-beautiful long hair was unevenly short, as if cut by a knife. A bow hung from her shoulders and her face proclaimed iron defiance. Her green eyes were icy windows to a cold and bitter anger. Madrazi felt her own rage rise in response as the discouragement of the past weeks began to bubble up.

But she reined it in at once. Anger would only magnify the problem. So she schooled her expression and welcomed the girl as if nothing were wrong. Flashing a warning look to her husband, she held out a hand. "Come with me, Jael, and let's get you cleaned up. The men can see to your horse." But even those innocuous words triggered an explosion.

"I can take care of my own animal!" flashed the girl. "As well as any man!" She spat out the last word and her dark look spoke volumes of her opinion of the men around her.

Madrazi caught her eyes and held them. "I did not say you could not." Her voice stayed level, but Jael shrank back at the power in that quiet reproof. Before she could rally, Madrazi pressed on. "These men have given much to bring you to my house. They have wives and children who missed them, and had to do their work… hard work. They deserve your thanks." Her voice then hardened. "And, young lady, you will respect my home."

Jael stared at her with narrowed eyes. Madrazi had imbued her words with all the authority she could muster as the wife of Jael's eldest brother, and the message was clear—the mistress of this house would brook no disrespect. Beneath the cold anger in the girl's eye, Madrazi discerned a desire; Jael wanted something. That was her one advantage. She said nothing more, but her own eyes made it clear that Jael would get nothing if she antagonized her sister. The men sat uncomfortably—their horses suddenly uneasy at the tension crackling between the two women. Finally, Jael looked down. She slid off the horse, tossing the reins to Shem.

"Zeb needs a few minutes of your time," Madrazi told Shem with a meaningful glance. Zeb was their most reliable messenger and would carry the news of Jael's safe return back to Noah and Wen-Tehrom.

Shem understood at once. "Of course, my love," he returned. "I may be a few hours. I also need to inspect the fields." His twisted smile told Madrazi that he understood her desire for time alone with Jael, but that he did not like it.

"Come, Jael," ordered Madrazi, gathering herself. "Walk with me." She offered her hand to the younger woman who hesitated, but then took it and let herself be led briskly up towards the house. The hand told Madrazi even more. It was already calloused and hard, and it felt like a bar of iron. A very cold, hard one.

A bath, some food, and some very potent wine sent the exhausted girl into a deep sleep. Then Madrazi checked her for wounds and vermin, cursing Nimrod under her breath. Noah had built a haven. His home had been a shadow of Eden—a refuge from all that was wrong in this new world. His fields and orchards were richer than any others and his daughters cheered the hearts of travelers.

Now it had all been ruined by an evil man and a wayward woman. She could see the echo of that ruin in Jael's face… even in sleep, it remained hard and bitter. As she stood there, staring at the husk of what had been a lovely young lady, tears seeped down her cheeks.

It was too much. She escaped to the meadow to pour out her complaint before the Creator. Shem found her walking with her young dog Saul. He fell in beside her, taking her hand, allowing their love to calm them both. As the emotions ebbed, Shem began to relate his story.

"We searched the lands southwest but didn't pick up her trail. We had to move west to find sign. She had wandered more north than northeast, and it was the seventh day before we caught her." He shook his head and laughed, "She had that old bow I gave her years ago. She was killing hares and squirrels, though only God's angels kept her from the lions, wolves, and bears."

He sighed and rolled his head to stretch his neck. Madrazi took the hint. "Sit down," she instructed, and she knelt behind him and began kneading the muscles in his upper back and shoulders. Shem sighed his gratitude and continued his story. "She was as you saw her and would say nothing of her flight. She was consumed with rage—worse than today—and would let no man but me near her. Some great fear lies at the root of this. I don't understand it… I don't think she does either."

He sighed again. "She was always so full of life and joy. It rends my heart to see that destroyed. We must heal her."

"Let her rest; then we can begin," Madrazi replied.

But sleep changed nothing. Her first words after a strained morning meal enraged Shem. "I came to you because you are the best," she said. "I want to learn to ride, to run, to shoot, to hunt, and to survive the wilderness... better than any man."

"You can't," replied Shem with an obvious effort to restrain his wrath. "You're not a man. God made you for other things. You lack strength and endurance."

"Is every man strong? Is every man fast? Does every man have the eye to put an arrow on the mark at a hundred paces?" Jael's sneer was certainly that of a man, thought Madrazi.

The girl continued. "Few men are natural warriors… otherwise they would need less time training." She drew herself upright. "All I want is the chance to show you I can learn."

Madrazi watched the vein in her husband's neck. Despite his neutral face, she could see it throbbing. Jael was moments away from a memorable explosion, but could not read the warning signs. She just kept on.

"After all, if I'm just a weak woman," she purred, "you shouldn't fear to teach me. You would only be afraid if you thought I might succeed." She cocked her head and gave him a thin smile. "Is that what you fear, brother?"

Her last jab was the last straw. Shem exploded. He stood, towering over her. "What I fear, little fool, is the wrath of God and of my father! How else should they respond to my corrupting what is good and beautiful in you?"

"You need not fear." She was not intimidated. "Nimrod, Father, and Mariel have already taken care of that!"

"You dare blame Father for what happened?" Shem's voice was low and menacing. Madrazi tried to interrupt, but Jael was too quick. "Yes!"

Shem stood abruptly. For the first time in their life together, Madrazi heard him scream in anger. Like a sudden thunderstorm, his anger broke and flooded the room. But Jael sat on the edge of her chair, hard and silent—impervious to her brother's wrath. Madrazi sat silent, too—it was too late for reason. Finally—with an obvious effort—Shem brought himself back under control. He stared balefully at the wayward girl. "I would cut off my hand before I would do what you ask."

Jael remained unmoved. She just shrugged. "Then I'll find someone else. I'll pay any price… any! I thought my own brother would want to prevent that." She spoke easily, as if discussing the weather or a meal. Shem's face darkened again and another torrent of words rushed over Jael, still leaving her unfazed. Madrazi let Shem's anger run its course and watched the girl closely. She was unmoved even by Shem's threat to bind her and take her home.

"I'll just run off again," she replied easily.

"You'll find only death… or worse." Shem's voice was growing hoarse.

"It's worth the risk to me," she replied. Her face was white, but hard as a stone. "But, of course, you will always wonder why you did not prevent it." Madrazi saw that shot strike home as Shem sagged back into his chair, and she quickly intervened.

"Why?" She spoke quietly, but in that moment Jael's self control slipped a little and Madrazi seized her advantage. She held the girl's eyes. "Being a student is not simply taking from a teacher. Since students cannot repay knowledge with knowledge, they must give of themselves—a part of their heart as a reward for what they gain. To ask my husband to teach you without sharing your soul is unjust and unworthy."

For the first time, Jael's brittle facade slipped. "You will do it?" she asked in a small voice.

Madrazi silenced Shem with a look and leaned forward. "You know that we seek only the will of the Creator. We will not sin in this, nor allow you to multiply yours, but I promise you this: if you will answer my questions honestly, I will seek a vision to guide us. If God so wills, we will petition your parents to place you under our care, and Shem will do as you request. But you *will* obey the commands of the

Creator, or you will be to us all like your sister. Is that what you want?" Jael recoiled at the suggestion, shocked that she might be thought no better than Mariel.

Madrazi saw it and softened her voice. "We love you, Jael, and you know it even as you harden your heart. We will not stand idly by and watch you destroy your soul. How could we? You are our sister."

Madrazi saw the war in Jael's eyes. The old Jael did not return, but some of the bitterness finally dissipated. "Ask your questions," she finally agreed in a flat voice.

It was a hard hour for all three; Madrazi and Shem had to drag each word from the young woman. They fought to contain their anger, sorrow, and despair as the story of Mariel's foolish betrayal unfolded again. Tears flowed, but none from Jael. She was beyond weeping. But through her own tears, Madrazi noticed a flicker of rage in Jael's eyes at several points, and she unerringly homed in on its cause.

"Tell me more of this Korac," she demanded. Jael flinched, then stiffened. "He is an evil tool of Nimrod; a man without a soul. His eyes are empty and hard, and he…" Madrazi interrupted with a raised hand.

"And he laid hands on you, took your innocence, and put this evil into your heart."

Jael recoiled visibly at Madrazi's insight. The dam broke, and rage spilled out in every word. "My father had three sons. They helped him in his quest to escape the old world. Afterward, one rebelled, and the others have followed their father…." She paused only a moment before letting the bitterness spew again. "They follow him in living in the past and ignoring injustice. Men like Nimrod should be destroyed, yet he lives to destroy the lives of others. Men like Korac should be sent to face the Creator, but they keep doing their evil deeds. Someone has to fight… someone must oppose these monsters. My father refuses, even for his honor and his daughter. If he will not fight and his sons will not fight, then his *daughters* must defend their home from *men*." The last word was uttered as a curse, and Shem recoiled at its intensity.

Madrazi kept her voice low and calm. "Jael, look at me!" Slowly the girl turned her face towards the woman. "Hate is a thief, and even as you thrill in its emotion, the eyes of your heart watch it steal your very soul." Jael started to speak, but Madrazi raised her hand.

"I speak from experience." She drew herself up, staring down the younger woman. "You think you are the only person to hate? I nursed it for long years and nearly destroyed my marriage." She looked over at Shem and caught his eyes. "If I had not married such a good man," she said softly, "I would have succeeded." She turned back to the younger woman.

Jael searched her eyes for a long moment. Satisfied by what she saw, she grudgingly nodded. Madrazi continued. "It is foolish to judge all men based on your hatred of two. Even a child can discern a good man from an evil one. Treating your brothers and father with contempt only hands another victory to Nimrod and Korac. Is that what you want?" She saw a flash of guilt cross the girl's eyes before they dropped.

After a moment, she muttered an apology to Shem. Madrazi ignored the manner of its delivery and continued in a calm voice. "You have kept your side of our bargain. As will I. Go walk the meadow. Let its peace ease your heart. Then come back, eat, and rest. We will talk in the morning."

Jael stood warily and left. Shem said nothing for some time, just looking at his wife; half in question and half in reproach.

"The sickness runs deep," she sighed in answer. "It will not be healed in an hour or a day; perhaps not even in a lifetime. There is more to this than meets the eye. Clearly this Korac was the key. He stripped her of innocence, of her safe, comfortable life. For that—probably more than his role in Mariel's abduction—she intends to kill him... and many more."

"Is there any hope for her?" Shem struggled to control himself. "My sister... I should have been there.... Is she right... about Japheth... about me?"

Madrazi was in his arms in a moment, holding on with all her strength. "No! Never doubt that! She doesn't understand! Killing is not the answer now. If it were that easy, you could have slain Canaan, Nimrod, and the rest of Debseda's foul brood long ago. This world is no Eden. The weeds grow with the grain, and so it will be until the world ends. Victory is simply staying faithful to the Creator's words—no more, no less. We will obey the command to replenish the earth and find lands far from Nimrod's reach. Shelah and the boys will find a way." Shem nodded wearily, and left to begin catching up with the work.

That night Madrazi did as she vowed, and sat before the fire, searching for guidance.

In the morning, Shem found her asleep before the fire, her face still bathed in the faint glow that marked the touch of vision. He pulled her into his lap after he sat down and then kissed her awake. There was a look of wonder in her eyes, and he waited patiently for the words to form.

"His ways are strange indeed!" she breathed. Shem raised one eyebrow. "You must do this," she replied. "It will be hard, but it is her only hope for redemption and... and...."

"And what?" he asked, gently.

"And it is my only hope, too," she breathed. "I don't understand how or why, but my life will one day rest in her hands... on whatever skill you can impart. Those hands must be strong. Teach her well; it is both our lives. But say nothing of that to her."

Shem sighed and stared at the floor. "What else?" he asked heavily.

"I can't hide anything from you anymore," she complained lightly, but her face clouded quickly. "This Korac is tangled in all this. Their paths will cross again; their destiny is intertwined. And he is dangerous. Ask Heth when he returns."

She reached up to touch his cheek. "Harden your heart. She is your sister, but has chosen this path. Drive her." Shem said nothing, and despite having spent nearly four weeks on a horse, he rode at once for Noah's farm.

Chapter 7
DESCENT INTO SHINAR

6-1-1754

Mariel was lost in a fog. Days had slipped away in a daze of new people and customs. They had come at her so fast that she was unable to find solid footing. Like a bad dream with no possibility of waking, she stumbled through… almost as two different women—one participating and one observing. She learned her duties, but with a dull heart. All saw her as Nimrod's chattel, not his bride.

Any residue of feeling for him withered under the bright sun of each day's travel, as the flocks meandered back south. She came to hate the way he forced his passion on her by night. Cruel comments by the other women deflated every attempt to rally her soul. She tried to keep some part of herself free and unsullied, but it was a losing battle.

Though her father's farm was isolated, she had never felt as lonely as she did now—a feeling ironically exacerbated by the crush of people. Debseda's three sycophants were the worst. One or more was always there, pushing her from one task to another. She had no time to herself. Her taskmasters filled her days, and Nimrod, her nights.

Only Graemea seemed to soften as the days went by, and eventually became guardedly civil. Celota was the worst; she gloried in her mistress' callous cruelty, and Mariel experienced her petty provocations at every turn.

There was no time to enjoy the pleasing grasslands or stands of acacia or locust. Even the proximity of moving water—always a delight—was nothing now. What was beauty to a condemned soul?

Today, a new humiliation waited. They were on the outskirts of Shinar, and Nimrod planned to exhibit his prize for the multitudes rejoicing in Noah's fall. Mariel woke to the three maids bustling about her bed. The women unwrapped bridal finery brought to the camp during the night. Mariel let her mind wander as she stood and let them encase her in the glittering prison, unable to find the will to resist.

When she once again began to take note of her surroundings, she was inside the city, riding Korac's horse. The animal had been groomed until its coat shone, with its mane and tail braided and decorated with flowers. Nimrod rode beside her, a triumphant grin lighting his face. It was no longer handsome to Mariel; she knew the hideous strength it masked. She sat stiff and expressionless, repelled by him and by the black spear he held in his right hand. She retreated back into herself to escape the jeers and cheers of the crowd.

As she did, she shuddered briefly. She was late for the time of women. She desperately hoped it was the stress—the alternative was much worse. It was bad enough to have been an unwitting pawn in a plot to destroy her father, but to produce an heir for the man who had done so was worse… far worse. She shook off the thought. She would face that problem later… she needed all her strength today.

Cheering crowds forced her back to an awareness of her surroundings. Most were young, throwing flowers and shouting praise for Nimrod. The older ones seemed more half-hearted. Passing down a broad street, she saw it open into a market square. She was dully surprised at the size and grandeur of the city. Its streets were well laid and the homes and shops that lined them were sturdy and solid. Nimrod rode straight across the market, turned north up a smaller street and followed it only a short distance before turning east again. People stood in front of their homes and shops; the adventurous climbed up on the roofs and showered them with flowers. Up ahead, she saw a tower, three times as high as the houses, standing as a sentinel in the middle of town. It was round, and looked strong. As they drew near, she saw that it was the center of a compound enclosed by a wall, eight or nine cubits high.

"Your new home," laughed Nimrod as they approached the gate. His eyes shone. Clearly he was proud of his fortress. It looked like a prison to Mariel and she shuddered. The feeling of evil was heavy here.

But if being put on display for Shinar was the nadir of her life, she suddenly realized that there was one advantage to striking the bottom of one's existence. It was there… a place to plant her feet and push back up. In spite of the oppression of the fortress ahead—or maybe because of it—Mariel felt her guilt and grief yield to something deeper; something fear had suppressed for days—wrath. It was as ferocious as it was unexpected. Every shout from the crowd fed its flames. At first it burned deep in the hidden corners of her heart, but it soon began to swell. As it did, she began to feel alive for the first time since her mother's dismissal.

The rage burned away the numb despair and seared her mind. Her hands trembled and she clenched them around the reins to try to hold back the rising tide… in vain. She sensed danger, but it felt so good to be her own person again—she was suddenly disgusted with her supine retreat from reality. There was only the undoing of her mind at the end of that path, and she vowed to die before walking it again. She would face the future as her own woman.

A great gate loomed before them with two small towers on either side. It was more than an entrance; the gate itself was a miniature fortress. A band of determined men could hold it indefinitely. It struck her as a sign that Nimrod was weak. If he felt the need of walls inside his own city, then how sure was he of the people's support? How did the people of Shinar really feel?

But such thoughts were fleeting, for the ride under the dark arch reminded her that this was the entry into the innermost cell of her prison. As she rode out into the light, she was saved once more from despair by the effervescing rage. It burst into her will, melting away fear and despair and leaving a residue of resolve.

In that instant, she vowed to change her circumstances or die. She would not live another day as the passive victim. Nimrod's casual use of her to destroy her family, Debseda's cold contempt, her maids' petty cruelties—all these fed her anger until she shook from passion.

A haze seemed to clear from her eyes as the procession halted in a large courtyard. As usual, the three women hurried to help her down, but seized by some perverse whim, Celota slyly withdrew her hand as Mariel dismounted and she fell heavily to the ground.

Some of the men snickered, but their humor vanished when Mariel leapt up. Her wrath had finally found an outlet. She snatched the hated veil off her head, shredding it. Then she rounded on Celota and the walls echoed with the slap that sent the servant to the ground. Everyone froze. Mariel turned to face them, her eyes blazing. After days of dull meekness, even Nimrod was left speechless. It was Debseda who pushed forward.

"What means this?" she hissed.

Mariel rounded on her tormentor, her fiery wrath wrapped around a cold core of determination. She knew that her future rested on this encounter and she was determined to control as much of her fate as she could. "What it is *grandmother*," she sneered the word as an epithet, "is change. I may be the wife of your… uh… *grandson*…" She let one hand trail down her belly and Debseda's white face and the dead silence in the courtyard showed that all understood her insult… "but I am also the eldest daughter of the patriarch of mankind, and I will be treated with the respect I deserve."

"And if not?" sneered Debseda coldly.

"Then take my life!" screamed Mariel. "For I'll not live another day as the plaything of you or your cows. Come, husband," she said, turning to Nimrod. "You have your silly little spear. Use it." She stood now, the wrath dissipating, but the cold certainty of her inner strength was finally hers once more. Her face was white, but proud and beautiful, and all the men murmured at its sight.

"Use it," she taunted. "Surely the great hunter can slay a defenseless woman!" Nimrod flinched, then half leveled his spear, his face growing red. Mariel bit her lip. *His face… had he really done it before… surely not….* Out of the corner of her eye, she saw Korac suddenly stare at Nimrod, his impassive face lit for the briefest moment with curiosity and shaded with doubt. She felt she had just seen a glimpse of the man he had once been.

"Use it," she repeated, her voice cold and cutting. "And destroy all your precious schemes. Having the daughter of Noah to parade on the plains as your wife is one thing, murdering her is another. Slay me now and Madrazi will see it in a vision tonight, and Noah will know within the week. My father might have withheld his hand at my abduction, but not because he is weak or foolish. You, Korac!" she turned to face him. "Was Noah weak when you dared lay hands on my sister?"

Korac said nothing, but under the force of her intensity, he shook his head in spite of himself, and the men around him saw it. Mariel turned back to Nimrod. "But you can find out." She ripped her robe, exposing the skin of her chest through the rent. "All you need do is strike and discover what was meant by the mark of Cain!"

Nimrod hesitated, his cunning restraining his anger, but Debseda, hearing the name of Madrazi, stepped towards the younger woman, spitting fury. "You little fool," she screeched. "There's no need! He can keep you alive and beat you every night. I'll show him how!" With that she surged forward, her fist raised… only to have it stopped short by a large brown hand.

"No one strikes my sister!" A large shadow fell across the scene as Ham loomed up behind her, his face set with a hardness that made even Nimrod flinch. "If you or your three slaves try, then I will repay you blow for blow… every night! After all… are you not saying that a man can beat his wife with impunity?"

Debseda blanched. She hadn't seen Ham like this since they had been banished from Noah's presence many years before. For years he had lost himself in building this city, immersed in each task, letting her do as she would with their family. It had been easy to forget his innate strength… he *had* built the ark. The hand around her wrist tightened casually, and she could not hide her wince. It has a hand used to metal and stone and its immense strength promised even more pain.

But Ham was not finished. Still grasping his wife's wrist, he turned to Nimrod. "And if my grandson does not treat my sister with the honor and kindness that she deserves, then all the spears in Shinar will not save him from my hand." He turned to face Nimrod. "Come, boy. Put down your spear and test your boast that you are the strongest man on earth. Let me show you the error of that claim!"

Nimrod sat frozen on his horse, stunned. He had never seen his grandfather like this, and as much as he wanted to leap forward and accept the challenge, his innate caution screamed at the foolishness of such an idea. Though not as tall, Ham was thicker and he was strong—Nimrod had seen those hands bend metal, break wood, and lift stones that other men could not move. He loomed up beside Mariel like an old cave bear, wary and dangerous. Nimrod's caution was quickly reinforced by the audible mutterings of the men pushing into the courtyard to see what was happening. Though he avoided the political posturing of Debseda and her sons, Ham was still the Patriarch of Shinar and everyone knew it. He had that aura of being an elder—a survivor of the flood—and Nimrod suddenly saw the chasm opening before him. He was not ready for this challenge, and Debseda's temper had almost pulled them both over the brink.

Instantly he dismounted and bowed, laying the spear on the ground. "Your word is the law of our household, grandfather." He kept his voice low and even. "It has been a long month and we are all tired and overwrought from our celebration. No one will lay a hand on my wife."

"Of course," growled Ham. "Just as you will treat her with honor and dignity." He tightened his grip on Debseda's wrist even more. "As will my wife!"

Debseda nodded through her pain and Nimrod bowed again.

"I think it wise that more suitable women be found to wait on the needs of the Lady Mariel." Celota shrank from the threatening glitter in his hard eyes.

"As you say," gritted Debseda.

"Good!" Ham released his wife contemptuously, pushing her to the ground, and turned to Mariel. The threatening mien was instantly replaced by a genial and unassuming smile. He completely ignored the frozen tableaux behind him and waved Mariel ahead of him. "Come, my sister. Walk with me and tell me of my parents while our *loved ones* prepare your *private* rooms." He turned, his face again hard and his eyes boring into Debseda's as he spoke, and though her face twisted in anger, her eyes dropped.

Korac turned quickly away. It would never do to let anyone see the slow smile he could no longer repress. So the old man had life in him yet. He had always been wary of Ham and was gratified to see his caution vindicated. Though he would never admit it, he also enjoyed Debseda's public humiliation. His memories of his own grandmother, Yaran, were quite different, and Debseda did not compare favorably. He resented her interference, wishing that Nimrod would break that bond and become his own man. Of course, such desires were best kept hidden.

But the episode had brought another troubling thought, and he quickly set his face back into its usual stony mask. He was willing to do many things for Nimrod, but there were still a few boundaries left. Murdering a woman was one. Yet a strange stillness had come over Nimrod's face at Mariel's challenge. Why? Had he actually killed a woman? Korac had been with him for years and knew more of Nimrod's deeds than anyone, but he had not heard a whisper of such a deed.

Was there more to the story of the accident that had killed Tabriz? There was no reason to think so. After all, she had been Nimrod's lover before joining Debseda's service, and all knew that Nimrod would not touch his grandmother's women. Korac felt uncertainty gnaw his soul. He needed to get away. Mariel's stand had struck him hard. There was something about her. Was it her plight… her courage in the face of overwhelming odds… her defiant beauty? Whatever it had been had unearthed shadows of old memories, and he needed time to shove them back into the black abyss where they belonged.

Mariel was no love-struck silly girl. Nimrod could pretend it had been a seduction, but Korac knew better, and he suddenly found himself hard pressed to justify it… even if it did take old Noah down a notch. Why not just challenge the old man and kill him? It might bring war, but war was coming anyway. Korac felt it… it was his future. But for the first time in years he felt uncomfortable. Was it the latent power in Noah? His wife's ability to see his soul? The plight of their daughter? Ham's unexpected interference? Things had been going well, but these were discordant notes. He needed time alone with his memories and time to ponder the events of the past weeks and their plans for the coming years. He turned towards the river. Nimrod might think him mindless as well as heartless, but that was far from the truth. Korac had always been gifted with an astute eye. Watching the endless water roll by would settle his mind and give him time to think.

Chapter 8
DISCOVERIES

Mariel laid a trembling hand on Ham's outstretched arm and let him lead her away. Knowing that every eye was on her, she straightened her back and held her head high. She would cry later, but only after ensuring solitude. Ham led her through several gates and gardens to an old low building just inside the northwest corner of the main wall.

"This is my workshop," he said. "It is open to you at any hour, as are my quarters." Mariel pulled back instinctively. Ham grimaced and stepped away to give her room. He held his hands up in the air. "No, little sister, I am not Nimrod. I offer you a refuge from the evil that will surround you here. No more, no less."

Mariel studied his face. She had heard the stories from her parents and brothers. But at that moment it was Madrazi's words that leapt into her mind, recounting the final days of the flood and Debseda's growing influence over her husband. "I pitied the conflict in him." Looking back over the past minutes, she understood Madrazi much better.

"My apologies," she murmured and extended her hand once more to his arm. "It was foolish to react so, especially after you had proven your worth."

"No apology needed," he returned softly, patting her hand. "I understand… and I understand your heart. You have cast your lot with those who turn their backs on God. They deny their souls, but you cannot let go of yours, though the weight of conscience sometimes makes you wish you could."

Mariel choked at his words and the unwanted tears began to flow. Ham sat still, extending a clean rag to her. After the first wave had passed, she twisted it in her hands. She could not meet his eyes. "I was such a fool. I sold myself and my family for a fleeting passion. He claimed to love me, but betrays that word every day. Don't I deserve misery?"

"We both sinned against our father," Ham sighed, "casting our lot with evil people. But I cannot let go of that part of my soul that tells me all is not lost. When I left years ago, Madrazi pulled me aside. I'll never forget it. She was weeping and I couldn't tell whether it was anger or sorrow."

Ham rose and Mariel followed him. He opened the door and led her inside. She gasped in surprise. It was a workshop—forge in one corner, neat stacks of curing timber lining the far walls, benches and shelves creating a maze of the large room, and tools she had never seen before arranged neatly on the walls. But it was cleaner than a kitchen, and nothing was out of place. The scent of curing wood and smoke reminded her of home. Ham led her across the room to a bench near the forge where they both sat. She felt weak and limp after the surge of emotion, but there seemed a strange peace within this room—a corner of the world walled off from Nimrod's domain. The two sat in silence for a moment, lost in thought.

"What did she say," Mariel finally ventured. "I don't know if I could ever face Madrazi… or any of them," she sniffed. "Mother cast me out… Mother!" she stifled a sob, wiping her eyes on her sleeve, and continued. "Jael called me a cheap whore…" Ham covered her hand with his. "And she was right," she whispered. "Even now I may be carrying his child—my body nothing more than a tool for his ambition!" Tears now flowed unhindered.

"She was not right." Ham spoke softly, yet with a strength that arrested her self-pity. "You are Mariel, just as she is Jael. You've made a decision that has stolen a part of your life and set your feet on the wrong path. Don't let it crush you. *Mariel* is still there. Don't let go of her. Only God knows our destinations. And only He can create life. If He has chosen to do so, then He has a purpose for the child."

He gathered himself and gave her a wry half smile. "Madrazi said just one word. She looked into my soul… you know that look?" Mariel nodded through her tears. "She looked at me like that," Ham continued, "and said 'hope'. It was like an offer." He looked down. "It still haunts my dreams."

"Hope?" repeated Mariel. She held her breath. Her world teetered. Could she afford that luxury?

"Yes," he replied. "So I cling to that word. I live with all that…" he waved his hand toward the door, "but still hold fast. One day," he said softly, "I will find a bridge and cross back over. Perhaps we could find it together."

"Please, God," she whispered.

"In the meantime," he said, "feel free to come here whenever you need a refuge. I'll teach you things—things that will make you more valuable to Nimrod. He'll treat you better—he values his tools. One day," he sighed, "I won't be able to control him. His power grows each day and I just grow old. But my birth and knowledge keep me precious to his schemes, and you need every safeguard you can find."

"What about your wife?" she asked timidly.

Ham frowned. "Wife in name only," he replied heavily. "Her heart is full of hate and a hunger to dominate. Keep your ears open. Over time you will learn things… things that may give you some leverage. Use them wisely. Few gain any advantage playing her game, and none defeat her."

"And those three…"

"She-jackals?" interrupted Ham with a short laugh.

Mariel laughed too, through her tears, not trusting her voice.

"I named them well," he said more seriously. "Celota is dangerous and will not forget or forgive your blow. But Oshetipin is more of a fool and Graemea…" he paused for a moment in thought. "That one still has some shred of conscience. The right person could lead her back. Treat her with respect, but do not open your soul to her. I may pity her, but I dare not trust her."

Mariel pulled herself upright and dried her eyes. "How can I ever thank you?"

"I won't be alone any more."

Those words struck Mariel like a hammer. Neither would she. Her smile lit the room and she saw an answering spark in Ham's eyes. "We can't be part of Father's world anymore, but that doesn't mean we have to be part of this! We'll walk our own road and see where it leads. Now show me your workshop!"

Hours later, Ham watched her walk away with Zerai—a daughter of Tubal and a girl of sense and decency. She would be a good companion, having escaped the worst corruptions of the town. Fair skinned and fair haired, she had an independent streak, and serving someone like Mariel might help her find her place. Ham only hoped she could remain faithful through the struggles that loomed before them. Would a mere servant have the will to resist Nimrod? The courage to cross Debseda?

He sighed as he turned back to his work. He would watch carefully, gather the gossip, and move to protect Mariel from all of them. He only hoped he remained enough of a man to succeed. But for the first time in many decades, he felt man enough to try.

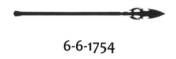

6-6-1754

A month after exiting the mountains, Shelah and Heth made camp beside a giant river. It was old and slow, meandering down from the north and forming a large delta at the northern end of the Qazvin Sea. Their progress had been frustratingly slow—the coastal area was flat, marshy, and infested with biting insects, forcing the men inland to higher ground. But the swamps extended well out to the northwest, and they had traveled far out of their way. The slow progress irritated Shelah. It was frustrating to have come so far, yet to have only reached the northern end of the sea. He wanted to cross the river and press east, but they were out of time.

From a high promontory on the outside of a large meander, they could see the grasslands continuing north and east as far as they could see. All around them was verdant country. Crops and herds could flourish, and there were fish in the sea. Heth leaned back against a sandy shelf. "Another time," he said in a soothing voice. "You'll come back. You have hundreds of years. Who knows? In a few centuries I might forget those gnats and be willing to come with you."

Shelah laughed. "By then it will be too late. Others will be living here and the magic will be gone. But at least I have finally topped Grandfather. We explored the southern shore of the sea when I was a boy. Now I can say that I've seen both ends—a boast he cannot make."

Heth grunted. "One for you and how many for him?"

Shelah laughed again. "Give me time. He had a head start of one hundred and thirty-five years!" He picked up his bow. "I'll find something for dinner. Back soon."

Within the hour, the aroma of cooking meat filled the camp. Heth sat and stared at the roasting hares and fingered his braid as he contemplated their journey. The world was wide and good lands could be found. He shook his head at those who huddled inside their walls in Shinar, ignoring the call of the wide lands. He liked the thrill of exploration, but that allure rested on him more lightly than on Shelah. For one thing, Heth had discovered that the earth was very large and he was very small. It made him uncomfortable.

Shelah understood his companion's moods and sat away from the fire, silently sketching a map in the dirt. It was his habit; the daily act of drawing the land they had explored locked it in his memory. Once home, he could draw an accurate map of all these lands. That map would guide those who would follow, men less hardy… men who would be bringing their women and children. They would need help to find their way.

Shelah glanced surreptitiously at Heth. A good man, he could easily have been something different. Fortunately, he had survived Debseda's poison. It was ironic; best of friends, the two were so different—Shelah was cautious, Heth, impulsive. Shelah listened; Heth erupted. Shelah was lean and quick, sure with the bow and silent among the rocks or trees. Heth favored the spear, his bulk and strength made it a fearsome weapon. But they had become close friends.

Sixty-one, Shelah was thirteen years older than Heth and nearly twice Nimrod's years. He had been wary of the boy for some time, having met him in Canaan's home fifteen years before. Shelah shuddered. Even then, evil had flowed off him like the stench of a corpse. He knew then he would need staunch allies. So when Nimrod bested Heth, Shelah sought him out, cultivating a friendship. And when Canaan finally drove him away, Shelah traveled south to bring Heth into his own home. The big man had proven a staunch friend, but there were strong currents beneath the surface. Years of watching Canaan lavish approval on Nimrod had left scars in Heth's heart that made him a very dangerous man.

No friendship could ever plumb those dark waters. That was why Shelah prayed for Heth every night. Only the Almighty could fix a wounded heart.

INTERLUDE 1

6-11-2161

"We can turn west any time. I can find a ferry across the Tigris," offered Lud quietly. Lydia shook her head, not trusting her voice. A weight had settled on her, growing heavier with each step south. Old nightmares had returned, and more than once she had woken to Lud's hand over her mouth.

Presenting themselves as a married couple, they had to sleep in the same tent. A perfect gentleman, he respected her privacy, never speaking of the words that probably escaped her mouth when she dreamed. And she would never volunteer anything about those terrible visions!

But her dreams were not the problem now. That he was offering to travel alone—a dangerous course in the wild—told her how desperate he had become.

It had been easy for a time. A cordial welcome followed them all the way to Tushpa. The Bianili revered the elders, and knew that 'Lydia' had been the Old One's close companion. "I'm traveling for Her," was all it took for the head of the council to offer men, horses, and even gold.

She had smiled, gently refusing. "All we need is the latest news and a small caravan heading south... one with people who won't know me." The next day they had left in the company of strangers taking highland wool to the cities of the plain.

Despite the headman being a fool, things had been easy. Most of the men were experienced traders, and all had accepted the couple as another family looking for a better life in Canaan. All that changed when a troop of Hatti soldiers overtook them a week out. They were going to the garrison at Carchemish, but instead of riding on, they stayed apace with the slower caravan. Lud avoided them, muttering, "I know two of them, but they won't know me. They fear neither God nor man," he warned, "and we'll have trouble. They'll probably demand payment for their escort."

Lydia still had not understood. "I have silver."

"No!" hissed Lud. "When they see your money, they'll demand more and more. They'll keep pushing until they have it all. None of us can live. Their superiors have a short way with caravan thieves, but if we disappear...."

Then she understood. Her heart had raced and sweat had gathered on her forehead. Lud was not the kind of man to misread danger, and his concern had shocked her more than the news.

"Have you talked to the headman?" she had asked.

He shook his head in frustration. "He's too friendly with them. And he's Hatti, despite his claims to be an Elamite. His accent's wrong."

"It's just bad luck," he sighed. "The wrong caravan. Why...?" His hand was white as it clenched the rein. "It will come to blood. Mark my words!"

She had struggled for self-control. "When?"

"A few days," he replied softly. "They won't do anything until we're into the wilderness."

"What can we do?" she had whispered. "Their horses are strong and they are seven spears." He had just looked away, saying nothing.

As those days passed, Lydia's fear mounted. They were far from civilization, and her mission was heavy upon her. It was not the thought of death—she had faced it before and now had knowledge of the next world to steady her soul. It was failure. That would be too much to bear. Her hands trembled all the time, now... what if she lost the scrolls? They were beyond value, and were her only link to one who had been a mother. It ate at her heart.

She wasn't alone. Tension crept upon the whole caravan, like the oppressive air before a storm. They sensed the danger; knew their helplessness. And it was more than their money. Lydia now wore a veil, but it didn't help. They had seen her face and she had to constantly endure and ignore their leers. The young captain was the worst. Brash and bold, he continually found excuses to ride near her, every appraising glance an insult. Lud almost lost control several times, but she stopped any rash words with requests for food or water.

The eighth morning after they had joined the travelers, one of the soldiers broke off and galloped ahead. Lud was instantly alert. "Listen and obey!" She bristled. There was a tone of command that angered her, but one that she couldn't refuse. She nodded as he murmured—lips closed and eyes always on the captain. "We'll stop in a few hours for the midday break. Act ill. Tell them the time of women is upon you. Insist on stopping. If they all stay, we'll think of something else, but maybe they'll keep going, leaving a few soldiers to 'help' us."

She felt as is she was seeing him for the first time. The humble shepherd was gone, and in his place sat a dangerous man with a fierce light burning in his eyes. He seemed to welcome a fight against seven of the world's best soldiers.

She shivered, but did as he said when they stopped, holding her belly and moaning. Lud was suitably abashed when the others stopped to see what was wrong. "It's her time," he mumbled, twisting his robe in both hands and keeping his eyes down. She marveled at the reappearance of the humble farmer; the embarrassed husband played to perfection. It was only then that she realized just how dangerous her companion was. It made her tremble, adding to the appearance of pain.

He kept his voice low and humble. "We must rest. We'll catch up tomorrow."

The headman nodded. He wanted nothing to do with the mysteries of women. "You'll be on your own," he shrugged as he strode off.

"As God wills," replied Lud. "We'll come when we can, but she can't ride when it's this bad."

The captain wasn't as easy. A false smile lit his dark face and he clapped Lud on the back, a threat even in a friendly gesture. "Two of my men will stay," he offered cheerfully. "No one would be foolish enough to attack Hittite soldiers in the middle of our kingdom. Our army would hunt them to the ends of the earth."

"How can a poor man ask for such consideration?" Lud mumbled, bowing his head. "I have nothing to offer."

The captain smiled. "Protecting trade is the duty of every Hittite officer," he declared in an officious tone. "I insist."

"As your duty demands," agreed Lud meekly. "We are forever in your debt, great captain."

He led her and the two soldiers back an hour to the mouth of a small gulch that cut north, solid rock walls rising twenty cubits on either side, providing shade. The flat sandy floor was littered with boulders, and a shallow pool lay against the western wall halfway up the canyon. A few trees had taken root around it, offering more shade. Lud led her around the pool, placing it between them and the soldiers. There he made a small camp, while the soldiers were content to sit in the shade on the south side, turning the oasis into a prison. Eventually, they lit a fire and huddled around it, talking quietly or casting bones to fill the hours.

As the afternoon wore on, Lydia moaned and did her best to look severely beset. It mattered little; the soldiers were men and studiously paid no attention, their eyes busy tracking Lud. He remained nervous, walking to and fro, looking like a husband helpless to relieve his wife's pain. He disappeared around the bend of the rock wall, then reappeared a few minutes later. He continued that behavior until the soldiers ceased noticing his erratic comings and goings. But Lydia saw deadly purpose in every step. He was throwing them off guard, spying on them, and preparing for the night. As the sun set, he built up their fire, leaving her well exposed in its light, but throwing the shadowed places nearby into deeper darkness. Remaining on her bed, watching the soldiers out of one corner of her eye, she heard him working quietly, appearing back in the firelight occasionally to fret for their benefit.

Despite his proximity, she felt alone under the pitiless stars. Lud was all that she had, but the man she thought she knew was a stranger. She was alone in the wilderness, at the mercy of merciless men. Now even Lud was nowhere to be seen.

But he had not abandoned her. "Get ready," he suddenly whispered out of the dark. She almost screamed in relief to hear his voice, but bit her hand to choke the cry. Lud spoke again. "They're coming for me soon. They have orders to save you for their captain, but they want to kill me and take our stock. Fix my bed so they think I'm sleeping."

Then he was gone, vanished in the dark. She quickly bundled packs under a blanket and shaped them into the form of a sleeping man. Then she lay down, listening, wondering if the stars shining down on her would be the last thing she would see in this life. For a moment she yearned for the release of death, but remembering the scrolls, she steeled herself against the coming ordeal.

Time passed slowly. Suddenly, she realized the night had gone quiet. Even the water was silent. As she lay, straining her ears, she could hear nothing but the crackling of the dying fire. Then, nearer than expected, she heard a faint scrape of leather on metal and the rasp of a sandaled foot on sand. Shivering with fear, she huddled in her bed and wondered wildly for a moment if Lud had come to his senses and escaped back out into the wilderness.

If so, she was completely alone.

Chapter 9
PATHFINDING

6-12-1754

Madrazi ran to Shem as he emerged from the barn. After weeks on a horse, he was dirty and distracted, weary and thin. New lines etched his face. Food, wine, and a night in a real bed helped, but he was still tired and discouraged in the morning. Madrazi did her best to cheer him, and he managed a short smile. But when she asked about his meeting with Noah, his face closed down and he just shook his head.

A few hours later, she tried to gently probe again, but by the end of the day it was clear that the subject was off limits. Indeed, it would be years before he would ever talk about it.

All he would say was that Noah had agreed, and Madrazi knew again the weight of her gift. It was the only reason her husband and Noah had agreed, though it was an unpalatable decision for both.

Jael had not wasted the days. While Shem was gone, she roamed the hills around the farm from dawn to dark, hardening her body and becoming attuned to the countryside. It was well that she had—from the day he returned Shem ceased to be her brother and became an unforgiving taskmaster. Driven all day, she often slept outside. No allowance was made (nor was any requested), in spite of days when Madrazi's skilled hands and salves were the only thing that kept Jael on her feet.

But Shem kept pushing; running her farther into the wilderness. If she was hard and stubborn, he was no less so. But her dark passions precluded any complaint. She obeyed every word, even when her body had long exceeded its limits. As she grew stronger, he only increased his demands, making her carry a pack as she ran. Each week, he added a stone to the pack. And he refused to let her lose herself in the pain; forcing her instead to learn—how to judge terrain, how to hide, how to find others hiding from her, how to identify plants—harmful and helpful—and how to hunt and avoid being hunted.

Though he offered no praise to Jael, Shem marveled to Madrazi at her progress. She was eager for knowledge and strength. Her body was fast becoming as hard as her heart. Already she was making her first bow: a complicated affair of horn, wood, and sinew, recurved for extra power since it would be smaller than a man's. She had yet to fire an arrow but had been drawing Shem's great bow to train her arm. Her inner demons pushed her hard and despite several attempts, Madrazi had been unable to break through the walls around her heart.

Madrazi did draw the line at wearing men's attire, helping the girl make outfits suitable for both the rigors of the wilderness and the demands of decency. Skirts slit for riding covering her leggings and a turban covered her head. She also put her foot down at Jael's efforts to hack away her hair. "Wear a braid. It doesn't impede Heth!" Challenged to do what a mere man could do, Jael appeared the next morning with woven hair, functional, but unattractive. Madrazi yearned for the day when it would be long enough to cut in a more feminine style.

Shem and Madrazi were eating a quiet summer breakfast when she asked—as she did every morning—how the girl was progressing. He just sighed and said, "If she doesn't kill herself or I don't kill her, she's going to be dangerous. I haven't started showing her how to use weapons yet, but she's got the eye for the bow and she's as quick as a weasel. Someone… maybe Zeb… showed her how to throw a knife and she's been sticking them in every tree and fencepost on the farm. If she's not careful, she'll end up killing someone."

"That's the idea," broke in Jael, standing at the door.

Madrazi put a restraining hand on Shem's arm. "An idea that will destroy your soul," she shot back.

Jael's lips tightened. "There's not much left to destroy."

"Yet from that portion will come the salvation of many!"

Madrazi was as surprised as the others at the echo of power in her voice. Jael's face went white, but she quickly turned away, slamming the door behind her.

7-5-1754

It was high summer when Shelah and Heth met the others at the foot of the mountains. Despite the remaining trek, it was a boisterous reunion. In the midst of their celebration, Shelah noticed that Anam seemed withdrawn. He resolved to have a quiet word with Ashkenaz. Jobaath's humor—though singularly inventive—often bordered on cruelty and Anam was a sensitive young man.

But everyone was absorbed in eating. They had fish from the river, wild grapes, and apples. Shelah brewed a strong tea from some blueberries. Afterward, Jobaath waxed eloquent about their travels. "I led these two on a far-ranging trek along the northern shore of the Black Sea. We kept the mountains to our south and followed rolling hills and green grasslands that will support thousands of herds and a bounty of crops."

Shelah's mind began to wander. *Both seas have a northern terminus. The way north is open—east and west. It's out there for me. Vast unexplored lands… and I can be the first!* His heart raced with excitement. Jobaath's voice was a faint buzz in his ears. When he closed his eyes he could see far-away mountains, rivers, and seas… vast stretches of forest, grassland, and plains. That was his destiny. Like his grandfather, he would seek out every hidden mystery of the Creator's handiwork.

He blinked and was back with the others. Light from the setting sun filtered through the western trees. Ash, Jobaath, and Anam were laughing at some remembered episode. Even Heth was smiling. The scene froze in his mind with incredible clarity. It was a perfect moment, one to remember for many years, but the pull of the horizon was strong—even now he yearned to leave the others, turn north, and lose himself. But duty drew him south. These lands offered more than the promise of his own dreams—they offered escape from the tyranny of Shinar. The moment ended, and the cares of the world attacked his mind once more. Would men choose freedom over the easy life between the Tigris and Euphrates? Too many had already been seduced by a promise of security, by the opportunity to herd together like cattle—the artificial happiness of the crowd.

It was time to report back to Shem and plan the next step. With a sigh, he turned back to the fire, now bright in the gathering evening. Seeing Heth lost in thought, he began to share his journey with Jobaath, Ashkenaz, and Anam.

Heth hunched by the fire, staring at its flames. Shelah was relating their travels, but Heth followed his own thoughts. Shelah could speak well; he didn't need Heth to tell the tale. And to be truthful, Heth had only half listened to Jobaath. For some reason, the past lay heavy on him and the fire drew forth memories. He saw himself on the training field, in the full strength of early manhood, condescending to give his young cousin a lesson with the bow, not knowing the boy's talent already exceeded his own. It was the first time Nimrod had made a fool of him, and Canaan's sneering laughter still rang in his ears.

Canaan—like his brothers—had trained all his sons to be conquerors and rulers. Heth was the strongest, the most promising—the object of his brothers' jealousy. His days had been filled with the mysteries of spears and swords. Early on, he found a passion for their making, and Ham had trained him in those secrets for many years.

Debseda had filled their heads with tales of an alluring world, his grandfather's estrangement from Noah, and the old drunkard's unjust curse on Canaan. As a hot-blooded boy, Heth had been enraged, preparing his arm for the coming war with the old man and the two brothers who had forsaken Ham in his hour of need.

But the tales wore thin over the years, and as a man, Heth came to see the deep flaws in his family. A few years of Shelah's friendship had completed the cleansing of those lies.

He knew the truth now, but he was an outcast. Despite turning his back on Canaan, Nimrod, and Debseda, most of the people in the North remained suspicious of "Canaan's son," even after several years living at the Lake of the Islands. Shelah assured him it would pass, but Heth wondered. Shelah saw great good in the human heart, but Heth was more cynical. People didn't change. Brave men had been brave boys and cowards were afraid from their cradle.

And much was changing. Each new generation vastly larger than the last, the earth would soon tremble under the feet of tens of thousands. Eight souls had come down the mountain; now there were twice as many clans. Soon they would become kingdoms, and old family ties would be renounced. A few, like Shelah, tried to hold men together—his passion had united this unlikely group. The five had built homes together near the lake, but they were the exception. Conflict seemed unavoidable, but after growing up in the midst of it, Heth wanted something more. Peace was the ultimate ideal. Heth the dreamer longed for it; Heth the cynical outcast thought it impossible.

Watching the flames, he recalled his first trip north with Shelah, years before. The looming mountain had been oppressive, but the welcome at Shem's home was warm. As usual, Heth had tried to prove his strength when gripping hands with Shem, but Shem had returned pressure for pressure. It was the start of a deep respect for the eldest son of Noah. The man was a study in contrasts: strong, fearless, a peerless archer, a cunning hunter… but at heart, a man of peace with a tranquility that Heth envied. A man to respect. Canaan had lied about him too.

If the reality of Shem laid bare the lies of his childhood, his wife banished them forever. Prepared by a lifetime of Debseda's dark stories for an evil witch, Heth was off-balance from the moment he saw her. She was everything that his grandmother was not. Even her appearance was different. Debseda was dark-skinned and dark-haired, her intense blue eyes creating a startling contrast that drew men's attention. Her shapely body—and the way she flaunted it—kept their attention by playing to lust. Madrazi needed no artifices. With modesty and grace, she presented a picture of womanhood that outshone her rival. Even in her modesty, her slim tall figure was just as attractive as Debseda's. Chestnut hair framed a soft and shapely face, and her green eyes seemed at home with her lighter complexion and soft features. But it was her soul that entranced Heth; the virtue and character in her eyes. Men might desire Debseda, but they would give their lives for Madrazi.

And so he had come to envy Shem. The man had a wife who put him first yet did not hide in his shadow. She was his helper, not a servant. Her eyes could sparkle with a quick joke or penetrate a man's mind with a glance.

But there was more. It surprised people who took Heth's physical presence at face value, but he was a perceptive man. And from the moment he met Madrazi, he felt an annoying buzz in the depths of his mind—a warning from some unplumbed depth. It spoke of power, though her gentle spirit disarmed him until it was revealed to him in a most disconcerting way.

On that fateful day he had been alone in the great room, enjoying the fire when a deep chill ran up his spine. The fire flared. He sensed that the flames had transformed into a curtain, hiding scenes not meant for his eyes. And then she was there beside him; her green eyes lost in the dancing fire. She saw beyond that veil.

Moments passed and she was strangely unaware of him. But the fire flared again and she turned to him. Feeling danger, Heth tried to leave. But her eyes froze his feet to the floor. He stood for uncounted moments, drowning in the green depths. Then, he heard a cold voice inside his mind.

> *Your sons will rule these lands. They will war with the sons of Shelah and be scattered to the far lands. After many kingdoms rise and fall they will return with blood and fire. Nations will be laid waste and men will tremble at the rumor of their coming.*

Heth could not breathe. Blood roared in his ears, and his sight was obscured. Then, as quickly as it had come, the storm vanished. Madrazi seemed to shrink, and the power that held him dissipated. His first reaction was anger at the violation of his mind, but it vanished at the sight of the tears filling her soft eyes, and the tentative touch of her cold hand on his cheek. For a fleeting instant he saw a vulnerable woman weighed down by a staggering burden. He blinked, and was back in the great room in the presence of the regal wife of Shem.

As he sought to regain his bearings he heard a voice of gentle sympathy. "These words are true. But take heart, son of Canaan. Shelah is your brother and will remain so all of your days. What I saw is far away and for your ears alone. A man is not responsible for the actions of his sons...." She looked at him shrewdly. "Nor does a son stand or fall by the deeds of his father. Each man must answer to the God of Noah. If you please the Judge of the Earth, you will find life."

Heth shivered. Those words had been from the Creator. He didn't know how he knew, but he would have bet his life on it. Heth acknowledged God, but always at a distance. He had turned to her for reassurance. "You see the things of God. Tell me what I must do!"

Then the words hit him. "War with Shelah?" he stuttered.

A light hand on his arm steadied him. "Not you. Not Shelah. Not soon." She swayed, and it was Heth's turn to help her. "Please, sit down," he urged.

"Yes," she smiled wanly. They sat on the large sofa. "What should I do?" he echoed.

"I am not wise enough to tell you what paths to walk," she replied. "But I can say this: I know you hate what is evil, but that is not enough. One day you will discover a greater power in love. When you do, follow it."

Heth considered those words again in the small campfire, as he did nearly every day. How could a man like him ever find love? Lost in contemplation, he did not see Shelah watching him closely, wondering at the troubled look on his face. His friend came over and tapped Heth on the shoulder, rousing him.

Heth looked up sheepishly. "Sorry. Just thinking…."

Shelah nodded. Words would have meant nothing.

The five gathered to plan the next step. As unlikely as it seemed, they would need to be certain they hadn't missed an easier path. Things might look different from the north… they might see a lower pass with a gentler gradient. If they split up, they could explore the side valleys and see if such a promising path could be found. There was no sense is coming all this way and not being sure.

Chapter 10
UP A TREE

7-17-1754

Heth stared at the wolf. The wolf stared at Heth.

It was disconcerting, he thought, how quickly a tree limb could become so hard. Danger had transmuted it into the softest cushion for a time, but tree limbs are less than ideal for sitting. Discomfort displaced the fear that had sent him ten cubits up a tree with no clear memory of climbing. But it was sit or stand; the grinning jaws and knowing eyes of the hungry predator leered up at him.

He swore loudly, wishing the creature could understand every word. His bow was back at camp, and though Heth was a large, well-muscled man—stronger than most—his thick arm and a long knife were no match for the crushing jaws on a wolf the size of a small horse. Forty-seven years was far too short a life to achieve one's dreams, and deep down—below the bubbling rage—Heth was still a dreamer.

He shifted uncomfortably, tugged at his thick black braid, grateful that wolves don't climb. He had been lucky; the only tree large enough to offer sanctuary was right beside the spring, just a few steps away when the overeager beast attacked. Camp and the now-useless bow were up in the rocks—too far for a sprint, though the rugged rocks called seductively. But it was fifty strides to the cliff face, and the wolf was curled up at the base of the tree. A chill wind across his thick, hairless face and hands presaged real problems, but there was nothing to do but sit, glaring at a wolf that had learned from its ill-timed rush. Heth sighed. Survival hinged on whether he was more patient than a dumb creature. He grinned back at the animal as he thought of all the lectures he had received about his impatience.

Then the smile vanished. A second son, Heth longed for his father's praise, but Canaan's constant criticism pushed him to rebellion. Early painful lessons only trained him to hide those feelings—deviation wasn't tolerated in his family. Debseda ruled the clan, demanding a cowed submission that he could not give. He came to hate them both, and despise any who lacked his stubborn independence. The only good memories were of Ham, who, recognizing a kindred love of metal and stone, had taught him many secrets of copper, bronze, and iron. Heth had endured several otherwise unhappy years solely for the sake of that knowledge.

But even Ham hadn't been able to keep him at home. He could never forget his last angry parting with Canaan. His dark brown eyes narrowed in anger and his full lips curled into a sneer beneath a prominent curved nose. It was their loss. He now stood beside Shelah, infuriating both Debseda and Canaan. Having inherited his grandfather's muscular build and strength, he was the most dangerous man in his family, save Nimrod. He sneered again as he recalled the day he knew he could best his own father—Canaan's shift from physical to emotional torment showed that he knew it too. Proud of his prowess—only his grandfather and his great-uncle Shem were better—he enjoyed life at the top. The older generation cared little for fighting, and that made him the best… until Nimrod had bested him in turn.

Even now that memory raised a red mist before his eyes. It was bad enough that Cush's son lived under Canaan's roof and stole Canaan's favor, but a day had come when Nimrod's strength exceeded Heth's. At eighteen, Nimrod was already a fierce foe; his supple strength and agility made Heth look clumsy. By twenty, he could outdo Heth in feats of raw power. His marvelous quickness and facility with a blade was unmatched; only Shem and Shelah remained better with the bow.

Heth clenched his fist. It wasn't a friendly rivalry. Nimrod's soul was twisted; he had an affinity for evil nurtured by Debseda. It had been time to go, and Shelah's offer of friendship had saved him. Ten years! Where had the time gone? Nimrod had always been a pure predator—like the wolf below. Men would serve him or die, but Heth refused that choice. He did not fear Nimrod—Heth had the heart and strength of a lion—but he had a foreboding that he must one day face Nimrod in a battle that would leave only one alive. He shied away, not from fear, but because hidden deep within his warrior's soul was a quiet dreamer who knew that killing would forever diminish his essential self.

Most men feared Nimrod. His early triumphs over wild beasts gave him a reputation, and men gave him a wide berth. There was a recklessness in him that screamed a warning at any who came in contact with him. He obeyed only two people—Debseda and Canaan—and he would probably slip the leash on them soon. Heth wondered idly if he feared Shem's wife. Debseda hated her, but there was an undertone of fear in her rants. Had she passed that on to Nimrod? Fearing Madrazi wasn't hard—the ignorant feared her reputed sorceries, and the wise respected her insight. It was rumored that if a man had the courage to hold her gaze long enough he would see the day of his death in her eyes. Heth no longer believed that, but having felt her power, he walked lightly in her presence all the same.

He shook his head. *Quit daydreaming!* Anger surged through his thick frame, and his grip on the branch tightened. He had no time to waste! They had been gone for months, and he needed to take the news home. There was a passage through the mountains and good lands to the north. Open grasslands and generous forests spread as far as the eye could see. There was a wide world, far from Nimrod's growing oppression, and Heth growled at the delay. But the wolf lay unmoving. He swore again. Then his rough sense of humor reasserted itself: at least his cousins would not see his predicament. The five men had split up a week ago to explore the twisted valleys of these confusing mountains. They were to meet tomorrow at the foot of the pass that would lead them back south.

That left one problem. They wouldn't reach the pass until tomorrow and Anam would probably be late again. It would take two more days for Shelah to track him here. Could he survive four days in the tree without water? No. And one cold night might finish him. How long would the wolf wait? Heth stared down at it again, and the steady yellow eyes looking back at him seemed to laugh; it had all the time in the world. In a flash of anger, Heth fingered his knife and was tempted to see if he could take one of those eyes.

But common sense prevailed and he cast about for a constructive alternative. Comfort seemed a good place to start. He climbed higher and began to cut smaller branches. At least the spruce allowed easy footing on its radiating limbs. One by one, he cut and trimmed several dozen of varying length; and one by one, he placed them across the larger branches below, forming a platform a few cubits wide. To complete the task, he swarmed up the tree as high as his weight would allow and cut thin limbs green with needles and laid them across the platform. It wasn't his bed at home, but if was infinitely more comfortable than a single branch. He had no rawhide strips to join the branches or lash them to the tree, but if he moved carefully, it remained steady.

The morning was half done when his arboreal perch was complete and still the wolf had not moved, eyes following the antics of its next meal. Then, as if to taunt his prey, he rose sedately and stalked over to the spring for a drink. Heth's newfound satisfaction vanished and rage boiled up. He laid hold of a short stick and hurled it at the wolf. Heth could throw stones or sticks with uncanny accuracy, and his eye had lost nothing after graduating to bow and spears. The branch struck the drinking wolf on the side of the head and it whipped around in a rage and sprang upward. Its great paws hooked a limb well up the tree, but it was too heavy to climb and fell back to the ground.

No longer the patient hunter, the beast snarled as it stalked back and forth, Heth taunting it with gusto. If it lost its patience so easily, then perhaps it could be convinced to search for easier prey. He glanced around and climbed down one step to a relatively thick, straight branch. It took some effort to cut it with his knife, but time was one commodity he had in abundance. The prospect of hurting the wolf added zest to his efforts. Once cut, he trimmed the twigs until he had a nearly straight stick, almost as long as he was tall and the thickness of a good spear.

Anticipation filled the next hour as Heth sharpened the narrow end to a needle point and smoothed a grip just back from the midpoint. Skilled with metal, he had made many spears and had no illusions of killing the beast with this toy, but a painful wound might convince it to leave. At worst, it gave him something to do while he waited for the others.

Climbing down carefully to a few cubits above the highest point the beast could leap, he searched for a position that offered stability and a clear throw. The wolf rose as soon as Heth started down and moved closer, staring up in anticipation. Just another step! Suddenly Heth cast his spear with all his strength. It almost worked— the wolf froze an instant, but its canine reflexes enabled it to twist aside just in time. The sharp point grazed its neck, slicing a shallow, but painful furrow.

It went berserk. Pain drove it higher this time and Heth later swore that he felt the teeth graze the bottom of his foot. Clambering quickly up, his foot slipped and he overbalanced. His instinctive grab missed the first limb, and he fell two cubits before his hand caught the next. In that instant he realized that he was within range of the great jaws. None of his vaunted quickness could possibly match it. His free hand darted for his knife—at least he would go out fighting.

In that instant Heth heard a meaty thud. The wolf hesitated before whirling in mid-air to snap at the feathered shaft in its side. Another magically appeared, before a third sank deep into its great neck, severing the spine. Heth watched it collapse and drew a deep breath before carefully setting his feet on the nearest limb and dropping swiftly down to the opposite side of the tree. The yellow eyes stared at him—disappointment plainly visible—before going blank.

From beyond the spring he heard a cheery voice, "That's another you owe me." Shelah emerged from a thicket, bow still ready, and advanced on the carcass.

"He's dead," Heth replied. "The last shot cut its spine—a lucky gust must have caught it." His humor was forced and off target. They both knew that Shelah could put an arrow into a rat's spine at that range.

"Of course," his cousin grinned. "I counted on that wind. That's why I sent the two others first. I thought if the beast was agitated, it would be a more challenging shot."

"A quicker one would have earned my praise!" Heth's humor was returning with the relief of his cousin's appearance. "What brought you? I was counting on several days up there—maybe more if Anam stayed true to form."

Shelah laughed again. "That's why I came. An extra day hunting with you is better than sitting around a fire in a cold, windy pass waiting on our young cousin. And I was right… you led me straight to a noble quarry!"

"Fine!" Heth returned. "Your arrows are in the beast; your knife can remove the pelt. I'm going to eat!"

"Fix enough for two. The least you can do is provide a meal for the hungry hunter."

"I almost did," grunted Heth as he walked back to his camp.

Chapter 11
NARROW WAY

7-18-1754

Anam locked his dark eyes on the gray rock, less than a span from his face. His mind replayed for an instant a picture of warm sun on calm water before a surge of fear shut it out. *Concentrate*! There was no sun here, only the chill gray of the mountains. There was no water except that frozen on the top of the steep mountain rearing above the narrowing ledge beneath his feet. His knuckles whitened as numb hands gripped the rough knobs of rock to either side of him and numb feet slid slowly back along the ledge, searching for firmer footing.

He cursed himself for coming this far; he had suspected earlier that the path was a dead end but had ignored that inner warning. He was not afraid! He would prove it… someday. He wondered—not for the first time—if this whole journey had been a vain attempt to find the courage he so admired in Shelah and Heth. He was the youngest and the weakest, and feared their bad opinion.

But the greatest fear was of the cowardice he felt inside. He could not hide from it, so he tried to suppress it with foolhardy stunts—like crawling too far along a precarious ledge. He cursed himself again, then clamped down on his emotion and slid his right hand over to a crevice, locking his fingers inside.

Proving himself had become a habit. His father, Mizraim, had favored the older, larger, and stronger Lud, but had never ceased pushing his second son. Anam had been constantly reminded that he was Lud's inferior—the harshest criticism coming in his teens. During one of his father's rants, he had cursed Anam as a coward. It struck deep; Lud appeared fearless in the face of any test. Anam—blessed with a quicker mind—avoided pointlessly foolish challenges.

Mizraim's jibe had festered in his heart. Was it wisdom or fear that prompted caution? Anam still did not know, but traced the beginning of a profound self doubt to that fateful moment. Soon the young man was finding weakness in his every circumstance. The more he doubted, the more he feared. The more he feared, the more he was determined to prove himself. And the more foolhardy chances he took to do so, the more he doubted himself. He was trapped in a slimy pit, constantly trying to leap out and forever unable to do so.

So once again he found himself in danger. Being the most agile of the five, it was not the first time he had set his feet on an unstable rockslide or narrow ledge just to master that bowel-clenching terror that seemed to haunt his steps. He slid his left foot back across the narrow crack to where his right had rested a moment earlier. Maintaining his balance, he slid his left hand across the face of the rock to the next knob before slowly turning his head back to the right and marking the locations of his next handhold.

He was ashamed of his fear. When the others were with him, he drew on their courage—but alone, it was different. Alone, he didn't have to hide the shaking hands or sweating brow, but neither could he draw on the quiet strength of Shelah or the bravado of Heth and Jobaath. Those qualities, combined with their willingness to accept him as a part of their circle—even as the junior member and the butt of their rough humor—had been the major reason he had been willing to leave home. It was a good trade: even Heth's acerbic jibes were delivered as a friend—a stark contrast to his own father's cold insults. He missed the comforts of home but seldom regretted the advantages of his new life. It was only in cold, uncomfortable perils like this that his mind returned to the hot food and soft bed of his youth.

He stopped for a moment, closing his eyes, frustrated that this valley—like almost all the others—was a dead end. There was no sense in killing himself to prove it. Ice was moving inexorably down from the heights, and the head of this valley would be impassible even if this path allowed passage. But Shelah had insisted that they explore the side valleys for alternate ways. There might be an easier trail—a shortcut that would save time or reduce risk. But it wasn't this trail or this valley, and at least he had done his job. Slowly, he moved his right hand over to the next crack.

Anam fought the temptation to look down. It was only a hundred cubits to the bottom of this narrow valley, but a hundred would kill him as surely as a thousand. Sure-footed and lithe, Anam could run for hours ahead of his slower cousins and was as graceful as a cat dancing, unlike Heth, who favored vigor, strength, and wild rhythms over subtle skill. But at this moment, Anam felt completely graceless; his feet and hands were frozen, uncooperative blocks. He focused on his goal—the ledge widened out just another ten cubits back and the path down was easy from that point.

So drawing in a deep breath, he moved each foot and hand in turn. It was easier now that he knew where the footing was firm and the irregularities of the dark gray rock offered a hold. Span by span he crept back along, sweat running down his forehead and cheeks, dampening his black, curly hair, and glistening against his red-brown skin in spite of the cold air. With only another foothold to go, Anam fought for his focus, knowing that premature relief could kill him too. After an eternity of sliding slowly along the face, the ledge widened into a path. Once there, he stopped and sat on the cold rock and bowed his head to his knees. He nearly vomited as the cold fear was released, and Anam swore that he would never ascend such a path again—an oath he had made and broken more than once over the past weeks.

A few hours later, he was staring into a small fire, still trying to shake his fear. He let his mind wander, seeing in the flickering flames a vision of sunlight on water. He had been a small boy, playing by the Lake of Many Islands on a beautiful summer day. Splashing in the cool waters had been interspersed with hours of lying on the warm grass, the vivid blue of an unusually clear day and the bright sunlight warming his skin. He remembered those hours as the best of his short life, and the past weeks had created a raging conflict beneath an easygoing exterior.

As the night closed in, Anam once more took refuge in his dreams. He had earned that much. Humans were made to have and fulfill desires. Evil or good, it was clear from his heart as well as from the actions of others, that all men were stirred to choice by their desires. Some were shared with others, some stayed locked in a man's heart. He loved his four cousins and was committed to their common goal—defeating Nimrod's evil. Though bound to him by birth, Anam (like Heth) had drifted away from his immediate family. His father, Mizraim, was certainly no friend of Canaan's, but he liked Anam's new friends even less, and not wanting to risk the censure of the town, had cast Anam out. In a perverse way, Anam actually approved of his father's action. It was clever—sheltering him from Debseda's wrath, scathing in its scorn for Anam and Heth, and their new friendship with Shelah.

At the time, Anam had vowed to hate his family, but now he did not care. Debseda's power in his life was broken; he saw her for the liar she was. Her tales of Shem and his wife were false, and probably much else too. Though a little fearful of Shem's wife, Anam saw the fundamental difference between the two matriarchs—Madrazi merited admiration… Debseda, contempt.

The lazy days he had spent at Shem's home had confirmed his decision. Nimrod and Canaan wanted to bring all men together on the plains of Shinar and to unite them with promises of protection and ease. But at a price—becoming tools of a tyranny that would spread across the Earth. Already they had many followers and were teaching them the arts of war.

Shem and Madrazi understood the reality of battle, and Anam approved; even Heth could not best Nimrod. But Shem's mind transcended swords and spears; seeing to the heart of conflict. "War is first fought in the mind," he had said. "You must understand the end of your enemy and find a weakness to exploit; a way to frustrate him with wisdom and cunning. Do not fight his battle; find one that ensures his defeat."

Through many nights of spirited discussion, the men found that "battle." The earth was wide and men would soon fill its lands as the Creator had commanded. Today people saw only "north"—the highlands above the Plains of Shinar—and "south"—those vast plains with their two great rivers, but in time those terms would come to mean little. There were wide lands beyond "north" and "south" that would one day be settled. And that was an advantage. Nimrod could enslave some in Shinar. But if many others moved beyond his reach, his triumph would be hollow. Once people tasted the fruit of freedom, they would be less susceptible to his enticements. But mountains blocked many paths. Controlling Shinar, Nimrod also controlled the easiest paths south and east. So the cousins had set off to find a way through the impassible northern mountains between the Black Sea and Qazvin Sea.

Anam feared heights, but he had gone. If men chose to settle distant lands, Nimrod would lose… and it would be because of Anam's friends, not Mizraim's schemes. That alone made the travail worthwhile, even if it was a little petty. Men subduing the grasslands and forests of the wide world would raise strong sons who, having tasted that good life, would never submit to his control. Nimrod might build a kingdom, but he could never conquer the desire for liberty of free, self-sufficient men—men tested by the rigors of the land itself.

Despite Anam's initial pessimism, they had actually succeeded. Shelah kept pushing them along until they had all stood on that last ridge, with green lands stretching north between the two great seas. The difficulty of their passage was proof that no army would ever disturb those who found freedom in those far lands. Now they must return with the news and stir others to begin the migration.

But there was more to be done. The wide lands must be explored and sites for settlements mapped and described. No man would risk his family to a vague promise of unlimited lands, especially if those lands would be swallowed by ice in the years ahead. Shelah might tremble with excitement over that journey; Anam trembled with dread—a burden to be endured for the sake of his friends.

For his heart lay elsewhere. He loved the thrill of discovery, but when he had looked at the northern plains beyond the mountains, he had not seen a home. How could a man explain his heart? Things felt the most deeply are always the most difficult to wrap inside mere words. Anam longed for something different, for a land where the sun shone all year long, where snow and ice never fell, and where fires were needed only for cooking.

Mizraim had little love for Canaan or the egotistical Nimrod, but neither was he enamored of Japheth and Shem. He had once talked of a land far to the south, beyond Shinar and south of the Great Sea. It was a land of warmth, green forests and rushing waters; he had wandered there years before. Deep down, Anam knew that if his father settled there, he would have to reconcile with his family and live there too.

His father's tales remained clear in his mind, as if told yesterday. The lands he described whispered to Anam even now; a haunting call no northern land could silence. Yet how could he abandon his friends? Maybe Shelah would understand, but the others would not, and Anam did not like the idea of losing their respect any more than he liked the thought of being apart from them. But why could he not live out his years in a land that *he* loved?

Clenching his fists, he looked across this cold, rocky valley. How could any man be happy here?

But paradise was far away and the small fire was no substitute for a warm sun. Anam shivered as he thought about the cold climb awaiting him to rejoin the others, and swore to himself that he would find his own home one day and find a way to reconcile that with his friends… maybe even his family. Compared to conquering his fears, it would be a small thing.

Chapter 12

RENDEZVOUS

7-19-1754

The sun was already behind the western ridge overlooking the pass when Anam stumbled up the rocky slope. Up ahead the peaks widened into a bowl, with the pass at the bowl's apex. Though still clear, there was ice on those peaks; summer melt sluiced downhill to join the river below. Anam grimaced. Icy water seemed to mark most of their trails through these accursed mountains and he hated the cold.

In the gathering darkness a bright orange fire blazed, uphill beneath a sheltering cliff. Anam was tired, cold, and hungry. Though probably the last to the fire again, he no longer cared about the heavy-handed ribbing he would receive from Heth and Jobaath. He was too tired. At least the quiet respect of Shelah and Ashkenaz softened the quips. He was not as strong as the others, but his quick mind—as much a part of him as Heth's strength—had proven itself many times.

But young men are young men, and Anam was the youngest. He thus was the target for most of the fireside banter. Hailing the camp, he trudged up, throwing his pack down on the ground nearby. Not waiting for the usual jokes about being the last to arrive, he looked to Shelah and asked, "Did you save any food?"

"Of course," he replied. Glancing at Heth, he added, "Not to say that it wasn't a struggle."

"Strong men need more," retorted Heth.

"Given the time, I'd say that Anam worked harder than any of us," Jobaath grinned, as he knelt by the fire and sliced a thick slab from the haunch hanging over it. He handed the knife to Anam and gestured toward a waterskin. "Take your fill and tell us of your adventures. We already had one good story tonight; Heth hid in a tree until Shelah convinced him to come down!"

Heth snarled a curse while the others smiled.

Shelah intervened… as usual. "Sit and eat, Anam. You can hear our tale while you eat and tell us yours after. We must make time tomorrow; we need to leave these mountains behind.

"Why push now?" growled Ashkenaz. "What are a few more days? Tired men make mistakes and this is unforgiving country."

Shelah merely nodded. "I know," he agreed. "But I feel the need to be back."

The others frowned, but kept their peace. Shelah's instincts had guided them to this point, and Ashkenaz merely grunted. They were tired, and although the distance as the crow flew was an easy day's walk, the way was rough with a descent of nearly 3,000 cubits. But if Shelah felt the need to hurry, they would hurry.

Anam longed for that kind of respect. Shaking his head, he sat on a stone near the fire and began to bolt down the meat with an occasional swallow of water. He had not eaten all day and was ravenous. Shelah gave him time without interruption. He turned back to Ashkenaz and explained. "We spent too many days north of the mountains. Nimrod has plans; we all know that. Do not mistake his patience for hesitation. The longer we delay, the more men he will lure to destruction. His designs are advanced; we are just starting. We should have done this last year! Our success will mean little if we linger."

"But you said that we needed to mark sites for settlement. That will take months if not an entire year," challenged Heth. "What do a few days matter now?"

"Those months are the reason," returned Shelah. "I would start people moving as soon as we get back, but few will come until we have more information. We have only cracked a door into a dark room. Few will go in until we light a lamp."

"You're right," admitted Ashkenaz. "But how many will attempt the mountains just because there is a way through? Few, if any, I'm sure."

"All the more reason to hurry," answered Shelah. Then he turned to the others. "We can be home in ten days if we push. Then we can rest." He smiled. "After tomorrow the way will be easier and we will be back in the lands that we know. Perhaps there is news from the south."

Anam started to groan, but then realized they would be leaving the mountains behind. It wouldn't be a warm, wide river, with the sun sparkling off the water, but it would be an improvement. Despite the verdure of the lands they had seen, the north wind was still chill. His paradise lay to the south, not the north. The others might love the mountains and upland forests, but they were not for him.

Jobaath laughed. "I'm going to spend days in hot water with cold wine! Call on me in a month or two if you want to travel back here."

"I hope that we all have that month," returned Heth, "but don't count on Nimrod to supply it. He's worse than the beasts he hunts! He'll come at your back and strike like a snake. And he has that witch to guide his hand."

Anam broke in, knowing that if Heth started, he would go on about Nimrod until the moon rose. "What did you find?" he asked Shelah. "Did you add anything to your map?"

"No. Every side valley ended in ice or rock walls. If there is another way through these hills, it is well hidden. What about your valley? Any hope there?"

Anam sighed. "Ice already covers its head. There was a ledge that I thought might skirt the edge of the rock and lead beyond, but it cannot be passed."

"It must be only a few paces wide." Jobaath laughed at his joke.

Anam burned at the memory of those moments on the ledge and rounded on Jobaath in unexpected wrath. "Then you go back and traverse it, braggart! The carrion eaters will thank you for the meal and we'll thank you for the peace!"

Everyone stared at Anam. He had always accepted their heavy-handed humor as his price for being part of the group. But weeks in the wilderness had changed him. Heth looked at him with new eyes. He had taken his own share of taunts about the wolf, and even though Jobaath and Ashkenaz were infinitely more careful with the words they threw at Heth, he had not enjoyed them. In a flash of insight, he found sympathy for Anam along with more than a little guilt for his past offenses. It was not too soon to make amends.

"Anam has a good idea," he stated bluntly, turning to Jobaath. "If you want to test the path, then go and do so. We can travel slowly for a few days and give you a chance to catch up." He paused and smiled, "Unless, of course, one of my wolf's friends happens to run across you far from a convenient tree!"

Shelah intervened before Jobaath could retort, "Anam, can you help me draw your valley?" He had traced information from the others on the bare rock with a burnt stick. Anam shot a look of gratitude to Heth and moved over to help him.

Ashkenaz stood and looked up the slope to the pass they would cross the next day. "I'll take the first watch and wake Heth in a few hours." Heth grunted and unrolled his blanket and Jobaath followed his example. Tomorrow would be another long day, and they all knew they needed sleep to face it.

7-20-1754

First light found the five climbing. Sunrise found them at the summit, gasping in the thin air and looking south along the rivers that would lead them through the lower slopes out onto the rugged country north of the great mountain. They were leaving the ice behind; the lower slopes were green. Farther down, the darker shades of evergreens were broken by the snaking line of the river that marked their path.

Night found them far below the pass. Anam slept well, happy to be leaving the cold heights behind. And the past months had given him strength and endurance he had never before known; he felt a new vigor. Lightly built and light on his feet, he was happy to lead, his staff prodding for any hidden danger on the trail. Next to the river, they had discovered several patches that appeared solid, yet gave way at the first pressure. Heth's firm grip on the rope around his waist caught any slips.

The next day the path was easier. Down among the trees, Shelah ranged ahead, hunting on the move to save time. And this day, like many others, Shelah met with success. They came upon him late in the morning gutting the carcass of a small deer. With practiced ease Ashkenaz moved to help and they soon had the hide off. Shelah selected the best cuts from haunch and neck and wrapped them in the still-warm skin after washing the blood from them in a quiet eddy at the riverbank.

Anam stood, grateful for Shelah's skill. There had been enough cold hungry nights on their trek. Tomorrow might bring another. But tonight would not. As they pushed on among the rocks along the bank, he dreamed of a bright sun on warm, calm waters, of hot food and cool wine.

7-29-1754

Madrazi woke one morning to find Shem sitting in the rocking chair across the room, watching her. She flushed. She knew she looked terrible, not having had time to wash her face or fix her hair. It always amazed her that Shem could see her looking like this and smile his satisfaction. Reading her mind, he chuckled. "Get up and walk with me. It will do the men good to see the real master of the house inspecting their work."

"Give me a minute," she murmured, knowing that it would be closer to half of an hour. He knew it too. "Breakfast will be ready when you are," was all he said.

Later, they talked over the life of the farm as they were wont to do in the cool of the morning. In the early years after the flood, Shem and Madrazi had learned much from Japheth and had become adept at producing crops and flocks. Madrazi pushed her knowledge further, working hard to share her husband's burdens. But crops were not on her mind today.

As they strolled out to the barns, watching the men prepare for their day, she stopped and asked him, "How is Jael doing? She still won't talk openly to me."

Shem shook his head. "She doesn't know how to quit. She has a ready mind and grows daily in strength. She'll never match men strength to strength, so I'll teach her to be elusive and to use their strength against them. In the end she'll be dangerous. In a few years, she might have a chance against someone good, though she'll never equal Heth or Shelah. But if she ever learns that her beauty and guile are weapons, she'll be more perilous than any of them." He paused and looked away. "It's hard, my love. Even with your fate in her hands, it wounds me to treat her like this. I hate the idea of turning my own sister into a killer."

Madrazi thought for a few minutes as they walked down the edge of the vineyard. "She need not kill. Perhaps the knowledge that she has the ability to take a life so easily will force her to consider the consequences, quiet her fears, and allow some sense to seep back into her head." Shem nodded. He was tired—it had been a busy spring and summer, and he wasn't getting any younger. Madrazi saw the lines around his eyes.

"Send her home for a week," she suggested as they walked on. "Tell her it's a part of her training. Tell her that she must be able to disguise herself as a weak woman to deceive her opponents. She'll go. She obeys your every command. Besides, her family needs to see her, and Zeb can watch over her from a distance."

Shem was silent, thinking. They walked out into the orchard, admiring the richness of the fruit that weighed down the branches. After a time Shem finally nodded. "I hate to interrupt her progress, but you're right. She needs to see them too… even if she doesn't think so. And I need time with you." He stopped and pulled her to him, and she threw her arms around his neck and kissed him fiercely. "I think so too." She pulled back, panting. "You've been a stranger these past weeks."

Suddenly she froze—a look of fear on her face. "Oh, no!" she breathed. "I forgot the day. Send her now," she urged. "The boys will be back soon. She's not ready for what passes for humor with them."

Shem stopped, stared at her in sudden understanding, and turned pale. "I hadn't thought of that," he admitted. Then he started laughing. "Jael and Heth. A spitting cat and a bad-tempered bear. The songs they would write about that meeting!"

Chapter 13
THE CAT AND THE BEAR

7-30-1754

Heth topped the hill to see the sun parting the morning clouds. Shading his eyes with one hand, he stopped to enjoy the vista. At the bottom of the long hill were the pastures and outer fields. He had ranged ahead of the others, swinging around to the west, while Shelah had done the same to the east. It allowed them to scout the land around the farm—something Shem had taught them long ago. "Stay aware of your surroundings," he had said, "and no one will surprise you." Heth grunted. No surprises today. He set his pack down and sat on it, determined to enjoy a few minutes of unspoiled peace before the inevitable uproar of their return.

The scouting seemed a waste of time, but Shelah had asked, and Heth would have walked a week out of his way for his friend. He looked back north. The lonely mountain loomed up, its crown covered with gray haze. He shivered. He had come around its west side, between the mountain and the chain of lower hills running off to the west. He had jogged most of the way and avoided looking up. There was something about this mountain that made his flesh creep. Quickly he averted his gaze. He was tired and thirsty, and didn't want to think about what lay on its peak.

A spring bubbled up from the black rock a few steps away from the road, so he strode over and stooped to drink. He was ravenous, but determined to wait for real food—fresh bread cooked by a woman's hand. He was sick of dried meat. Hunger and a vague menace from the mountain kept his temper on edge. He needed food, rest, and peace.

As he strode back over to his pack, he noticed two riders in the distance, walking their horses up the hill. The sun was behind them, so he shielded his eyes and looked again. Even now, he could see that one was Zeb. Good with horses, he had the makings of a fine man. No one sat a saddle as well. Zeb's companion was a stranger, thin like Zeb, but smaller. Heth watched the horses walk up the long incline. He still couldn't see the other boy clearly, but he grudgingly admitted that the lad handled the horse well… clearly he had been learning from Zeb. But his face was obscured by a rough turban—the top pulled down low on his forehead and the other end thrown over his lower face. His clothes were ragged, but Heth was quick to note two knives in his belt. He raised an eyebrow at that. A ragged boy shouldn't have such pretensions. He sat back down on his pack to wait.

As they drew closer Heth saw the feathered end of arrows peeking over one shoulder of the stranger and the end of a short bow sticking out from under his cloak. He decided it was one of the ragamuffins that tended sheep in the outer pastures, armed with a bow to fight off the wolves and jackals that ranged the rough lands. Young, full of himself, and not overly bright—Shem kept the smart ones closer to the farm and taught them well. He wondered idly why such a boy would be riding. Must be one of Zeb's friends, helping exercise a horse before heading back out to his flock. Whatever the reason, he would find out soon; they were only an arrow shot away. Heth stood, locking both hands on the spear just below the head. He leaned on his hands, weary but curious, waiting for the horses to make their way to the top.

Jael was angry. Just as she was beginning to discover the potential of her body, Shem had ordered her home. Her temper had flared, but she dare not argue—he was her instructor now. And she feared his anger—the first time she had triggered it, he had run her into the ground, and then left her to limp home by herself, not daring to remove the heavy pack, knowing that he was watching… somewhere.

She ground her teeth. Her sisters would think her repentant, but her parents would know better. Everyone would be uncomfortable. And Shem had added insult to injury by telling her that Zeb would accompany her part of the way, since he was (all too conveniently) going west to deliver messages to Japheth. It was galling to realize that Zeb was being sent to trail her home to make sure the "weak woman" got home without hurting herself. His lack of confidence hurt… she was sure she had been doing well.

At least it was Zeb. If forced to ride with any man, Zeb was acceptable. A superb horseman, he was willing to share his hard-won expertise, but he talked little unless asked. He seemed to understand her anger, tactfully ignoring it as they prepared the horses.

Preoccupied with her thoughts, she was surprised to see the heavily muscled man seemingly appear out of nowhere at the top of the hill, sharply outlined in the morning sun. She castigated herself for not noticing him sooner and sat a little straighter in the saddle. Her bow was under her cloak, but there was a knife hidden inside her sleeve and two more in her belt. Zeb shuffled in his saddle, suddenly nervous. He was always cautious on the start of a ride, and he had many long lonely days of riding ahead. But she sensed that this was different.

All of the sudden she grew cold and still. If her father's home could be attacked, so could Shem's. The man ahead didn't look like Korac, but he looked formidable and she didn't know him. The spear he was leaning on seemed to be an extension of his arms. Zeb stuttered for a moment, clearly wanting to say something but was unable to get it out. He might be afraid, she thought, but she was confident in her newfound ability. They were two and on horses, and he was one and on foot. If he was looking for trouble, he wouldn't have to search any further.

Zeb wasn't afraid of the stranger—he continued to walk his steed towards him— but as they neared, his tension was growing, and her senses were alert. As they climbed nearer, he began to fidget, glancing back and forth between her and the stranger. "What's wrong?" she finally murmured impatiently. "Is he a stranger? He is rather large… if he frightens you, ease behind me."

"Uh… uh… it's not that, my lady," he stammered. "That's Heth. No one else has such arms. And his braid… no beard… and that spear. I'd know it anywhere."

Jael relaxed. "So it's Heth. He's your friend. No reason for you to fear. Let's ride up and greet him."

Zeb swallowed. "He's never met you, my lady… he doesn't… he wasn't told…."

"Quit stuttering!" Jael shook her head, mistaking his nervousness for hero worship. Everyone seemed to think the sun rose and set on Shelah and Heth. "He's just a man... nothing special. Let's greet him and be on our way. It's a long ride to Father's farm... I mean, to Japheth's."

Zeb looked down at the ground, blushing furiously. "Please, my lady...."

"Oh, don't worry," Jael curled her lip. "I won't tell big brother. After we part ways, I never saw you!" She almost smiled.

"But... but... Heth..."

"Well, if you're afraid to talk to him, I will." She spurred her mount to a trot and slid ahead of the boy. He just shook his head and followed, bracing himself. Foremost among the thoughts racing through his mind was that they should have left the previous day. He braced himself and kicked his horse to catch up.

Heth watched the sheep herder ride ahead, boldly drawing near. The sun was to his back and the turban hid his face, but Heth thought he saw the hint of a smile in the shadowed features. "Hello big man," he called in a high voice. "Doesn't your spear ever grow weary of holding up so much weight?"

A frown darkened his face. After months in the wilderness, fighting cold, rocks, and wolves, the last thing he needed was to be mocked by some impudent herder. He slid his bulk into the horse's path and raised his hand. "This spear has taught lessons to man and beast," he growled. "For a little goat herder like you, the butt end should suffice. Come learn some manners from your betters. Your saddle will remind you of it for the rest of your ride!"

"You arrogant lout!" The boy's dark green eyes glared from beneath the turban. "Get out of my way before I ride you down!"

Heth's temper flared. He was tired, hungry, and footsore. He might have stepped aside for Shem or Shelah, but not for some rude little snot. Twirling his spear in his right hand, he grabbed for the reins with the other. As planned, the horse was frightened by the sudden flash of light from the spear and reared back, but to the boy's credit, he easily kept his seat. As it came back down, Heth seized the reins firmly in his left hand and stepped around its head to his right. At the same time he swung the shaft around, intending to knock the boy off his horse—a lesson in manners sorely needed.

But several things happened at once. The boy avoided his swing with ease, dropping off on the other side of the horse with surprising quickness and grace. Then he dodged uphill, putting Heth's thick body between him and the spear. A knife appeared in each hand, and his eyes flashed fire. Zeb was thundering up, and in a brief glance, Heth saw a look of horror on his face.

But his blood was up and he didn't care. He let the horse go; Zeb could catch it. He was going to deal with his angry young friend—knock the knives from his hand, turn him around, and let the spear's shaft go to work on his backside. He was looking forward to this.

But at that moment a quick movement of the boy's left hand—pulling his turban out of his way—struck Heth harder than a club. Despite the rough clothes, no one could mistake that face for anything but a very angry young woman. She was dark, but her oval face was bright with wrath; her lips parted slightly as she panted. Her hair was dark and ragged, caught up in back with a braid—very much like his own, but shorter. Thinking of what he had almost done, he felt the blood rush to his face.

She kept sliding to his left, keeping him off balance, but not nearly as off balance as her next words. "Lay a hand on me, you ox, and I'll cut it off and feed you the fingers. No man touches me!"

Flat footed, Heth stared. "Who are you, little one? I thought… I mean… you're no boy…."

"How observant," she sneered. "I am Jael, daughter of Noah and sister of Shem. I know you. You're that son of Canaan! You have the reputation of a warrior… and I can see that you're a man to be feared… by young boys and women." She spat and sprang back down hill to grab the reins of her horse from Zeb.

In an instant, she was up in the saddle. "Go spend some time with Shem and his wife. Perhaps they can teach you some manners!" She thundered off, disappearing over the hill, Zeb galloping to catch up. He turned and gave Heth an apologetic shrug, then was gone.

Heth stared after them for some minutes before shaking himself. "What a hellcat!" he muttered. "One of Noah's girls. I thought they were all proper ladies. This one slipped the bridle at some point!" He turned away, but couldn't get that fiery face out of his mind. A strange thought intruded. Given the proper clothes and absent the anger, she would have been pretty… in a rough sort of way. He couldn't shake the memory of those fiery green eyes. He shook his head as her words ran again through his mind.

Like any other woman, she knew how to flay with her tongue… *that son of Canaan*…. He bristled and felt his blood rise. Would he never leave his legacy behind? Anger took him and he turned and shouted at the road, "I don't care if you were Noah's wife; no woman talks to me like that! It might be worth marrying you, just to tame you!"

He laughed harshly. "As if I'd ever marry a hellion like her," he grunted, and started down the hill. "I'd sleep easier at night being married to one of Debseda's shrews!" He kicked a stone, anger turning quickly to depression. He wasn't going to marry her or anyone else. He had a war to fight and didn't need to leave any widows or orphans behind. There would be plenty of time for that foolishness after Nimrod was defeated.

But the eyes continued to haunt him.

He blushed as he thought of the others learning of this little episode. He needed to silence Zeb when he returned. Hopefully the wildcat was going home! If the others ever found out… if Jobaath ever heard of it…. Heth shuddered. Jobaath might be a good friend, but he had a rough sense of humor, and Heth knew he would never hear the end of it.

Chapter 14
COUNCIL OF SHEM

8-2-1754

Heth and Shelah stood silently together on the porch as the sunrise illuminated the line of hills to the northwest. Ice covered their crowns; it was a rare morning when they were not shrouded in gray. And though clouds were gathering on the horizon, light glittered off the lowland dew. Heth marveled at the deceptive beauty. But he knew that beauty would give way to the harsh reality of hard trails on their next trip.

With a half smile he put away morbid thoughts. Tomorrow might bring hardship or pain, but today was good. All five men were well-rested, having done little but sleep and eat for three days. Heth was a little shamed; his prodigious portions at table brought smirks from his comrades, but he did not care. Already he felt his thick body resuming its normal proportions. Ashkenaz and Jobaath had slept the days away, and Anam had wallowed in endless hot baths and the luxury of clean clothes.

But the time for indulgence was done; both knew it as they stood engrossed in their thoughts. And both nearly leapt off the porch when a firm hand materialized on their shoulders. Shelah began to laugh as Heth stopped his instinctive lunge for the absent knife at his belt.

Shem had become a farmer, but could still move as softly as a breath of air, and his broad smile told them that he enjoyed reminding the young adventurers of his prowess. "I hope you boys are well rested," he said. "We need to talk this morning. Much has happened and we have paths to choose." Shelah glanced at Heth. They shook their heads as they followed him back into the house. The holiday was over.

A bright fire filled the fireplace of the great room; evergreens and holly berries decorated the ancient timber mantel. As always, Heth felt the urge to run his hands across it—the wood was smooth and dark, a relic from the ark. Chairs were arranged in a rough circle around several tables laden with wine and food. Anam, Jobaath, and Ashkenaz were already seated, half-empty plates before them. Like young boys showing off their manners, they sat with serious mien, less than comfortable in the presence of Madrazi.

Heth frowned as he walked into the room. He, too, was wary of Shem's wife but despised that feeling as weakness. Though a great-grandmother, she looked as young as many women of fifty or sixty, just ripening into her full beauty. She was unfailingly gracious, but Heth was sure she harbored a secret amusement at the tongue-tied clumsiness that she inevitably engendered in the strongest men.

As a survivor of the ark, she was special—most people sensed the same aura in all eight elders. But with Madrazi, there was more... that cloaked power that only she and Noah possessed. He could never forget the harsh glitter of her eye as she had calmly spoken of the fate of his far descendents. Her ability to see the depths of time as if it were a deep lake—when everyone else saw their reflection in its surface—was disconcerting at best. During the trek north he had tried to convince himself that it was her beauty... her haunting eyes... or some music in her voice that had befuddled him. But walking into her presence now, he felt that familiar tingle. She was touched by power, and Heth was a man who respected it.

He envied Shelah—the only one of them truly comfortable in her presence. He was her blood and had her wisdom even if he lacked her other gifts. Having grown up here, his awe was tempered by years of love. Heth edged to a chair across the room, letting his friend bow to Madrazi and sit in an open chair beside her.

Sitting, Heth slouched down and crossed his arms. He was not one for talk but accepted its necessity. Glancing up, he was snared at once by her appraising glance. His face burned, but he sat up straighter and held her eyes, refusing to be intimidated. A small smile brushed her lips as she turned to her husband, who sat down on her other side. Heth flushed. Then he set his face and gripped his hands together in his lap, finding comfort in their rough strength.

Shem formally welcomed each man in the order of their birth, subtly reminding them that this was no social event. In his direct manner he moved immediately to affairs at hand. "You have much to tell us, but first you must hear our news. We said nothing until today to allow you a few days of peace after your travels, but Nimrod has already made his first move." He proceeded to tell them of Mariel's abduction. Heth's face hardened at Nimrod's effrontery. *How like the young whelp to wage war on women!* He was surprised to hear of Korac's role. It seemed beneath him.

Shem said nothing about the blow to Noah's reputation. He didn't have to. Heth shuddered at the thought of a generation growing up with no respect for their elders. No wonder Jael had been so angry when he met her on the road!

"Why did Noah not call down the curses of the Almighty on Nimrod's head?" asked an amazed Ashkenaz.

"Why did he not resist?" asked Jobaath, more thoughtfully. "Nimrod might have bested him, but laying hands on the father of us all would have made him an outcast. He's too smart to risk that."

Shem sighed. "I don't know. Father acted as his wisdom dictated... and his wisdom is informed by the spirit of the Almighty. While I don't understand, I know that he adhered to the will of the Creator... even to his own sorrow and loss."

He sighed and continued. "Nimrod will now present himself as the leading man of the plain, wedded to Noah's eldest daughter. Clearly Debseda has chosen him as her vessel for evil. It may be an affront to Canaan, but she'll keep him in line. When you combine his strength and her cunning... well, I fear we must move quickly."

He stopped for a moment as Madrazi laid a hand on his arm. "More evil has come from this deed," she added.

Shem grimaced and offered an abbreviated version of Jael's tale, watching the astonishment grow on the faces of the five cousins. Heth was surprised too, but it explained her behavior that morning. He felt a stab of sympathy and blushed slightly at the memory of his rude words. It certainly explained her rage. He found himself nodding in sympathy. Rage was something he understood. He hoped she could find a way to master it. Would he, had it not been for Shelah?

Jobaath interrupted his thoughts. "Little Jael… a warrior?" He chuckled.

Shem stared him down and the laughter faltered. "In a year she'll be dangerous. In five, she'll take you and be a threat to any man in this room. She's smart, fast, and growing hard. What's worse, she doesn't care." He glanced at Heth. "You know what that means." His words hung heavy in the room. "Give her a wide path and treat her with respect." He glared at Jobaath. "Am I clear?"

Jobaath swallowed hard as the others nodded. The implied warning was more than clear. Jael was Shem's little sister as well as his student. None of them had ever faced Shem's wrath… and none of them wanted to.

Madrazi spoke again. "There is more. She's become hard and we *must* find a way to restore her. We owe it to Noah. Nimrod has done grievous harm; we cannot let him succeed." She looked around the room catching the eyes of each man. "Do not strengthen the stone walls she has built around her heart. It will be enough to break through the ones already there."

Heth grunted. Shem's threat and his own encounter was enough. He wanted nothing to do with some angry girl who fancied herself a warrior. Madrazi interrupted, "Tell us of this man Korac. Who is he? Why is he attached to Nimrod? Wen-Tehrom told me that his eyes were cold and empty—like those of a cobra."

Heth nodded. "That's a good description. I know him… I mean, I knew him. A son of Magog, he spent time with our family, marrying Nimrod's sister, Timna. They were happy. But Korac loved to hunt with Nimrod. In time, Timna's jealousy led her to accompany them. She didn't return. Neither man would speak of it. Korac mourned for days, and that sorrow drained his soul. He became a shell of a man. But there's nothing wrong with his arm or his eye. He's dangerous—a sharp blade in Nimrod's hand. I could take him in a fair fight and Shelah might stand a chance. But like you said about Jael, he just doesn't care, and I wouldn't fight if I could flee."

Madrazi nodded. "Thank you, Heth." She paused and gathered the attention of all before resuming. "Know this! His fate is intertwined with Jael's. I have not seen why, but I know it to be true. All of you… beware this man!" The others glanced around nervously. There seemed no end of bad news. Heth shivered, recalling the power in this very room the last time she had "seen" something.

Thankfully, Shem broke the awkward silence. "We rejoice to see you back safely. Your trek was a first victory; one that gives us hope amid dark tidings. You have taken a large step toward defeating this new tyranny. With Shelah's help we are making new maps and it is time to decide our next steps."

Heth nodded. Now he knew why Shelah had been hard to find the past few days.

Shem continued, "Men, by nature, want the easy path, but you have found a different road, more difficult perhaps, but leading to a good end." He hesitated, and placed his hand on his wife's arm.

She stirred at his touch and sat up even straighter, letting her gaze brush from man to man, as if trying to read their hearts before she spoke. Heth coughed uncomfortably as she caught his eye, and felt an unreasoning rush of resentment. He was not his father's son—had not the past months proved his allegiance? He stirred, but before anger erupted, he saw a soft understanding in her eyes and caught himself.

"We are proud of you all," she said, staring at Heth as if in apology. "The seed of evil runs deep in the heart of every man. The best of us strive to stunt its growth and cultivate something better. The worst are destined for a bitter harvest that will consume others, leaving husks empty of joy and contentment. We escaped destruction in the ark, but not because we were free of that seed."

She faltered, and Heth did not miss Shem's hand covering hers. He wondered what stories of the voyage he had not heard. "We survived because of a light in our hearts that holds the darkness at bay. But that light is a gift, and not all desire it. The shame of Eden is in this world too, and it has begun to flourish anew… in Shinar."

She sighed. "We cannot win this war unless you understand that the battle is within each of you. You must vanquish your own evil to defeat the darkness."

She sighed and looked around the room again. "There is news from the south and I have seen things the messengers do not tell."

Heth stiffened. Talking about visions of Shinar as dispassionately as last year's harvest…. He felt his temper stir. How could a man concentrate, wondering what secrets she had seen in him? He flushed, thinking of several episodes from his youth he hoped were hidden from her sight. Sitting up, he set his face and looked about him. Except for Shem and Shelah, the others were uncomfortable too, and Heth was glad of the company.

He felt an urge to walk away, but then another thought struck him. If Madrazi could see him, she could see Canaan, Debseda, and the black heart of Nimrod. His lips curled up at the thought. Knowledge was power. He followed the thought on. She was not the source—she was merely the messenger. It was the Creator. He *was* interested in the affairs of men. Heth sat up. That meant that this was a far grander battle. He did not fight for Noah, for Shem, or even for Madrazi. He was a warrior for the Creator! That made Nimrod a warrior of evil, and made the fight of the utmost urgency. It also made the outcome inevitable. Who could stand against the King of Heaven? His eyes involuntarily turned north, towards the mountain. Who in their right mind could oppose the force that had covered that mountain with the sea?

Later in life Heth would look back on that insight as a defining moment. He had been the friend of Shelah for many years, but it was only now that he committed himself to something greater. He would fight for the Almighty. A sense of peace touched him. He knew this was right as surely as he knew his name. Madrazi was not someone to fear; she was a powerful ally—her gift was a sword for their side… for his side. He relaxed into his chair, feeling much more at ease.

Madrazi paused, fumbling for words, and Heth wondered if his revelation had just intruded on her thoughts. This time he met her inquiring glance with a grim smile. She saw it and inclined her head in thanks. Recovering quickly, she quietly asked Shelah for a cup of wine and took a sip before resuming her account.

"The Plain of Shinar. A flat, fertile land, shaped by the Tigris and Euphrates. An easy place to live and so men gather, ignoring the Creator's command to fill the earth. We have been a family—a large family with internal squabbles and spats, but ruled by the laws of family. With Noah's public humiliation and the numbers in each new generation, that restraint is gone. We have become clans; soon, kingdoms fighting for land and wealth. It happened once; it will happen again.

"A few short years ago we were eight. We had children. I held Arpachshad to my breast. Now his grandson Eber will marry and soon I will hold the great-grandson of Arpachshad on my knee. As men multiply, they cry out for government, creating opportunities for those who wish to lord it over others."

"What about Noah?" interrupted Jobaath. "Even if Nimrod has embarrassed him, he is still the father of us all and by rights should rule his descendents. Why does he not assert that authority? If he stepped forward, many would rally to him."

Shem replied sharply. "Noah spent centuries holding back the old darkness with his father and grandfather until it swallowed the earth. He watched those centuries of efforts come to naught—the earth was full of blood. He lost his father, his household, and his friends to that darkness. He carries those burdens, as well as those of building the ark and sailing it through the great flood. Most of his life is past. He lived it well, fulfilled his purpose, and now freely shares his wisdom with those that seek it. But this is not his struggle. In a way, it is not even his world. He will never assume the mantle of a great lord." Shem looked down and shook his head. "No doubt, we could use a man like Noah in his prime, but we must make do with what we have."

Madrazi nodded and continued. "Debseda has always lusted for power and has finally found her tool. Ham never wanted it. Canaan is weak, and Cush and Mizraim, not easily manipulated. In Nimrod, the blood of the Nephil runs true, giving him strength that few can resist. Even now he draws the weak and foolish, and binds their loyalty. The ranks of his 'friends' grow each year. Today they are a mob. Soon they will be an army. He will be a king… a dark, powerful king."

Ashkenaz broke in. "He cannot force everyone to his bidding. There are many who won't accept it."

"If only that were true," sighed Madrazi. "Few are like you, Ashkenaz. Force is the easiest path to power. If you wanted to rule and had an organized, armed group of followers, you could have it. Imagine yourself in his place. Someone speaks against you. You have him killed. Quietly… with uncertainty, so that you cannot be accused, yet men know your word caused the murder. Another becomes angry and speaks out. He too turns up dead. For every one dead, a hundred are reduced to obedience by fear. It's a powerful tool and just one of those that Debseda is teaching Nimrod to wield with skill. With fifty to kill for him, who would dare oppose him? Without organization and government, his enemies are easy prey. Yet with it, he can seize the reins of power with an air of legitimacy."

"So, our only hope is to organize our own army and fight back before he grows too strong," Heth blurted.

"That is one possibility," replied Shem quietly.

Before he could finish, Heth was up, speaking and pacing. "We six are a good start. Even Nimrod cannot match your skill with the bow and I have Ham's knowledge of metal and weapons. We could raise fifty men and march on Shinar within the season. Then…"

Shem's face darkened and Heth's flamed as he realized his error. He quickly sat back down and mumbled an apology. Shem took a deep breath and continued. "Actually, you are right. We could assemble a force and start a war with Nimrod." He paused and his eyes drilled into Heth. "We might even win... but at what price?"

Heth's brow furrowed. "A few dead or wounded," he stammered. "I am willing to risk my life to rid the world of Nimrod."

"What of the women and children?" Madrazi's voice was gentle, but insistent. "Who will till the land and care for the crops while these armies march and fight? How will they eat? They will take what they want. What if the forces are evenly matched? Years of ongoing warfare and destruction. That would suit Nimrod. Many would flock to his tyranny, forced to choose a side."

Her eyes flashed as she rose and spoke louder, with a strange echo in the room. "There will be an ocean of blood before the trail of man's years is complete." Then she seemed to shrink again as her voice eased. "Let us not add to it now... not if there is any other way."

Heth flushed again and looked down, the back of his neck still tingling from the outburst of power.

"I agree that avoiding conflict is the best course," interjected Anam. "But if Nimrod is going to use force, how do we defeat him without doing the same?"

"If you can't take a blow, deflect it," blurted Jobaath. "If your opponent is strong, stay out of his reach until you wear him down."

"Bah!" barked Ashkenaz. "We are talking of war. If we sit back, then we concede defeat and the earth is his. There's a way to avoid both. The six of us filter into Shinar, kill Nimrod and his key followers, and then escape. An easy victory."

"Yes!" barked Shem. "An easy victory for the evil one! Take six righteous men and make them murderers. Let that evil infect their families... let darkness roll down through the generations!" His voice rose to a thunderous shout. His face was dark and his eyes flashed. "What of your wives and children? At best they become the families of murderers; at worst they become widows and orphans."

Heth had never heard Shem raise his voice. It was impressive; Ashkenaz wilted. Heth felt a chill on his neck; he suddenly realized what he should have known long ago—Shem was the most dangerous man in the room. Sweat broke out on his brow when he recalled the times he had strutted and boasted before this man. Once again Madrazi's gaze bored into him... yet this time, with approval. She smiled. He shook his head. How could someone so beautiful be so wise?

Looking around, he saw everyone staring at the floor, so he broke into the strained silence. "Shem is right. One day we'll all stand before the Great Judge. I don't need any more stains on my hands. Yet Ash is not without insight. We need eyes and ears on the plain. We plan in ignorance, and that is perilous. Look what happened to Mariel and her family. He wouldn't have dared if any of us had been there." He paused again; then spoke softly. "What's Nimrod doing today? What plots are being discussed even as we speak? We must know."

He looked around the room for disagreement. There was none. Madrazi was smiling openly now. He felt like a school boy, some particularly bright student who had pleased the teacher.

Encouraged, Heth continued. "Some of us need to open the door to the northern lands. But we also need a man inside Nimrod's circle. One who can gain his trust, ferret out his secrets, and send them north. It can't be me—Nimrod hates me and I hate him. For the same reason, Shelah cannot go." He paused and turned to his youngest cousin.

"Anam," he said softly, "you are the one." He pointed his thick fingers as he made his points. "You are of his blood. Nimrod cannot afford to offend your father. You are not married. You have a way about you… people like you easily. And…" he hesitated, before plowing on, "people would believe you were easily led astray by Shelah."

"You mean they would believe I'm weak," Anam retorted, his hurt apparent.

Heth leaned forward. "Yes," he said steadily, "they would."

Anam slumped, his eyes cast down.

"But that is your sharpest blade. They don't know you! You're a man, Anam, and *I* know it. You were a staunch companion on a hard road. I would fight at your right hand, Anam, because I know you're a man of courage—and you'll need more than I possess to carry out this task."

Anam looked up, unbelieving. "But I thought you…" He faltered.

"No!" Heth sighed. "I once allowed pride to cloud my judgment, but now I'm proud to call you my friend. If you agree to this task, your life will hang by a thread every day. One false word, one false look, one mistake… and you will die. One false thought in the presence of Debseda, and Korac will give your body to the river. And yet," he sighed, "without information, we cannot succeed."

Anam's emotions whipped between fear and pride. Heth was right. To spy on Nimrod was to toy with his life. Yet Heth—fearless and formidable—was praising his courage before Ashkenaz and Jobaath. The larger man continued softly, "I will think no less of you for refusing, Anam, for if it were me, my heart would turn to water at the thought of what must be done."

Anam's heart swelled. Heth… *Heth* held him in high esteem. Then another thought struck him. This plan was an answer to his prayers. He could avoid the cold mountains and distant lands, and not fail his comrades. He could return to the sunlit lands and serve the Almighty too. And he could hold his head high… knowing that his courage was admired by the bravest man he knew. He sat straighter and looked around the room with a confident eye.

"I swore to serve the Almighty and serve Him I will. If the eldest son of the Patriarch agrees that this is my path, I will follow it faithfully." His smile broadened… the small voice of doubt that had been his constant companion silent.

This was his purpose. He had never been more sure of anything.

Shem nodded, his face troubled. "Heth is right, Anam. We do need information, but my heart hesitates to send any man into that snake pit. There is no stain in refusing, Anam. If you will go freely, then go with my blessing and thanks." Anam smiled confidently and nodded his assent.

Madrazi rose and walked over to the young man. Holding out her hand, she reached for his and he came immediately to his feet to bow his head. But she reached out and took his cheek in her hand. "Anam, son of Mizraim, your heart is bold. But there is a greater danger than discovery on the plain. Sin will seek to seduce your heart, whispering lies to lead you away from the Almighty. You will need another kind of courage to walk a path opposed to all around you."

She raised her right hand and laid it on his head. "Anam, child of Noah, walk in integrity of heart. Heed not the whispers of the serpent and his brood. Beware the leaven of evil. Walk in light, though all around succumb to darkness. Go with the blessing and protection of Noah's God."

She put an arm around his shoulder and turned to the others. "If brave Anam is to be our eye, then someone else must be his feet, to carry what he learns from Nimrod's inner rooms to our door. Which of you will help your brother?"

"How can it be done, grandmother?" interrupted Shelah.

"We already have men traveling to Shinar to buy and sell. Whoever gathers secrets from Anam can meet them outside town or in a crowd at the market. A secret word or sign can identify friends. But Anam must never be seen there—Nimrod knows our people come to trade. And if he succeeds, Debseda will have her spies watching his every move. We need a courier, working in a lowly, anonymous job—one that just happens to bring them near Anam on a regular basis...."

"Yes," breathed Shelah. "Like a guard, a builder, or an artisan...."

"Exactly," she replied.

Shem stood and walked over to them and put his arm around Anam's other shoulder—the two elders framing the smaller man. The three stood together looking at Ashkenaz. Shem spoke. "Jobaath has a wife and child. You must go south. When the time comes, he can go north with us."

Ashkenaz and Jobaath looked at each other and shrugged. "I'll care for your land and flocks while you're gone," offered Jobaath. "I'll treat them as my own."

Ashkenaz grinned. "Just remember that they're not. I'll have a full accounting when I return."

They all laughed. Everyone knew Jobaath would put his friend's profits ahead of his own."

"It's better that way," mused Heth. "Ash won't give himself away with some prank...." Jobaath glared at the bigger man. "And I won't have to listen to his snoring on the next trip!"

Ashkenaz and Jobaath looked at each other and grinned. "I'll teach him how before I go," said Ashkenaz to Heth. "It's all a matter of sleeping next to the ugliest... it brings dreams that make snore."

Heth shook his head and shot the pair a dirty look, but laughed with everyone else.

Ashkenaz stood and gripped Anam's slim arm in his brawny hand. "We'll make a great team! We'll get the information that you need. Nimrod won't surprise you again... you can count on us. Right, brother?"

"Without a doubt!" replied the smaller man, with a confidence that he actually felt.

Chapter 15
ANAM COMES HOME

9-4-1754

Ashkenaz leaned back against a boulder, his small fire keeping the night at bay. Two weeks behind Anam, he was near the edge of the plains. Within a few days he would strike the Euphrates, following it to Shinar. He thought idly about building a boat of reeds and floating downstream. But he was not much of a swimmer, and even the lions of the plains were less terrifying than the crocodiles that plied the river. He could accept being torn to pieces by a bear or lion, but had once seen a buck ambushed at the river—seized by the snout, dragged into the water, and then rolled over into the dark depths. He shuddered. Even an asp's poison was better than that!

He turned his mind away from morbid fears and considered the task ahead. In some ways, his task was harder than Anam's. Anam would blend in with the people of the plains. He was small, dark, and quick to make friends. His family lived there.

Ashkenaz snorted to himself… he would have never imagined that he might wish to be one of Debseda's offspring! But it would simplify his life; as Gomer's son and Japheth's grandson, he would be doubly suspected. Gomer and Javan were the only sons of Japheth who had so far refused the easy life of Shinar and his own cousins—the sons of Magog, Madai, Meschech, Tiras, and Tubal—would clamor against him to curry favor with Nimrod.

He would never fit in. He was large, though not as bulky as Heth, and his yellow hair and blue eyes would stand out among Ham's clan. Being a friend of Shelah and Shem wouldn't help either. He sighed. Madrazi had assured him that his story would be believable, and Anam had promised to drop a few hints about his defection, but if it didn't work out, he would be alone and surrounded by enemies.

But part of him didn't care. He had always been able to take care of himself. He wouldn't look for trouble, but he wouldn't back away either. And few men could move him once he dug his feet in. He must walk a fine line. If men feared him too much, they wouldn't accept him in Shinar. Too little, and they would walk over him.

He hoped Anam would be at his clever best setting the stage. The timing was right; a small caravan carrying wool and tin to Shinar was a week ahead, a week behind Anam. Its men had been carefully selected by Shem to carry the latest "gossip" from the north… all of it believable, yet none of it true.

Nimrod would hear about Shelah's failure to bring unity. He would hear of Anam's rebellion. Of hot tempers and angry accusations. Of Heth cursing Anam as a traitor and Ashkenaz' defense of the younger man. How Madrazi had expelled Ashkenaz and Anam, pinning her hopes on Heth in the coming conflict.

The story had been shaped to safeguard Anam and Ashkenaz, but more pointedly, it had been crafted to ignite Debseda's passionate hatred of Madrazi and Nimrod's of Heth. If those two focused on their loathing of ancient foes, then anything was possible. As long as they reacted rather than reflected, Ashkenaz should be safe, though probably never trusted. He would try to fan the flames when he arrived. Shem's obsession with freedom was a trick to avoid the laws needed by civilized society. Shem preferred to rule, and Ashkenaz would be sure to refer to Noah, Shem, and Japheth as the new barbarians of the wastelands.

He wouldn't be embraced. He anticipated being friendless, with a few years of demeaning jobs. Over time, a pretended apathy combined with a reputation as a hard worker at any task would earn him a place. He would survive, but never prosper. His pride was not the point, he reminded himself; he simply had to get close enough to Anam to accomplish his task.

He might never be trusted in the councils of Debseda and Nimrod, but all he required was a place in Shinar. To that end, the caravan traders had also been carefully coached to paint a picture of Ashkenaz. Stubborn, but not smart. A man desiring strict order and discipline. Loyal to anyone who could promise food, shelter, and order. A strong back and a weak mind.

"It's just a few years," he muttered to the darkness.

9-5-1754

Anam stared at the city ahead. It was easy to see; the land between the rivers was relatively flat and Shinar could be seen from a distance across the vast meadows. Whatever woodlands had existed near the city had been cleared for fields and timber. Sunrise glinted red off the bricks of the city, as if presaging a bloody destiny for its citizens. Anam didn't need any omens to trigger his desire to turn and walk in the opposite direction. During the journey down the plain, he had felt unusually alone in a vast dark world, and he knew it would be far lonelier inside. The soaring bravado of the past month waned with each step.

He did not fear his initial meetings. Heth was right. People thought him weak and even his father would think nothing of little Anam slinking home like a whipped cur. Shem and Madrazi had spent hours helping him create a story—from Jobaath's supposed promise of lonely women in the northern pastures to the self-righteous arrogance of Shem and his wife's witchcraft. He knew the story, but still… this new life would be difficult. Madrazi had tried to explain. She had told him that he must become two people: the real Anam, hidden deep, and the false Anam, disillusioned and disgusted with the sanctimonious hypocrites of the hills.

But how could he keep the role from becoming reality? If he survived the coming years, he suddenly realized *that* might be his hardest challenge. What would he do when his own heart accused him of deceit? Would he hate himself or would the God of Madrazi keep him from the worst of the filth?

He recalled Madrazi's advice. "Find a place to be alone—go into the wilderness if you must—and remember these past years, fast, pray for help, and anchor yourself anew in the memories of what the Almighty has done for you. Do it often."

It sounded so elegant in the clean air of the hills, but here on the plain there would be eyes watching his every move. Shem had assured him of that. "Always assume someone is watching. Establish routines. Be predictable, and eventually your watchers will relax. Don't worry about discovering or evading them—it will only draw suspicion. Never try to send a message. Be passive—let Ashkenaz initiate contact. You job is to watch, listen, and learn. Store up knowledge, sift it, and when the opportunity comes, give it to Ash. If it takes a year, it takes a year. That's not your problem. All you must do is stay alive and stay inside."

That's all.

Anam had slept poorly last night. He forced the fears down and took his first steps towards this strange new life. His appearance was in keeping with his story. Old, ill-fitting clothes. Matted hair and beard. Worn sandals. Few possessions. But the sun felt warm on his left side as it mounted the morning sky and Anam felt his spirits lift. The sun glittered off the water to his right. The land was pleasant. He could live here…. If not on these plains, then maybe south. Mizraim had found good land on the southern shores of the Great Sea, after a long march through rugged wilderness. A long trek to a fertile river valley.

Starting early, Anam reached Shinar before noon. All morning, riders passed him on the road, coming and going. Wagons creaked past, carrying grain, wool, and wood. Shinar was prospering. He felt its energy; he could see its progress in the road and the beginnings of a wall around the town. The city was much larger than he remembered. He saw a section of wall rising some distance north of the road. The reason for its sturdy appearance was plain in the distance. Smoke was rising from the kilns down near the river. Clay was being fired into hard bricks; set in the slimy mortar of tar, they formed dense, resistant structures. Even from this distance, he could see fields of finished bricks and an endless line of sledges hauling them to the wall and new buildings. People were working like bees to build their hive.

But why did they need a wall? His curiosity was piqued. There were no enemies to swoop down and seize the city; the men of the northern hills were mostly shepherds, miners, and farmers. It was then that the skin at the back of his neck began to prickle. If it wasn't meant to keep people out… there was only one other alternative. Anam exhaled softly. He wondered how many of those workers realized that they were building their own prison.

The wall had not yet reached the road, but there was a brick arch spanning the way, and it would soon house a strong gate. Men with spears funneled the traffic under that arch. Anam recognized several. One was his cousin Hiv, one of Heth's younger brothers. Anam recalled him as a follower, not clever but surprisingly friendly. Large and strong like Heth, he had little need to be otherwise.

Anam greeted him. "Hiv! New job?"

"Gate guard," grinned the larger man.

"I heard you were in the Legion," Anam responded easily.

"They ride up and down the roads, collecting silver from every trader. Easy work, but you have to earn a place. Another year and I'll be one of the lucky ones."

"You're sure to make it soon," encouraged Anam.

Hiv frowned. "I heard you were up north with Heth and his crowd. What happened?"

Anam returned the frown, as if recalling a bad memory. "They lied!"

He appeared to take a moment to control himself, but convincingly failed. His anger washed over Hiv. "They lied and treated me like a dog!"

Hiv appeared sympathetic. "How did you get away?"

"It took a while. They say the witch can see everything in the hills. But I made it to the headwaters of the river with a flock, left 'em for the wolves, and headed south. I've had enough of that lot... I'm back to civilization."

Hiv nodded in sympathy. "Sorry to hear it. I could have told you about Heth; he was always a hard man. And that Shelah gave me the creeps."

Anam nodded. "If I never see those two again, I'll die happy. Well, I'm off to find Father. I'll have to grovel a little, but he'll have something for me to do."

Hiv smiled. "Great to have you back, Anam. You were always a lot of fun. Look, your father's built a new villa, just the other side of the market. A golden staff is over the gate... you know—the one looped at the top."

Anam grimaced. "Yes. He calls it his "ankh," thinking it will bring him long life. Thanks. If you hear Mizraim shouting across the city, you'll know I found it."

Hiv laughed. "Let him growl for an hour. He'll get thirsty, drink for an hour or two with you, and all will be forgiven. Come back and see me tomorrow and tell me I was right."

"Of course, Hiv. Tomorrow, then."

Anam strode forward, following the main road, which became increasingly crowded. New buildings were everywhere. There was an intensity of purpose he had not seen before. If the road was crowded, the market was chaos. Anam found himself carried along in a human tide as it swept from stall to stall. He couldn't fight it, and after the emptiness of the mountains, he found the crowds strangely disturbing. He had always liked the bustle of the market, but today he felt like an alien. His pulse raced and he panted for air. He noticed that he was older than most of the people he saw. Many were little more than children, maybe fifteen or sixteen summers. But they were as many as the stars in the sky.

Finally the tide ebbed and he squeezed through onto the other side, only to find himself suddenly face to face with his brother Lud. "Anam? What are you doing back here? Does Father know? When...."

Anam held up his hand. "One at a time, brother. One at a time. I'm glad to see you. I'm home to face the rod, admit I was a fool, and become a dutiful son."

Lud gripped his arm. "You'll have some explaining to do. Father's still angry.... But here," he relaxed his grip and forced a smile. "No family business in the streets. Come, let's get you home."

Anam followed docilely, surprised that Lud's grip was nowhere near as strong as he remembered. Maybe the past months in the wilderness had been good for him after all. But he kept his arm limp and let his brother drag him along. A short block in front of him he saw a large villa. It rose in two levels above the ground, with an open airy look. Its grounds were surrounded by a wall higher than a man's head and Anam could hear the play of fountains beyond. If home had sun and water, he could face a few days' of his father's displeasure.

An hour later, he was no longer so sure. Mizraim had not hit him, but the haughty contempt he remembered so well had reached new heights. Anam felt like some loathsome insect and the words of his father flayed deeper than any rod. He kept telling himself it was just an act, but his heart felt the sting all the same. A compulsion came over him to bathe.

But another feeling was there amid the shame and chagrin. Success. His father believed him. All it took was a few facts scattered among a cascade of curses aimed at Heth, Shelah, Shem, and his witch-wife, and enough whining to convince him that the old Anam had returned… unchanged but chastened. A rebellious fling gone disastrously wrong. Broken promises of Japheth's brood, and no opportunity to escape until last month. In the midst of it all, an offhand observation that Ashkenaz was fed up with Heth too, paving the way for a comrade.

"So here I am, Father. I'm ready to accept whatever punishment you demand. I hate the northerners and want nothing more to do with them. I discovered one important thing, Father. Above all, I'm your son. It's time to grow up and act like it. That's all I ask."

Mizraim stopped his pacing and stared. Anam watched his eyes narrow, wondering what was passing through his father's keen mind. At that moment it struck the younger man how much his father favored Debseda. He was small, dark—more a dusky red than Debseda's olive complexion—with dark curly hair and piercing eyes. It was the eyes—in them, Anam saw Debseda's cunning.

His father curled his lip. "So. Maybe you have grown up. It's past time." He stared into Anam's eyes once more, grimaced and nodded. "Well, you've come at a good time. I have need of sons, especially clever ones. You haven't lost that, have you?"

"If I had, I'd still be under Heth's thumb," retorted Anam.

"Hmm." Mizraim nodded and suddenly smiled. "Get a bath and some clean clothes. You smell like the road. Then come to the garden and we'll have a drink and talk. It's hard to know which walls have ears these days."

Anam bowed and allowed Lud to lead him away.

Being clean felt wonderful. Anam was almost as fastidious as his father and the dirt of the wilderness had been disgusting. And Mizraim's garden was a welcome delight. Water played in two fountains, flowing in a little runlet between them. Fruit trees and herbs enjoyed the shade of the larger date palms, and small beds of flowers filled every corner. A small table sat beside the larger fountain. Anam took a moment to admire the beauty. Mizraim mistook his questing gaze. "Conversation is drowned by running water," he laughed.

Anam nodded. "Thank you for your hospitality, Father. I know I've been a disappointment. I've had several years to think about it. I'm sorry."

"Well, from what you say, it was a hard lesson. But maybe that's what you needed. But now you're home and we'll both start fresh. What say you to that?"

"I'm yours, Father."

"Good." Mizraim became all business—the shrewd plotter Anam remembered well. "Things have changed. I'm sure you heard the gossip up north. Nimrod's made his move, and a strong move it was. I saw that poor little thing of Noah's. She was terrified riding into town last month, though she hid it well. Not that I blame her. Caught between Nimrod and my wonderful mother (Anam wondered which one the scorn was aimed at), she should be. They'll suck the life out of her after she's given him a son. I wondered that he had the strength, between all the other men's wives and his own grandmother!"

Anam gasped.

"What?" Mizraim chuckled. "Surprised at Nimrod or your sweet little old grandmother? She fawns all over him—day and night. It's disgusting! Ham is blind, or weaker than I thought. He spends his time with his tools and ignores it."

"There's something about those women," countered Anam. "Japheth's wife doesn't seem a bad sort… just carries her nose in the air all the time, but Shem's wife made me shiver in my sandals every time I saw her. Her eyes are dead and even here I fear her curse. A horse threw her one day and the next it was down with a broken leg. Everyone knew how that happened."

Mizraim snorted. "Your grandmother's no better. There's talk in the shadows that she wants Nimrod to be king, as if the rest of us are just supposed to bow down and let him! Canaan and Cush are all for it, but Put and I see things differently. So do Magog, Madai, Tubal, and Tiras. But their sons favor Nimrod. So we must tread softly. Nimrod's gathered quite a gang of ruffians around him. Calls them 'Nimrod's Legion' and claims they will defend us against the barbarian hordes from the north."

He took a long pull at his drink. "As if they're any danger. If Nimrod can dance up the river to Noah's front door, drag away his daughter, and saunter back, there's little to fear from that direction."

"So what can I do for you, Father?" asked Anam. He needed his father's support, but he needed to be able to stay close to Nimrod too. It didn't sound like it would be easy. His father's lifelong suspicion of Canaan had evidently kept him distracted from the danger of Nimrod's ascendancy for too long, and he had to try and catch up. From a political point of view Nimrod's lead was daunting.

But Mizraim was no fool and could play with game with the best of them. He looked shrewdly over Anam once more. "You've been up north. You have information they want, or you can make up what they think they want. Everyone heard me shouting at you this afternoon. Only Lud knows we're on good terms now. In a few minutes we'll have a row and I'll kick you out. You can make your way over there seeking refuge with your loving grandmother. Nimrod's built a tower in the middle of town. Keeps fortifying it. It's a regular fortress already, and I'm certainly not invited there anymore! Go there and you'll find my sweet mother."

Anam stared, holding his breath. This was just the opportunity he needed.

Mizraim mistook the question in his eye. He spat on the ground. "You'll get in. You hate the northerners… just add enough to your story to keep them interested. Make them believe you have some really tasty news. And of course I treated you badly when you came home and you hate me too. You have nowhere to go. You know the enemy. And so on. Debseda's obsessed with spying. You'll look like a fat deer to a starving lion."

Anam grinned. "How do you know she's not listening to us now?"

Mizraim grunted. "She taught me well, and that's a risk *you* will have to take."

Anam's smile vanished. "Very well. How do I get word back to you?"

"Lud will be around. Soon he'll be wavering too. At least that's what everyone will think." Mizraim's lip curled and his eyes gleamed. "We'll find out what's what. Then we'll see what to do. If we can fight, we'll stay. If we can't, we'll slip away and take our wealth with us. Who knows? Maybe Ham will want to go when he finds out how his wife's spending her nights."

Anam shook his head. He knew Debseda was evil, but had a hard time with the idea of her sleeping with one of her grandsons. It was perverse.

Mizraim leaned forward. "Listen closely. You'll never learn anything directly from Nimrod or Debseda. See what you can do with her maidens—Graemea, Celota, and Oshetipin. She pretends they're just there to take care of her food and clothes, but there's more to it than that. They know things… maybe things even Nimrod does not. And they're dangerous. I'd sooner bed a cobra than one of them. Get close to one of them and you'll be fine. You were always smooth with the girls. Pray it hasn't deserted you." He leaned back and studied his son.

"Maybe Graemea. You used to play with her when she was a child. You remember… Put's girl. The one with the dark curls."

Anam nodded. He did remember. She had been a sweet girl, gentle and compliant. And he had been kind to her, protecting her from some of the others. Maybe she would remember. It was hard to imagine her as one of Debseda's crones.

He sighed. "Well, I'm home, Father. Let it be as you wish. I'll do this to atone for my foolishness, and we'll find a way to deal with their ambitions. Then we'll get a new start… all the way around. If we have to leave, we'll do it on our terms and build our own kingdom."

Mizraim nodded. "Maybe you learned something up there after all." He rose. "Use the side gate over there. Now come here." Anam stood. "We have to convince Debseda." Anam suddenly understood and felt ill to his stomach.

Mizraim's face softened for a moment, and in that moment Anam saw the father of his childhood. It vanished just as quickly. "Finish your drink. It will help." His face twisted for a moment and then set hard.

Anam swallowed the rest of his glass, ignoring the burn down his throat. The small voice of doubt and fear began to whisper in his mind, but he kept his own steady. "It must be done. I'm ready."

Mizraim pulled on a pair of fine leather gloves.

Chapter 16
GRAEMEA

9-5-1754

Korac was leaning against the wall, watching the lines of humanity scurry to and fro. There was much to learn from the observation of people's habits. Unfortunately, Nimrod lacked the patience to do it, and most of his men were too inept or too busy pursuing their own ends. Korac frowned. No more than one or two had any aptitude for it at all. His cousin, Jalam, was the only one who showed real promise. It took patience to stand still for hours, and a certain talent to blend into the background. So when Korac had time to polish his skills, he directed his efforts with care.

Right now, in his mind, there was no one that needed watching more than Mizraim. He was cunning and clever—more than most realized. He had discovered that water covered human speech and he had gone to the expense of installing fountains in his garden, where he often met with his sons and confederates.

He was there now with someone, and for a short time, he heard nothing. Then voices were raised and the sodden sound of blows carried over the wall. Korac tensed; Mizraim was not a man of violence. This was something different, and therefore something of interest. Indistinct shouting rose amid the blows and then he heard Mizraim's voice. "You disgrace… northerners… coward… home…." Then the words became clear; Mizraim's voice had become an enraged shout. "Get out. You are no longer mine!"

Korac tensed but did not move. His dark eyes were fixed on the back gate, which quickly opened. A cloaked figure, smaller than Mizraim, fell through—as though pushed violently—and ended up as a huddled mass on the street. The gate banged shut.

Korac was seldom given to indecision and was across the street before the sound died. As the figure on the ground unfolded and stood shakily against the wall, he realized it was Anam, his face bleeding. Korac froze for a moment as he weighed the risks, but then hurried forward and lent an arm to the stumbling figure.

"Anam? What happened?" he tried to color his voice with concern, but didn't succeed. He couldn't remember the last time concern—or any soft emotion—had colored his words.

The younger man's speech was slurred by the already swelling lip. "He's no better than Heth… no better than Heth…."

"Well, come with me. Others in this town remember you as a good man. Come find a welcome with them until your father sees reason."

"Reason?" laughed Anam bitterly. "His mind's consumed with other things. 'Canaan the favorite… Nimrod the chosen.' He's so obsessed with power that he forgets blood ties."

Korac put an arm around Anam's shoulder and supported him as he led him through several back alleys to another wall.

"Where are you taking me?" Anam asked suddenly. "You were never my friend."

"You can stay on the street if you want," returned Korac, casually, "but you'll probably find a better reception with your grandmother. "She can clean you up and get you some food, at any rate."

Anam hesitated, then nodded. "At least she'll understand… her precious brother and sister… the jackals of the north…." he laughed bitterly.

Korac steered him through the back streets and then around a high brick wall. Suddenly they were inside a side gate and crossing a wide courtyard. From under his hood, Anam saw this was quite different from his father's house. There were no plants or water. There was only dirt, well suited as a training ground for the pairs of men hacking at each other with wooden swords. Magog, Cush, and Tubal were wandering among the younger men, shouting criticism at each pair. Korac hurried him around the inside wall, avoiding the men, and through a smaller gate into a shadowed alcove. An ornately carved door stood before them. Korac stopped and knocked gently.

Anam stiffened when a lovely young woman opened the door a crack and peered around. He recognized the bright eyes and upturned nose. It was Graemea. He was suddenly embarrassed to be seen looking weak. But she took in the odd sight without raising an eyebrow.

Korac kept his voice low. "Tell your mistress her grandson is in need of help."

The gate shut and Anam stood impatiently. He started to say something, but glancing at Korac's iron lack of expression, he decided against it. He said a quick prayer and took a deep breath. The next hour might be the most important of his life.

No… it might decide his life.

The gate opened wider. Debseda stood before him, her eyes appraising each darkening bruise and streak of drying blood. Graemea and two other women were lined up behind her, staring shamelessly. A beautiful profusion of trees and shrubs filled the background… a stark contrast to courtyard behind him.

"So the prodigal returns," Debseda smirked. Anam just stared. He had forgotten how beautiful she was, her dark hair framing perfect features, distorted only slightly by the flat glitter of her blue eyes. She was his grandmother, yet it was hard to keep his eyes level. Her attire did little to hide her lush body. She noticed his glance and smiled knowingly. Anam blushed. "And it looks as if my ill-mannered son was not pleased to see you."

Anam looked down. *Be the weakling,* he commanded himself. He let a tear pool in his eye and looked back up. "No, grandmother," he stumbled. "He was… he was… I tried to apologize…. He's no better than Heth…."

She interrupted, one hand brushing back his hood, the other gripping his chin. "I can't let one of my grandsons wander the streets, dirty and hurt," she purred. "Especially a clever, handsome one like you! You're welcome in my home. You're among real family here. We'll see to your needs."

Anam felt the blue eyes piercing his. "Thank you, ma'am. I'll do anything for you… anything!"

"I suppose you will," she chuckled. "Graemea," she turned and spoke sharply, "see to my beloved grandson. Get him clean, clothed, and tended." Graemea bowed and took Anam's hand. "We'll talk this evening, Anam. I'm sure you have an interesting story to tell." He shivered as she turned and led the other two women back into the garden. He hoped it was interesting enough.

Graemea kept hold of his hand as she guided him through the maze of rooms and hallways. "Do you remember me, Anam?" she asked shyly as they walked along. "You were always kind to me as a girl. I remember you playing with me when the others would not."

Anam felt the heat rise to his battered face. "Of course, Graemea! Only you took me by surprise. You were a sweet young girl, but you've become a very beautiful young lady. I recognized your eyes, but the rest of you looks so… so… different." He looked away. There was a haunted look in her dark eyes that troubled him. His tongue almost betrayed his concern, but fortunately, Graemea seemed not to notice.

"Only different?" Her laugh was like a sweet bell and her red lips, full and enticing.

Anam recovered his balance. "Different as the rose from a weed; different as chalcedony from a mud brick; different as…."

Graemea laughed again. "You look older, Anam, but you haven't really changed that much, have you?" She leaned against him, letting his arm brush her breast. "But I always enjoyed your way with words, Anam. It's nice to see you again."

She led him into a larger room with a tiled floor. A small pool of water was set into the floor at one end, with sunlight rippling its surface through a skylight above. "You get a special treat, my old playmate. This is the women's pool. It stays warmer than the men's and will ease your aches. I'll return with some clothes in a bit. Go ahead," she pushed him forward. "No one will disturb you but me."

Anam nodded, not trusting himself. Graemea had grown into quite a fetching young woman. She was acting like an old friend… no, she was acting like a lover. Then he remembered what Mizraim had said about her and the other two. Her affection was a two-edged blade; she might be an impeccable source of information, but it would be a perilous relationship. A mere caprice could cost him his life. If she desired him and he spurned her… or if he pressed and she didn't… or if they both did but angered Debseda….

He suppressed his rising panic, fighting to keep an easy smile on his face. There was a chasm opening beneath his feet. Better to go slow and watch for hidden traps. "My thanks, my friend." He replied carefully. "And to my grandmother."

Graemea's smile tightened slightly as she sensed the formality. "Of course."

Anam's nerves were on the edge of a knife. His body felt better after a bath, a hearty dinner, several cups of wine, and the prospect of a real bed, but he did not forget who he was with for a moment. He raised his cup to his grandmother, speaking a little louder than necessary. "It's good to be home." It had been a cozy meal with Debseda, Anam, and her three maidens. Graemea reclined next to Anam, her foot brushing his leg too many times to be accidental. But for once, his innate fear served him well. It kept him focused in a setting exquisitely designed to distract.

His grandmother had been leaning back and observing him all evening, letting her girls carry the conversation—mostly questions about his recent years.

"You seem to have walked through many troubles, Anam," she finally commented. "What have you learned from your experiences?"

He let a frown wrinkle his brow. Slurring his voice just a bit, as if the wine had done its job, he pushed forward. "My woes would take hours to recount and would only put you to sleep," he began. "But the sum of them is this. Heth"—he spat out the name as a curse—"and his friends are treacherous liars. They tricked me into going north and threatened my life when I wanted to leave. And yet they have the gall to speak of freedom for all men."

"You must tell me all about your, ah, escape, some day, my child," she breathed, with a glint of humor in her eye.

Anam felt his heart skip, but pushed forward. He was on his path and must stick to his story. It was, Shem had assured him repeatedly, his only hope. "Shem is an arrogant hypocrite, using the disguise of a simple farmer to consolidate power throughout the northern lands. He teaches them all how to ride and use the bow. Even children. He could raise an army if he wished."

Debseda's lips tightened down at that, but Anam pretended not to notice as he plowed ahead. "But the one who scared me most was his wife. She's a witch!" he held his cup to his lips for several seconds, letting most of it slop out onto his tunic before setting it down with a shaking hand. "She tricks you into revealing your heart with her nice little ways, and then fashions a dagger from the knowledge to slide into your back."

Debseda was nodding openly now. Anam was surprised how easily she was satisfied with such trite insults, but Madrazi had assured him that Debseda would welcome any lie that fed her hatred. It was her weakest point. Anyone who hated Madrazi was halfway to being her friend.

So he continued, "It was terrible, grandmother. When that snake Shelah suspected that my enthusiasm for their little cause was waning, he dragged me into her rooms. There was a fire roaring and he held me before it, while she cut my arm and covered her hand with my blood." He held out his arm, showing a scar from one of Heth's overly-enthusiastic training sessions. Debseda nodded so Anam continued. "She gripped my hand with it and started muttering into the fire. She began to shake and drool... like... like a madwoman. I thought she would slit my throat then and there, but she just smirked and wiped my own blood in my face. 'Keep a close eye on him', she told Shelah, in that supercilious tone. That was when I knew I had to escape. Everyone up there is terrified of her curse."

"So you returned," she smiled, "to a fool of a father who lets his emotions cloud his good sense." Anam frowned, doing his best to appear hurt and angry.

"He always was a silly boy." She spoke in a throaty hypnotic voice that filled Anam's head with desire. "You should have come straight to me, my child. You know that I can fix these little family spats."

"Y-y-yes, ma'am," he stuttered, feeling like a foolish child.

"I think you should stay with me for a while until your father comes to wisdom."

Anam's heart leapt. This was the invitation he needed.

"You are not as foolish as your father, Anam." Debseda now leaned forward, her face inches away from his. He felt Graemea slide closer behind him, her body pressing against him and her hand now idly stroking his arm. He struggled to keep his wits about him, but the wine was going to his head and his senses were reeling from the proximity of two beautiful women, even if one was his own grandmother! He began to understand Nimrod's fascination with her. She might be older than every other woman in Shinar, but there were none as desirable.

She edged closer, sensing his turmoil. "Because you are no fool, you know as well as I that a war is coming: north and south. You have lived among the savages of a savage land and your head is full of things that might be of some small use. You can tell me the latest gossip about Shem, Heth, Shelah, and those sons of Japheth who dare to oppose Nimrod. You would do that for me, wouldn't you Anam?"

She leaned even closer. Her perfume filled his nostrils, and for a moment he thought she was going to kiss him. Her lips were parted and her eyes lidded. Her mouth moved close to his. Graemea had now molded herself to his back, her hands now insistent. But Debseda paused, less than a span away, smiled, and then slid back to her place. "I'm sure Graemea would like you to stay in her rooms for a while… after all, you are old… friends?"

Anam felt his world spinning. This was moving far too fast, yet if he refused, he would be dead before morning. He was sure of that. He recalled Madrazi's warnings. "She will keep you off balance; go fast when you want to go slow, or slow when you are impatient. Stay focused on your task. God will go with you, even when you are surrounded by evil. But always," she had emphasized, "guard your heart. If you do not let evil in, then it cannot destroy you."

He trembled and felt Graemea press closer, mistaking his fear for passion. "I-I-I would hate to be any inconvenience," he replied. "But your offer is generous and kind. I have no home. I've been in the wilderness these past years and I hated it. I want to live among civilized men and women and help build a new world where no one has to fear those who are not. And Graemea has always been a close friend."

"Good! It is settled," Debseda announced, relaxing. "There is much you can tell me of my enemies, and afterwards… well… I'm sure a clever boy like you can make himself useful to a feeble old woman like me."

Graemea's lips found the back of his neck as Anam fought the maelstrom of emotion washing over him. "I'll attend him well, my lady," she breathed.

Chapter 17
APPRENTICE

9-19-1754

Ashkenaz had taken his time following the Euphrates. He knew what lay ahead. Part of him was eager for the challenge, to prove he was a man fit to walk the earth with the likes of Shem, but another part dreaded having to live among those who had lost their way. His steps had been slow and heavy, and a premonition of danger lurked beneath the surface of his thoughts.

Eventually, he had cut due south, covering the last week on the grassy plains between the rivers. But even a leisurely pace could not keep him from the gate of Shinar. He wore ill-made and ill-fitting sheepskin leggings, with a sheepskin vest. His long blond hair was gathered into a greasy braid and his beard was unkempt. He had not bathed in any of the streams or springs between the rivers, and he stank.

The guard at the edge of town immediately stepped back, his face wrinkling in disgust. "Who are you?" he asked gruffly. "One of Japheth's clan by the look of you, but your face isn't familiar."

"Ashkenaz, son of Gomer," he returned placidly, keeping his eyes dull and his body lax, even when the man tightened his grip on his spear. But those dull eyes saw everything there was to see. Carts and men on horseback jostled past each other through the walls that were rising on either side of the large brick arch across the road. Though the bricks were only a few runs high, and not continuous for any great length, Ashkenaz could see the beginnings of a strong wall. There was no sign of men working on the wall, but there had been plenty of activity in the brickyards down toward the river. Ashkenaz eased over to the side to let a large cart past.

"Another of Shelah's gang, running off to the good life," sneered the guard. Ashkenaz allowed himself to look surprised. "Oh, yes," the man continued. "We've heard all about your group. Anam came slinking home a couple of weeks ago and some traders were laughing about you last week. 'What do you call ten men in a room fighting? Shemites!' Get it?" He sneered again.

Ashkenaz looked puzzled for a moment, then began to laugh. "Where'd you hear that one?" he gasped. "Shemites... that's funny!"

The guard looked at him closely, unable to decide whether or not Ashkenaz was mocking him. "So what are you doing here, Gomerite?" demanded the guard.

"Just looking for work," replied Ashkenaz, apparently puzzled that the man couldn't understand something so obvious.

"A bath might help," the man chuckled. "It would at least let someone close enough to ask."

Ash was sorely tempted to take the guard's spear and teach him courtesy, but it would have been out of character. The man was rude, but clearly not clever. But before he could reply, another figure stopped his horse in the middle of the gate and swung down. Ash stiffened slightly... it was his cousin Korac. Ashkenaz hadn't seen him for many years, but his face was distinctive, and Ashkenaz didn't forget faces. He forced his body to relax; he couldn't afford to give anything away in front of this man. Korac was a much different proposition than the guard, and, after hearing of Jael's story, Ashkenaz knew that he stood high in the councils of Nimrod.

Korac stepped over to the guard and touched him on the shoulder. "I'll handle this one," he ordered quietly. "Go about your business."

"Yes sir!" replied the guard, suddenly nervous.

Korac stepped forward, considering Ashkenaz for a moment. "Ash," he stated flatly. "What brings you here?"

"Just looking for work," he repeated.

"Why don't you come with me? After all, we're family. I'll see if I can help you."

Korac spoke evenly, but Ashkenaz could not help feeling a chill run down his neck, even in the hot sun. Korac had changed; his eyes were flat and lifeless, and the man Ashkenaz had known growing up was not the man standing in front of him. It was not hard to guess what kind of 'help' Korac intended.

With an effort, he kept a bland face and shrugged. "That's kind of you, Korac. You know anyone looking for some help? You know I can work."

"Yes. I know you." Korac's voice remained flat, but the subtle menace was not lost on Ashkenaz. Putting himself in God's hands, he followed his cousin who remounted his horse, reined it around, and headed back into town.

As they walked through the town, Ashkenaz marveled at the sights. He had been to Shinar many years before, but the small village it had been was becoming something much greater. Builders were busy on every street, and Ashkenaz had yet to reach the boundary of the old town. Planning was evident in the wide, straight streets; Ham's touch could be seen in everything from the outer irrigation canals to the elaborate new tower rising up just to the west of the old town.

Korac wanted no conversation, so Ashkenaz was free to take in the bustle of the town. A city was rising out of the wilderness. Buildings crowded the streets and people were in a hurry. Multitudes of children ran here and there in small gangs. More young hearts to be deceived by Debseda, he thought sadly to himself, and in a few short years, more spears for Nimrod. Korac led him around the market. Crowded and busy with people jammed into a small area, it would have to expand soon.

Ashkenaz followed Korac down several busy streets, always drawing nearer to the high tower. As they neared it, he saw a substantial brick wall cutting it off from the busy town. It was already a fortress, but people seemed oblivious to its threat.

Korac led him through a large gate, flanked by short watchtowers, out into a dusty courtyard. Several men lounged in the shade of the far wall. From the long sticks leaning beside them, it appeared that they had just finished training.

As soon as Korac dismounted, the men caught sight of Ashkenaz and moved over quickly, gathering like a pack of jackals.

"Where'd you find this desert goat, Korac?" called one. Though young, he looked familiar; Ashkenaz thought he might be one of Tubal's sons. He was short and stocky, with large hands and a cruel face.

Korac ignored him and led his horse through another gate. As soon as he was gone, the others began to gather closer.

"Do you smell that?"

"Something's dead!"

"Maybe he's a carrion feeder."

"Looks like one of those fierce barbarians."

"Nah! He's dressed up as a sheep."

"A dead sheep." Tubal's son again. What was his name… Turod?

Ashkenaz reined in his temper. He wouldn't have much trouble with any man in this lot… mostly boys… but that would give the game away. Nervously, he wished Korac would return. He shuffled his feet and looked down, trying to ignore the others. He felt a blow in the middle of the back and heard the stone drop to the ground. Turning, he saw one of the pack pick up another stone. "He's not dead," the man sneered. "At least not yet."

Several others picked up small stones. Ashkenaz feared that he would have to teach them a lesson, but a familiar voice cut through the chatter. "Put it down, boy."

Ash turned and recognized Ham's dark features frowning on the group. The older man strode over, and with deceptive ease gripped the stone-thrower's arm in an iron hand, before dragging him before Ashkenaz. "When a stranger comes within my walls, he is welcomed with water and shade, not foolishness. Before you draw water you can apologize." The grip tightened and Ash saw pain flit across the boy's face.

"I-I-I'm sorry," he gritted.

"Water. Now!" Ham sent him sprawling into two of the others.

Turning to Ashkenaz, he gestured towards the benches in the shade. "Come and sit. You look tired. Ashkenaz, isn't it?"

"Yes sir," replied Ash. He followed the older man over to the wall. Ham stopped and offered him a seat. "What brings you to Shinar?"

"Work, sir." Ashkenaz replied. "I'm looking for work."

"You seem strong enough," said Ham. "I doubt you'll have any trouble."

"Things seem busy," agreed Ash. He was on guard, pleasantly surprised, but surprised nonetheless at Ham's reaction. Madrazi had always kept a soft spot for Ham, but Shem and his grandfather both had a much different opinion.

He had just sat down on the bench when Korac came striding back through the gate. He stopped in front of Ashkenaz, a flicker of surprise showing at the sight of Ham sitting beside him. "I'm afraid there's no work in Shinar for you, Ash. Why don't you head back north… to your friends."

"No friends up there," replied Ashkenaz easily. "Shem kicked me out."

"What happened?" interrupted Ham.

"Well, I'm not clever like Anam, but it wasn't hard to see that Shelah's high-sounding talk was a way to keep people from being free to move south. Anam called him on it… surprised everyone that he had the stomach… and got himself banished. Heth wanted to work him over… to teach him a lesson. I didn't think it was a good idea and told Heth to stay off him. Jobaath backed me and Shelah took it to Shem."

He scuffed the ground with his foot. "Anam got away fast, so Jobaath and I took the brunt of it from those Shem. Jobaath knuckled under, but Shelah never was good at pushing me around. Heth could probably take me, but he'd get hurt doing it, so he kept off me. I took out south, figuring a man could probably find a quiet life down here. I don't care for all this arguing over who's ruling what. As long as they leave me and mine alone, I'm happy."

Out of the corner of his eye, he saw Ham's lip twitch, but no more. Korac stood before him, unmoving as a mountain. "I've got orders. You have no work; you need to leave. It's that simple." Ashkenaz' heart fell. The whole plan revolved around his ability to find work and blend into the background. It was bad luck to have run into Korac so soon. He flirted with the idea of taking his cousin down a notch on the way out of town. Looking up at the stone face, he wondered if he still could.

But the decision was taken out of his hand. "Simple is good!" interrupted Ham. "And the simple matter is this: I need a reliable man, someone strong and not afraid of work. Someone who won't let himself get pushed around by boys pretending to be men. Why don't you come to work for me, Ashkenaz? You'll be handy around the workshop."

He turned his dark face to Korac and in a less friendly tone said, "Go tell my grandson that this man has a job and will be a productive citizen of our city. And Korac," he continued in a lower tone, "Tell him that no one bothers *my* workers. *No one.*"

Ashkenaz was impressed by the strength of that command. Korac actually took a step back. He looked as if he wanted to say something, but his face showed nothing. He looked briefly at Ashkenaz and then at Ham, nodded stiffly, and turned away.

"He's a hard man, but predictable," said Ham. "For some reason, he lets Nimrod pull his strings."

Ashkenaz nodded. "I won't be looking for trouble, but I won't run away from it, either. I had enough of being pushed around up north."

Ham's lip twitched again and Ashkenaz had the feeling that his story was not as convincing as it should have been. But the older man just said, "There's plenty of trouble here."

He waved his arm at Turod. "Like I said, boys wanting to be men. Just remember that it's easier to deflect a blow than take it on the mouth. Come and tell me if you need to deal with something. If you're right, I'll back you up, if not, I'll stop it."

"Sounds just to me," returned Ashkenaz with a grin. "You have my word and you have a worker. If I satisfy you, will you teach me?"

"Perhaps," mused Ham. "If you can be taught."

Chapter 18
COMPLICATIONS

12-3-1754

Ashkenaz slid the billet back into the furnace, sweat rolling down his face in spite of the reach of the two-cubit tongs. He backed up and watched the lump of metal begin to absorb the surrounding fire. He never tired of watching it. In a few minutes it would reach just the right shade of red, so he took the opportunity to reach for the water bucket. Even stale lukewarm water tasted good, and it felt even better as he splashed some across his face and neck.

Ham had been as good as his word. A week of lifting, carrying, and cleaning had proven that Ash could work, and sensing Ham was a man of few words, he had kept tight rein on his tongue. Soon, he realized that they got along quite well. Then Ham began to teach the younger man how to work with metal: copper first, then bronze, and now iron. Though he lacked Shelah's insight or Jobaath's wit, Ashkenaz had a disciplined mind and Ham seldom had to repeat his lessons.

Months had passed, and Ashkenaz treasured the knowledge, storing it away for the future. It was something few possessed, and would one day be invaluable. Noah had attempted to bring some of the learning of the old world on the ark, but part had been destroyed and Noah had hidden much of what remained, fearing it would accelerate the slide to evil. But Ham had knowledge from the old world too and what he knew about working metal, stone, and wood would fill a hundred scrolls. So Ashkenaz struggled to fill his memory for the time when he would build his own city.

There had been no trouble in town. Word of Ham's protection spread quickly and Nimrod's bullies left him strictly alone. Ham gave him the use of a shed off the workshop, and after cleaning, it made an acceptable home. What hours were not spent working he occupied with wandering the city—learning its streets, watching the frantic building of homes, a new marketplace, and the wall.

He was doing what Shem had asked: burrowing into Shinar, learning as much as he could. His work for Ham precluded fading into the background, but it would put him close to Anam, although, it was impossible to have a quiet word. The younger man was surrounded by Debseda's minions every hour. Fortunately, Anam was a clever sort and Ashkenaz hoped he would find a way to make contact when needed. Otherwise, all of this would be for nothing.

He sighed and turned back to the furnace, the fire fading. He reached up and pumped the bellows, listening to the satisfying roar as it regained its energy. The iron was now a dull red. He concentrated on the subtler changes, ready with the tongs to bring it out. Working metal was challenging, though not something that roused any great passion. He grunted. It was better than baking bricks or laying them on the new wall, and for that Ashkenaz was grateful. Ham's knowledge was worth learning for itself. Ashkenaz knew he could become a skilled artisan, though he would never be the artist that Ham was.

The elder was a genius. Metal seemed to flow under his hand into whatever shape he desired. The basics were not difficult, but craftsmanship took enthusiasm and experience. Ashkenaz lacked the former but had begun to acquire the latter. And since he hid his passions well, Ham had accepted his stolid reliability in the place of an excitement he could not show.

Ham's craftsmanship was the least of the surprises Ashkenaz had encountered. His reputation as a craftsman was well known, even in the far north. What was more startling was his character. Ashkenaz had been amazed to see how much power he retained… perhaps because he was one of the few not scrambling to assert it, despite having the best claim. And men liked Ham—over and above his due respect as their patriarch and one of the elders. He had an easy way with most.

He also had their respect. Even Nimrod avoided testing the strength of his arm. Ashkenaz quickly realized why. Ash reckoned himself a strong man, but he might as well have been a youth compared to Ham. What escaped the notice of most was the mind inside that thick body—every bit as clever and quick as Debseda's.

The more Ashkenaz learned, the more he saw Ham as a mystery. He could easily have been the driving force of this emerging civilization, but he held to himself, nursing some deep loss, yet maintaining a simple dignity that Ashkenaz quickly came to admire. At times, he wondered if he should not unburden his heart and seek the older man's help. Only an innate wariness kept his tongue still.

Another discovery came as a relief. Nimrod might be the dark king of Madrazi's visions, but he and Debseda had not yet united the people of the plains under their rule. Factions abounded, and it was a popular sport in Shinar to keep up with the shifting loyalties of Mizraim, Put, Cush, and Canaan. Besides being a source of encouragement, it provided many evenings of entertainment for Ashkenaz, spreading rumors in the taverns to create new rifts. He spent his money buying drinks at the three inns, and he could always find someone willing to exchange gossip for a beer.

But none of these came close to the shock he had encountered on his second day of work—the twenty-first day of the ninth month. That was a date he would never forget! He had been sweeping an already spotless floor when he felt air on his neck. Expecting Ham, he turned…

His mouth had gone suddenly dry and his head spun. There, framed in the door by golden sunlight, old clothes unable to hide her beauty, stood Mariel. Years ago he had met her briefly, but nothing could have prepared him for the vision at the door. It smashed through every carefully contrived defense, and he felt himself falling uncontrollably into her gray eyes, wanting nothing more than to keep falling. The sun in her hair and the shadow in her eye made his heart race.

Mariel. Noah's eldest daughter and Nimrod's wife—carrying his child if rumors were true. Sudden fear yanked him back to reality. A woman who had betrayed her own family would think nothing of betraying him. She could easily endanger his mission and cost Anam his life. That sobered him… but not enough. Looking up, he was trapped by her eyes, and once again nothing else held any meaning.

"Good morning, Ashkenaz," she spoke effortlessly, with a small curtsey. "I'm pleased to see you. It's been many years." There was a slight smile that Ashkenaz didn't understand, and a question seemed to hover beneath her words.

His face was crimson and his voice stumbled for words. Finally, with an effort, he choked out, "Good morning, my lady."

"Come now," she smiled, "here in the shop, none of us are lords or ladies; we only want to master stone, wood, and metal, and only Ham can claim that now."

As she spoke, his heart turned over. He felt helpless against the flood of emotion, knowing that he would be walking the edge of a blade if he could not control it. She might have valuable information, but simply being together would make him the focus of Nimrod's attention. He wanted desperately to maintain some distance… to do anything to become a part of the background. "Ham is the son of the eldest and you are his sister," he replied, awkwardly. "I could never forget that."

She had a bewitching way of smiling with her sad gray eyes. "I'm just a stranger in Shinar with no family," she said softly. "As, it appears, are you."

He shook his head. "I'm just a servant, fortunate to be working for the master of this shop," he answered, shuffling his feet. He strove to keep his face impassive, but she seemed to see straight into his deepest thoughts.

"We are all servants of fate," she returned, with an intensity that brought his eyes up. Hers were moist and she strove to control herself. "I have found a friend in my brother…can you be too? I know you to be a good man…."

Ashkenaz inhaled sharply as his heart turned over. He knew the story of her betrayal, yet he was overwhelmed by the sorrow in those eyes. His first rational thought was to flee Shinar that hour. Nothing good could come of this. Yet his feet would not move. Distracting thoughts were already running free. He had to remain invisible. Yet Nimrod's wife… no… this lovely, lonely girl wanted to be his friend. No woman had ever looked at him like that before. What would Madrazi say? He tried to remember her face at that moment, but all he could see were the sad gray eyes of the beautiful woman before him. The light seemed to glow around her.

His mouth betrayed him. "Of course, my lady."

Her face lit and a real smile almost sent him fleeing that instant. He bowed and retreated to the far end of the shop to avoid saying anything else. What would a woman like that want with an ordinary man like himself? Nothing but trouble lay there, but while his trembling hands rearranged a stack of curing timbers, his eyes saw only that smile.

As the weeks passed, he became more accustomed to her presence, and by some miracle, he was able to maintain his self control, hiding his feelings beneath a bumbling incoherence. It became harder, not easier, when he learned that she hated her husband and took refuge from him in the shop each day.

If she truly regretted her actions… Ashkenaz dreamed of spending his days in her presence. Even the growing reminder of Nimrod's seed inside her did not seem to detract from her beauty—it only added the exclamation point to the feminine allure she exuded. He found himself living for the hour each morning when she would enter the door, transforming the shop into a garden of delights in the midst of a desert. He couldn't avoid her, and he no longer desired it.

They were both learning from Ham, but she was the better student. She had the passion for it that he lacked. But they made a good team. He handled the heavier tasks, and her precise touch and insight into metal and wood allowed them to make things of sufficient quality to earn even Ham's grudging praise.

Despite her position—Ham's sister and Nimrod's wife—she never failed to speak kindly to him, treating his as an equal. Yet he remained stiff of tongue, terrified of revealing his mind, and grateful for Ham's presence. He sincerely hoped the big man could not read his thoughts... she was, after all, his little sister.

He sighed, letting the resistance of the bellows absorb his frustration.

As she did each day, Mariel sternly crushed her feelings as she approached the workshop. But her heart betrayed her... again!... beating faster when she neared the door. It was the door to the only light in her world. Ham, the work, and... and.... *No*, she told herself. *I am Nimrod's wife. I carry his child. I belong to him*. But it did no good. Her mind had been repeating that refrain every morning for the past seventy-two days, but it did no good. Even the growing deformity of her figure did not quench her emotions. She could never forget that first terrible, wonderful morning.

She had heard that Ham had taken Japheth's grandson into his shop, and had been annoyed at the interference with her developing friendship with her older brother... at least until she had opened the door. To this day, she could not explain it. Was it the yellow hair, the piercing blue eyes, the calm confidence that reminded her of her father, or was it all of those... or none? Whatever it was struck her like an arrow, turned her heart over and caused her belly to tighten. The moment she saw him, she knew the extent of her foolishness. Here was her man... the one she would follow to the ends of the earth on her knees—yet she was bound to Nimrod.

It had been a bad moment... perhaps the worst of her new life. It almost crushed her; it took all her strength to stand—the room swayed and her vision blurred. The shame of her growing belly all but defeated her. She remembered little of that morning—the words that had somehow fallen from her lips, the courtesy, the calm façade that hid a storm raging within. She was glad he was a man; had Debseda or any other woman been in the workshop, they would have seen her turmoil and ruined what was left of her life.

She had no idea how she had been able to finish that day. Despite bracing her heart, the next had been nearly as bad; her resolve to ignore him melted away at first sight, and the only thing that kept her from throwing herself at him was the knowledge that Nimrod would kill him if he ever suspected... or if Debseda ever caught a glimpse of that part of her heart.

But as maddening as it was, the thought of seeing Ash made each new day bearable. The idea of losing him gave her a self control she had never known and a talent for deception she had never possessed. To preserve his life, she was able to go into the shop and pretend that he was merely Ham's servant, not the one man on earth she desired. Her mother's words haunted her dreams as she drank the bitter dregs of her folly—a slave to Nimrod, while the man God had made just for her slept a long stone's throw away. Many were the dark hours spent by her bedroom window, looking down from the tower towards the dark corner of the compound where Ashkenaz slept—unaware of her tears, of her longings, and her regrets.

At least Nimrod left her alone now. And that was a good thing. He might have discerned her distress and started digging for the cause. But since her perfect figure had become distorted by the growth of the child within, he had taken his lust elsewhere. Debseda and her three jackals also avoided her... to the point she had asked Zerai to keep her ears open for news of their never-ending plots.

There had been no shortage of nights when she wondered if she should not have tried to terminate the life growing within. Did she want to bear another Nimrod? But she could not. Her parents had instilled in her the precious nature of every life—only the Creator had that right. She hoped that she could raise the child, teaching it the same fear of God that her parents had taught her. Maybe Nimrod's son would end up his greatest disappointment.

Mariel paused at the door, composed her features, and entered. As usual, Ashkenaz was already up and working. Her lips went dry as she saw the hard muscles of his bare back work the bellows, and she was startled by a gentle cough—Ham was standing in the door behind her. How long had she been there, staring? Her face flushed as she turned and quickly stepped aside, murmuring a greeting and trying to gather her thoughts.

She wondered fleetingly if Ham knew of her infatuation or what he would think if he did, and for a moment she was tempted to confide in him and ask for his help; but as quickly as the idea arose, she knew it would destroy the tenuous balance in the shop she so enjoyed and would probably remove any opportunity to see Ashkenaz... to be with him... to trade simple words about their work... to be in love. She could not risk that and so asked Ham instead about the morning's tasks.

Ham simply nodded and told her to follow him. They approached the forge. Ashkenaz was studying the furnace. He wiped the sweat from his face and nodded to them both. He then turned back to the furnace, grasping the shorter tongs. The billet glowed. Smoothly, Ashkenaz gripped it, swung it to the anvil, seized the waiting hammer, and began to work the metal. Mariel's trained ear heard the thud of the hammer, watching it shape the metal under his strength. Feeling the hammer bounce with little effect and seeing the color fade, he swung it back into the fire.

Ham clapped him on the shoulder. "Well done! We'll make a smith of you yet. Next time, give the fire a few moments more and you'll get another three blows."

Ashkenaz nodded and wiped his brow, grateful when Ham took Mariel across the room to shape a beam. He risked a glance, drinking in her beauty. Another day had begun, and he had hours in her presence until the next lonely night.

Anam reclined in his blankets, watching Graemea brush her long hair. There was something hypnotic in the sure, easy strokes, and he loved seeing the glossy shine it imparted to her thick mane. Weeks had flown by. He remained in Graemea's rooms, marveling at how the awkward child he had once known had grown into such a graceful woman. After hearing his tales of the North (mostly wild exaggerations), Debseda had told him to stay and help but never said what it was she wanted.

He knew he was a hostage to Mizraim, but he hoped to become more. He had the freedom of the town and took it on himself to wander around, picking up gossip. The tidbits he heard were welcomed by Debseda and helped keep her leash loose around his neck. His increasing knowledge also gave him a background against which he could understand what he learned inside the walls of her home. When the time came, he would be ready.

With little work to do, much of his time was spent with Graemea. He suspected that she had been instructed to stay as close to him as she could. Not that it was unpleasant. Early on, they had discovered a mutual love of music, and they spent many evenings creating melodies for both singing and dancing.

His emotional defenses remained firm yet he wondered how long it could last. Graemea had said nothing for weeks about his past, seeking no information, asking nothing of him but friendship and love. She had become free in her gossip about the doings in the household, nothing of sufficient import to try to send a message, but enough so that he began to understand the undercurrents flowing around Nimrod and Debseda. He knew every person now; who was important and who was not. Having learned the players and the board, he was ready to being unraveling the strategies and plots as the game progressed.

He had only seen Ash twice, ignoring him both times as Ash had given the appropriate sign that all was well, a rock in his left sandal. At first, it had been disconcerting that Ash had taken work with Ham—the adoption of Mariel and Ashkenaz as apprentices had been the talk of the town. Ashkenaz was supposed to be invisible, working alongside numerous others and drawing no attention. At least he was nearby. Anam had already thought of a half dozen excuses to visit the workshop but was saving them for greater need. He was sure Ash was working on ways to make contact too, so he leaned back and relaxed, enjoying the way the brush flowed through the river of Graemea's dark hair.

Tomorrow would see a major move in the great game that was Shinar. Through Canaan, Debseda was calling an assembly to appoint a council for the city. It took no brilliance to deduce that this would be a significant step in Nimrod's ascent to power. He had his wife, his victory over Noah, and dozens faithful to his cause. Knowing Mizraim would be present, Anam had laid out his best robes. He couldn't wait to see the interplay between Canaan, Nimrod, Mizraim, Put, and the sons of Japheth. He wasn't sure what all Debseda had planned, but it would be entertaining and informative. He had his own ideas of what might happen and was curious to see if he had read the board correctly.

Chapter 19
WARRIOR & WOMAN

12-3-1754

As a rising sun began to break the gray mist of early morning, Jael sat still and silent on the branch, balancing against the short rope looped around the trunk and her waist. Her hands were occupied with her bow. Though shorter than the men's, it was still awkward in a tree. It didn't help that her seat was unconformable, but discomfort had become a constant companion over the past ten months and was easily set aside. With pain had come elation in a newfound freedom. Freedom from the limits of a weak passivity bred into her from birth. Freedom from the expectations of parents and sisters. Freedom from the stifling confines of her father's remote valley. She was strong and growing stronger.

Her body had become hard and she had (quite pleasantly) discovered a quickness of movement few men could match. Increasing skills brought interesting new ways to use them. She was becoming adept at the bow and knife, and was beginning to learn the rudiments of the spear. Most days and nights were spent outdoors, and she was learning to feel the rhythms of the world around her—changes in weather, danger, and the patterns of creatures. She was beginning to learn how to trail animals and men, and devise cunning stratagems for the hunt. The world lay open to her desire. Soon, she would be able to go anywhere, survive the vast wilderness, and kill any man who got in her way. Then Nimrod would begin to pay… and her retribution would be long and full.

But today was a different test. Shem had sent her hunting and would judge her on the speed of her kill. So she was forced to hunt near the farm, where the animals were fearful and cautious. But she had noticed that deer, for all their innate caution, never looked up. So dawn found her in a tree overlooking a trail that led to water.

Though chilled and stiff, she loved this new life. Discomfort and hardship were far outweighed by the benefits. Shem had taught her much and she eagerly attacked every challenge he posed… except one. At regular intervals he made her return home for several days. The first time had been the worst, but none of the other trips had been pleasant. They were nuisances that postponed knowledge she desperately wanted. What benefit could come from cooking, cleaning, and listening to her sisters gossip? It was the same every time. Her only consolation was in the fun of evading Shem's watchman, Zeb, on the trips down and back. She had actually succeeded for two days on the last one, much to Zeb's shame.

Her parents made it clear that they allowed her present life only in deference to Shem and Madrazi… as if they could stop her! Beyond that, they said little. Her sisters thought her mad. But the worst part of being home was not the recrimination of her family; it was the hovering fear that lingered over them. Their lives had been twisted and bent by Nimrod and Mariel. Noah—once an object of veneration—was now just another farmer. He had not been able to protect his home or his name. It was that fear that made Jael feel like an alien; her own fear had long been consumed in the purifying fires of anger and vengeance. But try as she would, Shem would not relent, telling her in uncompromising language that her days at home were as much a part of her training as running through the wilderness.

So like every other challenge, she endured and overcame. Hating every moment, she dressed like a respectable young lady, cooked, cleaned, sewed, and sang. By the end of the second visit, she was sure she was fooling her sisters—they expected her to stay home and become the old Jael. Her parents were wiser. Their disappointment remained palpable, yet unspoken.

She snarled to herself. What did they expect? Her father might be satisfied to allow the depredations of Nimrod and Korac, but she would not!

And yet… doubt crept in occasionally. Was she happy? Was it possible to be at war and be happy? There was danger in her new life, but there was also the zest of being able to face it squarely. She knew now the dangers of the wild, and realized that she should have died during those first days by herself. Something as simple as falling off a horse, days from help, could have killed her as easily as a lion or bear.

She thought of Zeb. He had followed her home each time, and they had reached an understanding. When she wasn't trying to lose him or ambush him, she would pretend he wasn't there and he would leave her alone. She appreciated his tact—he never mentioned her first encounter with Heth to anyone. He was a good man and good in the wild. She had managed to surprise him, but only twice now, and he was still a better archer. Yet she would surpass him soon; he was not driven by her demons. *Nimrod… Korac….*

Anger almost broke her concentration. Two does stopped just under her tree and pricked their ears. Jael controlled her breathing and did not move. Finally they eased down the path, offering a shot, but she refrained. She was after bigger game, and was not disappointed. A wary buck with a respectable spread of antlers came lightly down one side of the trail, ready to leap into the woods at the least sign of danger. He stopped under Jael and listened intently, but like the others, he failed to look up. As he walked forward, Jael noiselessly began to pull her bowstring, bringing it back to her cheek until the iron tip of the arrow sat just forward of the bow's curve. Another cautious step brought the buck's neck into her sight picture. Without thought she felt the moment and released, seeing the brief flight of the shaft before it buried itself between the shoulder blades with a solid *thunk*. The buck crumpled in on itself, its spine severed.

Jael grinned broadly. She had succeeded. It was barely after sunup. Quickly, she untied the rope holding her to the tree and wrapped in around her waist. Ready to leap down, she remembered Shem's teaching, and paused to search the area for danger. Satisfied there was none, she jumped down and worked quickly. The scent of blood would attract predators so she roughly gutted the animal, tied all four hooves together with one end of her rope, and lifted the buck to her shoulders, staggering under its weight. Not for the first time, she wished for the strength of Heth, who could have carried twice this weight all day with no effort. Unfortunately, a woman's body was not built like his.

Gritting her teeth, she set off as fast as she could, eager to present Shem with her trophy before the morning meal. She stopped only at the stream crossing to wash the blood from her prey and her own clothes before hurrying on up the meadow. There was a smile on her face as the sun cast its morning shadows out to the west. She felt alive and free. It was a good start to the day.

Jael was not smiling that afternoon. The sun was much hotter and the slight breeze carried dust into her eyes. She sat splayed in a most undignified manner on her backside, blinking away the tears and trying to catch her wind.

"You have the quickness, little one," laughed Heth, "but the spear and the sword require skill as well. Get up, now, and we'll see if you can remember which end to use."

His easy smile was a vast change from their first meeting (which neither ever mentioned). After her return from her first trip home she had been formally introduced to all four of Shelah's friends. Shelah had been a frequent visitor to Noah's farm and she knew him well—well enough to catch the disappointment he tried to hide. Jobaath and Ashkenaz she also knew on sight, but had not seen for some time, and Heth was a stranger, though his reputation was well known.

She had been unexpectedly uncomfortable at that meeting, but he appeared as relieved as she was when by some unspoken agreement they knew that their first meeting would remain between them and Zeb. And her second impression of Heth was far better than the first. She had time to take in his face. It was a little flat and broad for her taste, but she noticed something in his dark eyes she had not seen before…troubled currents that ran deep, and a hint of obsession that made him seem suddenly more approachable. She sensed that he, of them all, understood her.

Perhaps that was why Shem had asked Heth to instruct her in the ways of the spear and sword. "He's already better than I," he had explained, but Jael wondered. Shem usually had four or five reasons for any of his actions, and he rarely shared any of them with her. At any rate, Heth had proven every bit as skilled as his reputation. Strong and quick, penetrating his defense was as hard as going through a rock.

He was a good teacher. She seemed to instinctively understand his few words, and he quickly won her respect. It became easier over time, and in time, his sense of humor began to surface, coming as a shock to Jael, who had vowed to set hers aside until after she had killed Korac.

That was perhaps her most valuable lesson from Heth; killing was a serious business, and if you could not find something else to laugh about, it would eat you up inside. In time, she began to appreciate, and then share, his rough humor.

But not today. For some reason this session was only making her angry. Perhaps it was Shem's presence. He usually stayed away during these sessions, but today was standing to one side, appraising her every move. As she gingerly pulled herself up, she ground her teeth and took a few cautious steps. Her calf was no longer numb, but the growing pain forecast another uncomfortable night. Forcing it aside, she retrieved her stick from where Heth had casually knocked it away. It was a spear shaft with one end dipped in whitewash to represent the blade end. Heth sidestepped easily, twirling its twin from one hand to the other with a practiced ease that told her how far she had to go. She frowned. Her hands would never be large enough or strong enough for that trick.

"Come on, little one," he smiled. "Let's see how long you can stay out of the dust this time."

Jael felt her anger rise. He probably thought he was being kind, but she bristled at the slight. Her inner fury began to spill over the walls of self-discipline. It was time to show this oaf that the 'little one' was deadly serious about her work. He was treating it like a joke, and her like a silly boy wanting to play a man's game. Well, she had a surprise for him. Always cautious, she had never before shown him the extent of her quickness, and in her building rage, she decided that this was the time. She focused on his hands and chest, ignoring the talk that was designed to put her off guard…to let him force the timing. In the familiar place of Heth rose the face of Korac, ready to torment her once more.

Anger rushed energy into her tired limbs and she lunged suddenly forward, scything her stick in a short, sharp stroke aimed at Heth's mouth. Surprised at her speed, his reflexes took over and he snapped his shaft up and across, catching her blow and deflecting it aside. But Jael was a step ahead and she let the momentum of his blow pivot her around on her planted left foot as her right shot under his guard.

A part of her mind screamed to pull the blow, but passion won, and she rammed it into Heth's thick stomach with all her strength. Any other man would have folded and fallen at that blow, but Heth merely staggered. Jael's foot was numb—it felt as if she had kicked a stone wall. Suddenly she felt herself lifted by the stick she still grasped and swung through the air. She let go and tried to find her balance, but it was much too late. Her back struck the ground, forcing the air out of her lungs, and her head struck hard. Lights danced in front of her eyes and her chest roared in pain. She screamed at herself to get up and keep fighting, but her body would no longer respond. She felt hands under her head and through her blurred eyes saw Shem's face leaning over her.

"Relax and breathe," he ordered softly. She shut her eyes, trying to obey. She felt tears sting her eyes and angrily blinked them away. Warriors did not cry. But she had failed, and braced herself for a rough critique.

Neither spoke for several minutes. She didn't see the look of concern the two men traded as she gasped for air. Gradually, her lungs began to function once more and she began to feel the pain in her back and head. She tested it against what she had experienced before and knew that it would fade, leaving a few more bruises to color her body.

Chapter 20
LESSONS

12-3-1754

Heth picked up his staff and turned away, lest Shem see through his concern and into his heart. Jael was a conundrum—so exasperating, yet so easily understood. Nimrod had taken her innocence and happiness, and while Shem might condemn her vengeful spirit, Heth couldn't… not without condemning his own. And it felt good to know that there was someone else in the world as dedicated as he was to the destruction of Nimrod and his schemes. For that alone, he would have agreed to help her. He was willing to help anyone frustrate Nimrod's plans, even if it was a rangy young woman who should have been at home with a baby.

But his reasons had subtly shifted after the first few lessons. Her commitment to learning would have shamed most men, as would her rapid acquisition of skill to back it up. That last move had been worthy of any warrior; he was still trying to figure out how she had snaked in under his guard so easily. Had that been a man's boot, he would have been helpless to the follow up. As it was, his midsection would be bruised and sore for days—though he would never give Jael the satisfaction of knowing.

She was so easy to dislike yet it was so easy to feel… what? Sympathy? Empathy? Affection? He shoved that thought down hard—he wanted to marry a woman, not a spitting fury like Jael. With her volatile temper, he would have to sleep with a dagger under his pillow! And yet… there was something about those fiery green eyes that drew him like a moth to the flame. Maybe….

He turned back to help Shem. "Sit up and catch your breath," ordered the older man, as he helped Jael finally sit. She rested her elbows on her knees, her eyesight finally clear. Heth stood uncertainly looking on Shem, his face a mix of concern and anger.

Jael sighed and lowered her eyes. She deserved the latter, and knowing Heth, he would enjoy throwing it in her face. It was ironic—she could handle his wrath much easier than his condescension. But before he could speak, Shem silenced him with a quick look and turned to Jael.

"Tell me why you failed," he ordered.

"I underestimated his strength," she sulked.

Unexpectedly, Shem laughed. "You certainly did! Heth is like our brother Ham, as sturdy as an old oak. You'll never defeat him fighting as his equal. But that's not why you failed, is it?"

He cocked his head and gave her that knowing look she dreaded. She had never fooled him and probably never would. She had learned early on just to tell him the truth, no matter how humiliating. She bowed her head a moment and then met his eye.

"I let anger control me," she admitted softly. "I saw Korac, not Heth, and struck."

"It was a good attack," interrupted Heth. "Had I been weaker I would have been at your mercy." Jael recoiled from his generous words, alert for some hidden insult. Heth's sarcasm was impressive when he was mad. But he seemed serious now. She looked up again. He couldn't be praising her; he must be toying with her to make some point. She was still embarrassed by her behavior at their first meeting but could never bring herself to apologize.

However, he was the one who seemed embarrassed today and his next words surprised her. "I'm sorry I threw you so hard. You did much better than I expected and I just reacted as I would with a…." He tailed off, realizing too late his error.

Jael's anger blazed anew. "With a *man!*" she finished spitefully. "Well, *big man*, one day I will be better than all of you, and you won't have anything to be sorry for… except for your inability to defeat that poor, weak little girl who wants to play at fighting."

Heth backed up a step, trying to control his own rising rage. It didn't work. Jael might not be able to get past his spear, but she had an uncanny ability to prick his emotions with that abrasive tongue. His face reddened and he glared down, pointing a thick finger at her. "You can learn all you want and practice every waking hour for the next hundred years of your life, *little girl*…" His eyes burned into her. "But the end will be the same… come at me like that and you'll end up eating dust!"

He stalked off, throwing his stick down hard, hearing Shem's voice rising, and perversely happy that Jael was its target. Maybe he would feel some sympathy tomorrow, but not today. Today Shem could flay the skin from her wretched hide, and he would be happy to stand by and sharpen the blade.

He was angry at her and angry at himself. Why did she get under his skin? The idea of a woman warrior was ridiculous on its face. He couldn't understand why Shem would countenance such foolishness. If Nimrod or Korac learned of it, they would laugh themselves silly… at least Nimrod would; Korac hadn't cracked a smile in years—although Jael might be the one to change that. Heth frowned. If they learned that he had any part in it, they would be laughing at him too!

Not paying attention to his path, Heth crashed though a gate and nearly knocked Madrazi off her feet. He reached out to steady her and blushed. Now Jael had caused him to insult his hostess.

But Madrazi didn't appear upset. Indeed, she touched his arm gently and cocked an eyebrow. "Jael?" she asked innocently.

Heth didn't know what to say, so he simply burst out laughing, and was relieved when Madrazi joined him.

"She can have that effect, can't she?"

Heth nodded and took a deep breath. "I'm terribly sorry, my lady. There is no excuse for my clumsiness."

She smiled again. "I envy you for the freedom to express your feelings. I have to keep mine tamped down deep, lest I slap her every day! Some days I want to climb up to the ark and scream to the heavens, just to let it all out."

Heth laughed again. "At least I'm not the only one."

Suddenly Madrazi's smile disappeared and a look of concern clouded her eyes. "Heth… I know it's a lot to ask, but please be patient with her. Beneath that rage is a lot of pain—the kind that herbs and salves cannot touch. I know you don't see it, but she really looks up to you. You are what she wants to be… and cannot. And because of that…" she hesitated and looked down. "Because of that, I think she is attracted to you. Perhaps she thinks that if she can't *be* Heth, the next best thing is to be *with* Heth. Then she can laugh in the face of Nimrod and Korac, and make her pain disappear."

"But why?" he asked. "Nimrod bested me and I would hesitate to take on Korac. I'm a better fighter, but he doesn't care… and he's good enough that it makes him dangerous."

Then her words hit him. "Jael likes me?" He laughed again. "She has a unique way of showing her affection. She was trying to kill me five minutes ago!"

"You?" responded Madrazi with a keen look. "Or Korac?"

Heth nodded. Jael had admitted it, and it made the most sense. He remembered the look in her eye as she attacked… she had been somewhere else. Suddenly he understood. But Madrazi wasn't through. "You see things from a position of strength," she began. "Jael sees them a position of weakness and fear. If you can help her develop her strength, then maybe Shem and I can begin to deal with the pain that fuels it, and the rage."

Heth nodded. "But if we don't…" he paused and looked hard at Madrazi. "She's becoming dangerous. I don't know many men who could have come so far in so short a time. She'll never be able to face Nimrod or Korac, but she'll be good enough to defeat many others. And if she decides to lie in wait for someone with her bow, she'll kill them! I've never had to kill a man, but when it comes, it will change me… and for the worse."

Madrazi touched his arm again. "It's good that you see that; many others have not. And so you understand that with Jael it will be much worse. It would violate her fundamental nature. God made her to nurture life, not take it. Shem is trying to teach her to be good enough that she need not kill. Please try to reinforce that lesson."

Heth was intrigued. Madrazi had never talked to him like this before. He felt that he was seeing a part of her soul that was reserved for very few. He decided to take advantage of the opportunity. "Why do you allow it, my lady?"

"*I* would not," she shrugged, "but God showed me that we must." Heth shivered as he felt that deep tingle again. "It would be better if this evil had never come into her heart," Madrazi continued, "but the Creator is powerful enough to even use evil for His own good ends. I can tell you this… in the end she will need this. It's no game."

Heth nodded. "Fighting and killing never is, my lady. But if you say it's from the Almighty, then I will give her my best… both in skill and understanding. There's a good woman inside her," he mused, then blushed. He mumbled something respectful and stalked off as quickly as he could, fleeing Madrazi's knowing smile.

Chapter 21
SHINAR PLOTS ITS COURSE

12-4-1754

Nimrod sat at the head of the room between Canaan and Cush, watching impassively as the large room began to fill. Debseda sat behind him, her head covered, partly from propriety and partly to obscure the fact that she was speaking softly to him as each man entered the room. It was a struggle to hide his eagerness, but the black stillness that the spear had set at the core of his soul reached up and calmed his body. Even though it was not with him, its black spirit seemed to reach out across the town.

The soft chatter died as Mizraim walked into the room, followed by Lud. Smaller than most present, he still had an aura that cautioned his enemies. *He's no fool, that one!* Nimrod told himself, and his augmented senses knew that of all their potential rivals, Mizraim was the most dangerous. None of his generation possessed his foresight or his ability to see many moves ahead in the great game of power.

And yet Nimrod smiled. *He's just another mere man. Better than most, perhaps, but no match for his betters.* Proof of that sat against the wall—the son he had cast out was now a tool of Debseda. Anam sat in plain view with his three maidens around him—a display calculated to enrage Mizraim. But Mizraim was not given to emotional outbursts and his face didn't show a thing as his eyes swept over the display. Nimrod shrugged. It was of no importance. Just a prick against his pride.

Tubal entered with his four sons and Tiras with his five. "Those two must be included," Debseda hissed. "You will need their strength." Nimrod inclined his head so slightly that no one else would have noticed. The older men might resent his youth, but their sons were firmly in Nimrod's camp. The passage of time made them weaker and him stronger. Everyone knew that, and it was the only reason that a few of them were even in the room.

There was a buzz of excitement. Everyone knew what was happening. Years of tight family structures were giving way to a new arrangement; new loyalties would be forged today that would guide Shinar for generations to come. Canaan stood. It had been agreed that he would nominally be in charge of the meeting since he was the best orator and the target of Noah's curse.

"Friends," Canaan began. "Welcome, children and grandchildren, brothers and cousins. Our efforts to found a beautiful city have rewarded us many-fold. Out of the wilderness we have raised up a busy and prosperous home—a beacon for mankind." He talked at length about his family's heroic trek away from the cold and barren northern lands, of their finding the beautiful and fruitful plains, and of the courageous founding of their city in spite of Noah's opposition and his babbling about the Creator's commands.

Nimrod found his mind drifting. His uncle was supposed to rattle on for the best part of an hour, giving Debseda time to gauge the feelings of those present, to sense potential friends or adversaries. Maybe she could see something he could not, but Nimrod knew that most present felt as he did… bored. Canaan was not living up to his reputation today.

"We have made a home for ourselves and our children," droned Canaan, finally getting to the point. "Our success has now become our challenge. We are no longer a family settlement; we are a city. We need a strong government to protect us from the barbarians of the North, to establish justice within our walls, and to ensure that free men have a future free from the tyranny of the elders."

Nimrod smiled to himself. Canaan was doubly foolish. Everyone knew he would never speak like that in Ham's presence, and Ham would hear about it regardless. Many were still currying his favor, thinking that his support might tip the balance in their favor. Nimrod had to hide another smile. He wondered if Canaan appreciated the irony of his words, with Debseda sitting not ten paces behind him, ready to move the assembly towards *her* tyranny. But at least everyone was paying attention once more—the boasting had at least recaptured their interest.

This was what they had all come for, and they were ready to get down to business. But Canaan wasn't through. He still had a surprise to spring. "We are all wise in our own way, but lack experience in these matters." That brought mixed mutterings. The smart ones agreed, but saw no recourse. The fools thought themselves wise enough to not need it.

Canaan pushed on. "But there are those that do. Of them, six are unworthy of our attention, being our enemies and sure to lead us in the wrong path." A rumble of agreement flowed across the room, although Japheth's sons were noticeably silent. They may have wanted to share in Shinar's bounty, but lacked the visceral hatred for Shem and Noah that Debseda's children had imbibed from their mother's milk.

Canaan ignored their discomfort and continued, his voice growing stronger. "But there are two among us who saw how men once governed themselves. Unfortunately, my esteemed father was unable to attend." Several in the audience chuckled uncomfortably—Ham was still respected and none could argue his status in Shinar.

"And so," Canaan forged on, "we are left with only one person who has experienced human government on the scale we face." Another rumble spread around the room. Debseda was feared, but she was still just a woman. Politics was the work of men. A few thought otherwise, but saw it as a good excuse to bar her poisonous influence from their deliberations.

Canaan stumbled for a moment in the face of that dissension, but then recovered. "Therefore I have requested my beloved mother to share her insights." He hurried on to assuage the crowd. "She speaks not to *direct* our deliberations, but merely to educate us about the various paths along which wisdom may guide us." Nimrod sat up straighter. His move was noticed and the murmurs subsided. No man was willing to push the issue hard enough to be marked as Nimrod's enemy.

Debseda stood and began to pace the floor. Even with her head covered, her lush curves and fluid grace captured every eye. Nimrod knew that she had spent hours modifying her clothing so that it appeared proper while still revealing enough to entice men. Out of the corner of his eye he saw Mizraim frown. Here was one who would not be taken in so easily. But there were more arrows in their quiver.

Debseda spoke softly yet hypnotically, and Nimrod felt his skin quiver as she released a small portion of her power through her words. "It is true that I have seen many ways in which men see to their affairs. My father traveled much in my youth, and I saw everything from elected councils to despotic kings. Each form of government has its advantages and disadvantages."

She then proceeded to discourse for nearly an hour on the subject, and though Nimrod thought her words no more interesting than Canaan's, the continued ripple of her body around the room seemed to hypnotize the men, preparing them to follow. A few like Mizraim were smart enough to keep their eyes off her and their minds focused elsewhere, but the rest were like panting dogs on a leash.

Nimrod tensed. *Strike now!* he thought, and it seemed Debseda heard.

"We are a young town, with newcomers arriving almost every day. The children that play in our streets today will be our leading citizens in a few short years. Within your lifetimes Shinar will be home to thousands of people, then tens of thousands, rivaling the great cities of the lost world." She struck a sultry pose near the front of the room. "It will be glorious," she purred. "So as we lay the foundations, our need is for wisdom. There are no factions in our town; we are all in accord in seeking a life free from the despotism of Noah and Shem. We need no great general or strong king. You are free to choose your own way, but from my experience, a simple council of our best and wisest can guide the growth and development. Do as your wisdom leads." She swirled back to her chair with her dancer's grace, almost every eye locked on her body.

Nimrod saw Mizraim frown and knew Debseda had been right last night. With the others they could be obvious; with him, they needed a double game. Rumors that Nimrod would seize power had circulated among the younger men, and she had correctly predicted that Mizraim's fear of that would blind him to their real strategy until the trap was sprung.

Mizraim's participation on a council was a double-edged sword. A council would keep Nimrod in check… or at least Mizraim expected it to. But there would be a price for that "compromise," and Mizraim's immediate relief was keeping him from seeing the incongruity of putting someone of less than forty years on a council of "elders."

It was exactly as she had said, "Offer them the easy step. They will walk into our snare of their own will. Once they are caged we can break them at our leisure." He relaxed a moment and scanned the room. Anam was watching his father, too, the hint of a sneer curling his lip. *So he understands*, Nimrod thought. *Well, well. Maybe Anam really is as clever as Debseda thinks. Maybe he can be useful.*

Canaan stood again and bowed to Debseda as she returned to her chair. "Thank you, Mother," he intoned sonorously. "Thank you from us all." He turned back to the assembly. "I think this advice is like that of an angel," he said. "We need government, but only a little. A council would be my choice, and choosing our best instead of our oldest would be a welcome break from the traditions of a failed world."

He sat down and Cush immediately stood. "I agree with Canaan." He sat and Put stood. "I too. What say the sons of Japheth?"

Tubal stood, glancing at his brothers, who were nodding. "We agree too, as long as our clans are represented."

Canaan looked around. Most of the men were nodding their agreement. *The herd is following*, thought Nimrod sardonically. He caught Canaan's eye and glanced to his right. Canaan understood and spoke again, "What about you, Mizraim? Many would account you wise and yet you have said nothing. Gladden our hearts with your knowledge, brother."

Mizraim curled his lip. "I'm a simple man, Canaan. It's a struggle to keep all this wisdom straight in my head. But even a simple man can ask simple questions. Tell me, how many men will sit upon this innocuous council? Will any women?" He glared pointedly at Debseda. "What authority will they be given over the citizens of our fair city? Will they command an army? Pass laws without consulting the citizens?" He paused as he saw others in the room nodding, starting to think for themselves.

Nimrod grimaced. Once the momentum slowed, it would be hard to regain. And Canaan seemed oblivious to the damage Mizraim was wreaking with a few well chosen words.

But he wasn't through. "And of course, brother, the simple among us wish to know who it will be who chooses this council?" His sarcasm was less guarded now, but all the more effective as it caught the attention of those who had moments before been agreeing with Canaan.

"Strike now," Debseda hissed to Nimrod. "Shut him up!"

Nimrod stood forward, immediately capturing the attention of all present. "Forgive my intrusion, esteemed fathers," he started. "My tender years bid me to silence, but being young, I don't listen as well as I should."

The younger men laughed. Nimrod was their man. Besides, if the mightiest among them couldn't speak, they wouldn't support any arrangement, and their fathers knew it.

"Uncle. Father of my great friends, Lud and Anam." He waved in Anam's direction. Mizraim's eyes narrowed; but he was the only one in the room other than Debseda and Anam that discerned the threat in Nimrod's casual wave.

"I think that none of these questions could possibly be answered without the due deliberation of the fathers here today… foremost among them, the sagacious Mizraim. Nor could any council be considered complete without a man of your worth to this city. I could not countenance otherwise, nor support any proposal to the contrary. Nor should anyone else." The threat was less veiled now, and Nimrod saw the confusion on the faces of his younger allies.

Mizraim sat up straighter, his smile tight on his lips. Sensing his thoughts, Nimrod saw victory just before him. His uncle was being offered a place of power, virtually promised by the most popular man in the city…and the most dangerous. If he refused, he would forfeit any future voice. If he accepted, then he would be playing Debseda's game by Nimrod's rules. Too late he saw the trap, but even then he failed to understand its full danger.

Nimrod forced his face to remain neutral. It would not do to celebrate prematurely. But the power crackled inside him and he felt the answering echo from the small woman sitting demurely behind the so-called seats of authority. It felt good and he could not stop his speech.

"As to what this gathering of eagles might do… what else is there but to declare our independence from the elders, from the barbarians of the North, from the past that haunts their dreams and stifles our freedom. We must build a city that will become the mother of civilization on this new earth. We fear no floods; we fear no doddering old men. *We* are the future! We must show it in stone and brick. We must build monuments to the hope of the rebirth of mankind that will proclaim our defiance from one generation to the next. We must conquer the earth and ascend to the heavens. Who among us can refuse such a destiny?"

The room erupted and Nimrod saw Mizraim's glare of defiance attenuate under the weight of the realization that he had just lost a major battle. The smaller man abruptly rose and left the room. Nimrod turned and saw his grandmother staring hungrily at him.

Tonight would be special.

Chapter 22
LISTEN TO THE MUSIC

12-15-1754

Evening was casting long shadows when Anam led Graemea down the empty street toward the unfinished new market. It was a magical moment; the rainbow display of the setting sun and the warmth of the stones underfoot kept the evening chill at bay. They had to dodge men hurrying to finish their day's business. With people flooding into Shinar, trade and commerce continued until well after dark.

The couple dodged into the unfinished walkways of the new market to avoid the crowded street. Low brick walls separated the individual kiosks that were cleverly designed to funnel shoppers into the middle of the maze. Ambitious traders were already building permanent shops around the perimeter. Any man willing to work could make a comfortable living, and one with a modicum of cleverness could become rich. As Anam looked around he saw another indication of the energy and ability of Shinar's citizens. Nimrod was right—within a century, Shinar would be a great city, home to tens of thousands of people.

But Graemea's soft hand was a pleasant distraction from that depressing certainty. He gripped it tightly, and she squeezed in return. He glanced over and she ran her tongue lightly across her lips, her eyes dancing under her eyelashes. He gave her hand another squeeze and shook his head, thankful that no one saw the byplay. They received enough hard looks for holding hands in public. Most thought such a display inappropriate, but their disapproval was muted. Graemea often laughed that none would dare hurl a public accusation at one of Debseda's chosen. And Anam enjoyed thumbing his nose at their hypocrisy. Those who took the most offense were probably sleeping with their neighbors' wives. Such was the town of Shinar— obsessed with gnats while ignoring dragons.

He didn't bother to look around to see which of Korac's men were following this evening. He and Graemea enjoyed the game—who could spot the shadows without giving themselves away. It wasn't hard—they just looked for those who appeared to be following someone or those who were trying hard to avoid seeming to do so. The couple both enjoyed confounding their stalkers… letting them watch but not listen. While it wasn't much of a challenge to see who was following, they strolled leisurely through the streets, staying far enough from narrow alleys and sudden corners so as to keep their shadows from hearing their words. It was impossible all the time, so when eavesdropping was unavoidable, Korac's spies heard only saccharine endearments of two lovers… and an occasional giggle from Graemea. Being a flighty young woman, that was only to be expected. How could they know she was laughing at them?

That was one of Anam's problems. Graemea shared his sense of humor and they often laughed together. That compatibility highlighted Anam's greatest weakness. At first, having been thrown into her bed by the implied, but very real, threat of death and failure, he had hardened his heart against her ardor, only pretending to fall in love. But as the weeks fled by, he found that pretense wearing thin. She was hopelessly in love with him, and what man could resist the energetic affections of a beautiful and intelligent woman. And his affections—real or not—had begun to work changes in her behavior. A heart that had been hardening under Debseda's influence was growing softer again, shifting its allegiance from mistress to lover. Deceiving Nimrod and Debseda was fun… misleading Graemea was not.

It had only taken Anam a few days to solve the mystery of Graemea. Part of her was still the lovable young girl he had known growing up. The other part was the callous servant of his greatest enemy—a cold woman who had betrayed others to Debseda. In his first week in Shinar, Anam saw her at her worst. A certain young woman—working in their household while her betrothed saved towards marriage—had repeated an innocent jest about Debseda. Graemea overheard. The next day, the girl was back in her father's house, her betrothal broken by shadowy rumors of infidelity. Anam knew they weren't true, just as he knew that Graemea was at the bottom of the shameful episode. And she knew he knew by the simple expedient of his refusing to talk to her that night and several more afterwards, simply turning his back on her. Although his life hung by a thread, he didn't care. He wanted the girl he had known in childhood, not a cold avatar of Debseda.

Somehow he had won that gamble. The fourth night she had snuggled up to his back, her tears wetting his neck. She swore never to hurt anyone again and begged his forgiveness. "Be the girl you are, Graemea," he had said, "and I'll be yours forever. Become like Celota, and I'll never speak to you again." No vow had been too much for her that night. "I only want you, Anam," she had responded. "I swear I'll never do anything to make you hate me. Just give me the chance."

Anam rolled over and held her eyes with a softening stare. For a moment he thought Graemea was going to blurt out something else… the haunted look was back in her eyes and some of the tears seemed to spring from a more distant sorrow, but she shook her head slightly and shut it away. Anam hid his concern and decided that she had a dark secret that he would learn in due time—probably some similar abuse of power eating at her conscience.

That night had marked the first clear breach between Anam the spy and Anam the man. As time went on, her naïve trust created more cracks in that weakening wall. She assumed marriage was simply a matter of time—her ethos sufficient to desire marriage, but flexible enough to allow him into her bed before the vows. He did nothing to discourage her—partly because he needed her as a conduit into Debseda's inner sanctum, but partly because he had begun to allow himself to share her dream of a future together. Either way, he wanted to be with her.

And his efforts were bearing fruit. Little by little, Graemea's allegiance began to shift. She was beginning to gossip about her mistress. Oh, it was indirect. Celota, Oshetipin, and Graemea were always suspicious and jealous of each other—it was part of the daily vying for Debseda's favor. Their mistress clearly enjoyed the game, the constant tension of playing one girl against the others.

One night, after they had been together for several weeks, Graemea had begun to talk about Celota and a petty injustice. Anam had silenced her with a kiss and then breathed into her ear, "The walls hear, my love. Save your tale for the street tomorrow." That had started what had become an almost daily ritual—an evening stroll through the lanes of Shinar. Within a few nights Korac's spies had begun to shadow the couple. At first, the watchers were clumsy, and Anam spotted them almost immediately. From that day he began to imagine the steps he would take if he were doing the following, and quickly became adept at seeing all who trailed him. He trained Graemea to avoid meaningful talk unless they were out of earshot of any potential hiding place, and both became skilled at switching from real conversation to meaningless patter as they walked by dark doorways or narrow back streets.

Over time, Graemea became more open with her tales of Celota and Oshetipin, and in doing so, began to reveal subtle hints of Debseda's plots and plans. Anam pretended great interest in the mundane childishness of the three women, sifted away the chaff, and stored the grain in a locked storeroom in his mind, waiting for the day he would pass it to Ashkenaz.

Graemea was not his only problem. Living in such close proximity to Nimrod and Debseda began to take its toll. As the days passed he found himself changing. He had always been carefree and open but now his continued existence depended on being someone else. Worry ate at his heart, making him even more furtive. He feared discovery—through a slip, through Debseda's insight, or through plain bad luck. He began to wonder if Debseda already knew and was using Graemea to pass false information. Even his nights were not free of concern. What if he began talking in his sleep and betrayed his mission?

For a time, he worried about the effects on his heart. But as time went by, survival became the focus of his every thought, and other concerns were locked away in a corner of his mind to be dealt with later... if he lived. He couldn't afford the luxury of introspection now.

But at least he had Graemea, a beautiful young woman, a satisfying lover, and a good friend. She would make a fine wife. But even that haunted his conscience. If he truly loved her, how could he betray her now? And how could he marry a woman he was betraying or one so closely tied to Debseda?

Those questions gave him a new idea. He began to dream of going away—far away—and taking her with him. Away from Debseda, away from Shem, away from his father... a new life for the two of them. After all, the world was wide. But where could he go? She would never be welcome in Madrazi's house. Was there a home for them somewhere? His old dreams of a warm rich land with sunlit waters and lazy days began to resurface, and he found it pleasant to talk about this mythical future home with Graemea—first as a diverting fantasy, but then more and more as a tangible dream. She grew interested; Debseda's service was wearing and she liked the idea of leaving the conflicts of Shinar behind and making a home for themselves. Had Anam known, the desire occupied her mind more than his.

They were now in the broad open area between the rising city walls and the outermost homes. Feigning great interest in the construction of the wall, they were able to find privacy for a few minutes' open talk. Anam didn't even bother to look back and try to spot their shadows. He was determined to enjoy the few minutes that they had together, free of Debseda's distrust.

"Did you hear they finally reached agreement on the council?" she asked, knowing he had not. He shook his head obligingly.

"Your father is an elder now."

Anam stopped short and looked at her carefully. "Don't tease about this, Graemea."

"I'm not!" she pulled her hand out and turned away, her feelings obviously hurt.

"I'm sorry," he said quickly. "I just can't believe that he would accept it."

"He did," she said, "He thinks he has a place of power, but he's playing her game. Mistress has told me more than once that she keeps friends close at hand but her enemies in her bosom. He can't defeat her as long as he's on the council—he's only one of seven. She will see the nature of his opposition, and foil it through the others. His only hope is her making a mistake, and she doesn't make many."

Anam shook his head. In a master stroke, Debseda had just neutralized her most effective opponent. How had someone as clever as Mizraim allowed himself to be maneuvered into such a corner? He shook his head. Her schemes would be more easily accomplished now. Things were about to change in Shinar. Maybe not tomorrow or next month, but it was inevitable. The way was open for Nimrod. This was news that was needed up north.

Stopping and leaning up against a nearby building, he pulled Graemea to his side. Counting on one of Korac's spies being nearby, he looked pensive for a moment and sighed. Graemea leaned against him. "What's wrong, dear Anam? You look so sad."

"It's the music," he replied sadly. "Our new song is so perfect for the flute, but wooden pipes don't do justice to your voice. If only there was a way to make a better one." He sighed.

Graemea smiled up at him. "Why don't we ask grandfather, silly? He can make anything."

"I know," Anam replied. "But he's always so busy with weapons and buildings…."

"Which is why he would probably love to do something different," she beamed.

Anam smiled. "You're so clever! Next time we see him, you can ask."

Graemea frowned. "I don't want to wait." She skipped with excitement. "I want you to play for me as soon as you can. No one knows my voice like you. It will be the best song in Shinar!" She was already dragging him back towards the compound.

"Okay," he smiled. "You win."

He was smiling inside too. Anyone hearing their conversation would remember that it was Graemea—Debseda's trusted maiden—who dragged him into Ham's shop.

But as they neared the workshop, he felt his pulse race. He would have only one chance and Ash would have to be quick on the uptake. And if Mariel was there, she might report every word to Nimrod. He drew a deep breath.

Before he could gather himself, Graemea dragged him to Ham's door. It was standing open, and he could hear the voices inside. Bold as a lioness, Graemea pushed her head inside. Anam watched Ham begin to frown as he caught sight of her, and then another look flashed across his eyes as Anam came into sight. It vanished, and Ham welcomed them. "I fear we are busy now," he nodded to a very pregnant Mariel, sitting on a stool, holding one end of a string while Ashkenaz sketched a template on a wooden beam. "What is it you wish?"

Ashkenaz stiffened when he saw Anam follow the woman into the shop, then forced himself to relax. If Anam was willing to risk coming to him here, there must be something afoot. He was fairly certain that Ham and Mariel would keep any suspicions to themselves, so he schooled his features into a bland disinterest while keeping one eye on Anam as he pretended to arrange the template. It was Anam's move. He was ready to react.

He saw Anam put his hand on Graemea's arm to silence her. "We apologize for this interruption, sir, but we have need of your skill. Standing behind Graemea, he was able to catch Ash's eye and give him a short, sharp look.

Yes! Ashkenaz exulted within, keeping his face still. Anam had information. Ashkenaz felt his palms grow damp. Mariel was disconcertingly perceptive; he hoped she was too uncomfortable with her pregnancy to sense his anxiety.

Anam was speaking again. "We have need of a flute for a song; I know that is a trifle compared to the important work you do for the city, but we hoped that the change would be welcome and that for the love of art you might consider a few hours of your valuable time."

Ham pulled his chin and then looked suspiciously at Anam. He clearly didn't believe the story but seemed willing to let things play out. "You're right, son," he replied finally. "We spend too much time on practical things and not enough on beauty and pleasure. Have you been creating new songs?"

"Oh, yes sir," interrupted Graemea. "Anam is the best musician in the city!"

"Well," smiled Ham, "a master musician needs the best instruments. I haven't made a silver flute in many years. Perhaps you could stay and help me recall the spacing and size of the holes." Turning over his shoulder, he called to the others, "Come here, you two. You both need to learn the basics of musical instruments. It will be a welcome change from your work."

Graemea moved to help Mariel, and Ashkenaz saw Ham wink at Anam. The younger man swallowed nervously and let go of Graemea. He had to… his hand was shaking. He hid it quickly behind him. Ashkenaz smiled, hoping to communicate some confidence.

But it was Ham who bought time for the small man to relax. He pulled Graemea over to an empty work table, allowing Anam to regain his composure. "Bring some chalk and a measuring rod, Ashkenaz, and I'll show you the dimensions." Turning to Graemea, he asked, "Have you ever made a flute before, young lady?"

Her eyes were wide. "Oh, no sir. I can sing, but know nothing of instruments."

"Then it's time that you learned," he replied. "You sit here beside the Lady Mariel and I'll show you." He pulled two stools up to the table and as he helped the clumsy Mariel into one, Graemea cautiously climbed into the other. She recalled the day that Mariel came to Shinar and her fury at Celota. But looking sideways, she saw that she seemed composed enough. Perhaps the child in her belly had leached her anger. Graemea relaxed slightly and watched Ham begin to sketch the outline on the table's dark wood.

His maneuvering left Ashkenaz standing beside Anam behind the women. He knew that it was no coincidence and wondered just how much Ham suspected. He raised an eyebrow at Anam, then shrugged slightly and nodded. They would have to trust Ham. But now they had to communicate in the presence of Nimrod's wife and Debseda's maid. Ashkenaz felt his tongue freeze. He needed to speak, but didn't know what to say.

Again Ham solved the problem. Normally taciturn, he became almost voluble, rattling on to the women about the relationship between the diameter of the pipe and the size of the holes. As he talked he began to gossip about the doings of Shinar. "What do you hear about the new council, Anam? I understand your father will play a part."

Anam shot Ashkenaz a look. This was it. Ash stiffened slightly as Anam answered. "Oh yes," he returned in an equally casual voice. It was a testimony to his months among the vipers in this compound that he could speak so easily. Ashkenaz envied his apparent calm. "Grandmother lured him into a well-set snare."

"In what way?" Ashkenaz began to wonder if Ham was asking these questions for his benefit? But that would mean that he knew…. Ashkenaz drew a deep breath. He was committed now and had to play along.

Anam rattled on in the same bored tone. "He had to choose between evils. He could lose face by refusing service on the town council or diminish his influence by having his voice diluted among six others. I'm sure he's angry about the whole thing—he has certainly lost influence among many of the younger men." He paused and shot a hard glance at Ash, who winked back. "I imagine that with the opposition muted, Grandmother will be able to press forward more quickly with her plans."

Ashkenaz understood. Again, Ham took a hand. "Yes. I understand that she wants the council to vote on building a great temple near the center of town—a celebration of these many new gods that she has contrived. It will undoubtedly unify the men of Shinar and the plains in a manner that little else could… save war."

Ham shook his head and lifted the chalk again. "Now here, ladies, we must decide on the size of the mouthpiece…."

Anam waited until the women were engrossed in Ham's drawing, and caught Ash's eye once more. He nodded emphatically. Ashkenaz dropped a slow eyelid… he understood. Anam felt a surge of relief. The news would be headed north on the next caravan, probably within a week. He looked at Anam once more, glanced at

Ham, and then smiled and nodded. Their lives were in the hands of Debseda's husband, but it would have to do.

After the couple left, Ham turned to Ashkenaz and Mariel. "That's enough for tonight. We've stayed too long as it is. We'll clean up in the morning." He sighed. "I'm going to walk to the river tonight. Ashkenaz, would you please close the shop and walk my sister to her rooms?"

Ashkenaz grinned to himself. Ham was certainly in a helpful mood tonight. But an opportunity like this was one to be seized eagerly. "Of course, sir," he replied, keeping the excitement out of his voice.

Mariel was curious. There had been something false in Ham's voice, and she had never known him as a man of so many words. She began to wonder what had just happened, hoping it was something that would harm Nimrod. As they hurried to put away the tools she dared enough to ask, "I'm surprised your friend came to see you. He seems to have avoided you ever since you arrived."

Ashkenaz stopped and looked at her. She sensed a sharpness of mind he had not before displayed. Though she couldn't see his eyes, she felt the tension in his body.

"Well," he answered dryly, "he seems to have found a beautiful woman to occupy his days. In his place, I'm sure I would have done the same." But he added a bold look to the dry words that shot straight to her heart. It changed his face completely. The slow, stolid worker was transformed into an intensely alive… and intensely desirable man.

She flushed and daring greatly, she returned his look. "Even if the woman was… burdened?" Her hands rested on her swollen belly.

"Burdens are made to be shared… by people who love each other."

She almost stumbled from the force of emotion in his voice. She was a single word away from throwing herself into his arms out in the middle of the courtyard before her mind brought her back from the brink of sanity. This could only bring evil to them and to Ham. She strove for self-control, wanting nothing more than the privacy of her room and the luxury of tears. Attempting to force that control into her voice, it only came out low and husky, with an undercurrent of desire. "The lady would be fortunate indeed that would warrant such interest from you!" Then she rushed inside.

Ashkenaz was left standing there, wanting to curse himself for his words, yet relieved that he had finally spoken the truth… and dizzy with elation that he had heard his feelings returned.

As he walked back across the courtyard his heart was singing, even as his mind reeled.

Chapter 23
AN UNEXPECTED FRIEND

2-14-1755

Mariel woke sweating. Yesterday she had refrained from visiting the workshop, sending Zerai to tell Ham that her time was too near. In truth she knew that she could not face Ash so soon after their words two nights ago. And as the day wore on, her excuse began to feel more and more legitimate; her body felt horribly distended and uncomfortable. It was a struggle to rise from her bed, and eating was out of the question.

A bad day slid into an unpleasant evening. Debseda arrived after supper and insisted on examining Mariel thoroughly. "Who better to help with your delivery?" she laughed. "I have attended many and possess the knowledge."

Mariel refrained from the obvious—that her knowledge came from Wen-Tehrom, who had delivered all four of her sons and three of her daughters. But this was not a time to fight with Debseda; she needed someone's help and Debseda was probably the most knowledgeable midwife available. But there was something in the woman's barely suppressed excitement that unsettled Mariel. She acted as if it were her baby... like Mariel were merely a convenient womb and not really a mother.

It helped that loyal Zerai remained in the room, holding her hand. The girl had proven a faithful maid and good friend over the months. At first their relationship had been stilted—in spite of Ham's approval, Mariel knew that Debseda was wicked enough to find some leverage over her maid and exploit it. But the girl proved independent, and after her second screaming match with Celota, Mariel began to take her into her confidence. Not completely, of course, but Zerai was well aware of her attitude towards her husband's grandmother and her minions. She clutched Mariel's hand, offering what comfort she could.

Finally, Debseda pulled Mariel's skirts back down. "Sleep while you can, little one. Your time is close. Celota will remain with your servant." Zerai faced the sneer bravely, but looked warily at Celota. "Send her for me when the water of birth arrives."

She turned back at the door. Graemea will bring you something to drink soon. It will help you sleep. Don't refuse it. You'll need all your strength tomorrow to deliver the heir."

With that she had left and Mariel settled down as best she could. "Wait in the other room," she ordered Celota, to Zerai's obvious relief. Celota's face twisted, her eyes stabbing at Zerai. She seemed ready to argue, but Zerai spoke first. "You wouldn't want to upset my mistress and anger yours." Her voice was sweet, but her eyes danced. Celota glared, but edged out of the room. Zerai gave an exaggerated sigh of relief and Mariel giggled and squeezed her hand.

A few minutes later Graemea arrived, holding a cup. "It tastes bitter, but it's good for you," she promised loudly. Then under her breath she whispered, "What did you say to Celota. She looks like she swallowed a lemon tree!" Zerai clapped her hand to her mouth to keep in a guffaw and Mariel smiled briefly. "She wasn't happy with the view from the other room," she replied smoothly.

Graemea nodded, then pursed her lips as Mariel sipped gingerly. She grimaced, and drank it down quickly. Graemea hesitated, leaning closer. "My mistress wants Celota to help tomorrow," she began softly. "Would you rather have me?" She looked down. "Anam likes you," she murmured, "so I guess that makes you my friend too."

Mariel felt herself relaxing from the draught. "Can you?" she whispered.

Graemea smiled broadly. "Watch me." She winked at Zerai and left quietly.

As the day dragged on Mariel struggled to find a comfortable position. Every few minutes she would rise and walk around the room, but that wasn't any more comfortable than laying on the bed… simply a different kind of discomfort. Zerai, worn out from helping her up and down, was napping on a blanket spread on the floor beside the bed. The sun was low on the horizon when the first pang struck, wrenching an involuntary cry from her lips. She jammed her hand in her mouth to muffle the sound, but the pain grew rapidly worse. Just when she thought she must cry out, it was gone, leaving her feeling foolish. Zerai stirred and came awake quickly. She climbed on the edge of the bed and smoothed the sweat from Mariel's brow. "It's started, hasn't it?"

"Yes," panted Mariel. "But don't tell Celota."

"Of course, my lady," whispered Zerai, as she leaned close. "I wouldn't want that sow around me either." She winked and Mariel smiled… until the next pang struck. She bit off her cry and grabbed Zerai's hand. The girl winced, but wiped her forehead with a cloth. Soon, it too was gone, leaving Mariel self-conscious and tired. It would be a long evening. She knew from helping her mother that this could go for hours on end, especially for the first born.

Over the next hours the pattern repeated itself, with the episodes drawing closer together and the pain becoming more intense. Zerai had twisted a cloth to bite down on, and the faithful maid bathed her face with cool water. She even helped quiet the cries during the worst pangs. But it was a losing battle. During one particularly intense pain Mariel felt a warm wetness gushing down her leg. The pain shot through her entire body and she could not stifle her cry.

Zerai understood immediately. She slipped into the other room and roused Celota. "Fetch your mistress now!" She was pushing the poor woman out the door before she was fully awake.

True to her word, it was Graemea who followed Debseda into the bed chamber, carrying a leather bag. "Bring clean sheets and hot water," the older woman snapped, and Graemea curtsied and rushed away. Zerai turned to face Debseda. "She woke but an hour or more past," she lied. "Her water came just before Celota found you. The pain is intensifying and the baby is moving quickly."

Debseda raised an eyebrow. "I have witnessed six births, my lady," Zerai responded. "The Lady Mariel is progressing faster than any I have seen."

"Good," sniffed Debseda. "You may be of some use. It is no wonder the child is strong. He bears the blood of strength." As she spoke, a hungry look passed over her face. Zerai quickly averted her eyes, but her curiosity was stirred. There was something in the way Debseda said that… something to discuss with her mistress later. Now was the time to bring the baby into the world.

Without waiting for instructions she removed Mariel's skirt and underclothing, and threw the damp mess across the room. Rolling Mariel to the right, she pulled out the old sheet—damp with sweat and the first water of birth—and slid a clean one under her. Rolling her back, she completed the task, sliding a clean sheet over the bulging form of her mistress. Debseda curled a lip. "Perhaps you will be of use. Tell me what you know and I will teach you."

Zerai bowed her head. "You are too generous, my lady. I only seek the comfort of my mistress." She spent the next quarter hour relating what she had learned from her aunt. Clearly it impressed Debseda. "But it is such a privilege watching you, my lady," she simpered. "Everyone knows that you are the wisest woman in Shinar."

Mariel nearly choked, but Debseda took the words at face value. "Hold her leg up like this," she instructed. "Hmmm. You're right, little one. This one moves. We won't bother taking her upstairs to the birthing room. We'll deliver here." She turned as Graemea came in with an armload of linens.

"Good," Debseda stood for a moment. "I must fetch the leg supports. Help Zerai keep her comfortable. Prepare swaddling for the child. Build a fire in the fireplace. Heat a pan of water. When it begins to boil, drop my blade and needle in and pull it off the flames."

"Of course, my lady." Graemea bowed her head and moved to the other side of the bed to grip Mariel's arm. Another spasm struck her, and the moan drowned out anything else Debseda was going to say.

After she and the spasm were both gone, Mariel grinned crookedly at Graemea. "How did you do it?" she croaked.

"Do what, my lady?" asked Graemea with an innocent face. "I'm doing nothing but my duty. I can't help it if that oaf, Celota, cannot walk down the stairway without tripping. She twisted her ankle rather badly, but got no sympathy from our mistress. So I'm stuck playing midwife today. Poor girl," she sighed. "She's just so clumsy sometimes."

Zerai giggled with Graemea while Mariel shook her head.

"Thank you, Graemea. I like Anam too. He's a good man, and I think maybe you're a good woman. I'm glad you're here."

Suddenly tears began flowing down Graemea's cheeks. "What's wrong?" asked a troubled Mariel. "What did I say?"

"It's not you, my lady." She stifled her sobs and wiped her tears away. "I'm not a good woman. I'm not."

"We all make mistakes, Graemea," whispered Mariel. Daring greatly she whispered, "You're here today to witness mine." Holding back her own tears, she reached out for the young woman's hand. "We are not the sum of our errors," she hissed. "We are more. There is always hope! You have Anam. Cling to him and find hope together."

Graemea's eyes cleared. "Do you really think so?" Then they clouded. "You don't understand…."

Mariel looked down. "I understand. Why do you think I didn't cast myself in the river the first day I discovered this baby. I had a choice to make. I couldn't undo what had been done. I could only hope to do better the next day. Not all at once… not everything. Just one thing. One choice. One day…."

Her gray eyes bored into Graemea's. "Now you hold my life in your hands. What will you do with *that* choice?"

Graemea blanched. "Your words say the same as the quiet voice in my heart that no one hears. Anam understands it too." She nodded as if reaching some great decision, and straightened her back. It was Anam's Graemea who spoke next. "For your honesty, my lady, you have your life, and more." She paled, but met the question in Mariel's eyes. "I offer mine in return. When the child is weaned my mistress means to have him. She will raise him as her own, teaching him her ways… her arts… her desires. Your husband has already given his leave."

Mariel's eyes began to dissolve and her lip quivered. Just then another spasm struck and she cried her anger out with her pain. In the midst of the worst moments Graemea saw something take shape and form in her gray eyes. Mariel's face grew calm, even amid the pain, and a great resolve brushed aside the distress. At that moment, Graemea understood what it meant to be the daughter of the eldest.

"Forewarned is forearmed," she gritted out. "You leave me in your debt… friend. May the Creator give you the freedom to find your hopes fulfilled."

Graemea gripped her hand. "You call me friend, after all that I have done to you? If you can do that, then perhaps there is hope. Friend you have named me and friend I will be… until the world is undone!"

The women composed themselves just in time. Debseda entered the room, Oshetipin behind her, struggling with the clumsy leg supports. All she saw was Zerai hovering protectively over her mistress and Graemea smiling sardonically at her across the bed. Debseda smiled too. Things were progressing. Tonight the first heir of the new blood would enter a world being prepared for his rule. The line would expand and the Nephil would find their rightful place on the earth, lords over mere men; they would rebuild their empire and prepare to wage war against the god of Noah.

INTERLUDE 2

6-12-2161

Darkness pressed in on Lydia. She felt helpless in her bed. Stealthy footsteps drew nearer. Her mind screamed to jump up and run, but fear paralyzed her. Though her limbs wouldn't respond, her senses were preternaturally sharp.

Two soldiers were coming... large, well-trained, vicious killers. They would murder Lud and deliver her to their captain. She feared the pain and shame, but it was not that fate that froze her limbs. If she died, she would have failed—the last years of the Old One all for nothing. She lay still, shivering and trusting Lud's last whispered command.

"Wait for it," he had breathed, and so she waited.

She tried to keep still, but surely the men could hear the thunder of her heartbeat and the rasp of her uncontrolled panting.

She was near a pool at the base of a small cliff. The soldiers had pitched their camp in the gulch's mouth, bottling them inside. Lud had set their camp some distance away, on the opposite side of the water, ostensibly for Lydia's 'privacy' but in reality for his own. He had spent the evening preparing an ambush and now they must put it to the test against hardened warriors. Failure meant death.

Her dying fire reflected a dim red off the pool, but the ground around was in dark shadow. Lud was one of those shadows, and Lydia couldn't see him, even knowing the direction of his voice. Between her and the soldiers were scattered rocks and a few trees, but she couldn't see them either. She had to trust her heart that he was close and able to deal with the danger. There was no alternative. Gentle vibrations in the sand told her that the soldiers were near and she half-opened one eye.

The moon crested the shallow cliff, and for the first time she could see the two approaching shadows. They were close, and both were armed with spears. Lud had only a knife. They stopped for a moment and she held her breath. They must see two still forms. She moaned a little, as if in her sleep, so that they would know which form to attack.

But just before they struck, they stumbled over the cord Lud suddenly pulled tight up between their feet. They were trained men and didn't panic, but the moment's distraction was all Lud needed. Lydia saw him spring like a panther on the nearest.

In that instant she knew. He was no shepherd. He was a warrior—he had to be. There was a raging fire beneath his placid exterior she had never seen. Both her eyes were wide open now and she was sitting up—spectator to their struggle for life under the pitiless stars. She saw little but the blur of shadows, but her ears provided what her eyes could not see. A choking sound... a thud like an ax striking a side of beef... muttered curses... another gurgling noise... then silence—a quiet that was far more frightening than the quiet stalk. She bit her lip to keep from screaming. Scrambling to her feet, she heard a familiar voice.

"It's all right now," he whispered, though there was no longer any need. "They won't touch you... not now, not ever."

"What do we do now?" Her voice was like that of another person; steady and strong, when inside, she was coming apart. She hated the feeling of helplessness; it brought back bad memories.

"I don't know," he said. "We can take their horses and make our own way, but then we'll have that captain after us the entire way. And if he bumps into another patrol, they'll spread the word. To run, we'll need fast horses, but they would stand out anywhere we go. They're not the mounts of a poor farmer."

"What's the other option?" She already knew, but wanted to hear it from his mouth.

"We leave the bodies, catch up to the caravan, kill the rest of the troop, and push on."

"What about the headman?" she asked; a tremor in her voice. She realized now that Lud's simple declaration was a death sentence for those men, no matter how good they were. She had no doubts; he would do exactly as he said.

How could she have misread this man so completely for so long? Why had the Old One not given her some clue? At least she knew now why the old woman had chosen him to take her south. Anyone who could take two warriors so easily....

"He's a coward," Lud answered flatly. "With the captain dead, the headman will be easy to handle."

"Where did you learn how to do this?" The whisper leapt unbidden from her lips. She started to shake.

Then Lud was there. His hands gripped her shoulders and lowered her onto the blankets. "Sit and listen while I take care of things." He pressed a flask to her hands and she sipped the potent liquor, allowing its warmth to chase away the chill terror that gripped her belly.

She heard him unbuckling straps, salvaging armor and weapons. As he worked, he talked—for her sake, she realized. "I used to be like the captain," he said. She shuddered as two swords clattered near her feet. "I was almost as arrogant," he laughed grimly, "but a lot better at what I did. I became a member of the royal guard at Hattusa."

Lydia's mind could not absorb it. For a member of that elite group to say he was 'better' than the captain was like one of the elders saying that they lived a few years longer than other men.

Lud continued as he began sorting through the pile. "I saw a woman in the palace, and she saw me. I was a lowly lieutenant at the time, and her father was chief of the scribes and a friend of the prince. He found out and I fled, killing those sent after me. When I stumbled on the farm, the elder hired me as a shepherd. I told him everything before he died."

His voice tailed off as he began to dig. She understood. She remembered him. Even at death's door, he seemed beyond them all, as if this puny world did not deserve his wisdom and courage. The present age wasn't good enough for him or his wife—the Old One who had saved Lydia. She was silent for a moment, lost in memories of the mountain.

She shook herself. This was not the time. They were stuck with two dead Hatti soldiers. If discovered, they would both be tortured and executed. Lud seemed to understand her fear and began talking again. "These were just garrison troops. They didn't stand a chance."

She nodded to herself. Only the best were considered for the Hittite royal guard, the elite of their very formidable army. Lud had been a wolf among sheep. At least she knew him now... his mystery was solved. She thought for a moment to repay him, but could not. It might be unfair, but she could not speak of herself. She could never face him if he knew the truth of who she had been. But she felt closer to him than ever. They had so much in common—so much to leave in the past.

But the past always chased you down, no matter how fast you ran. She knew in her bones that hers would catch up one day, and prayed that she would be dead when it did. Death would be better than his contempt. He on the other hand retained his honor; she understood his courage, knowing that for every terse word, she would see a hundred more in his story. Under the tutelage of the Old One, Lydia had honed her natural insight to the point that she could understand with a few words what others could not in an hour of talk. In those few words, she could see all of Lud's past life.

Pain and fear filled her heart. But the panic was gone; her mind chewing on his story. Even if he decided to hate her, she couldn't let such a gift pass unrewarded.

When he returned from burying the bodies, she had their things packed and the fire built back up. Food sat beside it. He shook his head.

She was adamant. "Clean up and eat." He shrugged and sat down, but the food sat before him untouched.

"We both found a refuge with the Old One," she began, and struggled through the bare outlines of her tale—the priest, the trial, a shorn head, torn clothes, and banishment from Nineveh. She omitted only who she had been, unable to choke out those words.

During the story, he took up his plate, acknowledging her gift. "I'll never know how I survived the journey," she finished. "I guess the Old One's God protected me. She took me in, taught me, answered my questions, gave me her friendship...." She stopped, and wiped the tears flowing down her cheeks.

Lud stirred and looked at her across the fire. "You didn't owe me that," he said quietly.

"Yes... yes, I did," She forced a half smile. "I guess we're both orphans who found a better home than we deserved."

He nodded slowly. "And now that they're dead, we're orphans again."

"No," she shook her head slowly, "They gave us a new family, one that will always be there."

He nodded thoughtfully, and then sighed. "I'll get the horses."

Morning found her sitting astride her horse at the top of a long hill. Fast Hittite horses had carried them past the caravan, despite Lud's cautious leeway. Exhausted, but upright in the saddle, she sat in plain sight with two other horses beside her. She held their reins tightly and tried to suppress the tremor in her hand.

She saw the caravan wind into sight, and then saw excited figures on horseback pointing up at her. Even in the clear air they appeared as small as children's toys. She waited. After conferring with the headman for a few moments, the captain signaled his four men and all five advanced up the road, trotting abreast, just as Lud had predicted. As they drew nearer, she could see the captain's face, suffused with rage, his white knuckles gripping his war spear. He saw her sitting on one of his troop's horse, and understood perfectly.

The soldiers were still one hundred paces down the road when she heard the soft music of a bowstring—so fast that the two arrows seemed to fly as one. Just like that, two men were down, their horses faltering out of line as they rolled out of the saddle and onto the dusty road.

The captain froze for a moment and then kicked his horse just in time. Another arrow flew within a span of the back of his head, entering the side of the man just beyond him. Pointing the remaining man toward the ambush, the captain charged straight for Lydia. The soldier set his horse to the steep rocks that sheltered Lud's position.

Only he was no longer there. Taking his horse down a slope impossible for almost any rider, Lud slammed into the captain, throwing the man to the ground. His spear flashed down once. The last man was ready and waiting—obviously an experienced warrior who knew that flight was death. They stared at each other for a moment, then charged. The soldier feinted and lunged, but Lud had seen it before, and his counter was as smooth as it was deadly.

As Lydia and Lud rode down the hill, now leading seven horses, they saw the fear on the headman's face. He stood staring, clearly unsure what to do next. She drew a breath, but Lud cut her off. The sleepy, stolid expression was gone, and the man beside her was now the trained killer of the Hittite royal guard. He radiated danger and the headman was not *that* much of a fool.

"These men tried to take my property and my wife." Lud's voice was harsh. "You were a part of it... how much I don't know and don't care, but if you so much as look at us between here and Nineveh, I'll strangle you with your own guts."

The man paled; it was no empty threat.

Lud grated on, turning to the others. "In return, for your company and your silence, you may take five of these horses. You'll make a profit in Nineveh. They won't care where they came from." The men nodded, narrowing eyes flitting between Lud and the headman. A few of the more discerning glared at the latter, their respect—and his reputation—shattered by Lud's words.

Lud continued for their benefit, his voice now reasonable. "All we wanted was an honest company bound for the plains. Seven men died thanks to greed and treachery." He turned a baleful eye back to the headman. "Don't make it eight!"

Swallowing rapidly, that worthy shook his head vigorously. "Let it be as you say, my lord!" He bowed slightly and held his hands with the palms forward. "Let it be as you say. Only spare me, I beg you." The smarter traders turned away in disgust. Lydia nodded to herself—this headman was finished. Word would spread.

For a moment, a small voice inside told her to have Lud kill him. He deserved it. He would be desperate when he realized what he had just lost, and Lud would do it in a moment at her word.

But enough blood had been spilled, so she kept her silence as they resumed their place. It was a quiet cavalcade, and she could not wait to break free for Carchemish. Once there they could leave this nightmare behind and lose themselves in the hill country further south, finding the lost prince.

Perhaps then, they could both fade into another existence...a simple life together. She knew now...that was what she wanted...that was all she wanted. She just didn't know how to tell him.

Chapter 24
SHINAR FINDS RELIGION

3-25-1755

Canaan stood apart from the rest of the council on the platform as the crowds gathered before them—order coming out of crowded chaos by the heavy hand of Nimrod's Legion. Canaan had the most important task and was correspondingly nervous. Debseda, hiding behind the curtain, could see the sweat beading on his brow. She frowned. How could she have ever entertained the idea that this weakling could have anything to do with the line of new men? She had been fooled by Noah's curse… as if there were actually power in the old drunkard's rant. Her face hardened as she thought of the wasted years trying to teach Canaan to be something he clearly was not.

But at least that knowledge enabled him to become a respectable spokesman for Nimrod. His reputation projected a respectability of masculine age and wisdom that neither she nor Nimrod possessed. It still galled her to have to lean on so weak a tool, which was why she had ordered the platform built against the outer wall of one of her warehouses, facing the new market. No selling would take place today; a public assembly had been called by the council.

Debseda remained hidden from the crowd, standing in a window behind the dais, its opening shrouded with billowing curtains of an exotic pattern—one that she could see through, but that would hide her face as she watched the scene. Something about light and shadow… Nimrod was clever at such things.

The platform had been built to a specific height, placing her looking down, near enough to signal Nimrod if anything went wrong. They had an extensive set of contingencies… everything from tugging the thread that ran from his ankle to her window, to different noises designed to be drowned out by the crowd. Today was every bit as important as his abduction of Mariel. Then he had taken a wife from the great Patriarch. Today they would seize an entire city.

She had a performance to direct, but her involvement must remain unseen. Today was between the council and the people. Even Nimrod must remain in the background—except for one crucial performance—and she would stay completely invisible. She had heard all the rumors—mostly spread in the taverns. She was a puppet master, directing the council. While true, it was another inconvenient truth that must be eradicated. Women were not made to rule—that was still one of the prejudices of the old world that had successfully taken root in the new. She frowned to herself. *One battle at a time*, she thought.

And that was not a conflict she could fight now. In the future, the people must remember the men, those of the council proposing and those of the city responding. Nothing more. Even now her maids were busy spreading the story through the crowd that she was indisposed back in her tower.

Seeing the tremor in Canaan's hand, she willed power across the space between them. Mizraim stood uncomfortably to one side, clearly aware now that he had been outmaneuvered and played but unable to disengage without looking like a fool. Put and Tubal stood talking to each other, and Nimrod remained near the back, as was fitting for the youngest member of the group.

Finally the crowd was in place. As if in accord, everyone went silent and turned their attention to the council. They were curious—this was the first time the council had met with the city in this manner... and the first time they had presumed to do anything other than promulgate a few popular laws to keep order.

Cush, seeing the moment, prodded Canaan discretely, and so the younger man took a breath and stepped forward. Now that the moment was upon him, he seemed to relax. He had always been a natural speaker and knew how to connect with an audience. He did so today, gathering the attention of the men with a quip, a story, and a few flattering remarks about the great city of Shinar.

Debseda snorted to herself. She remembered the glory of Lamech, the strength of Taspar, and the exotic beauty of Y'tor before its fall. Shinar was a collection of children's huts in the sand... but the energy was there. If properly directed, Shinar could grow into a great city—a fitting capital for its future king.

Canaan's voice reached out to the far reaches of the marketplace. He had their attention and was enjoying the adulation of the crowd. Among his many weaknesses was his love for his own voice. Debseda hissed a nearly inaudible signal to Nimrod, who coughed twice. Canaan heard it and faltered. His role had been drummed into him for weeks and he knew the cost of failure. Quickly he resumed smoothly, but with the words he had been forced to memorize, not his own.

"Good men of Shinar. We face the coming of another season of planting, tending, and reaping our crops. Our lives rest on our ability to put bread on our tables, so we approach this season with concern. I know that each of you has been preparing your fields with care. It is well that we address the physical needs of the planting. The council has debated long and hard about the poor harvest of last year."

Debseda smiled. The "poor harvest" had been a direct result of Nimrod and Korac sabotaging enough fields to create a disappointing, yet not disastrous year. A little too much water on selected nights, and the yields had dropped noticeably.

The crowd murmured at Canaan's statement. Worry about this year had been a topic of many a marketplace discussion over the past months.

"We share your concerns, just as we shared your distress at the harvest. But we offer more than words."

At this the crowd went silent. Curiosity showed on the faces of everyone. No one had expected a council of wise men to address something as ordinary as tending soil or planting seeds. That was work for those of lesser minds.

Canaan continued. "We cannot tell you how to control your irrigation ditches or spread seed. What you learned from our father Ham, and what your own experience has taught you far exceeds our own knowledge of such matters. But we can offer something else. Crops grow as the sun shines on earth and rains water its fields. We do not control these, but make no mistake... they do not happen by chance."

The crowd was silent now, guessing that some portentous statement was coming. Nor were they disappointed. Canaan paused for emphasis before resuming.

"We have learned the legends of the old world, how one great god made the earth, exiled the first parents, and finally destroyed it by the flood. But something greater than cities and farms was destroyed—the knowledge of the ancients. Our father Noah was great, but he was only one man. He was no scholar or priest. He was an expert in the ways of government, not religion. So our knowledge of these areas is sadly incomplete."

Canaan assumed a pained look and tone, as if it grieved him to speak ill of the old man. Then he let fall the whole reason for the assembly.

"He only knew *one* of the gods."

Men looked to each other curiously. This was a new idea. Had not they always been taught that there was but one god? But then again, had they not also been taught that Noah was a less than perfect man? Surely Canaan was right. None of them could claim universal knowledge. Only a few—like Mizraim—were counted truly wise, but even he had his blind spots and limits. The crowd began to buzz as the idea took hold. It seemed imminently reasonable to most, especially to the youth.

They stared expectantly at Canaan, wanting to hear more. He let the tension build for a moment, then continued. "We of the council are wise in our ways, but there is always more to learn. We are fortunate to have men sensitive to the movings of the heavens and the meanings of the stars. Tubal and Tiras have shown extraordinary insight into this wisdom, and in their arduous studies have discovered the existence of gods we did not know before. They are beings of power and wisdom, and are not happy that men do not acknowledge their rightful rule."

From the back of the market to the front, the buzz grew louder. This was news! What an interesting idea... and discovered by Tubal and Tiras. It was no ploy of Debseda—it came from the house of Japheth!

Canaan held up his hands. "Men of Shinar. Please. I know this news is unexpected, but hear us out. Let these wise men tell you of the gods they have found, how they are to be appeased, and how they can bless our crops." Silence descended upon the multitude.

Then Tubal stood forward. He was wearing a long coarse robe, belted with a rope—the ascetic attire shouting, "holy man." A hood covered his face, adding a mystical air. He held a long wooden staff, adorned with holly berries. Turning to the west, he knelt and began to mumble, his face touching the wood of the platform at regular intervals. It was an impressive display of fervor and the crowd went silent, watching carefully. When he rose, he took a bowl from Tiras and dipped his fingers into the water, before ceremonially scattering it to the four winds. Only then did he push the hood back from his face and address the waiting crowd.

"My brother and I," he began, "have long been enamored of knowledge of the heavens. Some understand the movements of heavenly bodies but limit their understanding to their physical manifestations, ignoring deeper realities."

The crowd sneered along with him. Many northerners—taught by the witch Madrazi—were adept at predicting the phases of the moon and the passage of seasons, but no man in Shinar would admit that his ability to gauge the times of planting and harvest had anything to do with their arch-nemesis.

Tubal continued. "However, our studies have shown deeper things. It matters not how complex the numbering and calculation of the stars if one avoids the real questions. What actually makes the heavenly bodies move? What meanings do they convey? How do they guide our destinies? These and many other questions have wearied our minds for years."

His arms were thrust out dramatically and his voice cracked with excitement. "And we have found answers." A silence hung over the crowd. Tubal let it hover for a moment and lowered his voice.

"Noah taught of one god—the king of heaven. Just as there is the great light to rule the day, the order in the heavens tells us that there is a king to impose it, we have no argument with him in that regard. But what of the moon and the stars? Noah left his studies incomplete and made the fatal error of assuming that no other deities inhabit the grand panoply of the upper skies."

"We know better. As man is incomplete without woman, so a king is incomplete without a queen. So we understand that the king of the heavens must have a queen. Like any other woman, she is concerned with children and home. We are her children, and so she desires our love and adoration. We withhold them to her grief and to the displeasure of her great husband, who does not wish his wife to be dishonored by mere men.

Like any other family, they have borne children down through the long ages before the first man ever walked the earth, and these lesser gods have taken up their just occupations—just as the children of your own families do. There are gods that govern the fighting of wars, and goddesses that favor the conception and delivery of our children. There are those that govern the sea... that guide the courses of the great rivers... that bring bounty from our fields."

Now his voice could hardly be heard amid the uproar of the crowd. This was news! An argument supported by logic and common sense! It clearly showed that the teachings of old Noah had been anything but sensible. He had simply told them to believe his stories—offering no room for new knowledge. And Shinar was bursting with new knowledge. Every man there was proud to be a part of this rebirth of humanity; each imagined himself a great historical figure who would be revered by his children and their descendents after them.

Tubal gestured again and the buzz quieted. "We have much to learn, but have learned much. We will offer appropriate sacrifices to the gods of sky and field to bring bounty this season. Our cousins, Canaan and Cush, have generously offered twenty lambs for this sacrifice. My brother and I will build an altar on the eastern hill," he pointed to the rise just outside the new walls, "and perform those rites at sunrise of the seventh morning from today. If you wish for your fields to prosper this year, then be present to offer your praise and prayers to the Queen of Heaven."

Most men in the crowd nodded. Any opportunity to increase their yields would be eagerly seized. A lamb was an easy price to pay for a bumper yield. And who wanted to be the scapegoat for future calamities? Any man that failed to sacrifice to the gods would automatically be seen as the cause of troubles. Even those that thought Tubal's words nonsense knew better than to object publicly.

Tubal stepped back and lowered the hood over his face once more, making way for a new speaker. Several of the older men stepped forward and pledged their support to the brothers from the best of their flocks.

Finally Nimrod strode to the edge of the dais. Despite the time spent standing in the sun, the crowd cheered his appearance; many younger men screamed his name over and over, while their elders looked nervously at the one who commanded such power. He cast aside his robe, clad only in a kilt and sandals as a common worker, yet looking like a god—his perfect body glistening in the sun. He held a black spear as though it were a rod of wisdom. He raised it and smiled and the youth screamed even louder. Then lowering it, he let the crowd settle before speaking.

"Friends of Shinar. Brothers. Cousins. Uncles. We are all one great family, one people with one mind and one desire. We want to make a name for ourselves on this earth. To enjoy the fruit of its bounty. To live long, prospering in whatever trade gives us pleasure. To rule our households in peace and happiness. To worship together according to wisdom."

The youth in the crowd roared its approval, and the other council members glanced at each other nervously. None of them could elicit that reaction, and Nimrod had yet said nothing of substance. He raised his spear again for quiet, and it became so still that men could hear the faint noise of the wind in the fields.

"We are not animals to live our years, to mate, to feed, and to die without leaving a mark upon this bountiful land. We are men. We are made like the gods to rule their creation. Even my wife's father," he paused briefly with a knowing leer that brought a raucous response from the crowd, "acknowledges this."

Mizraim was frowning openly—if the boy did not respect the eldest of all, why should he respect any elder?

Nimrod spread his arms. He was the picture of perfect manhood—tall, strong, handsome. His flowing dark hair hung heavy over his broad shoulders and the sun played on his sculpted chest. He was the great hunter, master of beasts and men. Even the stout Heth had been unable to face him, and everyone feared Heth.

"Let us make our mark," Nimrod roared. "Let this city of Shinar become the capital of the earth—the first of many great cities to show the barbarians of the north, and their god, that our lives mean something! A great city needs a great symbol. Let us make one… here on these flat plains between the rivers. Build a monument to ourselves and to the new gods we have discovered! Build it high and strong! Let it reach to the heavens, forever binding the men of Shinar to the gods of the plain. Show them that we are worthy children."

His body glistened with sweat in the sun, his hair caught its light, and his face looked up to the sky, as if the gods were talking with him at that moment. If this was not one of the new gods, then it was certainly the finest example of manhood any had seen. A fitting symbol of the new, in that moment he cemented the allegiance of every youth of the city. He was no longer the youngest of the council… as far as they were concerned, he *was* the council. The older men were but props, and the other six councilors on the platform understood exactly what had happened, though none of them shared the enthusiasm of the crowd.

Mizraim relaxed his face, allowing no hint of feeling to show. Today had brought trouble, but it also brought a decision. Uncertainty was burned away in the crowd's fervor for the young whelp. It was time to begin planning the exodus of his household. It would not be tomorrow or even next year, but he and his would leave this insanity and find a land far away where they could build their own empire—a place in the sun, far from Nimrod.

Behind the curtain, Debseda hugged herself with joy.

Unnoticed in the shadows at the back of the crowd, Ham pulled the cloak further over his face and slid away, shaking his head. It was typical—grandiose plans with no thought to the cost in time, bricks, and labor. He knew he would be asked to design it, and toyed for a moment with designing for failure, but gave it up. He could no more do that than he could cut off his right hand. Then he smiled grimly. There was no reason not to *over* design—to give them something that would take ten or more years to build. Perhaps the city would grow tired of the demands on their labor and give it up. That would be a humiliating defeat for his wife!

No one knew her better. She was the root of this corruption—ruining a place that he had worked hard to build. He was tired of his labor being twisted for evil. It was time to free himself and start anew, a place far from her and her lover… where his gifts would be appreciated. Emancipation would not happen overnight, but he suddenly realized that he had taken the first step. He had decided to do it.

In the meantime, he sighed to himself, he would have to continue the passive role that he hated. He had made so many mistakes. His anger at Noah, his insane rebellion… throwing his father's weakness into the teeth of his brothers… all the while having been cleverly goaded by his wife, not yet seeing the depths of her evil.

Noah's curse and his exile had nearly crushed him. For a time, he had ceded authority in the family to his wife, and had never recovered it. Once they were down on the plain with sons and daughters, his subservience had seemed the easiest way to do the only things that brought him joy. He now realized that Debseda had played on his fear and he wondered darkly how he had been so blind.

What was unity if it only meant that men would be united in evil? But there were others to consider now. He had been able to protect Mariel—she was a valuable hostage to his acquiescence. Debseda was no fool. If he was going to challenge her openly, now was not the time. She would be ready, and quite frankly, he was not. He was tired… tired of this morass of spite, hatred, and the pursuit of power. He must take action, but with caution. Could he out-plot his wife?

At that moment he remembered the ark, his friend Meshur's confidence in meeting every challenge that the giant ship had thrown at them. And they had done it! If he could meet those challenges, he could meet these. But he missed Meshur—the memory was painful even after all of these years. Yet behind the pain was a quiet confidence that he had long left behind.

Perhaps it was time to seize it once more.

Chapter 25
NEWS FROM THE SOUTH

3-29-1755

Zeb rode hard through the night. It was three days of hard riding through rough country to travel between the Lake of the Islands and the farm, but by switching mounts at Arad's home in the late afternoon, he would arrive by sunrise of the third—now less than four hours away. It was tiring, but he loved to ride, and he loved the rugged land north of the Lake. It was exhilarating to ride alone under a half waxing moon, pitting his skill against the dangers of the night. His bow held tight in one hand; he could set an arrow to the string in a blink of an eye. More than one nocturnal predator had discovered that he hit what he aimed at, even in the dark.

Tonight there was more than the physical thrill. Important news had arrived from the south—so important that a scroll had been prepared and slipped to old Kezirin by Ashkenaz in the market of Shinar. It must be urgent news to have been risked to writing—discovery would mean death.

It hung unopened and still sealed in the saddlebag beneath his right hip, and Zeb was determined to place it in the hands of Shem just after sunrise.

Serving them was his greatest dream.

He smiled again when he realized how far he had come. He had been but a boy when Shem had seen his love for horses. Surprising everyone, Shem had taken the shy boy under his wing at an early age: first, teaching him all he desired about the noble beasts—how to care for them and how to ride far and fast. Though Zeb had not yet reached thirty years, he was already accounted the best rider in the North, and in achieving that, he had come to know the lands better than those many times his age.

He was now the chief link between Shem, Noah, and Japheth. So he knew all three. He loved best the nights spent with Noah's family. Noah was a walking legend—a man who talked with the Creator and who had built the great ark. His wife was like a second mother, and the daughters were as kind as they were beautiful, never once teasing the shy young man. Mariel's defection had broken his heart; she had seemed like a rock of virtue for as long as he had known her. And Jael… the extroverted, happy woman he had known had been replaced by the hollow-eyed, grim-faced parody of a warrior.

Zeb frowned. His skill forced him into the unenviable position of her shadow. It hurt to see her as she was now—to be reminded of the past and how much had changed. Her heart was as hard as stone and there was something in her eye that made him step warily in her presence. Her riding nearly equaled his and her skill with the bow was uncanny for someone so new to its ways. Soon, he would ask Shem to cease following her. There was no longer any need.

In the gray blackness before the dawn, he suddenly reined in. Something had disturbed him. He saw nothing and the night was quiet, but he was listening with the instincts Shem had taught him to heed. He sat, straining his ears and his nose for some sign. He felt his horse quiver, and knew that his first impression had been right. Dismounting, he let his eyes run back and forth across the ground behind him, but there was no track or disturbance. Springing back on his horse, he edged him quietly to the east. A faint sound, almost indistinguishable from the whisper of the wind, came from the ridge ahead.

Frowning, he nearly cursed out loud. This was no time for Jael to be playing her silly games! Kicking the horse, he set him straight up the ridge, directly towards a nest of boulders near the top. Just as he drew near, he kicked him again, and the horse responded valiantly, leaping forward to the top.

"I bring important news," Zeb said softly to the rocks, "and have no time for your silliness."

With barely a whisper of noise another horse pulled alongside him. "You take all the fun out of the night!"

Zeb could not tell whether Jael was being sarcastic or not. Her normal voice had affected that aggrieved tone for some time. He decided to ignore it. But she would not give up.

"How did you know?" This time she sounded more reasonable.

He answered in kind. "I felt something wrong. Then your horse brushed a rock." They rode on, saying nothing. Finally surmounting a hill, he looked down into the broad valley that ran all the way to the mountain. In the gathering light Zeb could just make out the farm—a distant checkerboard of fields with a faint gleam of white from the house in the midst of them.

Jael turned to him in the half light. He saw a brief gleam in her eyes. "You're very good," she said. "But I'll be better soon."

"You're welcome to it," he answered shortly. "I'm happy with my life. Can you say the same?"

His shot struck home, and with an angry glance, she wheeled her horse around, kicking him roughly into a gallop off to the west. Zeb nearly regretted his words, but anger drove him forward. He wondered—not for the first time—why Shem didn't beat some sense into her.

Irritated, he kicked his tired mount and cantered down the slope to the road. He had made one of his fastest trips ever, but the joy was gone.

Sunrise found him seated at the kitchen table, the precious saddlebag clutched in one hand. "Give me that," demanded Madrazi with a smile. "You need both hands to eat, and then it's off to bed." She still thought of him as a boy.

"I'm fine," he answered shortly.

"Ah," she returned. "I see you met Jael this morning. Did she try to surprise you again?"

Zeb smiled in spite of himself.

"So she failed again," grinned Madrazi. She allowed a mock frown to purse her lips. "Now she'll be impossible all day."

Zeb suddenly felt uneasy. "There's more to it than that, my lady."

Madrazi set down a cup of porridge before him and raised an eyebrow. Zeb looked at the floor, suddenly embarrassed. "I spoke sharply to her... told her I was happy with my life and asked her if she could say the same. She rode off mad."

Madrazi laid a hand on his shoulder. "Don't ever regret wise words, Zeb. You said exactly the right thing. No matter how thick the wall of hate and rage that she erects around her heart, words of light will always get through. She would never hear such things from me, but from you.... She will be thinking about it for a month of weeks and well she should!"

She turned and pulled a pan off the stove. The hot bread smelled heavenly, and she set honey and cream out beside it. Zeb smiled up at her; she knew his favorite food after a long ride.

"Shem will be here soon. Eat up. When he comes you'll be too busy talking."

Zeb grinned and turned to his food as only a hungry man can.

An hour later he was fidgeting in the great room. Facing him were Shem, Madrazi, Shelah, Heth, and Jobaath. Shem was fingering the scroll... still sealed... and staring with narrowed eyes at Zeb. "And you're sure that Kezirin said no more to you. Just that Ashkenaz drew near him in the market, said something to a young man that started a fight, and used the melee to slip this scroll to him without a word?"

"Yes. He said that the other man was young... Turok... Turoj... Turof? He wasn't sure of his name; only that he was a son of Tubal. Evidently he already harbored hatred for Ashkenaz—the fight only took a few words to begin, and the man clearly wanted to kill him."

Madrazi paled. "He wasn't hurt, was he?"

"No, my lady. After letting himself get knocked back into Kezirin, and slipping him this scroll, he had the youth on the ground in an unbreakable hold until his friends took him away." Zeb grinned. "Kezirin said that Ashkenaz forced the youth to apologize to everyone in sight for disrupting their market day."

Shem frowned. "He had no reason to needlessly make a bitter enemy like that."

Zeb shrugged. "I got the impression that they were far past that point."

Shem sighed and looked at his wife. "Then this is all the more precious. We must pray more diligently for the safety of the boys." He turned back to Zeb. "This was all?"

Zeb hesitated and coughed. "There's one more thing, sir. Uh, I mean, Kezirin thought you might, er...."

Shem frowned. "Spit it out, Zeb! I don't blame you for news you bear."

The young man flushed. "I'm sorry to have to tell this... I'm sorry that I even know it...." He sat up straighter. "Is Jael nearby?"

Shem started to speak, but felt Madrazi's hand on his arm. "She's not here, Zeb. Just tell us."

He drew a deep breath and looked up at her. "It is said in Shinar that the Lady Mariel is with child and was expected to deliver soon. I imagine the baby has already been born."

A pained look crossed Shem's face. "It's all right, Zeb," he whispered, then gathered himself. Speaking in a normal voice, he continued. "It's not unexpected, even though it is a sad reminder of the evil she embraced."

The others nodded and Zeb looked at the floor. He loved Shem and could see how his news hurt the older man deeply.

But Shem quickly hid his feelings and broke the seal of the scroll, unrolling the rough parchment before him. "Read it aloud, dear," whispered Madrazi. "It concerns us all."

Shem nodded and held it up.

Not much time. Working for Ham. Anam very close to D through her maid, Graemea. He stays out of things, doing small tasks for D. He is a hostage to Mizraim's behavior, and has burrowed deep into their household.

D has created a council for city. Mizraim, Cush, Put, Tiras, Tubal, Canaan, and N. D and N run things; others are tools, perhaps unwitting for now.

N has 70 men under arms; most are not much, but Korac has a small team—dangerous. Much talk about peril from north, but no action.

Council will announce new gods soon, break away from Noah completely. N has already hinted at the need for a great temple to D's new gods.

Mariel due soon. She hates life here and sees N infrequently. She is in Ham's shop every day. Ham befriended and protects her from D and N. She said N bowed to him! When they arrived, D threatened to have her beaten by N. Ham intervened and told D that he would repay her blow for blow! D backed down and N promised no harm. Very out of character for all.

D has taken N to her bed. He is her chosen one. She wants to make him a king. None of the others matter, but they think that because the council has formed, her scheme will not work. They don't see. Except maybe Mizraim. He's clever, but D lured him onto council, weakening him. But he probably has his own plans. Don't see Anam. It was hard getting this. Work on better contacts.

"Read it again," asked Heth and Shem complied.

"Seventy under arms," murmured Jobaath.

"But 'not much'," replied Shelah. "Except Korac."

"New gods... peril from the north." Heth shook his head. "This is ill news. She turns them all against us."

"We already knew that," interrupted Madrazi. "And the news is not all bad."

The men looked at her like she had lost her mind, but Madrazi just laughed. "You look for the bad and imagine the worst. Look at the good that is here." She waved the scrap of parchment. "First, our spies are doing their job and have not been caught... though I fear for Anam. Second, Mariel is safe, and if I don't miss my guess, Ashkenaz is quite taken with her. In a terse message, he included more news about her than anyone else. Did you notice how he implied that he sees her every day, but avoided saying so? Third, Ham is not directly involved in the evil there."

Jobaath interrupted. "But Ham is building the city!"

"Exactly!" Madrazi nodded. "He is doing what he has always loved to do. To build, to create, to subdue nature with his craft. He is not on the council, he is not a part of Debseda's plots, nor is he a part of her life if she is truly bedding Nimrod. That he has not killed either or both of them over what is apparently common knowledge tells me that he no longer even considers her his wife. Ham and Mariel are very much alike—they made bad choices but have not sold their souls to evil. I think there is a chance for both."

Shem frowned but said nothing.

Shelah spoke up instead. "If they intend blasphemy against the Creator—replacing His being, wisdom, power, holiness, justice, goodness, and truth with false gods—then this temple they are building will become a crucial focus of their fundamental plot. If they need to go to such lengths to bring people under their sway…."

Heth interrupted with rising excitement in his voice. "Then their control of Shinar is more tenuous than we have been led to believe!"

"Yes," agreed Shem, sitting up on the edge of his seat. "We have more time than we thought. We can more carefully lay our own foundations. We can begin to spread the news of the possibilities of new lands without appearing desperate. If we raise the opportunity before we explore those lands, then there will be a much greater interest and excitement over our travels than there would have been before. We won't have to press our case upon our return—many will be eagerly waiting to hear our tales."

"But won't that allow word of our plans to reach Shinar?" asked Jobaath.

"We cannot assume otherwise," Shem admitted. "Debseda has been thorough in developing her own spies."

"Perhaps that will be a good thing," Madrazi mused. "If they are truly feeling the need to go to these lengths to disobey the command of the Creator, then our pursuit of that plan will push them to take desperate chances, increasing the likelihood of some fundamental error."

"What if their 'desperate' error is to start a war?" asked Shelah. "Many innocent members of our line would die."

"They cannot fight a war, months from home in a rugged wilderness against people who know the land," said Shem grimly. "Especially not with seventy ill-trained men."

"What if they repeated Nimrod's initial gambit and attacked Noah and his family?" Jobaath had a worried frown on his face.

"Even Debseda would not be that foolish," Shem replied. "She and Nimrod would be outcasts if she did. Mizraim, Cush, and Put would use it against them to seize power and cast them out. No… that is the other side of her move to place them on a council. Even though they have no power now, any popular uprising against Nimrod would take them from the mere appearance of power to the real thing. Nimrod may not see it, but rest assured Debseda does. Whatever else you might say of her, she is no fool."

"Yet she has handed us precious years to prepare for an exodus to the far lands." Madrazi shook her head. "When evil has its way, sometimes wisdom and foolishness meet in odd places. That is one of the mysteries of those who choose to rebel against the One who is wisdom."

Far to the south Mariel was carefully pouring molten gold from a fired clay container into a hole in the top of a block of clay, its two sides bound together by cords. It was hard to control the pour at the end of one-cubit tongs, but even at that distance, her gloved hands felt the heat glowing from the liquid metal. It was essential to keep a steady stream flowing into the mold, but she could not finish before she felt another flow begin from her breast. Exasperated, she stopped—the goblet was ruined anyway—and swung the gold back to the furnace.

Ashkenaz looked at her quizzically. She flushed and turned away; there were some things you didn't discuss with men, even if you loved them to distraction. She quickly dropped the heavy leather apron and gloves as she walked towards Adan. The past two months had been hard, supremely happy one moment, and mired in the depths of despair the next. She knew that her body was playing tricks on her mind, but the knowledge couldn't stop the reality.

Surprisingly she had been as happy as Nimrod at bearing a son. Little Adan was the center of her life now. She did not think of him as Nimrod's son, but as hers. And she lavished all her attention and love on him. She refused Debseda's offer of a wet nurse, and brought the babe to the workshop as soon as she was able to return.

Ham had taken it in stride, constructing a cradle and a chair for her behind one of the larger work tables. Ashkenaz had been uncomfortable at first. Perhaps he had little experience with babies. Little did she know that his preoccupation was something quite different. The sight of a nursing woman rocking her baby stirred his feelings for her to new heights and he feared letting Ham see his desire.

She pulled the child from his cradle. Only two months old, he was now able to smile and laugh, and his eyes communicated a simple delight with life and with his mother that reinforced her protective instincts. She sat quickly and opened her tunic, grabbing a clean cloth to blot up the leakage running down her belly, and to preserve a bit of modesty. Adan ignored her contortions and seized a breast—once more all was right in his little world. Mariel smiled down at him, not seeing the two men who had stopped their work and were unconsciously smiling with her.

Finally Ham grunted and Ashkenaz started guiltily before preparing a new mold. Mariel sat, ignoring it all—her world at that moment was a baby boy and the unexpected pleasure of being his mother.

Chapter 26
RECOVERY

5-5-1755

The last rays of the sun bathed the hills with a reddish glow, made more striking by the play of shadow and light. Farm life has its own rhythm and the end of the day signaled contentment with another day's work. Horses plodded across the meadow towards the promise of warm stalls and full mangers. Sheep were huddling together under the watchful eyes of boys and dogs. Fields were green with the new growth of the year. A hint of the night's coming chill invaded the shadowed places of the main yard, and Shem took a moment to glance towards the setting sun.

Its glare could not hide the faint stirring of dust at the top of the west road, and that small interruption in the daily routine brought Shem from his reverie. Instantly alert, he shaded his eyes to watch a tired rider trotting slowly down the last long hill. The man was slumped in his saddle; he had come far and fast.

Shem saw Shelah walking towards the house from the vineyard. "Rider on the west road," he said. "See to his mount and bring him inside." Shelah nodded and trotted towards the road.

Shem stopped at the door long enough to wash his face and hands and beat the dust from his tunic. Shedding his sandals, he stepped into the kitchen. "A rider is coming," he told his wife. "Have something ready… something strong would not go amiss, unless I'm reading the signs wrong."

"And when was the last time you did that?" she teased.

"Yesterday, when you wanted me to take you for a ride," he returned.

"You didn't read the signs wrong," she stuck her tongue out at him. "You just chose to ignore them!"

"Is that why I had to fix my own breakfast?" he teased, taking a step closer.

"I'm overwhelmed by your insight." She started to say something else, but he silenced her with a kiss. It was just as good as the first time, and she let time slip away, giving herself once more to the thrill of his embrace.

Finally he stepped back. "It was easy to see that you needed that."

Her eyes danced. "Then why did it take you so long?" she retorted.

Before he could kiss her again, they heard Shelah's courteous cough from just outside the door. Shem realized that they had been quite visible with the late sun flaring through the kitchen window. He smiled at his wife, who shrugged and looked down.

"At least they'll realize we're not as old as we look!" she turned to the pantry to bring out a wineskin and cup. Shem opened the door.

Shelah was supporting a tired man. Under the dirt and sweat, Shem recognized Hiram, one of Noah's men. At once his face grew grim. "What news?"

He felt a soft hand on his tense shoulder. "May we refresh our guest, first?" Madrazi's reprimand was gentle, but he forced himself to nod. He watched while

Shelah lowered the man to a chair and Madrazi poured a cup of wine. She buttered a slice of bread and set it before him and refilled his rapidly-drained cup. Hiram nodded his thanks but ignored the bread.

"My master has taken ill," he blurted out. "It's not to the death, but the lady sent me to bring you to him. She requests you and your wife come as soon as you can." He took a slower sip of wine and looked down. "She also requests your sister."

"Very well," replied Shem. "Eat and rest! We'll start in the morning."

Shem turned to Shelah. "Call the men together. I think you and Jobaath should come too. You can visit the men of the outlying farms and speak of the new lands. Will you do that?"

Shelah nodded. "It's a good time. Your fields are planted and it would be an opportunity to check on ours." He started to say more, but was interrupted by Heth's face in the doorway.

"Is all well?" he asked guardedly.

"Heth!" exclaimed Shem. "Just the man I needed." Heth's eyes narrowed. "Can you take care of the farm for a month or two?" He explained the situation. "I need a good man here, one I can trust to protect my home."

"And you're taking Jael with you?" The big man's face was hard to read.

"Yes," Shem replied. "Her mother requested her presence, and I think she needs to be with her father."

"Good!" In spite of the exclamation, Shem noted a flicker of disappointment before Heth pulled himself up straight. "I will be proud to hold your home ready for your return."

"Then we'll be off in the morning as soon as Hiram has a good night's sleep."

5-12-1755

Jael hung back as Wen-Tehrom greeted Shem and Madrazi on the path outside their front door. "Hiram," she ordered. "See to the horses and baggage."

"Come, Shem. Bring your wife and sister. Your father is awake now, but he will probably be back asleep soon. His dreams disturb him."

The three travelers followed her inside, the couple eager, but Jael hanging back, hesitant and feeling defiant. It had been an easy ride but a hard week. That her father might die created disturbing thoughts; this house was the only place she had ever known happiness. Noah's loss of prestige had cost her dearly, driving her away from the rest of the family, but even in her rebellion, a corner of her mind was comforted by the knowledge that he would always be there, just as he always had been—wise, patient, and loving. Hiram's news had been disconcerting. Like every other human being, Jael knew about death in the abstract, but the reality of losing Noah hit her hard. A dark thought took root and chilled her heart; her father's death would eradicate any chance of ever regaining happiness.

Sleep had been difficult. She yearned to ride ahead at her pace, to see him alive, and alleviate her fears, yet at the same time she did not want to face those knowing eyes—accusing but full of sadness. Whenever she saw his sorrow, a small voice in the depths of her being whispered that it was her fault, not Mariel's, that the household had been so devastated.

And Zeb's simple words continued to haunt her—they had pierced her hardened defenses with one effortless stab. Ever since that night, memories had been haunting her—Mariel and Ashiel teaching her to play the harp... her envy of their voices... running in the fields with Bethsalom and Zeriah... rocking baby Sherzala, proud that she could calm her when the others could not. She had tried to fill her mind with other things, but those memories seeped back in unawares, ready to spring out at the most inopportune times.

As they walked down the hall, it happened again. She saw herself many years ago, following her father to hear another of his marvelous stories.

She shook her head, trying to bring up images of successful hunts, intricate moves with staff or spear, and the quiet night when she had first surprised Zeb. But they did not come, and receded with each step. The sight of Madrazi unconsciously smoothing her cloak and arranging her hair, reminded her of her own ragged appearance. Her face was tanned, her clothes more fitting for a shepherd than a lady, and the hilts of two knives dug into her ribs. It was too late to hide them. Her father would see them. How would he feel? Why hadn't she stowed them in her saddlebag?

She edged behind Madrazi, trying to hang back and blend into the walls. Let the good daughter be the center of Noah's attention. But it was not to be. As they entered his room, Madrazi ran forward and embraced the thin form on the bed. He had lost weight and seemed older; his hair seemed whiter and his face more careworn. But his deep brown eyes had lost none of their alertness; they swung immediately to Jael and took her in with a glance. She shuffled her feet and dropped her eyes.

"Leave us alone," he wheezed. Jael turned to go, biting her lip at his rejection of her in favor of Madrazi, yet realizing that she deserved nothing less. "No," the voice was stronger now. "I wish to see my daughter... Jael."

She turned, unbelieving. Shem slid past her, his face unreadable, but his dark eyes piercing hers. Madrazi could not hide the faint beginnings of a smile as she stepped past the younger woman. Jael stood rooted to the floor, hearing the door click shut behind her, as if she was now locked in a prison. She felt dampness on her brow, hypnotized by the old man's timeless eyes.

A moment of silence passed between them. Noah sighed and raised his hand from the coverlet. "Come sit with me, girl. It is time to talk."

Jael shuffled over reluctantly, her face red as her father's eyes caught sight of the knives at her belt.

Madrazi sat half listening to Wen-Tehrom's account of the planting and the prospects for the coming year. Something was making her uneasy... a tickle in the back of her soul. It was like a familiar taste that had faded, leaving only a memory of better times, but faint and distant.

After she had followed Shem and Wen-Tehrom out of the room, the three had adjourned to the kitchen. The other sisters hastily prepared food, and then peppered them with questions while they ate. But a part of Madrazi's mind was elsewhere, reaching out—questing for information. There had been an aftertaste of power in Noah's room, a familiar tingle that left her thirsty for more. She was intensely curious, but since neither Noah nor the Creator had seen fit to make her a part of that knowledge, it was clearly none of her business. She felt a tinge of jealousy, but then laughed silently. How many times had she wished her gift had been given to another?

Her senses were heightened, however, by the aura in the house and when Jael wandered into the room an hour later, Madrazi could sense a touch of power reflected from the girl. It shone as bright as her inner turmoil. Madrazi caught her eye and offered her assistance without words. Jael shook her head and turned her steps towards the door. Madrazi put her hand on Shem's arm and shook her head at Wen-Tehrom, and Jael passed through undisturbed. But all of them saw the redness in her downcast eyes.

Jael found herself near the barns before coming back to herself. She vaguely recalled Madrazi's sympathetic nod, but the rest was a fog. After… after he spoke…. Those words!

She stopped and took several deep breaths to center herself. She needed time, but there was none. Ashiel nearly ran into her as she strode around a corner of the nearest shed carrying a basket. Her eyes went wide with a hint of wariness, but then quickly joined her lips in a smile as she held out her hand.

"Want to help me gather the eggs?" Her smile lit the afternoon. Memories of that smile soothed Jael's troubled mind, and though part of her wanted to frown and walk away, a newly-awakened part took hold, and suddenly she found herself nodding and following her older sister toward the chicken coop.

They worked together inside, patterns of the past obviating the need for words. Outside, Ashiel sat on the old stump and set the basket down beside her. "Do you have a moment?" she asked.

Jael warily sat on the ground beside her.

"You look very good," began Ashiel. "Even just sitting and walking, I can see strength and grace that weren't there before. I don't pretend to understand this life you have chosen, but it's no passing thing. I…I…." She sighed and looked up at Jael. "It's harder to talk to you now. What I'm trying to say is that I love you no matter what. Are you well? Are you happy?"

Once more, memories filled Jael's mind and pushed her to answer. Ashiel had always been her confidant, and the old habits returned easily.

"In some ways, I am…but often I'm not. I lost something that day… maybe more than I understand… but seeing Father just now…." She bit her lip. "I can change what I do, but can't stop being who I am…." She stiffened. Ashiel wanted to talk and she was babbling.

Then, just as suddenly, all was as it always had been. Walls vanished and Ashiel understood.

"*What* you are now may be different, but *who* you are has not changed. Somewhere, all this—or its possibility—was always within you. Don't let the changes of life mask your true self. I know who you are… I've always known… and I think I always will."

She reached down, and for the first time in nearly a year, Jael let herself be drawn into her big sister's embrace. She forced back the emotions, but they battered her again, like the surf attacking, wave after wave. She stiffened, but Ashiel seemed to understand and she just held on tighter.

After a time, Jael felt her step back. Ashiel smiled. "Whatever Shem is doing is working. You nearly cracked my ribs!" They both laughed, as time fell back, allowing two souls to see each other without the masks of the years.

Ashiel put her hands on Jael's shoulders and looked at her. "I understand better than you think, Jael. It hurt us all. But I must tell you that the pain of losing you was greater to me than that of losing Mariel."

Jael hung her head. The words shamed her. She would have run away, but her father's words returned to steady her. She fumbled for a moment before meeting Ashiel's eyes. "You never lost me, sister. I may not live here now, but you never lost me. I lost myself for a time, and it will be a long path home, but you never lost *me*. Please believe that!"

Ashiel brushed away her own tears. "I will, Jael. But I've missed our talks together. So much has been placed on me now, but Madrazi was right—the Creator has not deserted us. I find him in the quiet of the hills, now…."

"Or in the memories of before?" prompted Jael.

"Of course." Ashiel suddenly grinned. "Do you remember the first time that Mother let us spend the night in the loft? We pitched a blanket over a rope between two posts for a tent, and slept on straw. And we talked of the men we would marry. I wanted a man of quick wit and a quicker laugh, but you wanted a big, strong…."

She stared at Jael's suddenly downcast eyes and clapped her hands. "You mean you've found him?"

Jael felt her face go crimson. She had never been able to hide anything from Ashiel, but why had that thought jumped out? Feelings she could not understand chased an image through her mind, racing to catch it and expunge it. Words tumbled out. "You don't understand! I'm with men constantly… working, hunting, fighting."

She caught Ashiel's impish grin and sighed. "Don't worry. Our elder sister— Mrs. Mother Hen—protects my virtue like a vein of gold. No man within a week's walk from the mountain would dare come close to me like that!"

Ashiel was not to be deterred. "You were thinking of one man… not many."

Jael frowned. "Yes, I was. But not like you think. He's one that instructs me in the spear, sword, and knife. He's a bully… an arrogant, conceited blockheaded man who treats me like an infant. I despise him. Well… maybe not despise… after all, he is a teacher. I should respect him, but… he's just infuriating and…and…."

Ashiel looked intently into her eyes. "You've got it bad, little sister. Who is this mystery man?"

"And you've got it wrong!" Jael snapped. "It's that Canaanite, Heth. You think I could ever fall for one of his brood?" She frowned. "I want to kill them... not marry them!"

Ashiel reached across and hugged her. Jael tensed, but forced herself to relax and return it. "Don't worry, little sister," whispered Ashiel. "Your secrets are always safe with me."

Jael felt tears sting her eyes again. Twice in one day! She had sworn she would never weep again, but first Father... now Ashiel. But her sister's words were as familiar as her face. She had heard them many times growing up and not once had Ashiel disappointed her.

Assaulted from all sides by emotions long suppressed, Jael sought to redirect the conversation. Still holding her sister, she asked, "Do you remember sitting on the edge of the loft that night, watching the moon go past the big window, swinging our feet in the air, listening to the animals breathe, and pretending we were on the ark?"

Ashiel hugged her tightly and let go. "I was Father and made you be Mother," she grinned.

"But then we realized they were too boring, you decided that I was Debseda and you were Madrazi."

Ashiel laughed. "I chased you around the loft and put straw down your dress. Debseda lost!"

Those words struck Jael hard. 'Debseda lost!' She had been so focused on Korac and Nimrod that she forgot the ancient origin of the conflict. Nimrod might be the focus now, but Debseda was behind him, poisoning all with evil. Nimrod was her tool, just as Korac was his. "Debseda lost!" she whispered, "And she will again."

Suddenly her father's words made sense. She smiled at Ashiel and reached for the eggs. "You look tired. If I can run all day across broken country, I guess I can handle a basket of eggs for my soft sister."

Ashiel smiled and bowed. "Just don't think that will get you out of telling me more, later. You know me... I want every detail."

Jael rolled her eyes. "Wish what you will. We'd better get these back to the kitchen." The two turned towards the house, and for a moment, Jael's heart sank as she thought that the moment was gone. But then Ashiel grabbed her open hand and smiled again. It wasn't lost, she realized... it had just been put away for another time. She squeezed Ashiel's hand as they walked towards the house. "

"*Some* of the details and you can't tell mother," she temporized.

"Welcome back, Jael," giggled Ashiel, her face reflecting a joy Jael suddenly longed to share. "Welcome home."

Chapter 27
FILL THE EARTH

6-10-1755

Glare from the morning sun shimmered off the surface of the lake, causing Shelah to shield his eyes. He shifted around, facing his cousin Uz and warning Jobaath with a quick glance to stay silent. He could see Jobaath's impatience, but an outburst now would only defeat their purpose. Uz was a hard, stubborn man. Shelah breathed a sigh of relief as Jobaath tightened his lips and settled back to watch.

Distracted, Shelah gathered his thoughts as he took a sip of the rough wine from the tin cup. Over the past weeks, they had traveled the area around the Lake of the Islands, spreading the news of the pass through the northern mountains and of the rich lands beyond. But telling someone to pick up their belongings and move into the vast unknown required soft words and subtlety—qualities that Jobaath lacked.

"It looks like a good year for you, Uz," Shelah mused. A sizable flock of sheep ranged the grassy pasture that ran from the shallow hill where the men sat down to the shore of the lake. They were sitting on the grassy hillside, in front of a dugout that housed Uz and two of his four sons for the summer season. It was a pleasant day, with the scent of fresh grass filling the morning air. "Your increase is a blessing and will provide warm clothes for us in the winter ahead. How much larger do you plan to grow your flock?"

Uz frowned, distracted for a moment by a barking dog chasing a stray. "It's hard to say," he pulled his beard. "They thrive on this grass, but we've already reaching the point of overgrazing. I'll probably have to keep this flock steady, a few short of two hundred."

"And your brothers Kittim and Hul face the same problem on the south shore," finished Shelah.

"It's good country here," protested Uz. "I could never keep this many sheep alive up in the wilderness where Shem farms."

"That's true enough," agreed Shelah. "Good land there is scarce, and Grandfather has the best of it up north. There's more wilderness to the west and the plains to the south are rapidly filling with our less hospitable family."

Uz looked troubled. He had been to Shinar during the winter and had seen the poor reception accorded to any of Shem's descendents firsthand. Had it not been for the quality of his wool, he probably would not have been welcome at all.

"Don't forget the mountains to the north," he grumbled. "We are hemmed into this land between the plains and the mountain." He stirred the fire with a stick and poured another cup of wine from a skin. Looking shrewdly at Shelah, he noted, "You were up in that country last spring."

"Actually we were on the far side of the mountains," Shelah answered casually, "wandering among the fertile grasslands of the plains on the other side. I saw pastures like this one that extended as far as my eye could see." He picked up a stick and started tracing some lines in the dirt beside the fire. "The Black Sea ends within a two week journey north of the mountains." He drew the border of that ocean, and then a rough line representing the mountains.

He pointed down with the stick. "On the east side, the Qazvin Sea extends north about the same distance. The land close to it is marshy and unfit for grazing, but once you reach its northern coast, good grass extends north, east, and west as far as we could see."

Uz grunted. "How's a man to get flocks through those mountains? I'm surprised you got through. Shem couldn't."

"Shem never tried," Shelah corrected. Then he shrugged. "It was a hike, but I wouldn't hesitate to take sheep, cattle, or donkeys through the pass. It wasn't that steep, though it did get high. I wouldn't try it in the dead of winter, but we did fine last year."

"That's a long way from civilization," observed Uz slowly. "I'd hate to get caught across the mountains if I ran into trouble."

Jobaath glanced at Shelah who nodded. So Jobaath refilled Uz' cup and leaned back against the wall of the dugout. "If enough people went, civilization would be north of the mountains. It's easier to get to the north side of the Black Sea from here than it is to get to the west side. Japheth and Javan could tell you that!"

Uz laughed shortly. It's an easy trip to the west side if you find Togarmah at home with his boats!"

"True enough," rejoined Shelah. "And it would be just as easy to get to the northern lands the same way. One of Togarmah's boats could take two families and their goods around the mountains while a few men took the animals overland."

Uz half nodded. "What you say makes sense. What are you going to do?"

Shelah smiled. "I'm going to be the first man to walk beyond those lands!"

"Unless Shem beats you to it," returned Jobaath.

"He's getting too old," Shelah laughed.

"Elders are different," said Uz seriously, shaking his head. "Shem's our grandfather, but he doesn't look much older than either one of us."

"Yes, they are," agreed Shelah. He stared thoughtfully out over the lake, nodding and letting Uz' impatience grow. Finally he shrugged. "I wouldn't be surprised to see Shem move north of the mountains eventually. He just needs to convince Grandmother to go. She's not the wanderer he is."

Uz frowned. "I'd hate to see her go. It would be a bad business here at the Lake. She spends most of her summers here, teaching the children, training the herbmasters, and charting the stars." He sighed. "If she went, I might consider going too, just so my children's children would have the benefit of her wisdom"

"We all need that," agreed Shelah. The seed planted, he stood and brushed off his tunic. "Thanks for the wine, cousin," he smiled. "May your flocks prosper!"

"Let us know if you need any help at your place," returned Uz. "I know you're trying to help us all, and we'll take care of your crops if they need you up north."

Shelah smiled and held out his hand.

"You're a good man, Shelah," said Uz. "You've got Grandmother's way about you, and most of the men look up to you. But I'll warn you... it will take more than that to get people to uproot their lives from a good place and go wandering off in search of something that may not be as good. I might follow on your say-so, but others would not."

"Even though the Creator told the elders to spread wide and fill the earth?" asked Jobaath.

"I've filled this patch," replied Uz shortly. "My sons can spread out a little more, and their sons can look to the north or west. Just not south. I don't want them to have anything to do with Ham's bunch."

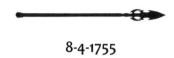

8-4-1755

Nimrod found Debseda angrily pacing her floor. The western sun through her window cast a black shadow at her feet, now leading her, now following. As always, it was an effort to force his gaze up from her barely-concealed breasts to her flashing eyes. But she did not return it—her face was fixed on the small patch of floor a few paces ahead of her feet. Her focus was far off.

So he stood patiently, letting her order her thoughts, but he frowned inwardly. When she had given him his spear and opened the door to the dark power that it held, she had given herself to him—a reversal of their previous roles. He had assumed he would evermore be her master. But as the months sped by she had begun to reassert her authority. Her methods were subtle and often well-disguised—even to his enhanced insight—but as he stood there waiting he suddenly realized that he had slipped back into the role of the supplicant.

Frowning, he strode forward and caught her by the arm. At first she hissed with anger, but as he gripped her other arm and pulled her to him, his eyes locked onto hers and he let the power build. For an instant she resisted, but then flung herself into his arms. Instead of kissing her he pushed her back and ripped the top of her tunic so that her chest was bared before him. Then he sat down in her chair and cocked his head. "Why did you request my presence?" he asked steadily.

She was panting, and he wasn't sure whether she was restraining anger or desire. His was certainly flaring. Holding out a hand, he pulled her into his lap and wrapped his arm around her bare back. He felt her quiver, then relax.

Suddenly she laughed. "Your awareness grows. Soon your mind will be the equal of your body, and all will bow before you."

"But I'll thank you not to tear my good clothes," she scolded with a smile as she wriggled in his grasp, rearranging the torn fabric. She sighed, and relaxed into his chest.

"I have news from the north." Her voice tightened and a crease reappeared between her eyebrows. "It seems that our enemies have a new strategy."

"What now?" he sneered. "Are they training their goat herders to fight?"

"No," she replied sharply. "Never underestimate Noah and Shem. You have power, but you have not yet seen half a hundred years. Noah has lived for nearly eight centuries! That time brings abilities that even I do not understand. And though young, Shem has seen two centuries. You are not the only one to grow in understanding as the years pass. They both see far ahead—and Shem has that cursed witch to feed him knowledge."

He felt her body grow tense at the mention of Shem's wife. Idly he wondered if he would ever know the whole story of what had happened on the ark—what had created such deep hatred.

She took a deep breath and forced her anger down. "If you challenge Shem to battle, you may be sure he is already thinking many steps ahead. Now I understand Anam's account of his travels north of the mountains with Shelah, Heth, Ashkenaz, and Jobaath."

"What of it?" Nimrod was growing impatient. "Young men like to wander and explore. It's in our blood. So they found a pass still open. I've found dozens through the eastern mountains."

Debseda pried herself out of his arms and began pacing again. "They mean to win without a fight. Shelah and Jobaath are recruiting men at the Lake of the Islands—not as warriors, but as settlers. They mean to lure as many as they can to the lands beyond the mountains... so far from Shinar that we could never rule them."

"Let them," laughed Nimrod. "It is easier to herd than to scatter. Men will travel north and see emptiness, harsh winters, no towns, no neighbors, and none of the pleasures of civilization. Then they will flock back to the easy life in Shinar, and soon our children's children will fill the land. If a few barbarians wish to stray far from civilization, let them!"

"What if it's not a few?" Debseda looked up at him with a tight face. "What if they open ways for many? What if a great kingdom rises there that may someday expand south to challenge ours?"

"We're too far ahead," argued Nimrod. "All they have is a brief trek by five inexperienced men. They will need to map rich lands to lure anyone away. Let Shem and his friends spend their years and strength exploring. In the meantime we will build a great city with a great temple. Shinar will be the foremost fortress in the earth. Then we will build other cities—a kingdom of fortresses that will control the plains from the hills to the gulf, and to the Great Sea. Let them go live in caves in the cold northern lands while we build palaces of ivory and gold. The plains will be the center of history for thousands of years."

"Fighting off the hordes from the northern hills," Debseda retorted.

"Successfully," replied Nimrod, just as sharply.

Debseda looked thoughtful. "There is much in what you say," she admitted. "And if Shem and the men leave their home...." A cold gleam entered her eyes, but she would say nothing more. Instead she slipped off the torn tunic and smiled up at Nimrod. A small cold part of his mind wondered what she was hiding from him, but it was quickly overcome by the heat of lust.

Chapter 28
A LEAN YEAR

9-16-1756

Ashkenaz gauged the weight and distance with a glance. "Easy, men! We don't want to lose this one. We'll be up here another week if we do." He eyed the tired men. "Short break," he ordered. "Get some water, stretch your backs, and then let's get this done."

The men nodded gratefully and sat in the sand by the river bank, leaving the rock balanced on its rollers. It wasn't all that big, Ashkenaz thought, just four cubits square and two high, but Ham had assured him that it weighed more than two hundred and fifty talents. It was just a short distance from the raft. Once secured precisely in the middle of it, the stone would slide downriver for another trip to Shinar. Ham was saving the larger blocks until the men grew accustomed to these.

Ashkenaz surveyed his crew. They were worn out. Ham had pushed the pace and done the impossible: quarrying, cutting, and moving more than one hundred blocks this year with men who knew nothing of the task. Another week and they would turn the work over to Canaan and his crew. Ashkenaz pitied them; Canaan made up for his own lack of skill by driving his men.

Ham had been the logical—indeed, the only—choice once the city had voted to build Nimrod's temple. He spent the first half of the previous year drawing plans, and watching him do it, Ashkenaz began to realize the true extent of Ham's abilities.

"It's magnificent," he had commented when the plans were complete, while wondering how the town could ever build something so large. "It's fitting," returned Ham, winking at Ashkenaz. "Even if it does take ten years of back-breaking labor. But if the city desires a temple they will never forget, who am I to stand in the way?"

Ashkenaz had managed to keep the smile off his face as he gravely agreed with his master. Clearly, Ham was beginning his break with his wife.

Ashkenaz wondered for a moment why he was being shown something that could endanger even an elder. He paused and replied carefully, "I am humbled that you would show me this glimpse of the future."

Ham had only nodded, and Ashkenaz began pondering the meaning of Ham's trust. What would he want in return?

Since the plans called for a stone foundation, Ham had spent the rest of the year searching for the right site to quarry it. Mariel and Adan were among the party that Ham took on that expedition—"she's got a good eye for stone"—was what he told Nimrod, but Ashkenaz knew better. It was a chance to get her and her son away from Debseda and Nimrod, and although he was glad that she was gone, it made for an empty workshop.

At first he feared that Ham's absence might place him in danger, and so he slept with a dagger under his blanket. But gradually he realized that with Ham and Mariel gone, he was one of the best craftsmen in Shinar. Ham had been stingy with his knowledge. Fortunately Ash had absorbed enough of it to attend to the everyday problems, like broken tools. He worked hard and kept away from the taverns during those months—being unseen was his best defense.

Once Ham had found his quarry, Ashkenaz was summoned, along with Korac and the men of Nimrod's Legion. Ham had placed Ashkenaz in charge of one crew and Korac, the other. Though his men resented working for "the outsider" at first, they soon changed their minds. Ashkenaz worked them hard, but treated them well and tended to their injuries. Korac drove his men as relentlessly as he drove himself, and few were up to that standard. As a result, Ashkenaz' crew stayed well ahead of Korac's, much to the amusement of Mariel and Ham.

Though difficult, the work was straightforward. Narrow trenches were cut around each block with chisels and hammers, and then the blocks were "floated" free by wooden wedges, hammering in tight and soaked in water. Their swelling cracked the bottom free. Once on rollers, the blocks were pulled down the light gradient to the riverbank where rafts waited. Blocks were secured to the rafts, then slid down to the water. Ropes secured each raft to a team of oxen, keeping them close to the bank and under control for the slow trip downriver.

Ashkenaz found that he had a talent for leading men and for finding small ways to make the job easier for all. His men appreciated it and went from grudging obedience to grateful acceptance. None would have called him a friend, but many promised to pay for a drink when they returned to Shinar.

But the best part of the expedition was the chance to be near Mariel again, catching glimpses of her as she might have been, free of Nimrod and Debseda. As with metal and wood, she learned quickly, and was soon able to take on the task of marking new blocks to be cut. And though he spent most of his time on her back, Adan was a favorite of the entire camp—even men steeped in evil loved children… and Adan was the heir of Nimrod.

They would have sent more stones to Shinar, but a third of the men had been called home late in the summer, and Canaan had replaced Korac. Rumors came up river that the harvest would be poor this year, and other work was being set aside to care for the crops and protect those remaining from birds and insects. More men were needed to catch and dry fish in anticipation of a hungry winter, and hunting expeditions were already ranging east across the Tigris.

At first, Ashkenaz and Ham had thought the poor yields might put the lie to Debseda's "new gods," but most seemed determined to believe in them, assigning their problems to a failure to recognize sooner the queen of heaven and sacrifice to her and her children. But if Nimrod needed Korac at home, some must be restless. Mizraim wouldn't waste an opportunity to cause trouble for Nimrod.

Ashkenaz braced himself for a lean winter, thankful that Mariel and Adan would have the finest of whatever food was there.

Heth stood leaning on his spear looking out over the fields with Shelah. A cold, wet spring had delayed the planting, and continued poor weather was going to minimize the harvest. At best, they would bring in half a normal year's return of grain, and men would be eating their sheep this winter as the bread ran low.

There had been no question of exploring this year; Shem was having just as bad a year under the mountain, and the younger men were forced to spend the summer tending their lands at the Lake of the Islands, laboring to get the most out of their pitiful fields. Heth—recognizing his complete lack of ability as a farmer—had worked out an arrangement with Shelah's son, Eber, several years back. Eber farmed Heth's fields with his holdings and they split the harvest. This year, there would be little to divide.

Rather than stay in the north, Heth spent the summer enlarging his forge and repairing tools for the others. He was a good smith, and men traveled days for his skill. When he wasn't smithing, he took the best of the young men hunting in the hills. They would need a large store of smoked meat for the winter ahead.

Shelah especially regretted the lost year, but a short message from Ashkenaz calmed him, confirming that Shinar's fields were no better. Shelah accompanied Zeb north to Shem's farm with the message and Heth traveled with them. "It's not safe to go alone," he grunted.

Shelah nodded wisely, but the twinkle in his eye told Heth that he guessed the other reason that might be motivating his friend.

"I'm sure they'll all be happy to see you," he said agreeably. "Perhaps you can stay on up there for a few weeks and help out." He smiled slyly. "I expect Jael has been neglecting her practice; maybe you can get her back on track."

Heth shrugged his broad shoulders. "Maybe," he agreed, looking off to the north, suddenly eager to see the mercurial young woman once more.

Shelah's grin grew broad. "Just make sure there's a good tree nearby. I won't be around to rescue you this time."

Heth frowned for a moment, embarrassed, but then laughed with his friend. "Who needs a tree? I've got Madrazi to protect me."

Chapter 29
FOUNDATIONS FOR THE FUTURE

1-1-1757

Canaan impatiently turned to Ham and whined, "Why must we dig so deep?" The two stood together on the outskirts of Shinar watching the dozens of men laboring under the morning sun. They were digging in lines marked out by string and stakes. Dirt was heaved into small donkey carts and hauled away to be stored for future use. The stakes littered a vast flat, marking ditches to be dug to create the sides of two perpendicular rectangles, each stretching 333 cubits north-south and 111 cubits east-west. Arcuate ditches connected the ends of the rectangles, as if a large circle had been divided into four equal parts and those pieces pulled apart.

It was a vast undertaking and Ham smiled to himself. If they choose to forge ahead, they would spend years of labor using their men. If not... he did not care. Canaan had begged him to design the great edifice, and if he asked for a change at this late date, he would be publicly admitting an error—something Canaan seldom did. The work had already begun. Any change now would show Canaan a fool, and he knew it.

Ham maintained a bland expression. "We're building with clay and pitch," he replied patiently, as if explaining something to a child. "Since we will not enjoy the inherent strength of large stones, we must make thick walls, stepped from one level to the next. All of that must rest on a solid, absolutely level foundation. That means we must dig past the surface soil and mud."

"But we strike water if we dig too deep," whined Canaan.

"Precisely," Ham replied evenly. "Water seeks its own level, which will show us that one end of the structure is exactly the same elevation as the other."

"But won't the water destroy our bricks?"

"That's why we're rafting enough rock from the north for the foundation." Ham sighed. "If you no longer require my help, all you have to do is say so."

"Oh no!" Canaan winced. His mother would flay the skin from his back if he were responsible for losing Ham's expertise. No one else could design or build the temple, and she had rather liked the design, caring little at the expense in labor and time. But he hated working with his father. Ham treated him like a youth, and he was a grown man... an important man.

Ham ignored his hapless son and watched the men work. It was a balm to his mind, still unquiet over this project. Normally, he would have been excited to take on such a challenge, but this was different. A foreboding lay on him he could not shake. He supposed it was from the degraded purpose of the building. He had stood by and watched many foolish and wicked things run through his family—the poison of his wife permeated the city—but the idea that they would pervert the truth about the Creator grated every sensibility. He shuddered to think of what his brothers and parents would think when they found out. They would never know that he was saving their lives... that the years and effort to build this monstrosity would keep Nimrod's army small and down in the plains.

And the truth was that he could no longer do much more. Mariel's plight had brought home to him the extent to which he had lost control. It had all started with his foolish fears on the ark. Failure followed failure. What had come over him that day? Why had he attempted to humiliate his own father? As always, his heart returned no answer.

He realized now that he had put so much energy into Shinar precisely because it was the one thing he could control. But grand buildings meant little if the people living in them were hardened in evil and subject to tyranny. That was the most fundamental problem—Debseda ruled his family.

Following that realization was another that had come early last year as he was drawing the plans for this monstrosity. As if a string had suddenly snapped, Ham decided that if he could not retake his rightful place, he would leave. Since then, he had been making subtle plans to get away with his life, his tools, and his sister. He would no longer build cities. If Debseda wanted Nimrod's bed, she could have the rest of it too. He was free. Let them do it themselves! This tower would be a parting gift... and a means to cover his escape and sabotage their aggression against his brothers. It wasn't enough, but any repayment for her ruin of his dreams was to be relished.

He would not go alone. Others feared the future. Mizraim was searching for a way out. He at least was wise enough to see what was coming. Ham toyed with the idea of going with him—at least Mizraim still respected him and valued his gifts. If they traveled south—around to the southern coast of the Great Sea—they could put enough distance between them and Nimrod to ensure their safety for many years to come. And in a few generations, they would have their own kingdom... one that Ham would ensure was well fortified and well-armed.

His mind made up, he turned back to Canaan. "Why don't you go inspect the brickyards? Make sure they are patient at the ovens. We cannot afford weak materials." Canaan clearly did not want to go, but slunk off.

Ham ignored his hurt feelings and began to walk around the perimeter of the ditches. On the far side, he strode past a gang of masons. Mizraim was in charge of this work, and as usual, it was being done well. Ham signaled Mizraim aside, leaving his crew hard at work squaring the stones.

"Do you like stone work?" he asked. Mizraim looked at him suspiciously, then shrugged. "Yes, I do," he admitted. "I wish we were building the entire structure of stone. It would be impressive in a white limestone, would it not?"

Ham smiled. "If we build with stone, we'll have a tower that will be stronger with less material and so will take a shorter time to build, even counting the time to move the rocks."

The shock in Mizraim's eyes lasted only a fraction of a moment before they were hooded once more. "I see." He turned and looked out over the building site.

"Well, the youth in Shinar are restless. I suppose they need something to occupy their hands."

"Something other than butchering their cousins?" Ham turned to his son, his massive arms folded across his chest.

Mizraim was much smaller than Ham, but he stood his ground and met his father's eyes. "Or dealing with 'dissidents' within their own family."

Ham nodded. "That too. Perhaps that animosity is a good reason to find another home. The earth is broad—too broad for such foolishness to mar our future."

"Your skills would be sorely missed here and greatly appreciated elsewhere, I'm sure." Mizraim looked down and kicked a loose pebble out of his way. "Do you wish to rule?"

Ham shook his head. "You know me better than that. My passion is making things for good people. I can no longer do it here. If I or my brothers desired dominion over men, would we not have it already?"

Mizraim nodded. "True enough." He looked around, noticing one of Nimrod's men staring at them. Pointing back at the stone, as if discussing the work, he looked up at Ham and said, "We must continue these, er... engineering discussions as the work continues. I think that you could find a better life doing this somewhere else."

Ham let his lips curl up briefly. "Perhaps, but there is a price."

Mizraim stepped back and narrowed his eyes. He said nothing, waiting for Ham to finish.

"I will not leave my sister to the mercies of her husband and my wife. She and her child must come too."

Mizraim sighed. "It will fuel a powerful fire. We will need to put many weeks journey between her and her husband, lest he come and take her back to Shinar."

"We will need that at any rate," agreed Ham. "If weeks of hard travel lie before them, it is unlikely that Shinar's armies will attack without years of preparation."

"I agree," Mizraim drew in a deep breath. "I suppose this tower will serve yet another purpose now. I will make sure that my family remains enthusiastically involved in work, but we are poor artisans. I suggest you keep us under your direct control and plan on many long hours of... er... supervision." He smiled thinly. "Building anything, be it a new religion or a new kingdom, requires foresight and planning... especially when there are those who would interfere."

Ham smiled and waved at the men working the stones. "A kingdom built with stone would be infinitely preferable to one of bricks."

"Or of fools!" muttered Mizraim as he walked back to his crew.

Ham hid his smile as he walked the rest of the way around the ground.

Canaan wondered why his father was in such a good mood as he trudged up later in the day to report on the progress at the brickyards.

Nimrod burst into the room. "The last rock has been quarried," he burst out. "All of the foundation stones will be here within the week, and will be laid in place by the end of the year. The kilns are ahead of schedule and soon the walls of our tower will soar into the sky, marking Shinar as the capital of our empire."

He was bubbling with excitement. It was hard not to share it, but Debseda waved it away with a flick of her hand. "Even so," she replied. "I'm still angry with my husband's petty dishonesty."

Nimrod raised an eyebrow. "I wonder what reason he might have?" he asked sardonically. "He made a fool of Canaan with the schedule, but you must admit that it's a grand plan—there won't be another building like it on the face of the earth!"

"I'm not sure if it was spite, and that's what worries me," admitted Debseda, waving her women out of the room. "Ham is many things, but whatever appearance he chooses to present to the city, he is no fool. The tower is twice the size we first envisioned; Ham knows very well the cost in time and labor of such a building. He knows that even with the young boys put to work that it will take many years to erect its walls. We are hard pressed to keep our spies at work in the north, much less begin to build our army."

She began pacing up and down and Nimrod, recognizing the signs of her agitation, stepped aside and let her pace. "You have taken everything from Ham but his precious craftsmanship," he said smoothly and laughed. "You have even robbed him of his manhood." She stopped and could not hide her smirk. Nimrod stepped closer and seized her arms, pulling her close. "He is using what he has to strike at you... that is all. But his spite will rebound back upon him. His overly-ornate tower may cost us more time, but what are a few years? We will have a few short years of hard labor and a small delay in our plans. But the northerners are wasting their time too—wandering the far lands—and we can spare a few years. Once the tower is built, and those fools Tubal and Tiras have eradicated the worship of the Creator, our people will need something to devote themselves to... if not god, then perhaps godlike rulers?"

He smiled and she smiled back. "The king and queen of heaven, perhaps? Gods come down to earth to rule with absolute power?"

"As we grow older, we will assume that part. The aura that surrounds Noah today will accrue to us in a few centuries. Until then we will lay the foundations for real power. When the day comes, we will use it!"

Debseda relaxed into his arms. "Yes. You're right. It's just so hard to wait. I want it so much!"

"That desire burns in my heart too, my love," whispered Nimrod. "One day we'll be rid of Ham and you and I will take our rightful places, watching all others bow the knee to us... to the power within us that makes us like gods. Those in the north will join them, be dead, or be huddled in some cold caves in some far mountain of ice. Trust me. Trust the power. And trust human nature. Noah can speak of some unattainable goodness all he wants, but we both know that the masses need this as much as we do. That's the mystery of humanity, and it works for us, not for him!"

"In the meantime," Debseda replied, "we need tools to build our empire. So may are flawed and weak!" They both thought of Canaan.

"Korac's no weakling," Nimrod argued.

"Not in battle or the hunt," she conceded, "but Korac lacks the wit to be a true right hand." She fluttered her hand. "Until we have a true line of superior men, we must make do... several are needed to do the job of one." She smiled slowly. "And right now, both qualities have their place. I have an idea...."

Nimrod shrugged. His lover had ideas like fields had weeds. Most were good; some were not. She would tell him when she was ready. Until then he wouldn't worry about it. He was content with Korac. A few more like him, and their plans would be years closer to success.

Chapter 30
AN ENGAGEMENT TO REMEMBER

2-15-1757

Anam forced down his fear, set his face in expressionless neutrality, and walked into Nimrod's outer room. He had been summoned from the courtyard just a few minutes ago—limiting the time he had to take counsel of his fears, but likewise limiting his time to learn the purpose of this meeting. Nimrod was seated before him in a large chair, relaxed, with his head cocked to one side as if examining a horse or an ox. In contrast, Korac was standing in a corner, his face its ordinary mask of iron, but his body tense and ready to spring into action at the first need. Anam looked left and saw Debseda and Graemea sitting together on a sofa. Debseda was leaning back, with her arms across her chest and a satisfied look in her eye, while Graemea was sitting upright on the edge of the sofa, her eyes fixed on her lover.

In the two and a half years he had been living in Shinar, Anam had learned to respect the abilities of both Debseda and Nimrod to read the minds and hearts of people. Survival demanded that he continuously practice a relaxed and carefree exterior by centering his thoughts on his most pleasant days as a boy and pushing the immediate concerns as far to the periphery of his heart as possible. So far, it seemed to have worked, but Anam knew that today would be a stringent test of his skilled nonchalance.

If he failed, he would be dead before nightfall and Graemea with him.

So he nodded to Nimrod and bowed to Debseda, hoping that even this small slight might irritate Nimrod enough to cost him his focus. But the smile never left Nimrod's face and he leaned back in his chair. Debseda on the other hand sat up, with a hand resting on Graemea's shoulder. Anam could see the tension in his lover's face, but it was accompanied by something more like… anticipation?

He stood silently, waiting for Debseda to speak. Anam knew that she hated useless words and had seen her use silence as a weapon many times. He let his mind drift across the sunlit waters that filled his imagination and waited for her to finish her little game.

"My grandson," she finally began. "Would that all my family had your clever mind and discerning ways! You have made yourself quite useful since you came to stay with us. You are a friend to all. That is a gift rarely bestowed."

Anam thought he heard a nearly inaudible snort from the far corner but ignored it. As deadly as he was, Korac was but a tool. The real power sat before him… or off to one side. He had not made up his mind about that, and wondered if Debseda and Nimrod really knew.

"You took me in when my father cast me out, Grandmother," he returned. "Any small service I can do for you is not only a pleasure, but an obligation. You have reminded me what family is and its importance in any civil society."

Debseda laughed and patted Graemea's shoulder. "And it *has* been a pleasure, hasn't it Anam?" Graemea blushed and Nimrod chuckled.

"Young Graemea is one of my closest friends," continued Debseda, "and her happiness is of great importance to me. I am pleased that she has been happier these past two years than since I have known her."

She paused and cocked her head slightly, a shrewd look darting across her lively blue eyes. Anam braced himself. "As you said, grandson... pleasure and obligation often go hand in hand. There has been much pleasure—or so I gather from her demeanor..." Nimrod laughed heartily and Debseda shot him a stern look. Graemea's face was cast down now, but her normally dusky neck was a dark red.

Debseda sat up straighter and her eyes bored into Anam's. "Now comes the time for obligation to play its part," she continued. "Your future here in Shinar requires that you be a part of a family. I have made you part of mine in your father's place, but you are growing into a man. A man needs a woman to bear his children and to carry his name down through the years across the great cycle of life that will turn our small city into a great empire."

Anam caught his breath, and knew that his own face showed a moment of shock. Debseda smirked at his loss of control. "Did you think, Anam, to take the pleasure without price?"

"Of... of... course not, Grandmother," he replied. "I love Graemea. She has been the joy in my life." He cast about for words; his ready tongue was tied in knots. "It's just that... well... I did not understand fully the nature of her obligations to you... and so did not wish to be presumptuous or to offend you after all your kindnesses."

Debseda laughed gaily. "See, Nimrod. Even at his tongue-tied worst, our Anam knows how to sweeten his words like honey. He deflects his duty to Graemea by offering a greater love for me!"

Anam interrupted. "Oh please don't misunderstand, Grandmother. I owe you my life and so you have my life. But I owe Graemea my heart and so barring your objection, she has it." He looked directly at Graemea and she lifted her head to him. Her eyes were shining and her smile pierced Anam. He suddenly realized that he had for once spoken the complete truth before Debseda.

"Oh, I don't object, Anam. As I'm sure you realize by now, it is quite the contrary. I want you and Graemea to be happy together... to be joined in the eyes of men, and bring a new generation into the world. That will be my reward—to bounce the children of my beloved grandson on my knee and raise them in my own home as if they were my own."

Anam's blood suddenly ran cold as he saw the trap. It was sweetly baited, but a trap nonetheless. For two years he had been in limbo; a spy for Debseda but at the same time hostage to his father's behavior. Now Mizraim would have more to lose. Debseda would have his grandchildren. Anam wondered what new move Debseda was plotting in the council that required this additional insurance.

Yet it was a trap he could not refuse. To do so would be the most dangerous course. No, he must walk into the pit and find a way in doing so to walk out, leaving his enemies in their own trap. The first move must be to warn Mizraim. But how?

The idea struck even as he opened his mouth and he silently thanked the Creator. "Your generosity never fails to overwhelm me, Grandmother," he began. "I came here with nothing and now you wish to give me everything that my heart desires. Yet..." he sighed. "It saddens my heart that such good news cannot be shared with my family because of my father's hard heart. Shinar needs unity among its families, especially those that hold such responsibility as service on the council." He nodded respectfully to Nimrod.

"Perhaps this happy occasion and Graemea's beauty and grace will soften him." He looked down and shuffled his feet. "He is my father, after all, and I owe him the attempt."

Anam had thought himself a fine actor, but he immediately saw how far he had to go. Debseda's eyes brimmed with tears and her face twisted into that particularly feminine mix of sadness and joy that only a woman's face could show.

"Oh, Anam," she began softly, with an artful sniffle. "You never fail to bring me happiness. No one that I know has such a depth of empathy for the feelings of others or for doing what is right in the eyes of the gods. Even after his harsh treatment of you, the duty of a loving son is foremost in your heart."

She turned to Graemea. "Didn't I tell you, my daughter? You are becoming the betrothed of the finest man in Shinar. He will treat you like a queen all of your days and your happiness will overflow like the Euphrates in springtime. Be worthy of such love!"

Graemea looked at Anam with shining eyes and nodded her head. "Oh, I will, my lady. You have given me my heart's desire!"

"Good!" interrupted Nimrod, standing. "As a member of my council, it is my happy duty to witness that Anam, son of Mizraim, takes Graemea, daughter of Put, as his betrothed, to marry and to raise up children for the glory of Shinar." He glanced over at Debseda and offered his hand to Anam. "I will announce the good news in the next council meeting. That's in three days. So, why don't you take your beloved to your father's house tomorrow and see if she cannot sway his proud heart."

Anam swallowed and nodded. He was saved from any further words by Graemea. She sprang up and ran to Nimrod and kissed his hand. "Thank you, sir. You are as generous as you are mighty." She stepped back and threw herself into Anam's arms. Her smile lit the room, and for once, Anam forgot his fear in the presence of Debseda, Nimrod, and Korac, amazed at the truth of his love—the only truth that had penetrated his careful disguise in nearly thirty months.

He led Graemea out of the room. He wanted to be with her, and far away from all the fears and pretense. He wanted to give her unimpeded access to his heart—to share the love that was the one thing in his life in Shinar that was good, true, and beautiful.

Chapter 31
NEW DAUGHTER

2-16-1757

The couple stood in the foyer of Mizraim's ornate home, staring at the intricate pictures carved into the wall, bright paint making them stand out in stark detail. Lud had met them at the gate and after controlling his astonishment at Anam's news, had cautioned them to wait until he had "prepared" Mizraim.

Anam nodded. His father would need a moment to adjust before his incisive mind began playing out the possibilities of the meaning of this news. They would need to communicate on a level hidden from Graemea without arousing her suspicion. Finding the proper balance between rage, cold contempt, paternal forgiveness, and a grandfather's pride in a new generation would be hard enough… adding the politics of Shinar to the mix made it much more challenging.

He was glad of the distraction. Last night Graemea had been on the verge of sharing something in her past—some dark secret that still haunted her, but at the last moment she had shut it back in. Before, her lack of trust had merely stirred his curiosity; after all, he had no formal claim on her and he was certainly not transparent to his betrothed. Yet he sensed a need to know what she hid and he could not shake the premonition. But the upcoming "confrontation" with his father required all of his guile, and so he put the distraction away. He would ask her someday soon, if she did not tell him herself.

They stood for nearly a quarter of an hour before Lud arrived and gestured them inside. "Before we see father," he said in a low voice, "allow me to congratulate you both. I remember the days when you played together as children; it's good to see that affection bloom into something richer. I must play the part of a dutiful son inside, but you both deserve to know my true heart."

Anam squeezed Graemea's hand and smiled at his brother. "Our thanks, Lud. One day perhaps, things will change and our family will be united and able to say what they feel without fear."

Lud grinned briefly and then resumed his solemn expression. He led them through the main hall and out the side door to the garden. Anam heard the splash of the fountains and remembered the last time he had been here. Even then there had been the necessity for layers of deception, but he had never envisioned anything as complicated as his life today. It did not help to consider that it would probably get worse before it got better.

Mizraim was standing beside one of the tables, watching them with his sharp eyes. His face was unreadably aloof, and Anam met his glare with a half smile, playing the guilty prodigal as best he could. He felt Graemea's hand tremble under Mizraim's gaze. He felt a sudden pang of sympathy for his lover. She had never been the focus of his father's piercing glare. He knew that it must be a shock to her to see a less veiled version of Mizraim's personality, but he was relieved. Graemea, fearful and off balance, would be more easily deceived by the necessary undercurrent of conversation that would mark the next hour.

Mizraim knew it too and his face suddenly changed to a welcoming smile. Holding her eyes, he spoke. "I am surprised, but pleasantly so, to see my son find a woman so obviously above his station in life. Your beauty is only exceeded by the reports of your loyalty and service to our city. Yet...." he paused nostalgically, "all I see when I look upon you is the little girl who stole my son's heart decades ago. That you would deign to extend your affections after he has failed to prove his worth these many years is a shock, but a pleasant one. For this, I could almost forgive his neglect of his family. But if I am to gain you and the fruit of your womb in the years to come, I suppose I must embrace him once more and overlook his failings."

Anam winced, thinking his father had overplayed his hand. A small voice questioned how much of that he really thought true, but he forced it down. Graemea stumbled, clearly not knowing what to say. She looked at him shyly and then back at Anam. With a hint of a smile, she replied. "Your son is a good man or I would not have accepted the proposal. Had I known that it might bring unity to one of the great houses of our city, I would have proposed to him myself... many months ago!"

Mizraim nodded and gestured for them to sit. He poured each a cup of wine and raised his. "Long life and many sons to you, my daughter." Graemea smiled again and Anam tasted the potent best of his father's stock. He took only a small sip, as did his father, he noticed. Graemea's anxiety blocked her inhibition and Mizraim casually refilled her cup as he asked her about the doings of her sisters and cousins—seemingly interested in the most trivial gossip of the city. After her cup had been refilled once more, he smoothly began steering the talk around to the workings of the council and the new temple.

Graemea's relief at his friendly welcome and her liking of his wine combined to loosen her tongue. Anam, seeing his father's tactics, added words as needed to keep the talk moving in the right direction, while maintaining an air of thinly-disguised hostility towards Mizraim.

"Oh, yes," Graemea giggled. "My mistress was not happy at first with the scale of the building. She thought her husband had multiplied it to spite her, but Nimrod convinced her that it was worth the effort and that Ham's spite would not hurt them."

"But surely we must keep our defenses up," protested Mizraim. "Our enemies to the north might take advantage of the distraction and launch raids on our flocks."

Graemea laughed out loud as she drained her cup again. "Oh no! My mistress has discovered that they are taking men over the far mountains to explore the ends of the earth. They will be caught up in that for years... building our temple will only bring more people to Shinar and weaken them in the end."

She giggled. "She heard that Shem himself will lead the group. His attention will be turned away from Shinar for some time."

Anam struggled to keep his face impassive. Debseda's spies were effective—he knew Shem had planned to go north, but had no inkling of when Shem intended to depart. Mizraim's smile did not change and he took a sip of his wine. "Well," he shrugged, "it's a relief to know that we won't be bothered by those barbarians this year."

Graemea nodded. "We don't want anything to interfere with our wedding. I think this summer would be a lovely time to get married. Don't you, Anam?"

Anam swallowed and glanced at his father. "Of course, my dear. There's nothing I would like better than to announce a ceremony next week!" He hoped his father understood his game.

He did. Mizraim frowned for the first time and shook his head sadly. "I know that you both are deeply in love, but please hear the voice of wisdom. Such an event must be planned with great care. As the boy's father, it falls to me to prepare a wedding celebration, and for you, Graemea, it must be one of the most memorable in our fair city's brief history. There must be feasting and music, merrymaking and wine. It will be expensive but well worth it. Every man will know that the families of Mizraim and Put are coming together for the common good. You must give me at least a year to save and prepare."

Graemea's face fell. "But I thought...."

Anam feigned anger. "This is some kind of trick to keep us from marriage," he began. "We don't need you! My grandmother will take care of this!"

Graemea grabbed his arm and pulled him back into his seat. "Hush, my love. Don't speak so to our father! We have waited many months to announce our betrothal. Though I grudge every day, we must respect his wishes. We want a family bound together by love, not torn apart by strife."

Mizraim nodded. "Listen to your beloved, boy! She speaks wisdom. Do you think that I'm a fool? I know you could have married her a year ago without my consent. Your grandmother will bend any tradition to suit herself. I am busy with the building of our temple now. Much of my fortune has gone to pay for the preparation of the stones for the foundation. I need time to recoup. I volunteered to take on that expense because it would be done now, and then over. Besides," he flashed a glance at Anam, "Ham and I both enjoy working with stone... building new things."

Anam settled back down. He understood his father all too well. Whatever he was plotting for the future now included Ham. That would be a coup that would shake Shinar to its roots when the time came.

He allowed remorse to color his face. Graemea was looking at him anxiously. "I apologize, Father." He assumed a look of embarrassed humility. "I misjudged you again. Perhaps you are right." He smiled at Graemea. "Perhaps having a wise wife will keep me from such foolishness again. You are our father. If you wish to wait a year, we will wear patience like a robe. I just want you to know," again he flashed his father a look, "that I love her very much and cannot wait to bring her out of her current family and into ours."

Mizraim sat up straight and looked thoughtful. Anam gave him a slight nod. Graemea threw herself into Anam's arms. "Thank you, my love. You could not make me happier! I wish to be married to you now, but I want our family to enjoy decades of tranquility and peace."

As they were walking hand in hand back through the city streets, Anam noted the cloaked figure following in the shadows. He gripped Graemea's hand twice, signaling her that their shadow was on his left. She immediately turned to him and asked loudly, "Can't we please stop at the market. Celota saw this lovely cloth yesterday, and I want to begin a new dress." She pulled Anam to the right and across the busy street into the market square. She turned and embraced him at the entrance, looking quickly back over his shoulder "Thank you, love!" she said aloud, then whispered in his ear. "It's only Jalam."

Anam smiled down at her and led her into the market. Jalam was clever, and with his smaller size and agility, he was a worthy adversary. But he was still no match for them. They spent the next hour leading him up and down, watching him dodge busy matrons and crowds of children. If it would not have given the game away, Anam would have laughed.

But he was glad they were here. Ashkenaz frequented the market square at the noon hour and they needed to set up a meeting. In addition to his betrothal, he must relay that Debseda knew of the upcoming expedition, that Ham was plotting with Mizraim, and that the temple was absorbing greater effort and expense.

He kept one eye on the crowd while he followed Graemea's lead. She finally stopped at a cloth merchant (they had passed by three times already) and pulled his hand. "Don't you like this weave," she asked.

"It's lovely, my dear," he replied, seeing Ashkenaz a few booths away. "That pale yellow brings out your eyes so well." He patted her shoulder. "Look, darling. There's Ashkenaz. I must ask him when Ham might have some time for us. I know the temple's important, but I've an idea for a harp and need Ham's opinion."

"Just a moment," Graemea told the merchant. "Of course, dear," she replied. "Let's go ask him."

Anam hid his disappointment, but quickly smiled at her. Maybe it would be better for her to be with him. They made their way through the crowd and found Ashkenaz fingering a pair of heavy sandals. Anam let Graemea do the talking and stood just behind her so that Ash could see his eyes as they talked. He said little, but his eyes passed the needed message along—"we need to talk!" Ashkenaz never changed his stolid expression, but he shook his head at Graemea. "I'm sorry, my lady, but my master is terribly busy. The only time he's in his shop is in the evening hour after supper."

Graemea put her hand lightly on Ashkenaz' arm. "Please tell him that we will be by tomorrow night. Buildings are important, but music is no less so."

Ashkenaz nodded reluctantly. "I will take your message to my master, but you must not be disappointed if he can't take time to help." He brightened. "But come anyway. If you can distract him, it would be a welcome relief... for all of us. He tends to be focused on his work and the Lady Mariel and I both enjoyed learning how to make the flute. We would like to learn more."

He waved as he walked away and Graemea led Anam back to the impatient cloth merchant. "Now," she said, "about this purple...."

INTERLUDE 3

7-12-2161

Carchemish reared up out of a hill overlooking the northern plains. A garrison town for the Hatti, it guarded the southern borders and reigned in banditry on the great roads. Far enough north from the great road to be free of corrupting bribes, it was close enough to respond to outlaw depredations between the Great River and the Great Sea. Its gentle hills relieved the monotonous landscape between the rivers, in turn eclipsed by the hazy line of the coastal mountains on the western horizon. The Hittites had poured resources into their southern outpost, and Carchemish was a rich, growing city—a check against the ever-expanding Sea Peoples.

Lydia sat resting her horse, glancing back at the slow, wide waters of the Euphrates flowing around numerous islands in the channel. Lud rode by, drawing her attention back to the walls of the city up ahead. It was a risk to ride Hittite horses—however dirty and bedraggled—into a garrison town, where a soldier might recognize a mount. Lydia shuddered at the thought of failure and steeled herself. There was no other way. They had to sell two horses, buy food, clothing, and information.

As they rode up to the gate, Lydia breathed a sigh of relief. Lud was right again—the guards at the gate had none of the disciplined rigidity of the great Hatti cities to the north, and let the crowd shuffle inside. This was an outpost, still rough around the edges. Its devil-may-care attitude infected soldiers and merchants. Perhaps it was the distance from Hattusa; more likely a fatalism stemming from their being the logical target of any attack from the Sea Peoples or Egypt.

Three companies of troops could keep the peace, patrol the road, and keep imperial messages moving, but if attacked, the city would be lucky to survive a siege long enough for a relief army to arrive. So the men of Carchemish lived for today. The guards waved them past with a larger group. A man and his wife were no threat and their wealth would profit someone—perhaps a relative of one of the guards.

Lydia found herself laughing softly as they dismounted and led their horses to a stable near the market square. Lud looked at her, smiled, and struck up a conversation with the stable keeper. Yes, he was interested in horses. Yes, he was sure they were remarkable animals, despite being from Nineveh. No, he was a poor man, forty-two pieces of silver was far too much for two nags near death's door.

Lud kept the man talking, using the patter to pick up news. He finally let the horses go for thirty-seven pieces of silver and an even trade for a fresh packhorse. Lydia took most of the silver and made quickly for the market. She knew exactly what she needed and was soon back, carrying a large bundle on her back. They had to push on, but took time for a hot meal at the tavern of the cousin of the stable keeper, while their horses enjoyed a rare meal of grain in the stable.

Lydia let Lud do the talking as they rode out the west gate in the early afternoon sun. They wound down the hill and forded a small river just south of the town. It would be late tomorrow before they reached Aleppo and the south road, and she could not wait to be beyond the reach of the Hatti garrison. A shrewd officer would ask questions that had no answer. The faster they moved south, the faster they would vanish.

And they needed speed. No doubt the headman and traders from their caravan were right now telling their wondrous tale of adventure and intrigue in some inn near Nineveh. One man killing seven Hatti soldiers was a story that would spread across the plain like wildfire, and their one hope was to keep ahead of it. They had done the best they could, leaving the caravan outside Nineveh, finding a faster one to Haran, and then driving their mounts up the eastern bank of the Euphrates to Carchemish.

The other half of their strategy was their new disguise. Gone was the poor farmer moving south and the wealthy merchant on the way to Aleppo. Instead, Lud had now donned the battered but serviceable armor of a mercenary bodyguard. A self-conscious Lydia was wrapped in the colorful silks of a Ninevite noblewoman. Lud's well-used equipment told of an experienced soldier not wealthy enough to refuse the silver of an addle-headed Ninevite.

Lydia had hated spending so much on clothes, but she had to be able to perfectly play the role of an eccentric, wealthy, and well-connected noble. Her tongue quickly recalled the distinctive accent of the city's aristocracy, and she practiced the haughty manners of its nobility, much to Lud's amusement.

He had been skeptical, but it proved an effective disguise, first blunting suspicion in Aleppo, and then in a succession of stops moving south over the following days. She treated Lud with contempt when they were in the company of any others, though it hurt her to do so. But the first time she tried to apologize, Lud laughed heartily. He was enjoying the whole charade; Lydia finally realized that he welcomed the chance to see another facet of her personality besides the tightly-controlled companion of the Old One.

When he laughed, she nearly lost her temper, but instead reverted to her new role. With a glint in her eye and in her haughtiest voice, she ordered him to prepare camp while she sat and watched, brushing her hair. He did so with alacrity, stopping to salute every few minutes. Both shared a long laugh over their meal, and Lydia felt the stress of the past weeks begin to bleed off.

By the time they passed Tyre, both had relaxed into their roles. Lydia's spirits rose with every day's journey; and wondered aloud if the heir would enjoy meeting a Ninevite noble. It was amazing how easy it was. The story was insane enough to be believable, and all knew that Nineveh protected her own. No officer or petty official wanted to offend the great city, and the few clever ones they met quickly concluded that beneath her disguise she was a secret envoy, making her life even more sacrosanct.

Their success convinced them to make for Gerar. Lud would find news of the heir and his family, while Lydia distracted the curious. From what the elder had told her, Lydia knew he was an old man, but a man who had defeated four kings should not be hard to find. As her confidence grew, she began to let herself dream of a life after this trek, and found herself looking at Lud more frequently.

So, when one afternoon they sighted a line of men on the road, she felt no premonition of danger. "Let's slip aside," urged Lud.

"Too late," she replied evenly. "If we can see them, they can see us. They look like soldiers. We'll have to rely on our wits. Perhaps they can tell us how far we are from Gerar."

"Perhaps." Lud's voice was full of doubt, but she was sure that her 'eccentric noble' story was safer than running. No civilized power would openly offend Nineveh. Its army had recently pursued one band of caravan thieves all the way to Egypt, dragging them back to the city to be publicly tortured and killed. That tale had spread throughout the civilized world, making Ninevites safe everywhere.

It was a company of soldiers...a large patrol. Their high helmets and scale armor marked them as warriors of the Sea Peoples, and the large man at the head of the column was clearly a high ranking officer. As he drew nearer, she grew apprehensive. He had a proud, hard face, with evil eyes. There was arrogance in his sneer as he looked them over.

"Who are you and what brings you to our land?" His command of the Ninevite language was adequate, though his accent harsh.

Lydia felt her only defense was to meet pride with pride. She looked him slowly up and down before answering. "I am Lydia of the family of Rabi of the great city, Nineveh," she sniffed. "I travel to Egypt to see its wonders."

"A woman alone?" He raised an eyebrow.

"Who would dare harm a noble of Nineveh? Her army would exact a terrible vengeance."

"If they knew," he mused. She sat stiff on her mount. "And who are you, captain," she asked scornfully, desperately trying to distract the man. The men behind him snickered.

"I am *General* Asak," he ground out. "Second in command to the Phicol, servant of the King of the Philistia." He leered at her appraisingly, and she cursed the styles of Nineveh that left so much of her flesh exposed. "And I've never had a Ninevite woman before!"

That was all it took. Lud spurred forward, but a group of horsemen surrounded him quickly. He fought anyway, but it was as brief an effort as it was violent, and a flashing spear shaft cracked the back of his head, limiting his tally to three men.

One month later, Lydia woke in the dark of the night. Dulled and broken, she seemed to be watching each day outside her body. Despair numbed the pain, but not enough. The troop that captured them had looped through the hills west of Tyre before heading back south. Only half awake, Lydia saw again the horrors of the first night, knowing they would haunt her for the rest of her life. There had been too many failures to count.

It had been a living nightmare, far worse than Nineveh. Allowing his men to keep their silver and goods, Asak had taken the scrolls and ripped them from their leather cases. Tearing one open, he had cursed—unable to read its markings, yet seeing the obvious craftsmanship and value.

"These are not of Nineveh," he shouted, knocking her to the ground. "And neither are you. Tell me the truth or I kill your friend." Lud had survived, but was concussed and lay as helpless as a child. Truth was the only weapon she possessed, so she wielded it as best she could.

Wiping the tears and dirt from her face and ignoring the rents in her clothing, she stood with as much dignity as she could muster. Almost, she could feel the Old One in the flickering flames of the fire, and her words had come into her mind. "Truth has a power of its own. Never be afraid to use it."

She had drawn herself up, facing the angry general. "I was born in Nineveh," she began calmly, "but have lived for many years as the companion to the wife of the eldest, far in the north, beneath the mountain of the great ark. These scrolls are her writings destined for her heir—a prince of the southern lands, Abram of Ur."

With a sinking feeling, she had watched Asak's face twist in rage. "Abraham again?" Spittle flew from his mouth and Lydia cursed herself for yet another mistake. She expected death at that moment. Asak had turned theatrically to his officers. "How many times have I warned my king of that man's cunning designs on our lands? He and his whelp have taken our best and grown rich at our expense."

He had glared at her. "You are full of lies. These rumors of the "elders" are tales told by old women to pass their days. These must be messages from Hattusa. The man is clearly Hatti." He paused for a moment. "That's it! Hattusa wants a treaty with Abraham."

He snarled as he turned back to her. "Well, little one... neither you nor your scribbling will ever reach him!" He had turned to the men beside him. "Hold her!" They had. Then laughing, he had taken the scrolls and began to slice them, piece by piece, and throw them into the fire. Two strong men had been unable to hold her when she saw his intent, but he knocked her to the ground once more. "Bind her!" he had commanded, and her embarrassed guards were only too happy to comply.

Rough ropes scraped the skin of her arms and legs, leaving her unable to move, except to shake in anger and a growing despair as he gloatingly fed the rest of the parchment to the fire. It was the worst hour of her life, worse even than the one that followed in his tent.

Now, a month later, she no longer wanted to live. Asak took her each night. His savagery had become mere habit, and she would have gladly destroyed herself had he not threatened Lud's life as a condition of her obedience. No longer worthy of Lud, she could at least save him as he had tried to save her. But this night was different, she noted dully. Spies had come after dark, giving her a few blessed hours of peace. But soon enough she heard a commotion at the entrance to the tent, and instantly prostrated herself as the general walked in.

"Good," he laughed. "I see you have learned your lessons well." He reached down and lifted her up by her hair. "You are the most interesting woman I have ever met. My spies tell me of a man and woman traveling together, who managed to slay an entire troop of Hittite soldiers." Her face showed nothing, but her heart sank. "Perhaps I should send the man back north," he began. "I understand Hittite justice is rather... strict." His smile made her shiver in spite of herself.

Then he smiled cruelly. "But any man who can slay seven Hatti might be of use... as long as his companion cooperated." She shuddered again, and her knees buckled in spite of the pain of her scalp. He twisted his hand casually, bringing tears to her eyes.

"I've had my fill, but I have better plans for you." He laughed again. "The king's kitchen always needs someone to scrub and carry. That seems a fit future for a Ninevite 'noblewoman.'"

Lydia no longer cared. Her ruin was complete. She had failed the Old One and herself. God had deserted her. The only spark that kept her going was the promise of preserving Lud's life. They could do nothing worse to her than they had already done. Painfully, she nodded her head. The vital part of her sank down into a black prison of her heart, yearning for the release of the grave.

Chapter 32
HUNTER & HUNTED

Ashkenaz slipped behind the building. He had eluded Korac for the moment, but it wouldn't last. Korac was too good a hunter. He took a breath and chanced a quick glance down the alley. He needed to throw his pursuer off the scent, find an opening, and escape. Then he would have to outrun the Legion… probably well into the northern hills. Glancing up, he saw a beam sticking out from a roof. Ashkenaz was agile for his size. Without a second thought, he leaped up and caught the end of the beam. It was the work of a moment to pull himself noiselessly up onto the roof.

He was not a moment too soon. Lying flat and with his hood covering the glimmer of his face and hair, he saw a dark shadow slip around the corner of the house across the street. Korac's size and stealth were unmistakable. Ashkenaz felt a thrill of fear. If Korac discovered him up here, he would have to fight. Yet it was that very quality that had attracted him to this hiding place. Korac would not expect so reckless a move from the cautious Ashkenaz.

Korac searched the area quickly and efficiently, but missed the dark shade on the roof. As he moved off, Ashkenaz let out his breath. Then he frowned. It was time to leave. After years of caution and success, Shem—of all people—had slipped up, sending a careless envoy. It was not surprising—there were not many older, wiser men that would come, and Ashkenaz never used the same man twice. Perhaps the famines of the past two years had kept the smart ones busy in their fields.

Whatever the reason, this one had been young and nervous, and Korac had been right there. Ashkenaz suppressed his anger at the young fool and concentrated on his surroundings. If Korac caught him, he would have to fight for his life. Even if by some miracle he bested Korac, he would never get out of town alive. The noise of the fight would attract too many. At least Korac had decided to take care of this problem alone; he had not yet roused the Legion. But that would change. Korac might be proud of his prowess, but it would never get in the way of his duty. He would rouse the town and instigate a search—one that Ashkenaz would not evade. With Korac's evidence, even Ham would be unable to shield him.

But he had three other pressing problems. First, he owed Ham an explanation. Second, he owed Anam a warning. And third, he owed Mariel… what? Truth? He wasn't sure, but he knew in his heart he couldn't leave her not knowing his love.

Ironically, all that required him to be inside Nimrod's home—the man who wanted him dead. He sighed quietly. His chances were slim, but they would be nonexistent if he did not run for the river right now. He wavered, and in a flash of honesty, he knew that Ham and Anam might survive his departure, but he could not leave Mariel without saying what was in his heart. It would be worse than death.

Having decided, he acted. He was back in the street in a moment. Feeling reckless, he followed Korac. If anyone else was searching, they would never expect to return to Nimrod's compound on the heels of Nimrod's deadliest killer. His heart raced and he forced calm into his limbs as he edged up the street. He could not see Korac, and every shadow could be hiding him, ready to spring to the attack. He tensed, bracing for the impact of Korac on his back. Yet still he crept forward.

Finally he reached a place of cover where he could see Nimrod's walls. He breathed a sigh of relief. There was Korac's shadow up ahead—challenging the guard and entering the gate. The hunt would soon be up. Ashkenaz slid around to the north side of the compound, staying under cover. Months ago, Ham had shown him a way in—footholds in the outer wall disguised as randomly broken bricks. He showed him how to identify the ones that would hold his weight and those that would not.

"You might need to sneak over the wall late one night after a late night in town," he had laughed. Ashkenaz recalled catching a hint of warning in the big man's voice, wondering then how much Ham suspected.

It was time to find out. He clambered up the wall, avoiding all the holes with bricks broken on the left side in favor of those with the bricks broken on their right. Soon he found himself on a rooftop, crawling towards the trapdoor. Testing it carefully, he found it open. He eased it back down and lay still, catching his breath and cursing himself for not having walked away from the market as soon as he had seen Korac. Years of success had made him careless. Kezirin and the others like him had been skilled at passing messages in public, and foolishly, Ashkenaz had assumed the same talent from this whelp. But the clumsy oaf had tried so hard to be discrete that his efforts had drawn the attention of the ever-suspicious Korac.

The man was no fool. In a glance he had known, his eyes burning with triumph. Ashkenaz had slipped away immediately, and only the size of the crowd had given him the moments he needed to elude his pursuer. Fortunately, it had been near sunset. But he had purchased a few hours, not his life.

Ashkenaz stiffened. He heard a faint scrape beneath him. Then a candle flared through the crack around the trapdoor.

His heart nearly stopped when he heard a quiet voice below. "Why don't you come down?" asked Ham. "I think it's time we talked."

In that moment of fear Ashkenaz wanted to run for the river, but something in Ham's voice gave him the trust to ease the trapdoor up and slide down. Ham was leaning against the anvil, his large arms crossed, looking intently at the younger man.

Warily, Ashkenaz brushed the dust from his clothes and backed up a step.

Ham sighed and sat down on the anvil. "Tell me the truth, boy. I'm too old for any stories and I get my fill of lies every day."

"I've never told you a lie," protested Ashkenaz.

"You've never told me the truth," Ham chuckled.

Ashkenaz found himself smiling in spite of his fear. In that moment he decided to trust the big man—Debseda's husband or not. He straightened up and looked into Ham's dark eyes. "You deserve to know. I don't know if it makes any difference, but I wanted to tell you before… I just…."

"I understand."

Ashkenaz wasn't quite sure whether Ham understood what he hadn't spoken sooner or why he was now, or both. He smiled again. "Your pardon, Elder," he began formally. "I am here to relay information to your brother and his wife. After the abduction of your sister they decided that they could no longer live in ignorance of events in Shinar." He took a deep breath. "I am the feet...."

"And Anam is the eyes," finished Ham.

Ashkenaz stood gaping at Ham. "How... how...."

Ham chuckled. "It wasn't that hard. I suspected as much when you both conveniently arrived within weeks of each other—shortly after Mariel was taken. You both told outrageous stories about Shem and Madrazi that only my wife would believe." He ticked his fingers at each point.

"And now Korac saw something and has vowed to cut out your heart by morning. I saw him come in a few minutes ago. There's something about him when he's on the scent... so I came over here to see if I was right. And here you are."

Ashkenaz nodded. Why was it so easy to underestimate this man? He fervently hoped Nimrod and Debseda did too.

"So you came back. You felt you owed me some honesty and owed Anam a warning." Ashkenaz just nodded. Ham stared a moment into his eyes and added, "But that's not all, is it?"

Once again, Ashkenaz felt cornered. Only this time it was by his heart. He wondered how far he could trust Ham. He took in a breath, hunting for a moment for a plausible lie, but then recalled the easy way that Ham had taken him in, all the days of patient instruction over the forge, and his antipathy towards Nimrod.

He smiled. How could one not trust a blacksmith? Besides, if Ham was as insightful as he was showing tonight, the news would come as no surprise. He looked down and smiled grimly again. His life was already forfeit... at least Ham would know the whole story.

"There's another reason," he admitted, his voice catching. "I could not leave without having words with the Lady Mariel. I cannot change her circumstances, but neither can I leave without speaking my love to her."

"In spite of the fact that she is a married mother?"

Ashkenaz looked up. "Yes. I cannot take her away now, but perhaps I can offer hope. I will await her freedom."

"For how long?"

"As long as it takes!" Ashkenaz let his heart fill those words with meaning.

"I see." Ham rose and slid the bolt on the door. "Hope is important," he mused. "We all need it. Can you truly make such an offer?"

"If she were free, I would offer her my life."

"You may not have one to offer in the morning." Ham crossed his arms and cocked his head.

Ashkenaz felt the test and responded sharply. "Perhaps. But if it is my time, my conscience will be clear."

Ham looked pensive. "That's a valuable commodity. I envy you." He spun around and began pacing by the anvil. "What do you propose to do?"

"I don't know," admitted Ashkenaz. "I hoped to find Anam tonight and see Mariel in the morning. After that, my life is in God's hand."

"You won't get in," replied Ham. "Korac has the household on alert."

"*You* could get in." Ashkenaz looked steadily at Ham and held his breath.

Ham laughed. "Your courage is great. Yes, I could. Why should I?"

"I suspect you have reasons of your own that have nothing to do with me, but I would simply ask you as a man to do it because it is the right thing to do." Ham stopped and stared at Ashkenaz, as if seeking some sign in his eyes. Ashkenaz kept his face steady.

"What would you have me tell them?" he asked at length.

"Anam should seek an audience with Nimrod immediately and denounce me as a traitor. He's clever. He can say that he suspected because he knew the people I was seeing in the market were close to Shem and Shelah."

"That would certainly solidify his position," mused Ham. "But how would his news reach the north?"

"I think his life is more important than his task at this moment," retorted Ashkenaz.

"My, my." Ham chuckled. "You're quite a passionate person, after all. You gave an amazing performance for the past six years!"

Ashkenaz smiled in return. "Actually, I found working with you to be quite peaceful and relaxing."

"It does have its compensations," agreed Ham. Then his face hardened. "What would you have me tell my sister?"

"I must tell her that myself," replied Ashkenaz. "Just ask her to come into the shop this morning as she always does. I can hide on the roof, speak my peace, and then try to get out tomorrow night."

Ham frowned. "You'll never make it. You need two things," he looked thoughtful. "A place to hide until you are ready to run, and then a way to get out of the city unseen."

Ashkenaz nodded his agreement. Ham sighed. "The first I can supply. The second I might... but it will be a great risk."

"Thank you," replied Ashkenaz simply.

Ham grunted and stepped to the anvil. The heavy iron rested on an old section of a tree. Ham pushed down on the anvil and then twisted it to the right. His veins stood out in his neck and Ashkenaz realized that several strong men would be needed to replicate Ham's efforts. Once loose from its catch, the wood slid aside, leaving a narrow dark opening. Ham gestured towards it.

"It won't be comfortable, but the ground at the bottom is soft and there is room to sit. Take this water and bread. You may need to be there until tomorrow night."

Ashkenaz climbed down. Ham was right. It wasn't comfortable and the dark confinement after he closed the top was nearly unbearable. Ashkenaz leaned back and tried to relax. It had been a trying day. But his heart felt much lighter for having finally been able to tell Ham the truth... all of it.

Within minutes he was asleep.

Chapter 33
BENEFICIAL BETRAYAL

2-20-1760

Anam woke to a soft tap on his door. He padded over and cracked it to see outside. Before he could resist, Ham pushed it open and slid inside, shutting it silently. Anam recovered from his surprise, following Ham's glance to the bed in the back room. Graemea lay unmoving, her face lovely in the moonlight. Ham leaned close to Anam, keeping his eyes on Graemea. "Go at once to Nimrod," he whispered. "Ashkenaz has been discovered. He sends this message: 'Denounce me and save yourself.'"

Anam's eyes narrowed. Could he trust Ham? But before he could ask him a question, the big man had ghosted out the door and was gone. Anam shook his head. Shelah would be hard pressed to have been any quieter, and Ham was easily half again Shelah's weight.

He stood weighing the elder's words, as the truth of the terrible choice dawned on him. Only there was no choice… not really. If he failed he would be dead before morning and Graemea with him.

He softly slid around the bed and slipped on his sandals and pulled on a robe. He had no idea what to say, but if Ham was right, time was important. He must appear as an independent source of information. Otherwise, Korac could kill him that very night. He shivered. Stepping out into the hall, he began to think feverishly. What lie could he spin that would have enough truth to convince Nimrod? Suddenly he stopped. There was a good chance that Korac was already talking to Nimrod. His only chance was Debseda. If she was not with Nimrod tonight, then he might still have a chance.

He breathed a prayer while making his way towards Debseda's rooms—the entire east end of the second level of the main building. A door sealed the hallway, but Anam knew that one of the women would be on watch. Debseda often received messages from her spies late into the night, and Anam almost smiled at the irony. He knocked softly and took a deep breath to calm his racing heart.

He didn't have to wait long. Celota appeared in the crack of the door, surprise clear in her eyes at the intruder. Anam didn't wait for her to question his presence. "Wake your mistress immediately," he snapped. "I have news that cannot wait." Celota's eyes narrowed, but while Anam had never come in the middle of the night, she knew that he was a valued source of information.

"Wait here," she replied. She was back before Anam had time to grow nervous. "Come with me."

She led him down the hall and into Debseda's private sitting room. She had obviously been awake, but there were fine lines of strain at the outside of her eyes and Anam knew from her imperious look that his news must be urgent.

Bowing before her, he began. "Grandmother," he began. "Please forgive my untimely intrusion. I would have waited until morning, but my dreams drove sleep from my eyes and added urgency to my news."

Debseda said nothing. *That was a good start*, Anam thought. *At least she isn't screaming at me*. Taking a deep breath, he forged ahead. "I fear Ashkenaz is here under false pretenses. I saw him earlier today, in secret conversation with one of the northern barbarian traders—a man I knew to be in the service of Shem and a tool of the witch, Madrazi. Since I had no reason to doubt his story that he followed me south after defending my name, I wanted to believe it was something innocent— perhaps he was making some small trade for himself. But it has bothered me all day and when I slept tonight, I had a terrifying vision."

Debseda showed little sign, but Anam knew she was interested by the flat glitter from her eyes. And, she would have thrown him out by now if she was not. So he continued. "I know that I am no seer like you, Grandmother, but we are all children of the gods, and sometimes they speak to those normally unattuned to their messages. At any rate, in my dream I saw a great and high tower rising out of Shinar… white and gold—the glory of all mankind. But a dark mountain began to grow in the north and a great stone came rolling down that mountain and struck the tower, breaking it into pieces. When I looked north, I saw the man in the market pushing another stone, as if to dislodge it and finish the job. I woke terrified. I could not sleep, thinking that one of those… barbarians might undercut our beautiful city and disrupt its path to glory."

He scuffed his feet. "I feared that Nimrod might have little patience with such an omen, Grandmother, but I knew that your wisdom would quickly discern whether this is an important matter or not. If not, then I beg your forgiveness for my intrusion, but if so…."

"If so," replied Debseda rising, "this must be investigated further." Walking to the doorway, she leaned out and called for Celota. "Go and bring Nimrod to this room at once."

Celota left quickly. "Sit down, Anam," purred Debseda. "You seem to become more useful each year. You have the potential of your father, but with none of his pride or temper. We might make something of you. Your insight is better than most."

"Thank you, Grandmother…" he began.

Debseda raised her hand. "That being the case, you surely see the problems for you and me both if Ashkenaz is truly a traitor."

Anam nodded slowly. "Of course. If one spy from the north, why not two? And if they came at about the same time…."

Debseda smiled her approval, but Anam felt the chill of the grave behind it. "You always were a clever boy." She sat watching him.

"A man cannot help but be concerned with his own welfare," he stated hesitantly. "But if a man cannot trust the discernment of his grandmother…?" He shrugged. "My best guess is that Madrazi sent Ashkenaz after me, thinking my defection might provide a convenient cover for her tool."

Debseda started to speak, but Anam boldly interrupted her. "I know," he said with a lopsided grin. "Ashkenaz spoke for me before I left." Debseda said nothing, staring at him intently.

"But my... um... sentiments were no secret those last months. I'm sure the witch woman could have foreseen my desire to leave." He stopped as if considering something new. "Perhaps that's why I was able to get away so easily. I should have thought about that more... you mentioned it the first night I was here."

Debseda was nodding too. "Yes, it makes sense. But we race ahead of our next step. We must ascertain the loyalty of Ashkenaz.

At that moment there was a knock on the door and Celota appeared, leading Nimrod and Korac. Both men looked suspiciously at Anam, but seeing Debseda's slight nod, Nimrod sat in his favorite chair, while Korac stood silent by the doorway.

"We have a pretty problem from young Anam," purred Debseda. "He has come to me with a tale of treachery and intrigue."

Nimrod leaned forward; Korac stood like a pillar, his cold eyes boring into Anam. Anam wisely said nothing, letting Debseda speak.

"He saw a suspicious meeting between Ashkenaz the Gomerite and one of Madrazi's tools in the market today." At that, Nimrod's mouth fell open and even Korac narrowed one eye. Debseda continued. "That, other evidence, and my own consideration of the events of his departure from the north throws grave doubt on this man."

Nimrod nodded vigorously. "There is no doubt... not any more. Korac saw the same meeting. Ashkenaz ran when he saw him and is hiding between the market and the west wall. We were about to take the men out...."

Korac interrupted, his eyes boring into Anam. "I did not see you there."

"Nor I you," returned Anam easily. "Perhaps we both possess some small skill at keeping to ourselves."

Nimrod laughed openly while Debseda smiled. Korac would not be deterred. "My men have followed you undetected for years," he bragged.

"Like the one lying on the roof of Terah's bakery day before yesterday?" asked Anam sarcastically. "Tell my Grandmother, Korac, just what have your men learned in these past years?"

Korac was stunned. He started to retort, but shut his mouth and glared at the smaller man. Nimrod laughed again. "Years of sweet nonsense between two lovers," he supplied. "You do it well," he added. "How did you train the woman?"

Anam shrugged. "It's a game for her, nothing more. Since I have nothing to hide, it's a game for me too. I just understand the rules a little better than Graemea."

Debseda clapped her hands. "Some small skill, indeed!"

"We are born with our gifts and so can take no credit for their use." Anam smiled "But what about the spy, Ashkenaz? Do you want my help?" he asked, turning to Korac.

"No!" Debseda's voice brooked no dissent. "You are too useful for such rough work. Much too useful." She cocked her eye at him, as if seeing him anew. "All of

Mizraim's intelligence, yet none of his stubborn rebellion.... Yes, we have more important work for you, my son."

"Don't worry about taking him alive," she barked at Nimrod. "We have all the evidence we need. Get rid of him tonight and give his body to the river. Put out a story that he went hunting alone. We all know how dangerous the wilderness can be." She laughed unpleasantly. "That should satisfy that oaf of a husband... I'm sure he'll not be happy to lose his aspiring student."

"Do you want me to keep an eye on *him*?" asked Korac quietly.

Debseda thought for a moment and then shook her head. Anam hoped no one saw the flicker of panic that passed over his face at Korac's question. "No," she said finally. "We have his sister. There's a fine balance there. If he does anything foolish, he can no longer protect her. If we anger him needlessly, then he might become a problem that we don't need now."

Nimrod grunted, recalling the scene when he had first brought Mariel here. Ham could be dangerous.

Debseda frowned, recalling the indignity she had suffered at his hands. At length she spoke. "If you can get rid of Ashkenaz quietly, there should be no problem. We can deny any knowledge of his demise. Ham just cares about his work... building his city." She sneered. "Building *our* city." She laid a hand on Nimrod's knee and smiled. "Just get rid of Ashkenaz. I'll keep Ham in line."

She stood suddenly. "I'm tired. Bring me news in the morning of his death. Tomorrow is a big day." She held out a hand to Anam. "We must discuss your future. It's past time that you married my Graemea. I don't care what Mizraim wants! We can't have open immorality flaunted in our city now, can we?" She smiled and gazed hungrily at Nimrod. "I think little Anam might be a valuable servant in the centuries ahead. Go now," she added, and waved them all away.

Nimrod and Korac began talking quietly about where to hunt for Ashkenaz, ignoring Anam, much to his relief. He trudged back to his room, his head whirling with the night's events. Suddenly the enormity of what had happened struck him like a club and his body began to shake uncontrollably. He leaned on the wall outside his door for a few minutes before entering his room to tell Graemea of their rapidly upcoming nuptials.

Chapter 34
ESCAPE FROM SHINAR

2-21-1760

Mariel woke to a soft tug on her arm. "Mama, I'm hungry," announced young Adan. At several months past five years, he was growing fast, but his smile never failed to elicit an answer from her. "Let's get cleaned up first," she replied.

As they walked out across the yard she noticed more activity than usual. She knew better than to ask questions of any of Nimrod's men, but noted as much as she could before entering the workshop. Ham was already in, and had a strange air about him. He was tense and alert, almost a different man. As soon as she had entered, he closed the door behind her and slid the bolt into place.

"Adan, go and play with your blocks," he ordered. Mariel sucked in a breath. Ham had never told Adan to do anything before, and certainly not with that authoritative voice.

"We need to talk," he explained quietly. "Keep your voice low… even the walls listen for my wife!"

Mariel felt a surge of fear but forced a small smile. "What is the matter, my brother? What else has she done?"

Ham began pacing back and forth. "It's not her… at least not directly," he began. He hesitated a moment, looking down. "Our Ashkenaz is in trouble."

Mariel leaned quickly against the anvil as her legs went weak. "Is… is he hurt?" Her voice trembled.

"No," replied Ham, with a strange smile at her reaction. "Not yet. Sit down. We don't have much time." She complied. "There is one thing I must know first." His voice carried an authority she had not heard him use since he had rescued her from Debseda the day she had come to Shinar. "Do you love him?"

Mariel gasped. She had worked so hard to hide her feelings. If Ham had seen, why not others? She cast about in her mind for a moment, tempted to lie, but then something inside suppressed the temptation. She had trusted Ham in everything else, why not in this? "Yes," she replied simply, looking him directly in the eyes.

Ham's face broke into a rare smile. "Good! That's the best news I've heard in years. Now we can move forward." He came and sat in front of her on the floor, looking up and grinning. "Ashkenaz has been working for Shem and Madrazi all these years—their eyes in Shinar. Korac discovered him and I'm sure the hunt is up. We must help him escape." He looked down briefly. "But I could not put your life at risk unless I knew that it would be your choice."

His words made her blood run cold. She knew all too well the vindictive paranoia of Debseda, the vicious cruelty of Nimrod, and the soulless competence of Korac. Ashkenaz would probably die anyway. Their help would only add their blood to his. Ham seemed ready for the risk. She could do no less. "My life is his," she replied softly, blushing. "It has been from the first. I would rather die with Ashkenaz than live with Nimrod."

"Even with Adan?" Ham's voice was soft, but his eyes penetrated her heart.

"Debseda wants to take him anyway," she sighed. "I *must* help my man. I must!" Suddenly she looked around the shop. "Where is he?" she asked, her fear rising. "Nimrod's men are stirring outside. They could come here any moment!"

"They could," shrugged Ham. "But they aren't here now. Ashkenaz could have fled last night, but he returned to warn me and to talk to you. The fool wouldn't leave!" Yet his smile robbed the words of offense. "Stand up, Mariel, and let him say his piece before leaving."

Mariel stood automatically but wrinkled her brow. Ash wasn't in the shop. She knew every corner. Ham was grinning as he motioned her aside. Understanding dawned as he leaned against the anvil and turned it slowly. As he strained, she began to appreciate anew the extent of his strength and took hope. The anvil and its wooden base swiveled aside, revealing a narrow opening. "I'm suspicious by nature," Ham grimaced. "I thought it might be a good idea to be able to hide things from my family—I never thought one of those things would *be* family." He chuckled and called down into the hole, "Come up, boy."

Within moments, a dirty and disheveled Ashkenaz clambered out, brushing dust off his clothes in a futile effort to clean himself. He was a mess, but at that moment, to Mariel, he was the most handsome man in the world. Her throat tightened as he turned his bright blue eyes on her. For five years she had only caught a few glimpses of their inner fire, but now she saw the flames and was consumed. The next thing she knew, she was in his arms, clinging to his neck and crying his name, over and over.

"I love you," he said as he gently pushed her back far enough to look into her eyes. "I know you belong to Nimrod now, but I pray the day will come when you are free of him and his evil. Until that day I will remain an unmarried man, if I have to wait a lifetime."

"And I love you," she returned. "I never knew what a fool I had been until the day I met you. If only it had been before..."

"Steady," warned Ham. "We are all in danger and we have much to do."

"Let me stay in your hole until dark," Ashkenaz urged. "I can make my way clear tonight."

"You don't stand a chance," replied Ham flatly. "And it seems that your life is important to my sister. If we can get you to the river, you can find a small boat. They're waiting to cut off your routes north, but if you go south first, you can circle around east or simply wait for a few weeks and then sneak back up the west bank."

"How can we get him to the river in broad daylight?" asked Mariel.

"Unless you have forgotten, we are carting those timbers," he pointed to the load by the large double doors, "to the river to repair the docks. It will involve some heavy work for you, but the wagon is just outside the door. We can arrange the load with space to hide a man at the bottom. Then we cart that man to the river, work slowly, and let him float away tonight." He winked at Mariel. "I feel especially hungry today. We must take enough food for a hard day!"

Mariel was impressed. It was a simple yet ingenious plan. She and Ham were the perfect cover for Ashkenaz. Few would be foolish enough to question either of them, and they had been preparing the timbers for more than a month. In fact the only suspicious thing would be to not do the work.

"Hide behind the forge for now," Ham instructed Ashkenaz. "When I whistle, come quickly. Take a long drink now—you won't get another until tonight."

Ashkenaz nodded, then surprised Mariel by gripping Ham's arm. "Is there any message you wish me to take north?" he asked hesitantly. "To your brothers… to your parents?"

Ham smiled slowly. "Just one. Tell Madrazi that I remember her last word."

Mariel interrupted. "Tell her that I have taken it to heart too."

Ashkenaz frowned slightly. "That's all?"

"She'll understand." Mariel laid her hand on his arm for a moment, and then withdrew it. "She always does."

Ham was as good as his word. Moving the lighter timbers aside, they soon had a small hollow in the middle of the wagon. Once longer timbers were loaded on top, it would appear solid. Mariel had to fight her fear with each step she took. During the short time they had been working, armed men had passed by three times but had fortunately ignored them.

"Twice an hour," grunted Ham. "The next two should be around any minute. After they leave, we'll get him in and cover him up." He grinned. "Then we'll get the next two to help me heft the heavier stuff on top."

Mariel tried to smile. Every time the men had come around, she had felt her heart race, fearing the worst. She didn't want to live if they found him. She imagined even now that Korac or Nimrod was hiding nearby, just waiting for Ashkenaz to show himself. One fear chased another in her mind until she could hardly concentrate on her work. Her hands shook and the sweat that covered her body was only in part caused by the hard work.

Finally the two armed men walked past again, not even bothering to acknowledge Ham. He waited for what seemed too long to Mariel and then whistled softly.

Ashkenaz was halfway across the shop when all three froze at the sound of a piercing scream. Mariel whirled to see Adan rooted to the floor. A cobra had found its way inside—probably last night—and was coiled up in the corner where the child had been playing. It was clearly angry, its head nearly as high as Adan's and its hood flattened. Its flat eyes were locked onto the boy and the head swayed back and forth, preparing to strike. Mariel acted, instinctively leaping for the boy. She heard something whiz by her shoulder and saw the snake knocked down by a hammer. She grabbed Adan and spun him out of the way, before being knocked to the ground by Ham as he sprang past, a length of timber in hand. With a swift strike he ground the head of the serpent into paste.

But the child's scream had brought the guards. She heard their footsteps just outside. Out of the corner of her eye, she saw Ashkenaz dive under a workbench. She realized that he had thrown the hammer that saved Adan… for her.

But the workbench was a poor place to hide. It had a low shelf, but the space was too small. If the guards looked carefully, they would see him. She did not know what possessed her at that moment, but she rose quickly and ran towards the door, keeping between the soldiers and Ashkenaz. She let her robe fall open, knowing that her sweat-soaked tunic was pasted to her body—hating herself for such a wanton display yet hoping against hope that the men were... well... men. She let her panic feed her fluttering hands and frantic words.

"Help us!" she cried as they ran past the wagon and into the shop. She waved her arms, letting her cloak slip further. "There's a serpent... my boy... Nimrod's son..." She was pointing and jumping, and as she hoped, their eyes were fixed on her chest. "Over there," she screamed, and they gathered themselves and strode over towards Ham, spears at ready.

"It's dead," he grunted. "My sister is a little excited. It was a near thing. But his mother saved him and I killed it." He picked up the dead snake and tossed it at the nearest man. "Put this outside so it won't frighten the boy."

The man jumped back instinctively as the snake fell at his feet. His partner grinned and slipped his spear under the snake's body. "Forgive my young friend. He's a little jumpy... Korac's keeping us all moving this morning." He turned, taunting the younger man. "Can't wait to tell everyone how fast you jumped for a dead snake!"

Ham moved up beside Mariel, holding Adan in her arms. His bulk further shielded Ashkenaz. "Thanks for the help. Come back soon and help us load the rest."

The older man frowned. "I don't think Korac would like that," he said, "but I'll ask."

Ham nodded. They both knew he would do no such thing, but at least he had replied with courtesy.

Ashkenaz rolled out and rose to his feet. Mariel was on him instantly. "You saved my son."

"Your smile is sufficient reward." He nodded and glided to the door. Looking both ways, he vaulted into the wagon and dropped into the hollow in the wood.

Ham roused Mariel. "Put the boy down and help me cover him, now. Someone will hear about this and be back shortly. If they find him and start asking questions, you don't know anything."

She shook her head. With the danger past, she was beginning to shake and felt tears welling in her eyes. Ham shook her, and then caught her eyes with his. "You don't know anything about Ash. Why should you? You're Nimrod's wife." He shook her again. "You must do this. Be haughty and angry."

Nodding numbly, she put Adan down and quickly helped him slide enough thin planks over the hollow. And just in time. Korac rounded the corner of the wall with the two guards and another two men. The men were anxious—clearly wanting to be anywhere but between Korac and Ham—but Korac looked as he always did... his face like that of a statue with no expression in his flat eyes. She picked up Adan and held him close. "Quiet, son," she whispered. "Don't say anything until these men are gone."

Then she walked over to stand beside Ham.

Before Korac could speak, Ham nodded to the two guards that had just left. "Thanks for bringing more help so quickly," he said. "The rest of the load is too heavy for the Lady Mariel," he now turned to Korac, "and you know how old and feeble I am these days."

"I fear we're busy right now," grated Korac. "But perhaps you can help us instead. It seems *your* man Ashkenaz is selling information to our enemies. Where is he?"

"I was not informed we are at war," rumbled Ham, folding his massive arms across his chest. "Be careful of how you speak of my family, boy." Korac did not shrink back, but Mariel saw the muscles in his neck tense. Ham leaned forward and Korac slid his feet apart as if ready for a fight. But Ham smiled grimly. "As for Ashkenaz, I've no doubt he found some woman last night and is sleeping it off in some hut on the edge of town. When you find him, bring him here. We have work to do and I need his strong arms."

"What about you? Have you seen him?" Korac suddenly whirled on Mariel and took a step forward. Mariel shrank back, but remembering Ham's words, she suddenly stepped right up to Korac and pushed him back with her free hand. "How dare you speak to me like that, you worm!" Her face blazed and she let all the emotion of the past hour pour out in a torrent of wrath. "You seem to forget who I am," she sneered. "I'm not some lackey who runs around doing dirty work for Nimrod. I'm his wife and this is his son. I have nothing to say to you, and if you ever speak to me like that again, I will *not* let it pass."

The men stood gaping at Mariel. Korac took a step back, suddenly disconcerted. He stepped right into the grasp of Ham. Now Korac was accounted a mighty man— many thought him the near equal of Nimrod, but Ham caught his wrist and had it up behind his shoulder blade before he or his men could react. The other giant arm was suddenly around his neck and the voice in his ear was reinforced by the pain in his shoulder as his left arm moved further up towards his neck. Korac struggled for a moment, but his wrist moved inexorably higher.

"Drop that blade or I'll snap your neck." Korac dropped the knife. His men stood uncertain, dumbfounded at the turn of events and clearly not sure what to do. But Ham was not through. He swung Korac off his feet and around facing Mariel. "Apologize to my sister," he breathed "or you'll never use this arm again!"

Korac felt flames inside his shoulder as the vice-like grip moved his wrist still higher. "My apologies, Lady Mariel," he grated out. "There was no excuse for my discourtesy."

"Better," said Ham as he spun him away. "Now get out of my sight and stay out of it. If you ever cause any trouble for my sister, I will not be so easy on you."

The men were goggling. All their lives Ham had been the quiet workman, letting his wife and sons run the community. Now they saw him with new eyes. He might be an outcast, but he was still an elder, and never in their wildest imaginations had they thought any man could handle Korac like a child.

Korac was rubbing his shoulder, keeping a wary eye on Ham as he stepped back. But Ham was not through. "As for the rest of you, load this timber on the wagon... carefully and neatly."

They scrambled to obey. Korac slunk away, while the four guards dropped their weapons and began a long hour's toil under a constant stream of sarcastic direction from Ham. Mariel almost giggled as she watched them. Not only was Ham setting them in their place, his unrelenting sarcasm kept them so preoccupied with their work that they had no chance to think about Ashkenaz. The hunters were helping the prey escape!

Finally the men were done and gratefully retrieved their spears before trotting away as fast as their aching bodies would carry them—each confident of one thing— a future... any future... that firmly excluded employment with Ham!

The remainder was easy. Word of Ham's manhandling Korac spread through the town like wildfire and Mariel saw a new respect in almost every face. They halted the wagon beside a tangle of reeds upstream from the damaged dock, facing the town. It was pathetically easy to persuade several of the guards to unload the heaviest pieces. Once they were done, Ham had the men carry them down to the dock, carefully laying them in place. After an hour sweating in the midday sun, the guards avoided that area for the rest of the day, finding other places that required their undivided attention.

Sitting and watching the wood moved to the dock, Mariel finally caught up the sack of wooden pins and a mallet before jumping down. She set her things on the ground and had Adan jump down to her. "Take this to Uncle Ham," she directed. With a lump in her throat she walked around the wagon, pulling out a waterskin. "I love you," she whispered.

"Remember my promise," was the whispered reply.

Fighting the tears, she trudged down to the dock. Not looking back was the hardest task of the entire day.

Chapter 35
ASHKENAZ RETURNS

4-5-1760

It was a weary, foot-sore, and saddle-sore Ashkenaz who topped the last hill on the road to Shem's home. He had ridden most of the night, and his mount was ready to drop. The mountain loomed before him in the late morning sun, its heights mantled in gray mist. But the greening of early spring had begun; the earth was taking on a softer, more pleasing appearance.

He had spent the first month running from Korac's searchers; drifting downstream to throw them off, then sneaking up the western shore of the river by night, risking the serpents, crocodiles, and other nocturnal predators that sought their prey along the river's edge. He had eaten everything from fresh bread—stolen from outlying farms—to dead fish found in the mud by the Euphrates. Twice, men had come within a hair of discovering him—the most terrifying being the night he had almost stumbled into an armed camp. He had run for hours after a heart-pounding hour working his way clear!

His most desperate need had been a horse, but in the end, his own two feet carried him all the way to the Lake of the Islands. Food, a night's sleep, and a mount had seen him on the last leg of his journey. And now his destination was within sight. He sighed, leaned over, and patted the horse on the neck. "Just a few more steps, old fellow," he rumbled. "A few more steps and we can both rest for days."

He kicked his heels into the shaggy flank, and the horse resumed its tired trot down the long slope. Perhaps he sensed the end too, for within a short time, his head came up as he broke into a slow canter. Ashkenaz steered him off the road and cut across a field towards the barn. Let Shem fuss; he didn't care. His appreciative horse picked up his pace as he scented the barn ahead.

People were hurrying to meet him. He saw Zeb run out of the barn with Enoch, while Shem and Shelah strode down from the house. Heth and Jobaath followed, and several of the women trailed behind. As he pulled up short of the crowd, he saw Jael step out of the barn door, lowering her bow. Had she been prepared to shoot him?

He laughed to himself as he reined the horse in. Why not? He probably looked like a wild vagabond, his clothes dirty and torn; his long yellow hair and beard matted and filled with dust and grit. He was grinning as he pulled to a halt and stepped stiffly down from the saddle. It was an effort to straighten his back and stand up, and he was thankful for Zeb's quick grip of the reins. "I'll take care of him," the boy said, already leading him away.

Shem shook his head. "Hard night?" asked Shelah.

Ashkenaz shook his head. "Last night was easy. It was the other forty-five."

Shelah put an arm around his shoulder. "Come in and sit and eat. The faster you tell your tale, the faster we can get you cleaned up."

Ashkenaz grinned tiredly. "An even trade. Are you sure the lady will let me into her kitchen like this?"

Madrazi pushed forward. She eyed him up and down. "Just this once." Her eyes twinkled. "But don't make a habit of it."

Leaning back from an empty plate and a steaming cup warming his hands, Ashkenaz looked over the room. The small kitchen was crammed to overflowing. He knew it was time to talk. "Have you heard from Bela yet?"

Shem shook his head. "He's not expected for another week. He'll be surprised to see you here."

"Sorry, more likely." Ashkenaz' face went hard. "The young fool gave me away to Korac!"

The room went still. Jael pushed forward, her face bright and hard on hearing the name of her nemesis. Ashkenaz shook his head. "He tried too hard. Acting secretive in a public place defeats the purpose of the exercise. But, then again, it could be my fault. I knew Korac was following me... Anam was so eager to get his news north."

Shem interrupted. "Start from the beginning and tell us your tale."

Ashkenaz nodded slowly and began. It took an hour to tell of Shinar, the new temple, Ham's role in delaying its construction, Anam's betrothal to Graemea, Mizraim's enmity with Debseda, and the myriad other details. He took a deep breath. "Korac found me out. I eluded him and escaped downriver before making my way back to the lake. They gave me the horse and here I am."

He noticed Madrazi staring at him. She clearly knew that there was more to the story but was leaving the decision up to him. He held her gaze then let his eyes circle the room. She understood immediately and softly whispered into Shem's ear. He cleared his throat. "I think that's enough for now," he said. "We have work to do." The room cleared, until only the elders, Heth, Shelah, Jobaath, and Jael were present.

He looked dubiously at Jael but decided to trust Shem's judgment and picked up his story. This time he told of Anam's desire to wed Graemea, assuring them that it was Graemea who was changing and not Anam. "I trusted him with my life, and he delivered me from their hands. I have no doubts of my friend."

Taking another deep breath and keeping his eyes down, he told them of Mariel and Ham, of his love for Mariel and of his trust in the patriarch. "He helped me after he knew what I was doing," he concluded. "I think he relished the opportunity to hurt Nimrod and Debseda... and...." His voice wavered.

"Go on," urged Madrazi softly.

"He approved of my intentions toward his sister. He has protected her as much as he could and has kept her from a life that could have been much worse."

"A waste of his efforts," sneered Jael.

Ashkenaz glared at her. "You speak as a witless fool," he snapped, showing real anger. "You know nothing of your sister for the last five years and your vision is warped by your own petty anger. Grow up, Jael! Your sister has... and she is the better for it. God grant that one day you will know remorse... and God grant that you deal with it with the grace and courage of the Lady Mariel."

Jael started to retort, but Shem gripped her arm, grinding his fingers deep into the muscle. "Silence!" Ashkenaz saw the desire on her face to lash out, but Shem tightened his grip and she shrank back.

"There is one more thing," sighed Ashkenaz. "Debseda knows you are leaving soon to explore the wide lands and mark them for settlement. Although they sneer at your effort, they know too well all that is happening here. You need to find her spies and root them out. What if they discover that Anam is helping us? He and Graemea would both be dead within the hour."

Heth nodded and spoke. "Maybe it's time to get Anam out—no information is worth his life."

"How are you going to do that?" asked Jael sarcastically. "Have Bela smuggle him wings so that he can fly him away?" She sniffed. "It's not very helpful for Anam to have all this wonderful news when he can't tell it."

"What do you know?" retorted Jobaath. "You're just a foolish young girl. We can make contact with him somehow."

"Using Bela?" sneered Jael. "He nearly got Ashkenaz killed. Do you think Korac and Nimrod fools? Even a *foolish young girl* like me knows that every merchant we send will be followed by at least three people every moment in Shinar."

"Children," warned Madrazi. "This is not helpful. We must have time to consider what we know and avoid rash decisions. We cannot solve this problem now."

After the others had left, Ashkenaz lingered with the elders. Shem shook his head before walking away. "It's good to have you back, young man. You've proven yourself worthy of my sister. I hope God allows you both that joy." He shook his head again, chuckled, and walked out.

Madrazi sat beside him, her eyes an intense green fire. "Go ahead and tell me what you've been bursting to say," she said softly.

Ashkenaz looked at the floor. "I'm glad I wasn't that obvious to Debseda!" He sighed and looked back into those disconcerting eyes. "Ham asked me to tell you that he remembers your final word to him." He paused, amazed at the tears that suddenly filled her eyes. "And Mariel wanted you to know that she keeps the same word close to her heart." He paused, intensely curious at what the message meant.

But Madrazi was openly weeping. Not sure what he had done or what to say, Ashkenaz gently set down his cup and quietly walked away.

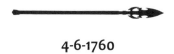

4-6-1760

Jael ran the brush across the mare's flank. The horse shivered in appreciation as she repeated the long, slow stroke. It was easy to lose herself in such an easy task and needed the distraction. A difficult crosswind had combined with her resentment of Mariel and disappointment with Ashkenaz to ruin her archery practice. After missing several times, Shem sent her home, his disappointment palpable. Enraged at herself and him, she had taken it out on her mount. But the hypnotic brushing of her horse was leaching her anger and calming the animal.

She was between the horse and the wall of the stall and so invisible to anyone else in the barn. She heard Heth walk in with Ashkenaz, talking with him of Shinar. Jael strained to hear. She was intensely interested in Heth's past—he had refused to say much. He seemed such a mystery at times, but one that she wanted to solve. It was only because she wanted to understand the source of his courage and skill… or so she told herself. They were drawing close, so she paused and slowed her breathing, standing perfectly still. Shem claimed that talent as the most important for remaining unseen, and she had worked hard to perfect it.

The men were passing her stall. "…during the night. But I was able to see her most days. I tell you, Heth, the day I first saw her, my heart was lost. In some ways it was torture to have to be with her, knowing she was beyond my reach…."

Heth grunted. "It's a sad thing to be brought low by a woman. We have important work to do. Your heart needs to be set on that, not on some unattainable dream—especially that of a woman who has already betrayed her family!" Jael's respect for Heth rose. At least someone saw how foolish Ash had been!

Ashkenaz' reply was low with danger. "Watch your words, Heth. You don't know her. And who are you to instruct me? I heard the rumors in Shinar of your youth—of your dalliance with Celota!" Ashkenaz stomped away, leaving Heth swearing softly to himself. Then he too turned and stalked out of the barn.

Jael reeled against the stable wall. Heth with Celota? One of Debseda's closest friends? The brush dropped from her nerveless hand as her horse turned to see why the brushing had stopped. But Jael's mind was far away as she slipped down to the stable floor. Hot tears flooded her eyes as a wave of emotion swamped her body.

It was only then that the truth broke upon her. She loved him… or at least she had. Shem and Shelah were good men and would both have made fearsome warriors, but they lacked the inner rage that made Heth so dangerous. And it was the danger that drew her. She shared his rage—a connection that she could never feel with her brother or great-nephew… they had too much self control. She now looked forward to her training sessions with Heth… had it been for more than the skill and knowledge? Had Ashiel been right?

Had it been, perhaps, that she had wanted to be with Heth… to be close to him… to see his strong face, to hear his rough laughter, to feel the touch of his calloused hand on hers as he pulled her up? Ashiel had accused her of as much several years ago, but she had pushed the idea down into the recesses of her heart, afraid to face that possibility. She shook her head.

It was nearly too much—the discovery of deep feelings for a man by their very betrayal. For the second time in her life a red rage took her. Instinct caused her to grab her cloak and weapons as she slipped out the door. Ignoring the stares of the workers, she ran across the newly-turned fields. One thought to accost her, but one look at her blazing eyes turned him away and she pounded past him, heading for the wastelands to the west. She needed to get away from people before the urge to kill overtook her.

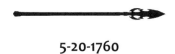

5-20-1760

Heth stood out in the dawn mist watching Jobaath tighten the final straps around the packs on the mule. Shem had decided to allow a pack mule for the long trek. beyond. "We're going to probably be gone for two years or more," he had said. "A few luxuries will make the mule worth the trouble."

"As long as I don't have to handle it," muttered Heth to himself. He had been in a bad mood the entire month. It had started the day Ashkenaz had repeated Korac's old lie about Celota. As if he would ever stoop that low… she looked too much like Debseda! He could have had any woman in Shinar; why would he choose the worst?

Then Jael had disappeared for a week and returned in such a sour mood that Shem almost sent her home. Hoping to snap her out of it, Heth had volunteered to show her some of his more advanced techniques with the knife. Over the past three years they seemed to have grown closer together, but this time her eyes and tongue rebuked his advance—treating him as though he were Korac or Nimrod. "Women!" he muttered to himself. "I'll never understand them!"

He was glad they were going. His rage at Ashkenaz had pushed their friendship to the breaking point. He had blistered his cousin… though to Ash's credit, once he learned the true story, he apologized immediately. Though heartfelt and sincere, it had still been a week before Heth would speak to him again.

On top of that, his troubles with Jael brought on a dark depression. Worried when she stayed out for more than two days, those fears were accompanied by his old desire for a wife and home, and he was mortified that those thoughts kept turning to Jael. It was ridiculous… especially after her irrational behavior, but the more he thought about it, the stronger his feelings became. In spite of her flaws he was attracted to her… or maybe it was because of her flaws. He understood her. He knew all about betrayal… and the rage it ignited in one's heart. He understood the single-minded drive to destroy the evil to the south…they shared the same enemies.

Madrazi's words had come back to haunt him—Jael wanted to be *with* him because she could not *be* him. He did not understand the workings of the female mind as Madrazi did, but he knew that over the past five years he and Jael had created something that was much more than a simple teacher-student relationship. Yet if her attraction rested only on some unattainable selfish desire, what hope could they have together?

So it was that when she returned, he was eager to see if this something more was really there… only to be met by scorn and a seething anger.

"Women!" he muttered again, bringing himself back to the present.

He stared again at the mule, as if it were to blame for Jael's temper. Fortunately Jobaath had volunteered to take charge of the animal. Heth was eager to be off. He wanted distance… to be able to forget Jael and enjoy the wilderness and the companionship of his friends. But the others were dragging their feet. He was ready to go, but Shem and Shelah were talking to their wives. The entire household had turned out to see them off, and Heth felt like a fool under the gaze of so many people. He feared that Madrazi would see him standing apart and see into his heart. He wanted nothing to do with her or her counsel.

He glanced around. Ashkenaz was standing alone too, looking up at the mountain. His mind was probably back in Shinar. Heth had been astounded at his tale, especially as he had pondered it over the past weeks. It had been comforting to know that the memory of his grandfather's goodness was true. Heth's respect was grudgingly given, but Ash's harrowing escape was a feat worthy of any man. Once he had been able to see past the tale of his love for Mariel, Heth had found that his estimate of Ash had risen considerably. He smiled grimly at the thought of Nimrod's rage at Ash's escape.

Of course everyone else had been moved by his tale of Mariel, and Madrazi had wept when Ash had related her selfless risks to save him.

Only Jael seemed to share his suspicion of the woman who had betrayed Noah. She clearly had little sympathy for her older sister's plight, and was only interested in the parts of the tale in which Ashkenaz had outwitted Korac. When Ash had begun to talk of plans to rescue Mariel, Jael had risen with a sneer. "She chose her bed; she can lie there," she said before stalking off. It had been the only time that Heth had seen a look of pure rage on Madrazi's face.

As Heth looked again, he saw Jael standing apart from the others, with her hood pulled up, hiding her face. Like Heth, she clearly had little time for the crowd or the extended farewells. She was standing some distance away from the household, her eyes scanning the horizon. The sun was not yet up, but the gray was fast dissipating as a yellow glow began to fill the eastern sky. Looking back over, Heth caught Jael's sharp glance as the light increased—her face tight with anger... and with something else. But before he could read her, she intercepted his stare and curled her lip in contempt before deliberately looking aside.

"Women," grumbled Heth once more. "No wonder I never married!"

Shem waved the men on. Madrazi stood back, a frown on her face, but Shem was smiling. His pack rode high on his back and his bow was in his right hand. Raising the bow and his empty hand, he blessed the house and charged the men with its protection and productivity during his absence. "If there is any question that you cannot resolve, look to the wisdom of the Creator through my wife. She shall speak for me in all matters. When we return we shall have a celebration such as has not been seen in this new world."

The small crowd cheered—except Jael—and Shem turned north towards the mountain. Shelah caught up his bow and followed. Heth shifted his pack and stepped up behind them, with Ashkenaz at his side. Looking back, he saw Jobaath leading the surprisingly docile mule. He turned his eyes back north—he had set out on a quest and would not turn aside until he had completed that task.

But as he walked down the meadow towards the river, he could not shake the memory of Jael's hard young face. For years he had imparted his skill with weapons.

He had followed Madrazi's advice, maintaining a patience that would have done Shelah proud… and Heth was not a patient man. She was a good student. But was she more than that? Had the years allowed something else to grow unawares? Over time the iron had softened and they had begun to trade a few sentences about other things. She had even laughed with him when he told her about being treed by the wolf. It had transformed her face, and he would never forget that flash of what she might have been.

But the easy camaraderie had vanished soon after Ashkenaz' return. Was it the talk of Mariel, Nimrod, and Korac? Then why had she seemed so angry with *him*? He tried to turn his mind to the trek ahead, but the questions kept nagging. She had avoided him for the past weeks, and when she could not, the face of iron was fixed in place. He had offered his friendship—something he never did lightly—and she had spurned it, discarding him once she had gained the knowledge she needed.

He sighed. The road ahead was long and he was free of her. Let Madrazi deal with her. For the next months he could savor the companionship of friends… as long as people like Shem and Shelah desired his company, he was content.

Chapter 36
PATERNITY

5-25-1760

Mariel was sleeping heavily—exhausted, as usual. Since Ashkenaz had fled, she had thrown herself into her son and her work to escape the heartbreaking loss. The light had left her face. Her time in the shop kept her sane, yet its memories were torture… Ash working the forge, Ash laughing with her as they re-marked the curve of a beam for the eighth time, Ash leaning on a broom staring at her when he thought she wasn't looking. Despite the pain, she kept returning because memories of Ash were better than the presence of Debseda and Nimrod.

To be married to a man she hated; to have lost the man she loved—even the opportunity to be near him—had nearly crushed her. She was convinced she would never see him again… never touch him…. never be with him. Her other consolation was Adan. Ash had promised her that Adan would be his son when the time came… he loved her so much that he did not care that Nimrod's blood ran in his veins.

So Adan became her world. He was growing into a happy companion and could bring a smile to even Ham's dour face. Only five, he was observant and intelligent. He would talk to Ham, and was already learning the names and purposes of many tools. He was old enough to help clean and young enough to think it a great adventure. As he grew, she rejoiced in the innate happiness he displayed. He could bring a smile to the lips of the most hardened man in the Legion. His laughter saved Mariel from despair. Everything was a joke, and he often reclaimed his mother from the verge of tears with a smile.

Her work no longer brought her joy, but it filled her days. Her natural gifts with metal and wood were obvious in her work, and she was only slightly less gifted with stone or brick. Ham no longer inspected or supervised her tasks. He just told her what to do. Her favorite medium was metal—she saw Ash's face in the glow of the fiery forge.

As she drew herself awake, she consoled herself with those thoughts. She had Ham, her work, and her son. It would have to be enough. She struggled towards full wakefulness, realizing that something was pulling at her shoulder. She rolled over, expecting to see Adan urging her into another day. Instead, she saw the terrified face of Zerai. Instantly sleep left her and she leapt up, grabbing a robe to wrap around her.

"He's gone," the girl kept repeating. Then softly, "They took him."

Mariel grabbed her shoulders, fear coursing through her. "Who, Zerai?"

"Adan."

A red mist obscured her vision. Dimly she felt herself sinking back onto the bed, and then knew nothing.

She woke again to a damp coolness on her forehead. A weak hand fluttered up to brush it away. "I had a terrible dream, Zerai," she began, not fully awake. "They had taken my son...." Memory returned. It was no dream. She drew a breath to scream, but a strong hand covered her mouth. She struggled, knocking aside the damp rag that obscured her vision, but the hand was immovable. It was Ham's.

Mariel saw the mixed fear and rage on his face, confirming her worst fears. She wanted to die, but first to scream out her grief and rage at the evil that had twisted itself around her life. She felt strength return, but Ham's grip was unbreakable.

"Silence!" He hissed. "I know this is hard, but you must gather yourself. Nothing good will come of hysterics." Mariel nodded her understanding and he withdrew his hand. "Speak quietly," he cautioned. "The walls hear. Graemea has brought news. Her life is forfeit if she is found here. Do not give her away."

Mariel looked beyond him to see Graemea trembling behind him. She shuffled forward, tears glistening on her cheeks.

"I don't have much time, my friend, but I'll tell you all I know."

Mariel caught her breath and forced back her panic. She needed news now. Tears would come later, where Nimrod could not hear and gloat. A fierce hatred rose inside, beating back the weakness. She clutched at the strength it offered. Sitting up, she nodded to Graemea. "I'm in your debt again, friend." Her voice was like stone grating over stone, but Graemea didn't seem to notice.

"I learned this morning from Anam that they have taken Adan to a village up the Tigris. He will be kept safe, learning to watch flocks until he is older. He is in no danger now, nor will he be for some years. Nimrod will take no time with him, nor will my mistress until his twelfth year. They intend to hold him hostage until then. It is not so much for you, my lady, but for the Lord Ham. Korac was shamed in front of his men. Nimrod must assert his control before some begin to realize that he can be challenged." She glanced at the windows and pulled up her hood. "I will tell you more as I learn it," she whispered, "but I must leave now. I will be missed."

"Go with my friendship," whispered Mariel in return. "May God grant you happiness for your kindness."

Graemea bowed and slipped away. Ham came and sat down on the bed. "Keep watch on the door," he ordered Zerai. She nodded and slipped into the other room.

"Mariel," he began. "Know this. I will restore your son to you or die in the attempt. But we must bide our time. Any action now is an open trap, and we are not prepared to spring it. Give me time, I beg you."

Mariel wavered. She wanted to rush to Debseda's quarters and tear out her eyes, but in the midst of that rage, she knew that Ham was right. Regaining control was perhaps the most difficult thing she had ever done. But Ham deserved better. He had been her protector for years, shielding her from a life that could have been much worse. Seeing his anguish, she put a hand on his arm. "You have been as an angel of the Almighty to me from the day I came," she whispered. "My life has been in your hands over and over again. Once more I put myself in your care. Just tell me what I must do." She faltered. "I don't know if I can go on without him... without Ash...."

"You must," he replied simply. "Adan will need a mother when we rescue him. A broken woman will only be a burden. Be strong for *him*."

She stared at him for a moment until the import of his words broke through the fog that threatened to take her mind. Nodding slowly, she forced it away again and stood. "I'll try," she choked. "For him."

"Good girl," he said with a hint of a smile. "Get dressed now and come down to the shop. Work will be better than sitting up here alone. I'll send Zerai back." He matched actions with words and waited in the outer rooms.

Mariel was nearly dressed in her drab work clothes when she heard a commotion at the door. She threw on her cloak and told Zerai to bring her sandals. Striding into the room, she saw Ham blocking the door. Nimrod was already inside, Debseda and her maids outside. She heard Debseda's shrill protest. "Let me in!"

Ham refused her. "He is her husband," he said, nodding at Nimrod. "He has a right to these rooms. You do not. Nor do these others. If the Lady Mariel wishes your company, she can send for you. Otherwise, go away. We have much to do today."

"Get out of my way," screeched Debseda. From what Mariel could see of her, she was livid. Instantly her own anger rose in response. This witch had just kidnapped her son. She strode past a surprised Nimrod and stood beside Ham.

She turned to Ham and let contempt drip from her words. "I have no desire to see your wife in my private rooms. Ever!" Her cold voice echoed out into the hall. "Or her lickspittles." She looked disdainfully at Debseda. "Now leave!"

Nimrod began to interrupt. "I'm your husband and I demand that you let her in."

Mariel turned on him like a lioness. "You have no rights here other than your own presence, which would not come unannounced except for extreme discourtesy! If you want me in the same room with that… that…." Her curse shocked even Ham. "Then summon me to *your* rooms. I'm sure she's there often enough!"

A silence hung in the room. Mariel was panting slightly, her white face graven like stone, proud and defiant. A white hot anger burned through her and she cared no more for life. Thoughts of murder danced around the sides of her mind—murder of both the people who had dragged her away from her home, who had kept her as a slave in this mud-rubble fortress, who had chased away her true love, and had taken her son. Everything that had been light was gone; if she was to be left in darkness, then it would be on her terms, not theirs.

"Where is my son?" she refused to slink around in the darkness any longer.

"He was becoming weak," countered Nimrod angrily. "I have taken him to a place where he can learn to be a man, as he should."

"You mean a heartless murderer, don't you?" Mariel's face was white and cold. "Return him to me at once!"

"You may see him some day… providing that you can control yourself and submit to your husband as you should."

"Why?" she returned in a flash of anger. "I have learned from you, oh husband, and from your grandmother. I see how the two of you respect authority," she sneered. "Since you admire her so much, I'll offer you a bargain. I'll treat you with the same respect that she offers to her husband." Her voice trailed off in contempt and then she raised her hand to her mouth. "Oh, but then I would be spending every night in a different room, wouldn't I?"

Debseda's face was ashen with shock, but her body shook with rage. Nimrod stepped towards his wife. Raising his hand, he saw Ham tense and turn. Once again, he was reminded of an old bear, cornered and ready to sell its life as dearly as possible, and fully able to exact a terrible cost. He had heard of the ease with which Ham had handled Korac, and he knew that he could not take Korac that easily, even with surprise on his side. He lowered his hand, but let a sardonic grin light his face.

"Do as you will. You women are all alike… weak and given to fits of passion. My business here is brief. I was simply extending you a courtesy," he said, bowing mockingly to Mariel. "I have a journey to take, and in the course of it shall be seeing my son. Is there any message you wish to send?" But he misjudged Mariel's rage and her anger carried her away.

"Yes," she ground out. "Tell him to learn the bow and learn it well."

Nimrod was taken aback. "Of course, my dear," he sneered. "I was planning to instruct him in the use of weapons. After all, why shouldn't he learn from the best?"

"I hope he does," she replied with her own sneer. "That way, in God's good time, when he is looking down his arrow at your putrid heart, he will not miss!"

Nimrod's face blackened. He wheeled to leave, but as he did, he turned back to her, his face hot with wrath. "I'll be back tonight, *darling*, to exercise my rights as your husband."

"No you won't," replied Mariel calmly. "You forfeited those rights long ago, if indeed you ever had them. You have had every woman in Shinar." She was staring at Debseda, whose shocked expression showed that she continued to misjudge Noah's daughter. "Since you have such a wide selection," she turned back to Nimrod, "there's no need for you to be here. You have taken everything. Leave me in peace."

Nimrod drew himself up and hissed back, "I have a right to be here and I shall!"

"If you come tonight," replied Mariel calmly. "Only one of us will walk through this door alive in the morning. Think well. Is an hour of spite worth it?"

His face suffused with rage, Nimrod shoved his way past Ham and stormed down the hallway. Debseda glared at Mariel and opened her mouth.

"Leave now," rumbled Ham. "The day I hear that you have entered this room uninvited is the day that you will no longer enjoy the privacy of your own rooms. I will be there every night. And since I have no further interest in your body, I will treat it harshly."

She glared at him and followed Nimrod down the hallway, her three maids scurrying behind as if caught in her vortex. But Graemea turned and winked before they disappeared around the corner.

Ham turned and started to say something. "We have work to do," she interrupted. "We'll talk in the shop." Turning to Zerai, she said, "I have put you in danger. Leave my service this hour and you will save your life."

Zerai bristled. "I am sworn to your service by your God and my God," she returned. Mariel stood stunned. She had never known that Zerai was a worshiper of El Shaddai. "Only death will part us."

Mariel felt a softening. She embraced the younger woman. "You are my servant no longer, Zerai. You are my steadfast friend. I choose not to lose any more today.

At least return to your father's house for a week, until the wrath of those two subsides. Please."

Zerai shrugged. "As you please, my lady. Send for me at any hour."

Ham waited with her until the maid had gathered her belongings. Brother and sister walked her to the front gate and bid her farewell in the hearing of the guards. They then trudged to the workshop. Once inside, Ham said nothing. He threw charcoal into the forge and began to pump the bellows. Soon it was roaring—far too loud for any eavesdropper to hear their conversation.

He had a strange smile on his face. "You made me very proud today, my sister. Yet I fear that your life is now in great danger. The balance has shifted. We must both beware the machinations of those two. They will want us both dead—it is merely a matter of when would be most convenient."

"Then so be it," she returned. "They have taken my son. I can no longer live as his wife or as anything subservient to that...." Ham put his finger over her lips before she could repeat her earlier curse.

"Such words do not become you," he said gently. "Do not let them make you into their image."

"They already have," she whispered. "I stood up to them in rage, not in faith. It's the only thing that keeps me from falling apart."

Ham looked at her closely and shook his head. He sighed. "What are you going to do today?" He tried to resume a business-like voice.

"I'm working with metal today," she said, cryptically.

He shrugged and sighed again. "I'll be here if you need me," he replied. She nodded and moved over to the far worktable, where the exotic metals were kept.

Her threat to Nimrod had been very real and he had known it. What he did not know was that she had every intention of being the one to walk out alive in the morning. She might not be able to match his strength, but his overconfidence would be his downfall. He would not suspect that a mere woman could be every bit as ruthless as he, and she was determined to show him just how wrong he was. Blades were not the only way to kill. Her arm was weaker, so she must slay from a distance. That meant poison. She knew very little about toxins from plants and animals, but she had not spent six years with Ham for nothing! Other things in nature were dangerous to man, especially some of the more exotic metals.

She sat thinking. Quicksilver... too hard to work. She suddenly remembered the problems they had encountered two years ago, making brass. A new source of zinc had been found near the southeastern shores of the Black Sea. Despite its plentiful occurrence, it had proven too dangerous to use. The ore had been found intermixed with a malleable blue-white metal,[2] and attempts to work that alloy had killed two men. Ham had investigated and declared the ore unusable. His tests with animals had shown that it produced deadly vapors when heated. Even a slight exposure resulted in debilitating sickness, while a heavy dose killed every time. He had removed

---

[2] Cadmium

several samples from exposed veins to study further, but that work lay many years in the future. He simply had too much to do now. The metal was safe if kept cool, and most importantly, it was soft enough to shape easily with tools.

Mariel glanced up guiltily, but Ham was busy. She put her head in her arms, as if weeping silently, but thinking instead how to do it. She would have to shape the metal into something that would be heated in Nimrod's presence. As she thought about it, she recalled the appearance of the ore. It was silvery white....

Suddenly she smiled and was glad that her head was down. If Ham saw that feral look, he would have read her heart in an instant.

A lamp reflector.

She could carve a small plate—it was soft enough. Replacing a lamp reflector would be innocuous and it would look enough like polished tin to fool most. Ham would eventually know, but would he say anything? Probably not. It was a good plan, but it would take time. Better yet, it was a reason to keep living—maybe her only one right now. In a few months, she would be done. She would place the reflector on the oil lamp in Nimrod's inner room. No, she would replace the entire lamp. No one would think twice. She was constantly making useful things.

She smiled to herself as she imagined hanging it in place. She could see the events in her mind. It would hang there; a subtle trap for the mighty hunter. Unaware of the danger, Nimrod would light it. The flame would heat the reflector, slowly releasing the poison into the air. There were no windows. He was often up late at night, working on his schemes. Within weeks he would become sick and weak. She would tend him as a good wife should, making sure he slept with another of her special lamps. He would continue to breathe the fumes and would quickly die a horrible death, despite her best efforts. Debseda would be left without her right arm and Adan would be restored to the grieving widow.

In a moment of weakness she considered confiding in Ham. His help would be invaluable, but he wouldn't agree. He had once given in to Debseda to avoid bloodshed in his family. And he wouldn't understand. He was a better person than she. No, better to keep this to herself. They thought they had taken everything. But they were not as clever as they thought. She had her anger. Soon she would have vengeance.

She was now a murderer in her mind and—thanks to Nimrod and Debseda stealing her son—she had the will to make it real. In a way, it frightened her, but not enough to stop. Her husband's threats and torments had pushed her to a place where anything was justified. Had she the size and strength or Korac, Nimrod would not have left her room alive this morning.

But Nimrod had other weaknesses. Primary among them was his foolish idea that she was helpless. He had taken her future. He had taken her virtue. He had taken her son. Soon she would repay him for each of those indignities.

She hoped he suffered cruelly.

Chapter 37
SORCERY

Nimrod grew increasingly impatient as Debseda paced the floor, muttering to herself, and occasionally stopping and cursing with clenched fists. Her three maids had been dismissed and so the meeting was important, but he did not know why. Part of him wanted to pick up the maddening woman and throw her onto his bed, but this was not the time for pleasure. She was enraged, and he felt those echoes.

Finally she took notice of his presence and turned to him. Her ire was apparent in the flash of her eyes, but he thought he saw a tinge of fear too. Over the past three months they had put out several stories to circulate through the town's rumor mill. First, some of the men whispered that Ashkenaz was dead. When word had leaked that Korac suspected him as a spy, another rumor was released that Ham and Mariel knew he was a spy, feeding him false and useless information.

But word from the north was trickling back to Shinar. Ashkenaz was alive and well, last seen heading to Shem and Madrazi. Instead of confusing the issue, the earlier rumors made Nimrod and Debseda appear inept. Ham had openly laughed at his supposed role, and word of that had spread.

Mariel was also becoming more difficult to control. Since the removal of Adan, she had grown sullen and distant but had been heard to sneer at all the stories, declaring that whatever Ashkenaz was or had done, he had at least succeeded in revealing Nimrod and Korac as inept fools. Nimrod had been tempted to retaliate, but with Adan gone, there was little left but force to keep her in line, and that would incite a potentially lethal response from Ham. Worse, the members of the council were "interested"—politely hoping that Nimrod's loss of face would rebound to their advantage.

Debseda knew all this and didn't waste words. "This situation is serious," she began. "One of us should have sensed the presence of the traitor. And then he should never have escaped. Your "Legion" is a joke; you would do more with a dozen like Korac than with a hundred like them!"

"I know, my love," he answered softly, "but there is only one of Korac. He is valuable. But we also need a hundred fools to keep our enemies at bay."

"Did they keep our greatest enemy at bay?" sneered Debseda. "She sent one of her men right into our midst… that fool of a husband made it all possible."

"So what can we do?" asked a wary Nimrod. "We cannot challenge him openly. He's too useful. And even if he wasn't, the others would side with him as an excuse to be rid of me."

"There are two urgent needs now." Debseda was drawing back from her anger, allowing her cold, calculating mind to work unimpeded. "First we must cover these rumors with a better lie. We let him go… no," she smiled suddenly and Nimrod felt drawn to the raw evil it represented. "He ran because he fought Ham… over… over your slut of a wife!" Debseda's face shone in triumph. "It will give people a more salacious story to tell about Ashkenaz and it will weaken Ham. Our enemies take hope that Ham and Mariel defy us. We cannot allow that!"

Nimrod smiled as he lifted her into his embrace and twirled her around.

"Wonderful! Ham may be an old bear, but even a bear cannot stand the pricks of too many arrows. This one will sink deep. His own sister..." He chuckled cruelly. "I can't wait to see the look on my precious wife's face when I share my... concern for her virtue." He laughed again.

Debseda interrupted him. "There is more. We must determine whether or not Madrazi has been strengthened by her spy or not. We must know that we can still prevail." Debseda began pacing again, this time apprehensively. "And there is only one way to do that!" She straightened her back and tightened her lips. "Stoke the fire and prepare yourself," she ordered. "I *must* know."

Nimrod went cold inside but hastened to do as she asked. Debseda's propensity for sorcery had always enthralled him, and since coming into possession of his spear, his sensitivity to her power gave him greater insight. But it was dangerous. The power was dark and fierce, and if not carefully controlled it would consume them both. Yet her logic was unassailable; they could not consolidate power in Shinar if Shem and Madrazi could penetrate their security with impunity. At least it wasn't his blood that was required....

Debseda continued to pace, her face outwardly calm, but her body tense as she prepared herself for the coming ordeal. Nimrod added wood to the fire, set a lamp on the mantel, and passed his knife through the flames several times before laying it on a nearby table. He then retrieved the intricate wooden box from Debseda's rooms, noting the frightened looks on the faces of the three women huddled outside the door as they saw it in his hands.

Back in the room, Debseda had arranged herself before the fire. Her clothes were folded neatly on the bed and she faced away from the flames. Nimrod did not hesitate. He set the box before her and watched as she brought out two candles. He lit them for her and handed them back. She dripped wax on the floor and set the burning candles upright in their precise place. She then handed him the jar of blue powder. He sprinkled it on the blade of his knife and set it aside. Then he shook some out onto his spear. He began to feel it pulse as he held the blade over the fire. The powder began to burn, emitting a sickly odor that made his head swim. Debseda was chanting softly; Nimrod could not catch the words.

He did what he had to do, quickly and expertly. The tip of the smoking spear carved a small circle on her lower back, just above two others. She did not move, but began chanting with greater intensity. Blood flowed out onto the spear blade, and as it accumulated, Nimrod used it to draw a circle around her. Dip and draw; dip and draw. Finally the circle was complete and Nimrod set the spear on the floor before her. He knelt and shoved the blade of his knife into the fire. Debseda's head was beginning to roll and her eyes were white. He waited.

She mumbled and began to drool. Blood flowed from her nostrils and stained her lips before dripping onto her breasts. Suddenly her head stopped and she bowed it low. Nimrod steeled himself. On any other person, he would not have hesitated, but this was the flesh that he worshiped. Nonetheless, he drew his knife from the fire, held her long hair out of the way with his left hand, and used the hot knife to sear the bloody circle on her back. Debseda stiffened, but did not cry out.

The fire flared green and then the power was gone. Nimrod felt it go, and without hesitating, he gently lifted the naked women up and laid her face down on the bed. He hurried outside and motioned. Oshetipin and Celota jumped up from the floor and pushed past him. He let them go and looked at Graemea, raising one eyebrow.

She smiled tentatively and shrugged. "Three of us just get in the way."

He nodded and followed the other two more slowly. He trembled as he felt the strength leave his body. He would be weak for several days. If the power did this to him, he shuddered to think of the toll it took on his grandmother. But she was in good hands. They would tend her body and give her a sleeping draught. She would be in pain for several days, but she would bear it without complaint, as always. And by the time she had recovered, he would be ready for her. They would take their pleasure and only then would she disclose her knowledge.

When the night finally came, Nimrod was leaning back against his pillow, his arm sheltering Debseda's warm body as she lay beside him, her head on his shoulder. The light was back in her bright blue eyes, though now there was a shadow of new pain. He waited patiently; she would tell him in her own good time, just as she always did. His free hand stroked her flank, enjoying the contours of her soft skin. It had been a week since the ceremony, and she had remained in her rooms the entire time.

She sighed her pleasure at his touch and snuggled closer, reaching her hand across his chest. "It was hard this time, my love. I'm sorry that it took so long to recover."

"Was it worth it?"

"Yes. It was… but the news is not good."

"Tell me. Let us devise a counter together." To emphasize his words, he drew her closer, wrapping his strong arm around her lush body.

"She pursues a different course. I was a fool to underestimate her."

"We both did," he replied, soothingly, "Tell me plainly what you saw."

"We are seeing only Shinar… a great tower… a new civilization… all under our rule. She sees further and seeks to entice men to the far ends of the earth, far away from our dominion. People will go. Not all at first, but the lands are good and much wider than even the entire plain. Even now her men are marking lands for settlement—good lands, far from here, beyond our reach. She will lure many to her folly if she is not stopped. If Japheth settles the coastlands of the Great Sea, they would hem us in eventually."

"How will you stop it?"

"The key has always been that witch. Her people believe that their god speaks to her in visions, and so they follow. Without her, they would be like blind men; perhaps strong, but unable to direct their blows."

Nimrod stirred uncomfortably. "So you think the best course is to kill her? None of my men are eager to trek through enemy territory all the way to the mountain, face Shem's bow and Heth's spear, and be ambushed by every shepherd as they try to fight their way back south. After our victory over Noah, the northerners are alert to our movements, and they know that country."

Debseda smiled. "But what if the men are gone? Searching for these new lands? What if she is alone in her house?"

Nimrod's eyes narrowed. "That would be a different tale." But then a troubled look passed over his face. "Still… who would undertake to murder her? Men fear her power, even as they fear yours."

"As you said before, there is only one Korac. He has no soul. He has no fear. Let him bring her head to you; if he succeeds, I have seen that the earth will be yours."

Nimrod nodded slowly. "He would do it, but I would hate not having him here watching our other enemies."

"No one will openly oppose you now," she replied. "But Korac will need help to overwhelm her household, even with Shem gone."

Nimrod nodded. "Four should be enough. A small enough group to slide past their watchers and large enough to overwhelm the few men who are still there." He paused as he thought for a moment. "Korac's cousin Jalam brags about crossing arrows with Shem. He would go. We need not tell him that Shem will not be there."

Debseda interrupted. "If there's slaughter to be done, those perverse twins should be included. I'm sure they would go."

Nimrod grimaced. "Dishon and Dishan? They're madmen."

"But useful madmen," purred Debseda, her hand playing with the hair of his chest. "Every tool is useful," she sneered. "At least, that's what my husband swears!"

They both laughed at that, and further talk was put off until morning.

Mariel was grateful that Ham had been needed out at the tower. It was nothing new; as the bricks were laid and the levels began to rise, problems continually cropped up that were well beyond Canaan's limited capacity. Of course, any problem that could not be solved with empty words was beyond Canaan's capacity! It was difficult to keep bricks plumb and true, but as Ham had emphasized hundreds of times, it was essential in a building of this scale. A miniscule error on the lowest levels would multiply weakness up into the succeeding ones. But Canaan's incompetence was Mariel's blessing.

With Ham gone, she had the workshop to herself many days. Ham expected her to complete a day's work, but her skills had reached the point where it was easy to find bits of time for her own project. The hardest part was hiding it from Ham. The now-round block of metal spent its nights atop one of the rafters; she could just reach it standing on her toes on the highest work table. And the metal scraps were carefully gathered into a small bag sewn inside her tunic. Though small, they were distinctive in color and luster, and Ham would know them immediately. And they were easily disposed down the privy shafts.

Today was little different. There were many small tasks to complete, but she found some time for her own work in the cool of the evening before Ham returned. She was starting to shape the front of the reflector with careful strokes of a chisel. She could not afford to break it, so each movement of the tool took all her concentration. Each sliver brought her one step closer to Nimrod's death. Her rage had become cold, though no less dangerous; she was precise in every movement. She had time… it was all she had left.

After weeks of effort the reflector was finally taking shape. Soon it would be just another lamp—one of dozens—an innocuous piece of the background. Yet as soon as the lamp was lit and heat began its magic on the metal, this unassuming reflector would be the slayer of the world's greatest hunter. She grinned crookedly. Slayer of lions and bears defeated by a lamp! And a lamp made by a woman! He would never suspect. And if he did, it would be too late.

With a start she looked up. Time had flown by and Ham would be back soon. Hastily she scraped the metal shavings into the sack and tied it off under her tunic. Then she replaced the tools. Ham would see a tool out of place before he would notice ten naked women dancing around his forge. With practiced ease, she stepped up on her stool and then onto the worktable. Reaching up, she shoved the metal plate on top of the rafter. She had just stepped down and resumed her seat when Ham strode in the door. His face was flushed from the sun and his clothes were covered in dust, with stains of bitumen spotting his cloak.

Mariel composed her face and got up to offer him some water. Deceiving Ham hurt, but no sign of that pain was visible on her face. Why was it so easy to learn the skills of wickedness, but so hard to take the simplest steps towards good? That was a question for another day… a better day… a day when her hated husband would be dead. She would have her son and her freedom. As she walked back to her rooms, she saw in her mind the face of Ashkenaz. What would he think of her plot? She quickly turned her mind to other things—she knew what he would say and it made her very uncomfortable. Better to think about Ashkenaz as she lay by herself tonight in her cold, lonely bed.

Chapter 38
PLOTTING

9-1-1760

Nimrod sipped wine as he watched Debseda stare out the window. His rooms were near the top of the tower, where they could observe the growing city. Ever since her "seeing" she had been irritable and impatient... driving events forward. Korac was working as quickly as he could to train his team, but no effort seemed fast enough.

At first, had proposed going alone; he had been reticent to work with his cousin and the two brothers. But Nimrod had insisted on the team, not a lone assassin, and, as always, Korac had acceded to his wishes. Now he was pushing them as hard as he habitually pushed himself. Debseda had wanted to send them at once, but Korac pointed out that training together was essential for success, and Nimrod had tactfully convinced Debseda to let Korac run the operation.

The mission required the four to work as one; the men following Korac without question. Penetrating the northern hills without being detected would be no mean feat—any stray shepherd or hunter would spread the word and the mission would be over. So Korac had been working them hard. Tonight the others would finally be told the full extent of the plan. They would be given their target—the wife of Shem. All they knew now was that they would have to move undetected through enemy territory for weeks, kill someone, and then escape unseen.

A low knock on the door marked the men's presence. Debseda assumed a seat in her favorite chair. The transition was impressive; from a pacing, nervous woman, she instantly became a regal, serene queen, down to the goblet held in a very steady hand. She looked slightly bored. Nimrod was tempted to laugh, but that would spoil the illusion, so he contented himself with standing beside her, his hands holding his black spear in front of him.

Celota bowed, ushering in the men. Korac had been here often; he stood easily, watching the three others. They, on the other hand, had never been allowed into these private rooms and their attempts to keep their eyes on Nimrod while surreptitiously gawking at Debseda were almost humorous. Nimrod rapped the spear on the floor. Instantly their eyes were back on him; their arms stiffly by their sides.

He let the black power of the spear fill him. "You are here," he began, "for a very special purpose." He frowned suddenly. "Which of you has been talking about this mission?"

Their stunned and ashen faces told him all he needed to know. The secret was still safe. Korac's eyes glittered; he was familiar with Nimrod's tricks.

"No one knows," he grated. "My life on it."

"That's very good," purred Debseda. "Loyal to your men... are they to you?"

The twins looked like they wanted to speak, but Korac's instructions had been clear. Keep your mouth shut unless directly questioned. They remained still, glancing toward their captain.

"We will accomplish the task," he replied steadily.

Nimrod shifted and coughed lightly. These were his best men. There was no need to subject them to petty games. Debseda frowned, but said nothing. Nimrod drew himself up straight. The four men looked to him expectantly.

"If Korac is confident, then success is assured," he said with a smile. The men relaxed. "But the task before you is one worthy of all your skill. You must penetrate deep into the precincts of our enemies and strike at their heart. We face a formidable foe—having humbled Noah, we must now take on his sons."

"You mean for us to kill the other two elders?" blurted out Jalam.

"No," replied Nimrod. "Killing Japheth is of little use. He stays off to the west, and many of his sons are loyal to me. It would not do to repay their trust by killing their patriarch. No… Japheth is not the problem."

A strange light glowed in Jalam's eye. "Then we get to go after Shem?"

"Do you really wish to cross bows with him?" Debseda leaned forward.

"Of course, my lady," answered Jalam. "Is he not reputed to be the best? Would not the man who could put an arrow in his heart then be the best?"

"If you see him, you can shoot him," Debseda laughed. Korac shifted slightly. He knew that Shem was nowhere near his home, but if Nimrod wanted the others to know, he would tell them.

"But!" Debseda's face was now hard. "Killing him is not the goal. He is not the heart of the northern rebels. We all know who is!"

Nimrod was watching Korac's face carefully. Asking a man to kill was one thing; asking a man to kill a woman was something else entirely, and Korac had a history. But the iron mask didn't slip; he only cocked his head and stared at the small woman whose face was lit with an unholy light.

"We must slay his wife," she breathed.

Jalam shifted uncomfortably but felt a slight pressure in his back as Korac nudged him. He froze his face and stood still. But Debseda's attention was fixed on the twins. Their faces were alight with possibility and Dishon was nodding.

"Can you do it?" She asked. "If you do not, all our plans will ultimately fail. I have seen it in fire and blood. Only her death can bring us the victory we all desire."

Jalam and the twins looked down uncomfortably, but Korac looked at Nimrod, pulling himself stiffly erect. "I have a good team. We *will* get the job done."

Nimrod grinned. "That's all we needed to know. And now," he continued genially, "the best of my men deserve the best of my table. I know you've been training long and hard. Tonight we celebrate because the task is as good as done."

Debseda clapped her hands and her three maids appeared. "Prepare a feast for these brave men!"

Mariel glanced furtively around the empty workshop. Not six weeks after Ham had corrected one of Canaan's near-disastrous errors, he was back at the tower, fixing another. Despite its evil purpose, even Mariel had to admit that the growing tower was a grand sight. Under Ham's guidance she saw the dimensions with a different eye; as a craftsman, she recognized a grand harmony in the rising edifice. The dark red bricks would be covered with lime plaster, but even without the white façade, the building continued to excite all who watched it inch higher. Its base was as big as the new market and it had now reached sixty cubits above the plain, dominating the skyline of Shinar. Within a few years, it would attain its designed height of two hundred cubits, and with the sun shining off its white face, it would be visible for miles.

But Mariel cared little for the tower's beauty right now—she was hypnotized by that of the metal disk before her. After months of surreptitious efforts, it was nearly finished. All she had to do was polish the face and fix it to the lamp—one of a stack of three dozen on the far wall. Soon Nimrod would begin feeling the weakness and instability of his limbs. He would lose his keen mind. Breathing would become difficult. After a short time in bed he would breathe his last, and she would regain her son.

"But at what cost?" Ham's quiet voice interrupted her reverie; she jumped up, scattering the tools and turning quickly to face him, hoping against hope to hide the thing behind her. Ham stood silent, watching her carefully, waiting for the initial shock of his appearance to fade and the weight of his words to register in her mind.

She began breathing rapidly, her hands shaking. "Sit down," he said gently. She watched as he crossed the shop and returned with a small flask of brandy. She hated the taste but welcomed the heat as it burned down her throat and into her stomach.

"Sit down," he said again, and this time it was an order. She lowered her still shaking body back onto the stool and clasped her hands before her. He reached around her and picked up the silvery white plate. "How long have you been working on this?"

"A few months," she whispered. "I started when he… when they…."

"I know," he murmured. "There were days I was tempted to do the same." He held her eyes. "But you cannot. He could; she could…." He sighed.

"But you are *not* them, and I will not stand by and watch you destroy your soul."

"Have I not done that already?" she flung back. "Just ask our father or sisters. 'A cheap whore.' That's what Jael said. Why shouldn't a whore stoop to revenge? What soul has she got to lose?"

Ham's face grew dark. He seized her shoulders and shook her. "Never speak those words again! They aren't true. There is yet hope."

"How?" she flung back. "They chased away the only man I'll ever love and stole the only light in my life." Tears were flowing down her cheeks. "How can I live without my son, knowing that your wife is bent on corrupting him before he is old enough to know the difference?"

Ham took the rebuke without flinching and pulled the sobbing woman into his arms. "Answer me one thing," he whispered. "If Adan is such a precious child, how can your marriage to Nimrod be so completely black?"

Mariel stiffened, but Ham was relentless. "God gave you a beautiful child out of the worst thing in your life. If something that good can come from something that evil, how can there not be hope? How many days did the sight of Adan keep us both sane after Ashkenaz left. He was a joy to us both. We will get him back. I swear it. But until we can, you must believe that God will protect him. Murder is no answer."

Mariel shuddered. "I never thought...."

"You're no murderer, my sister, and you'll become one over my dead body. So put this back with the other samples and turn away from your hate. It makes you cold, like Debseda. Come back to me. Hope in God and leave vengeance to Him."

A strange feeling entered Mariel's soul. It was as if she suddenly woke up and saw what she was doing. Repulsed by what she saw, she was terrified in a way that far exceeded anything Nimrod had been able to do. How could she be worthy of Adan if she took the life of his father? She pushed the cold rage away, and in its place she felt a soft, faint warming in her heart. Ham was right. If there was a God in Heaven, then He would care for Adan, just as He would condemn her if she took evil into her own hand.

Tears still flowed, but now they were cleansing, washing away the cold hatred that had governed the past months.

"I feel so weak," she whispered. "I don't know how to go on."

"One day at a time, little sister," Ham whispered. "One day at a time. The day will come when we will have an opportunity to rescue Adan and flee this evil city. Maybe north; maybe south." He hesitated. Secrets shared quickly became market gossip, but Mariel needed all the hope he could supply. "I have spoken with Mizraim," he said softly. "We will leave at the first chance. I agreed to go only after he promised protection for you and for Adan. I need not tell you that if you breathe a word we are all dead!"

Mariel nodded, and managed a smile. "I'll keep it hidden deep. May the day come soon." She looked up at Ham and hugged him suddenly. "Thank you! From the day I arrived, every good thing in my life has come from you. Once again I owe you everything. You are all that a big brother should be, and I'm proud to claim you as mine. One day Father will hear and be proud too."

Ham's crooked smile was at odds with his shaking head. "Go in peace. Spend your evening praying for your son. Hope in God and let your heart be at rest."

Mariel nodded and wiped her eyes. Wordlessly she handed Ham the reflector. Ham said nothing, but he broke it in pieces, put them in a drawer with the other samples and shut the door. She grimaced but let her face relax into a smile before she left for her rooms. She lived in the midst of evil, but that did not mean she had to embrace it. Her head was high and the light back in her eyes as she strode across the courtyard, up the stairs, and down the hall. She swore to herself that she would not risk her soul like that ever again.

Chapter 39
VALLEY OF DEATH

10-6-1760

Korac peered around the base of the boulder at the meadow in the small valley below. Sheep were beginning to feed on the dew-soaked grass, and the first hints of the sun were sending the promise of a pleasant day. Winter was late this year, and the days seemed more like those of late summer.

But Korac was not like other men; his only thought of the weather was a professional assessment of whether it helped or hindered the day's work. In this case it helped; the sun was behind him, making detection by the shepherds in the valley impossible. With the light breeze in his face, it was unlikely the dogs would spot them either. He saw no beauty in the scene below—that capacity had been erased a decade before. All that mattered were the positions of the two shepherds and their dogs relative to his men.

He blinked as a stray shaft of sunlight flickered off a rock just down the slope. Without warning his head began to throb. He knew what was coming and ground his teeth to stop its unwelcome return, but his clenched jaw could not shut out the vivid images his mind threw before his eyes. A far off corner of his mind registered surprise—it had been many weeks since the last one.

He saw another valley... rougher and bare of vegetation. Boulders littered its rocky floor and steep cliffs capped with ice reared up behind it. Narrow... but there were still many places for a wounded bear to hide—even one this large. A foreboding struck him; the place stunk of death. Yet Nimrod was even now clambering over the downwind ridge to the right. Soon he would be in position to see the valley floor; his great bow ready to slay the great beast.

That strategy had worked many times, though Nimrod had left it close once... the lion falling literally at Korac's feet with Nimrod's arrow in its throat. They had laughed, as men will after a crisis, and the tale enhanced Nimrod's reputation as a hunter.

But his was different. She was here now. He glanced to his side. She looked up at him, her beautiful green eyes as bright as the sun off her chestnut hair, smiling with a confidence that seemed misplaced. Yet that smile lit his heart and he could not help but smile back. She took his hand. "Nimrod will protect us. I want to see you finish this."

How could he refuse? He knew it was foolhardy, but his faith in his friend... no, his brother now... was absolute. So in spite of every instinct, he started forward and let her follow, a few paces behind, walking silently as he had shown her....

A dog barked below. The scene faded, leaving only a sweat-soaked forehead and the taste of bile in the back of his throat. He swallowed harshly; it would not do to empty his stomach in front of his men. He blinked again and looked around. Jalam was looking at him with a curious expression, but he made no move except to raise an eyebrow in question.

Korac scanned the scene before him once more, no expression breaking the stone-like mask of his face. All was as it should be... no more, no less. He tensed himself for action and then raised his right hand. In answer to his signal, he heard the whiz of the three arrows, the sharp yelps of the two dogs, and the choking rattle of one of the shepherds as an arrow suddenly transfixed his throat. By then Korac was already bounding down the hill, reaching the bottom before the dead man fell, and hurtling across the grass towards the campfire. The other shepherd stood frozen, staring at his comrade's crumpling body. Shock was only beginning to register on his face when Korac leaped, crushing him to the ground, a knife at his throat.

Anger and shock flitted across his eyes before fear overcame them. The shepherd felt the cold iron blade against his neck, and the implacable dark eyes staring down at him were empty. The rest of the face was wrapped in black cloth, but before he could take in anything else, he felt the blade at his throat move, followed by a warm trickle down his neck that he belatedly knew was his own blood.

"Where is *The Woman*?" The voice under the black cloth sounded like it came out of a deep pit. It was not angry, not loud, not even harsh—it was just there, as unforgiving as the harsh, rocky wilderness. No threat was uttered, but the promise of pain was clear enough from the blade breaking his skin.

"I d-d-d-don't know," he whispered. "W-w-we were sent h-h-here last week."

"Then you are of no use to me," he heard as he felt more pressure on his throat and then the gush of blood... his blood... and no more.

"Get anything from that one?" Jalam nodded at the still-bleeding body as he retrieved his arrow from the other. Iron heads were valuable, and he would not leave one to rust in the body of some insignificant herdsman. Carefully he wiped the blade clean with the dead man's tunic. It was typical; Jalam was meticulous with his weapons. It provided focus to his great dream—for years he had heard that *The Woman's* husband was the best archer alive, and for years he had longed to prove otherwise. He dreamed of the time when they would face each other across a broad field, arrows to the ear, and may the best man win. For years he had devoted himself to that dream—hours of practice every day—and he hoped it would be fulfilled tomorrow.

Korac knew that it would not—Debseda had been quite clear on that point. Korac hated lying to his cousin, but Jalam was too useful to leave behind. He would be disappointed, but there would be another time. Nimrod and Debseda might shrug it off, but Korac knew that if they succeeded, Shem would hunt them implacably to the end of their days.

"He knew nothing," Korac grunted, as he wiped his knife clean on the tunic of his victim. "We'll have to scout in close ourselves tonight, and then finish it at dawn."

Jalam nodded. More skilled than most, he lacked Korac's utter ruthlessness, and was happy to take orders. And he was loyal… they were cousins, after all.

"Get the others. We eat and move."

"That'll please Dishon and Dishan," laughed Jalam. I wager they'll kill every animal in the valley just to get one to eat." He chuckled and pointed. "See. They're starting already." Then he looked back at the fire. "What about them?" Jalam waved at the shepherds. "You want me to move them?"

"We need something to sit on," grated Korac.

Jalam nodded warily. He was as close to his commander as anyone, but would be the first to admit that Korac was closed to all. He knew more of the story than most… except Nimrod, of course… but his cousin remained a mystery.

Why had Korac lost his heart? Others suffered loss and recovered… regained happiness. All he knew was that years ago, Korac had gone hunting with Nimrod. His wife had gone too, but only Korac and Nimrod returned. The one time Jalam had dared to ask what had happened, Korac had beaten him senseless. Jalam fancied that even Nimrod avoided that subject, and he idly wondered if Nimrod could meet those dark, empty eyes.

He turned to hide his face as he went to retrieve the other two arrows, happy for anything that would let him hide the question in his eyes before Korac saw it and killed him.

"Tell me we aren't going to swim this one," Heth growled. Large rivers seemed as regular as the sunrise in this land; though they would be useful arteries to move goods south to the Black Sea, they were all tired of crossing them—especially Heth.

"Why don't we just go back," suggested Jobaath? "I'll be the first to admit that this land is ideal for farming or grazing. Thousands of people could inhabit this land and never see each other. The days are long and warm, there's no forest to clear, and the soil is rich. If these rivers empty into the Black Sea, we have a way to take goods from the rich plains here all the way to the Great Sea." He sighed. "But I've never been so bored in my life!"

"You're always bored," argued Shem. "And we're not here for your entertainment. I'm not going to waste four months of travel just to turn back now. We came to explore the land—all the land—to map it and blaze trails for future settlers." His dark eyes bored into Jobaath's. "You're welcome to go back now if you want… alone."

Jobaath smiled wanly and shook his head. None of them would abandon this quest. It was the adventure of a lifetime. Heth noted that Shelah couldn't hide his look of satisfaction. If possible, he was more eager than Shem to continue and Heth knew why. He looked at the river again and frowned, but knew he would go with his friend to the ends of the earth.

"Very well," Jobaath interjected. "I'm looking on the bright side. Eventually, we'll walk around the whole world and end up back here again. Then maybe we can go home."

The others chuckled as they began to prepare for the crossing. Ashkenaz and Jobaath unloaded the two skin bladders from the mule's pack. It didn't like crossing rivers either, but the two bladders would keep it afloat, and it had proven to be a better swimmer than expected. Shem and Shelah helped Heth secure all their packs to a raft, hastily lashed together from a few pieces of driftwood.

"Very well," said Shem when they were done. "You two go ahead with the mule." Ashkenaz and Jobaath nodded. "We'll swim the raft over. First one across light a fire and we'll camp there tonight.

It wasn't that hard, Heth tried to convince himself. The water was chilly, but the day was warm. But his heart beat a little faster as he surveyed the far bank. This was the biggest river they had encountered, and he knew he was the poorest swimmer of the group. But he was also the strongest... except for Shem, he reminded himself... and his legs could kick for hours as long as he had a solid raft to support his body and keep his face out of the water. But looking out across the rolling expanse, he saw some choppy waves; the current in this one would be worse than the last. But even if they were carried a day's walk downstream, it was only a day, and anyone coming to live in this country would want to know how fast the river flowed.

Keeping the grumbling and fear both locked inside, he walked resolutely into the river with the others, pushing the raft into the current with a willing arm. At least Shem and Shelah were considerate. They took positions on either side of him, ready to help if he experienced any problems. As one man, the three began to kick and the raft moved swiftly into the river. Upstream, he saw the other two with the mule. With the air bladders to support it, it swam better than the men, and forged ahead of the raft, staying somewhat upstream. As they crossed the midpoint of the channel, Heth looked out across the remaining water. The raft was drifting south at a good pace now, and the three of them would need to hike back upstream most of the afternoon; at least Jobaath and Ash would have a fire going. And maybe Ash would even have a meal cooking. Game was plentiful—everything from hares and squirrels to ungainly elk and hairy elephants.

Despite the younger men's enthusiasm, Shem had the good sense to avoid the larger creatures. With such abundance, there was no need to risk injury or to waste meat. They couldn't carry much. But their strategy would change soon. In a few months, they would find a winter camp and what they killed would stay frozen for weeks. Heth wondered if the hairy elephants tasted good. They would certainly be fun to stalk and to hunt... and probably safer than the ill-tempered oxen that roamed these plains in tight herds.

A rogue wave splashed his thoughts away. They were only halfway across the river and the cold was starting to sap his energy. Gritting his teeth, he kicked harder. Already the mule, Jobaath, and Ash were far upstream, and nearly two thirds of the way across. Well, he decided. It was worth it. He hated the mule with a passion and a half day away from it was nearly worth the discomfort. How could a man feel so cold when every muscle in his legs was on fire?

He sighed and kicked... and kicked... and kicked.

Chapter 40
MASSACRE

10-8-1760

Eight eyes glinted in the waning moonlight as the four assassins huddled in a nest of rocks on a low hill overlooking the southeast corner of the white stone house. Darker shadows beyond the house showed the positions of its barns and outbuildings, and they could even see the dim outlines of the near fields. The noise of the river drifted up through the trees of the meadow below the house.

The rocks were cold in the pre-dawn chill, but the men ignored them and listened carefully to Korac's whispered instructions. He had circled east and brought them upon a servant hurrying along the road to the Lake of the Islands. He had babbled for nearly a quarter of an hour before they finally discarded his broken body.

Korac had watched Jalam carefully, as he tried to hide his disappointment. If the boy was right, Shem and his young friends were gone. His dream would not be fulfilled today. There would be no challenge worthy of his talents. Korac showed no surprise—he had already known—but no one noticed… Korac rarely showed surprise at anything. But it helped to be sure. This was what he had envisioned all along. No distractions. Easy in. Easy out. Job done.

This one was important to Nimrod and Debseda both, and Korac was not foolish enough to think that they would countenance failure. And, unlike Jalam, he had seen Shem with a bow, many years ago, and he had no wish to face that uncanny skill. And then there was Heth…. A small shudder rippled across his shoulders at the memory of their last meeting. Heth was like a bear… strong, cunning, fearless to the point of recklessness, and deceptively fast. Korac was good, but he knew that only fate or luck would give him victory over Canaan's son.

He pulled his thoughts back to the house. "We sweep down at first light and hit this corner. Ignore anyone who isn't a threat. Encircle the house. Dishon, Dishan—you enter through the front and kill all within. Jalam and I will stay at the northwest corner, taking any who escape through that door, and any workers who feel like heroes."

He paused, cocked an eyebrow, and watched the men nod. The twins' eyes gleamed with anticipation. "Can we have *The Woman* before we kill her?" asked Dishon, daring greatly.

Korac stared back at him and frowned. His past pushed hard against the walls in his mind, but he beat it back. The twins were sick, unable to be satiated by any amount of blood and pain, but he knew that they had been sent for that very reason. So he kept his voice even as he unclenched his hands. "Just bring me her head in a sack," he whispered. "He wants proof. Find some salt and fill the sack so it will last long enough for him to see."

Dishan licked his lips, his mind clearly not on the matter at hand. Korac's large hand struck like a cobra, pulling the smaller man across a rock until they were eye to eye. "Do... you... understand?" The flat menace in that voice burst Dishan's sick fantasy. He nodded, his eyes focused and afraid.

"You mess this up and the black spear will take your soul when we return," he grated. "If I leave anything for it to take. No woman's worth that. You can have what you want after you take care of business. After!"

The other men carefully looked away, readying their weapons and tightening their boots. They were hunters; the prey was in sight and the kill was theirs.

Madrazi woke with a start. A hooded figure loomed over her in the predawn darkness and she inhaled sharply, ready to scream. Similar figures had haunted her dreams and fear gripped her. A hand touched her shoulder again.

"Wake up, Madrazi!" whispered the figure, and the shadows shrank as she heard the familiar voice of Jael.

"Don't scare me like that," she whispered.

"How would you prefer that I scare you?" came the sarcastic reply.

"I thought you were off hunting this morning," Madrazi murmured. She had no strength to address Jael's manners right now. "Let me go back to sleep."

"I was on my way, but Enoch sent me back. Your mare is having a hard labor, and he's concerned. Hurry, now, and maybe I'll still have time to make a kill."

Madrazi sighed, but rose and began throwing on some clothes. Jael handed her a pair of fur-lined boots and her heaviest cloak. "There's a chill," she explained. Madrazi saw she was dressed heavily too, leather leggings and a woolen poncho. She picked up her bow and gestured sharply. "Let's be gone!"

Madrazi slipped on the second boot and turned to pick up her hairbrush. "I won't be a minute," she said softly, but Jael grabbed her arm and began pulling her towards the door. "Do it on the way, if you think your horse cares about your appearance!"

It took all of Madrazi's will not to snap back, but she pulled away from the younger woman's grasp. Jael might be younger than Shelah, but she was still unintimidated by Madrazi. It was refreshing in a way—so many treated her with fear and awe, but Jael went too far in the other direction, pushing her treatment of her older sister far past the bounds of discourtesy. She was different with Shem—he was her teacher. But she still gave him no due as Noah's heir, caring little for convention. Madrazi had often rebuked her for her lack of respect, but she was too tired this morning. She contented herself with a hard look. The girl had been difficult when she came to them, but her hard-won prowess made her nearly impossible now.

Madrazi didn't want to start her morning with a spat; so she simply began to brush her hair, ignoring Jael's impatient looks while walking to the kitchen. There she made Jael wait while she quickly brewed tea—braiding her hair while she waited for the precious leaves to steep. "Enoch will be cold and tired," she explained as she filled a large horn. "Besides, I'm not taking my good brush to a horse barn, and that's final!"

Jael paced the room like a caged cat but kept her mouth shut. She didn't have long to wait; Madrazi soon was ready and the two women were on the way to the barn, a hundred paces northwest of the house. The morning was cold. Harvest was upon them, and winter would follow hard on its heels. The moon had disappeared, but the darkness offered no impediment to either woman. Jael could see like a cat in the dark and Madrazi knew every step between her house and barn. Neither spoke. The barn loomed up and they entered the small side door. A small lantern shone from the birthing stall in the back corner.

"Enoch," Madrazi called as they neared the light. A man grunted from the shadows behind the mare. "I have some tea. Take a moment, drink, and tell me her problem."

A slight man with light hair, Enoch appeared, washing his arms in a bucket and wiping them dry with a rough rag before accepting the horn. He took a sip and smiled. "The little one was crooked. When I straightened him out, the cord caught. I think I've slipped it off, but the mother's restless. If you can keep her quiet, I can bring out the colt."

For the next quarter hour, the attention of all three was dedicated to the task at hand. Talking softly to calm the mare, Madrazi kept a firm grip on her bridle, holding her soft eyes with her own. Jael leaned against the wall—her thoughts on her morning hunt—birthing foals was none of her business, but she was curious enough to delay. Enoch was skilled, and some day she might have a mare in similar circumstances. But observing was all she would do; no thought of helping crossed her mind.

Enoch worked quickly and soon he laid the new colt on the straw. Madrazi stepped out of the stall, taking a sip of the warm tea. She nearly spilled a mouthful when Jael gripped her arm.

"What's that?" the young woman hissed sharply.

"I didn't…" began Enoch.

"Quiet," whispered Jael. "Keep the horse quiet, too." Enoch grumbled softly but moved back into the stall.

Jael extinguished the lamp and slid over to the door, gesturing Madrazi to follow. In the dim early morning, they saw two shadows appear around the corners of the house and stop outside the kitchen. Madrazi froze and began trembling… they were the dark shadows she had seen in her dreams. Jael pulled her face around to her own. "Wait" was all she whispered, and Madrazi waited.

Almost instantly two other shadows leaped up onto the porch and burst through the door. A scream inside the house was cut short. Others rang out, only to be extinguished one by one.

Jael turned and gripped Madrazi's arms. "They're here for you! We need to get out now!"

It had been many years since Madrazi had faced so immediate a threat, but the familiar feelings returned with Jael's words: the raw taste in the back of her mouth, the feel of her blood pounding through her body, the sharpening of her senses. "There's a small waste hatch in the back of the barn," she whispered."

Enoch joined the women and took in the scene with a glance. "You must leave now, lady," he whispered. "They'll be here as soon as they search the house. I'll try to steal some time when they reach the barn." Turning to Jael, he simply said, "Her husband has trained you well. Repay his trust."

Madrazi let Jael drag her back into the barn, but then her mind began to operate once more as she pushed the fear back.

"Stop," she hissed. "If they're Nimrod's men, they won't stop. Wherever we go, they will follow and it will be a long trip. Take what we may need."

Jael was already shouldering her pack and lifting her bow. Madrazi glanced around. She seized two old blankets and a coil of rope. A small ax was sticking out of a block of wood and she tossed that onto the blankets, followed quickly by an empty waterskin. Jael was pulling her on as she bundled the blankets in her arms. As Jael quietly opened the hatch and looked out, Madrazi ran back and slung the horn of tea over her shoulder. A box by the stable had a few old iron nails rusting on top of it, and Madrazi thrust them in a pocket and hurried after Jael. If needs must, they could be shaped into arrowheads.

The younger girl was already outside. The hatchway opened over a low waste dump next to a corral. Manure and straw were piled to one side. The corral's wooden rail fence joined another that surrounded the garden. Madrazi kept hold of her bundle and jumped down, aiming for straw. She landed lightly and Jael seized her arm.

"Walk on the lower rail of the fence until you get to the head of the gully," whispered Jael, "Hide there until I come." Madrazi pulled herself up, hanging uncomfortably over the upper rail, trying to balance her bundle. She started sliding along as she watched Jael shift straw and dung to cover signs of their exit. Voices could now be heard coming from the workers' quarters, and in the gray half-light of dawn, Madrazi saw young Zeb running towards the house. He halted, an arrow suddenly materializing from his chest.

Fighting tears and stifling a scream, Madrazi shuffled clumsily along, barely felt the splinters pushing into her hands. She started down the second fence towards the gully, expecting any moment to see more shadows appear, but all she saw was Jael, bent over at the back of the barn. A wisp of smoke rose, and then Jael was hurrying along the fence, moving quickly.

Madrazi dropped into the gully, wanting to bury her face and weep, but instead she rearranged her bundle into a loose roll wrapped with rope, leaving a loop for her shoulder. Jael dropped beside her and began pulling her back along the gully.

"We don't have long," she said softly. "We need to find a place to hide, now. These men are good—I saw four but there might be a dozen—behind us or ahead." Madrazi fought down panic at the thought of other killers waiting in the trees at the end of the gully. Jael saw her fear and stopped. "Take a breath and think. Where would you go if you had to hide from Shem?"

Madrazi looked back. She barely heard Jael. Smoke was billowing from the barn. "Why did you do that?" she accused.

Jael's face hardened. "We needed a distraction. If we're fortunate, they might think you're still inside. Enoch had an old bow; he was going to defend the door."

"Why would they be that foolish?" asked Madrazi. "Especially if they are as good as we both fear."

"Because Enoch was going to rush the horses out in the smoke and hope they thought you were trying to ride away. If they don't find you with the horses, the barn is the next place to look. You were scared, knocked over a lantern, the horses stampeded, and you were left to burn. I hope they're that stupid."

"You would burn Enoch alive?" Madrazi's eyes blazed.

Jael didn't back up an inch. "Enoch will be dead before the fire reaches him!"

Madrazi's retort was interrupted by shouts ringing on the other side of the barn. The thunder of hooves followed as the terrified stock escaped the fire and ran for the river. Then an angry shout rose above the others. "Enoch got one," whispered Jael. "I hope he was smart enough not to kill him…. Come on." Madrazi crouched over and followed.

"Why not kill him?" she asked sarcastically. "I thought *you* of all people would take pleasure from that."

Jael frowned. "We saw four. Enoch kills one and we have three after us. He wounds one and maybe we have two after us.

"It only takes one that's good enough." Madrazi replied. Jael frowned again. "If he's better than me," she snarled. "Maybe the Creator will smile on me and it will be Korac." Madrazi shivered at the raw hate that accompanied that name.

"Make for the river," she whispered. "If we can get across, there's a cave near the ford."

"These men are good. They'll find it," hissed Jael.

"They won't find the back door," retorted Madrazi. "It took Shem fifty years."

Jael suddenly grinned. "Lead on, then."

They heard nothing as they continued towards the river. The gully floor began to seep water, but by then the trees were near and the meadow grass was high. Following Jael on hands and knees, Madrazi had to fight the urge to look back and see the destruction being wrought on her home. Jael urged her forward, but both women froze when they heard the grass rustle behind them. "Down," breathed Jael, and both women froze. Madrazi turned her head and saw a knife materialize in Jael's hand.

The grass rustled nearby and Jael tensed. But it was a canine face that pushed through the grass. Sirus—still a young dog—was a descendent of Sorga, her canine companion aboard the ark. Memories brought tears; she longed for Sorga. Sirus was usually playful but was now subdued, as if he sensed the danger. He stood beside Madrazi, the fur on his back ruffled and his ears back, looking towards the house. Jael slid her knife quickly away and sighed softly. Madrazi cocked her head and lifted an eyebrow, then started off again for the river, the dog padding quietly beside her.

INTERLUDE 4

5-22-2162

Lud loosened his grip ever so slightly, and let the shaft slip down a span in his hands while pretending a thrust. His opponent stepped back and raised his shield, but the spear was already scything in a circle, sliding forward through his hand as it swung, slowing it as it impacted the man's unprotected shoulder. It instantly reversed, but halted, this time stopping a span from the man's surprised face. He dropped his shield and began massaging his shoulder, a rueful grin breaking through the shock and pain. "You did it to me again," he complained. Lud merely nodded.

Far better than any of the palace guard, he had been careful to show only a part of his skill. He walked a fine line between proving his value and insulting their pride. But over time his skill and stolid compliance began to earn him the trust of some of the better men, though it took all of his iron self-control to play his role he had been assigned. But he made very sure that any of Asak's troops always carried heavy bruises away from the practice field.

Fury still filled him when he remembered Asak's threats. When confronted with the story of the Hittite troop, he thought he was dead. The Hatti messenger system had proven its speed once more.

But the general had only laughed. "Seven less to deal with," he smirked. "But what do we do with you?" He had looked thoughtfully at his captain. "Kill him or use him?" The captain had shrugged. "If the story is true, he has tricks he can teach us. If he knows Hatti tactics, he could teach us more. We can always kill him... later." He had slid his sword under Lud's chin. "Cooperate and the woman lives. Try anything and you'll watch her die very slowly. I promise you that!"

And so he had assumed a strange career. When not teaching the younger men, he was assigned the lowest of jobs—guarding the small door that led from the kitchen to the dump outside the wall. It was a punishment detail, but Lud never complained.

They intended it to hurt him... letting him see Lydia's abject slavery, and it did. How many ways had he thought to kill Asak as he was forced to watch her suffer? But, in the end, it only mattered to him that she still lived. There was always hope. But he swore to himself that the day he did not see her that he would kill Asak no matter what the cost. He had not yet been able to speak to her—she was always accompanied by one of the viragos that ran the kitchen—but he tried to encourage her silently the rare times that he could catch her eye. He had been terrified when he first saw her. The vibrant, self-assured woman he had known for years was gone. In her place was a defeated, dirty shell with empty eyes. It was as if her soul had fled while her body continued to go through the motions of life. But as the months passed, she grew no worse, and Lud began to see some small signs of life. Her face remained dull, but she began keeping herself clean. It was something.

But time had slipped past, and she was going downhill once more. She looked unhealthy and wan, and as hard as he tried to find an escape, no plan survived the harsh realities. It was nearly time to kill Asak and be done with it; having seen her the day before, he knew she would not last another winter.

He had hoped her life would improve, giving him time to make himself valuable enough to someone powerful enough to free her. And his feelings were mixed. Most of the men would have made good comrades. Asak was an anomaly, but unfortunately, he was powerful, and his spies were everywhere.

Warriors were men who faced death at the call of their king. Such men had a code and Lud understood it, just as he understood them. Even given the lowliest of tasks, he had their respect—none of them could brag of taking an entire troop of Hatti. The veterans who had killed in battle treated him better than the others—they understood him in a way that idiots like Asak never could.

Somehow, Lydia had to survive. They wouldn't deliberately kill her—even a slave was useful. But each week, she seemed to shrink further into herself, her eyes dull and listless. He knew she was beaten regularly by the woman who ran the kitchen, yet even when she came to the gate with bruised face, walking stiffly upright to keep the coarse clothes from rubbing her back, he could see no fire in her eyes. That frightened him more than the abuse. He had to find a way soon, but for now there was none. He was watched, day and night, and even if he could elude his watchers, he was in the middle of the capital city of the Philistines—an alien with no way out.

He wiped the sweat from his face. This one would never make much of a fighter but he was big and strong, and would serve to stiffen a shield wall. Another man stepped up. He was old—older than Lud—and did not look familiar, but something in his carriage and eye warned Lud that he was not a man to be trifled with.

"You teach well," he said quietly. "Could I practice with you?"

Lud nodded. He had no choice. "Spear or sword?" he asked.

"Sword," replied the other. "I'm too old to be dancing around with a spear." But instead of taking up a wooden practice sword, he drew his blade. "I think we're both good enough to have a bout without killing each other."

Lud simply nodded and tossed the spear aside, drawing his own sword. He had a feeling that he wouldn't be holding back with this one. Probably some old noble, yearning to relive his days of glory.

Or… maybe not.

His questions vanished immediately. The old man came in hard and fast, as only a confident warrior will, pressing Lud to the defense. His blade flashed in an intricate dance and for a moment Lud forgot to watch his eyes, and a thrust suddenly drove over his shield, halting less than a span from his throat.

"You can do better than that," chuckled the old man, and Lud was suddenly angry with himself. He searched his mind for a moment for his best tricks and found one that might work. Focusing his mind, he held his shield a fingerwidth too far to the left and slid in sideways, as he had learned from his old Hatti weaponmaster. The old man hesitated, sensing a trap, but unsure of himself for the first time. Lud slowed for a moment, letting him recover. It was too good an opening; the old man sidestepped abruptly, his sword flashing just past the edge of Lud's shield towards his exposed chest. Except Lud was no longer there. As soon as his opponent began to move, Lud dropped to one knee, drew his shield in close to deflect the blow, and slammed the point of his blade into the dirt between the man's feet.

The old man stepped back, smiling. "I've heard of that one, but never seen it," he admitted. "Hatti Royal Guard?" he asked, in a voice that no one else could hear.

"A lifetime ago," admitted Lud.

"Well it seems you have found a new life." He paused for a moment, thoughts flashing across his face. "You're the Hittite that Asak captured." He chuckled again. "I'm surprised he took you. He can't find his armor without his bearer," he sneered. Lud went still. There were not many men who would speak ill of Asak, even if it were the truth, and this man did not look the least worried.

His question must have flashed across his face, for the older man sheathed his sword and held out his hand. "I am the Phicol," he said. "Unfortunately, I've been in Egypt for some time. And you are...?"

"Lud."

"That's a simple name for such a complicated man." The Phicol chuckled again. "Well, Lud, I'm sorry that I wasn't back sooner. I'd like to practice with you regularly. There are too few here that can give me a good workout, much less show me anything new. Fourth day, fourth hour, every week?"

Lud nodded. The old man was polite, but both knew it was an order.

"Fine! I'll see you then." He walked off, erect and proud, and Lud felt the eyes of the others on him. He didn't know whether to smile or frown. They would treat him better now, but they would watch him more closely too. Powerful friends meant powerful enemies, and Lud had a soldier's appreciation for how easily the common soldiers got left holding the blame for their betters. But for the first time, he had made contact with someone powerful enough to free them from Asak. It was something, and he hoped he could quickly cultivate a friendship. But time was not on his side.

He sighed and picked up his spear. "Next."

Chapter 41
ESCAPE COMMITTEE

10-8-1760

Shivering from the knee-deep water at the ford, the women glanced nervously behind them. Anyone near enough to the river would have seen them crossing, and their wet footprints would remain on the rocky path at the foot of the mountain for several hours. But they were now flitting between jumbled boulders, and the shadows of the mountain's rough surface provided further concealment.

Both women remained tense until Madrazi led Jael down into one of the caves that littered the foot of the mountain. With one hand on Madrazi's shoulder, she followed the older woman some distance into the pitch black before they stopped. "We left some torches somewhere nearby," whispered Madrazi. Although whispering was probably unnecessary in the bowels of the earth, Jael felt the oppression and whispered back, "I have a striker if you find one."

Soon they were walking in a small pool of yellow light that penetrated a few cubits of the surrounding cloak of heavy darkness. "Here we are," said Madrazi at last. They had followed a solid wall to their left and Jael could see nothing.

"Give me a moment. It's been a few years since I was last here, and it's hard to see, even when you know what you're looking for."

Eventually, the older woman began walking slowly along, running her hand lightly over the dark rock until she found the overlapping narrow fold—nearly invisible even when they stood before it—that marked some trick of the mountain's formation. She heard Jael sigh with relief as they entered the low tunnel that led to an antechamber. But that relief was short lived; as they emerged from the other end of the tunnel Madrazi felt the younger woman tense. Jael was frowning at the sunlight filtering through a hole at the opposite end of the small cavern. Before she could erupt, Madrazi put a hand on her arm. "They won't find it. Trust me. Sit and rest."

Jael eyed the opening suspiciously, then shrugged and sat. "We don't have time to wait here," she argued. "We need to keep moving, gain distance while they're still busy." Neither woman wanted to think about what was presently keeping the killers occupied.

"No!" Madrazi made her voice purposefully sharp and watched Jael bristle. Madrazi held her hand out. "I'm sorry. You're right; we need to run. But we need to stop and think before we do. We… I can't outrun them. We must make good choices before we start." Jael reluctantly nodded. Madrazi went on. "We both know why they're here. If they're from Nimrod, they won't stop until I'm dead. And there's only one place I will be safe."

"But they'll be expecting us to head south," Jael countered.

"Not the lake," sighed Madrazi. "The only place I will be safe is beside my husband."

Jael didn't bother to hide her astonishment. "We don't know where they are! And even if we did, it would be many months' journey through untamed wilderness. You'd never make it. I don't think *I* could."

"We know where they are going," countered Madrazi. "North of the mountains, then west. Yes, the land is vast, but they are the only other people there." She sighed and sat beside the younger woman. "I know I can't survive alone, but together…." She hesitated and saw Jael look closely at her, sensing something. How would she take the news?

"Jael. There is something I must tell you… I wanted to before, but you're not an easy person to talk to."

Jael bristled, but then looked thoughtful. "It's been hard," she admitted. "You're the lady of this house and I'm an interloper. You're the perfect daughter and I'm the rebel. You hate me for what I've become."

Madrazi felt the tears flooding her eyes, realizing that she had mistaken a part of Jael's hard exterior for a long time. The younger woman looked uncomfortable at the sight of the tears.

"I'm sorry," she muttered. "I didn't mean to hurt you."

"Oh Jael," Madrazi wiped the tears away. "Please understand this if nothing else. I *don't* hate you. I never have. I *love* you! You're my sister." She flung her arms around the girl and felt a tentative response under the stiff exterior.

"But there's more." She drew back, feeling the blush mantle her face. I wanted to tell you before, but you've been so hard…. Do you remember when you first came to us… when you asked Shem to teach you? Do you remember why he did?"

Jael looked suspicious. "He told me it was the will of the Creator. Nothing more."

Madrazi nodded. "That's true, Jael, but there *is* more. I saw a vision. A dark king was hunting me in the wilderness. He has haunted many of my dreams... ever since Debseda conceived her firstborn during our last days on the ark. She wanted to forge ahead… even at the end of the Flood, she had delusions of dominance in this world."

"So the dark king was Cush?" Jael shook her head in disbelief.

"No." Madrazi shivered. "He is our old enemy, Sechiall, reborn into this world."

"Nimrod?" Now the younger woman was nodding.

"Probably," returned Madrazi. "Though he haunts my dreams, I've never seen his face clearly. But I feel his evil." She shivered, then gathered herself. "In my vision, he had trapped me in a ravine. I was about to die, but you appeared and fought him back, and helped me escape." She hung her head. "I told Shem to train you well, Jael, because I knew that one day my life would rest in your hands. This is that day. I'm sorry I didn't tell you sooner. I just didn't know how."

Madrazi expected outrage, sarcasm… anything but what happened next. Jael began to laugh. "That must have been a shock to your proper decorum!" Jael saw the older woman's frown and laughed again.

"Don't worry, Madrazi. I know your power. I'm Noah's daughter, too." She chuckled. "So the Almighty didn't choose Shelah or Heth or even Ashkenaz to protect you… He chose me."

"Yes," returned Madrazi stiffly.

"Oh sister! It makes you wonder about divine irony." She laughed again. "I did wonder why my big brother changed his mind so quickly. He *is* the second most stubborn person I know…." Madrazi blushed and started to speak, but Jael forestalled her. "How can I not help you? I owe Shem…." She smiled, but it was the smile of a wolf about to spring. She reclined back against a rock wall and crossed her arms behind her head, looking for all the world like a child who had just outwitted her parents.

Pausing to gauge Madrazi's reaction, she landed her blow with as much nonchalance as she could muster.

"I knew." She let the words hang between them, watching the shock chase understanding across Madrazi's face.

"You knew?" Madrazi's voice came out as something between a squawk and a squeal. "You've known for all this time and you didn't say a word to me? But… but how? What did I say? How did I give it away…?"

Jael laughed and sat beside her. She reached out and patted her hand, like an indulgent aunt with a sulking child. "You told me nothing. But your memory is starting to fade… and here you are, not even two hundred years old!" Madrazi frowned and bit her lip.

Jael laughed again. "You're forgetting that you aren't the only person in this world who hears the Creator's voice."

The words struck Madrazi like a blow. "Noah? Father told you?"

Jael nodded smugly. "Five years ago, when he was sick…"

"He sent us all out of the room… all except you… I felt the shadow of his power, but never thought…." Madrazi recalled the stunned look on Jael's face when she had come out of the room. Now she understood.

Jael's face was serious. "Father told me many things that day. He accepted what I must become but told me I had a choice. Once I knew about you… he said that I could continue my course out of hatred for Nimrod and Korac or that I could become better than that—saving life instead of taking it… that I would need the same skills to do either. That if I chose the wrong path, I would never be happy again."

She sighed. "So I decided. I redoubled my efforts. I determined that if I could protect you from Nimrod and Korac… that if they wanted you dead and I could frustrate them… it would hurt them more than death. Not really a worthy motivation, but it was the best I could do at the time."

Madrazi found her voice again. "You made a good choice at a hard time. It was not wholehearted, but your heart was not whole then. It was noble, and the Creator will honor it."

Jael shrugged. "We all have to live with our choices, don't we? I do… Mariel does… and so do you." She stumbled, and looked apologetic, but Madrazi seized her hand. "You're absolutely right, Jael. Perhaps over the next few months, I can tell you of some of my past, and you can learn from my errors. But right now…."

"But right now you need some rest." Jael's lip curled. "Perhaps you can dream us a way out of this mess!"

Madrazi tried to frown, but Jael's grin was infectious and she could not help smiling. "Have some respect, Jael!"

But her words were tempered with a hug. "Thank you, little sister! You've already saved me once." The embrace tightened and both women were content to hold each other for some minutes as the stress of the morning began to recede. Sirus whined softly and Madrazi reached down. "You poor dear. Feeling left out? You have a long journey ahead of you."

She sat on her blankets and pulled her knees to her chin. "We'll never catch the men if we follow over the mountains," she mused. "We need a shortcut…"

"Well, unless you can arrange an angel to fly us, we're in trouble," answered Jael. "The country south of the Black Sea is rough."

"We don't need an angel," answered Madrazi, suddenly excited. "You've given me the answer… the Black Sea! If we can make our way to Arkaz, we can sail across and save weeks. I doubt Nimrod's killers are mariners."

Jael nodded. "Togarmah wouldn't refuse to take you. But when Nimrod's men find him gone, they'll know he helped, and they will slaughter his family."

"That's why we go without him. We'll take a boat and make our own way. I want no more death in this."

Jael paled. "Shem taught me much, but he never took me on the water. You know how fast storms can rise on that sea. You'll just be saving Korac the trouble."

It was Madrazi's turn to laugh. "I haven't told you much of my childhood, Jael. My father sailed the wide seas of the old world for centuries, and taught me his craft. You're not the only rebellious woman in the family! Who do you think showed Togarmah how to build and sail ships?"

Jael's eyes narrowed and she crossed her arms in front of her. "So you are the world's foremost mariner?" Sarcasm coated each word.

"Yes," answered Madrazi simply. "Far and away."

Jael frowned, but sensing the calm assurance beneath it, she broke into a hard grin.

"Very well. We'll go to Togarmah and see about a boat. This might actually be fun. Our assassins will expect you to flee south to the Lake. If we leave tonight, we'll be in Arkaz within ten days."

Unaccountably, Jael rose and began to pace, her face twisted with worry and her knuckles white on her bow. Madrazi wondered if she slept with it in her hand. The cool and confident Jael of the past hours seemed to waver in her vision; Madrazi caught a glimpse of the young girl she had known before Mariel's treason. Then, just as suddenly, the hard warrior woman was back and she turned abruptly around, as if bracing herself for an attack.

"I know you are an elder, a seer, and the mistress of these lands," she began harshly, "but…"

"But I need to submit to your judgment in the days ahead," finished Madrazi calmly. "Don't worry on that score, Jael. I know the task that lies before you. I've known it since that day that Shem brought you to stay with us. I will follow you willingly." She paused. "I know that it will be difficult to keep us both alive. I'll try not to make it harder."

Jael went rigid for a moment, another hard smile bending her lip. "I forgot that you know my thoughts before I do," she said, half sarcastically, half admiringly.

"Only those that your face and a modicum of common sense make obvious," retorted Madrazi. She winced. "Just as I know I must push myself beyond my strength. I accept that, and will do my best."

"Very well," breathed Jael as she sat beside the older woman. "It will be hard, but you can do it. You're strong where it counts. Survival is more about the strength of your will than your body." Madrazi hid her smile at hearing one of Shem's adages coming from his young sister's lips. Jael pretended not to notice. "We're in for a long journey. We must balance our need to fly from these killers tonight with the need to still be able to do so in a week, a month, or a year."

Madrazi nodded. "If we reach Arkaz in ten days, you may be dragging me the last day, but once we set sail, we can both rest. Do we travel by night or by day?"

"Night." Jael didn't hesitate. "They have to track us and it will be harder at night." She looked now with a little sympathy at the older woman. Even the journey to Arkaz would be a nightmare. "Sleep now; I'll wake you when it's time to leave."

Madrazi shuddered as she considered the journey before them. "As you say," she breathed, and settled herself on a blanket to try to rest and prepare, trying unsuccessfully to erase the picture of an arrow sprouting from Zeb's chest, before she drifted into an exhausted, but uneasy sleep.

Chapter 42
NINE DAYS TO ARKAZ

10-8-1760 *(day 1)*

Korac kicked the dead horse, and then suddenly kicked it again. The others stepped back—that seemingly minor outburst from Korac was like another man lost in a raving rage. Korac was dangerous enough when coldly sane. They eyed one another uneasily. Jalam sighed and took the risk.

"Maybe she died in the barn. Two fresh sets of women's tracks go in and none come out. That little jackal that shot Dishon gave his life to defend the door, and the horses were a distraction. If we had fallen for his trick, the woman might have slipped away. But we didn't. And she didn't."

Korac weighed his words. "Then why burn the barn? She's not the kind of woman to immolate herself. No," he paused looking around, "she's out there right now."

"But we found no tracks around the barn to suggest she fled," dared Dishan.

"I could hide my tracks from you," sneered Korac. "And Shem could probably hide his tracks from me. He could have taught her the same." The iron face returned. "It won't be easy, but we will keep looking. Unless you would rather report the failure to Nimrod?" Korac eyed Dishan, who wilted and looked down at his feet.

"Then we continue our search."

"Won't she be headed for the Lake of the Islands?" dared Jalam. "She has people there to hide and protect her."

"That's the logical choice," Korac agreed. "But I don't like it." He stood in thought for another minute, the others not daring to speak.

Finally Korac made up his mind. "You're right as usual, Jalam. Something is tickling the back of my mind, but I can't fault your logic. We hit them hard. She's alone or with another woman. She has nothing and she's frightened. A man might stop and consider a ruse, but she's no man. Doubtless she's fleeing for the Lake… probably by some hidden trail." His eyes squinted against the southern skyline, the midday sun highlighting every hill.

"Dishan. Take your brother and quarter the ground to the south. Start to the east and move west. Find her trail. Jalam and I will take the rougher ground to the west and work east. We'll meet at sundown. We finish the job and head back for Shinar."

It was nearing sundown when the men met. Jalam had said nothing for several hours, watching his cousin grow sullen and angry as the afternoon wore away. They found no fresh trail, despite a diligent search. And when they met the twins, it was clear they had been equally unsuccessful. More and more, Korac would stop and look back to the north, muttering to himself.

Just as Jalam thought he would explode, Korac simply turned to him with the faintest grin on his iron mask of a face. Just a twitch of one side of his mouth, but Jalam had known him for years and read the sign correctly.

"What are you thinking, cousin?" he asked.

"She kept her head. Why shouldn't she. She's been in tight situations before. She went north to throw us off. Maybe she thought we would kill who we could and leave. Either way, it doesn't matter. She's a woman, alone in the wilderness, with one of her servants or family. Two women. We can find them inside a week, no matter how well they hide or how fast they run."

"So what now?" asked a much relieved Jalam.

"Eat, sleep, and go find her trail tomorrow. It's been a long day."

From practiced habit, the men quickly and efficiently set up camp. Dishan tended his brother's arm. The wound was deep, but the men had trained to ignore pain. Their sleep was uneasy and Korac tossed about, some vague fear haunting his dreams.

Timna edged up closer until she was beside him. He wanted to warn her back, but dared not shift his attention from the narrow valley floor ahead. A trickle of water coming down the far cliff sounded like a waterfall, and effectively hid any breathing from the wounded beast, or the brush of its coarse hair against a rock. And the wind didn't help either. Blowing from behind them and up the valley, their scent was being carried to the bear, and Korac could not hope to catch the odor of the beast, undoubtedly laying in ambush for the two humans. That advantage was all with their prey, and he hoped that Nimrod was in position. He also hoped that it had been hit harder than it looked—maybe it was even now slumping behind some rock at the far end of the valley, having come to the end of its race.

Every sense on edge, he crept along the narrow path, scanning each boulder or nest of boulders... every potential hiding place. He carried his bow in front of him, arrow set to string, ready to draw and fire in one smooth motion. Nimrod was somewhere up to his right. He would whistle if the bear was near.

Regret distracted him momentarily. Why had he ever given in? Why had he let Timna out of the house? This was no place for a woman... no place for a sane man, either. His head swiveled, scanning from side to side. She walked confidently on his left, as cool as if going to the market. Was she foolish or did she have that much faith in his ability? A sixth sense pulled him back to the valley. He shivered in anticipation.

And then... he saw it.

10-8-1760 (night 1)

As the four assassins prepared a quick meal before sunrise, Madrazi stumbled over the rocky path after Jael. A hint of light behind them told her that the night's journey was nearly done... and not an hour too soon. They had cut across the shoulder of the mountain and turned west. None of the climb had been hazardous, but all of it had been hard, even with the stars and half moon providing an uncertain light. But Jael knew the country well, and Madrazi was grateful for her uncanny ability to find the easiest path.

There had been one terrifying stretch. Walking through a narrow defile, the sandy ground before them became solid rock. Jael had taken advantage of it to change direction; they had been traveling due north, but she forced Madrazi to clamber up the steep slope and start west. It would have been a difficult climb in the daylight. It was steep, and there were two stretches where Sirus had to be hauled up with the rope. Fortunately, the dog didn't complain—he seemed to sense the need for silence. Madrazi was tired, but it was not fear that caused Madrazi to drag her feet in the waning hour of the night—it was Jael's relentless pace, hour after hour. They had covered more than a day's journey and Madrazi was both ashamed and afraid of her body's reaction. She had let herself grow soft, and she shuddered at the thought of the days that would follow. Her body would regain its strength, but without time to rest, the process would be painful. She gritted her teeth and pushed her weary feet another few steps.

Jael continued to alternate between the trail and her companion. Recalling her early days with Shem, she knew Madrazi's pain. The numbing shock of the previous morning's attack was starting to wear off. Jael knew that her sister was weeping inwardly for every member of her household, while forcing her body onward. She remembered how it felt to be soft and then suddenly pushed—and pushed hard—to become fit for wilderness travel. And there was a difference; she had welcomed the pain and the hardness. Madrazi wanted neither.

It was more than that. In the years she had spent in Madrazi's house, Jael had come to admire her elder sister, though she would never openly admit it. Her brazen disrespect was the best way to hide it; she could not afford any softness in her quest to become as hard as Heth and as swift as Shelah. Madrazi was too much like Noah; she was always composed and always right, able to read the thoughts and intents of the heart, but able to maintain an easy way with everyone from Shem to her servants.

Her household idolized her. Jael knew that her sister was a good woman. She even felt an occasional twinge of guilt for her cavalier attitude. As the initial rage of the first years of her quest abated, she had wanted to change their relationship, but had no idea how to start. Something always stood in the way. Maybe she saw in Madrazi a shadow of Mariel. Maybe she resented Madrazi's unstated disapproval of her new life. Whatever the reason, they had never become comfortable around each other. But with the men gone, they were now together and dependent on each other for their lives.

She smiled in the darkness. Madrazi had passed her first test; the climb up the cliff face in the dark would have given Shelah pause. Jael shook her head. There was no room for regrets now. Their existence hung by a thread. Madrazi needed Jael to survive, but Jael suddenly realized that she needed Madrazi too. Saving her would validate the past few years—bringing redemption from rebellion.

Her mind raced. *Maybe*, she thought, *if I save Madrazi, I can save myself. What better revenge against Nimrod and Korac…* she was certain the pursuing murderers were their tools. Perhaps she could have her revenge without sinning against her father or his God—a God that had become an uncomfortably small part of her life since she had come to live with Shem and Madrazi. Maybe for the sake of Madrazi, He would be kind to them and allow Korac to be one of their pursuers. If she could be the instrument of his greatest failure, then her cup would be full to overflowing. Why kill him when she could make him suffer for the rest of his life?

She forced those thoughts down. They needed to survive right now and she scented water. "Up here," she said as Madrazi and the dog trudged up. "There's a small spring hidden in this hollow. We'll drink and wash, and then find a place to sleep. There's a nest of boulders up ahead. We can hide there. I'll try to confuse our trail while you sleep." Madrazi was too tired to respond; she just nodded and moved forward. Jael watched her for a moment, sighed, and then moved to help her climb the shallow slope to the water.

10-9-1760 *(day 2)*

Jalam shouted and waited. Within minutes Korac had joined him and the twins were jogging across the fields. Dishon lagged behind. He had tried to shrug off his wound, but the arrow had pierced his left arm, and his body had little opportunity to heal. He was obviously in considerable pain and held his arm close to his body. With each step, Jalam could see the jarring pain imprinted on his face. But Dishon was the least of their worries. Jalam had searched for hours until finally stumbling over the women's tracks in a gully northeast of the barn. He had been lucky, finding the tracks accidentally, after walking down the gully to find fresh water.

Korac came running to his call and his lip twitched when he saw the tracks. It was as close as he could get to a smile, and Jalam felt a surge of pride. Korac leaped lightly down and clapped his cousin on the back. "Well done! We have them now. She's better than I imagined... she kept her head and must have thought to draw us north and then slip back to the Lake of the Islands. We only need find the place where they doubled back. Spread out! Fifty paces apart and find me that trail!"

It was nearly sundown when the four men crowded through a narrow defile on the west shoulder of the mountain. The tracks had been clear for most of the afternoon. Jalam was grateful; although they had lost them crossing the river, the trail had reappeared around the southwest side of the mountain. He wondered idly how they had hidden their trail over that stretch, but there was no time for that puzzle. They were full of surprises. He had been mildly surprised to find a dog's tracks with the women's. It might try to protect them, but even the fiercest dog stood little chance against a well-aimed arrow.

Dishan was in the lead when suddenly he stopped. "More rock here," he called back softly.

"Keep going," Korac replied. "They've been heading northwest for some time. They may be smart enough to swing east around the mountain. That would keep them away from the main road back south."

But the sand on the other end of the little gorge showed no tracks. Darkness was falling and Korac was growling to himself. Jalam sought to ease the tension. "It's no different than the river," he said with a confidence he didn't feel. "They can't fly. We'll sweep around and pick them up in the morning, just like we did today."

"No." Korac's flat voice brooked no dissent. "We keep going. I think they went east around the north side of the mountain. We travel tonight and perhaps we'll be on them in the morning. We need to finish this and get back to Shinar." Jalam didn't agree, but Korac seemed driven, and Jalam wondered what orders Nimrod had given to spur him so.

His thoughts were interrupted by Dishon's whine. "But I need to rest and wash my arm." His voice reflected the miserable day he had endured, and Jalam was nearly tempted to sympathy until he remembered the screams of women and children inside the house. Korac just stared at him and Jalam wondered if the injured man understood how close he was to death. Obviously not… he kept on, "A night's rest won't hurt and it will go far to getting me back to fighting form."

Korac's voice was almost conversational, but Jalam felt the menace under each word. "Let it hurt. The pain will teach you endurance. And if you can't keep up, then perhaps you are of no more use."

"It's just a scratch," quivered Dishon, sensing the threat in Korac's words. Without a backwards glance, Korac led them off at a brisk pace, while Dishon cursed under his breath. He was hard pressed to keep up. Jalam glanced over with some sympathy; he remembered the time he had been hit with an arrow. It had not been bad, but he still remembered the fiery pain shooting through his leg. Dishon must be suffering incredible pain, but Korac still set a brutal pace, clearly wanting to pick up the trail on the east side of the mountain and run the women down. As the night closed in around them, Jalam thought how much they were like a pack of hungry wolves. Having chosen their prey, they would now literally run them to death.

10-9-1760 *(night 2)*

Madrazi woke to a hand on her shoulder. "We need to travel. I have food ready." Jael was standing over her. For a moment, Madrazi felt guilty, knowing Jael had foregone sleep to let her rest, but as her stiff back and tender feet made their presence known, guilt fled.

"There's no sign of pursuit so far, but we must hurry. Trained men can travel further and faster than we can, and we need a big a lead if we hope to beat them to the Black Sea."

Madrazi nodded. She agreed, but her body was rebelling. Another night of forced marching! Could she last? She rose slowly, trying to stretch the tight muscles. Jael shoved some hot meat impaled on a stick towards her and Madrazi began to tear at it, suddenly ravenous. She glanced around for the fire. "I found a cave up the slope," explained Jael. "It hid the smoke long enough to cook this."

Madrazi's guilt rose again. Clearly the girl had not slept very long. If she had hunted, gathered wood, made a fire, and cooked her kill, her day had passed quickly. Madrazi nodded. "Thank you, Jael. But you must let me help. If you wear yourself down, I'll have no chance at all."

Jael grinned. "I'm a long way from worn down, Madrazi. As you gain strength, I'll give you more to do. Trust me; I know what I'm doing. Just remember who taught me."

"No meat for Sirus?" Madrazi asked.

"He can learn," Jael replied. "Hunger is his best teacher. If he can learn to hunt for himself, then perhaps he can hunt for us when we really need it."

"My life is in your hands," replied Madrazi. "I would rather it be you than Heth or Shelah." She caught herself short. The last part had just come out, but when she examined it again, she knew it to be true.

Jael heard her sincerity and was equally surprised. She was encouraged that Madrazi didn't fight her over the dog. She almost blushed, but instead she began gathering their meager belongings and rolling them up in the blankets. "I filled the water bottle and horn," she remarked. They had finished the tea the previous night. "Tonight will be easier. We'll be walking downhill and tomorrow morning will find us in a fertile valley. We need more meat, but I can't guarantee a kill every day. Be ready to go hungry."

Madrazi picked up her roll and settled the rope over her shoulder. "I could walk all night for some green meadows and trees," she said, forcing a smile.

Morning found them in the valley Jael had promised. As she came over the low ridge and walked down the grassy slope, Madrazi remembered it from a trip with Shem long ago. It had changed so much. The trees were now mature, with fruit still lingering on a few. Harvest was over and winter was coming earlier every year. How would they survive the wilderness in the bitter cold? One step at a time, she reminded herself. If they didn't hurry, cold would be the least of her worries.

The night had been easier than she expected… at first. She had cut strips off her blanket to pad her feet and her muscles had loosened in the first few hours. But then the pain and stiffness returned with a vengeance, and her feet began to complain despite the padding. The volcanic rocks were unforgiving, and she knew it was providence alone that prevented a twisted ankle.

But they finally entered the valley and it was all Jael had promised. Its grass felt like the softest carpet to her feet, and the early sun revealed a pleasant green vale. Jael found shelter among several downed trees, and was even able to build a small fire in a hollow trunk. She left Madrazi with Sirus, caught up her bow, and went to find game. Madrazi was asleep before she returned.

10-10-1760 *(day 3)*

Morning found the four assassins on the northeast side of the mountain, looking up at the smaller sister peak and wondering why they had not yet found the trail. Jalam had a nagging feeling that something was wrong, but Korac had been in no mood to listen during the night. Jalam gathered up his courage and tried again.

"Cousin," he began in a placating tone. "Your guess was inspired, but who can judge the minds of women. I think that whatever they did, it was not here. Let's go back and find the trail. They are frail women and cannot travel far or fast. They're probably hiding in some valley or wandering in circles. It should be a simple matter to pick up their trail and follow them."

"Two days," muttered Korac. "We've lost two days. We must rest and retrace our steps. What power is thwarting us?"

"It's a small matter," Jalam murmured. "Even with two weeks start we would run them to ground within a month. It's only two days; we'll have them within the week."

Korac wavered and Jalam pressed. "Let me go hunt while you rest. We'll sleep a few hours, eat, and be ready to move quickly back to their last prints. It will be a simple matter to pick up their tracks. They're just women."

Korac finally nodded. "Very well, cousin. There's wisdom in your words. Tell the twins to make camp and rest. A fire will feel good."

Madrazi bathed her feet in a cool streamlet while Jael slept. The younger woman had reached her limit early in the afternoon and had wakened her companion to keep watch. Two hares provided enough meat for two days, and Madrazi had found clean leaves and grasses to wrap tomorrow's. Even she knew better than to leave the scent of meat—even cooked—on their clothes or blankets. Jael had been right about Sirus. He had wandered off earlier and returned several hours later, content.

Once everything was done, she settled down to watch. In the solitude, the images of that morning returned, and she took time to weep for her household. She couldn't rid her mind of the picture of Zeb running into an arrow. It haunted her now and she imagined that it would for the rest of her life. The thought of what must have happened inside the house made her shudder. She could still hear the screams. She was grateful that only four women had been inside that day, and hoped the others had escaped into the fields. What kind of evil could fill men to do such a thing?

But evil was not the sum total of men—Zeb had run courageously into enemy arrows and Enoch had probably sold his life holding the barn door to buy her precious minutes. Would those sacrifices be for nothing? The pursuing killers could be entering this valley right now. She shivered. Jael might escape, but she would not. What had possessed her to fly west into the vast unknown? What had she done to Jael? Had it been wrong to encourage the training that had turned a bitter young woman into a bitter, dangerous warrior?

She shivered again. The evenings were growing chill. Even if they made it to Arkaz and found Togarmah, obtained a boat, and sailed across the Black Sea, how would they survive winter in the bleak wilderness on the other side? How had her life gone from the quiet order of her beloved farm to this chaos? Where was her husband when she needed him? Tears wore tracks down her cheeks.

At some point she remembered Noah's resolute face on the eve of the flood. Surely the same fears and worries had assaulted him. How had he found courage to continue? She knew, of course, but her mind did not want such a simple answer. He had believed the word of the Creator. A soft stirring inside brought it all back. Noah had faced an impossible journey. He had been assaulted by evil men. His chances of survival seemed next to impossible. But he had kept faith and survived.

The tears now marked the release of fear and the beginnings of peace. Noah had completed his journey and defeated his inner demons. She would do no less. All she must do was travel in his footsteps. As his faith had been a beacon for her during her darkest days aboard the ark, she vowed that she would be no less for Jael. She watched her companion sleep and prayed that she could meet that challenge.

It was well that her heart had found peace, for the night pushed her body to its limits. Pain returned on the ascent out of the valley. They followed a stream up to the west and then turned north, scrambling along the sides of the running water over rough ground. Hills reared up on either side; the dim light of the moon and stars barely reached the valley floor. Madrazi added bruises to her collection of aches as she stumbled and fell several times. The muscles in her legs were as unyielding as stone and each step jarred her from the soles of her feet to the top of her head. She soon reached the stage of unthinking plodding, unable to see anything but the ghostly form of Jael ahead, mechanically obeying her occasional whispers to stop, start, turn, or sit. She barely remembered curling up next to Sirus in a small cave before dawn as exhaustion claimed her.

10-11-1760 *(day 4)*

Korac felt an uneasiness building, though there seemed to be no obvious reason. But past years had taught him to pay attention to such things and he was alert. He scanned the ground ahead. It was rough and rocky, but he could see nothing. Behind him, Jalam and the twins pushed on at a steady jog. They were all relieved to be heading back west; Jalam's council had been good. Dishon was better, though his wound still seeped blood. The rough bandage was stained red. The sight of that bandage finally connected Korac's instincts and mind. Blood! He cursed softly and picked up his pace. There was a nose of rock just ahead and uphill. If they could reach that….

Jalam had also sensed danger. He shot a questioning look, and Korac pointed at the rocky promontory, unlimbering his bow as he ran. Jalam did the same and his head began to swivel back and forth as he ran. The twins, obviously puzzled, followed. Dishan was running with his brother, encouraging a pace to match Korac's. As they neared the promontory, Korac dropped back and barked, "Get up the rocks! Move!"

Dishan looked startled for a moment, then seized Dishon's arm and pulled him up the steepening slope to the foot of the rise. Then they began to clamber up. Jalam dropped back beside Korac. A few hundred paces back, the wolves burst out of a dip in the rock. There were at least a dozen of the brutes; the leader was as large as a small horse and every bit as fast. Korac looked both ways. The wolves were closing and the twins were nearly up the small cliff. "Up, then shoot," he grated and the two cousins shouldered their bows and sprang up the rock face, using the handholds and footholds that they had unconsciously noted the twins using. They were halfway up the face when the wolves reached the base, leaping futilely behind them. The men slowed their pace, careful now not to fall. Another twenty cubits and they were safely up at the top with the twins.

"Don't give them time to find another way up," ordered Korac, suiting actions to words and putting an arrow into one of the larger animals scrambling at the bottom of the face. Shooting down on the beasts allowed him to sever the spine with one shot, and the animal collapsed. Jalam's arrow found a similar target and another one went down. Dishon could not shoot, but he handed arrows to Dishan, who quickly put two into the back of another. Neither found a vital spot, but the creature yelped and ran back down the slope. Another volley of arrows saw another beast dead and another wounded. Now the rest began slowly to back away from the cliff face. "Kill more, or they'll hound us for days," ordered Korac.

Jalam lifted his bow away from an easy shot at an ugly black wolf still leaping against the rocks and killed a more intelligent pack member fleeing down the slope. It was a good shot and he was momentarily proud. But there were still wolves to kill so he pushed pride down and lined up his next shot. Korac was content to leave the distance shooting to Jalam and killed the black beast. Dishan finally killed another that was backing slowly down the slope, sinking three arrows into its chest. Decimated, the remnants of the pack broke and fled, seeking easier prey.

Within minutes the men had scrambled down and retrieved most of their arrows. Then they fled west. Korac pressed the pace for an hour, hoping the surviving wolves would feast on their own dead and seek easier prey. He finally slowed at a small freshet, where the men slaked their thirst. "Leave your bandage here and soak your arm in this cold water," he ordered Dishon. "Then wrap it again. We don't need the scent of blood bringing every wolf in these mountains down on us." Dishon was about to protest, but seeing the hard glitter in Korac's eyes, he quickly did as he was told.

They pushed the rest of the day, stopping only at dusk. Jalam found a small cave. Though there was no wood for a fire, the opening was small enough to be easily defended, and the men spent an uneasy night, eager to be away from the mountain the next day.

10-11-1760 *(night 4)*

Madrazi trudged on as though walking through a nightmare. She no longer felt pain in her feet or thighs; her entire body hurt. The terrain was similar to the night before; so she stumbled along the stream in the dark, pushing upward, step by step. Just when she thought it could be no worse, it was. Jael found a ford and led them across the stream. The icy water swirled around her legs, filling her boots, and halfway across, she slipped off a stone and fell. Jael pulled her across, where she sat shivering on the ground, unable and unwilling to rise.

"Get up," hissed Jael. "Out of those clothes!" She suited actions to words and pulled Madrazi to her feet. Her legs swayed and her fingers shook. The night air that had seemed merely cool now cut to the bone. She commanded her hands to work, but they would no longer obey. Jael sighed and began to pull clothing off her, wrapping her in the blankets and pulling her into a tight embrace, her own heat penetrating

Madrazi's chilled flesh. After a few minutes, Jael guided her to a rock where she sat huddled in the blankets. Jael spread her clothes out, wringing out as much water as she could.

"You're going to have to wear them damp the rest of the night," she whispered, "but we have to climb out of this valley so you'll stay warm. Eat something now, while I fill our waterskin."

Madrazi mechanically chewed and swallowed a few bites of meat. They sat in silence for a few more minutes before Jael began to gather up the damp clothing. "If we stay any longer, your body will tighten up and hurt more. Just a few more hours. I know it's bad, but you can do this. You must."

Madrazi nodded and rose, too weary to speak. She shrugged back into the cold uncomfortable clothes, shivering as they chilled her skin. But Jael was right. As they began to climb a side gully up to the plateau, her blood began to pound once more and the clothes began to dry. But the return of circulation brought the return of pain, and she bit her lip as she pressed forward. It was easily a half a thousand cubits from the stream to the top of the plain above, and Madrazi was beyond thinking by the time they reached the top.

The rest of the night passed in a blur of pain as she pushed herself to put one foot in front of the other. Sirus walked beside her, leaning his body in to steady her when she stumbled. She had passed her limits hours ago, and only some stubborn kernel of will kept her body moving. Jael was a pale shadow before her; her occasional whispers of encouragement sounding like the passing of the wind. Madrazi turned inside herself, re-living the death of her mother, the voyage to Lamech, her early years with Shem, the flood, and the birth of Arpachshad. She was only dimly aware of Jael leading her into a small cave, giving her water and meat, and covering her with a blanket before the bliss of nothingness overtook her.

10-12-1760 *(day 5)*

Jalam felt relief course through his body when he saw the indistinct tracks on the lip of the shallow gorge. It had been a tense morning; they had worked back to the last sign of the women and wasted several hours working back and forth at the end of the gorge searching for the trail. Jalam had climbed the gorge as much to distance himself from the growing wrath of Korac as to search for the women. And then, just like that, the trail was right in front of his eyes. Looking down, he saw Korac berating the twins, and he was tempted to keep silent and let him continue—the twins had proven useless in anything but sadistic butchery. But time was pressing and so he threw a rock down to catch the attention of the others before waving them up the wall.

Korac's face gave nothing away, but Jalam could see the tightness in his neck ease as he studied the tracks. He was not surprised that Korac took time to study the tracks and think; he had always believed that you could successfully trail a man only by gaining the ability to put yourself inside his mind and to understand his tricks, his habits, and his weaknesses. And a cold, thoughtful Korac would lead them to success. While the twins wandered off to rest in the shade of a boulder, Korac tilted his head and nodded Jalam over to his side.

"I don't like this. It's the move of an experienced man, like Shem, not of two frightened women. But I have never heard that he trained his wife or that she ever shared his love of the wilderness. If not her, then who… who is this other woman?"

"Perhaps it is a boy, one who has learned the rudiments from Shem or Shelah," Jalam mused. "A boy with a small foot might appear to be another woman."

"No." Korac muttered, "The stride is wrong. It is a woman's stride, yet different from any I've seen. Confident. Controlled. Dangerous."

"But a woman at home in the wild? Next thing you'll tell me is that she is an expert with the bow and sword!"

"Maybe she is," shot back Korac. "There's no reason a woman could not draw a bow. We need to start looking for signs of hunting. We know now that she is learned in the ways of the trail. Did you notice how far they have come? She is strong to be pressing a pace like this. Look for any sign of hunting. They must eat just as we must. If she can feed them, then we must assume some skill with weapons too."

Jalam shook his head. "You're right. The signs are before us, but the idea seems so… unlikely." He looked at Korac again. "But that's not what's bothering you, is it?"

"No." Korac grimaced slightly. "This trail leads northwest. Why go there? We have been foolish in assuming they would flee south to the Lake of the Islands. But they are not. Why?"

"I don't know, cousin," replied Jalam. "But we have a trail to follow again and no woman can outrun us in the wild. We've lost a few days, but we'll be on them inside the week."

"I want you out front, following the trail," ordered Korac. "No more assumptions. You find the sign and follow. If you lose it, we stop until we pick it up again. No more mistakes."

Jalam nodded. Korac's earlier anger had evaporated. They had a clear trail. They were once again the hunters—like the wolf pack that had almost taken them on the mountain. Only there were no warriors to deal with this pack. "We still have a few hours of sunlight left," he answered and began to trot northwest, noting the smudges in the sand or the occasional scuff of a rock, faint marks indeed, but each one leading him closer to their prey.

10-12-1760 (night 5)

Madrazi woke with a start. She was sore and stiff but felt refreshed and clear-headed. Jael sat in the cave entrance, hunched over her knees and looking out. "What do you see?" she asked softly.

Jael turned quickly and crawled over. "Good! I was afraid to let you sleep much longer, but afraid to wake you too. I have pushed you hard, and that's the path to failure. It's better we travel a little less each day, but keep up the pace. I don't want to run you into the ground."

She handed Madrazi the water skin and a hard lump of meat. "No kill today."

Madrazi smiled. "This is fine, Jael." She looked shrewdly at the younger woman. "Have you eaten?"

Jael dropped her eyes. "I had some while you were sleeping." Madrazi saw the obvious lie. Jael shrugged. "It doesn't matter. We'll both know hunger in the months ahead, unless we are caught and killed first. Personally, I prefer hunger."

Madrazi rose experimentally and stretched her muscles. "I feel better than I expected. But I don't know how far I can go tonight."

"We won't push as hard," replied Jael. "There's a lake ahead and we'll follow the shore for a ways. It will give us drink and a bath, and probably food. We'll make an easy night and let you regather your strength. Then we must push hard for the sea."

"What about our pursuers?"

"I followed our back trail for a ways this morning," said Jael. "Even looking over the rim down into the valley, there was no sign of pursuit. We may have a greater lead than we think."

"Even if we fooled them, they'll make up ground quickly when they come," Madrazi said, watching Jael yawn into the waning sun. "You didn't sleep today, either," she accused.

Jael shrugged again. "Shem made sure that I knew how to function without food and sleep. It's nothing I haven't done before."

Madrazi gave her a look that made Jael smile. "Tomorrow, you will catch up on both," she declared in her best mistress-of-the-house voice, and she was relieved to see Jael smile.

"Yes, mother!" she laughed.

Madrazi laughed back. "Mother! Do I look seven hundred years old?"

"Not a day over six," returned Jael with a straight face, dodging the blanket Madrazi threw.

True to her word, Jael eased the pace and Madrazi felt merely exhausted when they reached the lake later that night. A light wind in their face smelled of fresh water, and both women enjoyed bathing their faces and hands in the cool water. The bare rocks of the wilderness gave way to shrubs and trees—a fringe of life around the water. Soon they were crossing a meadow and Madrazi smiled her appreciation of the soft grass beneath her tired feet. Jael set a leisurely pace along the shore, which allowed them to move quietly. Sirus stayed beside Madrazi, having made his kill earlier that night.

In the waning light of the moon, Madrazi stopped as Jael froze in front of her. In a blink, she had set arrow to bow. Sirus stayed quiet, hugging Madrazi's side. They watched Jael smoothly draw and fire. The solid sound of an arrow striking told them that Jael had killed her prey—a fat doe coming to drink. Sirus wagged his tail, but did not bark. Madrazi leaned over to scratch his ears. The dog was smart and learning every day.

"Go find shelter under those trees," whispered Jael. "We'll risk a fire at daylight and cook as much as we can. This may last us the rest of the way."

Madrazi limped off with Sirus. At the edge of the trees, she found one that had fallen, covering a dip in the ground that was big enough for both women. She poked a stick into the leaf litter, but nothing was there. Shoving her blanket roll in ahead of her, she wriggled under the trunk, remembering her warm bed with regret.

And no tea for breakfast either.

10-13-1760 *(day 6)*

Korac stood looking down at the hole in the ground. He marveled that Jalam had found it. His cousin had great instincts. The women had cut out a circle of turf, dug down into the ground and buried the remains of two hares. Then they had laid the turf back in place. He would have missed it… he *had* missed it… but Jalam's nose was more sensitive. He had smelled the faint odor of decaying offal. Circling around, they found cold ashes inside a hollow trunk, well covered by leaves and debris, seemingly there for decades. Once again, Jalam's nose had found the trace.

"This changes everything," he said to Korac, his voice low. "Man or woman, whoever is doing this is good! We can't trail at night. One good trick and we'll be wandering in circles. And we can't stay here forever. Once the locals see what we've done to their precious elder, we'll have every man and boy in the hills after us."

"Peace!" Korac's low voice seemed to rumble up from his shoes. "This is for you and for me. The twins aren't along for their minds, after all."

He paused to think. The sun was high in the morning. They had made it to the valley at nightfall, but lost the trail at dark. It had taken several hours this morning to find these traces and get back on the trail of the women. He called the twins over.

"We run. We have to catch them and kill them quickly; I, for one, want to be back in Shinar as soon as possible."

"How long," asked Dishon. "I'm better, but I don't know if I can run all day."

"Then I'll kill you, and the rest of us will run. We run until we catch them. We can't afford to lose more time, so we only travel with light. You can rest at night. But during the day you will run and you *will* keep up with me!" Korac pushed himself right up against the wounded man, his dark eyes implacable—his threat clear.

"We run," agreed Dishon quickly. "I'm good for it."

Jalam held back by the injured man as Korac started off. "Here," he said, tearing a strip of cloth away from Dishon's jacket. "Wrap your shoulder like this." He bound it and passed the end of the strip around the man's back. Now hold this with your right hand and keep the arm close to your body. It will help."

Dishon nodded his gratitude and gripped the cloth tightly before springing after Korac. Jalam grinned and ran beside him. "We'll catch them, get this over with, and get you home to Shinar. Just a little effort now. We'll be back in our own beds inside the month!"

10-15-1760 *(day 8)*

Jalam glanced back at the twins as he jogged along beside his cousin. Dishon continued to run, but his steps were heavy and his face drawn with pain. Korac had set a hard pace. It was almost as if they were the hunted and not the hunters. There had been times late yesterday when Dishon had staggered, but his brother had spurred him on. "When we catch them, you and I will get the women," he promised. "You can make them hurt more than you do and take them before we kill them... slowly!"

Jalam winced at that. Any sympathy he felt for Dishon evaporated. This was a job, pure and simple. Korac understood that. There was no need for rape and torture. All they had to do was kill the women and go home. For a moment he wondered what his mother would think if she knew what he was doing. She was proud that he had risen high in the ranks of Nimrod's Legion, but if she knew that he was a party to rape... to abusing innocent women... she would disown him and spit on his memory. Hopefully she would never find out.

Since they had left the valley, their progress had been rapid, and the signs showed that they had narrowed the lead of the women from three days to less than one. The trail continued to lead northwest—straight for the Black Sea.

Korac had figured that out yesterday. Though not well known outside the circle of survivors of the great flood, he had told Jalam that *The Woman* was reputed to have knowledge of ships and the sea. If she found a boat, their task would become much more difficult. All of them had been on small boats on the rivers, but none of them had ever been at sea on a real ship.

If she made her escape across the Black Sea, she could go anywhere and it would take years to find her. The twins' hope that the chase would be abandoned then was crushed when Korac had made it clear that they would spend the next decade chasing the women if that was what it took. Jalam wanted this to end; that was all the incentive he needed to run and run hard.

The trail had become difficult. After climbing out onto the plateau, it had passed a lake, then headed straight for the Black Sea. But it had then reached the broken lands where the uplands dove down to the sea in a series of rugged hills and deep chasms, descending thousands of cubits. It was devilishly difficult to follow, but Jalam had become accustomed to the skill of the guide and his eyes marked the faint signs of *The Woman*. Had it been just the guide, he had no doubts that they would have lost her long ago.

Thankfully, the women had known the easiest trails and Jalam was happy to follow their lead. His respect for them rose each day—Nimrod himself could not have picked out a better path. But the men were stronger and more enduring, and they were closing in. On the horizon the blue waters of the sea loomed ahead.

Jalam put his head down and ran.

10-16-1760 *(day 9)*

Madrazi watched the sun rise across the dark waters of the Black Sea, filling the air with new light after another hard night. Her knees ached with the constant strain of climbing downhill. She was amazed how quickly Jael had moved through the rugged hills, but now they were down on the narrow strip of flat land that circled the eastern shore of the sea. She was glad they traveled at night, having seen the dizzying drops beside the paths years before. It was far better to not see as they made their way, literally sliding down several of the worst stretches. Her faith in Jael's judgment soared.

The hills behind them were just beginning to catch the sunlight and Madrazi was searching the ground nearby for a place to lay her weary body and lose another day in the forgetfulness of sleep. Sirus clearly shared her desire; he was lying across the trail, too tired to drink in the clear water of the stream that had grown into a small river beside their path.

Jael was tired too; her steps were heavy now, and she no longer took time to try to hide the trail. Nine days of little food and less sleep had taken their toll. But her innate caution had not been dampened. Madrazi watched her scan the back trail, looking for any sign of pursuit. For the past two nights, she had been growing increasingly impatient, constantly looking back, as if she sensed the nearness of the two-legged wolves that haunted their trail.

Suddenly she stiffened. "What do you see?" asked Madrazi.

"Something stirred up that ridge," she replied. "It could have been a rock fall, but we cannot take that risk. We push on. Togarmah and his people are only a few hours away."

Madrazi's face fell. "Couldn't we hide and sleep for a few hours instead?"

"Of course," Jael sneered. "If you want us dead by noon. In that case, why did we ever bother to start? If I'm to die, I would rather have done it last week and saved myself the trouble of dragging you all the way here."

Madrazi almost snapped back, but Jael was right. So she turned to hide the tears gathering in her eyes and started down the riverbank, calling Sirus to follow. She had not gone ten paces when she felt a tentative hand on her shoulder. "I'm sorry, Madrazi. I know you're at the end of your rope. You've been magnificent. To have come so far, so fast… the men could not have done better. But I don't want to lose you to Nimrod. We can't let him win."

Madrazi wiped the tears from her eyes. "You lead; I'll follow. You were right before and you're probably right now. We'll make it, won't we Sirus?" She reached down to pat the dog on the head. "If we can borrow a boat from Togarmah, we'll leave these devils far behind. Then we can find the men at our leisure."

Jael urged her forward. She started to speak, but quickly closed her lips. What if Togarmah was not at home? What if he was out on the water and no boats were there? They had spent so much of themselves to reach his little settlement of Arkaz that the possibility of no boats was too cruel to contemplate. They must be there! With a hand on Madrazi's arm to steady her, she led the older woman down towards the beach.

Chapter 43
OUT TO SEA

10-16-1760

Jalam hurried back to the others. "Down there!" he cried. "I can see them! They can't be more than three hours ahead, and they're moving slow."

Korac glanced back at the twins. "Come at your best pace. Jalam and I will run ahead and overtake them. We can't let them escape."

"There's Togarmah's settlement," said Jalam, pointing to the tiny buildings right on the coastline. I don't see much activity. Maybe they're out fishing. If so, we have them cornered. There's no place for them to run!"

"Then hurry," grated Korac. "I want this finished."

Dishon cradled his arm as Dishan supported him. They stood and watched Korac and Jalam spring forward, oblivious to the steep slopes, rushing to the pursuit. Dishon sat down. "Let them run as fast as they can. I'm going nowhere for an hour. We can afford that. Our leader," he spat, "has the situation in his grasp. He can have them."

Dishan pulled him back up. "What if they slip away? Do you want to be responsible for holding Korac back if we must continue the pursuit?" Dishon grimaced, but followed his brother slowly down the hill, cursing every step.

Togarmah looked up from his net. Stretched lovingly over its own frame, it was his pride—his best yet—it had taken him three months to weave. It was strong, but catching fish would strain a net made of bronze and one made of mere rope needed constant repair. Fishing had been good this year, but one weak point could rip a hole that would lose him a boatload of fish. Success meant hard work and meticulous attention to every detail. So he checked each knot, and then checked them again.

His relatives thought him mad to live in isolation by the sea, but it provided its bounty readily enough. There was no challenge like the sea; its winds, waves, and currents could change from hour to hour, and it took a man to dare the deeps. They lacked nothing here. The ground was rich, and even sheep could be grazed on the nearby hills. Best of all, this was a refuge from the turmoil between the clans. There was no North and South here, only the sea. He didn't care for Nimrod and his crowd, but neither did he want to live under Shem or Noah, though he owed Madrazi a great debt for his knowledge of ships and the sea. Let others engage in the political struggles; Togarmah just wanted to be left alone. He was content to remain here, in his own little corner of the world.

He looked up again. Some motion had caught the corner of his eye. He stared up the trail into the hills. *Strange that a wolf would venture in the open during daylight.*

He caught up the spear leaning against the side of the frame. But the animal trotted forward fearlessly, and Togarmah finally realized that it was a dog—one clearly comfortable with humans. Had one of the migrant shepherds wandered this far west? Just then two figures appeared out of the vale, one holding the other upright, stumbling behind the dog. He ran towards them, but stopped, astonished, as he recognized Madrazi. Her clothes were torn and dirty and her face was drawn with pain, but there was no doubt. Her companion looked even stranger. At first, he thought she was a boy; her clothes were a man's, her hair was pulled back from her face, and she held her bow like someone who knew how to use it. There was a fire in her eye that burned through the exhaustion and pain.

He had never seen such a sight and he drew up short, looking past the women, expecting a company of others. Remembering his manners, he hurried to help the women, stopping suddenly when the dog laid back its ears and snarled. Madrazi spoke and the dog relented but its eye followed his every move.

"What brings you to our desolate shore, my lady?" he asked. "Are you hurt?"

Jael interrupted him abruptly. "Men from Nimrod—at least four—have sought our lives these past nine days. They killed everyone at Shem's farm and we barely escaped. They're an hour behind and closing fast."

Togarmah felt a twinge of annoyance beneath the shock of this news. It seemed the war had come at last, and his refuge was not as remote as he once thought. He wanted nothing to do with that conflict. Then he shook himself. Madrazi had taught him most of what he knew. He owed her, and he was a man who paid his debts. He put Madrazi's arm over his shoulder and helped her along towards his home. "Who are you, young lady?" he asked.

"My name is Jael," she snapped, and said nothing more. Togarmah hesitated. Noah's daughter? Here? Dressed as a shepherd? What more might this day bring?

Madrazi drew herself up. "I am sorry to bring this trouble at your door, but we had nowhere else to go. Only on the water can we outrun these men. Can you loan us a sturdy boat, Togarmah? One that the two of us could handle? The men behind know nothing of the sea."

Togarmah nodded. "I have two at the dock, my lady, and either is yours, of course. Do you need my help? Where are you going?"

Jael pulled Madrazi forward. "We can talk as we prepare," she snapped. "There's no time to lose."

The man looked again at Jael. Women were for the home, tending the hearth and raising children. But this one… she had the look of a wild animal. It was not just the clothing. It was not even the ease with which she handled her bow or the long knife at her waist. It was her eyes. They were dangerous eyes, and he turned away from her predatory stare. Madrazi shot him a wry sympathetic smile. "You can see who will be captain," she remarked dryly. Jael gave her a dirty look but continued to pull her forward.

"Remind me of your vessels," Madrazi continued, as they walked down towards the beach. Three houses sat on the bench above high tide and several sheds littered the area. Drying fish hung on racks scattered mostly downwind of the houses. But prominent before them was a pier stretching fifty cubits out into the water. Two vessels lay against it; a smaller on the right and a larger on the left.

"The old *Kef* is a fine craft," he replied, waving at the smaller ship. "She's handy in any breeze and with her centerboard down, she rides the waves much better than her size suggests." Madrazi remembered advising him to add the centerboard years ago. He smiled with her as he shared that memory.

He waved over at the larger craft. "The *Jez* is newer and able to hold more fish, but it is a rough ride in hard waters and takes three able men to handle. Must you leave right away? The women and children are down the beach collecting mussels and will be sorry to miss you."

"Togarmah, my son," she answered, staring into his eyes. "These men are murderers. We will take *Kef*; handling *Jez* would be impossible. But these men will take *Jez* after us, even if they don't know how to sail her. They will probably threaten your life and those of your family to force you to go with them. Whatever happens, do not go! That would seal your fate. If necessary, dive off and swim away. They cannot. Be thankful that your family is not here to offer hostages."

Togarmah paled. "What kind of men are they raising down south?"

"Evil men," replied Jael shortly. "Just give them what they want and let the sea deal with them."

Madrazi looked back as they stepped out onto the pier. "Send a runner to the Lake of the Islands and another to Noah. Tell them all that has happened here and tell them to give you a hundredweight of silver to pay for your ships."

Togarmah started to protest, but Madrazi gripped his arm. "It is only just. You need to live while you rebuild them. Give them this necklace as a token of my pledge." She removed a golden chain with a tarnished tooth attached that was easily the length of his finger. "This is precious to me," she said. "Tell them that Shem made it for me after killing a great lizard long ago. By that, they will know that you obtained it freely."

"What shall I tell them when they ask where you go?" asked Togarmah. "Will you seek Japheth at the straits?"

Madrazi shook her head. "Tell them that we go to find Shem and the boys. I'll send word when I can. Tell them I said to keep faith and look to Noah for wisdom."

Togarmah drew up amazed. "But Shem and the men are in the middle of all that," he waved his arms north. "How will you ever find them?"

"Good question," Jael muttered under her breath.

Madrazi ignored her. "Jael will guide me and God will protect us." Jael snorted as she began to untie the lines from the posts of the dock.

Togarmah roused himself, slid the necklace into his pouch, and began to help her. "Here, let someone who knows how," he growled. "There's bread, water, and wine aboard… enough for five men for a week. There are also a few lines for fishing, some spare blankets forward in storage, and leather for boots or gloves. Here," he thrust his spear to Madrazi. "You will need this more than I. May it protect your life."

Hesitantly she gripped it and thanked him with a wan smile. Then she turned to the ship. Sirus hung back, but at Madrazi's call, he slunk onto the pier and down into the boat. Madrazi followed. She looked around with an experienced eye. *Kef* was twenty-five cubits long, with a sharp bow and stern. Its single mast was short and stout, and held a large triangular sail. The proportions gave her a handy ride, even in rough seas. He saw Madrazi frown slightly at the steering oar on the starboard stern; she liked a central tiller and rudder, but the oar had been easier to make.

Jael finished untying the last rope and threw it haphazardly into the boat. Togarmah sighed. Madrazi would have much to teach that girl. He seized the side and began to walk the boat forward along the pier, grateful that it moved easily through the water. At the end of the dock he gave it a good push and it floated out onto the water. "Remember," she called across the widening gap. "Give them the ship, but do not go with them!"

He stood watching as she turned her attention to the ship. If she didn't get the sail up, the waves would soon take them back into the shore. Fortunately, he had installed a winch to raise and lower the sail; it made fishing easier and would enable the two women to manage that evolution with their limited strength. He watched over the gap as Madrazi walked forward and wrapped the line around its barrel.

"Help me, Jael," he heard. "Crank this... no, the other way... until I say to stop." The sail began to flap as it caught the northeasterly wind and Madrazi ran back to the steering oar. Jael looked helplessly around. Madrazi called out to her, "Coil that rope carefully and then come back here."

Togarmah chuckled to himself. The warrior who had been so fierce on land looked as helpless as a child on the boat. As the ship gathered way, it slipped out onto the calm waters. He saw Jael point back towards the coast. Turning, he saw two dark figures, sprinting towards him, their angry cries flying past him out across the water.

Korac pumped his feet as fast as he could. He could hear Jalam's labored breathing above his own, but the men had seen the women embarking in the small ship and were sprinting at full speed. They ignored Togarmah as they flashed out onto the long pier. Jalam pulled his bow as they thundered down the wooden planks. By the time they stopped at the end, he had an arrow notched and drawn to his cheek. He planted his feet, breathed out, and let fly. He cursed. His hands were shaking from the run and his arrow fell a few cubits short. He pulled another. The ship was moving, but slowly. Doing his best to control his breathing, he adjusted the arc and let fly.

The second arrow flew through the sunlit air and embedded itself in the railing near the stern. He fired again, but the arrow fell into the water behind the fleeing boat. One of the figures pulled the arrow from the side and held it up, mockingly. Then she snapped it contemptuously and threw it in the water, but not before spitting on the pieces.

It was an enraged Jalam who turned on the staring Togarmah and pulled his knife. "Who was that with *The Woman*?" he demanded. All the frustration and anger of the past weeks welled up in him and he drew back his blade to strike.

"If you kill me," replied the man easily, "I can tell you nothing."

Jalam started to lunge forward, but Korac blocked him. "Then start talking," he said softly to Togarmah, "or I will withdraw my arm."

Togarmah's courage held in the face of Jalam's fury, but it withered before the empty blackness in Korac's eyes. "It was the Lady Madrazi and her companion, Jael, the daughter of Noah," he replied, trying to keep his voice from shaking.

Korac stood, stunned. Jael! After all these years! He had heard vague rumors of her vow of vengeance. He had laughed at first, but he laughed no longer. No mere female should have been able to outdistance his men, especially having to shepherd *The Woman* across the wilderness. He thought back over the past days, remembering how faint her trail had been, her choices of shelter, and the carefully hidden remains of her kills. She knew exactly what she was doing.

Shem must have trained her and trained her well. Even if she couldn't fight, she had proven dangerous, and Korac began to suspect that she could fight as well as she could travel. A curious thought struck him; while acting as a monster, he had created another—one who had stolen his prey and would cheerfully and skillfully turn on him and take his life too.

Wen-Tehrom's words came back to him.

> *You think you cannot feel because you have lost your soul. But it is not gone. Only hidden. One day it will find you again. When it does, the consequences of your lost years and especially this day will haunt you and cost you another loved one. When that day comes, only my children will be able to help you, and they will despise your very name. I could almost pity you that misery.*

Was this what she meant? Had she cursed him, knowing that her daughter would one day exact retribution? He shook his head slightly, distracted as Jalam pushed against his arm once more.

"And you just gave them a boat?" Jalam was still in a killing mood. He clearly didn't care if the man was Korac's cousin or not.

"Of course," Togarmah shrugged. "She is an elder. I would have *no* boats without her knowledge and help."

"Where is she going?" demanded Jalam. He had stepped back, but his knife was waist high, in close, its point steady. Korac knew he could strike like an adder, and kept himself ready to intercept it if necessary. They needed Togarmah alive for the time being.

"I don't know," lied Togarmah easily. All she said was that she could outrun you on the water, and that you would never find her."

"*Never* is such a long time." Korac's face was hard and his voice soft. "But if that's how long it takes, then we'll still be at it."

Togarmah started to open his mouth. Korac watched, reading his face. He wanted to ask why, but then realized that asking would seal his fate, cousin or no. After all, these men were willing to kill an elder…. His mouth snapped shut. Korac smiled to himself. It didn't matter, once his usefulness was over... but for now the illusion of life better served his purpose.

"There's still a ship here," mused Korac. "And an experienced sailor. This one is larger; it should be able to catch that small craft."

Togarmah kept his face neutral, hiding the contempt he felt. Korac's stubbornness was impressive, but his knowledge of ships was not. *Jez* might be nearly forty cubits long and rugged in heavy seas, but even with her two masts, she handled like a pig. She was for moving large loads of fish, nothing more. But if Korac was ignorant of ships, he was decisive.

"Jalam," he ordered. "Go find the twins and bring them here as fast as they can run." He turned to Togarmah. "Get food and water aboard that ship!"

"It's already provisioned," admitted Togarmah. "We were going out fishing in two days."

Korac turned his dark eyes full on his cousin. "No, we're going hunting... today!"

They stood in an uncomfortable silence, watching Jalam sprint back up into the hills. Korac broke it suddenly. "Where are the others?" He tried to sound casual, knowing his cousin was canny, but Togarmah did not confuse anything Korac said for small talk.

Togarmah held his voice steady. "The men are cutting timber up in the hills. The others are far down the coast, gathering and smoking mussels for the winter."

Korac stared back up towards the hills. Jalam disappeared behind a fold in the ground. "When my men get here, you will sail us after the women. If we don't catch her, you will die, but only after we come back here, wait for your family to return, and kill them all before your eyes.

"My men will be back in a few days," replied Togarmah. "If they find you here, they'll kill you."

Korac's lip twitched upward. "You have no *men*. Only sheep. If you had a hundred, the four of us would still slay them all." He saw with satisfaction that Togarmah believed him. *Good! He would do as told.*

Togarmah held the tiller, trying hard not to laugh. Korac, for all his boasting was worried, and Togarmah silently wished Madrazi favorable winds. *Kef* was out of sight now, coasting easily off to the west; *Jez* would never catch her, even if he knew her course. But just to make sure, he steered a point or two north of west; if the men kept this course, they would eventually run aground on a harsh, barren peninsula on the north coast. Madrazi knew the Black Sea; these men did not, and so could not know of the large rocky cape, a little more than half the length of the ocean. If they landed there, Madrazi would have a month's lead. It was the best he could do.

It had taken nearly an hour for the other three men to come panting into the yard, and Togarmah had tried to delay by offering to care for the injured man. "We'll tend to him later," Korac had answered. So he had done the best he could, taking valuable minutes to get the men aboard, explain the different lines, cast off the ropes, raise the sails, and get underway.

Outwardly, Togarmah remained the picture of cooperation. He had considered setting less sail and reducing speed, but he reasoned to himself that if the winds rose, they would have more trouble with too much sail than with too little. The houses and pier were receding in the distance. He must jump soon. Korac and the twins were forward, tending to the injured man, but Jalam was too close. He was suspicious, in spite of all Togarmah's bluff cooperation. Just then, the mainsail flapped as the wind gusted by. Togarmah pointed at a rope. "Pull that line a little tighter and lash it off," he told Jalam.

"Why?"

"Because if you do not, we will go slower, and if I go to do it, your inability to steer a straight course will slow us even more."

Jalam frowned. He struggled with the idea for a moment, then shrugged and turned away. As soon as he began pulling the rope, Togarmah put a hand on the railing and vaulted over the side. He took a moment to shed his robe, and then dove deep and began swimming steadily east. He had seen Jalam shoot and wanted to be far away when he came up for air.

Korac was roused by Jalam's shout. He ran for the stern, where Jalam was standing looking back along their wake. "He jumped! The miserable son of a goat sent me to fix the sail and then jumped over. Let's turn around! When I get him back, I'll lash him to the mast and flay the skin from him!"

"How are we going to turn around," asked Korac quietly. "The wind is blowing from the shore and I don't know how to sail into it. Do you?"

Jalam deflated. It was clear that he did not. The twins looked terrified. Neither could swim and neither could sail.

Korac knew he must regain order quickly. "I've sailed smaller craft on the rivers," he said confidently. "We'll follow the women. They're sailing with the same wind. Jalam," he seized his cousin's arm, "climb up the mast and see if you can spot their vessel. Dishon," he nodded at the stern, "take the tiller and steer a straight course. You can do that with one arm. Just watch our wake to stay on course."

"Dishan and I will see to the sails. This ship is barely twice the size of river boats that I've piloted," he lied. "We'll be fine. Besides, I think I know where she's going."

It was the final sentence that got the others' attention. The coast had receded and the sight of water as far as the eye could see was unnerving.

"Where?" asked Dishan.

"Japheth, Gomer, and Javan are exploring across the straits at the other end of the Black Sea, where it flows into the Great Sea. She's running to them. We'll follow and kill them all!"

The men nodded slowly and turned to their tasks, confident in their captain in spite of their fear.

Chapter 44
TEMPEST

10-22-1760

Madrazi felt a chill in the morning wind as the sky gradually lightened. The sun felt good as it crested the horizon, but in its light she could see clouds building in the east. They had been very lucky. The Black Sea was unpredictable at its best, but with winter approaching, avoiding storms and squalls had been an act of a gracious providence. *Kef* was a good ship, but even two experienced men would have been hard pressed to ride out a storm, and Madrazi was under no illusion that she and Jael could survive one.

Despite their need of rest, neither had been able to sleep for more than a few hours each night. She knew exhaustion was clouding her mind, and even Jael seemed worn down. Nine days fleeing through the wilderness and six days on the deep had taken their toll. At least on board ship she didn't have to walk! But running a ship, even a small boat like this, used muscles that she had not used since she was a girl, and her body cried for relief. Jael had learned fast and had the sense to let Madrazi command the ship, but she was clearly uncomfortable on the water. Only Sirus really enjoyed the voyage. He spent hours curled at Madrazi's feet as she steered the vessel, regaining his young strength quickly.

Jael had insisted they save as much of the hard biscuit and wine as possible for harder days ahead, but they didn't go hungry, as Madrazi had been able to catch a few fish along the way. Fortunately the sea was calm enough to use the small brazier to cook them. Madrazi wrinkled her nose—they both smelled like fish… among other things.

Jael's voice rang down from the masthead, interrupting Madrazi's reverie. "I can see land. Low hills and the mouth of a large river." She pointed her right arm. Madrazi steered a little to starboard until the bow matched Jael's direction.

"Come down," she cried. "This will be difficult, and I need to tell you what to do. We won't have time later."

Jael slid down and walked back to the steering oar. Her face was tired—thinner, but harder. Madrazi got the impression that privation would only toughen Jael, not defeat her. Pointing behind them, she told the younger woman, "Those clouds are the front of a storm. Winter rides those winds, and we must find shelter before they catch us. I intend to sail right up the river, find a sheltered bend, and ride out the storm. Look out for shallow water where the river enters the sea. Sand bars appear and disappear easily in those waters and we cannot afford to run aground. As soon as the water shallows, come down and raise the centerboard. Then hurry back up the mast and keep a sharp eye. Find the biggest channel and direct me through its twists and turns."

"How much sail will we need?"

"Normally, I would only show enough for steerage, but with the storm coming, we'll have to risk more. Lower the sail half way as soon as we hit the river and be prepared to move fast if we must trim more."

Jael nodded, then pointed. "Look! You can see the land from here. Another hour or two should see us to the river."

The day was growing dark rapidly as the *Jez* plunged up and down the rising waves. There had been no sign of the other ship since the afternoon of the first day, when Jalam had caught a glimpse of her bearing west. Korac knew that the women could have turned north or south anytime afterward. In which case, they were losing ground, not gaining it.

But sailing this pig of a ship had taken all their efforts and attention. They had learned many lessons in the calm water and steady winds of the first five days. From the look of the gathering clouds, they were going to need all their newfound skill. There was still nothing but water all around; the wind had carried them west with a slight northerly drift. And now the wind was shifting slightly, pushing them further north.

Korac and Dishan feverishly reduced sail as a gust heeled the ship over. Wind beat the growing waves into foam. In a moment the water and sky had transformed from merely threatening to immediately deadly. Though only a fraction of the canvas was showing, the squall's breathtaking fury split the foresail to tatters. Even so, the ship that had been slower than an ox was now hurtling through the water. Korac could see nothing beyond the rain and the waves.

Jalam joined them on deck. "You nearly lost me," he panted. "I can't keep my place up there any more!"

"Did you see anything?" Korac grunted.

"I'm not sure," Jalam admitted. "But I might have seen land up ahead. If so, we're headed straight for it."

"That's good news," spat out Dishan. "I'm sick of the water."

"Think about how we would be introduced to the land in this storm," suggested Jalam sardonically.

"Oh." Dishan's ruddy face was suddenly white.

"Yes. Oh." Korac sighed. "Prepare for the worst. Hope for the best. If we strike, try to seize a piece of wood and cling to it with all your might." He stumbled as a rogue wave smashed into the side of the ship and reached out to steady Jalam with his strong right arm. Dishan was thrown to the deck and slid to the opposite side as the water threatened to wash him overboard. Korac turned to Jalam, "Lash your bow to your body," he urged as he quickly did the same with his spear. "If we survive this, we'll need our weapons. Go drink and eat now, and take food to the others. We may not get another chance."

Jalam stumbled forward to retrieve skins and bread, while Korac fought the wind back to the tiller. "Can you manage?" He was shouting now as the wind was shrieking across the deck. The corner of the mainsail exploded as an even stronger gust tore across the ship. Dishon was pale and his arm was bleeding again. He clenched his teeth and nodded.

"Try to keep the waves to our stern," cautioned Korac. Before he could utter another word, both men heard the thunder ahead. Terror filled Dishon's face and even Korac's iron mask cracked. Jalam came stumbling back, burdened with a water skin. "That's surf!" he shouted. "We're...."

His words were torn from his mouth as the ship lurched. The crash of wood beneath them was followed by the crash of water behind. The raised stern protected them from the full force of the wave breaking over the ship; it slewed the ship around on its grounded keel, and the next wave loomed high over their heads.

Korac remembered that moment as if it were an hour. He saw the wave rising impossibly high over their heads as he felt the ship swing around. Acting by instinct, he grabbed Jalam with his left hand and leapt over the side just as the wave arrived. Water was suddenly all about him; he lost his grip on Jalam. He was tumbling through the water, no longer knowing up from down.

He felt the wave's power; he was moving faster than he could run, and there was nothing he could do to control his body. Water filled his eyes, his nose, and his ears, and his chest began to ache. Before his mind could decide what to do, his head broke the surface. He drew in as much air as he could. In spite of the water in his eyes, he saw the coast rushing at him at a terrifying speed. It appeared to be a beach, but slanting steeply up. In the next moment, the water had pulled him down again, hurtling him forward. He wrapped his arms around his head and forced his body to go limp. It was just in time. The wave struck with awesome force, slamming him into the sand and pebbles, and then dragging him further up the strand. As it did, the terrible force diminished, and he was able to move his arms and legs. Frantically, he scrambled forward, desperate to avoid being pulled back into the maelstrom of the sea. Then his head was again out of the water and his limbs were moving as fast as he could pump them.

He looked back. Another wave was rushing towards him at frightening speed. His limbs felt like blocks of wood, and he cursed his lack of speed. Turning back to land, he put all his remaining energy into propelling himself a few cubits further up the slope. He did not need to look back; he felt the explosive crash of the wave breaking onto the shore and felt it surge about his thighs. It began to retreat, pulling him out to sea. He fought back, but it was like pulling against an ox. All he could do was slow his retreat by ducking beneath the water and digging his hands into the earth. Just as his chest threatened to burst, the water left him, and fear propelled him forward.

This time he made the bench above the beach and found a rock to cling to. When the next wave broke, it only lapped his knees and did not dislodge him. Suddenly, he could hear the wind again. Another wave was coming. He scrambled a few cubits higher. He desperately wanted to lie down and rest, but that path led to death. He must get higher. Somehow he did, and found himself sitting against a large rock face, shivering—equal parts of fear and cold—as his body fought to recover from the struggle. It was some time before his mind began to function once more. A voice inside was telling him to get up. If he went to sleep now, he would probably never wake up, but his weariness whispered "so what?"

Gathering his strength, he loosened the straps that still held his spear across his broad back and used it to pull himself to his feet. The wind seemed colder now, and his hands could hardly feel the shaft. He needed fire. He staggered along the rocky face looking back at the scene of disaster. He could just make out the outline of the ship—much farther offshore than he had first imagined—and saw how lucky he had been. The beach was narrow and bounded north and south by rocky hills that came down to the water. Had he been cast up on those, he would certainly be dead.

He looked up and down the bench. Two figures were stumbling towards him. Jalam and Dishan grew near. Their clothes were in tatters and both were bleeding where the water had dragged them across sand or rock. But both were alive and walking. He was suddenly aware that his own clothing was no better, and that blood was dripping from his hands, arms, and face. But he could walk, so he staggered to meet them.

"We found a cave and some wood, although it's wet. Do you still have your striker?" Jalam sounded even worse than he looked.

Korac felt under his tunic and found the cord around his neck; the pouch still resting against his chest. He pulled it out and showed the others. Jalam tried to smile, but the best he could manage was a wince. He turned and led Korac back to the north end of the bench and along a rocky defile heading inland. Within a few steps they were at the cave; wood had washed down the gully and lined the walls, mixed with rocks and pounded to splinters in some cases.

Each grabbed a load and carried it inside. Dishan trudged back out to get more wood, while Jalam and Korac knelt down. Jalam began shaving the smaller pieces and Korac pulled out the striker. It had been a gift from Ham years ago, before.... He shook his head and untangled the cord that held the small piece of steel to the flint stick. Within minutes, and despite the damp wood, there was a small blaze going. Korac begin to think they might survive. The cave was beginning to warm up and the wind, blowing up the defile, sucked the smoke outside. Dishan returned with another load of wood.

Korac gathered his thoughts. "Two hours on. Me first. Then Jalam. Then Dishan." Korac leaned on his spear, feeling his fingers grip the shaft once more.

"Shouldn't we search for Dishon?" Dishan stared at the entrance.

"He's gone," grated Korac. "Even if he made it off the ship, he would have needed two strong arms. He didn't have a chance. Curse Togarmah! We will pay him a visit some day. But not now! If you stumble down that beach, the chances are good that you will never return. We still have a job to do, and I can do it easier with three than with two. Sleep!"

Dishan glanced out the entrance and glared back at Korac. "He served you well, and you make no effort to help him?"

Korac stared at him until Dishan dropped his eyes. "If there was any chance at all," he conceded, "we would all be looking. But there's not. Jalam and I got clear of the ship before the first wave struck. Dishon did not. He was probably gone before he knew what was happening. You can take your vengeance on those women and on Togarmah. But we can do nothing unless we stay alive. Sleep!"

Dishan turned his back and curled up on the floor. Jalam glanced at Korac and raised an eyebrow. Korac shook his head slightly. Dishan was no threat. Not today. Tomorrow was another day, but tomorrow would take care of itself. He tended the fire and staunched his cuts. When Jalam woke to take his turn watching, Korac fell to the stone floor. It felt as comfortable as a soft bed to his exhausted body and he was asleep within moments. But deep memories arose to trouble his dreams.

The bear was far too close; it had been hiding in a nest of boulders that seemed far too small to shelter its vast bulk. It moved awkwardly, but quickly enough for its size. They had hit it hard, but there was vitality enough for rage and revenge. Blood stained the coarse brown hair down one side and across its right shoulder, but its ability to kill was undiminished. Especially in this enclosed valley. He felt a surge of fear and dimly heard Timna gasp. The reality of a cornered monster was much different than the boasts around last night's fire. She stood frozen, unable to run.

Where was Nimrod?

He saw every hair, every fleck of blood on its chest… he even noticed the broken claw on its near paw. But most of all he saw its red, porcine eyes— cunning, hate-filled eyes—as it rose up in front of them, barely twenty paces away. If it had charged immediately, it could have killed them before its presence even registered clearly. He had no illusions about the speed of even a wounded bear. But it was angry too, and took the time to heave its bulk up on its rear legs… to defy the puny humans who dared challenge its supremacy in this corner of the wilderness. Fully erect, it was easily twice a man's height; its dirty brown coat was stained with bright blood from two arrows in its neck. Its yellow claws were spread, each one as long as his hand. Those claws could rip the life from a bull with one blow, and a comparatively puny man stood no chance.

Surprise dulled Korac's reactions, and as he raised his bow, its end bumped into Timna, slowing his response. He would never get it up on time. Terror made his hand tremble. He despised his weakness….

Where was Nimrod?

Chapter 45
CHAINS OF COMMAND

12-3-1760

Jael sat on the deck, ignoring the cold northwest wind. More snow was coming; she could feel it. All the more reason for this work—the deer had been the size of a horse, and its hide would be invaluable. They needed warm clothes and shelter, and soon. There was no time to properly cure the hides, but rawhide would serve for everything from boots to blankets. She wrinkled her nose; in the absence of lime or salt, she had resorted to their own waste to preserve the hides.

But as much as they needed it, the skin was the least of her worries, and she wouldn't have bothered if she didn't need the time alone to consider her many dilemmas. Two were particularly troubling and weeks of trying to solve them had proven futile.

The first, and most disturbing, was Madrazi's attitude. She lacked the constant fear needed to stay alive. Not a moment passed that Jael did not think about their pursuers. Were they an hour away or a month? She always assumed the shorter and so stayed continually alert. But Madrazi had grown complacent, thinking the men had died in the tempest.

Two months of precious time had been wasted on this cursed ship. Cross-country, they would have been so far ahead that their trail would have been completely untraceable. But two months of uncooperative winds and an-even-more uncooperative sister saw them barely fifteen days' march upstream. Whenever she raised the topic, Madrazi would roll her eyes and give the same answer: "We barely beat a nasty storm. Those men are dead or marooned, no longer a problem."

Jael had finally lost her temper the day before, and shouted at her sister. "Then why aren't we sailing back home?"

Madrazi had clamped her jaw and said nothing, but her eyes had been emerald fire. Showing her the inherent contradiction between her fears and hopes had only hardened her to *any* words, no matter how reasonable. Now she was afraid, but at present, she was angrier at Jael. It was clear that Shem had never taught her the harsher lessons he had imparted to Jael. Not an hour went by that Jael was not imagining the men catching them unawares: how she would fight, which weapons to choose if cornered, how she would react if injured. Madrazi never gave those issues a moment's notice.

Jael cursed her temper as she worked the hide. If only she could curb her tongue! It seemed that every time she opened her mouth her inner rage broke through in words that she longed to unsay. She rubbed the stone fiercely across the pelt. Madrazi was caught in a vortex of uncertainty. She wanted to believe that the men were dead, that God had taken retribution for the lives they had snuffed out at the farm, but she didn't know. And Jael's pungent comments about wishful thinking and the need to see the dismembered corpses hadn't helped either.

But she knew she was right. Shem had taught her well. *Never underestimate your enemy. Never assume his actions will conform to your desires. That's how to get killed.* But Shem wasn't here to explain that to his wife.

Jael knew her fears were well founded. She had recognized her deadly foe on the pier as they sailed away. She hate him, but would never sell him short. If she had been Korac, she would have headed for shore—any shore—as soon as the storm began to gather. Even marooned days east of the river, he would still be alive. And as long as he was alive, he would come. And he could have covered a lot of shoreline in two months.

Madrazi's misplaced logic had only grown more convoluted. If Korac was alive, she argued, he would have caught them already. It took all of Jael's self control not to scream that reinforcing one bad assumption with another was foolish... not to mention that the consequence of a horrible death for both women.

She had let Madrazi talk her into this insane quest to find Shem, but then let her hamstring their chances of living long enough to try. They should have been another month upstream, moving forward on foot.

And that was the second problem. Madrazi did not want to leave the boat. It had provided a haven from the blood and death that had burst into her world so terribly. First Korac and his men... the death at the farm (she was still having nightmares)... and the terrible chase to the Black Sea. It had only been that first afternoon aboard *Kef*, watching *Jez* fall slowly astern and finally out of sight that the women had been able to relax—and then, only Madrazi. For Jael, the dangers and hardships of sailing across the Black Sea had seemed just as bad as Korac.

Jael understood. Everyone wanted the illusion of control and Korac had yanked that away from Madrazi, just as he had years ago from her. In some strange way the ship had restored a measure of that illusion and Madrazi clung to it with a tenacity that had to be seen to be believed.

Jael dared not mention the other reason Madrazi wanted to stay with the ship... partly because she feared her sister's rage and partly because she feared her own. Madrazi had promised back in the cave on that terrible first day to follow Jael. And she had done so with perfect humility on the race to the sea. But once on board the ship, something had come over her. Maybe it was memories of days before the flood. Maybe it was necessity. For whatever reason, Madrazi had taken control of the trek in seizing command of the ship. Her orders had at first been entirely about running the ship. Pull this line. Hold the steering oar just so. Tie this knot.

But as the days passed, that command had pushed the boundaries, and the orders began to touch on other things. It had been innocent... perhaps in the beginning she hadn't even realized it was happening. But there came the day when Jael wanted to abandon the ship and make their way on foot. Madrazi had flatly refused and insisted they stay with the ship. Her arguments were all reasonable and delivered in that sweet tone of voice that had the men eating out of her hand, but Jael was no man. All the arguments in the world about how convenient and safe the ship was were nothing compared to their rate of progress.

It was simple. They were slow. Korac was fast. Eventually he would catch them. Then they would die.

Now Madrazi was using the weather as an excuse. It had snowed a few nights ago and the sky promised more. "We need to moor the ship, find a comfortable cave, and let the winter storms blow past. In the spring we'll have favorable winds and can ride *Kef* to the head of this river and find the men." When Jael began to demur, she had been abruptly cut off. "Even if Korac is alive and pursuing, he will have to take shelter too. No man can survive the storms and the cold."

Jael had wanted to say something then, but things had gotten so far out of hand that she hadn't known what to say. She was right and knew she was right, but her tongue felt like lead, and the only words that came to mind would have been angry and offensive. Was God repaying all her provocations over the years?

And that was yet another problem. Strife was a luxury neither woman could afford. Their survival rode on their ability to work together, and Jael had sworn to the Almighty and to her father that she would preserve Madrazi's life. Madrazi had broken her word, but that was no excuse. Jael would keep hers. She gritted her teeth. She had hoped at least that they might keep sailing upstream, but within a day Madrazi had found the perfect spot to hole up. In other circumstances Jael would have admired her eye for the terrain. A small tributary flowing in from the north offered a safe mooring for the ship, and the hills overlooking that stream had contained an ideal cave. It was snug, had water seeping inside, and best of all, it had a back entrance that would be hard to find and was too small for men to squeeze through.

So, ignoring every screaming instinct, she had given in. Madrazi had tied the ship to trees on both sides of the stream, letting it swing free in the deeper channel. She was now up in the cave, building a stove, laying furs down for beds, gathering wood, and preparing for a long, cozy winter. Jael could have been up there, enjoying the warmth and comfort, but in her present state, she deemed it better that she work the edge off her anger on the boat.

She took a deep breath. Shem had also taught the importance of self control, but that seemed to be the most difficult lesson of all. What was she going to do?

She did something she had not done for many days. She put the tools aside, got onto her knees, and prayed. How many minutes she spent there, she never knew, but during that interlude, something like a sigh breathed through her heart, and she felt her tensions ease. She sat up abruptly, knowing what she must do. She would honor her word, but for now she would also honor her sister and stay. She could not drag Madrazi out into the winter wilderness against her will. And perhaps Madrazi was right… perhaps Korac and his killers were dead.

She shook her head. Even this newfound peace could not erase the deeper instinct that told her he was alive. She would kill Korac without compunction but would never underestimate his ability. The two of them had a destined part to play, and it would not be as simple as the man dying in a storm. But it was also true that there had been no sign of them for weeks.

Jael sighed. She would stay in the cave for a time, bringing in food to keep them alive. But while hunting, she would continue to scout the approaches from the north and east. She would build up their supply of smoked meat, add to their furs and pelts, and make warm clothes. Madrazi could enjoy her rest; Jael would be preparing for the inevitable day that would see them fleeing into the unforgiving wilderness, maybe only a step ahead of their pursuers. She hoped Madrazi was right, that they wouldn't have to leave until spring. But somewhere down in her belly a small voice was laughing at that idea, and that was the voice Shem had taught her to heed in times of need or peril.

Madrazi had usurped command of this expedition, but the day would come when circumstance would realign that chain. When it did, Jael would be ready. Madrazi might not like it, but at least she would be alive to protest. Jael swore again that she would not fail. She would never give Korac the satisfaction of hurting her family again... ever! If it came down to life and death, then she would die, but so would he. It would be enough.

She gathered the hide up from the deck, threw it over to the shore, climbed up on the rail and leapt across the dark waters. Gathering up the hide and her weapons, she made her way up the hill to the cave, forcing a smile. It looked more like a death mask, but it was the best she could do.

Heth gripped his spear a little tighter and dared not move a muscle. These leopards might not be lions or even the great dagger-fanged cats, but any cat was dangerous. They were smart, instinctive killers, and even a small one could tear a man apart. Unfortunately, they were also near... very near. His back was to a large tree and his eyes scanned the underbrush around him, looking for anything out of place—any flicker of color or movement that would locate his prey.

After crossing the giant river they had made good time. A range of mountains appeared far to the south, drawing nearer day by day before gradually fading into the south once more. It seemed to run in a great curve from east to west along the southern edge of the plain; at its apex, they were close enough to see the snow glittering on the higher peaks, and Shem had thought them well over two thousand cubits. Though breathtakingly beautiful, the mountains stayed to their left, never impeding their westward progress across the plains. When they began to curve back southwest, Shem had veered southwest too, following the edge of the foothills.

As they traveled further west, the grassy plains gave way to a forested land of thick, dark woods, but with large meadows providing relief from their confining closeness. The men had found a large river running east-northeast and followed it upstream until the winter storms had begun to blow. Cold winds followed them, rushing unimpeded from the east, bringing bitter cold. Eventually even Shelah admitted the need to stop, find shelter, and wait out the winter.

It was Jobaath, of course, who had spotted the cave. It was nicely situated on a bluff above the river, but it was already inhabited by a pair of white leopards—a point that somehow escaped Jobaath's attention until the five men and two cats had arrived at the entrance at the same time. All of the men had been tired and unwary, the two white leopards had loomed out of the snow like fierce ghosts in front of them. For a moment, it appeared the cats might attack, but the mule started braying and kicking, and the cats had spooked, disappearing before even Shem could loose an arrow.

So here we are, thought Heth, *hunting two cats probably hunting us.* For his failure, Jobaath had been left at the cave with the half-crazed mule, with stern instructions to get a large fire started to keep the rightful residents as far away as possible. Even with the burden of settling the cursed mule, Heth would have traded places with him in a heartbeat… he could have killed the mule and then built the fire. Instead, he was sitting out here in the snow, trying to find two angry cats that blended perfectly with the white landscape.

A slight sound just to the left drew Heth's attention. His eyes tracked around; the point of his spear automatically followed. Then there was the hiss of an arrow, the meaty sound of its strike, and an enraged snarl just over his head. Without thinking, Heth dove to his right, rolling with his spear. It saved his life. But it wasn't over. The other cat had been waiting in a nearby copse, and seeing their ambush fail, it streaked straight towards Heth like a white lightning bolt.

But Heth was on his feet, ready. Now that he could see his foe, his body reacted even as his mind registered the scene. His spear came up and then flew at the cat with all the force of his powerful body. Straight into the onrushing leopard it tore. Even as it halted the cat in mid-air, an arrow struck its side, but the cat was already dead. It plowed into the snow a few paces from Heth, and the fiery anger in its eyes slowly burned away to glassy nothingness.

At the same time, other arrows were sinking into the first cat, and it too fell dead, right on the spot Heth had been standing. In a moment, it was over. As Heth stepped forward to retrieve his spear, his body began to shake. He had to force his hands to remain steady—he didn't want to show fear to men like Shem and Shelah. Both stepped out into the open, Shem off to the left and Shelah to the right. It had been Shem's arrows that killed the first cat and Shelah's that had pierced the second, although its heart had been ripped apart by Heth's well-thrown spear.

Crushing his fear, he turned to his friend. "Why did you have to put another hole in such a fine pelt?" He was proud of the steady, slightly-aggrieved tone that his voice managed. Turning to Shem, he held out his hand. "Thank you," was all he said. Shem hid his half smile and nodded before taking the big man's hand with a sharp grip.

"You make good bait," he drawled, but Heth could see the worry fading in the back of his eyes. "And that was a mighty cast of your spear. I thought you would hold it and fight in close."

"Only a madman like Jobaath would let something like that get that near," Heth laughed. "It was *too* close."

"Yes it was," agreed Shem. "We all need to be careful. My wife would skin me alive if we returned with less than we started."

"Would she miss the mule?" asked Heth.

"Would you rather carry its pack?" Shem was leaning on his bow and chuckling; the tension and terror of the hunt was fading. "Why don't you and Shelah carry your cat back to the cave? Its skin will make a nice blanket in the months ahead. I'll show you how to preserve it, if you would want."

Shelah interrupted. "Surely it was my arrow that killed the beast. Maybe I should take the pelt." Heth turned and glared at him. "Maybe you should have shot sooner," he snarled.

Shelah smiled. "All right. I concede the pelt. But the next one is mine. Let's get back to the cave. If Jobaath doesn't have it warm by now, I'll use him to bait mine!"

Chapter 46
WHITE DEATH

2-25-1761

Jalam drew up against the giant tree at the meadow's edge and leaned against its bulk for support as he eyed the withered, ice-rimed grasslands leading down to the river. He was wearier than ever before—the past months felt like centuries and their weight lay heavy on him. It was cold. The river—far larger than the Euphrates—was half frozen, and only its strong current kept the middle of the channel clear. Cold had been a part of life ever since the disastrous shipwreck, yet Korac led them on, caring little for their comfort and not at all for his. They had crossed the rugged mountains of the peninsula, and then followed the unexplored shores of the Black Sea, making their way west, then south around the vast ocean.

But Jalam did not grumble. Korac had kept them alive. Fire, food, caves, weapons, pelts crudely fashioned into warm clothing—he had done the lion's share of providing these necessities. For three men facing winter in the wilderness with nearly nothing, it was only his inner fire and outer iron that had kept them going.

It seemed impossible that he still wanted to complete the mission. With no idea of where the women had sailed, they were hunting blind, relying on Korac's instinct. But those instincts were better than the reasoned contemplations of the wise. He had latched onto the river; the first time he had seen it, a light had come back to his eyes. And he had been proven right just a few days later when they began to find tangible traces: the remains of an old fire, a few sticks cut by metal blades, and rope scars on tree bark. The women were still on their boat, and still moving upstream. Best of all, they were only weeks ahead. Each day shrank that lead.

As Jalam thought back over the past months, he realized that he had changed since the shipwreck. What had started as a silly desire to face Shem had become a test of loyalty. But after the shipwreck, rage had pushed him forward. He blamed the women for the storm, the wreck, and ensuing hardships. This was a personal vendetta. Hatred drove him, fueled by frustration.

Two *women* had escaped elite assassins who had penetrated the heart of their enemy's territory and executed a perfect raid. An impossible mission completed without loss. But by a twist of fate, their target had been in the barn, escaping into the wilderness. Ordinarily that would have meant a short delay; he and Korac could bring any man to bay in the wild lands. But with a lead of just two days, the women had outraced them to the Black Sea and outsmarted them by taking to the water. The memory of Jael casually snapping his arrow only fueled his rage. Then they had led them out on the sea and nearly killed them in the storm. *But we survived*, thought Jalam. *We survived the shipwreck, found your trail, and we're coming for you!*

And yet… he could not help but concede a grudging respect for that whelp of Noah's. He frowned at the thought of her name and cursed it under his breath. For a man to have outstripped a hunter like Korac would have been a notable achievement.

For a woman to have done it was incredible. But to have done it burdened by a woman unaccustomed to the wilds was nothing short of a miracle.

It was also a sore blow to Jalam's ego. Women had survived what men had not. Jalam didn't know whether his hate stemmed more from the shipwreck or from its result—endless days of trudging around the accursed Black Sea. The loss of Dishon should have hurt more, but Jalam couldn't find that emotion inside. Dishon was not a man who would be missed by many.

But as he pondered it now—several months later—he suddenly found the heat of his hate dissipating in the cold of the oncoming winter. There was simply no room for such extravagance in this wilderness. He needed all his focus just to stay alive. Let Korac worry about the quest; Jalam was worried about something else… returning to Shinar in one piece. So he had withdrawn into himself, letting Korac take the lead each day, facing the brunt of the danger from land or predator. Jalam just followed. He pulled his share and fought when fighting was needed, but no more. After all, Korac *was* his cousin and he would remain true to that blood tie, but any enthusiasm for the job seemed to evaporate in the freezing air.

In fact, in those quiet moments at night, when the fire was the only thing that kept off the predators lurking in the darkness, pieces of truth began to seep through his conscience. One night, he woke startled, realizing that he had come to respect the women. Their accomplishments were magnificent, worthy of Noah's daughters. Despite Nimrod's despoiling of the old man's house, Noah was a name that evoked something in every man. *The father of all.* And one of these women was also an elder—a survivor of the great flood.

Now as he leaned against that tree, the twisting paths of his deepest thoughts suddenly met. He would follow Korac, but he would not lift his hand against either of them… not for all the gold in Shinar. Let Korac or Dishan do the dirty work.

He sighed. Dishan blundered up behind him, as unquiet and uncaring as ever. Something vital had left the man in the past months. Maybe it was the loss of his brother… maybe the hardships of the daily struggle for survival. Whatever the cause, the core of him was gone. Even his mind wandered. His eyes were not attuned to the wilderness; they were locked on some inner dark palce only he could see. It was as if life was slowly draining away, leaving a husk to wither and vanish in this vast forest.

Jalam watched quietly as Dishan sat down with his back to a nearby tree. His breath came in great gasps of cloudy vapor that drifted away on the probing wind. His normally fleshy face had melted into a collection of sharp ridges and gray skin above a lank beard. Sunken haunted eyes stared unseeing at the river. Jalam grimaced and turned back to the north. For weeks, they had escaped the teeth of winter; snow had been sporadic and light. But the dark clouds following hard on their heels promised to make up for those easy days. He swung his gaze south and west. Low hills called to him from the horizon. A tight cave and blazing fire might be all that stood between life and death within a few hours. Though only midmorning, the light had faded, and the forest assumed a gloomy twilight aura. The silence was palpable.

Every instinct urged him forward, but Jalam stood and waited. Korac was scouting ahead and they needed to wait for his return, especially if a storm was in the offing. So he waited, ignoring Dishan.

Finally the large gray figure loomed out of the gathering gloom. He hurried across the meadow, heedless of any potential ambush. Waving his arms, he urged them over. Jalam shouldered his pack and pulled Dishan to his feet. "Time to move," he grunted and Dishan looked up, staring at Jalam with those bleak eyes. But he followed out into the meadow.

"There are caves in that ridge," grunted Korac, panting. "The women may be there too." Jalam raised an eyebrow. Korac's mouth twitched in what for him was a wide grin. "I saw the ship's masts among the trees at the river's edge up ahead. Ice probably forced them to take shelter. We'll just march up and join them."

"Finish the job," agreed Jalam. "It would be nice to start for Shinar instead of to the far ends of the earth. Maybe we could use their ship and save the walk around the rest of the Black Sea."

His biting tone was not lost on Korac; his eyes hardened. "We need to hurry. That storm will be on us in an hour."

Jalam glanced back. The clouds were lower and thicker; an icy wind was blowing consistently now, driving the clouds south. He nodded and began to trot after Korac, looking back every few minutes to make sure that Dishan was following. The man began to fall slowly behind, but remained within a spear cast, and so Jalam pressed on. The trees began to thin and the land began to rise slightly as they neared the ridge. It was now visible in the half light ahead. Another half hour… maybe more… and they would be there. A cave, a fire, and hot food. Jalam could almost picture it….

Then, without warning, disaster struck again.

The wind rose suddenly, whipping forward and nearly throwing them to the ground. The blizzard had finally come. Snow filled the air, and for a moment Jalam was alone. He froze. Korac was only a few paces ahead, but he couldn't see him. He looked back. Dishan might as well have been in Shinar. He jumped when a hard hand gripped his arm. Korac loomed up out of the whiteness like some dark specter. He had to shout to overcome the wind. "Hold arms. Don't get separated. We'll try for Dishan. If we don't find him in two hundred paces, we turn back and make for the caves."

Jalam nodded. He was reluctant to turn back at all, but they owed Dishan that much. He had come all the way from Shinar with them, and although Jalam did not particularly like him, you did not leave a comrade. Carefully he counted paces, trusting Korac to keep them straight. It was a terrifying feeling to be so blind. They could have passed within a few paces of Dishan and never known it. When they reached two hundred paces, he tugged at Korac's arm. "That's it," he shouted, the words freezing on his lips, barely passing his chattering teeth. "We're in trouble," he added needlessly.

Korac nodded, his face battered by the freezing winds. "We can try to find the caves or go back to the meadow and look for a deadfall." That he would offer an option told Jalam just how desperate he was. He calmed his mind. Their lives depended on this decision, and he did his best to drive the fear away and let his mind find the solution.

"If we start walking, we're liable to wander into the river," he shouted. Korac grimaced, and nodded. The swirling winds made it hard to estimate their direction of travel, and with the limited visibility, they would not know they were headed for the river until they fell in and drowned. The snow drove against them, already drifting above their ankles. It was going to get much deeper. Much deeper. That was when he suddenly recalled the story Ham had once told them about surviving a blizzard on the mountain many years ago. He gripped Korac's arm. "Look for a hollow in the ground. Dig in. Let the snow cover us. We'll live if we're careful."

Korac's eyes narrowed slightly in comprehension, and then he nodded. They turned halfway around and probed forward, doing their best to avoid the river. Luck was with them. Within a few paces, they stumbled into a small depression. Frantically they scraped the snow into low walls and let their packs fall at their feet. Korac drew out a blanket he had fashioned from a lion skin and laid it on the ground. Jalam drew out another from his pack, and the two men stretched out on the ground, pulling other skins over them. With their hands they reached out and pulled snow back on top of the blankets. Their efforts were feeble, but the sky was dumping it at such a rate that they were soon covered anyway. As it accumulated, the banshee howl of the wind gradually died until they found themselves inside a quiet cocoon.

Surprisingly, Jalam began to feel warmer. With no wind, their body heat, and the insulation of the skins and snow, the icy numbness retreated. "Use our packs to make more space." Korac shoved gingerly upwards, but the snow roof held, moving up slightly. He set his pack at their head, and Jalam cautiously maneuvered his down at their feet, gaining them a few extra inches of breathing space. "As it gets thicker on top, we'll dig out and pack it against the sides." With some difficulty, Korac slid his spear around and used it to poke a hole out to one side for air.

"Do you think Dishan was smart enough to dig in?" asked Jalam tentatively.

Korac shook his head. "He might if he wanted to live, but he's been dying a little every day. I don't think he wanted to go on."

"And you never gave him much choice," blurted out Jalam, suddenly angry and weary at the same time.

Korac studied his face for a moment in the gathering darkness. For a moment he tensed, but then relaxed. "No, I didn't. But Nimrod never gave me one either."

Jalam seized on the opening. "Even Nimrod can't fault you for this," he exclaimed. "*He* couldn't catch them in this wilderness. The forest goes for years in every direction. We're marching across land that no man has ever seen. We never know what river or mountain range may lie ahead, and we're lucky that we haven't become a meal for some wandering wolf pack or cat." He took a deep breath. "I say we survive and go home. Let the wilderness slay these women. They've been lucky too, but everyone's luck runs out eventually… especially if you push it every day."

Korac snorted. "There's wisdom in your words, cousin. You always were one of the smart ones. I don't deny I would like to take your advice, but you don't understand Nimrod. He's a powerful man who will shape this world. We'll either be with him or against him, and I don't relish opposing his spear. If we go home now, he would nod and pat our backs and tell us that no man could have done better. It was just hard luck."

Jalam nodded. "As well he should."

"And then we would both be dead within weeks," Korac added bleakly. "Just as soon as he found someone else. He's not a forgiving man."

Jalam sighed.

"Look," said Korac. "I'm sure the women are just ahead. When this storm blows itself out, we'll sneak up on those caves and finish this, once and for all. Then we go home."

"What if they aren't there?" Jalam let a little sarcasm tinge his voice, but Korac chose not to notice.

"That's a problem for tomorrow or the next day. If they aren't there, we'll talk about it again. But I feel it... they're just ahead. I can't walk away knowing I was this close."

Jalam took a few minutes to dig snow out from on top of the skin and pack it against the walls, moving their ceiling slightly higher. Finally he sighed. "As you say, cousin. I've followed you this far; I won't desert you. But know this. *You* can do the killing. From Shinar to Togarmah's dock I would have killed them because that was our job. After the shipwreck, I would have killed them out of anger. But now… there's something wrong with this business. We should be hunting Shem and Shelah, not killing women or children. I haven't felt like a man for weeks, and I don't know if I ever will again. But I won't make it worse. I won't raise my hand against either of them. That's all."

Korac let the silence stretch between them. "Fair enough," he sighed. "You've stuck with me this far. But I'm warning you. When we get back to Shinar, you get credit for the younger one, and you keep your mouth shut and take it. If you do, Nimrod will owe you for the rest of your life. He's going to be a king someday, and having a king in your debt will take care of you for the rest of your life. I'll make sure you don't have to do any more killing. Trust me."

Jalam sighed. "You know Nimrod better than I do," he admitted.

"Good!" Korac pushed the roof a little higher and packed some more snow. "Stick with me and we'll stay on top of this rotten world."

Jalam nodded and rolled over. He was tired and needed to think. Every hour or two, Korac stirred him and the men enlarged their cave, packing the snow tight and keeping the air hole open with the spear. They filled their tin cups with snow and placed them carefully under their furs. The water was cold, but they needed moisture as much as warmth and they sipped it slowly. Hours passed uncounted, and Jalam lost himself in the routine. Sleep. Wake and drink. Pack snow. Talk a little of the days gone by… the good times they had enjoyed together. Then back to sleep.

In reality, it was a good time. Months of travel, short sleep, and irregular meals had sapped their strength. Over the three days that the storm blew, they caught up on much of that sleep and found new strength. Though not hungry, they chewed dried meat to keep their bodies warm.

Jalam thought hard about Korac's words and gradually came to accept that the hunt would go on. Despite his misgivings and his stubborn insistence that he would kill neither woman, his fate was linked to that of Korac, and he would not desert him. It was really that simple, and the days in their icy cocoon crystallized that commitment. But he wondered at times what might have been, had he been born into a different family.

Chapter 47
NEAR MISS

Madrazi stirred from sleep, suddenly aware that the gale which had roared over the past few days was no longer blowing. It was desperately cold inside the cave, even with a fire, and she shivered at the thought of being outside in such a storm. This cave would be a cozy home as long as winter lasted. Jael had quit badgering her; Madrazi assumed she had finally seen the wisdom of a shelter against the elements. It would be foolish to sever all connection to the ship. Sailing upstream was far better than walking… at least once the wind shifted and they were able to make headway west. Unfortunately there was no sign of the wind shifting, and the ice in the river grew thicker every day.

As she drifted awake, she heard the soft scrape of rope against leather. Rolling over in her furs, she saw Jael hard at work packing. Two packs. Madrazi sat up and began to protest. "What do you think…?"

Jael's face was as hard as the icy wilderness outside. "Back at the beginning, you agreed that I would lead us," she said tightly. "You used the voyage to take back control, and I was stupid enough to let it happen. It was actually nice, not feeling the weight of your life on my shoulders every day. But we both know that we're not getting any closer to Shem, sitting in this cave."

Madrazi started to protest, but her conscience chopped her words short. Jael was obviously enraged, but just as obviously, she was keeping it under tight rein. It made her accusatory stare that much more convicting.

Madrazi deflated visibly, and then sighed. "I'm sorry, Jael. I did promise and have not kept that word." Jael only nodded. Madrazi tried to lighten the tension. "I hereby relinquish command to Captain Jael." Jael's face remained hard. Madrazi rose and sat down beside the fire. "Please forgive me, Jael. And tell me, why now? I'm not questioning that we need to go… I just want to know why today… why now?"

Jael relented. "I can't explain it. I just woke up this morning and knew it was time to leave. Can you accept that?"

"Accept and understand," replied Madrazi. "You are attuned to nature. Perhaps God speaks to you through those perceptions." She paused. "Do we have time for a hot breakfast?"

Jael narrowed her eyes, but finally grunted. "There's a cup of that bark tea you like, by the fire. We'll eat as we walk."

"How are we going to walk in this?" Madrazi held up her hands. "Just curious again."

Jael's face lost its edge as she shook her head and turned away. "I always wondered why Shem let you have your way in everything," she laughed. "You nudge him this way and that, so sweet and subtle."

Madrazi felt her face flame. "I do not! I'm an obedient wife... I... I...."

"Save your innocence for the men, big sister. Your feminine wiles don't have the same effect on me."

"Hmmmph! Maybe you should try some wiles on a man sometime."

Jael glared at her, then laughed. "Nice try. But we're going. Get ready, now. We'll use these," she said, pointing to a stack of wood and straps. As Madrazi looked closer, she saw small hoops that had been contrived for stretching furs. But these were different. They looked stouter and surrounded a web of hide strips. She remembered Jael working on them for the past two nights, but the younger woman had only grunted when asked what she was doing.

Now she deigned to explain. "Animals with large feet seem to move well in snow by walking on top of it. We'll try to mimic their behavior."

"Why so many?" asked Madrazi.

"Want to stop and make another in the middle of our march when one breaks?" Jael snapped back, her patience obviously used up for the morning.

Madrazi hastily drank her tea and let Jael show her how to strap the contraptions on her feet. "We'll put them on outside."

Madrazi moved towards the front entrance.

"Stop!" Jael gripped her arm and pulled her back abruptly. "I've set traps for our pursuers. We're leaving by the back door.

Madrazi sighed but knew better than to argue. It was a hard climb and a tight squeeze, but Jael's back door cut a half day's travel from the march across the ridge. Even better, it led them along a windswept face that would help hide their tracks. Knowing that the men would expect them to follow the river, Jael had decided to cut north away from the river and then west. So she re-gathered her load and slid into the narrow passage at the back of the cave.

Jael stayed behind to finish setting her traps. Madrazi questioned their need—the men would never be able to follow them through the tight passage in back, even if they were within a month's journey, which she doubted. Given the intensity of the storm, they were probably dead, but it was no good raising that objection. Jael would just say the same old things about planning for the worst. And God help her, the girl had been right about the issue of command. Madrazi shook her head and moved down the dark tunnel.

Four bone-chilling hours later, Jael joined her near the end of the ridge. They slid down the last incline to the forest floor—both doubly grateful for the tough hides that now formed their clothing. Madrazi's face was red from more than exertion; she had lost her balance on the last little bit and had provided an indecorous show that had Jael bent over laughing, which did nothing to help her injured pride.

Jael's shoes worked better than expected and the women were able to make good time through the forest. Though after a few hours, both realized that there were different muscles involved in this form of locomotion. But Jael was inflexible. She continued to look back and pushed on into the late afternoon before stopping under a windfall. "No fire tonight," she commanded, and Madrazi wished she were back in their wonderful little cave as she rolled herself into her furs.

2-28-1761

Jalam balanced on the branch, staring down into the boat. Lines moored it to trees, bow and stern on both banks, but neither man felt inclined to brave the icy water. Korac remained on the ground, his size making it impossible for him to follow his lighter cousin. Jalam just stood, letting his eyes take in the details of the deck. Then he jumped down to search more closely. Anything might be a clue that would help them get to the end of their mission. There was no doubt that this was the women's boat, but he saw no recent signs of activity. However, Jael had proven adept at masking their activities so he looked carefully for any tricks that he would have used to increase the appearance of disuse. He nearly missed the artificially frayed rope—it was hard to make it look completely natural.

He grinned across at Korac. "They've been on board within the past week."

He leaped back to shore and Korac's powerful hand pulled him back up the bank. He glanced back. The last thing he wanted now was to get wet. They stood together at the tree line, scanning the ridge. Jalam spoke quietly.

"Up there!" He pointed to the ridge. "If they chose that cave, they could have seen anyone coming an hour away. There's some rough climbing lower down."

"It'll be worse in this snow," grunted Korac. It had taken them half the morning to fight their way from their impromptu shelter to the boat. The snow was past their knees. It had been blown off the exposed rocks of the slope, but there were still deep patches dotting their path, hiding potential perils they could not ignore.

Carefully they made their way up. Jalam had half-expected traps along the way—there were several places he would have done it—but for some reason Jael had not bothered. No arrows whizzed through the morning air—in fact, no sound could be heard from the rocks above. The absence of any threat made the ascent more nerve-wracking, but two interminable hours later, the men stood at the entrance. The women were gone. There had been several places where Jael could not have missed with her bow, but no shot had been fired. The scent of smoke lingered, but was stale. Their prey had eluded them once again. But now they had a fresh trail, and the women were the ones fighting the wilderness. Jalam grinned. The game had just turned in their favor.

But games are tricky things, and take interesting turns. Korac could never explain to him afterward why he let down his guard. He had lived with caution for decades but for one insane moment, he cast it aside, impatient to be done. Jalam froze for a fateful moment, in shock that Korac would simply push past him, and before he could speak a word, it was too late. Jael had set no traps outside for a good reason. It made them complacent and susceptible to those she set at the entrance. Her strategy worked perfectly. It was not an elaborate trap—Korac probably would have seen it, had it been. Nor was it lethal... by itself. But in a wilderness where any weakness was a death sentence, it was enough. The rock that appeared so steady under a small weight—enough for a man's questing toes to verify—proved false under his full weight, and Jalam heard the unmistakable crack of bone as Korac's leg slid into the small hole cunningly disguised in the entrance.

To Korac's credit, he froze quickly. Jalam knew it hurt; he saw the sweat beading on his cousin's face. He stood awkwardly stiff, not moving a finger's width in any direction. "Check for others," Korac grated out, and Jalam hastened to comply. A few minutes later, he had Korac reclining on the floor; a small fire beginning to warm the cave. Korac was pale but said nothing as Jalam ran his fingers along the ankle and lower leg. He had a sensitive touch and knew almost immediately that the injury would heal, if kept bound stiffly for a few weeks.

Korac seemed to read his mind. "Go now!" he grated. They're no more than a couple of days ahead of you. You'll be on them in less than a week."

"And then what, cousin," Jalam asked? "Should I sit and join them for tea? Or ask Madrazi if any of Debseda's tales of the early years are true?" His face turned hard. "Or need I remind you of your word to me? You promised that you would handle the killing."

Korac's eyes narrowed. "This is different. I'm done and they're close. What would you say if you ever returned to Shinar with them still alive?"

Jalam grinned. "That wouldn't be any of your concern, would it, Korac? I doubt the pieces of you that were still fattening the worms in this part of the world would really care. And you needn't worry about me. I'll have months to create a tale of a terrible shipwreck, with all lost but me. All due to your foolishness, of course. I protested, but you wouldn't listen. After it was over, I wandered half crazed for months up and down the Black Sea, until god—oh, it's 'the gods' now, isn't it," he sneered—"finally granted me a restored sanity and a path home, weeping every step for my dear departed cousin."

His face grew hard again. "No, 'dear cousin,' I've done enough weeping this trip. You'll be fine. If you shut up and do exactly as I say, you might even heal quickly enough to catch the women. You'll have lots of time."

"You fool!" snarled Korac. "How would you know?" They'll be down among Japheth's clan in a few months!" He hammered his fist into the stone floor.

"You're the fool." Korac looked up at him, stunned, but Jalam seemed to have lost any fear of his cousin, and he bored in. "You've forgotten the first rule of the hunt. You've been chasing yourself... or another man nearly as good... not the daughters of Noah. Just because you chose long ago to set your heart aside, don't imagine that they have! Ask yourself this—where does a woman feel safe?"

Comprehension began to dawn on Korac's face. Jalam chuckled. "Yes, fool. As soon as they turned west with the river, I suspected. I just never thought you had missed something so obvious."

Korac's face was white. "But that's impossible. How could she possibly find... it could take years... why would someone as smart as Jael...?"

"Perhaps because Jael retains something you and I lost long ago—faith in God and in the wisdom of a woman who is the matriarch of the rightful line of Noah. I may love the thrill of the hunt and of having few rules to follow, but don't ever think I don't know what a lying egotistical vixen Nimrod's grandmother is... nor that there are still virtuous women in the world... nor that we are trying to kill two of them!

Don't take *me* for the fool. Having Nimrod's favor is one thing… believing the tripe he feeds the masses is beneath us both. Madrazi even talks with the Creator, so they say, just as Noah once did. Have you ever heard Ham deny it? Who knows? They may be guided by an angel even as we lie in this cave in the middle of nowhere."

As he talked, Jalam pushed a curiously unresisting Korac back down to the floor and began to wrap strips of cloth around the leg before binding it tight with rawhide. "We'll need warmth for the first few nights," he said. "I'll be back with wood before dark. You just lie back, keep the fire going, and think about your world."

Heth struggled into the cave. His arm bulged around the log on his shoulder—it was twice his weight—but only the half melted ice at the entrance made the task difficult. Once he had danced across it, he straightened up and unceremoniously dumped the section of trunk to the floor. Jobaath jumped away, spilling a hot cup and cursing.

"Can't you find anything smaller?" he snarled.

Heth brushed snow off his chest as if he hadn't heard. He had quickly mastered the game of 'gather firewood.' Logs the size of a man burned for a long time—time he wasn't out thrashing his way through deep snow scrabbling for more. It wasn't his fault that he could carry twice the load of Jobaath. "That should keep us warm for the night," he observed, his lip twitching almost involuntarily at Shelah's obvious effort to suppress laughter.

Shem sat up in his furs. "Jobaath, you're first on tonight, then Heth, then Shelah."

"Don't you get tired of sleeping?" Jobaath tried to keep his voice neutral. Shem had slept long hours the past two months… once the weather had become harsh enough to require a winter camp."

"Catching up on the last few months," he replied evenly, "and getting ready for the next few."

Jobaath shook his head. He craved novelty and the enforced boredom weighed most heavily on him. Once the beds and fire pit had been built, their days consisted of little but gathering snow to melt for water, hunting, and the never-ending collection of firewood. Fortunately they had only to walk a few paces outside the cave for wood. Even so, Jobaath had toyed with the idea of cutting down one of the forest giants. "It would give me something to do until we can start again," he complained. "I can't stand this sitting around, doing nothing."

"We'll be doing plenty in a few weeks," answered Shem, rolling back up in his furs. Despite the fire, the cave felt cold, but it was a hothouse compared to the temperature outside.

"How do you know?" asked Jobaath.

"When you're as old as I am, you'll understand," assured Shem.

Heth smiled and shook his head. He had once thought his knowledge of survival in the wilds was better than most. After a week of watching Shem, he realized that he could live ten lifetimes and still not understand it that well. The older man invariably found water. He always chose the easiest path unless he had reason not to. He could bring game back when everyone else returned with excuses. Heth no longer sought to equal Shem; he was simply content to learn as much as he could.

He knew Shem had reason for the extra sleep. It kept the body fully functional, better able to fend off cold and sickness. So he climbed into his own furs and lay down. His watch would come soon.

Hours later, Jobaath woke him quietly. Most of the others were asleep. Heth checked the entrance, the fire and the others. All was at it should be. Jobaath had let the fire burn down; he didn't want to move the log further into the fire pit. Even with a cubit or more burned off, it was still heavy. Heth frowned for a moment and stretched his back and shoulders. Then in one easy motion, he lifted the log and eased the end of it out the other side of the fire. He sat back into the rough chair that Ash had made weeks ago, and watched the flames lick up around the new fuel.

It had been an easy trip so far—a leisurely six months' walk around the Black Sea and across endless grasslands, interrupted by narrow strips of thick forest around the all-too-many rivers and streams. There was room for millions of cattle and sheep just in those lands alone. Perhaps some enterprising man might even tame the ubiquitous wild oxen.

A cold wind blew outside; more snow was on the way. Heth could feel the heaviness. He was thankful Jobaath had found this cave, even if it had required them to dispossess the two leopards who also wanted it for a winter home. Heth grinned fiercely to himself... *dispossessed* was certainly a much nicer word than *slaughtered*.

But his leopard skin made for a comfortable bed, and he would soon be back under its warmth. It was more than just a pelt; it was a reminder of one of the finest throws he had ever made with his spear. When they finally cut the weapon free—not even Heth could pull it out—they discovered that it had penetrated deep into the cat's chest, shredding the heart before piercing deeper into its vitals. The animal had been dead on its feet before Shelah's arrow had struck—a point that Heth brought up repeatedly over the winter. Shelah always responded with a laugh, and Heth learned something else—how to maintain peace in trying conditions. His respect for Shelah rose ever higher.

But that was all the past. As he stared at the fire, Heth thought to the months ahead. Shem intended to continue west for at least another season. How many months of this forest loomed ahead? He sensed that Shem and Shelah would be happy to wander for years. Heth could feel the attraction, but there was something about the grasslands that called to him more. He liked the wide horizons and the feeling that the sky was big enough to contain God. Perhaps he would push back east someday. Maybe the grasslands went on to the ends of the earth. It would be fun to find out.

For some unexplained reason, his thoughts turned back to the farm. He wondered if Madrazi and Jael had been able to manage the year's harvest without them.

Like it often did, Jael's face came to him in the fire. He liked the visions; her face was bereft of the rage that drove her, and her green eyes were wide and filled with happiness. Months of adventure had not erased her memory from his heart—if anything, he felt closer. He wondered if he could pick up the pieces of their fractured friendship when he returned back to the mountain, and being in a good mood this night, he let himself wonder if it could ever be more. Madrazi would help.

He thought of them now, probably enjoying the warmth of the great room, a warm fire burning and hot drinks beside them. It was a soft life, but then, they were women. Wandering the wilderness in the winter was a task for men. He roused Shelah softly and climbed back into his bed. Yes... leopard skin made a *very* comfortable blanket.

Chapter 48
FAMILY TIES

3-25-1761

Korac hobbled over to the fire, pulling a couple of sticks out a half cubit. The fire waned, allowing the meat to cook instead of burn. Swiveling gracefully on his crude crutch, he pushed the arm on the tripod, moving the small pot over the fire. Jalam had found clay on the stream bank that could be fashioned into crude dishes.

Already, his leg could bear his weight, but having exercised it enough today, he was using the crutch to save his strength. The first week had been hard—the realization of weakness and dependence had hurt more than the leg. But over time and under Jalam's watchful care, his natural strength asserted itself and the bone began to knit back together.

As the water boiled, he added the spruce needles and dried willow bark; the former for taste and the latter to ease lingering soreness. He heard Jalam on the ledge outside, laboring under a load.

"Hello, cousin," he called. "A change of meat today." He pushed inside the cave carrying two large fish, strung together by a cord through their gills. Korac almost smiled. After a month of living on an elk that had blundered into a snowdrift, he was ready for the soft meat of fish, although it came at a price. He had argued that Jalam's fishing through the ice of the river was a waste of time, and now his cousin would be crowing about this achievement for weeks. Carefully laying the fish on a clean rock, Jalam slipped back outside to retrieve two large, thin pieces of bark, both waterlogged. "You haven't been walking on those, have you?" Korac asked suspiciously.

"Of course not," Jalam returned. "I prefer more delicate flavoring! No, these have been soaking up the river water. I cut them from a partly-submerged tree on the bank." He slid one of the fish on top of one of the concave sheets and covered it another slab. Damp cords of rawhide bound them together, and formed a loop which was hooked over the top of their tripod, letting the damp wood and fish dangle down above the fire. Soon another bark vessel joined the first, and Korac retreated to a stone seat to watch them cook. As he did, he looked surreptitiously at his cousin.

Jalam had changed much over the past month… or maybe it had been coming on before. Either way, he had lost his hard edge and would be outmatched by a dozen men back in Shinar that he had before handled with ease. The fire was gone, but he seemed not to care. It was crazy. For years he had dedicated himself to the art of war, learning all that Korac could teach him. All he wanted was to be one of the elite of Nimrod's Legion. He had stayed drunk for a day when Nimrod had chosen him for this mission. Korac remembered the day well. It hadn't taken more than a few drinks for Jalam to start bragging about crossing bows with Shem and making his name in the new world. It was more than a drunken boast—the idea had consumed him for years, and his ability matched Korac's. That had been his motivation for this trek, and for the first time, Korac felt a twinge of guilt over his deception. He had known Shem would be gone, but wanted Jalam's steady presence to counter the instability of the twins. It was well that he had. Jalam had held up his end, killing the man in the barn who had shot Dishon, accounting for most of the wolves that had attacked them on the mountain, holding to Jael's trail, and helping hold things together after the shipwreck. And now Korac owed him his life.

But it was not the same Jalam. Korac remembered the fire in his eyes when he nearly killed Togarmah on the dock. That man had all but vanished into the mists of the wilderness, and a better man had emerged. Maybe it had been the shipwreck or maybe those three days buried by the blizzard. Whatever the reason, Jalam was more at peace with himself. Perhaps he had become weary of war and had decided to grow up and enjoy life.

Korac settled back, his mind uncomfortable with the direction those thoughts led him. But his cousin had stayed with him when others would have left him to die, taking his place as Nimrod's favorite. Instead, Jalam cared for him, making sure his leg knitted correctly to regain all its strength. These past few days he had gone without food, making sure that Korac had meat to give strength for healing. Korac's mouth twitched. How could he deny the man the simple joy of a successful idea for catching fish? How could he now deny him anything?

It never occurred to him that Jalam was not the only one being reshaped by this journey.

Jael struggled through the snowdrift, fighting her way through the fringe of smaller trees out to the edge of the meadow. It was all covered by snow... the whole world was white and barren. She found it an effort to remember warm, green lands. She eyed the meadow. It was open ground—easier to traverse, but lacking concealment. Both women now knew more than they ever wanted to know about snow—hard, soft, wet, dry... what kind to tread and what to avoid. Hours had been spent improving their snow walkers by firelight, and more hours in learning the strange sliding pace that seemed most effective. Once they had strengthened the right muscles, they could both walk all day.

She stood quietly, letting her senses absorb the meadow. Both women had grown stronger this month. Those first days had been terrible—struggling hours to cover ground she could have run in a few minutes in the summer, and harried by a growing panic that she had failed.

Korac and one of his men still survived, and had not Korac been careless, they would have won their dark victory weeks ago. Jael would have sold her life dearly, but she was a realist... only the most favorable circumstances would ever allow her to slay Korac and another warrior.

Their only hope was to lose themselves in the vast wilderness, and they needed distance to do it, as well as snow to cover their tracks. The snow had come—whether or not the distance was sufficient would only be known later. Every day that they stayed alive and kept moving increased their chances—chances still low by her cynical estimate. It was small comfort that her instincts had been right.

She had taken an awful risk that first night, slogging back to the cave and sliding noiselessly into their back passage to confirm her fears. Despite her certainty, it had been a shock to find other people so near. Her anger had boiled at the though of those vile men living in their cave, but the shock of discovering that the mighty Korac had been hurt had almost given her away… she had nearly laughed out loud. Her simplest trap, right at the entrance, had felled the mighty hunter.

A potent desire had nearly overpowered her. She could wait in the darkness, slip into the cave, and kill Korac—ending his threat for good. She had actually begun the vigil—knife in hand—quivering with anticipation, but as the hours passed, the wisdom of Shem returned. There were two, and if the second was good, she would be hurt or killed, leaving Madrazi alone. She saw the face of Enoch inside the dark barn, the shadows on a face that knew death was coming soon. *Her husband has trained you well. Repay his trust.* Shaken at the memory, she retreated, inch by inch until she was clear of the cave. She had returned to their camp at sunrise to find a very angry Madrazi.

Knowing the men were close, they had both struggled hard those first few days, Madrazi as much from guilt as from fear. Jael kept telling herself that Korac would be down for a month, but her fears offered different council. It was only after a cold night that she realized that unless they conserved their strength, they would do Korac's job for him. So she slowed the pace and took time to hunt. They settled into a routine and grew accustomed to the cold. As the weeks passed, they grew lean and tough. Meat was adequate—many animals were still unwary of humans.

Over the past few days she had felt her strength waning, despite adequate venison. It had been Madrazi who had realized that they were eating no fat. They needed a bear or a boar. Jael shivered at the prospect of facing one of those terrible forest giants without someone like Heth to watch her back. Even Nimrod would hesitate to take on a bear alone.

She shuddered at the thought of failure in that hunt—not at death, but at leaving Madrazi alone in the middle of creation, with Korac only weeks behind. She looked back. Madrazi stood waiting quiet and still beside a forest giant, the dog sitting beside her, guarding from any unseen peril. Sirus had grown hard too. He was smart, knowing in some inexplicable fashion that it was his responsibility to detect danger. He could do more. Standing as high as Madrazi's hip, only the largest predators were a threat to him now. He had even learned to lead the women over treacherous snow; his instincts keener than his mistresses' reasoned experience.

Jael stood pondering their course for a while, letting Madrazi wait. They didn't talk much any more; Madrazi had retreated inside herself, finding determination and strength from the power of her spirit. She did her tasks, spoke no word of complaint, and huddled over their little fires by night. On rare occasions Jael caught a bright intensity in those mysterious green eyes and wondered what she saw in the fire.

Korac was not the problem. Jael had a decision to make, and a wrong choice could kill them. They were following the river, but keeping a few hours from the banks to maintain a straighter path. To pursue a bear meant straying away from the river, north to the edge of the hills. If they lost their way, they would lose precious time. Even if successful, they would lose days. And who knew what the next valley would bring? For the first ten days from the cave, the river had rambled through a broad plain, much as it had since the sea. But then they had encountered a small mountain range, and the waterway led into rough country with steep slopes right down to the bank. Those had been hard days. At the end of the worst day they had been able to see their previous night's campsite, even after hours of grinding effort. Only their increasing skill with the snow walkers kept them moving. It had taken sixteen days to clear the mountains, and as much as she wanted to push on, she knew they needed food and rest.

Frowning, she motioned Madrazi forward. They must talk. She was still quietly angry at Madrazi's usurpation of her authority during the weeks on the ship. It was foolish, but she couldn't help it. If the past years had taught her anything of her shortcomings, she knew now that she could hold a grudge as well as any man. She also knew she needed to let it go. Madrazi *was* her sister. Sisters fought. But they also made up. Biting her lip, she decided reconciliation would have to wait. They needed to stay alive now, and she couldn't afford to worry about anything else. She forced down the simmering resentment and summoned an encouraging smile.

As she waited for Madrazi to work her way through the soft snow, a corner of her mouth turned up. Madrazi moved so differently now. The farm wife who had started the trek had given way to a wilder, almost feline human. Her body glided over the ground now with hardly a sound and with an economy of motion learned through hard days of wasted strength. Her quick eyes flitted back and forth, missing nothing. The heavy spear helped maintain balance but was ready for instant use. She had lost weight—they both had—but despite the leanness of her face, Madrazi maintained an austere beauty that Jael could never match. She wondered idly if she was catching a glimpse of how her sister appeared on the ark… if so, no wonder the vain Debseda hated her!

It was early afternoon, and the wind whipped a small gust of snow across the meadow as Madrazi drew up under the shade of a bare chestnut tree. She was panting a little from the exertion. Jael spoke softly as she always did—sound traveled far across these bare meadows, and neither woman wanted wolves or worse to hear.

"We need to eat and rest. We need fat." She waved her hands up at the hills. "We might find a young bear in a cave up there. If we killed it, we would have both fat and shelter for a few days."

Madrazi's eyes twinkled. "And it might find us. Or we might find a great cat. Or a wolf pack."

"We need a bear or boar," Jael insisted, "and I haven't seen any sign of boar in the woods."

"And you need my permission?" Madrazi kept her face unreadable, but a glint of laughter in her eyes gave her away.

Jael's next words were no lady's. After she stifled her anger, she replied more reasonably. "Yes, I do! This is a hard choice between evil on all sides. We can move into the foothills and lose time. Or we can stay nearer the river and lose strength. Spring may come next week or not for many weeks. Korac will be on the move soon."

Madrazi nodded. "I've been thinking of Korac. Let's move off and look for a bear for three or four days. If we see no sign, we'll press on, trusting God to bring us what we need."

"What about Korac?" Jael whispered, not to be distracted.

"We cross the river now... well... after our hunt." Madrazi waved downhill. "This is a mighty river. In the spring melt, it will be difficult to cross. If we're on the other side before the ice breaks and they don't know before spring, we'll have the river between us for weeks. Our trail would disappear."

Jael cocked her head. It was a brilliant suggestion. It irritated her that she had not thought of it sooner. "I suppose we will need to be on the west side eventually."

"Hard to say," Madrazi allowed. "It might bend to the west up ahead."

Jael shouldered her pack. "Right. Wait 'til I'm well out into the meadow to follow. Watch Sirus...."

"I know," Madrazi grinned. "Just go find us a bear."

Jael nodded, glad for the support.

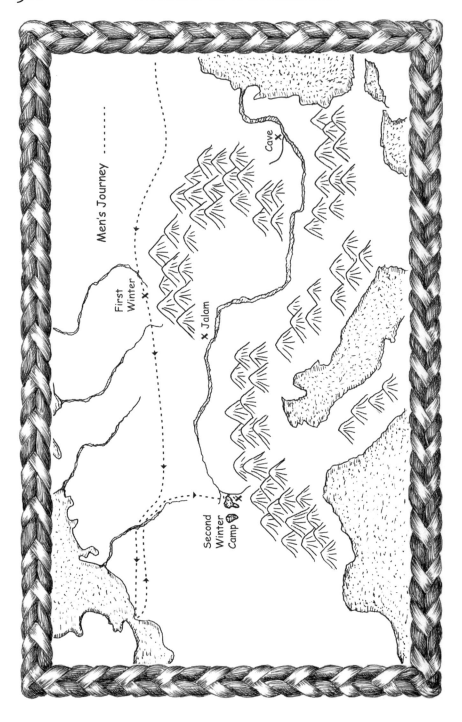

Chapter 49
THE FAR END OF THE WORLD

Sunrise spread its rosy light across the long grass, casting shadows off to the horizon, merging with the distant dark waters of the sea. A steady wind blew from the west, carrying the scent of salt into their faces. They were still an hour's walk from the ocean. *Maybe more*, thought Shelah. For the past few days the land had been deceptive; it gave the appearance of a broad plain, but the green fields hid marshy folds or small streams.

For days, they had smelled the sea—a distinct odor; not unpleasant, and carrying a salty tang. All of them were excited; even Shem's eyes were shining. This was not the Great Sea... it was too far north and didn't have the right smell. It was another, maybe even larger. Shelah tried to calculate how many days' journey they had come but quickly gave up. There had been a time, in the depths of the forest, when he had wondered if they would ever reach the end of the land. It went on forever, day after day of nothing but forest or plain. All the children of a hundred generations would never fill this land. And who knew how far it extended east of the Qazvin Sea?

Shelah shook himself, then labored to catch up with the others. It was time to quit daydreaming and finish this trek. A growing discontent was coalescing in the corners of his mind, an almost instinctive call to start back home. He pushed it down and took in the vista. If this truly was the edge of the world, then he needed to cement as much as he could in his mind for a future map. Perhaps Shem would agree to his plan to return by a southerly route... if they could find a way through the two vast mountain ranges they had passed, they would have a good feel for the whole region. Maybe there were fertile lands there too. If not, they might find the northern extent of the Great Sea... if it carried so far west.

He came over the rise to see the others. Jobaath was snarling at the mule; it was stuck in mud or quicksand in the stream at the base of the swale, quivering with fear. Heth, Ashkenaz, and Shem were laughing on the bank. Somewhere back down the trail, the mule had become Jobaath's pet. He complained about it every day, but wouldn't let anyone else near it... not that any of them wanted the task! No one could remember quite how it had come about, but Jobaath alone loaded, unloaded, fed, watered, kicked and petted that animal, grumbling about the unfairness of his lot. Now he was carrying part of its load to the other side, mud staining his legs and stomach.

Shelah slipped down the grassy slope and sat down on the bank beside Heth to watch the struggle. Ashkenaz was laughing so hard that tears were flowing. He tried explaining but couldn't speak without falling into fresh gales of laughter. Heth was chuckling too, though his eyes remained alert on the far bank. "Fool animal bolted for the water, didn't like the taste of it, and then couldn't get out. I told Jobaath we could pull it out, load and all, but he mumbled something about breaking another rope; I think he was afraid we'd snap the beast's neck."

"Was he right?" Shelah asked innocently.

"Probably," admitted Heth. "I sure would have tried. It's not carrying much anymore, and it's more trouble than it's worth."

"Oh, I thought digging under the winter's snow for dead grass was good exercise," laughed Shelah.

Heth frowned. He had hated that particular task more than any of them, complaining even more than Jobaath. "We'll be roasting his haunch over a roaring fire before the next snow falls," he growled. He rose and held out a hand to Shelah. "We'd best get the rest of that load over and pull the sorry thing out of the mud. I, for one, want to see the end of the world before I grow as old as Shem."

"The only end of the world is death," interrupted Shem, rising. "Land or sea, it doesn't matter. It goes on and on and on. This world's a big place, big enough even for you."

Shelah nodded as he set to work; it was only a matter of minutes until the load and the mule were reunited on the far bank. Jobaath was still washing in the shallow brackish water—he could catch up. Shelah strained his eyes ahead. There were still some low hills to climb, but they should soon find the final slope down to the ocean.

Ever since their start late in the winter, Shem had been pushing relentlessly—driven by some inner need. Heth stumbled on the slick grass; like him, they were all tired. After the cave, they passed through dense, hilly forest for weeks. From the high meadows they had seen more mountains to the south, capped with the flashing glare of ice in the sunshine. Shem had guessed that some of those peaks reached as many as five thousand cubits above the land.

Many streams and rivers had been crossed, but several weeks ago they had encountered a river nearly as large as the one north of the Black Sea. It had been another long swim and even longer hike back upstream. More importantly, this river flowed north. Shem had been excited, then impatient, as he explained that it must end in an ocean other than the Great Sea. He considered following it downstream, but whatever was driving him kept them all pressing west. For a time, the land became rougher and the evening grumbling louder. It wasn't mountainous; but it was a rugged land of sharp valleys and hills that only gradually gave way to smoother ground. Grasslands once more appeared amid the trees, and just a week earlier they had begun to see gulls and smell the salt air.

Shem was trotting now, and though tired, the others joined him, unwilling to be thought weak by the older man. As the sun rode higher, they toiled up one last long slope. Reaching the top, Shelah stopped with the others to admire the sight.

At long last, they saw the sea. There was something about that first glimpse of endless waters that stopped a man in his tracks and caused even the most jaded to marvel anew at God's creation.

From their elevation, they saw green waters near the shore merging further out into a deeper blue. They were on a cape or broad peninsula—water was visible to the south, west, and north. Straight ahead there must have been a low cliff above the beach; all Shelah could see was the abrupt end of grass and then greener water.

Looking north, he saw white beaches extending as far as he could see, broken only by a small inlet halfway to the northern horizon.

But his attention quickly shifted to the west. Looking almost like low clouds in the distant haze was another land. It hovered like a vision above the waters, with a bright white strip that could have been low cliffs, perhaps made of the same cream-colored chalk that kept showing up in the faces of hills and stream valleys, littered with bones preserved in the great flood.

Despite the shimmer of the distance there was no doubt that a whole new land lay before them. Was it a large island or the start of another landmass like that they had followed since the Black Sea? Shelah suspected the former; the sea went on to the horizon to north and south. Even so, it was a large land, green and verdant in the distance. Shem grinned at him. "I told you it just goes on and on." Shelah just nodded, still absorbing distances and direction for the map he was drawing in his head.

"That's the land for me," exclaimed Jobaath suddenly. "Away from the rest of you—a nice cozy Eden for my sons to cultivate."

"Where you and your mule can laze around under the sun," finished Ashkenaz.

"The mule couldn't swim that ditch," scoffed Heth. "But maybe you can take a deep breath and carry it across on your shoulders… unless, of course, the bottom's muddy."

The others laughed as Jobaath feigned a hurt expression. "You're right as usual." His sly eyes glittered. "I guess someone else will have to take care of the poor beast on the trip home."

Heth hefted his spear. "I'll be glad to take care of it… right now!"

"Grow up, boys," growled Shem. "We camp here. Get some rest and be ready to head back in the morning." He wandered a few hundred paces down the hill, leaving a buzzing behind him.

"Tomorrow?" began Ashkenaz.

"Start back?" continued Heth.

"He's getting too old for this!" grumbled Jobaath.

Shelah just shook his head and followed his grandfather. Standing respectfully behind him for a few minutes, they shared the spectacular view. "It always makes you feel small," Shem said softly.

Shelah said nothing. After a few minutes, Shem continued. "My own grandfather told me that when he first took me out into the Great Forest. I was younger than Eber then, and proud of my strength and speed. But when you look outside yourself and see all that God has made, you realize how small and weak you really are." He sighed. "I'm glad we live forever after death. We'll need every one of those days to explore His wonders."

"But not now," said Shelah, his brow raised in question.

Shem shook his head. "I can't explain it. I felt drawn west; I guess I knew that I would know when it was time to turn back. Today it is."

"Which way shall we return?" Shelah tried hard to keep the yearning from his voice.

"I don't know." Shem smiled briefly. "I feel a need to hurry, but I can't pin it down."

"But you always listen to that voice." Shelah remembered his boyhood lessons in the wild lands around the mountain.

"Yes." Shem turned to him. "But there's more. You've felt it yourself, haven't you? Like home is calling...." Shelah felt a rush of understanding. "Yes," he admitted. "I just hadn't heard it clearly until you pointed it out. But you're right." He was suddenly confident. "We need a faster route."

Shem nodded. "Aye, boy. It's a risk, but we need to move faster than we did. We'll go upstream along the river and follow it toward its headwaters. If we can get south of the mountains, we can make for the Great Sea or the Black Sea, and sail back."

"What if the mountains extend all the way to the water?" Shelah asked.

"Then we find another way," Shem answered. "God will lead us."

"The others will be angry. They're already tired. Not everyone moves as fast as you, grandfather."

"They're men," Shem retorted, before softening with a sigh. "I know they're tired. I'm tired...." He shook his head and frowned. "But if you dare mention it...."

Shelah just chuckled and shook his head. "I'm too exhausted to remember what you just told me."

Shem smiled briefly, but then turned and looked south. "We'll take today and then rest again when we reach the river. It's a shame it flows north... we could have made some rafts and saved a few weeks."

"That's what Grandmother would do," replied Shelah. "But you're right. We're men. We'll run and keep running for as long as it takes."

INTERLUDE 5

6-8-2162

She dragged herself off her thin blanket, splashed some water on her face, and wrapped the rags of her clothes about her thin, bruised body. Another day. Work hard, eat scraps, and probably be beaten. Another day. She wondered why God let her live when she longed for death so much.

But He *was* keeping her alive… that much of her old self remained. Maybe it was her cursed memory; she kept recalling the Old One on her bed. A few more days and she would have been here for a year.

She had lost flesh, her hair was lank and greasy, and she no longer cared about the vermin that infested her bed and clothes. Without being told, she immediately began to bring in wood for the fire. When the box was full, she lifted the water buckets and trudged towards the door to the courtyard to fill them from the well. While she shuffled along, she kept a watchful eye for Abigath, the headmistress of the kitchens. A large coarse woman of indeterminate age, she was well-practiced in cruelty. Had she been weaker, she would have died long ago, but none dared lift a hand against her. Some gave in, becoming her toadies, bring her every rumor of discontent. And she dealt harshly with every rumor.

Today seemed strange. There were no blows or harsh words. Abigath was distracted. Lydia took a chance and glanced over, keeping her head lowered. Abigath had pulled the cooks aside and was speaking to them loudly. Slowing her pace, Lydia eavesdropped, having perfected her command of the Sea Peoples' language months before.

"The king is back," Abigath was saying loudly, "and he has an important guest. There will be a feast tonight and probably another tomorrow. We must make ready. We must…." She continued, detailing all the extra work that would be required. Lydia grimaced to herself. She would be forced to bear much of that burden. She slipped out the door and trudged to the well, not daring to look up. She never looked for Lud; it was painful enough to meet his eyes when he was guarding the gate. Her sole remaining happiness came from the knowledge that he was safe and well.

The buckets were heavy as she headed back, not paying attention to those around her. She had sunk into herself again, as she had been doing more and more. But the sudden loud gasp snapped her back.

Looking up, she saw the reason. Two men had entered the courtyard, followed closely by two soldiers. She had never seen him before but knew at once that the one to the left was King Abimelech, patron of the man who had despoiled her. Months ago, she would have wished to kill him, but now vengeance required too much energy. His rich clothing and noble face told her much, and her old habit of reading people thrust conclusions upon her before she could think about it. Surprisingly, she liked the face, and that of the man beside him.

She tried to rally hatred, but the effort was beyond her strength. And by then she was too distracted by his companion. A little larger than most, he was clearly no warrior, but he seemed confident in the midst of warriors, nonetheless. A man accustomed to authority.

But what caught her eye was something in his face she could not immediately define... like a faint memory of better days. It had a strange effect on her; she felt doors in her heart cracking open that had been locked for months. Something about him took her back to the house of the Old One... nights by the fire, reading the scrolls, and watching the Old One's eyes lost in the flames, wondering what she saw beyond. At that moment, as if she had called aloud, his eyes turned towards her and she saw amazement cross his face, to be replaced by wrath. "What is the meaning of this?" he barked to the king, looking directly at her.

She had learned her lessons well over the past months. Not knowing what she had done to incur this noble's anger, she certainly knew what was expected. She dropped the buckets and threw herself flat on the stony ground, ignoring the water soaking her garments.

She heard a muttered curse and the two men drew near. She flinched and braced herself for the blow.

It never came.

Instead, she felt one of the men kneel beside her. She covered her head with her arms in an instinctive protective reaction. Another muttered curse. Then a clear voice, barely containing its wrath. "I wouldn't treat a dog like this!" She cowered, feeling the cold water soak through her rags.

"I have not been aware of this, my brother," the other voice replied. "But it shames me both as a man and a king."

The first voice changed. It was gentle and soft. "Young woman," it said. "What have you done to deserve this?"

She did not know where the words came from, but they forced aside her sobs for a moment. "I tried to serve the living God." She heard a sharp intake of breath. Strong hands lifted her to a sitting position, and one caught her chin, forcing her face up. She found herself looking into the eyes of the guest... clearly some great noble. There was compassion there, but the anger still lurked behind it, though now she sensed vaguely that it was not directed at her. But what held her eyes was a light in his—one she had not seen since she started this disastrous trip.

"There are many gods in each land," he said, and his eyes burned into hers. "Which do you serve?"

She felt her body weaken, and grew dizzy and faint. "The God of Noah, Shem, and the elders," she whispered before her world went dark.

She woke lying on a bench, her head in the lap of the stranger, a wet cloth in his hand. She felt the cool dampness on her forehead where it had been. Her first thought was to get away; she was dirty, infested, and smelled. But strong hands gripped her thin shoulders and eased her back down.

The king stood uncomfortably behind the man with a semicircle of soldiers gathered round. Her first thought was that she would be severely beaten or killed, but the stranger interrupted her thought.

"What does a kitchen slave in Gerar know of the Creator?" he asked, and she heard the intense curiosity in his voice. She prayed for strength, and dredged up memories of the Old One.

"I served the wife of Shem at their home beneath the mountain, until the day of her death," she whispered. "I was on an errand for her when I was taken into slavery here."

His eyes narrowed. "And what errand was that?"

"The Old One spent her last two years, after her husband died, writing her account of the lost world, the great flood, and the early days of this world. I was to deliver her account as an heirloom to one of her descendents, Abram of Ur, a prince living in Canaan, and a man who knew the Creator."

The man's face went pale, but the king's was ashen. The stranger drew a breath and continued his questioning. "How did she know that Abram followed the true God? Many of her descendents do not."

She nodded. "It was a source of great sadness to her. But she saw him in the fire... that was how God revealed visions to her... and she saw the light of the Holy One on him."

"What became of these scrolls?"

Tears began to flow down her cheeks. "I failed," she whispered. "They were taken from me and burned when I was captured." She was sobbing openly now. "I owed her my life and I failed her!" She curled up into a tight ball and wept, hardly feeling the hand resting on her head.

Anger was back in the man's voice. "Who did this?"

"G...G...General Asak," she sobbed. "Just before he took me to his tent and...." She wailed out loud, unable to continue.

A hated voice broke through. "That's a lie! You would believe some wretched slave? I took her because she was an outlaw—accused of complicity in the murder of Hittite soldiers."

Recognizing the voice, she went stiff with terror. Strong arms began to gather her in, and suddenly she felt safe. Her spirit began to rise from the depths of its prison and she sat up abruptly, and wiped her hand across her face. A righteous rage coursed through her veins, and she turned to her accuser.

"It is true that Hittite soldiers were killed," she said with quiet dignity. "They tried to take the scrolls and to do what you did, you animal!"

Asak went white, then red with rage. He pushed forward but was halted by a heavy hand on his shoulder. "Who dares touch me?" he barked.

"I do." The ominous voice was soft, but Asak wilted. "I am the commander of the king's armies, Asak, not you, and there is a witness who can testify about these matters." He stepped forward, bowing to the king, dragging Lud with him. She could not meet his gaze. He looked ten years older, but a hard light shone in his eyes.

"This is my weaponmaster," said the Phicol, and a murmur went up from the surrounding soldiers. They knew the man well, mostly from their time learning the lack of their own skills by the casual exercise of his. "He was trained as an officer of the royal guard of Hattusa," the older man continued, "which is why he was able to slay seven renegade Hittites. One against two, and then one against five."

A murmur of respect ran through the soldiers. "It has been my experience," the Phicol added dryly, "that men of such valor also have the courage to tell the truth." He pulled Lud before the king and his guest. "Speak, weaponmaster!"

"It is as the woman says, my lords," he replied. "I too served the household of the son of Noah for some years, and this woman was the chief steward of the house after my master's death. She is respected by the Bianili and Hatti alike, because she was like a daughter to the old woman, the wife of my master. Seeing this," and she heard the hammered iron of his anger as he pointed at her, "would be like any of you seeing your queen as a slave to some wandering tribe of Amorites. Asak took her against her will and destroyed the priceless words that our mistress had sent to this Abram."

"He lies," screamed Asak. "He has no proof!" Spittle flew from his lips and his eyes were wild. "I am your cousin, my liege, and this murderer has no proof!"

She saw the Phicol step between Lud and Asak. Clearly he expected a killing rage from Lud at such words, as did she. But instead, she saw his lips curl up into a smile, though his eyes remained as cold as the ice on the mountain.

"Would the words of my old master be proof enough?" he asked the king, ignoring Asak.

As her awareness returned, she began to see as her mistress had taught her to see, reading the thoughts behind the faces of the men there. The king was troubled, the man who supported her was caught between anger and excitement, and Lud was supremely confident. After a long moment, and a sideways glance at the other man, the king nodded sharply. "We have a treaty," he muttered, "My word must be honored."

Lud stepped forward and unbuckled his belt. Handing the dagger hilt first to the Phicol, he removed the old leather sheath and began to pick at the edge of the leather while talking in a conversational tone. "My master taught me how to read and write his language—the old speech that men used before our words were confused at the great tower years ago. My first lesson was to read the words that he wrote of the great flood and his father's ark. It is my finest memory of him, and his words will be an heirloom for my house."

As he spoke, the men saw that the sheath had been made of two thin pieces of leather cleverly sewn together. Between them was a piece of parchment, weathered and very old. He held it carefully in his hand and extended it to the king. "Can you read the words, my lord?"

Abimelech looked at it curiously, handling it with the same care. "Some of the characters look familiar, but I cannot read the writing."

"Give it to the woman," Lud said softly. "If she can read the writing, then her story is true."

The stranger beside her interrupted. "He speaks reason, my brother. Let her read the words." Abimelech nodded hesitantly and extended the parchment. Trying to seize it, Asak leapt forward, but a heavy hand dragged him back. The Phicol held his neck with one brawny hand, while the other snaked up to twist Asak's arm behind his back, his wrist near his neck. Pain and shock battled in his eyes as the Phicol dragged him back several steps. "Let the woman read the parchment, your majesty," he grated. "If this story is true, then we have broken our treaty with Lord Abraham, and we must make reparations to preserve our honor."

Lydia was amazed to see fear now cross the eyes of the king. They darted between her, the stranger, and the Phicol, undecided. Abruptly, he nodded. "You are right, as usual, old friend." He extended the parchment again but was looking at the stranger. "You have my word," was all he said.

With a shaking hand, she took the parchment. She had never even known that Lud could read and write, but it was a day for surprises. As she took it, she recognized the hand of Shem, and she felt a return to the days under the mountain—to the love of the Old One, and to an assurance that she had not felt since the first two Hittites had been killed to save her.

She sat up straight and began to read. As she did, power came into her voice, holding all the men in the courtyard captive.

> And it came to pass, when men began to multiply on the face of the earth, and daughters were born unto them, that the sons of God saw the daughters of men that they were fair; and they took them wives of all which they chose. And the Lord said, "My spirit shall not always strive with man, for that he also is flesh: yet his days shall be an hundred and twenty years."
>
> There were giants in the earth in those days; and also after that, when the sons of God came in unto the daughters of men, and they bare children to them, the same became mighty men which were of old, men of renown. And God saw that the wickedness of man was great in the earth, and that every imagination of the thoughts of his heart was only evil continually. And it repented the Lord that he had made man on the earth, and it grieved him at his heart. And the Lord said, I will destroy man whom I have created from the face of the earth; both man, and beast, and the creeping thing, and the fowls of the air; for it repenteth me that I have made them.
>
> But Noah found grace in the eyes of the Lord.

As she read, the courtyard went quiet. Even Asak ceased struggling. All the men were looking at her with a mixture of rage, shame, and fear. All except Lud. His eyes were shining, and she realized that in spite of everything, his love remained steadfast. She could no longer accept it, of course—she was degraded... but it comforted her and she felt her back grow straighter.

But of all the men there, the one who held her was looking at her with mixed wonder and compassion. There was also an intense curiosity in the back of his eyes. "You really knew them," he breathed. She felt his hands on hers, shaking. "You actually talked with Shem and his wife?"

She nodded, her head high. "And these words that you read... they are truth?"

"The scrolls told the full story, but yes, these are true." She looked down. "But alas! The scrolls are no more, and I failed the greatest test of my life." She looked down, but his soft hand pulled her face back up to his.

"Do you know the one true God?" he asked softly.

"Yes," she murmured, the tears starting again. "That was her greatest gift."

"Then your life is no failure," he replied.

She shrugged, glancing down at her bedraggled appearance.

His brow suddenly wrinkled. "Do you know who I am?" he asked quietly. She shook her head.

"I, too, know the one true God," he smiled slowly. "I learned of him from my father... Abram of Ur."

She heard, but understanding lagged behind. When it caught up, darkness took her again.

Chapter 50
DEATH IN THE MORNING

10-8-1761

Jalam crouched in the thicket, waiting for Korac's return. For a moment, he thought about trying to stop his cousin. Throughout the spring and summer, his heart had continued to change… far beyond the epiphany of the previous winter. It was no longer that he would not help kill the women—now he opposed Korac's intent to do so. He was torn between the demands of loyalty and those of his conscience. While the former never wavered, the latter grew stronger, whispering in his heart that he should be helping them.

But Korac was his cousin and deserved the truth, if he could give nothing more. So Jalam had finally spoken the night before, "If you take me with you, I'll do everything in my power to see that you fail. It's wrong to kill them and you know it." Then daringly, he added, "Things are going on inside you, Korac, though you try hard not to show it. Give it another year and you'll be fighting Nimrod."

In the light of morning Korac had said nothing until they were ready to move. "Stay here," he had ordered angrily. "I'll take care of this myself and come back for you. They're in the next valley… it won't take long."

Jalam had laughed as he backed into a thicket. "Longer than you think." But as Korac turned away, he spoke one last word, "You have denied yourself for too many years and used Nimrod as an excuse. Find your heart and start to live again… as your own man. Spare the women… for me if not for yourself." Korac had stomped off and Jalam smiled to himself. If his cousin was angry, then he was starting to feel again. And if he was starting to feel… well, anything was possible.

The thicket was comfortable and the late autumn sun was warm. Jalam half dozed as his mind drifted back over the past months. After his injury in the cave, Korac had been off his feet for several weeks. He insisted that he could have walked with a crutch, but the snow came heavy during those weeks; it would have been suicidal. Jael had picked a good cave—it needed only a small fire, even in the coldest weather, and the smoke blew out a narrow passage in the back. Even the lithe Jalam could not fit through it, but he finally found its exterior opening and evidence that the women had left that way. His respect for Jael rose another notch.

By the time the snow began to melt, they were on their way again, covering ground at a distance-eating lope. Once the weather warmed, game was easily found, and so Korac insisted that they travel as long as there was light. Neither expected to find any sign of the women for weeks, and so it had proven. It wasn't until Korac found a ford and crossed the river that he realized Jael had tricked him again. Faint signs began to appear—nothing obvious, but to Korac, clear enough. He cursed Jael, but there was an undertone of respect in his voice that Jalam had not missed.

The women had crossed over and been traveling on the west side of the river. It was a good ploy, but the men were faster and continued to closet he distance. A month ago they found a few charcoaled sticks, indicating a fire within the past week. From that day Korac redoubled his pace. Always a good runner, Jalam had taken it in stride, spending his days admiring the beauty of the countryside around him as they ran. In the far distance, they had seen mountains to the north and had passed the end of another range in the east. Then they had come into a broad valley, circled by far mountains to the east and north.

It was a beautiful plain, and Jalam dreamed of coming back and settling there. There was water, game, and soil. All a man would need to start a home. He knew it was impossible—once back in Shinar they would be under the thumb of Nimrod, but it didn't cost anything to dream. Signs of the women were becoming more frequent, though still hard to find. But they had learned much of Jael's habits from all the puzzles in the trail over the past months, and Korac was able to predict her movements more and more frequently. And the signs were fresher—the hard pace had cut the distance between them.

Jalam had not been immune to the skill of their quarry. He began to mention Jael's skill in selecting campsites, choosing trails, and avoiding danger. That a woman could do so was unusual enough; that she could drag an untrained woman along with her made her arguably better than her pursuers. He often spoke of it just to irritate his cousin. Ironically, most of the traces they found of the women were from the growing dog, who gave no thought to hiding his prints. The beast was now larger than many wolves. "Watch out for that dog," Jalam would tease. "You get close enough, it'll tear your throat out." Korac would snarl and moved on.

But that summer together had also carried both men back to their youth. Though neither would admit it, they had grown close once more. Korac respected Jalam's growing skill in the wild, and he was deeply in debt for the weeks in the cave. Jalam sensed deep waters stirring within his cousin, but Korac would not speak of it though his sleep was often troubled by dreams.

The great river turned sharply west across the fertile plain, running parallel to a line of mountains to the north. There seemed to be two ranges, a lower forested range and distant, snow-capped peaks beyond. But the river ran across the flat plain, interrupted occasionally by a small run of hills that it easily cut.

They were back on the north side of the river now; the women—evidently sensing the closing pursuit—had crossed back over in a desperate attempt to throw them off.

Now they were drawing near to another low range of hills running down from the north. The river dodged around their southern end and continued west. Scouting the ridge the day before, Korac had caught a whiff of wood smoke and had come back to plan his attack. "We end it tomorrow," he had said confidently, but Jalam's declaration of support for the women had drowned Korac's satisfaction.

Jalam remembered their parting. He was glad that he had finally found the courage to oppose Korac to his face. "I am your friend, Korac… maybe your only friend. But I won't be a part of it. I'll wait here, praying that you fail. I'll be here for you, even if you won't heed my wisdom. God is in this. Two women could not have survived the past year, otherwise. You fear crossing Nimrod; I fear crossing God. If you had any sense, so would you."

Now the morning was passing and Jalam woke suddenly. He had not realized he was dozing. Something was moving in the woods, uphill to his right, and he heard the distant, heavy snarl of a dog or wolf. He grabbed his bow. Time passed with nothing disturbing the silence but the buzz of insects. Then suddenly, it was closer. He heard something larger. It was close… too close….

He glanced around for a tree to climb. He needed to see and to act. As he slithered out of the thicket, he cursed the leaves. They had been comfortable, but now they were making noise. Something caught the edge of his vision. He froze, letting his eyes wander the terrain, trying to see the smallest disturbance. There was something over to his left. With difficulty he drew an arrow and fitted it to his string. Something was moving behind the trees, just a few tens of cubits away. There was a scrape of fur against wood. Without warning, a large wolf… no, a dog… burst into his vision. Instinct brought the bow up, but the dog was not attacking. It was fleeing.

Hard on its heels, a giant cat burst into view. Jalam had time to see its long, powerful fangs and to release his arrow before it was on him. He felt nothing but a heavy pressure on his chest… he heard the solid *thunk* of a spear and a horrible scream as the cat fell over and tried to drag itself away. Then Korac was there, his hand under his head and his mouth moving. Jalam couldn't hear. He tried to speak, but there was too much blood in his mouth. He began to feel the pain, but ignored it. There was something he needed to tell Korac, but he was too tired. He would just go to sleep….

Korac brushed the tears away as he prepared to bury his cousin. It had been decades since he had wept. He once thought he was done with tears for the rest of his life, spending them all on Timna. He had wept for weeks then, and it seemed at the time that those tears had burned away any trace of feeling. Maybe he had been wrong. Maybe they had been fighting the black despair. Maybe they had lost the battle, allowing the slime of that desolation to cover his heart.

These tears were different. They were washing it clean once more, uncovering something long buried by its dark muck. Feelings, long forgotten, began to filter through. He was standing on the sharp peak of some great divide. He could fall back into the old hardness and exist as a hollow half man—a blade in Nimrod's hand—for the remainder of his days. Or he could become once more the man who had loved Timna so much… the man that Jalam had believed was still hidden inside.

If he followed that path, he would have to face the pain of Jalam's death. It was his fault. He had seen the whole incredible incident from the hill top. Just as he had sighted fresh smoke, he had heard the dog on the slope behind him. Perhaps it intended to defend the women; perhaps it had just been hunting. But it had blundered into the great cat instead.

Korac wiped his brow when he thought of his own stalk up the hill. He must have come within a hundred cubits of the cat. Maybe it had been stalking him as he stalked the women. But when the dog interfered, the cat retaliated. A deadly game of chase had taken place, the desperate dog finally leading the creature to Jalam's position. His cousin had managed to get off one arrow, and it had plunged deep into the monster's chest, but not soon enough.

Korac had been running full speed down the hill; never before had he put that much strength into a throw. It had gone true, his spear doing what Jalam's arrow could not, but not before the monster's claws had opened Jalam's chest.

Korac wiped another tear with his dirty hand. He could blame the cat, now dead a few dozen cubits away. Or he could blame the dog for leading the cat to Jalam. But those options were false and he knew it. He had killed Jalam—he was the one who had accepted this insane quest. He had selected Jalam. His stubborn pride had led them halfway around the world, despite Jalam's warnings. For the first time, he saw what his life had become. Murdering innocents, pursuing women with the intent to murder, and getting his men killed, one after another, along the way.

Maybe Jalam was right… maybe God was protecting the women.

If so… then perhaps the old stories of his grandmother, Yaran, were true. And if they were, and if Timna was alive on the other side of death, what did she think of him now? That thought nearly crushed him.

A sudden resolve struck him. If Timna really was watching… he couldn't serve Nimrod any longer. Not another hour. Jalam's fresh blood on his hands erased that bond, just as Timna's had forged it.

He remembered his role in taking Mariel from her parents and his part in stealing her boy. For the first time in decades, Korac, the great killer, felt something, and even more incredibly, he felt shame. For a moment he was tempted to retreat back to the iron cage that had comforted him once before. But that would be cowardly, and that was one thing he was not.

Suddenly, unbidden, the words of Wen-Tehrom leaped into his mind.

> *You think you cannot feel because you lost your soul, but it is not gone. Only hidden. One day it will find you again. When it does, the consequences of your lost years and especially this day will haunt you and cost you another loved one. When that day comes, only my children will be able to help you, and they will despise your very name. I could almost pity you that misery."*

Misery indeed. He had found his soul again, but at too high a cost, and only to bring heartache, remorse, and loss. Her words had been fulfilled in part, and the remainder would undoubtedly bring worse. He needed a way of escape, but the memory of his bloody past came rushing up to overwhelm him. But had she not said, *"my children will be able to help you"*? Her children? Ham had not, Japheth was far away, and Shem would probably kill him on sight.

Then it hit him. The women! One was Wen-Tehrom's daughter by birth and the other by marriage. He wrinkled his brow. How could women help him? But those had been her words. He remembered them as clearly as if they had just been uttered. It was a slender reed to bear so much pain, but it was his only chance. Jael would probably kill him on sight, but at least then he would be free of the years of pain promised by Wen-Tehrom.

Kneeling there before the body of Jalam, he felt self-disgust welling up within him. His tears flowed easily now. "I swear to you, Jalam, that I will fulfill your final wish. I will abandon this terrible hunt. But first, I must give you a decent burial. It's all I can do for you now."

He looked around. At the base of the hill was an outcropping of stone. It would do. Tenderly he carried Jalam over to a glade near the stone face. He would build a cairn to keep the creatures away. Rock after rock he carried and stacked into a fitting tomb for his cousin… his friend. He did not rest until it was done, not realizing that the sun was nearly down behind the hills. The cat lay over in a small hollow, the arrow and the spear still visible.

With that sight, something like reason returned. He suddenly wondered if the cat had a mate. He ran over and tried to pull his spear out of the body. It caught on a bone, and he had to cut it out. In the end, he cut out Jalam's arrow too. "I'll keep this always, to remember your wisdom, cousin," he whispered. "It was so much greater than mine."

Jael crawled carefully over the rocky ledge. It was a short drop to the floor of the ravine below, but it was jagged with rocks and undergrowth. She was trying to leave no sign of her passage, having covered the slight scrapes that Madrazi had made going before her. Her keen eyes saw another, an almost imperceptible scrape of some moss, but Jael carefully eased it back into place. A handful of dead leaves finished the job, obscuring the small bruise. A handful of dust covered the smudge in the loam. Selecting rocky surfaces, she moved her hands and knees carefully towards the cave's entrance.

She wasn't quite sure what had happened this morning, but Sirus had left the camp at a dead run and had been gone for hours. She had hidden Madrazi under a deadfall and then edged into a thicket that gave her the best view of their camp. She held an arrow ready, cursing her trembling hands. She knew the hunters were not far behind but thought they were at least three or four days back.

An hour had passed. Faint sounds of Sirus' barking came over the hill. What to do? Shem had taught her to be patient, but he had also taught her that knowledge was the deadliest weapon. So she slid towards the crest of the hill, keeping low and stopping every few steps to listen. Movement always attracted attention, but she had to know what was happening. Finally, she found herself prone, looking down into the valley a few hundred cubits below. The forest was not thick here; she could see well down into the valley… and what she saw amazed and terrified her. On the valley floor, she saw vultures weaving their funeral dance. Was it Sirus?

Then movement caught her eye to the left. Out in plain sight, but some distance away, she saw the broad back of Korac straining as he tottered away from her. Following him with her eyes, she saw him place a large rock on a growing pile. It took a moment to realize what he was doing, and in her shock, she almost gasped. He was building a cairn. His partner must be dead… but how? Had Sirus killed him and then been killed in return? Sirus was a large, strong dog, hardened by more than a year in the wild, but these were Nimrod's trained assassins. But the vultures were feasting in a hollow beyond her line of vision, and Korac was burying his friend.

Or was he? Suddenly Jael felt naked. What if this was a cruel deception, designed to bring her out of hiding. What if the "dead" man was sitting in a tree, an arrow aimed at her, right now? Sweating, she moved her head slowly, searching any possible ambush. She saw nothing… but then if he were good enough to have made it this far, would she?

Move or stay? Risk being killed here or lead them to Madrazi? There were no good choices. Panic was rising. The idea of defeat after all these months… they had come so far… what if Shem and the boys were just up the river? What if they were not? What if they were back at the farm? She and Madrazi were stranded in the middle of a vast wilderness, with her deadliest enemy a long bow shot away, and her friends and family, months of hard travel distant.

Ruthlessly she forced down her fear. She recalled Shem's teachings. There were only three choices. Fight, flee, or hide. She couldn't fight. If the man was dead and Korac truly distracted, then perhaps she could kill him. But if it were an elaborate ambush, she stood no chance, and Madrazi would die before the sun set. She couldn't flee. They had been running for months, yet the men had proven faster— making up lost ground in spite of delays from shipwreck and injury.

That left one choice. She must hide. Now. Korac was busy, either setting his ambush or burying his dead. Either way, she had to act. And she would have to break their trail well enough to elude a man who had followed them all the way from the farm, never losing the scent, in spite of snow, rivers, distance, and every bit of her skill. She could not have kept to a trail as well as Korac, and he was easily Shelah's peer.

To break the scent, she would have to be at her best and hope he made a mistake. It was then that she remembered the small cave on the ledge of the ravine, in the valley leading down to the river. She had noted it yesterday, scouting the ravine. It was the kind of skill that had become second nature. If they could get into that cave without a trail, and hide for days, leaving no sign… perhaps Korac would move on, and they could slip away once more. It was a slim chance, but their only one.

So it was that she found herself inching down the ledge on hands and knees, studying the ground before moving, and careful to cover the few marks that Madrazi had made. She was upon the entrance. There had been no sign of Sirus. If he was still alive, he would have to fend for himself. She hoped he could. One of her greatest fears was that Sirus would find them and Korac would be following the dog.

"One problem at a time," she sighed to herself and finally dragged herself over the threshold of the cave. Looking back out, she saw a light scar in the loam. With exquisite care, she slid a few dead leaves over it, and backed into the cave. Madrazi's hand guided her back. It was musty, but she could hear the drip of water further back. They could live without food for a while, as long as they had water.

She allowed the older woman to pull her further in. Madrazi had spread their bedrolls and pushed Jael gently back on the pelts. She knelt in front of her and began to unlace her damp leggings, drying her feet with her own clothing and rewrapping them in the remnants of their remaining blanket. "Rest a bit," she mouthed into her ear. "I'll rouse you if I hear anything."

Jael nodded. She had been moving on nervous energy for the past six hours and as it bled away, she felt incredibly tired. She leaned back, resting her head in Madrazi's lap, letting the older woman's fingers stroke her matted hair. "I'm sorry I failed you," she whispered, trying to keep the tears at bay.

"There is no failure, little one," whispered Madrazi, still stroking her hair. "I'm so proud of you. Shem will be too, when we tell him of your exploits." She rubbed Jael's temples, easing the aches. "And so will Father." Jael nodded, and let the tears leak from her tired eyes. She fell asleep, crying.

Chapter 51
STONE TO FLESH

10-8-1761

Korac sat with his back to a tree, staring into the gloom at Jalam's cairn. The fire burned high; he no longer cared if the women saw him or not. He was exhausted. The shock of Jalam's death, the labor of building the cairn, and the punishing pace that he had set for the past six months all seemed to strike him at once. He felt listless and tired. If Jael came upon him, she could have killed him with a stick… a small stick.

He had to think. But his eyes were heavy. He…had…to….

Once more he was back in the dreaded valley. Timna by his side. The great bear lunging. His fingers fumbling the arrow as Timna bumped the bow. Her involuntary scream of fear. It was nearly on them before his arrow struck its throat. No time for another. He reached for his spear, knowing he was too late. Timna shrieked and turned to run, stumbling. The bear swerved, one great paw swept Timna aside, hurling her against a boulder. He heard the sharp crack of her head striking the rock. Then it turned. One paw hung loose, but the five great claws of the other were reaching for him. He was hemmed in by the narrow path, no place to run or climb.

Mortally wounded, the bear had enough strength left to destroy its tormentor. The arrow had penetrated a vital spot, but it was not enough. The monster had a purpose, even death could not forestall it.

He stared at his arrow, cursing his aim. Without warning, another arrow appeared beside his. The bear halted and looked up, roaring its defiance. Another arrow seemed to grow out of its mouth, piercing the skull. Angry eyes dulled. It staggered but fell forward.

He stumbled back to avoid the great body.

Then he was running to Timna. His hand felt the spongy pulp where the back of her head had once been. Nimrod's hand was on his shoulder. Words roared in his ears like a storm. Finally he understood them. "Let me tend to her, brother. We'll bury her out here… build a cairn to her memory." Nimrod guided him back down the valley to a seat by their packs. He wrapped a blanket around him, and seizing another, he walked by, up into the valley of doom, the drying sweat streaking his broad back.

Korac woke, screaming. Another comrade. Another cairn. He glanced in the fire; in the glowing coals he saw once again the broad back of Nimrod, sweat drying in streaks…. Suddenly he sat straight up, his fists clenched. Nimrod had apologized for his tardiness, telling of a perilous scramble over the rock ridge, just in time to get a shot at the beast before it could kill Korac. But if the climb had been that desperate, the sweat should have been pouring off him, not drying on his back. There was only one explanation—he had been in position all along, just as they had planned. But he had been slow to shoot. Why?

Korac had no false pride. He knew that he would have been a powerful ally for Nimrod, especially if bound by the chains of family. Yet had he not proven far more useful as an unfeeling husk? A shell of a man with no heart, no conscience, no woman to restrain his basest instincts? Had Nimrod foreseen the limits of his conscience, fearing that it might be nurtured by Timna? Had he gambled that grief would unite Korac's will to his with chains stronger than love... chains of an emotional surrender to the emptiness that could keep the sorrow of Timna's loss from destroying his mind?

Was Nimrod *that* evil? He thought back over his deeds of the past two decades, as if waking from a long slumber. He saw them as a man now, not an animal or a machine. He shuddered, and again recalled the words of Noah's wife.

He knew she was right. A conscience—slumbering since the death of Timna— had been reignited by Jalam's death. It did not burn brightly, but it did burn. Remorse hammered at his heart. Jalam had not been killed by the great cat. He had not been killed by the dog. No, Jalam was dead because he had been dragged away from a happy life in Shinar to murder women and children. Refusing to admit failure, they had come into a wilderness vaster than imagination. Jalam had recovered his senses months ago. He had refused to raise his hand against the women. And yet... Korac shook his head in wonder... he had stayed, protected him while his leg knit, and then followed him for months, just because they were family.

Korac finally wondered why *he* had ever come this far. Nimrod wanted these women dead. No... that wasn't right either. Debseda wanted Madrazi dead. It was an ancient feud, and none of his business. He knew there had been conflict, and he knew he couldn't trust Debseda's account. She would say anything to further her purposes. Maybe he should ask Madrazi. That was a thought!

Korac shuddered. Nimrod was just going along for reasons of his own—mostly to satisfy his lust for his own grandmother. His own grandmother! *How could I accept such evil?* It was time to turn around and go home. He had a score to settle with Nimrod. He would probably die, but at least—like Jalam—he would die an honorable death. The professional part of his mind weighed his chances. Nimrod was the better man; he was stronger, quicker, and his black spear seemed a part of his arm. There was a chance, but only a chance. Korac had not been as good as Heth, and Nimrod had bested Heth years ago, before he had grown into his full strength.

If there was any hope at all, it was in the two women up ahead. Even if he gave up his hunt and left them out here, it would be no different than driving a blade into their breasts. They had survived this far; but there had been an element of luck, and luck always ran out. If seasoned men like Dishon, Dishan, and Jalam fell to the wilderness, why should it not claim the women?

He needed them... and Jalam had wanted them to live. Maybe that was the answer. Jalam had given his life for Korac. It was a blood debt. He could not just leave... he must save the women.

The more he thought about it, the more convinced he became. Jalam seemed to be calling from the cairn, in the shadows beyond his fire. *Save them!* How could he do it? They expected nothing from him but death. They would rightly view any offer as treachery. If he came upon them unawares, demonstrating his power over them, and then let them live, would that not be enough? It might for Madrazi, but he shook his head at the thought of Jael.

Jael hated him. His face burned as he remembered his rough handling of her in her father's house. It had been disgraceful. And it had obviously triggered a raging hatred that had warped her life. She had become a warrior for one reason alone… to kill him. Was she good enough? Probably not, but one never knew. She was certainly no longer the innocent young daughter of Noah. He pulled his beard in frustration… another life he had wrecked.

Was she like her sister? He admired Mariel. She was a woman any man could respect… making the best of a bad situation… living with dignity in the midst of evil.

He was the cause of so much suffering. Nimrod had driven him hard and used him for deeds no other man would do. His hands were black with blood and deceit. How could he ever atone for that?

But whatever Korac was, he was no coward. If he was going to atone, then he would atone. He would start here, by preserving the lives of these two women and guiding them back home. He must approach them in weakness, not strength. Anything else would kill their trust before it had a chance to take root. And yet… Jael might kill him on sight. He certainly would in her place.

Maybe *that* was something else that needed to change. If Jael took his life, was it not just payment? He would have to trust the women… no, he would have to trust their God to stay their hands. Perhaps that was the best solution. For years he had been fighting against God, blaming Him for the death of his wife. Now, through his dream, he realized that Nimrod was to blame, not the Creator. And he could not simply ignore Him. That was the essence of Debseda's grip on Shinar. A city for the godless. If he was going to stop fighting godly people, then maybe he needed to stop fighting God, first.

Memories of old Yaran's stories flooded back into his mind. What better way to surrender to the Almighty than to put his life in the hands of his enemies?

Korac suddenly felt a sense of relief; a load lifted off his shoulders. He finally knew he had the right path. All that was needed was to walk it. No Nimrod. No Debseda. No evil. Just Korac, naked and alone before the Almighty. It seemed appropriate to be all alone here, far from any others. He was truly alone before God.

"You judge tomorrow," he breathed. "Take my life if you must… I can't complain if you do, but I ask that you let me live to keep them alive." The stars shone brightly.

"I can change, Jalam," he whispered. "Nimrod killed her, not I." A tear rolled down his cheek. "You were right, cousin. I will frustrate his plans. I will save these women. If God sees fit to let me live after that, then I'll war against Nimrod the rest of my days."

A wind blew through the tree tops, rattling the dead leaves still clinging to the trees. It was as if Jalam was giving approval. Korac nodded as the fire flared.

"East?"

Heth ground out the question with less respect than Shem deserved. He was tired, weary of this whole business. They had followed Shem without question, driving themselves across a vast, rough wilderness, all the way to this western ocean. It was exhilarating, but exhausting. Heth had been fascinated by the sea, at first wondering if Shem would take time to build a boat and sail across to the enticing shore across the water. They had all summer.

But Shem had abruptly turned back. Without the benefit of even a full day's rest, he had reversed their course, pushing back east as if a demon were driving him. Not only could the old man outsprint a deer, over many days he could run a wolf into the ground. And Heth could sympathize with that wolf! Despite his age, he often ran ahead of the younger men, meeting them in the evening, meat roasting on the fire.

It annoyed Heth. Though he knew better, it gnawed at his idea of himself as a man. He should be able to keep up with someone older than his own grandfather, but he could not. He told himself that he deserved to be tired… he was larger than the others, and stronger. But it had never slowed him before. Despite his bulk, he could run for days. Unfortunately, Shem wanted them to run for weeks! He wasn't just tired. There was weariness deep in his bones that would take weeks of leisure to leach away.

Shem just looked at him with those inscrutable brown eyes, the lack of expression telling Heth how close to the edge of anger he was. But suddenly, he was past caring. He squared his shoulders and stared back. "First we head east. Then we follow that cursed river south, searching for a way around those mountains." He waved his hand. They were close enough now to see that they spread as far as the eye could see, east and west. The highest peaks were closer to ten thousand cubits than five, and the passes were blocked by snow and ice. No man could cross them and live.

"Now we have to cut back east." He caught his breath, realizing that he was nearly shouting.

"Sorry," he mumbled.

Shem nodded a slow acceptance. "But I don't understand," continued Heth in a more reasonable tone. "The nights are starting to get cold again and the higher we climb, the colder it will be. If we stay moving along the north slope of the mountains, it will be a cold winter."

"It will be a cold winter no matter which way we go," replied Shem evenly. "But we need to head back." He sighed. "I can't explain it, but I know what I feel. It's never let us down yet, has it?" His voice was soft, but firm.

Heth glanced around. The others were nodding. They all respected Shem's uncanny instincts in the wilds. Many times they had been saved hardship, hunger, and time by following them, and Heth realized that if he chose another direction, he would be going by himself. He shrugged. "I guess not," he returned. "But I would still like to know what you're trying to do."

Shem smiled for the first time. "We know now we can't get through these mountains," he said. Everyone nodded. "But there were *two* ranges that we followed. The first swung southwest before the second began curving north. They might be the same or they might not. If we can find a gap, then perhaps we can find a shortcut to the Black Sea. It would save a couple of months, and I fear we need that time."

"All right," sighed Heth. "The way's not getting any shorter. At least we were able to swim the river before the cold set in."

He picked up his pack and shifted it higher on his shoulder. Shem led off. They had been following a river east, but Shem cut away from it, actually heading even closer to the mountains—more southeast than east. He turned and smiled at Heth. "We'll have to stop for the winter in a month or so," he explained. "There's probably more game in the foothills. Creatures that graze the high pastures in the summer will retreat to the low pastures in the winter, but not much further."

Heth almost smiled. Shem was not given to explanations of his actions. Perhaps his flash of anger had touched the older man's conscience. He thought for a moment.

Or perhaps not.

Chapter 52
AN UNEXPECTED GREETING

10-9-1761

An early morning fog drifted up from the river and hung over the hills, filling the valleys and ravines with its damp grayness, another clue of the coming winter. Jael had slept for hours, waking only late in the night as Madrazi shifted her into her bed and lay down beside her, one arm hugging her close. She woke to the fog filling the cave and felt the lassitude of exhaustion in her bones. She slid a wolf pelt over Madrazi and lay back down beside her. No one could find them in this fog, hidden away in this cave. With that thought, she drifted off again.

It was late morning when she woke once more. Madrazi was up, filling her horn with water. It was a tedious job, the water dripping ever so slowly down the stone face at the back of the cave. But Madrazi crouched, intent on her task, as if it were the most important job in the world. Jael bit her lip. Madrazi had been a great help all summer, deferring to Jael as she had promised, and doing more than her share.

As the snow had thawed, so had the coldness between them since the cave. Gradually, they grew close. After the successful hunt for the bear, Madrazi had begun to talk to her again. Over the months had told her much of her life, a chapter at a time around innumerable fires—everything from her childhood nightmare to her struggles to keep her family together. Jael found the accounts fascinating, not missing the similarities between herself and the young Madrazi. The tales had been strictly honest—unsparing in their description of Madrazi's disbelief in Noah and her passive rebellion. The more she told, the closer they became.

Noah had related only the bare outlines of the flood to Jael, but Madrazi made it come alive… made Jael feel like she was on board the ark. She finally understood the ancient enmity between Madrazi and Debseda, and in doing so, she understood that the evil in Nimrod extended far beyond her petty injury. A few weeks earlier, when Madrazi had related her final vision on the ark, Jael had shivered, unable to sleep for wonder and terror.

Watching her now assume the menial task of refilling their water supply made Jael felt guilty… somehow disrespectful… but, as always, she chased the feelings away.

She was loath to crawl out of her bed; a delicious laxness filled her body. There was nothing more to do than to abide with her decision. No hunting for food. No searching for the next path. No scouting the back trail, filled with worry over leaving Madrazi, yet filled with greater worry over not knowing where her enemy was. All that was past. All they had to do was stay quietly in this remote shelter, waiting until hunger drove them out and back to their search for the headwaters of this river—an accursed torrent that showed no sign of lessening, despite months of travel. But Madrazi kept insisting that was their goal, so they had pressed forward.

Her lip curled in a grim half smile. At least the men would have no better tale of exploration. In the months that they had followed this river, they could have traveled to Shinar and back, ten times. She wondered what her mentor would have to say about that—about keeping his wife alive through many challenges. She relaxed on the furs, thinking of the rare words of praise he would speak…

"Hello the cave!"

Those three words drove all thought of praise from her mind, turning them instantly into bitter defeat. It was only numb shock that kept that bitterness from overwhelming her. Without thinking, she was out of her blanket, bow in one hand and quiver in the other. She recognized her enemy's voice, and fear and hatred warred within as her fingers went white, clutching the bow. Silently, she waved Madrazi back, but the older woman shook her head, quietly set down the horn, and picked up the spear.

Jael's mind was awhirl. Should she answer, try a lucky shot from the depths of the cave, or belt on her blades and go out to meet him in combat. None of those options seemed good, and for once, her decisiveness deserted her. All she could see was black failure. She wanted to scream. After all the months, all the effort, all the suffering, she had failed in her trust.

She turned to Madrazi, expecting to see her own despair mirrored in her sister's eyes. Instead she saw a calm resignation—a peace that she did not understand. Before she could say anything, the call was repeated.

"Hello, the cave! I come to talk. I have no weapons. I want words, nothing more." The voice hesitated. "Please…."

Jael turned to Madrazi in open-mouthed amazement. Madrazi smiled slowly and nodded. Then Jael remembered his rough hands on Noah's porch. Her face hardened. She owed this man much. If he was without weapons, it would be easy to extract payment. She gripped her bow and turned to the entrance. Madrazi dropped the spear and grabbed her arm. "We will hear what he has to say," she said softly, but there was steel in her words.

"It's a trick," hissed Jael. "He wants to kill you. If he can get within twenty paces and has a hidden knife, he will. Or he'll kill me and take you at his leisure."

"If he wanted to kill us, he could already have done so," whispered Madrazi. "Talk to him. Let me hear his voice. If I hear deceit, I'll warn you. But give him the chance."

Jael frowned, but realized that this was Madrazi's decision. She nodded and relaxed a bit, letting Madrazi move toward the entrance.

Drawing a deep breath, the older woman replied, "I know you as a liar, murderer, and kidnapper, Korac, son of Magog. What words can you offer in the place of those deeds?"

"None," he returned. "But if you look out, you will see that my hands are empty. Jael is skilled with the bow. It should not be hard for her to kill me if that is your wish. I only ask that you listen first. What harm can it do?"

Jael felt harsh words in her throat, but before she could spit them out, Madrazi walked past her out onto the ledge. "I will listen, son of Magog, for the sake of my love for your grandmother. But your reputation precedes you, and evil hangs about you like a stench from the pit. It will take power to overcome it."

Jael slid out beside Madrazi, an arrow drawn half way to her ear. Instinct kept her within the cave entrance, flattened against the rocky side. But as she took in the sight, she saw that he spoke the truth. Korac stood in the ravine below, his hands held out to his side. She scanned the ground around him, looking for a hidden spear or bow, but saw neither. "No blades, either," he said softly, following her eyes. He stood well out in a clearing—it would take five or six steps to reach cover. Jael knew she could kill him easily. It was tempting to just let go of the arrow, but something in Madrazi's manner stayed her hand.

Korac must have sensed how close those fingers were to releasing the arrow; he sat down slowly, with his hands in plain view. Jael relaxed slightly, but the arrow remained on the string and the bow up.

"What would you say to us?" repeated Madrazi. "For the past year all we have heard were your actions. You murdered my household. You drove us across the wilderness. You followed, seeking our lives… all on the whim of a woman who is no closer to you in blood than I. And before that, you have been a blade in Nimrod's hand, aiding his evil, to the point of helping him kidnap our sister. I could go on, but why pollute the morning?" She drew herself up, and suddenly Jael saw another woman—a matriarch of the chosen line, not the meek companion of the past months. Korac must have sensed it too—he held one hand in front of his face.

"All that you say is true," he admitted. "But I have seen the last of those days. I will tell you my story. I admit freely that I deserve to die for what I have done. If you think my offer of no value, then kill me here. I only ask that you bury me beside my cousin… in the valley over there."

"What happened to him, and what was his name?" Madrazi still stood on the ledge, proud and erect.

"His name was Jalam. He ran afoul of the evil that follows us all in this wilderness. He was killed by a great cat. It stumbled on his hiding place while chasing your dog." He shook his head. "Is your dog that clever, or was it just bad luck?"

A spasm of sorrow twisted his face. "Jalam was hiding because he refused to help me, calling our task evil and naming us dupes of Debseda. For months he had been hounding me to turn back; I refused, and because of his loyalty, he stayed. If I am to lie here in the wilderness, I prefer to be beside him."

Jael found her tongue for the first time. "The cairn of stones?" she asked.

Korac nodded, but looked up at her with a questioning eye. "I saw you carrying rocks yesterday," she said. "You killed the cat?"

Korac nodded again. "Jalam got off one arrow that would have killed it eventually; my spear finished the job… but not before it had torn him open. He paid for my evil."

"And the other two?" Jael still suspected a trap.

"One died in the shipwreck. The other in the blizzard just before we found the first cave."

"Where you broke your leg?"

Korac looked up at her with a half smile. "Yes. I was foolish. It was a simple trap... yet it only takes a moment of inattention." Then he nodded slowly. "You were there—the back passage?" Jael nodded back. She still wanted to kill him, but curiosity stayed her hand. "How did you find *this* cave?"

Korac twisted his mouth in a half grin. "Don't worry. You left no tracks. I looked even after I knew you were there. Your friend repaid me for the life of my cousin. He is up on the top of the ridge, guarding you."

Madrazi called and Sirus came down the narrow trail, growling softly at the man in the ravine below.

She turned back to Korac. "I ask you again... why should we let you live?"

The man slumped. "Because this wilderness contains dangers that we all have been lucky to escape. You will be safer in my company than alone. And I will take you home. I will protect you with my life. If you still want me dead, then your husband can do it, and you won't have blood on your hands." He looked down at the ground and shook his head. "It is a hard thing for a man to bear that stain... I would not wish it on any woman." He paused, looking down. "It changes things."

Jael was astonished. Words would not come, but Madrazi appeared as unflappable as if she were discussing the harvest with a retainer. "Why should we trust you, son of Magog? By your own words, you admit seeking our lives for more than a year. Why should we believe you have changed your mind?"

Korac shrugged. "I know of only one way. Some say that you see visions from the Almighty in your sleep. The men of Shinar call you a witch. You cannot trust me. Trust Him instead. I felt a power in Noah when I stood before him. I feel the same power in you now. Ask your God. Would you not trust His word?"

Madrazi stood silent, appraising the man for some minutes. Jael wanted to speak out but felt a constraint on her lips. This was between Korac and Madrazi. Finally, the older woman spoke. "Kindle a fire and I will come down. Jael will stay up here. If you threaten me, she will kill you. Do you agree?"

Korac nodded and immediately began gathering wood. He raked the leaf litter into a pile, clearing a space around his fire and piling the kindling at the same time. Within minutes he had a blaze burning in front of him. "If you let yourself down over the ledge, there is another narrow way that slopes down to the ravine floor," he advised.

Madrazi paused and turned to Jael. "Whatever happens now is in God's hand," she said. "Thank you for my life and for much else, my sister. I love you. Watch well."

Jael felt the tears gather. "I love you too. He will not harm you. Not while I live."

She watched as Madrazi slid over the side. Her feet found the ledge and she followed it down to the valley floor. Jael felt her tension easing; he had told the truth in that. Madrazi had to cross the stream, but it was small, with rocks choking it from some prior flood. Sirus followed her, staying right on her heels. As she strode to the fire, she kept her head up and did not hesitate. Jael's fingers tightened on the string and she brought the arrow up. The string was digging into her fingers, but she would not let down her guard. Once again, she thought to just release and end it all, but she could not.

Madrazi sat down before the fire. Jael kept the arrow aligned with Korac's heart. But he did not move or speak. Time passed. Jael did not know whether it was moments or hours, but her aim never wavered. As the moments slid by, Jael felt a tension build within her. All the memories of her first encounter with Korac came rushing back. What might she have been if he had never touched her? Would she still be happy in innocence? Like Ashiel? Or would something else have destroyed it?

Finally Madrazi stood and turned back to her. "You can come down now, Jael. It's safe."

Sliding the arrow back into its quiver, she shouldered it and slung the bow around her other shoulder. Yet the inner turmoil only increased. Following Madrazi's path, she hurried down, but each step brought a building rage. Once across the stream, the bow snapped back into her hand with an arrow on the string. All she could see was the black place in her heart that harbored her hatred of this man. A red mist obscured her vision.

When she strode into the clearing, it was Jael the huntress who arrived, not the daughter of Noah or sister of Madrazi. Madness was upon her. Her voice sounded like that of a stranger. "He may be safe," she growled, "but I cannot forget the past. He owes me a debt. I lost a sister and nearly lost a family. My father was humiliated and my mother driven to the edge of the grave. His life is mine. I claim it now!"

A tiny part of her mind screamed to stop. But the years of bitterness that had driven her to become what she had become—unloved and unloving—rose up like a great wave to swamp it. She hated herself in that moment, but she didn't care. This was what she had lived for all these years… the goal that had sustained her through so much pain and suffering. The body pushed beyond all reasonable limits. The disappointment of family. Jobaath's taunts. Heth's temper. All for this moment… all for her vengeance.

Her face crystallized into something harsh. She saw again the slumping defeat on her father's face. Heard the wails of her sisters. Felt the grief as she rode away from her home, the dutiful daughter lost forever. Her bow came up; the feathers of the arrow brushed an icy cheek. Korac did not move. She saw acceptance in his eyes… and pity. Through the haze, she heard Madrazi's shout. "No, Jael! Don't destroy yourself!"

Suddenly, she was back in the clearing, her fingers releasing the arrow. Madrazi now stood before her, shielding her enemy. Frantically, the girl swung the bow up and away just as she released, and the arrow flew off into the woods after ruffling Madrazi's hood. She stared in shock, the voice inside now screaming. Her sister's life had been spared by a fingerwidth.

Her hands began shaking. She collapsed to her knees, all strength gone. Her stomach recoiled, and her next clear thought was of Madrazi holding her, rocking her to soothing words she could not decipher. For all the anguish of the past years was pouring out. Sobs wracked her body. Dimly she was aware of being sick once more. Madrazi still held her. After a time, the roaring in her ears subsided and she felt herself tremble... felt the tears flowing down her face... tasted the bile in the back of her mouth.

From out of the haze came a calm voice. "Lie down, Jael, and drink this." Madrazi let her down onto a pile of furs and handed her a hot cup. She took a sip, recognizing the Chamomile flowers that Madrazi was hoarding for the winter. Soft hands washed her face with cold water from the creek.

Finally she found her voice. "I'm sorry, Madrazi; I'm so sorry," were the only words she could choke out. She kept saying them over and over, as if the repetition might expunge her guilt.

"I know, Jael. We're safe and we're together."

That brought back memory. Jael tried to sit up, but Madrazi pressed her back. "What of... him?"

"He's away, retrieving his things." The voice was soothing, and Jael almost relaxed. But a picture of Korac bringing weapons back into the ravine forced her upright on the bed, spilling the tea. "You can't... it's not safe... you...."

"Hush, Jael." Madrazi seized her shoulders and forced her to stare into her bright green eyes. "It's safe. I promise. I have seen it."

Jael felt a wave of power wash over her and she relaxed. When Madrazi used that voice, there could be no doubt. "What now?" she asked. "I'm so tired, Madrazi. I cannot protect you if he's close."

"God will protect us both, Jael. I saw something else in the edge of the vision. Shem and the boys are not far away. If we follow the river, we'll find them soon."

Jael relaxed again. "I trust you." Her face twisted. "But I don't know how you can even bear to look at me." Bitterness began to reassert itself... to resettle itself into its accustomed place in her heart. She felt the hardness coming back to reclaim her.

"Stop!" Madrazi seized her shoulders and shook her. Jael wanted to drop her gaze, but she could not. Madrazi's eyes held hers, reinforcing the words that flowed between the women. "Hear me, Jael." Though said in love, the words were permeated by power. "Life has taken you down a twisted path. But it has not made you another person. You are still Jael. You are still my sister. I love you. Shem loves you. Our parents love you. Do not let bitterness crush that love. You nearly let it add a burden to your life that you could not have carried."

Jael began to sob again.

Madrazi smiled. "But you did *not*. In the end, that's what counts. Rid your soul of bitterness and hatred. You battered your body into that of a warrior. Use that determination to overcome your true enemies. Start praying again. Only God can grant the peace you seek."

Jael dried her eyes. Memories of every harsh and disrespectful word she'd ever spoken to Madrazi washed over her. It took all her strength to meet her sister's gaze. "I've been awful, haven't I? Especially to you. It was because you were right, and I hated that I was not. I know it, and I'm sorry. From this day, I'll try to treat you as I should. Thank you for holding on to your love even when I would not."

Madrazi hugged her. "I forgive you, Jael. We all love you." She released the girl and a glint of mischief sparkled in her eyes. "We'll be with Shem soon... and the others too," she added slyly. "Even Heth...."

Jael felt the heat blaze in her face and neck. "Madrazi!" She paused a moment as the idea took hold. Heth.... It was a pleasant thought. She lay back and let herself drift. Dimly she realized that Madrazi had put more than chamomile in the tea.

They stayed in the ravine for three days. Korac staggered back into camp late on the first afternoon, weighed down by a load of fish he had speared in the shallows of the river. Jael and Madrazi cooked several while Korac built stands to smoke the rest. It would give them a supply of food for days, speeding their travel. Jael was still uncomfortable in his presence, but the blind rage was gone. He seemed to understand. Though he said nothing, he stayed as far from them as he could, even sleeping up on the top of the ravine.

He said nothing to her, and said only what was necessary to Madrazi. It was stilted and curt. Jael noted it and frowned, and when they were alone, she commented on it to Madrazi. "He's a rude man. I hope you're sure of what you saw."

Madrazi chuckled. "He's not rude, Jael. He's terrified."

"Afraid? Him? He may be many things, but a coward...."

Madrazi continued gently. "Of you."

Jael stammered and went silent. "Why...? How...?"

Madrazi saw her confusion and explained. "For years he has brought pain to many, and now, for the first time, he is beginning to feel that guilt. For some reason, he feels it most deeply around you. When I stopped you, he didn't move an inch. He was ready to die and fully expected it. In some ways, I think he welcomed it. There are a flock of words bottled up inside him. He'll release them when he's ready, probably a little at a time. And the day will come when he will ask you to forgive him. That will be your decision, but you must think very hard about it—it will define the rest of your life and the rest of his."

Her eyes narrowed. "Are you *telling* me to *forgive* him?" She was indignant. "How could you...?"

"No," interrupted Madrazi. "I'm telling you to consider it... for your sake more than his." Jael clamped her mouth shut. She knew exactly what Madrazi meant, though she didn't want to admit it.

By the end of the third day the sense of strangeness had lessened, though Jael's suspicions remained. They were eating supper when Korac ventured to speak. "My lady," he nodded at Madrazi, "perhaps it would be worth the effort to build a boat or raft to return downstream. It would be faster and safer."

Madrazi shot a look at Jael, in part warning her to keep silent and in part a small gloating over her prediction. "Thank you for your consideration," she replied evenly, "but we are headed in the opposite direction. Shem, Shelah, and their friends are only a few weeks west. I would like to find them before the winter strikes."

Jael almost giggled at the look of slack-jawed amazement on Korac's face. He stammered and blushed. "But I thought…."

Madrazi interrupted him gently. "I know they are close, Korac, in the same way that I know my life is safe in your hands, now."

Jael suddenly thought of Heth and Ashkenaz, imagining the looks on their faces when they met with the women, guided by Korac. She frowned, and heedless of Madrazi's warning, she blurted out her first thought. "They'll kill him."

Korac looked uncomfortable and would not meet Jael's eyes. He sighed. "That is my thought too," he admitted. "But I swore on my cousin's body to keep you alive. I will fulfill that oath. As for the rest of it…."

He chuckled to himself and leaned back to enjoy the fire. Jael looked at him. His black eyes, for so many years dead and empty, seemed crowded now with many things. He chuckled again, reading the question in Jael's look. "You'll get your answers—someday." The look she gave him in return was curiously devoid of animosity.

Chapter 53
ENEMIES & FRIENDS

10-21-1762

Winter kept holding back, but the days were colder—water froze at night. Their progress had been rapid. Thanks to the smoked fish, they had not stopped to hunt. Both women had commented on how much faster they could move; they were no longer evading pursuit… though it still felt strange to be walking behind the pursuer. Also, they had seen how good Korac was on the trail. Jael had grudgingly admitted to Madrazi (in a whisper) that his skill exceeded hers… slightly, of course. But the man certainly could find easy paths, good campsites, and quiet water. Finally, they had discovered that with Korac carrying the lion's share of their supplies, the women could travel much faster, often at a ground-eating lope. The past year had made them all strong and enduring.

Jael was beginning to relax, but she always stayed between Korac and Madrazi and never walked in front of him. He refused to take offense, and had given her an approving half-smile when he first noticed.

It was hard to believe it had been eleven days. Jael ran back over them in her mind to make sure. The river had continued out over the plain for two days before bending northwest, heading around the north side of a range of hills that threatened to become mighty mountains in the distance. They had lost most of the second day crossing to the south side of the river. Even though Korac bound two large logs together, the women still were thoroughly wet, while Korac was soaked to the skin, swimming behind and pushing the raft with all his considerable strength. They were in the water a little less than an hour, but Korac was exhausted and stiff from cold when they abandoned the raft a half day's journey back east. The current had been placid until they were within a spear's throw of the south shore; then the flow had carried them quickly downstream.

Korac had wanted to keep moving, but Madrazi demurred. "Fire and food," she ordered, "Or we'll all be sick." They made a few more hours that day, and then the days fell into a routine. Rise, eat, run. Rest at noon. Walk, make camp, eat, and sleep.

The river continued a little north of west. Although the ground had been slowly rising, it seemed as big as ever. Over the following days, the hills—now more south—rose higher and higher, with snow-capped peaks in the distance. They were all happy to follow the river, now… those mountains looked rough, even from a distance.

On the fifth day, the river had bent a little further north, angling away from the mountains. There was a brief discussion; Korac suggested that they would find the river again if they continued along the foot of the mountains, but Madrazi insisted on staying their course. Jael had supported her out of spite, even though she privately agreed with Korac, but there was no argument. He had quickly deferred to Madrazi's wish. "Be careful," he had warned, however. "The country is getting rougher, and the snows could come at any time."

Korac's prediction had been as accurate as always. Over the past week, hills had risen, and the river had sunk down into a valley that grew larger each day. After experimenting, they had found travel easier along the top of the ridge paralleling the river, which now rose more than five hundred cubits above the stream. As with most things in the wild, there was a price to be paid for the easy travel. Whenever a tributary entered the river, they had to cross ravines, usually tangled with brush. Stream followed stream; hill followed hill, but still the river snaked to the northwest, farther from the southern mountains.

They were all tired when Madrazi called a halt near the end of the day. Korac picked up his bow and went out to hunt. Jael was preparing hers when Madrazi waved her over. "Don't, Jael," she ordered softly.

"Don't what?" the girl returned, with a touch of aggrieved innocence.

"First, don't take me for a fool!" flashed Madrazi. "He is very good at what he does. So are you. Don't make it a competition. There is enough between us already without adding new tension. You have nothing to prove to me or to him. So quit trying."

Jael let her quiver fall to the ground with her bow. She could not believe that Madrazi was taking sides with that… that….

Madrazi sighed. "I know you hate him. I know why… probably better than you do. But when you wear it like some badge of honor, all you do is create friction, and that only serves the evil one."

Jael frowned. "He promised to talk to you: to tell you why he went from wanting to kill us one hour to wanting to save us the next. Yet he's said nothing. It's been days. Why shouldn't I be suspicious?"

Madrazi tried to hide her smile, but couldn't.

Jael felt her blood begin to rise. "There's nothing funny…."

"Oh, Jael. Do you really wonder why? I wouldn't speak either, not sitting across the fire from some perpetually-scowling woman looking for the least excuse to rub my guilt and shame in my face." She snickered softly. "Especially if she were beautiful."

Jael felt like she had been struck by Heth's spear. Her mouth fell open and her eyes bulged out like a fish. She tried to speak, but all that came out was an incoherent gargling. Madrazi was giggling now, with a sparkle in her eye that Jael had not seen for many months.

Finally she regained control of her voice. "You must be joking," she hissed. "Him? Me? Me? Him?" She shook her head violently.

"Not you, Jael. I know who you're thinking about when you get that dreamy look on your face." Jael blushed and looked down. "But I've seen the way he looks at you… half in wonder, half in terror. I've seen it before." She sighed. "Just try to be civil. That would help start him talking."

Jael was dazed, but nodded at Madrazi's insistence. Despite misgivings, she was as good as her word. She put her bow away and helped build a fire. Then she built a small shelter, leaning branches against a deadfall, and covering them with thick pine boughs to keep out the wind. She cleared the area around the fire. At Madrazi's insistence, she even washed her face and hands, though she drew the line at releasing her hair from its tight braid.

When Korac returned with two hares, she forced herself to compliment him for his kill and ask courteously if he had seen signs of any predators. After a hesitant start, he began to talk, though he did not meet her eye. Jael glanced at Madrazi, who was smothering her best I-told-you-so-grin. Getting more than a dozen words out of the man was an achievement, but his relief at Jael's new attitude began to bring words out in a tumble. He relaxed as he cooked and sat at ease during their meal.

Madrazi rose and threw some dead branches on the fire. It flared and danced, offering some relief against the cold that was rushing down upon them. "Thank you for the meal, Korac," she said warmly. "It was kind of you to bring in something different. I'm weary of venison and fish."

He nodded, embarrassed, glancing sideways at Jael. But she just smiled too. "Yes, thank you. It's so much easier with your help."

He shook his head, clearly out of his depth, and sighed. "It's the least I can do," he grunted.

"It's so big, isn't it?" asked Madrazi, waving up at the sky. "It reminds me of watching the sky grow as the waters shrank down off the mountain… slowly receding week after week."

"I would like to hear the story," Korac admitted. "When I was young, my grandmother would tell us, but we moved away and I've forgotten most of it."

"Don't they tell it in Shinar?" asked Jael, an edge returning to her voice.

"Not really," he said, ignoring her tone. "Ham refuses to talk of it and I fear the only other source might not be… objective."

Madrazi interrupted before Jael could retort. "I will be happy to relate the entire tale to you, Korac, though it will not be as well done as your grandmother. She has a way about her that makes stories come to life."

Korac nodded, lost in old memories. Madrazi let the silence hang, shooting Jael a warning glance. Jael sat back and forced her face to relax.

"Jalam was like that," he sighed. "He could brighten a night by talking. You didn't really care what he said… it was pleasant to hear him." He flexed his right leg. "When we were stuck in the cave for a month, he talked a lot about our younger days… about grandmother and her stories and songs." He paused and looked down. "I should have listened more carefully. You never know how much you'll miss someone until they're gone."

"Tell us more about him," prompted Madrazi softly.

"Jalam was an archer. He was better than… better than anyone except Nimrod." He frowned and bit his lip. "He was always small and quick, with his hands and his words. We played together as boys. When we became men, he told me that he was going to become the greatest archer in the world." He looked down embarrassed. "He always dreamed of competing against your husband, my lady. It became an obsession… not to kill… just to compete. He never knew what killing was until last year, and he quickly found it not to his taste. He didn't like the way it changed him.

It stole something precious, he said. Taking the life of another does that." He looked down.

Jael started to stir, but a sharp look from Madrazi silenced her. She turned to Korac. "I know. The old stories tell us that man was made in God's image. A sin as terrible as murder destroys that image, diminishing the murderer." She looked at him keenly. "Is that why he wanted to turn aside from your mission?"

Korac nodded. "Once he saw death and thought about what it had done to him, he wanted nothing more to do with it. He even quit talking about your husband. In fact, he quit talking at all for a time. It was only in the cave, and after that it began to come back. He was my best friend... and I killed him."

The man sank down, his shoulders hunched as the memories flowed over him. Jael was amazed at how fragile he looked at that moment. Nimrod's great assassin... just a broken, sad, man... old before his time.

Madrazi broke in again. "He must have been very good. Few could have reacted at all against the speed of one of the great cats, and yet Jalam managed to loose a deadly shot before it struck. I don't know if Shem could have done that," she said softly. "Maybe there at the end, he really was the greatest archer in the world."

Korac stirred. He looked at Madrazi for a long minute, as if searching her eyes for something. "Thank you," he choked. "I couldn't have done it. He was a better... a better man than I'll ever be."

"God put us on this earth to effect change," Madrazi added. "Small men make small changes and great men make great changes. If Jalam could bring about such a change in your heart, then he was a great man."

"Yes," Korac was gloomy again. "He showed me that I was not." He sighed again. "I know how the Almighty must see me."

"The Holy One is just," replied Madrazi, and Jael felt a tingle of power in the air. She noticed Korac sitting up straight. He noticed it too. "He destroyed the works of man... indeed, the entire face of the earth... with the great flood. It placed no strain on His power."

Korac frowned, but nodded.

"But He is also a God of forgiveness," she added. "He saved Noah and his family from the same flood. Look at me, Korac," she said, sitting forward. "God did not save me because I was righteous and holy. He spared my life in spite of unbelief and a hard heart. When I walked up the ramp of the ark, it was not in faith of His promises, but in fear of the forces of Sechiall. The ark changed me. Even that was the mercy of God, coming in the midst of His great anger. Over those months, He became the joy of my life. Guilt is powerful. Yet forgiveness is greater. I hope that you learn that one day... just as I did."

"But you are a great lady," he countered. "The wife of Shem." He looked down at the ground. "You were not born into a family cursed by the Patriarch."

"Neither were you," she replied coolly.

"But I have made it mine."

Madrazi sighed. "Heth was born the son of Canaan, yet he discerned good and evil, leaving to pursue what was right."

"After enjoying its fruits," muttered Jael. The memory of Ashkenaz' words in the barn still rankled.

Korac stared at her. "What do you mean?"

Jael flared. "It is well known in Shinar that Heth enjoyed the pleasures of Debseda's maid Celota, even as he was preparing to forsake her mistress!"

Korac choked and shook his head. He tried valiantly but unsuccessfully to hide a smile. Jael's face was growing red with anger. "Why do men always think fornication funny?"

Korac shook his head again. "No, wait! Hear me." He gathered his breath and looked at Jael, his dark eyes deflating her anger. "The humor is irony. Heth hated Debseda and her maids. I spread that tale on Nimrod's orders years ago to discredit Heth. It didn't work in Shinar—men knew Heth and knew Celota; therefore they knew it to be a lie from the beginning. But it seems to have taken root in the north."

Jael rocked back, dumbstruck. How could she have believed the worst of Heth so easily? She blushed as she remembered her anger before their departure. Any chance she ever had of winning Heth's regard and affection had been destroyed—all because of her own stupid lack of self control! How easy it would have been to simply ask the man. He was no liar.

But a part of her heart was singing in spite of her dismay. Heth *was* a man of honor. He was worthy of her admiration and her…. No, she stopped herself. She belonged to no man. Her lot in life was to war against Nimrod, not to churn out babies for Heth or any other. Yet the idea stirred something deep within. She ruthlessly suppressed it.

She lifted angry eyes at Korac. Another sin to place at his feet! It was all very well for Madrazi to speak of mercy, but it was not for him… never! She could never forgive Korac, she reminded herself… not after all he had done. Only blood could do that.

Korac stared at her as if reading her mind. Finally, he shook his head. Turning to Madrazi, he spoke, "Thank you for your words. I just don't think it's possible for me. I've gone too far… done too many evil things. Jalam is dead, yet I was the one who deserved death." He laughed shortly. "I expect that Shem, Shelah, and Heth will correct that oversight when we meet them."

"Perhaps," said Madrazi. "But what counts is right now. And how you stand before God will define your fate in the next life too. If God is speaking to your heart, then listen and follow His voice. You will be happier, even if your days are fewer."

His eyebrow quirked slightly. Madrazi smiled. "I was at Methuselah's side when he died," she said. Jael saw moisture pool in her eyes, making them glisten in the firelight. She saw a glimpse of ineffable sadness and loss. Madrazi blinked and it was gone.

"He died a happy man," she told Korac, "but it had nothing to do with his years. He died as he lived, with faith in God and the new garden with no mighty angel to bar the gate. He would have been as content with nine days as nine centuries."

"How do you overcome hate?" muttered Korac, with a side glance at Jael. "For many years I felt nothing, but Jalam's death seems to have broken the lock that imprisoned my heart. Yet the first feeling after shame was hatred… a bitter loathing of Nimrod for what he has done to me. He took away my happiness, and then he used it to make me something she would have hated."

"You speak to God in the fire, my lady," he said, looking hard at Madrazi. "Does He speak to others? In dreams or visions? Sudden insights?"

"God is close to every man," replied Madrazi evenly. "There is nothing special about fire. I have had dreams and visions since my youth—before I knew His touch. One only has to look up to the heavens to see the stars or the course of the Sun and Moon to hear something of His voice. In a way, every star is singing… if we choose to listen."

She trailed off for a moment, lost in thought. Then looking back across the fire, she spoke again. "Did God reveal something to you in a dream, Korac?"

"I don't know!" He got up and began to stalk up and down. "I saw something in a nightmare I had never seen before. It was a little thing, but it changed *everything*. How can I know if it is from God or not?"

"Is it true?"

Korac paused at that and sat down. Staring into the fire, he nodded abruptly. "I believe it to be."

"God is truth," replied Madrazi. "He reveals what He will. Tell me what you saw. Perhaps I can help."

Korac looked away. "Not now. Maybe not ever… but thank you for the offer."

There was stillness for a time. The fire crackled and began to die. Even the forest was quiet, as they were left with their own thoughts. Suddenly Korac broke it again by standing and looking at Jael. Her heart tightened within her; she felt her blood pounding. His face was twisted in pain. "I… hurt you and yours," he began, "and it pains me to see the extent of it, just as it tears at me whenever I think of the Lady Mariel. I know that I deserve your hatred, yet I ask for the mercy of your forgiveness."

Conflict rose up inside Jael. Part of her wanted to embrace what Madrazi had said. But the past years had made her hard in spirit as well as body. The old bitterness raged like a storm in her heart, crying out for revenge, not mercy. The turmoil blocked any words. She stood abruptly and strode off into the darkness. As she walked away, she heard Madrazi's voice.

"Let her be, Korac. You have asked, and now the battle is hers. Let her fight it."

Jael did not go far. Common sense had not vanished, in spite of the emotional maelstrom that swirled inside. How dare he ask for mercy? Yet the memories that sprang to her mind were not those of Korac, Mariel, and Nimrod, but those of herself, running from home, multiplying her family's pain. She remembered Shem's face when he found her in the wilderness; recalled her curses and hysterical ranting. And she remembered her treatment of Madrazi—her spite and harsh gibes. And she remembered the terrible moment when her arrow had come within a span of killing her sister.

Yet Madrazi had been willing to overlook it all… to help her… to love her. To forgive. Jael wavered, but the old habits rose up. She was not Madrazi, nor could she ever attain that standard. Her sister was one of the elders—a survivor of the great flood… someone who had seen two worlds.

Though she lay quietly with her thoughts that night, sleep proved elusive. She listened to the regular slow breathing of Madrazi and wondered long about righteousness, mercy, and sin.

Chapter 54
DEEDS & WORDS

11-4-1761

Korac steadied Madrazi as she crossed the small stream. She winced at the icy water on her bare legs but said nothing as she climbed out onto the other bank. Her feet were red with cold; a small dusting of snow had fallen during the night. "Use the snow to dry your feet," he advised, sitting beside her, matching actions to words. She followed his example before pulling on the deerskin shoes and wrapping long strips of hide around her lower legs, tying them in place with rawhide cords.

Korac politely kept his eyes fixed in the other direction, glancing upstream. Jael had crossed by herself and was attending to her own feet. He glanced at her again. Over the past two weeks she had said very little to him and maintained her distance. He longed for her words; that one evening when she had… he hadn't felt like that since Timna died. It had felt as if another wall had crumbled in the fortress around his heart. He had hoped for some acknowledgment to his request, but was realistic enough to know better. She would never forgive him. Had he been in her place, he never would. By default, Madrazi had become his counselor, warning him to give it time and to demonstrate his repentance with acts of kindness.

Jael remained quiet and withdrawn, so Madrazi had talked to him. Every night she would draw something out, probing ever deeper until he was remembering things forgotten for years. Slowly she learned more of his youth, his family's break with Japheth, and their fateful migration to Shinar. Over time, he told of his frustrations at taking second place to Heth at the martial skills the men of the plain worshiped. He even told of his delight when Heth was bested by Nimrod. That event was the beginning of his friendship with the younger boy.

In all of these tales he had said nothing of Timna—their marriage, her death, and the sorry aftermath. He couldn't bring himself to speak of his recent revelation of Nimrod's role in her death… he barely believed it himself. But it was changing him inside. The icy prison of service to Nimrod and his schemes was being melted by the ever-growing fires of hatred.

Those things he kept from Madrazi; he knew that any desire to slay Nimrod would upset her. In spite of his evil, she would not approve of his revenge. To compensate for his silence on that subject, he began to tell her of the plans and strategies of Nimrod and Debseda instead, but was surprised to discover that she did not care. After living with the perpetually-scheming Debseda for so long, he naturally assumed that the other elders would be much the same, trying to twist the world into their version of what was best. But, as he was learning anew each day, Madrazi was not Debseda. And he had no measure of comparison except faint memories of his own grandmother. Like her, Madrazi had no desire to rule or control, just the normal impulses of a matriarch to see her family come to good.

Feet dry and shod, they shouldered their loads and headed west. True to Madrazi's words, the river had turned back southwest and the distant peaks grew closer every day. The land was rougher now; they were by no means in the mountains, but hiked up and down hills every day. Korac took the lead—his eye for terrain kept them on the smoothest paths close to the river, but they often cut across the uplands to avoid its many bends. It was getting easier—the river was following a straighter path, cutting across country instead of looping around obstructions as it had in the plains behind them. He turned to watch Madrazi struggle up a short slope.

"She's nothing like Debseda," he muttered to himself. "She just wants to be a good mother." He shook his head and turned back west, stopping for a moment as if gathering his bearings, giving her a chance to catch her breath.

He was grateful for her acceptance of the changes taking place inside him. It would have been awkward if she had treated him with Jael's bitter silence, and he was smart enough to realize that her advocacy would be the only thing that might keep him alive when they met the men, slender as that chance might be. He never stopped to think they might not meet them—she was sure... just as she had been immediately sure that he no longer harbored any murderous intent towards them. How could he not believe her?

Jael was a different story. She pulled his heart in almost every direction. He resented her aloof hostility yet could not blame her for it. He admired her ability to lead him on a chase halfway across the face of the earth, and yet wondered why she despised herself for not having done better. She had injured him gravely at the first cave; if she had been alone or had decided to hunt him, she might have killed him from ambush.

He knew that it was only her concern for Madrazi that had kept her from doing so, and he admired her all the more for the discipline it took to be a shepherd when at heart she was a predator. She was the first woman since Timna that ever stirred any kind of feeling. Lacking the soft, curvaceous appearance that was popular in Shinar, she had an austere beauty; her face was perfectly formed and the flash of her eyes would draw any man.

But today she was nervous; she kept looking back over her shoulder and staring at the sky. He took a chance. "Do you sense danger?" he asked, careful to keep a neutral tone. Her habitual frown answered him first, and then she shrugged and pointed back with her chin. "I feel a change in the air... maybe a storm hiding behind the horizon."

"It's past time for a big one," he agreed.

"What can we do if it hits?"

"The lady is certain we are close. She spoke of seeing two large lakes, of seeing the men on the south side of the western one. I would like to get there before winter gets too bad. If we don't find the men immediately, we can find a cave or build shelter and wait. The land is full of game. Between the two of us, we should be able to find enough. If we can kill a large boar or a bear after the freeze sets in, we can survive for weeks."

He wanted to say more... to ask her how she felt about him... but he knew better than to press. Madrazi had warned him often enough.

"You have a better feel for the weather than I do," he answered instead. "Tell me if you think it draws closer."

Jael nodded and despite her continued suspicions, she took the lead, vowing to keep her eyes on Korac as well as the trail ahead. He watched her back for a moment before sighing and turning back to walk with Madrazi. At that moment, Sirus bounded out of the woods to his right, headed straight for Madrazi. Korac's instincts began to scream and he called out as he sprinted back for her, dropping his pack and unlimbering his spear. Madrazi was in the middle of a small clearing, just now realizing something was wrong. She too dropped her pack and fumbled to pull her spear off her shoulder.

It was too late. A boar was running at full tilt towards her, its small, red eyes on fire with hatred, and its ivory tusks ready to slash the intruder. It was easily thrice the size of Sirus, but the dog didn't hesitate. Voicing its battle roar, it sprang at the pig before it reached his mistress. Korac winced as he ran. Sirus was a big, powerful dog, but even striking the boar at full speed, he barely slowed it at all. But he saved Madrazi's life, knocking it aside just enough to miss her.

Angrily, the boar whirled and slashed back at the dog. Too stunned by the tremendous impact to dodge, Sirus slumped down, blood pouring from his side. Free from the dog's threat, the boar turned on Madrazi.

Korac ground his teeth. He couldn't cast his spear. If he missed, it might kill the woman. There was only one hope. He saw it instantly and didn't hesitate. His life for hers. It was more than a fair trade. Shifting his grip to point his spear downward, he gave a mighty bound. Somehow, the creature heard him and began his turn to face the new enemy. That slight movement was enough. Even in mid-air, Korac could see he would miss. And he was right. Instead of striking the shoulder above the heart, his spear entered the pig's side further back. In his anger he drove it in hard, and then felt a line of fire on the back of his leg. But fear drove the pain from his mind. His thrust would eventually be fatal, but in the meantime, he was facing an enraged boar with nothing but a knife. Rolling aside, he felt his lips twitch. *You won't be alone much longer, Jalam.*

But he had a short and unexpected reprieve. The boar was whirling round and round, trying to bite the bloody shaft. Korac took that gift and shoved Madrazi sprawling to one side. Sirus was staggering up, but was disoriented. He would be no help. The pig squealed its rage, unable to select a victim. Some instinct turned it towards the most dangerous, and it charged Korac. He saw Madrazi up and running for a tree. *Smart woman*, one part of his mind thought, while another thanked Jael for teaching her to be so. But most of his churning thoughts centered on how to stay alive long enough to strike a killing blow with his knife. He couldn't match the strength behind those tusks; despite its bulk the animal was too fast to sidestep. The only path was over the top.

Sirus growled and gave a feeble leap just as the brute charged. It hesitated, giving Korac the opening he sought. He leapt again, but not as high—his right leg seemed weak. But it was enough. Up over the razor sharp tusks he soared, diving forward and thrusting awkwardly with his blade at the spine as he flashed past. But his blow was defeated by the thick fat, and before he could strike again, he landed heavily, his knife lost—stuck in the boar's back, but not deep enough to cripple it.

As he prepared to die, he saw with satisfaction that Madrazi was scrambling up a tree. At least she would live. He could die knowing he had succeeded.

Squealing with pain and rage, the boar whirled again on its tormentor. Korac could see the intelligence in those red eyes… and the hate. There was no fear. Nor should there be. He had no weapon. The savage beast began to stalk him, creeping close enough to prevent any escape. Korac calculated. If he leapt high enough, maybe he could retrieve the knife. He gathered himself. The boar moved…

…and slumped to the ground as a feathered arrow drove deep into its neck. It rose and tottered forward, half-paralyzed, as another shaft and then a third hammered into its neck within a finger width of the first. After another half step it fell, the spear pointing straight up in the air like a banner of victory.

Korac felt the world speed back up. His leg was on fire now, but he ignored the pain. Hobbling over to the brute, he seized his spear and shoved it down hard. Trying to pull it out would waste effort. He yanked the shaft back and forth, tearing great gashes in the animal's vitals. It shuddered once and lay still. Korac yanked his knife from the beast's back and slashed around the shaft until he could pull his spear free.

He backed off a few steps and suddenly collapsed to one knee as the fire of his wound overcame his will. He clung to his spear and watched the animal closely. He heard footsteps behind him. "Stay back, lady!" he barked, keeping his eyes on the boar. Jael ran into the clearing, her bow ready. Keeping it trained on the pig, she sidled over towards Korac.

"Give me your spear, Madrazi," she ordered, not relaxing her bow until she had the spear. Korac felt dizzy. He looked down at his right leg. There was a deep slash across his calf, dripping blood on the ground. His vision blurred. Over beyond the boar, he saw Sirus slump to the ground, his eyes glazing.

Madrazi was there for him. He saw her look over at the dog, a spasm of sorrow twisting her face, but then it turned back to him, full of concern. He knew in that instant the difficulty of her choice. She leaned over him as she lowered him to the ground. "Build a fire, quickly!" she commanded Jael. Korac felt a tug at his spear and reflexively tightened his grip. "Let go," he heard faintly. "I'll take care of you." The voice sounded like his grandmother, so he relaxed his hand and let go. Darkness took him.

The dream struck him at once.

Step by step he walked again up the canyon, Timna by his side. He whispered caution to her, but her bright eyes disdained the advice. Nimrod would be coming over the ridge line and they would have the beast surrounded. Once again, he saw the bear lunge out. Once again he fumbled his shot, enraging it further. It charged. He screamed as Timna was cast aside and the bear turned on him. Then the arrow appeared in its throat and the other emerged from its mouth. It tottered and fell. He rushed to Timna, watching her life bleed out. Felt the hand on his shoulder; saw the drying lines of sweat on the broad back of Nimrod. He wanted to leap up and stab him, but he couldn't move. Nimrod turned to him, holding the bloody rags of Timna's clothing. Grinning, he wrapped them round and round Korac, securing him in a bloody tangle that held him fast. The dead bear shuddered and rose up on its hind legs... staring at Korac.

He wanted to scream, but the rags covered his mouth and he could no longer speak.

Korac woke to a sharp pain in his leg. Jael was staring down at him, looking at him oddly. He glanced down. Madrazi's back was to him and he felt another jab in his leg. Then he saw her hand come up, holding a needle. He grunted as it all came back to him. The boar, the slash of its tusks....

"You lost a bucket of blood," observed Jael flatly. "You'll be weak for several days."

"The dog," he croaked. "He saved us both." Jael shook her head and he saw Madrazi's shoulders shudder for a moment before she resumed her work. Another sorrow he had inflicted on this woman. He must divert her.

His mind replayed the incident. He looked up at Jael. "Thank you. They were worthy shots."

Jael sighed. "You put yourself in peril to save my sister. I should thank you."

"I swore I would protect you both."

Madrazi jabbed again with the needle. "Two more," she said. Her voice was hoarse. Korac maintained an iron face.

When she finished, she spread her bedding over him. "You lost blood. Your body will not fight the cold. Lie still and heal." To Jael she said, "Start a fire and a shelter. We stay here tonight."

"The blood will attract predators," she objected.

"Then build a *big* fire," retorted Madrazi sharply through her tears.

He watched as the women set up camp quickly and efficiently. Jael roasted meat, but Madrazi prepared broth in her small pot. While it was cooking, the two women took the spears and loosened the ground. With tender care, they wrapped Sirus in their only spare blanket and buried him as deep as they could. He saw the tears streak Madrazi's dirty face and wondered if she would have shed them for him... or if he deserved them. He thought of the sorrow his life must have brought to his grandmother... to so many others. She was much like this one... and he had been ready to kill her. What madness had controlled his life? Looking back on the nightmare that had been his life, he shivered in fear of having to face her God.

After the broth had cooled, he sipped it slowly. It was salty and full of fat. He tasted winter mint and sage. His leg ached, but Madrazi had bathed it, smeared honey on the wound, and bound it. He was accustomed to pain. But he shook slightly, fearing the return of his nightmare. But Madrazi sat beside him, tending the fire and singing softly as he faded away.

The dream did not return.

Korac woke to a pale sky, with bands of high clouds rushing to the southwest. He could smell snow in the air and knew that the long-expected winter was finally coming with the fury of a delayed storm. Jael was cooking strips of the pig, and he saw from her worried glances to the sky that she felt the same. Keeping his face impassive, he rose and tested his leg. It hurt, and he would not be able to run or leap, but he could walk. It was enough.

Within the hour the three were back to the ridge overlooking the river. Its course ran straight as far as they could see, and the ridge seemed to be falling. Korac felt a small rebirth of hope. If the land ahead was gentler, they could move faster. Maybe the snow would hold off for another day or two. Maybe more. Madrazi kept looking back, her eyes full, as if expecting Sirus to come ranging back up for a pet and praise. He could think of nothing to say.

At noon they stopped on a small rise of the ridge. "Look!" exclaimed Jael. She was pointing southwest. "I can see water. You were right, Madrazi. There *is* a lake. If we head straight for those two peaks, we can make it tomorrow."

Heartened, the travelers started off again at once, eating as they walked. Korac now needed his spear to support his leg, but he pushed the pace, fearing the weather behind them more than the pain. He was grateful that the land became gentler as they abandoned the ridge. But the woods were thicker, and it was difficult to keep on track. Distracted by the pain, he let Jael set the course. They walked until dark, and once again, he had to sit while the women made camp. It was a fire in front of a deadfall, but the bedding was warm. He forced down a few bites of meat, and they shared the water in the horn. His bandages were stained red, but he fell asleep in spite of the throbbing.

Morning was gray and ominous. Madrazi knit her brows at the sight of his leg and unwrapped it to make sure the stitches held. Satisfied, she wrapped it again, shaking her head. "You need to rest it, Korac, but I fear…."

He tried to smile. "We need to move fast today," he interrupted. "Look for shelter. We'll need it. The storm will catch us before sunset. Plenty of time to rest, then."

They pressed on, eating cold pork and drinking from cold streams. All about them, the land was still. They saw no creatures; all had taken shelter. The gray sky behind them grew darker, but they kept their eyes locked on the two peaks ahead. Off to the right they could now see the iron gray surface of the lake, reflecting the ominous sky above.

"Get out your rope," grunted Korac as the morning wore on. "When the last storm hit, I nearly lost Jalam, even though he was only a few steps behind. Tie short lengths between our belts. They stopped long enough to do so and then struggled on. Korac took the lead. If another beast came upon them, he could blunt the attack. But Jael moved up beside him, helping mark their course.

Miraculously the storm held back and the travelers hurried down the length of the lake, losing track of time. The sun was hidden and twilight blanketed the wilderness, even though the trees had thinned and it was at least an hour short of noon. They pushed forward, Korac ignoring the growing pain in his leg. It was bleeding again; he could feel the bandages wet against his skin. But he kept the pace, his vision locked on the two peaks. Time rushed on yet still the storm held back.

Suddenly Jael gave a cry. They had been crossing an upland meadow. Off to their right the lake was dark and smooth, like the iron lid of a giant cauldron. On a warm summer day it would have been breathtakingly beautiful, but now its darkly threatening appearance only inspired speed. Jael pointed—far off in the distance Korac saw the intermittent spark of a fire. Madrazi saw it too and gave a soft cry of excitement. Jael was grinning. Korac smiled to himself. He wouldn't last much longer. Maybe that was for the best. He would fulfill his vow and join Jalam.

He looked back. There was a white shimmer to the dark gray and knew that snow was already falling on their last campsite. Another hour… all he had to do was keep pushing for one more hour. He bowed his head, refusing to feel the pain, and started forward, leading the women towards their salvation.

Going downhill though the woods, they lost sight of the fire, but Korac could no longer keep the course. His vision seemed blurred, and he could only see the next few steps. Jael had to direct him more than once. For some reason, the downhill grade hurt more; the pounding of his feet with each step sent waves of pain shooting up his leg. His face never showed it, but he knew Madrazi was watching him. His suspicion was confirmed when she called out to Jael.

"Please slow down just a bit. I can't take this pace anymore."

Jael looked back at her then ahead at Korac and nodded. "Yes, Korac. A little slower. We can still make it."

He was leaning on his spear more, and letting Jael guide him with quiet words. The trees arched over them and the dead leaves beneath their feet gave out little sound. A hiss of wind struck their backs, and then another. Korac no longer looked back; he knew what was coming. If he could only last a little longer, he would have fulfilled his oath to Jalam. He staggered forward.

He was barely aware when the women stopped suddenly, nearly pulling him to his knees. Dimly he saw Shem materialize before him, bow drawn, an arrow aimed at his heart. His eyes were blazing and his face set in hard lines. Korac knew that he had never been closer to death. He smiled. At least he had kept his vow. He was ready. He drew himself up. He barely heard the cry behind him and a slender vision flashed in front of him. It was Madrazi. In his daze he saw a light around her head. He heard words, but could not understand. A gust of snow struck him from behind and his knees buckled. He dropped his spear and fell face forward to the earth.

Chapter 55
MYSTERIES

11-6-1761

Madrazi had never seen Shem look as dangerous as he did when he rose up before them. His fury broke through her shock at his sudden appearance and quashed the ache of not seeing him for months. As his bow came up, she instantly realized that all he saw was Nimrod's assassin, leading his wife and sister by a rope. The flame in his eyes left no room for thought, and his hand was white against the bow as the arrow came back to his cheek. Dropping everything, she leaped in front of Korac. "Don't shoot!" she screamed, and spread herself as best she could against the man. Shem's expression flickered and she saw his fingers tighten their grip on the arrow. "Help him," she cried. "He helped us."

Immediately he lowered the bow, the killing rage gone, but wrath still dancing around the edges of his eyes. Then Madrazi saw the realization that he had nearly killed his wife. He let his bow drop slowly out of a suddenly lifeless hand. Madrazi fumbled at the rope to run to him, but was pushed to her knees as Korac fell against her and then to the ground. She stumbled up, but her eyes were locked on her husband as his were locked on her. She wanted to laugh and cry at the same time. They had made it! She knew she looked like a wild animal yet Shem was staring at her as he had that very first time she walked down the path as his bride.

She did not see Jael shake her head at the two, staring at each other, frozen in the moment. In an instant, a blade was in her hand and it severed the ropes that bound the three together. Her action wakened Shem, and he sprang forward, enfolding Madrazi in his strong arms. She buried her head in his chest inhaling his familiar scent and clinging to him for all she was worth.

"What...?"

His words were cut off by Madrazi as she saw Korac, face down in the leaves. "I'll explain everything later," she promised. Shem gave her one more hug and stepped over to the man.

"Jael," he ordered, "Grab his other arm." They lifted him between them. "Leave your things," said Shem, as he pushed her away and took the man's arm. "We'll come back for them. Madrazi nodded, but caught up Korac's spear along with her own and followed behind.

"Our camp is just ahead," said Shem. "I don't know whether I'm more surprised to see you or to see you with him."

Jael laughed. "It's nice to know the student can keep the teacher off balance."

Madrazi slid around beside them and slid a hand through Shem's arm. "His leg is cut and might be infected. He killed a boar the other day, and saved my life. If I can tend him quickly, he will heal."

Shem grunted. "Just ahead." He struggled down a shallow slope with Jael and then turned sharply left. A well-defined trail led up to a rock face, sheltered by large trees. Madrazi could see a small wooden hut up against the rocks. It looked far too small for five men.

"There's a cave behind it," said Shem, seeing her puzzlement. His breath was labored. "The boys are out… they'll be back soon with the storm coming. Open the door," he ordered. Madrazi hurried forward and pulled it back. The men's equipment was neatly stacked against the walls. Shem led them deeper into the cave, where a fire smoldered. They could hear the faint sound of water deeper inside, and the smoke rose up through a hole high above. Beds were spread around the fire pit and Shem lowered Korac onto the nearest. "He's a big man," he sighed, stretching his back.

"Feeling your age?" asked Jael innocently.

Shem ignored her. He set a pot of water onto some flat stones at the edge of the fire and added more wood. They rolled Korac on his stomach and Madrazi shed her outer clothing. After washing her hands, she carefully peeled the blood-soaked cloth away from the wound. Two of the stitches had ripped, and though blood still oozed out of the wound, there was no redness around the wound or smell of corruption. Breathing a sigh of relief, she applied herself to the task. Calling for water, herbs, and clean strips of cloth, she cleansed the wound, sewed it back shut and rewrapped it. Then she covered the man back up with pelts. "He lost a lot of blood," she commented, "but the wound is clean and should mend in time."

"Good!" Shem looked from one to the other. "Now perhaps you can explain what you two are doing at the back end of creation."

"Walking," replied Jael flippantly.

Madrazi smothered a smile, seeing Shem's normally phlegmatic face darken. "Don't forget, Jael…" she added just as flippantly, "…we sailed part of the way."

"Of course, Captain Madrazi, Sir!" Jael stood and offered a sketchy salute. Both the women giggled, then laughed until the tears ran down their faces, the relief of finding the men finally upon them.

Shem grunted. "Women!" he grumbled.

Madrazi leaped up into his arms. "Wait for the boys, dearest. I only have strength to tell it once. The important thing is that we are now safe with you. God has brought us together."

"But how did you follow us?" asked Shem. "Two women…?"

Jael looked at him darkly. "We didn't follow you," she returned with more than a little sarcasm. "Though I don't doubt that it would have been just as easy to trail a stampede of oxen or elephants. We simply chose a more efficient path."

"Then how did you find us?" He frowned at Jael, his eyes narrowing.

She wasn't intimidated. "You're the only men in these parts," she shrugged. "We're women."

Madrazi intervened, seeing the red rise to her husband's face. "God brought us to you, my love. Don't fret about Jael… she's become rather bossy this past year. You just have to know how to deal with her." She turned to Jael and said sweetly. "The boys will be back any minute. *All* of them… shouldn't you wash your face and brush your hair?"

Jael reddened and stuck out her tongue and Madrazi laughed again. She was home. Shem looked back and forth between them and just shook his head again.

Heth strained against the rope. It was not yet midday, but they were all tired, having risen early to hunt down near the lake. Shem had stayed in camp, once again outguessing the rest. With the approaching storm, every animal had sought shelter, and it was a subdued group that had gathered around a fire near the shore—they could at least be warm when reporting their failure to Shem. All agreed that Jobaath had the best excuse; he claimed that the hairy elephant he had tracked for an hour was too large to haul back to the cave. As usual, his humor lifted the spirits of the others, and they were joking and laughing as they neared their encampment.

It was Shelah that stifled the laughter. Seeing the approaching storm, he insisted on stopping and dragging a fallen tree to their wood yard. Judging from the leaden sky, they would need the extra supply. It was enough to burn for a few days yet small enough for them to move... though with some effort. They dragged it uphill, dropping it finally in the hollow just below the cave. All four were sweating freely, in spite of the cold weather. Snow flakes were already beginning to fall. They had arrived just in time.

Shelah took charge. "Jobaath... coil the ropes. Let's get inside and dry off. Grandpa's probably wondering where we are."

Ashkenaz snorted. "He's probably been following us the whole time. Just like him to sneak up on us about now."

The others laughed and tossed their ropes to Jobaath, who grumbled at the tangle. Snow began to fall faster and the men hurried up to the door. Heth and Ashkenaz pushed into the wooden room and up to the cave entrance. There they stopped short, the others banging into them. "What's the idea..." began Jobaath, but he was interrupted by Shem's droll voice.

"Come in boys and say hello to the ladies."

The men pushed forward, all sharing the same open-mouthed, wide-eyed face that set the two women laughing. Heth was the first to notice the man lying on the other side of the fire. He pushed Ash aside and recognized the face. An inchoate roar broke from his throat and he lifted his spear, hearing the rising rumble behind him as the others saw Korac sleeping before their fire. He leaped forward only to find himself looking down into Jael's blazing eyes. "Sit down, you oaf!"

Ashkenaz stepped forward, his face like stone. He too was stopped short as Madrazi stepped in front of him, looking up at him with an infuriatingly serene, yet quizzical smile. "If you have that much energy," she said, "I'm sure there's firewood that needs cutting."

Heth looked from Jael to Korac and back to Jael. Shelah stepped around him and hugged Jael. "You're a prettier sight than spring, Aunt Jael," he said warmly. He repeated the hug with Madrazi. "And you're prettier yet," he smiled. "Welcome to our humble home on the shores of Lake Shelah under the scenic slopes of the Shelah Mountains.

"No place for a lady," added Jobaath, slyly. "You can tell by the names!"

Even Heth laughed at that, and he saw Jael's face relax, though it was still staring strangely up at him. He backed up a step, suddenly uncomfortable, remembering her irrational anger at their parting.

"This has the appearance of a long tale," he said. "Let's get some wood inside the cave and some dinner inside us, and then...."

The question hung in the air. "Then we can all share our stories." Madrazi's voice had the soothing motherly tone that they all knew, and it helped calm the still-ragged tempers of Ashkenaz and Heth.

The men nodded and sprang to work. Shem took Jobaath and went to retrieve the women's packs. Heth and Ashkenaz began hauling wood up into the cave, building the already-respectable pile in the back into a veritable mountain, watching the skies blacken and the snow increase as they worked. Shelah helped the women with the food, and the welcome aroma of hot food filled the cave. Shem and Jobaath arrived just ahead of the storm—a shrieking wind could be heard down on the lake as they brought the women's packs inside and laid them on a shelf of rock to one side.

Heth could not keep his eyes off Jael. She had changed in some indefinable way; for the first time he saw her as a woman not his equal, but his superior. She was a daughter of Noah and sister to Shem. No longer the temperamental, raging girl wanting to learn how to kill, she now possessed an aura of confidence. The months had transformed her; the fire of all her trials had burned away the dross, leaving a person whole and free. He felt suddenly very inadequate yet at the same time, he knew—in some indefinable instant—that he loved her and that he always would.

It tore him apart. His common sense that had kept him from the evil influences of his family told him that she was beyond him. His love would forever be a secret thing he carried inside. But his heart was light at her simple presence, here at the far end of Creation.

As he glanced around, he saw the others felt it too—that light and warmth the women brought with them. Shem was smiling broadly, sitting beside his wife, his hand resting on her shoulder. Everyone turned their attention to the hot food; it was some time before they leaned back satisfied, with cups of hot chamomile tea warming their hands, while listening to the howling wind outside.

But the sight of Korac sleeping in the back of the cave stirred Heth. He stood and looked down at Madrazi. "Why do you want him to live?"

Madrazi stared at him across the fire. For a moment he saw a glint in her bright green eyes and remembered the power he had felt in her presence when she had told him of the far future. He dropped his eyes, but she was not angry. He heard her sweet, even tones. "Korac is my guest. As to his ultimate fate, I will bow to the will of my husband." She looked pointedly at Heth and Ashkenaz, and neither could meet her gaze.

"In the meantime," she continued, "We will tell you our tale and hear yours. When Korac is recovered, you can hear his too. Given the weather, I expect we will have plenty of time for talk and contemplation."

Heth bridled for a moment at her assertion of authority but was immediately distracted by the sight of Jael, sitting across the fire on the other side of Shem. Her eyes were on him, and in their bright mysterious depths, he saw a question. Her lip curled, and she turned away. But was it his imagination, or was her glance returning to him more than to the fire? He nodded to Madrazi, resumed his seat, and settled in to listen to her account.

As he listened, he glanced at the other men to make sure this was no dream. Like his, their emotions ran the gamut from rage at Nimrod's cowardly, brazen attack on the farm (it took a sharp word from Shem, and Shelah's grip, to keep him from slaying Korac then and there) to amazement at the women's successful flight to Togarmah, their voyage across the Black Sea, and the great hunt over the past year. He smiled broadly when Jael told of her trap in the cave that had broken Korac's leg, and found himself holding his breath when Madrazi told of their discovery by Korac months later, and their strange salvation. His frown grew as they told of Korac's help over the past weeks in their journey upriver, and his rescue of Madrazi from the boar just two days ago. He even felt his eyes fill as Madrazi wept unashamedly over the loss of their faithful Sirus. But as he glanced around, he saw that none of the men were immune from her story, although Ash was grinding his teeth at the idea that Korac should meet with anything but a spear through the heart.

"And so it must have been your fire near the lake this morning that brought us to you." Madrazi finally stopped. She and Jael looked at each other. Heth looked on, and felt the moment—like an outsider looking in—when the women realized what they had come through together. Their eyes locked; for a long moment, Heth knew that they were sharing something on a level he could never reach. This was the first time that they had the opportunity to sit down and reflect on all that had happened… all they had endured together…. He saw in that moment the bond they had forged— one that could never be shared by anyone else.

The silence lasted a moment longer and then all the men began talking at once. Jael was basking in their admiration. Shem—her mentor—had been nodding with approval for some time; her eyes were full of a well-deserved pride. Jobaath and Ashkenaz were looking at her as if she were some creature from another world, some great hero of the lost days. Heth was staring at her for another reason, hoping she wouldn't see his heart but unable to turn his eyes away.

Madrazi drew a breath and took a sip of her cool tea. "So here we are," she said lightly, "with many things to consider."

"Yes," interrupted Ashkenaz. "Like why I don't take that thing outside and slit its throat! After all, was it not the Almighty who told Noah that if a man sheds the blood of another, by men would his own blood be shed?" He sneered in Korac's direction. "By that measure, he should be killed many times over. He kidnapped Mariel. He tried to kill me. He has killed others, including people of your household. If you're squeamish about it, then let me cast him out into the storm, and let the Almighty deal with him."

Madrazi rose, her face suddenly as dark as a thunderstorm. Her voice rang out, and Heth heard power in her words. "How dare you, son of Gomer! You seek to justify your murderous hatred with God's holy words? If you want justice from the Creator, then bare your own breast for His first blow!" Her voice subsided; it was now full of anguish.

"Do none of you understand?" She was openly weeping now, to the consternation of all present, but they sat frozen at the power that hung in her words.

"What do you think of the mystery of lawlessness, son of Gomer?" she stared him down despite her tears… or maybe because of them.

"Well," he mumbled. "It is as you have taught us before. It's the profound mystery of how men—not yet four generations removed from the great flood—have forsaken the Judge of the Earth and turned to evil."

"That's the part I teach to children, young fool!" Her voice was tight, and Ashkenaz shrank from her wrath. "As they mature, I hope that they come to see deeper—understanding their own hearts and the black stains that mar them." She drew a breath and let it out slowly, her anger again forced down. "Tell me this, Son of Gomer. Am I righteous? What of my husband? What of our father, Noah?"

Ashkenaz turned red. "My lady, who am I to judge…."

Madrazi hissed at him. "Who are you? You are a man with a mind and a soul. You condemn Korac—another man made in God's image—easily enough. Speak!"

Ashkenaz licked his lips. "Well, of course then. We all revere our father, Noah. He was chosen by God. He built the ark. You were spared from judgment. God preserved you and your husband through the cataclysm."

"As He did Debseda," Madrazi flung back in his face. "Explain righteousness to me now, little boy."

Heth was glad that her eyes were on Ash. He would have wilted at the anger and frustration that darkened her face and her voice. He could not answer her question; he had never before considered things in that light. God had spared Debseda with the others… why? She was so different from Madrazi!

Ashkenaz stuttered and shook his head. His logic in tatters, his rage started to fade. An embarrassed silence fell upon the travelers. Heth glanced up surreptitiously; the others were looking down too. He was trying to understand the question—it seemed somehow urgent, yet the answer was beyond his grasp. God was righteous; everyone knew that. And he had always drawn a simple line between people. Madrazi was good; Debseda, evil. Nimrod was evil; Shelah was good. It no longer seemed that simple. And the more he thought about it, the more he realized that people like Korac and Jael were harder to put in either group. Was he? He had done good, he thought defensively. He had forsaken his family, helped Shem and Shelah… he was even willing to fight for them. Then a disturbing thought entered his mind. Was *doing* good the same as *being* righteous? His head began to hurt.

He wanted to ask Madrazi, but she was still weeping softly. "Do you not see?" she asked in a broken voice. "Even now, I sin by letting my temper control me. Am I righteous?" Heth held his breath, bracing for the blow.

It came. "Of course not! Sin stains my every day. The closer I grow to the Creator, the greater my sin—the increasing light of His presence reveals the darkness in the deepest corners of my soul. My evil would fill the seas!" Madrazi slumped and wiped her eyes with trembling fingers. Heth sensed an ineffable sadness in her face that mirrored his heart. If Madrazi wasn't good, then what hope had he?

But then her face changed. She was looking at Jael. The girl was nodding, a new light in her eyes. Heth could see that she understood—had found the truth that seemed determined to remain just outside of his grasp. But he would not give up. It was there—Jael's face was proof.

Madrazi saw and her face now had an expression of pure joy. She dried her eyes and laughed out loud. "Jael sees." Heth's lips tightened. What did she see?

As if hearing his thoughts, Madrazi answered the question. "The best of us, the oldest of us, the wisest of us, the kindest of us… we are all irretrievably stained, unfit to stand in the presence of our God." Heth felt a surge of panic. Was all that he had done for nothing? Then Madrazi spoke again.

"*Yet He does not give up; He continues to draw us to Him.*" She paused again, holding the eyes of each man in turn. Heth felt a glimmer of excitement, a stirring in his heart. God had not deserted him!

"That is the true mystery of lawlessness." She shook her head. "How the One who is perfect in His justice can stand the very sight of any of us… much less claim us as His children."

"Then how can anyone be saved?" stuttered Jobaath. "Don't the sacrifices we offer atone for our sins?"

Shem snorted. "Do you believe that the blood of goats and sheep—creatures lacking even an immortal soul—can purchase your righteousness before the Creator?"

"Then why do we offer them?" Jobaath looked puzzled. He looked to Madrazi. "How are we made righteous?"

She sighed, but smiled again. "We cling to a thread—in ignorance yet in faith," she returned. "He made a promise to Eve in the garden. One day, one of her descendents will break the head of the deceiver and accuser, and free us from our slavery to Adam's rebellion." Her eyes were far off as she relived the past. "There came a day in the ark when I forsook all my wisdom and put my hope in that promise—clinging to it like a drowning rat."

She laughed suddenly. Shem was standing beside her, his arm around her. Heth saw them trade a glance—perhaps the memory of that morning. She laughed again. "That was the day that I made peace with the Creator." She dropped her head. "It was a long struggle… to my shame."

Heth looked at the others. Shem was eyeing Jobaath and Ashkenaz, seeing their attempts to hide a polite skepticism. He chuckled, pulled his wife close to him, and let a false smile play across his face.

"Female sentiment," he drawled. Before they could hide it, the two younger men's eyes betrayed them in a flash of agreement. Shem just looked at Madrazi and both burst out laughing.

Then the humor vanished as he turned back to them. "You boys are too young to have learned the sin of underestimating your betters." His indulgent tone turned suddenly hard.

"Fools!" His eyes flashed and the two men quailed. "In the old world there was no greater name than my wife's father. Millions of men envied my fortune in gaining the hand of his daughter." He smiled slowly. "Though most of them also thought me imprudent for violating the first rule of marriage—never join yourself to a woman so much smarter than you!"

The men laughed uneasily but looked at Madrazi, eager to hear more. She had always been reticent about her past, and only Shelah and Jael knew more than the bare outline of the story. Shem continued. "If there had been no flood... if you had been raised among the men of my day, you would know me not as Noah's son, but as the man fortunate enough to have married the daughter of Pomorolac."

"And she was no ornament in his house. She was the reason for much of his success. Before she became my right hand, she was his. Even before she surrendered her soul to the Almighty, she was accounted one of the wise of our world, chosen for me by the foresight of Methuselah."

Jobaath and Ashkenaz were blushing, but Shem wasn't through. "Afterward, God gave her—not me—the gift of Noah. So heed her words. They are both wise and true. The thread she speaks of may be slender when measured by your wisdom. It may even fade before your earthly understanding. But it is infinitely strong, as evidenced by the fact that I stand alive before you, instead of lying buried under these rocks with all the others of my generation. That promise is all that we have to answer the riddle of lawlessness. Cling to it. It is the only path to life."

His face grew serious. "As to Korac, we will deal with him when he is healed, and when we have heard from his own lips what has happened. Until then, he is our guest and will be treated as such. It will be hard enough with two women in our cave; we will not fill our home here with retribution and blood."

Almost against his will, Heth nodded thoughtfully. His thoughts were confused, but something deep within him was screaming that he had just heard the most important words of his life. He concentrated on preserving them in his mind, burning them into his memory, already thinking of questions to ask Madrazi... later... in private. He wanted what he saw in her spirit, but did not understand her words in the depths of his heart. He swore to himself that one day he would.

With that thought, his eyes strayed to Jael. He was jealous of her great adventure, but he felt like a foolish young boy, searching for words to say to the first girl who had captured his heart.

His mind was now at peace with a certainty he had never known before. He loved her, but for now his lips must remain silent. He cursed the memory of the past—his arrogant dismissal of her determination and skill, his condescension of her quest—all because she did not possess his strength or skill. Yet he wondered... could he have kept Madrazi alive? Could he have led her through the great wilderness and brought her to her husband?

And that was now the frustration of his new knowledge. Yes, he loved her, but now she was out of reach, a woman to be admired and adored... from afar. His heart sank.

The men were quiet, but Jael broke the silence. "May I say something, my brother?"

Shem looked at her with curiosity. She had not called him that, in that tone of voice, for many years. He simply nodded.

"As most of you know, there is no one here with greater cause to hate that man than I. You know how it has eaten at my heart and driven me to do things that every one of you thought unseemly and unnatural. Yet now we all know the reason God allowed these things to come to pass. Had I failed in the smallest detail, Madrazi and I would not be here tonight. And now I understand—really understand—what my sister and my comrade has said… what she has tried to teach me for years. Only now do I see… it is now *my* truth." She looked down. "There is much for which I must repent—not the least, my offenses against my brother and sister which they bore with patience for many years."

Madrazi nodded at her in encouragement, as if she guessed the words that were coming.

Heth just stared. There was a light in her face—the full radiance of what he had sensed before. It was as if she were being reborn—once again the daughter of the great Patriarch. He saw the woman behind the warrior and was again aware of his unworthiness. Yet he could not tear his eyes away from the vision that was her face.

"In the light of these truths," continued Jael, "I can only offer the same to Korac. He asked me many nights ago to forgive him, but my pride kept me from answering, though even one as hardened as I could hear the sincerity of his plea. In the presence now of all of you, my witnesses, I will grant him that request as soon as he wakes."

Heth held his breath. He heard the small crackle of the coals, so silent was the cave. His eyes shone with pride. Jael had broken free of the chains that had enslaved for these past years. She would spread her wings and become one of the great people of the new world… a queen. His chance of ever possessing such a woman dissipated like the smoke from their fire—she was beyond him now. But perhaps, if God smiled on him, he could someday be worthy of her friendship and regard. If so, he would count himself the luckiest of men.

He glanced around. Most looked as stunned as he felt… and aware that this was the daughter of Noah. Ashkenaz seemed as a drunken man, his eyes wandering this way and that, while seeing nothing. But Shem and Madrazi glowed with understanding smiles, as did Shelah. He knew… a warm smile lit his face. He knew.

Heth sighed. He had seen so much, but felt as if the parts did not quite fit together in his mind. Something eluded him… probably something simple. A prize waited. He would wrestle with the words he had heard, talk to Madrazi, and perhaps one day soon he would see as Shelah saw… and as Jael now saw.

Chapter 56
KORAC'S STORY

11-7-1761

Korac woke slowly, a strange lassitude filling his limbs. Hearing came first; low voices filled the air about him. He felt warm, both from the crackling fire and the pelts that covered him. He opened his eyes and saw the flicker of flames. Then, as his eyes came into focus, he saw a familiar face smiling down at him. Madrazi held a tin cup. "Drink this slowly," she said softly.

He sat up, cursing his weakness, but his leg was no longer on fire. He felt the ache and throb of healing flesh, but that was all. He took the cup and drank, grateful for the warm tea that flowed across his parched tongue. He glanced around, seeing the others staring at him... Shem and Shelah appraisingly, Jobaath and Ashkenaz with a wary, yet veiled, hostility, and Heth with a look he could not decipher.

Jael came and sat beside him. He instinctively flinched when her hand reached out and touched his arm. She had never initiated contact before. Her face was different; it was softer, the lines of bitterness smoothed. "Do you remember the question you put to me, Korac?" Her eyes were bright with a light he had not seen.

Not trusting his voice, he nodded, holding his breath.

"My answer is yes," she said simply. "It can be no other."

His tears surprised him as much as they did the others and he felt intensely ashamed. Shem, understanding, stood. "Let's get some more wood, boys," he ordered. The men turned and followed him out. Madrazi held up a rough cloth, and he wiped his eyes. "I'm sorry," he mumbled.

"Never be sorry for tears," Madrazi scolded. "Not when they reveal the truth of your soul."

"Thank you," he croaked, dragging his arm across his face. He turned to Jael. "And thank you. It's the best... the greatest gift I ever received."

Madrazi interrupted. "You have one last thing to tell us, son of Magog," she said, and the power once again crackled in the air. "You have told me much of your life—good and bad—yet you have kept one door locked. It is time to open it."

He choked. "You know I can't, Lady," he pleaded. "You know I can't."

She was relentless. "You must." She tactfully restrained herself from reminding him that he owed it to Jael, but the thought flared in his mind, nonetheless.

He slumped in defeat, tears once again filling his eyes. Madrazi held one arm and Jael the other, and he felt their strength uphold him. When he spoke, his voice was hardly audible. "When I was young, Nimrod was my friend. Others envied me; he was well-liked by all... his cruelty then hidden. All the years he was building his reputation as a hunter, I was there. When he killed the two tigers of Segret, I was there, keeping the one at bay while he slew the first and stepping aside to let him have both kills. I thought that I was as happy as a man could be until I met his sister." He shuddered slightly at the memory, but the strength of the two women beside him carried him across the chasm. His voice grew stronger.

"Timna added so much more to my life. She gave me love, unselfishly, and she was my joy and light. Yet she had one weakness. She resented the time I spent with her brother. One day, she insisted on going with us, thinking that she could share that part of my life. We wandered among the eastern mountains for a few days until Nimrod found the tracks of a gigantic bear. They were the biggest he had ever seen, and he demanded we pursue it. It would have been a mighty trophy, but I refused—it was too dangerous. But when her voice joined his, I relented, unable to refuse her anything. We came upon it in an open valley and wounded it with arrows, but it retreated into a ravine filled with jumbled stone and hid."

Korac took a deep breath and continued. "Nimrod was to go into the bordering ravine, climb the ridge and descend to a position to kill the beast. I was to advance just inside and draw him from hiding. Despite my pleas, Timna followed me into the ravine. The bear was hidden much closer to the entrance than I expected...."

His face was twisted in anguish, but Madrazi held his arm. "It's just us, Korac. We shared the wilderness together. We are your comrades," she whispered. "You can tell us. It will go no further without your consent."

Korac sat up straighter. "Yes, I owe you that." He took a sip of tea and composed himself, something of the old iron mask slipping into place. "I fumbled the bow when it rose up before us and my arrow missed its vitals. It charged." He paused for a moment, shuddering.

"Timna was overcome by terror, and I was trying to get my spear around. But it was fast... too fast. It struck her, throwing her against a boulder and then it came for me. That was when Nimrod shot... two arrows... one in its throat and one in its mouth. When I ran to Timna, the rock had crushed her head. She probably was dead as soon as she struck."

"Tell us the rest," insisted Madrazi.

His face hardened in hatred; his heart felt as cold as the ice on the mountain. "Ever since that day, night visions of those minutes have haunted my life. When Jalam died, I dreamed of it again. But this time I saw something new... something I had not remembered. When Nimrod came down into the valley to help me with Timna his back was streaked with sweat from the climb, but it was nearly dry."

He felt the women grip his hands. Jael understood at once and horror filled her face. His voice cracked.

"He had been in position the whole time. He let it happen! He destroyed the light in my life and took advantage of my grief to draw me into darkness."

Jael was shaking her head, crying freely now.

Korac gave a twisted smile. "He'd been destroying families long before he took your sister."

"I'm so sorry," she said. "I think I understand a little. I know what I felt these past years because of his evil; if I had been in your place, I would probably have done the same."

Korac shook his head. "No, little one," he said. "You have a core of steel inside that would not allow you to be what I was. You're too good for that. You're like your sister... the Lady Mariel. Nimrod has done every evil to her that a man can do, and yet there is a part of her that he can never touch. She is the noblest woman in Shinar."

"That's not saying much," muttered Jael, her face darkening.

Madrazi simply stared at her until she dropped her eyes.

"You would grant forgiveness to this man but not your own sister? You think your life has been hard these past years? You know nothing of tribulation. She has endured more than you could imagine, and it is my sincere hope that we may one day rescue her from that evil. Who knows? Maybe she was sent to save Ham."

"My brother Ham is the problem!" Jael's old sarcasm had returned.

It was Korac who caught her up short. "No, my lady," he replied, with a frown. "Ham's a good man... the best in Shinar. He could be great, but he hides it to avoid open warfare within his family. My guess is that he is planning to escape with Mizraim and take the Lady Mariel with him."

Jael looked down. "I don't understand...." she began.

"Exactly!" snapped Madrazi. "So extend some mercy in your opinions until you do."

"My usefulness is coming to an end," sighed Ham. They were working in the shop for a change, having spent the last week on the tower, and Mariel just nodded. She was tired, both in body and spirit. For over a year, they had both avoided any conflict with Nimrod and Debseda, and curiously enough, those two seemed content to let them work. Mariel thought it was because they were useful; Ham was more inclined to the cynical view that with Korac apparently dead, Nimrod was short an assassin. And though hardly anyone knew what Korac's mission had been, word had filtered south about an attack on Shem's farm shortly after Korac and his team had disappeared. Few dared risk Nimrod's wrath with loose talk, but someone as notorious as Korac could not simply disappear for two years and not have people talking.

Ham worked the bellows until the fire was roaring. It was a simple way to keep anyone outside the door from hearing their conversation. "I can't believe how fast the work has progressed. I didn't think Nimrod could rally so many people so easily."

"Having the women and children work the fields certainly didn't hurt," replied Mariel in a low voice. "After the lean years, the land had been kind to them once more. No one is very happy about the work, but it is offset by pride in the structure and fear of Nimrod. Even without Korac, all knows what happens to troublemakers."

"I know," he returned softly. "There's no one to lead them. I might have done so a few years ago, but if I tried now, all it would do would be to get a lot of good men killed for nothing."

"Then why do you stay? Why keep building this abomination? You know that's what it is."

Ham looked troubled. "Yes, I know." He sighed. "I'm trying to keep you from harm. As long as I'm needed, you're protected, and Nimrod can't cast you off or kill you. But he has too many men watching. I can't get you out."

"Then you must leave without me." Mariel finished. "Please, brother, I beg you. Flee while you can. Stop multiplying our sins before God by working on this tower. I know you want to leave with Mizraim. Leave then, and be done with Shinar."

"You know what they will do to you if I go," he said. "I could not face myself if I let that happen. You're my sister, and without Father here to protect you, the responsibility is mine. I must." His shoulders slumped. "I must."

"I will not leave here without my son," she returned fiercely. Ham held up his hands. "I know. That's what makes it so hard. Mizraim is working on it." His voice carried little conviction.

Mariel stirred the fire half-heartedly. "You should have let me poison him. It would have worked."

"Perhaps," Ham agreed. "It was a clever idea. But it would have cost you your soul. If you ever got your son back, would you want him raised by someone with blood-filled hands?"

She bowed her head. "You know that I wouldn't."

"Then trust the Almighty to work for you," he started, but his words trailed off as the door slammed open.

Nimrod stalked in, his black spear in his right hand and a dozen armed men flowing in behind him, filling the shop. Mariel saw Ham's eyes stray towards the massive hammer at the forge, but put her hand on his arm. She would not let him commit suicide.

"Quite a cozy arrangement you have here, grandfather," he spat out. "My wife seems to like it here."

"Not as much as mine likes your bed chamber, boy," retorted Ham. Nimrod didn't flinch. He simply laughed in acknowledgement. "There must be something there that she can't get elsewhere," he mused.

"She seems drawn to evil," agreed Ham, with a sneer.

"Power," corrected Nimrod back. "She likes strength." He waved to the men. As one, they leveled their spears. "And now, dear wife and grandfather, you will come with me." Mariel was frozen with fear, not for herself, but for Adan. If she died, he would certainly be at Debseda's mercy.

"You can't kill us," grated Ham. "Your precious tower will fall over tomorrow with Canaan in charge."

"I don't doubt it," chuckled Nimrod. "His uses are so… limited. But not everyone is as inept as Canaan, and I know as well as you that the hardest part is done. If the lower level is solid, the upper will follow in due course… even with someone as incompetent as my dear uncle in charge."

"You'll find out different after we're dead," shot back Ham. "You don't think I would have shared *all* my plans with Canaan, now do you?"

Nimrod paused, but only for a moment. "I think he will do. After all, he can consult you if he has a problem." He laughed. "Not that I wouldn't like to rip your heart out now, old man, but we're saving that. Perhaps after the tower is complete, the Queen of Heaven will reveal her liking for human sacrifices on her altar." His eyes flamed with a blue fire. "My lovely wife would make another good candidate!"

With a roar, Ham caught up the hammer and rushed at Nimrod. So quickly did he move, that the others had no chance to react. But Nimrod was ready. As Ham swung the hammer, he brought up the shaft of his spear and caught the downward blow.

Now Mariel knew Ham's strength and knew the strength of every wood that grew within a three month journey of Shinar. None of them would have slowed the terrible blow of that great hammer, but Nimrod's spear not only stopped it, but broke the head of the hammer as if it were clay, not the hardest iron.

She blinked, trying to understand what she had seen, and the mystery froze Ham for a split second—long enough for Nimrod's casual backswing to send Ham to the floor in a welter of blood. Mariel tried to spring to his side, but two men grabbed her arms and lifted her off the ground. She kicked and had the satisfaction of feeling solid contact with a shin, but the man held on, and two more seized her legs. Another crammed a cloth in her mouth, stifling her scream.

"He's alive," said Nimrod negligently. "Bring them both." Four more men bent to lift Ham, but Mariel saw no more. She was already outside, being carried toward the tower. Nimrod caught up with the men who were still straining to hold her struggling limbs. He glared into her face. "A few months in prison will cool your temper, my beloved," he sneered. Then he pulled the rag from her mouth. "You can beg for your life now, if you wish." Unable to lash out, she spat in his face, but he wiped it away with a smile. "I hope you face your death with such courage," he whispered. "It will be a comfort to know that blood runs in the veins of *my* son."

Now they were inside, climbing the spiral stair that wound around the inside of the tower. "Think on this, my love," Nimrod whispered. "You have six months to live. You'll be treated well as long as you behave. If you don't…." he glanced around at the men carrying the prone figure of Ham. "I'm sure that we can make things very uncomfortable for your brother. You wouldn't want that on your conscience, now?"

Mariel sagged in defeat. She felt a numbness descend to cloak her, and said nothing when the men locked her in what she had thought was a storeroom. It didn't matter. The door was solid wood, the walls brick, and the only window was too high to reach and too narrow to admit her body. There was a wide bench, almost a bed, with a blanket and pillow. A bucket of clean water stood in one corner and an empty bucket in the other. She wondered if her maid had escaped. Had she found a way out, or was she now drifting deep in the cold waters of the Tigris? Mariel did not bother to restrain the tears, now that she was alone. Everything she touched turned to evil.

She feared for Adan too. Nothing hurt more than the thought of her sweet-natured son warped and twisted into something as evil as Nimrod. But what did it matter, she thought? She had finally been overtaken by her own sin. She cursed the day she had first kissed Nimrod, selling her soul for a moment's pleasure. She would never have the chance to explain to her family… to apologize for all the harm that one act had done.

She would be dead soon. It was ironic that her sins would catch up to her at the top of the tower that she had labored to help build. Her thoughts turned to Adan again. With her death, his fate was sealed too; and that hurt more than anything else. In a way, she welcomed the idea of death. She had taken a good life and thrown it away. She deserved to die, just as she deserved the innumerable small deaths that had dogged her days in Shinar.

In a way, she had been dying, a little bit each day, ever since she had met Nimrod in the hills behind her farm. What would her family think when they finally heard of her end? Would they mourn her or simply nod their heads, knowing that she had earned her fate? She wanted to think that her sisters would at least shed tears for her, but after all these years, did they still care? Did anyone? She sank to the bench, a defeated woman.

The hard part was the wait. Better that Nimrod had killed her today and had it done. But that was part of his revenge. He wanted her to have lots of time… he wanted the fear of death to be far worse than the reality. But he would have been disappointed. Fear was something she cast aside. She simply did not care. Weary in body and spirit, she lay down and slept, numb, but curiously at peace.

Chapter 57
WAY HOME

11-22-1761

A pale blue sky reflected off the placid surface of the lake and the brilliant white of the snow. Everyone was sitting around a fire in the wood yard below the cave, enjoying the clear weather and sunshine, after several weeks of unremitting storms.

Korac had gradually become more talkative; he spoke easily now with Shelah and Heth, though there was still friction with Ashkenaz. Shem had talked with him at length, but it was clear that Korac—once unperturbed by anything or anyone—still was unaccustomed to trading speech with an elder. His reticence was sharpened by the knowledge of what he had done and been.

But today Shem had called for a council, and Korac faced the distinct discomfort of being center stage. He was questioned at length of what he knew of Nimrod and Debseda's plans. Though he had told much over the past days, Shem's careful questioning elicited information that even he had forgotten. It filled in gaps from what they had learned from Anam and Ashkenaz; Korac was able to tell of Nimrod's motivations and long-term goals.

Despite the free exchange of information, Shem remained cautious, saying nothing about Anam's mission in Shinar. The other men followed his lead. Their trust did not yet extend that far.

Talk soon turned to the lands they had traveled over the past year. "We have found inexhaustible lands for anyone who has the courage to settle them," Shem concluded. "But getting them to move will still be hard. The question remains: do we take as many as we can and flee to these lands or do we also challenge them on the plains? What about the land along the Great Sea? Or to the south? Or even to the east, beyond the mountains?"

"There is dissension among Nimrod's allies," Korac said carefully. "Even his father, Cush, has his own plans. Nimrod's words seek to bind men together, but his example encourages every man to take for himself at the expense of his neighbor." He leaned back and looked thoughtful for a moment. "Something changed after he took the Lady Mariel. Before, he had always treated me as a brother—a younger or weaker brother, perhaps, but still a brother. After that, he began to act is if he thought himself superior to everyone… except perhaps Debseda. I don't know if his victory over Noah brought it out, or something else changed. But part of his power comes from a firm belief that he is better. He intimidates most, and the others are too smart to challenge him directly. I have no doubts that he will achieve his dream of an empire, but I think it will be smaller than he imagines. Other men have ambition too, so other empires or nations will populate the world—up on the eastern plateau, in the highlands between the Lake of the Islands and the mountain, and in the lands along the Great Sea."

Everyone stirred uncomfortably. "We've been gone too long," interjected Shelah. "We need to know what's happening now."

"Have you grown wings?" growled Jobaath. "With all due respect, we're facing a trek of at least five months just to get home," He shook his head. "And we cannot start safely for another three or four months." The others sighed and looked down. They could add the days as easily as Jobaath.

Their silence was broken when Madrazi laughed suddenly. "I can cut that time in half," she said. Jobaath stared at her as if she were crazy, but said nothing. Jael suddenly laughed too. "Do you think these ham-handed men can do it?" she asked Madrazi.

Ashkenaz frowned. "Do what, little girl?"

Suddenly Heth began laughing too. "Too bad you don't have your brother's skill, Ash. He'd know what to do."

"What does Riphath have to do with getting home?" Ashkenaz frowned.

"Wrong brother," drawled Jobaath.

Understanding flared in Ashkenaz' eyes. "Boats!" he exclaimed.

"There's a well-explored river just a pleasant morning's walk away," laughed Madrazi. "If you men can build a few boats, we'll be down to the *Kef* in less than six weeks… less than five if you can make decent oars. We'll need a week to make sure the Kef is seaworthy, and then we'll be back to Arkaz in less than two. That gets us home in less than three months, plus whatever time it takes you to build the boats."

"But we know nothing of making boats," frowned Jobaath.

"That's all right," smiled Jael, with more than a touch of condescension in her voice. "I'm sitting next to the foremost mariner in the world. If you big strong men can do the heavy work, I'm sure she can provide the brains."

"How long," interrupted Shem impatiently, trying hard not to grin.

Madrazi tangled a finger in her hair and tightened her lips. "Two months if you want one large vessel to carry us all," she said finally. "Maybe half that for two small boats. That includes time to build a forge and make tools."

"Can we start shaping timbers in the cave if we do the smaller boats?" asked Shem.

"Yes," she admitted. "That would save time… and we do have lots of strong backs to carry them to the river."

"Then that's our course," decided Shem.

The work began slowly. While Shem and Madrazi scouted and marked trees for felling, the younger men built a forge and began to reshape their axes and knives into the tools Madrazi described: adzes, chisels, drills, and planing blades. Heth and Ashkenaz came into their own—the skills they had learned from Ham stood them in good stead. Within days they had forged the necessary tools, while the others felled the marked trees and began to cut them into manageable lengths.

But the weather refused to cooperate. Soon after they started, a storm roared in from the northeast, and others followed behind. For a short stretch the men were hard pressed to find enough food. Korac gained a little more acceptance during these weeks. His ability to make kills was second only to Shem, but Shem was occupied with helping his wife begin work on the boats, and so Korac became their best huntsman.

Not able to forget their enmity in Shinar, Ashkenaz still refused to go out with him, but Shelah and Heth hunted with him often. Jael refused to be left out, and since Ashkenaz was the odd man out, she went out often with him.

In the bitter weather survival was the first priority, but despite a few hard days, game remained unusually plentiful. Madrazi turned all her attention to shaping the timbers. There was no time to season them, but the boats would only be needed for a short voyage. Green wood would do.

Lacking drawings, she was forced to first build the boats in her mind; each peg and plank was assembled in sequence in her head before the first cut was made. Then she started with the easier things—the rough-hewn keels, bow and stern strakes, and planking.

As the slow work progressed, she found old memories stir and the tricks she had learned in her youth returned, speeding the work. But there was only so much that could be done in the caves; the boats would have to be assembled outside and the weather still refused to cooperate. Just when a clear day or two raised their hopes, another blizzard would blow in and smother everything in snow once more.

But Madrazi used the weeks well. By the time they were able to finally assemble the pieces outside, every plank had been carved, shaped, drilled, and smoothed.

One morning, Madrazi watched Jael invite Korac out for a hunt. Madrazi said little, but shook her head as the unlikely couple slipped outside. She was proud of the grace that Jael had shown after her declaration of forgiveness. Her actions had largely backed her words, and more than that, she had treated him with courtesy, if not kindness. Jael's growth had become evident in the past weeks—the angry girl who had fled the farm had been replaced by a confident young woman.

But she was an unusual woman to be sure—not many of her sex could ride, run, fight, and shoot better than most men—but those physical skills no longer defined her. Her heart was awake, calling her back to her heritage.

Madrazi had seen the way she glanced at Heth when she thought no one else was looking and knew what lay behind those glances. But Jael was reticent to speak to him at all, probably from the shame of believing that he had been Celota's lover in his youth. And Heth was unsure and hesitant—qualities one did not associate with the young man. Evidently, the changes in Jael had forced a re-evaluation of their relationship. Heth had become accustomed to being the master of their relationship… and in the years he had taught her, that was true. But Jael had proven herself the equal of any of them, and was no longer a student. And Heth was unsure just exactly what that made her. Though conditions were not conducive to romance, there was more holding him back.

This morning Madrazi saw him watching Jael. He had stayed late into the night helping her shave planks. Feigning sleep, he was still watching when Jael left with Korac. Madrazi watched his eyes dim with sadness. Did he really think she would join herself to Korac? It was frustrating to see two people so well suited for each other and clearly in love, be kept apart by their own foolishness. Madrazi promised herself that as soon as they were home, she would take whatever steps were needed to bring them together.

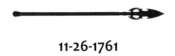

11-26-1761

Mizraim uncovered his face at the guard's command. The flare of torchlight revealed heavy armor and a ready spear. It also reflected off a hard young face, lacking any trace of respect for his elders. But Mizraim had dealt with arrogant youths before. His cold stare met the hot eyes of the guard, and his words dripped ice. "I'm a member of your master's council, young fool. Out of devotion to him, my family has volunteered to perform any task that would contribute to the completion of our great tower—even one as menial as this. Can your family say the same?"

Mizraim kept his face impassive, but he watched the predictable calculations flit across the eyes of the now-wary guard. Mizraim had opposed Nimrod in the past, but it was true that he was on the council. He was carrying out the work of the city—which meant no less than the will of Nimrod. No mere guard—and this one was hardly twenty summers—wished to risk Nimrod's rebuke or the cutting tongue of Debseda.

Besides, they were leading the oxen south, to the bitumen pits. It was a dirty job; Nimrod must have assigned it as a punishment. Any guard that stood in the way of Nimrod's pleasures, might be the one loading pitch on the next trip. So he pursed his lips and stepped aside.

"Wise decision," purred Lud, but no one else spoke as they walked out into the night, the oxen plodding along the well-trodden path.

It was an hour before Lud spoke again. "Good thing he decided not to search the panniers."

Mizraim laughed shortly but then frowned. "We might get a smarter one next time."

"If he's smarter, then he'll not delay as long for your 'arrogant-elder-serving-noble-Nimrod' story."

"Maybe," Mizraim sighed. "But it only takes one dolt willing to get his hands dirty and inspect the oxen."

"But who would ever suspect that the wealth of your house was hidden inside those dirty, oily packs?" Lud grinned again. "If we have to leave, we'll at least leave rich. And if we don't, it's just a day's ride to retrieve what is ours."

"I'll regret leaving my house to that jackal," snarled Mizraim, finally showing a hint of his true feelings.

"We'll build a better in a new land," encouraged Lud. "And if you can figure out a way to free Ham and take him with us, then we will build a nation whose splendor will make Shinar look like a hovel in the desert and Nimrod's precious tower like a pile of rejected bricks!"

Chapter 58
TIME IS SHORT

Anam stood with the rest of Nimrod's court, at the front of Shinar's great hall, worried and afraid, but showing neither on his face. He smiled as the others smiled, and laughed when they laughed. It had become second nature over the years in Shinar, and as talented an actor as he had been when he first came, the years of constant practice had honed his skills. He could make his face and words say whatever he wanted without a slip. But in spite of his expression and words, his mind and heart remained his own, and he granted them full rein to be miserable and afraid, even while laughing at one of Nimrod's jests.

The council had degenerated into a mere group of advisers—second in influence, of course, to Debseda. With the enthusiastic support of the people— especially the youth—Nimrod now ruled Shinar in everything but name. Anam had been surprised. He had anticipated some anger and resentment over the way that Nimrod and his Legion drove the work on the great tower. It had been unremitting, hard, and had gone on for years. Yet even when the women and children had been sent to the fields so the men could continue laying bricks, the people had not complained. It had taken him too long to see the reason: people admired the growing grandeur of their landmark. It said a lot for their civic pride, though something less for their common sense. But even Anam had to admit that it was quite a sight.

Though the lower level still lacked a few months, the tower stood nearly eighty cubits above the plain. It would rise higher still in the coming years, drawing all men of the plains to Shinar. Nimrod may have taken a gamble, but it had paid handsome dividends. Men were too busy to complain, they were welded together in a great enterprise, and those that once might have obstructed Nimrod's rise to power were thwarted by the resulting rise in his popularity. He had been the first to suggest the tower, and he had pushed it in the face of opposition from his elders. But as Shinar began to take its identity from the growing edifice, its citizens began to see Nimrod as wiser than his fathers. Their one advantage gone, there was no sane reason for the elders to oppose his continued rise to power.

Anam heard Canaan drone on about the greatness of their city but paid no attention to the words. He was looking around the hall for his father, finally seeing him in a corner, surrounded by Lud, Lebah, and Naphta. Mizraim caught his glance and brought his hand to his mouth to stifle a cough. He had been successful! At least something was going right.

When Nimrod had taken the bold step of imprisoning Ham and Mariel, Mizraim knew that his days were numbered. From that hour he had begun implementing the risky venture of smuggling the bulk of his wealth out of Shinar. Debseda (through one of Anam's snide comments) had been maneuvered into assigning her recalcitrant son the dirty job of hauling tar into the city. He was able to hide most of his wealth among the oxen trains that made their regular trips to the pits south of town. Coming north, the oxen hauled baths of the sticky bitumen that served as mortar for the vast tower. But going south, they hauled all of his gold and silver. No guard in his right mind would dig through empty wagons and pack saddles that were caked with bitumen; for the past months Mizraim had accompanied caravans carrying fabulous wealth out from under Nimrod's very nose, hiding it far from town before returning from the pits. When the time came to flee, he would keep what was his. Nimrod would be sorely disappointed; he was counting on that gold to build his army.

Anam breathed a sigh of relief in the recesses of his mind. The signal meant that his father had hidden enough to guarantee a new start. A few more trips and he would have enough to begin his own city, far from Shinar. Anam wanted to laugh out loud at the thought of Nimrod's rage when he discovered that his army would not be funded by Mizraim's vast treasure. Anam ached for the day they could all leave, especially now that Graemea feared the unexpected arrival of a son in eight months.

Amid all the shocks that had come to him over the past years, none had affected him more than the quiet night the week before when Graemea had breathed into his ear that he would be a father in the course of time. There was much laughing and crying by both—they were overjoyed at the prospect of parenthood but terrified of creating another hostage of Nimrod's will. He knew then that they must escape before the other women found out. Once Graemea could no longer hide her pregnancy, Debseda would tighten the guard around them, and even if she didn't, Graemea's condition would preclude the ability to travel far and fast.

He had managed to get word to Lud in the marketplace, amid a dozen of Nimrod's legion. Had someone as cunning as Korac been there, it would have been impossible. But with Korac gone, Nimrod was relying on quantity instead of quality. And now Mizraim knew… they must escape soon. In three or four months, Graemea would show and it would be too late. Behind his smile, Anam's mind rushed over all the possibilities once more. With one ear, he listened while he watched Graemea standing serenely behind Debseda.

Nimrod now stepped forward. "Friends and citizens of the great city of Shinar," he boomed. Shouts of adulation interrupted him even then. "We are rapidly coming to a momentous day in the history of our town. We are proving that when we pull together and work as brothers should, that there is nothing under heaven impossible for mankind… once freed from the foolish superstitions of the north! Noah and his kind tried to keep us enslaved with their laws and curses, but we have broken free. We have built a city unlike any that has existed before. We have discovered that Noah hid from us the knowledge of the pantheon of heaven. We have remedied that ignorance with the construction of our great temple to the Queen of Heaven…." More shouts and cries. Anam stirred nervously.

Nimrod held up his hand and silence returned to the hall. "And now, dear brothers," he announced, "we will dedicate the completion of the first level of our great landmark with a public sacrifice. In two months we will know the triumph of our efforts, another great victory over the enemies to the north who would have us groveling at their feet and the feet of their god. The council proclaims a feast for three days following the dedication of the tower. Join us in lifting our hearts together, rejoicing that we are men, that we have been granted strength and peace, and that we live in the glorious city of Shinar. Henceforth, our beloved town will be known and revered forever as the real birthplace of men because it is here that we have learned to live in harmony and prosperity."

Anam was surprised that the following roar didn't collapse the timbers of the great roof. Despite his hatred of Nimrod and knowledge of his schemes, even he was swayed by the eloquence and power of his words. It wasn't surprising, he thought. All men wanted to be known... to be appreciated... to leave some mark of their lives. Building the world's first great city and becoming the heart of the world's first great empire was certainly something to brag about.

The world was young and the men in this room were laying its foundations. Yet should the price have been so high? Why would a man accept enslavement as the cost of some tenuous claim to greatness? Nimrod understood the reality of the equation; the man who ruled got a disproportionate share of the adulation without any of the sacrifice. Unfortunately, it seemed that Nimrod and Anam were the only two in the room who did. Then Anam glanced over and saw the crease on his father's forehead. That made three that understood. He shot Anam a hard look. "Soon," it said, and Anam hoped the promise of that look held true.

Heth grunted and lifted the pole lashed crossways across the heavy stern of the boat. Korac was on the other side and Heth was pleased to feel him holding up more than his share of the weight. Ashkenaz and Shem had lifted a similar pole lashed to the lighter bow. Jobaath looked on with the women; Heth saw the hard line of his mouth. It had been a blow to his ego to be told that as the weakest man, he would stand ready to step in for one of the others. But from the tension in his shoulders and legs, Heth realized that Jobaath would have ample opportunity to help. It was a long trek across uplands to the river, a little over twenty thousand paces as counted by Shem. Jobaath would get his turn. For now, he carried an arrow set to his bow in case they met a starving or particularly foolish predator.

Heth grimaced as they started off. They had all walked the trail to become familiar with the rough spots and the dangerous patches of mud and ice. Had they been ready a few weeks earlier, they could have simply dragged it over the snow, but a warm spell had melted much of that cover, leaving just enough to impede their way through the wooded stretches. He straightened his shoulders and kept one eye on the ground and one eye on the others. Though only twelve cubits long, the boat was heavy. It might have been easier to carry on their backs, but if one of them slipped, they might all go down under the weight. It was worth a hard day's work to avoid a crippling injury, and the men had shrugged off the effort as men will do when women are present.

Shem set an easy pace and called out the obstructions in the path. After a few hundred paces, Heth felt his arms begin to burn and heard Korac's heavy panting. "Stop," growled Shem. "Down... easy... and rest."

The four looked at each other. They had known it would not be easy, but this was going to be a *long* day. Heth could already feel his muscles burning. The women hoisted their packs and forged on. They would make sure a fire and warm meal was ready up ahead. The men picked it up and started off again. Heth swore as he nearly stumbled over a patch of ice, trying to control his breathing and prove to Korac that he was still the stronger man.

Once they were in the upland meadow, the way became easier and it was well that it did. By that afternoon, Heth no longer cared who was strong and who was not. His arms felt like leaden weights, and his back and shoulders were knots, relieved only by the burn of overworked sinews. His only consolation was that Korac seemed too tired to notice. Jobaath had spent plenty of time relieving each man in turn, and even the women had even taken one of the places for a stretch, combining their strength to take the place of one man. Heth shook his head. It shouldn't have been this hard. Fortunately, a welcome line of trees that marked the river bank was just a short stretch downhill. Heth traded a relieved glance with Korac and gritted his teeth as their knees took the stress of the downhill grade. Shem called for another rest, and all four men slumped down against the side of the boat.

"One more push," the older man panted. The river was tantalizingly near, but the ground was wet and the wet grass slick.

"Wait a moment," called Madrazi. She uncoiled a rope from her pack and tied a secure knot through a hole drilled in the bow. "We wouldn't want it to float away after all this work." The light, teasing tone was just what the men needed. They laughed, and wearily rose to their feet. "One more short one, boys," called Shem.

"You just keep up with us, old man," called Jobaath, who was now on the other side.

"Shall we run back and see who gets there first, boy?" growled Shem.

"Only if the winner is cooking tonight," laughed Jobaath. Shem smiled. "I expect the women will beat us all back, then."

"The women will be only too glad to fix a meal for you big, strong men." Madrazi winked at Jael. "After all, you're the ones who have to do this again tomorrow. We need to keep up your strength."

Jobaath groaned. "Did you have to remind us?"

Chapter 59
A TERRIBLE RESOLVE

2-19-1762

It took two more days to get the other boat and their equipment to the river, and it was seven exhausted people who camped on the bank that night. But they were eager to start, and left at first light. Heth found himself with Ashkenaz, Jobaath, and the bulk of their packs in one boat. He was content to let the others row while he sat in the bow, calling occasional directions as he followed the other. A light fog lay on the water in the morning chill, so they stayed close. The men were rowing easily, and they were all happy to be going downstream. They could have simply let the water carry them, but all were too anxious to be home.

Heth was particularly troubled. He had been thinking about Shinar ever since the women had joined them. The city that had been perched over the abyss of evil was now sliding inexorably down into that chasm, led down the path to irretrievable ruin by Nimrod. He recalled the hours talking to Korac, trying to perceive any weaknesses in the man who had bested him long ago. He had been forced to conclude that as much as he had grown in strength, Nimrod had only increased his advantage. It galled him, yet knowing was a small advantage.

If Korac was right, Nimrod was even more dangerous with his new black spear. It sounded like an extension of his arm; Nimrod would not allow any other man to touch it. Heth recalled the night Korac had told them what little he knew about it. Madrazi had been especially curious, and her probing questions forced Korac to recall details long forgotten. She and Shem had been greatly troubled when Korac casually mentioned overhearing his old master calling it the spear of Sechiall.

Both had both been shocked when they heard that name. Heth recalled the scene vividly. Shem had explained the significance of the name and Madrazi named it an evil from the old world that should have been buried with all the rest. "I wonder how it came to Nimrod?" mused Shelah. At first the older couple shook their heads. Then, at the same time, they sat bolt upright and stared at each other in horror.

"Sechiall cast it at Noah," breathed Shem.

"God blew it aside and it struck the doorpost instead," interrupted Madrazi.

"Just before the door shut," finished Shem. "It must have been trapped between the door and the lintel," he frowned slowly, his forehead wrinkled in thought. "If the door struck it right, it might had sheared the shaft and driven the head all the way into the post. But how did Debseda find it?"

"Its evil called to her," replied Madrazi, shaking her head. "We should have seen it, but we were too busy. She must have spent weeks digging it out without our noticing. That whole area of the deck had become a refuse heap."

"I wonder if Ham knew?" Shem's face had been hard.

"No!" Madrazi had been equally emphatic. "He would never have allowed her to have it. He would have given it to Father."

"He was already falling into evil," muttered Shem in return, but Madrazi had disagreed. "Ham has done much wrong, but he is not our enemy," she had insisted. "And neither are all his kin," she had said quietly, looking at Heth. That look had reached deep within the younger man and planted the seed of a thought—dealing with Nimrod's evil. Was it his responsibility? He was Canaan's son, yet accepted by Shem and Madrazi. Nimrod had been his enemy from the beginning. All of his life he had been preparing to fight, but there was no one that he wanted to kill. No one except Nimrod.

Was that a sign from the Almighty?

An eddy ahead brought Heth back to the present, and he called out a course correction to follow the other boat. After hearing the tales of Madrazi's youth, he trusted her direction in all things pertaining to this voyage. He only wanted to set his feet on the dry land beyond the Black Sea. They needed news—the tales of Korac, combined with the old news from Anam and Ashkenaz were ominous.

During the days that followed, a terrible resolve began building inside Heth's heart. From early manhood he had known that he was the adversary of Nimrod—the only logical choice. It was his fate, and as he thought back, he realized he had known it all along. There had always been animosity, though Nimrod had sensed it first. It was the only explanation for his behavior under Canaan's roof. Heth bit his lip. It was one thing to be destined to fight Nimrod, but another to win.

It took courage to admit that Nimrod was the better warrior, but perhaps the difference was less than Nimrod believed. That would be one advantage, however small. But it wouldn't be enough. He needed something else, and even after wracking his mind for days, he could think of only one. A man willing to trade his own life to insure the death of his enemy was a man to be feared. There were many moves available to a weaker man willing to impale his own body in order to do the same to his foe. Heth was a skilled fighter; he knew most of the tricks. Nimrod did too, so the challenge was to choose one that would fool him—only for a moment—and then... then Nimrod would be dead. But, of course, so would he. The cost made him shiver; only by abandoning his own life could Heth hope to defeat his foe.

He didn't want to die. He had centuries before him, a world to subdue, a wife and children... and that was part of the problem. He couldn't keep his eyes off the other boat. Jael floated ahead of him, beautiful now in body and spirit, but she was unreachable now, separated by much more than a few boat lengths of water. He wanted her, but even more he wanted her to be safe and happy. How could that happen in a world ruled by Nimrod? The man had already ruined one of Noah's daughters, and as soon as he found out how another had thwarted his will by saving Madrazi, he would not rest until he killed her.

And he would. She was good, he admitted, better than most. In a straight fight, she might hold her own against Jobaath, and with a little luck, she might take Ash. But she wasn't as good as Korac or Shelah, and she wouldn't stand a chance against him. And he wasn't as good as Nimrod. The only way to keep her alive would be to make sure that Nimrod was dead. It all added up. For Jael to live, he must cast aside his life. He looked longingly at the other boat. If he couldn't love her, he could at least protect her.

And so that terrible resolve began to take form. He was careful to hide it deep, and glad that any slip was put down to his preoccupation with Jael. Now that he had purpose, he began to plan his path. Many times in his head he fought Nimrod, first from the memories of his youth, and then from the accounts of Korac. Move and countermove—he thought hard about the possible ways to take his enemy down, and began to narrow his options to his best deceptive moves.

To kill Nimrod, he first had to get away from his friends. They would surely try to stop him, and he trembled to think of how easily he might be swayed by Jael's importunities. He also had to get to Shinar. He was not the only man who wanted Nimrod dead—Korac had good reason to slay his old master. If Korac beat him there and tried… Nimrod would be alert, and Heth would never get near him. So he must forsake his friends as soon as they landed. If Togarmah had a fast horse, he would steal it and ride for Shinar that very hour. If not, he would run all the way to the Lake of the Islands at his best speed and find a horse there. That would be harder. He doubted that he could outrun Shem or Shelah. Maybe if he left at night, giving him a few hours start….

Once in Shinar, he would seek out Nimrod and taunt him. As the warlord of Shinar, he could not refuse a public challenge or he would be branded a coward. And if his hot anger could be roused before his cold mind had time to consider the possibilities, Heth would have his fight. Once Nimrod was dead, Shinar would cease to be a threat. Without him, Debseda's spite and hatred would have no tool. Shinar would become just another city. Other cities would be built and mankind would live out the years in an uneasy peace. Anything, however, was better than the terrible unity of tyranny—the whole world under Nimrod's heel.

He said nothing of his troubled thoughts, but as the river bank rolled by, he became preoccupied with the impending fight. Over and over in his mind, he lunged, dodged, sidestepped, and thrust… every possible move considered and reconsidered. He planned counters to every possible attack that Nimrod might launch. He continued to talk to Korac, trading tales of Nimrod to dig out any missing details of his enemy's style and preferences. Korac had the eye, and he was able to describe them in detail. Though Korac might be as good as his old master in the wild—setting an ambush or detecting the same—if it had ever come to a straight fight, he was Nimrod's inferior and wasn't afraid to admit it. Nor did he seem bothered any longer that Heth was also his better. The two took to sparring in the evenings with spear, sword, and knife. Korac appreciated the practice, seeing his own considerable skills improve by fighting an opponent of Heth's caliber, but Heth knew he had the better of the lessons. Korac had sparred with Nimrod, and this was as close as Heth could come to fighting Nimrod himself. A skilled warrior, he deduced a few more of Nimrod's abilities from the residual imprint they had left on Korac's style.

The others thought that Heth was showing off for Jael, but they joined the play—it was diverting entertainment. Shem even demonstrated his prowess in unarmed fighting—taking down every man present, even Korac and Heth. They clamored for his secrets, but he refused to show them. "I'll save my tricks for my sister," he joked. "She'll need them to handle you stalwart warriors."

But Jael's absence was a surprise to all. At one time she would have been in the thick of the sparring, absorbing new skills and reveling in every point scored off the men. But months alone with Madrazi, the achievement of her purpose, and her forgiveness of Korac had done their work. Instead of fighting, she spent her time talking to Madrazi. When invited to join the men, she just shook her head and continued talking with her sister. The new Jael had come into full bloom. She was at peace with herself, content to help Madrazi around the camp. Her drive and heart were still there, but the berserker rage had been left behind, scattered across the vast wilderness. Heth envied her change. Peace had displaced her old restlessness, and that had been their greatest point of commonality. It made him more determined to slay Nimrod, though he despaired of ever having the chance to know that same peace. There was no peace for him—just an opportunity to give his life for her.

So the days passed. They had to hole up for two days soon after they started; one last blizzard gripped the land, but as the days sped by and the river carried them south and east, a tinge of spring came into the air. Snow-encrusted banks turned brown with mud, and then to green with the first shoots of the new year's grass. Hints of green also appeared on trees and shrubs, and the game became less wary as they sensed the return of a new cycle of life. Korac would mutter to himself at times, reliving his trek as they sped along. He covered his head and sat hunched in the back of the boat for a day as they floated past Jalam's cairn. The women saw and comforted him that evening, warning the men away with sharp glances. Heth had no idea what they said, but he saw something he had once thought impossible... more tears flowing down Korac's cheeks.

Korac was silent the next day and the next, but he finally began to open his heart to Heth, talking to him about Jalam—his loyalty, good sense, his knowledge of good and evil, and his final refusal to continue their quest... naming it and Nimrod immoral and evil. His eyes narrowed and his lips thinned each time he mentioned Nimrod, and Heth knew he would have to move fast when they returned. For a time Heth considered bringing Korac into his confidence. Perhaps they could go together. Nimrod would be hard pressed to fight either; fighting both, he would be at a distinct disadvantage. But at last he decided that this was his fate. He could not use Korac as a crutch to avoid his duty.

Time passed and the river widened. Melting snow fed its tributaries, and they began to dump great volumes into the main channel, raising the level of the river. They were riding a surging wave down to the Black Sea. Heth welcomed the flood. It carried the boats along at a speed equal to a brisk trot, hour after hour, taking them a day's journey in just hours. Madrazi had been right. Soon they would be near the stream which hopefully still held Togarmah's ship. Then they would be on the last leg of their journey back home... the last leg of his life's journey. He shuddered.

Chapter 60
HOMECOMING

3-20-1762

Heth's wishes were realized one fine spring morning. Rowing around a bend in the river, Madrazi suddenly signaled them to make for the northern shore. It was hard rowing into the tributary against the current, but they made it and soon found *Kef* where Madrazi had left her. She rode low in the water, but a quick inspection of the outside of the hull revealed no damage from ice. Madrazi's foresight in tying lines from all four corners had kept the ship in the middle of the stream where the current had kept it clear.

But a year of inattention had led to innumerable small leaks. "We'll have to re-caulk the hull," Madrazi explained after rowing completely around her. "Moss would be easiest. It won't last long, but we only need a few weeks to reach Arkaz." She and Shem went on board after they pulled the ship over to the east bank. Then everyone began the hard work of bailing out the icy water, revealing many small leaks.

Heth was sent out with the other men to gather moss, while Shem and Madrazi worked to plug the leaks and replace other deteriorating seams. Shem had to drag Madrazi off the boat after a few hours, forcing her to sit in front of a roaring fire to dry off. She seemed driven, and despite her chapped and numb hands, she continued to press on with the job for hours each day until the interior of the ship was once again secured from the waters outside. Heth shook his head as he watched Jael care for her bleeding fingers each night. He knew he had just seen another kind of courage, and it spurred him on towards his own terrible goal.

Soon Madrazi pronounced the ship ready. Some of the ropes were beginning to rot, and it took every cubit of line to splice replacements. Fortunately the ship had only one short voyage to make. Heth joined the others in praying for gentle winds on the Black Sea. Even he could see that *Kef* could not take a storm.

Seven was a full load for the small ship, but she seemed to handle well. She slid across the water as the wind and current cooperated to carry them north, down the last stretch of the great river and finally out through the treacherous, shifting sand bars of the delta into the deep waters of the Black Sea. If any doubted Madrazi's mastery of ships and the sea after building the boats, they were convinced by her ability to navigate the maze of the delta; she invariably chose the right channel and *Kef* responded to her touch at the tiller like a well trained horse following the nudges of its rider's knees.

3-30-1762

Anam slipped silently through the night. Ham had shared the secret of his way over the wall outside his shop months before, and the now-unused corner of the compound was seldom watched. It was an easy way outside the walls for one as small and quick as Anam. Tonight was going to be hard, though. He had little time. He was being watched closely and had only a few hours. Even the dull Turod wouldn't sleep all night, so Anam took the risk of running down some of the darker streets, keeping to the walls and hoping no dog began barking.

Soon he was at one of Mizraim's outlying warehouses near the brickyard. A slight hiss attracted his attention to a side door, and he slipped inside. A hand clutched his and led him through several rooms, up a flight of steps, and out onto the roof. Dark shadows rose in the starlight and surrounded him. A motion revealed the face of his father, though the others kept their hoods up.

"What's your news?" whispered Mizraim. Anam began to talk in low tones; there was no time to waste. "We have to leave soon," he began." One of the shadowy figures began to mutter, but Mizraim stilled it with a sharp hiss. "Everything is set for this ceremony," he continued. "They will encourage the town to eat and drink. When all are drunk, selected men will act. Grandfather and Mariel will be killed, as will you and Lud. I probably will be too, along with Graemea and our child. Debseda can always find another attendant."

Mizraim nodded. His mind moved at its usual speed; he needed no deliberation. "Then the ceremony will be our sign too. I'll announce a feast and bring in wagons of wine. But while a few present the illusion of eating and drinking, the rest of us will start under cover of night. The others will have fast horses and will come as they can." He turned back to Anam. "Will they let you and Graemea attend our feast?"

"Probably," murmured Anam. "That would put us with you; their assassins would have an easier job."

"A servant will be there tomorrow with an invitation." Mizraim pulled his hood up over his face "Safe days, my son, and better ones ahead." He turned and vanished down the steps. Anam shook himself for a moment and was soon climbing the wall back onto the roof of Ham's workshop. He hoped Turod was still asleep. Just one more month and all the lies and deception and risks would vanish. They would go south with his family to the home he had always wanted. A tiny part of his heart was still able to hope, though a much larger part doubted he would survive that long.

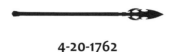

4-20-1762

It was a fine spring evening when the voyagers finally tied *Kef* to the dock at Arkaz. The sun and a gentle wind were dead astern, and the sea, uncharacteristically calm. Men, women, and children swarmed out to meet them, and Togarmah was openly weeping at the sight of the ship he thought lost. Madrazi understood at once, and leapt lightly out to greet him. "She's a wonderful craft," she said softly, kissing his cheek. "She needs a little work, but she'll be as good as new!"

"She's my first... my best...."

"You don't need to explain, child," she whispered. "I understand."

"Thank you for that precious gift," he returned, wiping his eyes and smiling down at her. "And I have one in return for you." He reached inside his tunic and lifted out a gold chain with curiously-designed gold wire embracing an even more curious tooth as long as his finger, yellowed enough to match the gold. Madrazi's hand reached out for it, her eyes shining. "Thank you," she breathed. "It is precious to me."

"And to me," interrupted Shem softly from behind her. "Allow me." He took the chain and gently laid it around her neck, kissing the tooth before letting it settle down between her breasts. She looked into his eyes and saw the years of love they had shared since he had first given it to her; their surroundings faded for a moment as they walked back through their memories together.

Shelah broke their reverie with a respectful cough. "Let's get unloaded," he suggested. Suddenly Togarmah saw Korac and his eyes went very hard as his hand snaked down for his knife, but Shem's was on his wrist before he got it out of its sheath. "Everyone," Shem emphasized, staring with authority into the man's eyes, "in the boat is a friend."

Togarmah nodded with a jerk, eased the knife back into its sheath, and composed his face. "I see we have many tales to trade," he said tightly. "Come to the main house and we will have supper. Then there will be time for news."

The crowd parted and the travelers made their way to the shore. Jael and Madrazi traded a look as they both turned to look back at the ship rolling gently in its moorings over the darkening sea. Jael smiled and gave her sister a quick hug. "You were right all along, Madrazi. God carried us across the wilderness to those we sought. When I was too weak to save you, He changed the heart of our enemy and made him our friend. I hope one day I have your faith."

"You have your own, Jael," she replied with a hug, "unmarred by my many sins. Be content with it." The two women lagged behind the dwindling crowd. Stars were just beginning to make their appearance in the blackening sky. "Though I think you need to speak very soon with one of these young men."

"He hasn't said one word, Madrazi. Not one word!" There was an undertone of hurt in her voice.

"He thinks himself unworthy, Jael. But I've seen his eyes on you. He would give his life for you without a second thought. You're a woman. See through his reticence and bring him around. One word from you, and he's yours for life. Trust me on this."

Jael looked suddenly thoughtful. "Are you sure?"

"Yes, child. I am."

The younger woman brightened and straightened her shoulders as they followed the stragglers to the well lit doors of the stone house before them.

It was nearer morning than night. After a hastily prepared feast, the travelers had told tales to an astonished audience. Interested murmurs rose as Shelah waxed eloquent about the vast forests and plains to the north, and even those on the verge of sleep followed every word of Madrazi and Jael's account, and an excited buzz broke out when Korac's story was heard, rising in volume when he stood and apologized to Togarmah, vowing to repay him for the lost ship.

But the news was not all from the north that night. The men of Arkaz traded with Shinar and one party had been there a bare four months earlier. So Togarmah related all that he knew of events there. It took some time, but his voice hardened as he summed up his words. "So they have imprisoned Ham and the Lady Mariel," he sighed. "This tower continues to rise. I have not seen it with my own eyes, but it is large… very large. And there is more to come. Rumors are rife that Nimrod and Debseda will dedicate their tower to this Queen of Heaven soon. Very soon. Once that is done, and the people of Shinar are sold into their service, they will make sure that Ham and Mariel will no longer be needed.

"That we must stop," growled Shem.

"We know," sighed Togarmah. "There was nothing my small party could do at the time, and even if we had enough men, we couldn't run fast enough to get there in time. It cannot be done."

Heth had been staring at the walls absorbing the news, his face growing darker and darker. All of his worst fears were coming true. Ham was the only worthy man in Shinar and Nimrod wanted him out of the way. His eyes burned with rage. All the evil he had feared all his life was coming to pass. All his plans from the trip down the river crystallized in an instant. Sins no one thought possible were really happening. Nimrod was going to kill his wife and grandfather, just to marry his grandmother. What greater evidence could be given of Shinar's utter depravity?

Togarmah could do nothing… but Togarmah was a fisherman. Heth was a warrior and he knew abruptly that the time had come. His destiny lay plainly before him now.

But because he was a warrior, his plans to sneak off during the night seemed unworthy and cowardly. Togarmah had no horses here, and he knew he could not outrun Shelah and Shem, but he also knew that they could never stop him, even if they desired to deny him the path he had to take. So he could no more help what he did than he could stop breathing. Standing abruptly, he seized his spear and pack. "This abomination must not continue," he said in a low, hard voice. "And there is only one way to stop it. Nimrod must die. That had been my fate since the day I met him. Farewell!"

Everyone sat stunned, but Jael rose, her face angry. "Why throw your life away for nothing? You cannot prevail, not even if… if…." Sudden understanding flared in her eyes.

"Not for nothing," said Heth softly. "For you. For your children. For theirs." Finally, he let his heart shine through his eyes. Jael stepped back, her lips trembling. Her throat tightened convulsively and the words in her heart could not find their way to her tongue. She shook her head, but Heth was suddenly gone, vanishing through the door like a puff of wind off the sea.

Jael went pale, staggering back. Shelah caught her and guided her to a seat. She looked beseechingly at Shem. "I can't let him go," she finally breathed. I can't."

Shem nodded, but pursed his lips. "We'll start after him in the morning. We'll catch him at the Lake."

"No we won't!" With a flash of anger, the old Jael was suddenly back. "He's tireless and burning with rage. He'll outrun us to the Lake, take a fast horse, and be in Shinar, while we're up here trying to decide what to do. If you won't go after him, I will."

"All right," said Shem evenly.

Like everyone else at the table, Jael just stared at him—his easy permission as much a shock to her as to the others.

But Shem wasn't fazed. His dark brown eyes gleamed with a strange light. "You're ready." His lopsided smile made her almost as proud as his words. "And you appear to be highly motivated," he said. Jael blushed, but Shem wasn't through. He winked at her. "If you catch him, you can keep him."

"I'll pass that along when I do," she answered back tartly. "Maybe he'll even stop long enough to ask you for my hand."

Ashkenaz started to protest. "You can't go alone. Let us come with you. Give us an hour to prepare."

Jael was already shouldering her bow and a waterskin. The rest she left on the floor. "Feel free to follow," she said. "If you can keep up," she taunted. With that, she sprang out the door into the night, her challenging laugh floating back on the wind.

Madrazi put her hand on Shelah's arm as he started to rise. "Let her go. Only you or Shem could catch Heth, and neither of you could convince him to let go of his foolishness. She can."

Sudden understanding flared in Shelah's eyes. "You're sure?" he asked.

"Yes." Her face was serene and Shelah relaxed. His eyes took in her ragged clothing. "We still need to follow tomorrow."

"Of course." Her eyes twinkled.

"It will be hard. You could stay here…" his voice trailed off.

"I had two lovely weeks on *Kef*, and days of restful boating before that," she replied. "A little walking and riding would probably be good for me."

Shem laughed and the men joined him. Even Korac shook his head and chuckled.

Chapter 61
JAEL'S HUNT

4-30-1761

Jael ran, panting as the rising sun hindered her view over the low divide and out onto the Lake of the Islands. At first, she had thought to catch Heth in a few hours—she didn't think such a large man could outrun her over a long distance. But he had. He had to be exhausted; she was ready to drop. Settlements dotting the coast of the lake glimmered in the morning sun, calling to her. She needed a mount and news. And she had to move fast. Only hours ahead, Heth would already be stretching his lead, riding south and she was less confident of catching him mounted. If he was smart, he would have taken two horses. Switching between them, he could ride fast and far… and she was still a half day behind.

She cursed the first night. In her excitement, she had allowed her mind to dwell on Heth's last look at her—the unveiled love making his angular face a thing of rough beauty. Distracted, she had run into a blind canyon, costing her the six hours—the same six hours she still trailed him. Such a small thing for her future to hinge on, but there was nothing to do but keep going. So she pushed herself hard. But it couldn't last—game had been sparse, and hunger, combined with the grueling pace, slowed her down. Her only consolation was that Heth, too, had been slowed.

She would have to eat and sleep for a few hours before she could take up the chase again. The farm of Uz was just down the valley, but she expected little help from him. He was one of those who thought her a scandal, and only the direct command of Shem or Arpachshad would force him to give the help she needed. Eber's village was her best hope, but it was another hour south. At least it was in the right direction. She pulled in another gulp of air and then ran down the hill, shivering at the cold water as she crossed the small river, and then warmed again as she sprinted the last stretch to Eber's home.

Night found her far from the lake, cursing her bad luck once more. Eber had given her a horse—a fast one, but the second one she needed had been lame, and it would take a day to find another. She had eaten and slept… had even bathed quickly before she slept, and Eber's wife, Rachel, had spent the time altering clothes to replace her rags.

Heth had arrived in the middle of the night. He had taken the shortest route and roused Uz, taking his two best horses at midnight. So he was nearly a day ahead and had the advantage of two mounts. Once out on the plains, she would stand no chance; he knew the country there better than she did, despite hours of description by Shem. So she would have to make up time in this rougher country, hoping that being a little more than half his weight would help her horse handle the strain better than Uz' favorites.

She grinned for a moment as she imagined the man's discomfort—Heth would have set his spear to Uz' stubborn neck and demanded the horses.

Now she faced a hard choice. The fastest route lay a little to the west. Once she descended the mountains bordering the south side of the lake, the land became smoother, descending evenly all the way to the upper reaches of the Tigris. Crossing at one of the many fords, she could then follow the way between the rivers down to Shinar.

Just ahead the path split, offering the choice of two valleys. The longer was the more traveled way, because the shorter saved only five or six hours, and its steep trail had injured more than one horse and man. But time was working for Heth now, and risk was no longer a choice. Heth had prudently taken the longer route; his tracks were clear in the moonlight. She said a brief prayer, hoped Eber's mount was nimble, and reined him to the right before plunging her heels into his side.

Debseda paced back and forth across her room. "You're sure about this?" she snapped at Celota.

"Yes, my lady," the servant whimpered. Debseda was nervous and angry, and Celota had been beaten enough to recognize the warning signs. She went down to the floor. "They are preparing a giant feast. They've killed two oxen, and there were at least ten large urns of wine delivered to the house." Daring greatly, she looked up. "It will be a great opportunity, my lady. Your enemies in one place, sated with food and wine."

Debseda frowned, but then nodded. "You're right, my child. This is an opportunity. Go and ask my grandson to attend me at his earliest pleasure."

Celota scurried out of the room, happy to have escaped a beating. Running down the hall, she found Nimrod's door shut. She hurried down the stairs into the courtyard, seeing him there giving last minute instructions to a troop of his men. She would have to wait for him to finish and hoped he would hurry. Her mistress was not the most patient of women!

Finally she was able to deliver her message, and to her surprise, he nodded and followed her immediately. It had been some time since he had taken her to his rooms, so she pulled her robe close to her body and added a slight roll to her hips. He laughed behind her. "Not today, little one. Soon, though." She smiled to herself as she opened the door and bowed him in. Her mistress was not the only attractive woman in the house!

Nimrod was still smiling as he walked into Debseda's room. "You have news?" He leaned against the wall, forcing her to come to him.

"Yes," she said, gliding across the floor to him. With all the preparations for tomorrow, they had not been together much in the past week, and he could see the flame of desire was upon her. Every last measure of her self-control was needed to keep from throwing herself at him, but she stood in her place, quivering.

"Mizraim is acting in his typical manner," she reported. "He's holding his own feast for his own family instead of joining ours for the council."

"Well," Nimrod grinned. "That will certainly make our gathering more pleasant! And it puts our enemies in one place, drunk and gorged." He wrinkled his brow. "Will Anam attend?"

"Yes," she replied hesitantly. "His invitation was seen by Celota. That was our first indication of the feast. She has been investigating ever since." She shook her head. "Are you sure about Anam?" she asked. "He's been quite useful. I know he is no warrior, but with Korac gone, we need clever eyes and ears."

"Blood will tell," he replied sharply. "The boy has been useful, but he's fulfilled his use. Better to be sure and not leave any loose ends." He fingered the hilt of his knife. "And if he's as clever as you think, that can cut both ways. I just don't trust him completely. I never have." He shrugged his shoulders. "We'll just have to find another musician."

Debseda nodded. "Very well. So we do the ceremony tomorrow, enjoy our own feast the rest of the day, and send your best men to Mizraim's house after dark?"

Nimrod nodded. "Two days from right now, you and I will control this city. Anam has played his part. Our empire is finally within our grasp!"

Chapter 62
TERROR AT THE TOWER

5-1-1762

Sunrise found the citizens of Shinar abuzz with excitement. The day was finally upon them! Everyone had been up for hours celebrating and most had not slept at all. Tonight, the feasting would begin in earnest.

Nimrod had napped for an hour and had the good sense to eat well; he probably wouldn't get another chance until the next day since he would be skipping his own feast to lead his men against Mizraim's house. With Korac gone, there was no one he trusted with that job.

But now he was focused on the morning. He had poured himself into the preparations for months and found that his patience for this kind of work was lacking. *A ruler must be able to deal with running an empire as well as building one*; his mouth twisted as he thought of the discipline he needed to learn in the decades ahead.

If only Korac would return! Vague rumors had put him on a ship sailing across the Black Sea, and then there was nothing. Unfortunately the few competent men left in Shinar couldn't be spared to search that vast shoreline, and Debseda's vaunted spy network had proven useless. As the months had dragged into years, he found himself wondering if Korac was truly gone, killed by any of the innumerable things in the wild that could snatch a man's life—even one as good as Korac. He hoped not. The longer Korac and his team had been gone, the more he realized how much he needed him… even Jalam would be an improvement over the current lot.

He slammed down the goblet and began to pace the floor once more. Today was important. He had to keep focused on making it work. If everything went to plan, Shinar would be his. With Ham out of the way and Mizraim dead, he could begin the next phase—key fortress cities up and down the length of the rivers, tying the whole of the plains to Shinar to his throne.

He looked up as his door opened and was struck dumb with astonishment. Debseda glittered in her costume. She would make no overt claims, but most would be unable to see her as anything but an incarnation of the Queen of Heaven. As long as that association remained unstated and vague, in the realm of emotion, the illogic of that impression would not matter. And no one who saw her like this would be able to escape the force of her appearance. Gold, finely hammered into thin flexible plates, and connected with nearly invisible wires formed undergarments that hid… no, emphasized… her body. They were covered by a tunic of exquisitely fine gold mesh, which suggested more. Tiny gold plates made her slippers shimmer in the light, and an elaborate headdress of peacock feathers mounted the ivory crown that held her hair in place. Cosmetics highlighted her eyes and lips; the colors seemed garish in the confines of the room, but Nimrod knew that they would have their desired effect atop the tower.

Her smile conveyed her appreciation for his surprise and the following flare of desire. She struck a pose. "Will this do?" she cooed. He began to laugh out loud. "There won't be a man not drooling down his beard today," he chuckled.

"Nor a wife that will notice," she finished, eyeing him lasciviously. She snapped her finger. Celota hurried in from the hall with an oversized cloak and hood. Debseda slipped it on and the two women cautiously lifted the headpiece off her brow. It would be hidden in a box to be carried to the tower later. Celota took it carefully away. "Aren't you ready?" Debseda crooned. "You'll catch every eye today. The women will be too distracted to be angry at their men for staring at me."

He laughed again. "My preparations are easier than yours. The armor is already in the room atop the tower. I'm going over now to check on security. With Korac gone, I have to do it all myself."

She shrugged. "He's still alive, my love. I don't know what is keeping him, but he will return to you. I have seen it." She glided over and leaned against him. "I won't be able to do this properly again until tomorrow night," she breathed, and lifted her lips to his. For a few heartbeats their passion merged and flared, but Nimrod finally pulled back, shaking his head. "It cannot come too soon!"

Tubal, Tiras, Canaan, and Cush met Nimrod at the tower's foot a few hours later. The sons of Japheth were dressed in their 'priestly' garb, each laden with an armful of powders and plants that would bring color and smoke from the fire to impress the young and simple. Canaan was richly dressed and looking a little too proud of himself. Nimrod had spent more than one night pacing the floor, wondering if they had made a mistake in jailing Ham too soon, but Canaan had finished the first level without mishap and had been boasting that the rest would be done within three years. Cush stood silent, solid and proud. After all, it was his son whose star was on the rise. Nimrod made a mental note to keep an eye on his father—no need to let that pride pull him in the wrong direction!

As one, the men began climbing the great steps, Tiras swearing softly to himself as he almost tripped over his long robe. Nimrod ignored them all, feeling the shiver of excitement as he neared the top. No god was needed to make the platform at the top a sacred place. From there he would issue the proclamations of his coming kingdom. His spear sang in his right hand as they continued up. He could feel the power within it, trembling with anticipation, in tune with his deepest desires.

They finally reached the top and looked back down. Nimrod felt the same thrill every time he stared down over the city. He loved the view from this height and looked forward to the completion of the next levels. He couldn't wait until he could look down over the wide plains with all the little men scurrying around like ants to do his bidding. Even at this height, the view was magnificent. Each step was a little less than a half cubit, and the two hundred steps put them eighty cubits above the plain. He could see to the far side of the Euphrates valley to the west, and far beyond the city walls in every other direction. Maybe when the tower was complete he would be able to see all the way to the Tigris! This was his domain—he knew it in his bones. It was merely a matter of plucking the fruit from the tree… and today would see it torn halfway from the stem.

Nature had chosen to cooperate. Scattered high clouds covered enough of the sky to keep the crowds comfortably shaded, but enough sunlight shone through, to reflect off Debseda and dazzling the people below. While Tiras and Tubal lit the fire beneath the altar, Nimrod slipped into the small room behind it and donned the heavy pieces of his armor. Made of pure gold, they would have been of little use in a battle, but combined with Debseda's attire, they would leave an image in the minds of everyone that would last for centuries. He wore golden greaves, a wide golden belt with long flat plates hanging down over his linen skirt, a bright breastplate, and golden vambraces on his forearms. His thick black hair was the only crown he needed, matching perfectly the distinct black spear.

He strode out and took his place beside Debseda. As expected, most of the crowd stared up at the golden couple. Most of the men paid little attention to his appearance—Debseda probably seemed naked from a distance, her skin a glowing gold instead of its usual olive tan. For long minutes, the crowd roared its approval. Behind them, Tiras and Tubal slew the goat and laid it on the fire. Smoke curled up into the sky. They stayed near the fire, well in the background—as instructed—but Canaan edged closer to the steps, though Cush remained back in his rightful place.

Finally, Nimrod stepped forward, and raised his arms. Debseda stayed beside him but kept her hands linked in front of her—a counterpoint of modesty to her decidedly immodest finery. As the roar subsided, every face turned towards the man that was clearly born to lead them to a great future. Nimrod smiled as he imagined Mizraim down in the crowd, gnashing his teeth, helpless to alter the course of the great river of destiny that was rushing towards him. An eerie stillness descended on the tower and the people gathered before it. It was almost as if the earth itself had decided to take a hand, the air creating a hushed vacuum to hear what its new lord and master would say.

Nimrod kept his voice level. He was prepared to speak over wind, the dull roar of the river to the west, and the murmur of the people below. He could project his voice as well as any of his elders, but today it was not needed. "My friends and brothers," he began. "Today we come together before our great tower. It is a fitting symbol of what we can do when we work together."

Everyone began shouting and cheering, forcing him to raise his hand again. Silence again.

"We are the kings of creation—sons of the Queen of Heaven. Just as this tower belongs to her, this good earth around it belongs to us; soon we will make our mark up and down the length of the rivers, from the sea in the south to the mountains in the north. By the time your grandchildren are born, this plain will be an empire that will be remembered for as long as men will walk the earth. Her name will be praised in every city. From here we will spread throughout the lands, until the entire world will echo the praise of our glory up to the very heavens above."

He paused dramatically before raising both hands wide. "We have defeated Noah and his sons. Nothing can stop us… no one can stand in our way!"

He stared down at the crowd. He heard gasps of amazement, and for a fleeting moment he allowed his pride to tell him that they were because of his words. But an instant later, he knew better. Tiras and Tubal cried out behind him and he heard them throw themselves on the ground. He turned instinctively, sensing danger before he saw it, and felt Debseda's sharply indrawn breath as his eyes saw what at first they refused to believe.

Smoke from the altar had been ascending up to the clouds as he spoke, forming a thick column. A golden light was permeating the smoke, moving slowly down from the clouds. It had an evil feel to it, and as Debseda shuddered beside him, he knew she felt it too. "I felt this on the ark," she hissed, one hand on her breast. "It is the hand of the Creator!"

Her words only reinforced what Nimrod instinctively felt... the touch of his greatest enemy. It was the fire he had felt banked within Noah, but now burning bright and clear, breaking forth in roaring fury. All he could see was a golden glow inside the smoky column, but he raised his spear in an instinctive defensive motion. It sang to his heart as black answered gold, but the same intimate connection enabled him to feel the frisson of terror beneath the black rage and power. As powerful as the darkness was, it was no match for the light, and Nimrod's fury mounted at that realization.

He staggered back, dragging Debseda with him. He shoved her towards the room behind the altar. "Stay there!" he commanded, and she scuttled into its depths, glad to be sheltered from the descending fire. The other men were retreating back down the stairs, led by Tiras and Tubal. Nimrod was left alone to face the danger. He sneered inwardly at the others.

Sheep! He was the one destined to lead mankind. That was worth more than his life. With that thought, he stopped retreating and stood his ground, wishing only that he could slip out of this ridiculous golden armor and put on the real thing. A part of him wished too for Korac standing by his side, but another rejected it. As useful as Korac had been, he was, in the final analysis, just a man, and this was the place for a superior man—the child of the Nephil. He raised his spear and waited.

Waves of panic ran through the crowd below. They surged back and forth, as if wanting to flee, yet unable to tear themselves away from the awful spectacle. All felt the power in the alien light; all felt the same fear and rage at the invasion of their city, but all eyes remained locked on the light as if chained. Lower and lower it sank. Clouds now obscured the sun completely, but the noon light was not diminished—if anything, it was brighter. A few fools in the mob began to cry out in a vain hope that the Queen of Heaven was descending on her children, but their cries seemed to make the light pulse in anger, so their voices quickly went silent. Nimrod was trying to shield his eyes with one arm, cursing the golden armor that reflected the painful light no matter how he held his arm. Only the faint shadow of his spear protected him from blindness.

Gradually the crowd grew still; they were paralyzed in the realization that their glorious day had become something far different. One or two at the far edge were able to tear themselves away and slink back into the shadows of the city, but only one or two.

As it drew nearer to earth, they could see that the light had a source, and that small blazing sun soon settled atop the altar, its purer flames overpowering the puny fire still smoldering from the sacrifice. Nimrod sensed a pulse of power that threw him to his knees and the solid stones of the altar crumbled, leaving the near-intolerable light atop a formless heap of dust and ashes. The very floor of the tower began cracking slightly under its feet, as though some unimaginable weight bore down upon it.

As Nimrod gripped his spear, the light began to take shape, shimmering into a large, man-like being. It was clothed in golden light, making Nimrod's armor look like badly tarnished brass, and great wings spread from its back. There was no face, just a light that could not be borne. Shielding his face with the head of his spear, Nimrod caught a glimpse of many eyes watching out of that light; more than one was riveted on him. He could feel their displeasure, and the power of the spear—which had been such a source of pride—seemed as inconsequential as his armor before their gaze. Yet it was still power of a sort, and gathering his will, he stood his ground. If it killed him, then it would kill a defiant king, not a fleeing coward.

Suddenly the air was clear of smoke, and the angel stretched out his hand. It held a rod, larger than a scepter but smaller than a spear, which struck an odd contrast. Instead of gold, it seemed to be made of polished iron, dark and forbidding. Nimrod knew immediately and instinctively that if he attacked, his dread spear would be shattered against its impenetrable hardness, so he maintained a defensive stance, ready to fight if attacked, but wise enough not to seek certain death. After all, he recalled, the Almighty had pledged his own word that the flood was unique, that no destructive judgment would ever come upon the earth. Perhaps this was just an elaborate threat, an attempt to cow the people. His mouth tightened. He would not back down.

His resolution grew. He was no mere man to fear the terrors of the abyss!

As if it could read his thoughts, the thing tilted the iron rod slightly towards Nimrod. A wave of power buffeted him, though his connection to the power of the spear told of its greater pain. Nimrod felt a weakening of its power, as if it had been halved… or more. It cut him to the quick to feel that weakness, especially now when he needed all its strength.

Then the monster spoke.

Your unity is broken!

The words thundered over the city, audible to both rivers, driving Nimrod back to his knees in pain. But the thing had not finished. Once again the angry voice roared.

By your tongues you blaspheme your Maker. Therefore, by your tongues will you strive against each other!

It held out the iron rod and Nimrod felt a blast of pure energy wash past, knocking him down to the rocky floor of the platform. There was one last burst of light, and then the dread thing was gone. Clouds parted, and the sun shone once more. The tower was intact. Its whitewashed glory shone again, though dingy compared to the memory of the angel's golden hue. Fearful of another attack, he hurriedly cast off the golden greaves, vambraces, breastplate, and belt. Picking up his spear, he rushed into the building behind the altar and found Debseda quivering in the far corner. Her arms were wrapped around her face. "Take it away," she sobbed. "Take it away!"

He rushed to her and gathered her into his arms. "It's gone, my love. We still live. The Creator can do nothing but frighten the people with his angel. He has no real power here. We're safe!" He said nothing about the lessening of his spear's power.

Debseda clung to him, molding herself to his strength. He felt her golden garments dig into his flesh and he gently held her back. "Come," he commanded, "we must settle the crowd. They are frightened. Our loyal priests and aides have fled. We must regain control."

She nodded, the fear receding, the need of the moment settling her. Nimrod smiled encouragement. This was the woman for him! She composed her face and dried her tears. There was strength in her that the others lacked. Her blood ran true.

He suddenly realized that only she could bear him the sons he deserved. Mariel had been too weak. She must die, and Ham with her. Only then would both be free to join and start a family that would produce the kings of men for all time. He could place no trust in Adan. The child must die too… although a small part of him trembled at that resolution. He must harden himself, though… a ruler had to be firm.

He took the time to buckle on his iron breastplate and slip his feet into his heavy boots. His bow and quiver were slung, and his helmet settled on his head. It would be a deliberate message to his people—he was ready to fight for them, against the forces of heaven if needed.

Debseda was back on her feet, her cloak about her and her feet now wore her comfortable leather sandals. Hand in hand, they stepped out where the monster had stood, and faced the crowd once more. But something was wrong. All were looking up to them, but their faces were full of anger, not adoration, and a murmur was turning into a roar. Men were shouting up at them, but Nimrod could not hear their words. They sounded almost like children in a fit of temper, with meaningless sounds replacing rational speech. He began to lead Debseda down the steps, but as they descended, the roar grew louder.

Suddenly it struck him. *By your own tongues will you strive against each other.* Nimrod had been so relieved to be alive that the words had not penetrated. He glanced down at Debseda. She looked back at him, understanding in her eyes. "It cursed us," she hissed. "Instead of sending the waters of doom, the Creator is playing games with our speech."

Nimrod paled. He looked again and saw the mob breaking up into small groups, each with men facing outward, as if expecting attack from every quarter. Panic was overtaking them. Would any heed his voice?

"To me!" he shouted, but to his dismay, only a tithe of his legion came pounding up the stairs. They were only two dozen, but with relief he saw that he had the hardest and most ruthless of the warriors around him.

"This is some trick," he said loudly. "The sheep panic. Back to the fortress! We will protect ourselves and let them settle down. Form a circle around the Lady Debseda and protect her with your lives!" The men growled their assent. "Let those who attack us face our full wrath," he continued, seeing fights breaking out before them. "Show no mercy!" He moved to the front, his black spear leading the way, still terrible, even in its diminished wrath.

Men parted in the face of it, but the shouting continued on every side. Out of the corner of his eye, he saw Mizraim, his face pale, shouting imprecations and pointing at him. Though the words were nonsense, there was no mistaking his intentions. Nimrod thought for a moment to bring his bow around and deal with that enemy once and for all, but the crush of the crowd forced him to clear a path with the threat of his spear. "Death to Mizraim and his brood," he shouted. "If you have the chance, don't waste it." His men growled their approval; they had no love for Mizraim.

Rocks began to sail through the air, and two of his men went down, blood flowing from their heads. Mizraim had gathered his family about him and was organizing an attack, using the confusion to offset the advantages of numbers and weapons. Nimrod saw Anam standing with his father, and his blood began to boil. The slick-tongued boy had deceived them all—loyal to his father all along. He grabbed a spear from the man next to him and sent it hurtling towards Anam, but a man was pushed into the way and took it through the chest. Anam stared at Nimrod and the dead man, fear clear on his face.

He began to run. Nimrod was ready to spring into pursuit, but a rough hand pulled him back. "We need to keep moving, sir," urged Esar. Nimrod nodded. He led them off, but not before they had gathered the weapons of the dead. Firuz had one of the extra spears and he cast it with all of his considerable strength at Mizraim, but thanks once more to the crush of the crowd it pierced a lad instead.

Seeing the blood, the crowd went insane. Nimrod had seen animals do the same. He had seen a pack of wolves, goaded by hunger, suddenly turn on their pack leader and pull him down. He gritted his teeth. "We'll have to run for the fortress," he shouted. "Pick up the lady, Firuz," he snapped. Firuz obeyed, handing his spear to another. He was a large, strong man, and Debseda was like a child in his arms. "Now," snapped Nimrod, and they set off at steady trot, spears bristling all around.

As a whole, the crowd would have torn them apart, but individual men flinched and dodged that deadly wall of spears. Nimrod glanced around. "Back through the weaver's alley," he ordered. Its narrow way would protect them and funnel them back towards their front gate. "Erech," he ordered one of the younger men. "Run ahead and prepare the men still at the fortress. They must hold the gate at all costs." The man saluted and sprang ahead, while the group kept a measured pace. They entered the alley just in time. Rocks were beginning to rain down on them, and Nimrod's men tore out shutters and broke chairs to use as shields. Timuz, the giant brother of Firuz, actually tore a door from its hinges and sheltered himself and several of his comrades, who cast their spears into the trailing mob, slowing them down just enough for the small legion to break clear.

Nimrod kept calling out encouragement to his men, keeping a tight fast-moving formation all the way to his gates. Twenty still were alive when they flowed back inside the high walls, and he ordered them up onto the ramparts. Firuz let Debseda down, and she scuttled off into the tower as fast as she could run. Nimrod smiled grimly. Erech had done well. There were two men at each gate with bows, and the crowd withdrew a distance after two went down to their arrows.

"Good work, Erech!" he smiled. "Now bring the youths out. They will fetch weapons and help the wounded. We will need every man." The walls were high, but they stretched a full block in all directions. Even fifty men would have been hard pressed to hold them, but the area around the main gates was built as its own fortress. They must hold that, trust in the strength of the tower, and hope the madness of the mob subsided.

Heth cursed the mountains. He was a man of the plains and knew that gentler lands lay just a few more hours south. He suspected that Shem had sent Shelah after him, and so he had pushed the pace to stay ahead. If Shem had come himself, he would have caught him within a day; even Nimrod couldn't match Noah's son on foot. But the possibility of pursuit—Heth knew that Shelah couldn't stop him, though the effort might destroy their friendship—was nothing compared to the driving necessity of killing Nimrod as quickly as possible.

Hatred burned like a furnace in his heart and drove him forward at reckless speed. It was a killing rage—something Heth had fought for years. In his early years, he had felt its power, but fortunately, something deep in his heart had warned him of the danger of yielding to its control. Even when Nimrod had humiliated him, he had managed to keep it at bay... though he could never explain how. Perhaps that distraction was one reason that Nimrod had been the better man on that fateful day when he had bested him. One thing was certain... Nimrod had no such inhibitions.

Now things were different. In less than two weeks he would be dead and his self control would matter little to the worms of his grave. And his berserker rage might give him an edge when facing his evil cousin. He had seen the terror in Uz' face when he demanded his horses. He hadn't even needed his spear to make the point. Uz had stared into his eyes for just a moment and stuttered at him to take whatever he needed. Rage made him a different man... not better, his conscience reminded him, but certainly a more efficient killer.

A distant part of him mourned for the life he would never lead, for the chance of a family. For the hurt he would cause to people who had made him a friend when they had every reason to hate him. A deeper and sharper part grieved for what might have been with Jael, had she ever lowered herself to consent to marriage. He would miss her... that was the worst part of this journey. Every step that took him closer to Nimrod took him farther from her. But since it would never happen, he was free to dream of what might have been, and a half smile appeared on his face as her face drew into focus in the pathways of his mind.

When his horse stumbled on the steep trail, Heth dismounted and threw the saddle on the other. He would have to stop at the next water and give them both time to rest, but he was making good time, and as soon as they were on the relatively level ground at the foot of these mountains, they would make better time. But at that moment, he wished he had been born with the lithe—and much lighter—body of Shelah.

Jael nodded in the saddle. After a hair-raising ride through the narrow valley, she reckoned that she had gained a few precious hours, and her knowledge of these mountains kept her at a pace that was continuing to ever so slowly cut into Heth's lead. Unfortunately it was doing so at the cost of her mount. Even with her light weight, it had limits, and she needed to watch her pace. It might take days to catch Heth. Every time she thought she had done something clever to cut the distance, she discovered that he had done it too. She had always known that he was her superior in combat, but had harbored the thought that she was his in traversing the wilds. Now she was learning the error of that assumption.

It was disconcerting in one way. This would be a race between equals, and the smallest factor would tilt the board to one or the other. Maybe his possession of two mounts. Maybe something as stupid as a rock in a hoof or a serpent spooking a steed. In any case, she would have to marshal the strength of her horse and exert every last iota of her skill. She had even begun getting off and running alongside her horse for stretches, giving him some small relief. Maybe Heth would be the one to lame a horse. Maybe he would miss the trail or…. *Yes indeed*, she thought. *Maybe lightening will strike nearby and spook his mounts. And maybe he'll just ride into Shinar, kill Nimrod, and die with him. The fool! Why would he give up my love for petty vengeance?*

She frowned at the momentary distraction, and turned a professional eye back to the trail. *Can I make it down here?*

Chapter 63
CHAOS AT SHINAR

5-1-1762

In the aftermath of the terror, confusion and chaos fell like a cloud of doom on Shinar. The once unified city was disintegrating. People scurried from one street to another, desperation driving apart those who could not communicate, to be replaced moments later by a pathetic relief when they found someone else who could understand them. The latter gathered into homes or neighborhoods, wary of anyone who spoke another tongue. Lifelong friends became instant pariahs, and lifelong enemies became close comrades.

It could have been worse. The angel's curse seemed to flow mostly along family lines; for the most part, young children could receive parental comfort and assurance—if there was assurance to be found in a terrified mother or father. Fist fights broke out all over town, and several men were killed. The more intelligent families were frantically packing their goods. Shinar was cursed and anywhere else on earth suddenly looked like paradise. But some—even though they spoke disparate tongues—were united in one purpose. There was no doubt who had brought this doom upon them, and before they left Shinar, they intended to repay that debt.

Nimrod and Debseda must die. So gathering weapons, many of the younger men hurried off towards Nimrod's home with vengeance in their hearts.

Anam sped through the streets, dodging the flotsam of the city. His emotion drove him forward. Anger at his father was uppermost. Mizraim was leaving immediately with all who would come. Anam had begged for help to rescue Graemea, but Mizraim refused. A part of him understood Mizraim's fears and his argument that the whole family must be saved. But wasn't Graemea a part of the family? What of the child she carried? Why couldn't Mizraim see that?

Fear permeated and dulled Anam's anger as he drew nearer to the compound. Nimrod had failed, and failure was something he had not yet faced. If he lashed out in anger, Graemea—wife to a man he now knew as a traitor—could easily be the one to feel the brunt of his wrath. Anam had no doubt that Nimrod would kill a woman. Nor would he hesitate to kill Anam.

He shuddered as he remembered the black wrath on Nimrod's face upon seeing him with Mizraim. He had immediately understood; but for that fellow stumbling into the way, his spear would have killed him. Given another chance, Nimrod would not miss, and then Graemea would be next. But Anam was no fool; he feared the mob more than Nimrod. The people of Shinar would be out for Nimrod's blood, and in their fury, they might raze his home, killing everyone inside.

Including Graemea.

Anam's heart sank as he saw men gathering in the marketplace. It was already happening. He dodged north, avoiding the worst of it, and headed for the north wall of the fortress. Ham's secret entrance would once again be his path inside. Looking around, he could see no one nearby, so he picked out the right holes and skipped lightly up the wall. Within moments he was inside Ham's workshop.

Dim and musty from disuse, the shop seemed to mourn the loss of its owner. Anam cracked the door and looked out into the courtyard. His only hope was that the confusion would have affected Nimrod's coterie too. He hoped that Nimrod had lost most of his Legion to the angel's curse. Fewer men meant fewer guards—with luck, he and Graemea could escape before anyone was aware of their absence.

Dashing across the courtyard, he could hear the sullen rumble of the crowd gathering closer outside the walls. His heart sank when he saw Nimrod and his men already on the ramparts—they had run faster than he expected. Had the order to slay Graemea already been issued? Anam hesitated. Fortunately none of the combatants were looking at him. He prayed that confusion would draw out the assault, keeping Nimrod occupied at the gate for some time. Hurriedly he slipped into the small door at the base of the tower. He hesitated a moment—Ham and Mariel were locked in rooms nearby, but they were more likely to be guarded... but by whom?

Sliding noiselessly up around the circular staircase, he dropped to his knees and looked down the hall. Just as he feared, there was one of the younger men nervously walking up and down, carrying a spear. Anam hesitated. Would Nimrod and Debseda have the nerve to murder their spouses? He shivered. Then his face set hard. The answer was easy. What better way to consummate their adultery than with the death of Ham and Mariel in the chaos?

He wanted to find Graemea, but duty and common sense kept him kneeling there. With Ham, he would have a better chance to rescue Graemea. He was no warrior, and after the curse on the people, he didn't know if his clever tongue would gain him anything. What use were silver words if no one understood them? Ham's strength would be of more use.

Then he froze again. What if Ham and Mariel had also been affected and couldn't understand his words?

As he debated what to do, he thought of all the compromises he had been forced to make over the past seven years. He had slept with Graemea outside of marriage. He had lied, stolen, and tricked nearly everyone he knew. He remembered the words of Madrazi.

> *There is a greater danger than discovery...sin will seek to seduce your heart....You will need another kind of courage to walk the path.... Walk in light, though all around succumb to darkness.*

He had not really done that, and although he had remained faithful to his mission, he felt his heart tainted by all the compromises he had made.

It was time to do something right for a change. Squaring his shoulders, he stood and marched down the hall. The man turned to face him... it was Gatar, Sidon's youngest. Anam plastered a smile on his face and raised his hand in greeting. He knew that speech would only panic the boy, so he waved him over, trying to ignore the spear, still partly pointed at his chest. If the boy had been here during the curse, he would not know that Nimrod had vowed to kill him. So he held a finger to his mouth to enjoin silence. Gatar nodded suspiciously. Anam pointed at Gatar. He pointed outside. Made an angry face and ran the fingers of his right hand over his left to suggest running men. He then pointed down the hall, frantically.

For a moment, Gatar stood dumbfounded. Then it struck him. *Enemies. That way!* Anam pointed to himself and then at the ground. *I'll stay here. You go fight.*

Straightening his shoulders at the opportunity to prove himself to Nimrod, Gatar nodded and trotted down the hall, disappearing around the staircase. Anam ran to the end of the hall, thankful that Gatar was both young and foolish. He stood on his toes and began looking in the peepholes. Ham was in the second cell. Hesitation gone, he drew back the bar.

Ham shielded his eyes for a moment and his mouth dropped open when he saw Anam. "Can you understand me? Oh, please God, let him understand me... please...."

"Quit babbling, boy, and tell me why you're here. An errand for your master?"

Anam leaped into the air. "You can... you can... you can...." He danced over to Ham and hugged him.

Ham drew back, looking at the younger man as if he had lost his mind. Then his face hardened and he seized Anam by the cloak and lifted him off the ground. "What does your master want today?"

The scowling face restored Anam's wits in a flash. "My master is necessity," he replied. "God has struck the city with confusion. No man can understand the words of his neighbor. Nimrod's power is broken... I'm here for Graemea and the child she carries, but I couldn't leave you and the Lady Mariel."

Ham lowered him, but kept a tight grip on Anam's tunic. "Where is the guard?" he rumbled.

"I sent him away. There's a mob coming against this house, and I doubt there will be one brick standing by tomorrow. They'll kill everyone...."

Ham searched his eyes, his craggy face suddenly thoughtful. "I knew that you had come from Shem, but you really have kept faith with him, haven't you? In spite of Graemea, you remain faithful."

Anam knew the time for lies was over. "Of course! I'm sorry about you and Mariel. I tried, but couldn't...."

Ham smiled grimly. "It doesn't matter, my boy. We seem to be friends after all... in spite of your problems with your father."

"Father and I are long reconciled." Anam realized it was pointless to explain the complexities of his relationship with Mizraim now. Ham seemed to grasp that there was more behind the words, but just nodded. "Then we must rescue the women."

It took but a few moments. Mariel was pale and wan. An ineffable sadness was etched in her face, but when she spoke, Anam and Ham could both understand her words. Ham led her gently out behind the younger man. But they stopped short when they heard a noise. Turod running down the hall... his spear up and his face twisted with rage.

Anam never knew what inspired him to do it, but instead of cowering back, he sprang at Turod. The larger man slowed and hesitated, not believing that an unarmed man would charge into a spear. He recovered quickly, a gleam of anticipation in his eyes as his spear came level with Anam's chest. But his hesitation was enough. Anam dove under the spear and threw his body into Turod's legs. They felt like trees, and the larger man stumbled, but did not fall. Anam waited for the downward stroke that would end his life and his dreams. He wondered if Ham would help Graemea and his child.

But the killing stroke never came. He looked up to see Ham's right hand locked on the spear shaft and his left on Turod's wrist. He bore down and Anam heard the crunch of bones as Turod screamed and released the spear. He turned to run, but Ham was faster. His hand caught the scruff of his neck and drove his face into the wall. Blood spurted from a ruined nose, but Turod never knew—he was unconscious. Ham dragged him down to Mariel's cell, flung him in, and locked the door.

He trotted back, a look of grim satisfaction on his face. Anam swallowed. "Thank you."

Ham interrupted him, clapping him on the shoulder. "That was bravely done, little Anam. You're a worthy grandson indeed! Now where's Graemea?"

Anam led the way up the staircase, alert for other rampagers. But none appeared, and he was able to lead the others to his rooms without interference. He knocked on the door. He heard the bar drawn back and led the others in. Graemea ran soundlessly into his arms. He started to speak, but she put her hand over his mouth and shook her head.

Suddenly he understood. She feared that they would be affected by the curse… doomed to separation by their own tongues. He shook his head and smiled, gently removing his hand. "We will always be together, my love," he whispered, and watched the joy and relief flood her face. She burst into tears. "I heard the others… I was so afraid."

Ham interrupted. "We need to leave now!"

Graemea looked around, as if searching for what to carry. "Leave it all, love." Anam pulled her to him. "We start anew, now. I want nothing of this old life. Leave it all."

A hint of humor crept into Graemea's smile. "Even my clothing?"

Anam grinned back, and shrugged. "No time."

Graemea suddenly turned back. "Only one thing!" She was back with them in a flash.

Ham led them back down the hall, the two women following him and Anam bringing up the rear, glancing back to make sure no one was following. They were nearly to the stairway when they heard a noise. Someone was coming up. With no time to hide, Anam stepped up beside Ham, conscious of his lack of ability with the spear they had wrested from Turod. But Ham was not waiting. He stepped back into the hallway and seized the first door, ripping it off its hinges in one great lunge. He raised it high and stepped out into the stairway.

Nimrod's brother, Sabteca, saw them just as Ham hurled the door down the stairway. His mouth opened to shout a warning, but no sound came out. Throwing himself back and sideways, he tried to evade the missile, but it struck him on the right shoulder before caroming down to the base of the tower. Sabteca dropped his spear, his arm numb and useless. He opened his mouth to yell once more, but Ham was already on him. One blow from his great fist dropped the man where he stood. Ham seized the spear and turned back to Anam. "Let's move while we can."

His voice was remarkably calm and it helped Anam shake himself free of his fears. He grabbed the hands of the women and led them down; Ham's great bulk shielded them in front. But no one else met them. Anam assumed that Nimrod's men were busy elsewhere. As they stepped into the courtyard, he could see why. Men were coming over the walls—Nimrod's company was too few to guard it all; they were making their stand at the main gate. The rabble could not contest the black spear, but soon, dozens would fill the courtyard and Nimrod would be cut off from the tower.

Ham led them toward his shop. They were nearly in the shop when they heard a roar behind them. Nimrod had seen them. He had been leading a knot of men back to the tower but had recognized the broad back of his grandfather and the long hair of his wife. But before he could charge, another wave of outsiders flowed between them. Some came running for the fugitives, but Ham pulled everyone inside the shop and slammed the door, dropping the bolt. Immediately, blows began to rain down on it, but Ham had built that door carefully and it would not give way easily.

"We're trapped," cried Anam. He could hear other men outside the wall and beating at the door.

"Not yet," replied Ham. He threw his spear to Anam. "Protect the women!"

He turned to his anvil, pressing down and turning it until they all heard a latch engage. Then he slid it aside. "Ashkenaz hid here," he smiled, "and I decided that it might be handier if it led somewhere. Get in… get in," he chided. Mariel understood first and led Graemea down. "There's a lamp on the shelf, and a striker," called Ham. "Down with you, Anam. Leave the spears. No room." But Anam noticed that Ham seized two daggers from a worktable before he followed the others down.

Anam slid down the ladder, making sure that the women were out of the way. Mariel had the lamp alight and was already starting down the passage. Anam stepped back as Ham descended. The large man strained at a lever at the base of the ladder, and the anvil slid back into place. "Keep going," he called to Mariel, and the four followed the light.

Anam began to count. He had reached two hundred and sixty paces when Graemea stopped in front of him. Mariel called back softly, "How do I open this end?"

Ham pushed by Anam, and then by Graemea. "I'll have to do it," he rumbled softly. "Just stay there and hold the light. Anam put his hands on Graemea's shoulders and looked around her. Ham was climbing another ladder. He reached out near the top and pushed down on yet another hidden lever.

The four were soon standing in a dim room, wooden shutters obscuring the view, but more importantly, keeping them hidden. "We must wait for dark," Ham rumbled. "Too much nonsense out there right now."

Anam interrupted. "Father's leaving tonight."

Ham nodded slowly. "You're right. You must take care of your own. I'll take my sister home."

Anam bit his lip. "I suppose you're family too, my lady, and our lives were in your hands. You could have traded us for your freedom… or for your son."

Mariel shook her head. "Nimrod's word cannot be trusted. You owe me nothing. Your wife's many kindnesses have repaid any debt."

It was then that Graemea began to weep, choking and wailing. Anam caught her to him to stifle the noise. "Hush, my dear. We're safe now. You're finally free of your years of bondage to that woman."

With an obvious effort, Graemea suppressed her sobs, though tears streamed down her face. She pushed Anam away and sank to the ground. "I cannot go with you. I'm cursed forever! I'll never be free of her. Never!"

Mariel sank down and pulled the younger woman to her, warning the men away with a look.

"Why do you say that, Graemea?" she asked kindly. "You have shown a good heart in the midst of great evil."

"I'm not good," wailed Graemea in answer. "I'm forever stained by the evil of my mistress. Nothing can take away the black stain."

"What stain?" Mariel ran her hand down Graemea's hair. "You can tell me. I'm no stranger to evil. I betrayed my own family to aid Nimrod in his wickedness and gave him a son out of my own body. Nothing could be worse than that!"

Graemea shook her head. "You don't understand. The blood of Tabriz haunts my dreams. I'll never be free."

"Tabriz?" Ham rumbled. "She was lost to wild animals in the wilderness. Seven… eight years ago, wasn't it?"

"No!" Graemea turned a tortured face to Ham. "We killed her… sacrificed her to the darkness that fills Nimrod's spear and his heart. And I helped them do it!" She collapsed into Mariel's arms, weeping inconsolably. Ham and Anam traded looks. Then Anam knelt down beside his wife, making sure he did not touch her. She had always responded to his love, so he spoke softly to her.

"Tell us," he commanded in a low voice. "You cannot be rid of the evil unless you confess it openly."

Mariel joined in. "There is great forgiveness with the Almighty, as well as great wrath. I know. Tell us all and let us help you. You cannot bear the burden alone. We love you, Graemea. Let us help you."

A faint hope flared in the tear-filled eyes. "I will do as you say, my lady." She sniffed and shuddered, and then looked at Anam. "I release you from your vows," she said haltingly. "I know you can never love me after you know the truth, but I love you and owe you that much." Anam had the good sense to say nothing, hiding his feelings as best he could and just nodding.

It seemed to lend strength to the young woman, so leaning on Mariel's arm she told of the trip into the valley, the nightmare in the cave, the giving of the spear, and the death of Tabriz. Words rushed from her mouth and her eyes remained fixed on the ground. When she finished, there was silence in the dim room.

Ham broke it first. "Sechiall's spear!" His anger grew and Graemea shrunk from him into Mariel's arms. But his rage was not directed at her. "That foolish cow! How could she have found it? How could she have hid it from the rest of us? Why would she have kept it?" He shook his head and lowered his voice. "No wonder evil has haunted my offspring and filled the hearts of my descendents. Her lust for power has ruined this world and brought this judgment upon us."

Anam wavered. The woman he loved had participated in the ritual murder of a friend. He started to open his mouth to accuse, but a hard look from Mariel shut him up. "Graemea, look at me," she whispered. The girl complied. "You have learned a hard lesson for one so young and innocent. It has been eating your heart all these years, has it not?"

"Yes," sobbed Graemea. "She comes back to me in dreams. I cannot rid myself of the stain!"

"Yes you can."

Mariel stared at Ham. The big man was now kneeling beside Graemea and put a hand on her head. "You have confessed your evil, young one. Do you turn away from it, from Debseda, from Nimrod, and from all their ways? Will you turn to the ways of the Almighty and keep His commandments?"

Graemea nodded. "I hated myself for what I did. I know that I had little choice, but even little is some. I would have died in the place of Tabriz, but there would have been no stain." She seized a handful of dust from the floor and laid it on her head. "I repent before you and before the Creator. Let Him judge me as He will."

Ham lifted her to her feet with an easy tug of his right arm. "If you truly turn to the Creator with a contrite heart, then you will find His mercy is even greater than His ire."

Mariel rose, and embraced Graemea. "So my father—the father of us all—has said many times."

For the first time, hope flared in Graemea's eyes. Then they dimmed again. Anam remained crouched on the floor, looking down at the ground, his shoulders stiff. He was clearly deep in thought. Mariel warned Graemea with a look and held the younger woman to her bosom. Tension built in the room. All eyes were on Anam. Though it was only a few minutes, it seemed like hours before he rose and dusted off his clothes.

"The evil was great," he began softly. Graemea's face fell. But Anam was not done. He looked up at her and for the first time she saw the trail of tears that ran down his cheeks. "But I understand what it is to do evil under the compulsion of Debseda and Nimrod. I know its stain… how my heart has been darkened in spite of all my best intentions. You have offered the truth at great risk and offered to assume punishment by granting me release from my vows. We all know what this would mean." He stared at her and she dropped her head.

"But evil is present in us all. None in this room can claim innocence; we have all violated the commands of the Holy One. We are all in the position of placing our very souls at His mercy and hoping that it exceeds His anger." He sighed and took a step towards Graemea. "Let us both trust in that and go forward together to fight the evil within and without. It is all that we can do."

As he spoke, he took Graemea into his arms. "You have been my light in the middle of eight dark years. I choose to put the night behind me and cling to the star that guided me through it all. My wife you will remain, my love, until death claims us, and my only wish for the life after is that you remain by my side."

He wiped his eyes with his sleeve. "And now we must find our way to Mizraim. He will wait two days at the bitumen pits and then start south.

Ham frowned. "I must take care of my sister and our path lies north."

Anam shook his head. "*Our* path lies north. You need my help. If you can hide here for another night, I'll take Graemea to Father. She's family now. He'll take care of her and I can meet up with him after Mariel is safe. He's going south to the great river beyond the desert."

"I know," replied Ham. "And *we'll* catch up," he nodded. "After I take my sister home, I intend to settle in the south with Mizraim. "We have been planning this for some time. I'm surprised he said nothing to you. And after today, I think I can convince some of the others to join us. I doubt that Cush or Put will want to stay... though some of the younger ones will stick with Nimrod."

Anam remembered the terrible light from the angelic judge and shivered. "Anyone who stays in this city is a fool!"

Chapter 64
FUTURE OF EVIL

5-1-1762

Nimrod sprinted up the stair, chest heaving. Black rage coursed through his veins. Ham and Mariel escaped. Who would have thought that the little worm Anam would have the courage to do it? Had it not been for that last rush of the mob over the wall, he would have had them all at the end of his spear. It had drunk deeply today; more than a dozen had fallen before it. It had taken the fire out of the crowd in the courtyard. They were even now filtering off; his few remaining men were out holding the gate, while he would stay and command the defense of the tower. They would be safe, but they were too few to protect the entire length of the walls. Soon the mob would be laying siege to both gate and tower, and his two companies would have to fight separately. Nimrod could not afford to lose any more men.

He headed up. Debseda would have gone to her secret room at the top of the tower, knowing the crowd would tear her to pieces on sight, matriarch or not. Nimrod couldn't understand the words shouted at them as they defended the wall, but their intent was clear. They wanted his blood and hers. She wouldn't be safe alone in the tower; there were too many seeking her life. Nimrod wrinkled his brow; there was no place on earth she would be safe for the immediate future, and she couldn't defend herself as he could. People would leave Shinar, but not all at once. If anyone found her, she would be dead.

He stopped outside her doors. Fearful, he pushed them open. His relief was immediate. She was reclining on a sofa in the hallway, Celota and Oshetipin standing at either end, knives in their hands. Nimrod rushed forward, but the two servants sprang in front of their mistress. "Easy, my dears," drawled Debseda. "It's just our consort." She laughed, and Nimrod suddenly wondered if she was completely sane at that moment.

"Don't touch me until you're clean," she purred. "You made quite a mess." For the first time, Nimrod noticed the blood smearing his body and still dripping from his spear. "Fetch him hot water and clean clothes, Celota," she ordered, and the woman bowed and left.

"What now?" he asked, amazed at her indifference.

"What now? She repeated, chuckling darkly. "What can one do when Noah's dark god amuses himself by destroying the careful plans of those who threaten him? All one can do is begin again. I've done it before."

Nimrod was astounded. "But…."

"Dear Nimrod. Do you have any idea what it means to live for nine hundred years? We almost triumphed today. Don't you see? If HE had to interfere directly, we were on the verge of victory. HE doesn't usually do that. We'll keep trying, and eventually HE will tire of this game and we'll have all that we want."

"How?" He was practically dancing now. "We've lost nine men out of every ten we had. People are fleeing the tower... the town. They'll scatter from sunrise to sunset."

"You must build a kingdom here in the plain. It will be a solid foundation. Then you can begin the conquest of the rabble, one by one."

"Not we?" He stammered. "But I thought you...."

She smiled and rose. "Dearest, you'll always have my heart, but for a time, I think you will be better off without me. You can blame all of this on me, and dissipate the anger. Soon people will forget, and we'll be back together. Then I'll do my part—I'll give you sons to build an empire. Within a hundred years, we'll rule the most powerful kingdom on the face of the earth!"

"How can you give me sons?" he grated. "Every man in this city wants your blood. Even those that are faithful to me would slip a dagger in your side if they could."

"Then suppose I die," she suggested lightly. She leaned back, baring her breasts. Do you want these to suckle your sons?"

"You know what I want," he sputtered.

Debseda smirked. "I do, my son, I do."

"Oshetipin," she ordered. "Go to my bedroom and bring my best clothes." The girl scurried away.

Debseda leaned forward. "If I died today, I could be born again as whoever you wish. Perhaps a daughter of the gods, come to earth to help you build your kingdom."

"How?" Nimrod quivered. He recognized the tone. She had a plan... a good one by the way she was smiling up at him. But the idea of living without her....

"Have you ever noticed how Celota bears a strong resemblance to me?" She cocked an eyebrow. "Add my best clothes... an unfortunate fall from the top of this tower... the wrath of the mob below tearing at the body...."

Nimrod nodded. "It could work. But when you re-appear, people will know."

Debseda shook her head. "You overestimate their intelligence. If I stay away for years, memory will dim. And I know how to change my appearance. Different hair, different cosmetics, different coloring. A new name... a new lineage. Things will be confused for some time. We will use the chaos created by the angel to help us, not to defeat us."

"You're sure?" Nimrod's heart contracted at the thought of separation... even for a few years.

"Trust me," she said. "You need to start building your kingdom. I'll pop up later... things will work out, my son. After all, we are superior men, even if subject to the whims of Noah's god."

"How shall I know you?"

"Listen for the name," she said, rising and pacing. "Daughter of the great goddess... a harbinger of peace and prosperity... hmm, maybe doves...." She turned and paced for a moment. "Semiramida," she announced. When you hear that name, you will know that our love has survived this chaos."

"How will you escape town?" he asked.

"If the mob believes me dead, it shouldn't be too hard. I'll use Oshetipin to get away, though I'll have to cut that link soon. Don't worry about me. Just make sure there's a throne waiting for me when I return."

Nimrod shook his head and grinned. "You can count on it," he promised.

In spite of her progress, weariness filled Jael. By pushing hard as she left the northern hills, she had managed to pull closer to Heth, but the strain on her steed had proven too great and now she was falling behind. Two hours! She had been that close, and both his mounts were tired. But he still had two and she only had one.

She had two choices; she could rest her mount and hope to regain time further ahead or run it to death and continue the pursuit on foot. Neither offered much hope, and although her emotion screamed to push on now, the horse was not hers and she could not do that to Eber.

Anger threatened to consume her once more, but Madrazi's words from long ago leaped to the front of her mind. *Hate is a thief, and even as you revel in it, the eyes of your heart watch it steal your very soul.* She drew a deep breath and slid down from the grateful horse, slowing her pace to a walk and letting him blow. While they walked, her helplessness made her think of other old memories—her father's prayers and her mother's love.

"I know I have not done as I should these past years," she bowed and prayed, "and for that I have already asked your forgiveness." She stopped and lifted up her hands towards heaven. "But I ask your help now to stop a good man from going needlessly to his death. Please help me save a life… my life… my future."

Tears were running down her face now, the release of dependence on the Almighty was almost too much to bear. He had kept her from destroying herself for eight years, and had brought Heth into her life. Surely He would not let her lose that chance of happiness. "Please," she whispered.

Drying her eyes, she looked down the valley. Running across it, parallel to the hills, was the east road, and a small dot was moving off to the west. Hope flared and she remounted the weary horse and trotted slowly down towards it. As she grew nearer, it grew too, and she her heart leapt when she saw five horses in a string behind a rider. She kicked her heels and spurred forward.

Elishah, Javan's son, was traveling west with goods and horses for his father. All his mounts were strong and healthy, and the black mare looked nearly as good as Eber's.

"Jael!" he exclaimed. "What are you…?"

She raised a hand abruptly. "This is life or death," she said simply. I need a fresh horse. I'll give you this one for the black mare. She's Eber's and better than yours, but I'll make up the difference to Eber. Let her rest a day and she'll be fit to travel."

He opened his mouth, but she raised her hand again. "There's no time. Yes or no?" She swung down from the saddle and began pulling it off. "In the name of the Creator, I beg you do this for me now!"

Elishah shook his head and smiled slowly. "How can I refuse? Take the mare and if Eber is foolish enough to want more in return, my father will repay him when we come back to the Lake."

But Jael already had the blanket and saddle on the mare's back. She dashed back for her weapons and water, not noticing the bemused expression on Elishah's face. But before she turned south, she reined the spirited mare around and smiled warmly at the young man. "You were an answer to prayer," she said, and was gone.

Jael cantered across the plain, her eye once again scanning the ground ahead, looking for signs of Heth's passing. Never again would she doubt God, she swore to herself. Always she would remember this day.

As she rode, she lifted her thanks for His mercy and asked Him to protect the man ahead. A new confidence flowed through her. Heth had two steeds, but both were exhausted and he was a large man. Her heart sang as she studied his tracks. By the end of the day, she had closed back to within a few hours. Barring some terrible accident, she should catch him well north of Shinar. Maybe even loop around and surprise him. She grinned at the idea and began thinking how she would do it.

As she rode, she absorbed the details of the land—hills, streams, wooded swales of pine and acacia, and the slowly-changing landmarks on the horizon. Shem had taught her thus, telling her over and over again that she could never be too familiar with too much territory. The intersection of knowledge and need popped up in strange places and at unexpected times. It was better if you were ready. Content with her progress, she rode far into the evening before stopping at a spring, happy in the knowledge that Heth had dipped his hands into the same water only a short time before.

Chapter 65
ANOTHER MYSTERY

5-14-1762

An early moon dipped to the horizon, and Heth stumbled to his knees. He could smell the river; when dawn came, he would be able to see it. He had run straight south from the northern plains, staying well away from both rivers to avoid the water traffic and the caravans that followed their banks, sticking to the fields and pastures that occupied the land between the rivers. With the line of trees marking the Euphrates curving east to meet him, he knew that Shinar wasn't far away.

He was tired. In six weeks, he had come what should have been a two-month journey—more, counting the added days for avoiding the main routes. He would rest for a day outside of town… he would need his strength. He had no illusions. His only hope of a killing stroke was to offer himself. When the time came, he would have to ignore Nimrod's spear and focus on planting his own in his enemy's vitals. His only advantage was passion—he would die, but so would Nimrod. Yet was that enough? As he neared his goal, doubts had begun to creep in; the pure rage that had sent him on this quest had cooled, distilling into disturbing questions. Every night in the fire, he saw once more the disappointment in Madrazi's face and the shock in Jael's.

He found her intruding into his thoughts and dreams even as he traveled. Her rare smile, her hard frown, the tight lines of determination around her mouth. He was a fool. Had he taken Madrazi's advice years ago, he could have wooed her and perhaps turned her from her bitter hatred. Yet his pride had stood in the way. And now, after her exploits in the wilderness, she was no longer that driven young girl… she was an accomplished woman, far beyond him. He sighed. It was good that he had not married. He would leave no widow or orphans. And yet, what good was a man's life if he couldn't leave a legacy of children to preserve his memory?

He saw a grove of acacia trees ahead, probably signaling one of the small springs that seemed to erupt from the cream limestone where it occasionally broke the ground surface. There was shade and shelter here. Fresh water and food. He could drink, sleep, and drink again, ready for the last leg to Shinar. He would enter the town at night, find a hiding place near the tower and challenge Nimrod when the crowd was thick the next day. In front of his own people, Nimrod would have to answer his call to combat.

Not abandoning his caution, he rode all the way around the spring, looking for any new tracks. A horse had come from the east, but judging from the dust filling the prints, it had been at least a week past. There was no one here; he was safe. He swung off the staggering beast and relaxed, leading both horses between the trees, and spotting the pool that marked the spring.

"It tastes delicious."

Heth whirled at the voice, spear up and ready to throw.

"Do you want to kill me now?"

He dropped it from suddenly nerveless hands. Stunned, he sank to his knees. "Jael," he breathed. "What… how… where…." He stammered, unable to make his tongue form words.

"Been waiting here for days," she lied cheerfully. "But you were always a bit slow."

His mind was racing. He had said good-bye weeks ago, meaning it. Yet here she was. His dream, here… and death just ahead. The pain was too great.

The pre-dawn gray paled as the earth prepared for a new day.

"Why did you follow?" he croaked. "I have this to do… then I'll be out of your life… for good. Nimrod will be no more and you can be happy."

Yellow rays soared through the sky. The sun edged up, throwing its fire across the plain. Shadows stretched out to the west as the rich green of the earth shimmered in the first light of morning.

"What if my happiness depends on keeping you around?" She was sitting, lounging back against a tree, one knee thrown over her other leg—her leggings unable to hide their slim beauty. Her hair was free, framing her face perfectly, bright green eyes against olive skin. White teeth and red lips formed a perfect smile, and the light in her eyes was undimmed. Her lithe body stretched just a bit, as she rested her hands a little behind her shoulders, stretching forward, arching her chest, while studying him from under dark eyelashes.

Heth stared at her through narrowing eyes. She was a vision… surely just a vision. No, she was real… all too real. She stretched again and smiled up at him. His eyes drank in her beauty.

Not knowing what to say or do, the old familiar anger rose in his heart. He tried to regain control, though he felt forces beyond him at work. Something else… something deeper than the rage… was forcing its way to the surface.

"Why are you here?" he blustered.

"I thought that was obvious," she replied coolly. "Why else might an unmarried woman meet a man alone?"

Heth stood again, trembling. He could not believe that she would stoop to toying with his affection simply to divert him. Madrazi must have sent her. His eyes narrowed. He would not be swayed. Crossing his arms, he grated out, "You know what I must do. Why do you seek to turn me aside? Do you want Nimrod to succeed?"

Jael examined him for a moment. She shook her head sadly. Then a hint of the old Jael returned, as anger flashed in her eyes. "What you *must* do," she sneered. "Did God tell you? An angel? Noah? Madrazi?"

Heth bristled, but his rage was turned inward—a heart at war with itself. "I don't need them," he blustered. "I have my own good sense. I know the man. He's a liar, a thief, and a murderer. He must be stopped."

"And God told *you* to take care of it for Him all by yourself?"

He could not stand the cool mocking tone. Nor the morning sun lighting her face, revealing a beauty he had never really seen before. Not like this. Unattainable, yet calling out to him. His heart wanted to love, but that was the very reason he needed to face Nimrod… to keep him from ever harming her again. Part of him wanted to seize and kiss her, but there was another bride waiting in Shinar—a cold grave. He dropped his eyes.

"Don't mock me," he begged. "I'm sorry, my Lady," he started again, then faltered. "Don't you see? I'm doing this for you… so that you can grow up happy, without the threat of him hanging over your head… it's what I can do for you… and I want to…I love…."

He blushed and looked down. He had gone too far. He looked up again, expecting to see haughty disapproval, but instead he saw her shaking her head with a rueful smile. She rose, and he thought he had never seen anything so graceful in his entire life. Each step she took towards him gave strength to the awakening in his heart, and rage was being swallowed up in love. She her hand on his cheek, and he flinched.

She stared up at him for a moment and lowered her eyes. "There are other things that you could do to make me happy, Heth… but to do them you must be alive."

He jerked back. "Don't torment me," he cried. "I would give my life to you if I could, but you're the daughter of Noah, and I'm a son of Canaan. I'm not fit to look at you. But I can fight, and so I will!"

"Can you fight this?" She leaned forward and lifted her lips to his. Their cool fire made his legs go weak, and he sank once more to his knees, stunned.

"You are not Canaan's son," she breathed. "Your heart has never been a part of that family. Leave them forever, now. Become *my* family."

It was then he remembered the words of Madrazi from all those years ago: *I know you hate what is evil, but that is not enough. One day you will discover a greater power in love. When you do, follow that path.*

He stared at her, finally understanding what had eluded him in the cave when she had forgiven Korac. His path lay open before him, and it was no longer the cold, hard road to Shinar. He shook his head, still not able to believe that God could be this good to him.

"Do you know what you are saying? What would your brother say?"

Jael grinned and Heth saw a flash of the old, sardonic smile. "He said that if I could catch you, I could keep you," she laughed, and her smile changed to match the one he could not see on his own face. Its radiance burned away the last of the hatred that had driven him south.

In her love and in the beauty of God's gift, he felt new strength… new purpose. Yes, he would fight Nimrod, but he would do it by affirming life, not embracing death. He would raise strong sons… worthy of their mother. He would build a kingdom in the north that would be a shield for the elders.

He found his strength returning at last as he pulled her to him, and the wonder of her lips drove all else from his mind.

Chapter 66
SISTERS

Anam slid quietly back into the small hollow. Mariel was slumped against the dry sandy floor—too tired to move. He glanced at Ham, who grimaced and shook his head. After an easy hike with Graemea to Mizraim's camp, Anam had hoped the journey north would be as simple. But it had proven a hard two weeks of running, hiding, and avoiding the many small, but belligerent, groups of people filtering out of Shinar.

It was a difficult adjustment. In years past, people were eager to meet and exchange food and news in the wild. That habit was hard to break; courtesy was common because it was the way of the world. But the first two groups they had met outside of town had threatened them with wild-eyed suspicion and unintelligible belligerence. Had it not been for Ham's presence… as well as his size and spear, they might easily have been attacked.

So they began to travel by night. Both men feared that if Mariel was recognized, that her relationship to Nimrod—despite her suffering at his hands—would draw unreasoning violence. She seemed to understand without forcing them to bring back those memories, and she had traveled with a hood pulled well down, leaving her face in deep shadow.

She was eager to get away from Shinar and Nimrod, and kept the pace for a few days. But she had been a prisoner for months, and her stamina was limited. She kept on, uncomplaining, even when it was clear that she was on her last legs. She needed rest… they all needed rest… and Anam had just found the perfect place.

"There's a spring and thicket ahead," he whispered. "It's just what we need. I saw some recent tracks, but didn't hear anyone. We can rest for a few days and regain our strength. There's water and palms—plenty of life. If they have no fruit, I can go hunting tonight."

Ham winked at Anam. "Sounds good. I'm not as young as I used to be; I could use a rest. Let's regather our strength. I think we're far enough from Shinar now."

He lifted the exhausted woman to her feet. "Just a little further, Mariel. Anam's found a place."

She nodded wearily, caught his arm, and started off. The sun was just over the horizon now, bathing the landscape with gold. Up ahead, a green blur shimmered in the early light. The three travelers made their way towards it, drawn by the prospect of clean water, shade, and rest.

Heth broke their embrace. Jael stiffened at the same time. Mutual warning flared in their eyes; there was no need to speak. Something was out there, coming toward them. Heth faded behind a tree with his spear, moving like a great cat. Jael slid the opposite direction, snatching up her bow and quiver. She knelt to present a lower target and set an arrow to string. She glanced over, a smile lighting her face. She couldn't help it. If they had to fight, she was still content. She had found the love of a good man... her man. Shaking her head, she forced her attention back to the southern horizon.

Suddenly Heth stepped out from behind the tree, in plain sight. He waved his spear. She darted out beside him, determined to share his fate. Two men and a woman were struggling towards them. One of the men was small—not much larger than she was, but the other was bigger than Heth. There was something familiar about the woman... her hair, her gait....

A gust of wind seemed to clear the air, and then she saw Anam, leading Mariel and a big man who looked strangely familiar. Heth was running towards them, shouting.

Jael followed, hesitating just a step or two. Her heart felt the pull of the old anger. It welled up out of nowhere and threatened to swamp her happiness. But the sorrow and exhaustion on Mariel's face drove it away. An older, more basic emotion seeped up from the recesses of her memory... Mariel singing her to sleep, Mariel helping her finish her cleaning, Mariel taking the blame for the cattle in the fields. On top of that, the sight of Heth's broad shoulders reminded her of the happiness she had just found. Suddenly she was running forward, wanting nothing more than to share it.

Mariel stopped abruptly when she heard a familiar cry. At first she thought it was a small man from the manner of dress. But her sight cleared and she saw Jael— older, harder, different... she looked dangerous as she ran, but there was serenity in her countenance that seemed out of place with the practiced ease with which she held her bow.

Mariel felt her heart race. All she could remember was the scene on the porch, ending in Jael's bitter denunciation. She shrank instinctively back towards Ham. She knew she deserved her sister's scorn, but she was so tired. Was there no refuge from her past?

Jael stopped short, seeing the reaction and reading it correctly. "Mariel?" she started tentatively. "Is it you?" Her voice broke.

Mariel's face changed from fear to uncertainty. "What's left of me," she answered dully.

Jael slung the bow over one shoulder with a polished ease and strode forward, her hands down and a look of concern on her face. "I don't care what's left or what's not," she asserted boldly. "You're my sister, and always will be."

Mariel's disbelief kept her from answering. Ham prodded her forward. She stumbled towards Jael, the question still in her face. "You can say that, after...."

"We have both sinned against the Creator and against our family," Jael's head came down, but her eyes held her sister's. "But God has shown me great mercy... how can I not do the same? After all, we are made in His image."

Wonder and tears came together into Mariel's eyes. "I thought you despised me," she sobbed. "I thought you all despised me."

Jael reached out a hand and clasped hers. It was warm and strong, and Mariel felt a rush of life enter her heart at its touch. Jael looked down. "I did, Mariel… for a time. Then I found that I despised myself even more. It took a year in the wilderness with Madrazi to help me understand that it was all so wrong…. My family loves me in spite of many sins. We can love you, too."

Hope finally kindled in grey eyes that had been so long without it. "Can… can *you* forgive me?" she asked tentatively.

"With all my heart!" It was Jael's confidence, as much as the words, which caused Mariel to open her arms. As they embraced, Jael winked at Ham. He nodded, pride shining in his dark eyes.

Heth and Anam were not far behind. The big man lifted Anam off the ground in a fierce embrace. "You're alive!" He swung him around and set him down, holding him at arm's length. "Let me see you." He shook his head. "The bravest man I know!"

Anam basked in the sincerity, grinning from ear to ear. Ham strode forward. "Hello, Grandson." Heth gripped his forearm and bowed his head. "Hello, Grandfather. It seems we have much to say to each other. Why don't we find a nice shady spot by the water?"

"You were always smarter than the others," laughed Ham. "Have you any food to go with it?"

"Not much," admitted Heth, "but we saw a herd of wild sheep a few hours back. I'll go get one if you're hungry."

Ham shook his head. "Let's talk first, then sleep. Then we'll see to dinner."

He matched actions to words, leading the women back under the trees, Anam and Heth following behind. Mariel was clutching Jael now, tears blinding her. But it was a much stronger Jael than she remembered who easily supported her weight and led her unerringly to a soft seat by a quiet pool.

"What are you doing here?" asked Ham when they had all drunk deeply. "We have news from Shinar that needs to get to Father and Shem."

Heth frowned with embarrassment, recalling his rage that had vanished like dust in the wind with a few simple words from Jael. He shrugged. Nobody here was perfect—it was a good audience for him to confess his foolishness.

"Korac was sent by Nimrod to kill Madrazi. It became a hunt; Jael protected Madrazi and led Korac and his men halfway to the far western sea. All but Korac died during the hunt, but Jael's skill preserved Madrazi."

Ham, Anam, and Mariel were all staring in amazement at Jael. She was blushing furiously and Heth was filled with pride at their reaction.

"The Creator was not idle," he continued. "Korac began to change. By the time he caught up with the women, he had forsaken his purpose and his service to Nimrod, and he helped them find Shem and the rest of us in a land far away. That was just a few weeks ago… we returned by boat down a long, powerful river to the Black Sea, where we sailed to Arkaz. During the trip Korac told us all he knew of Nimrod's plots. Then Togarmah told us of your imprisonment."

He paused and looked down. "It was too much for me. I was overcome by rage and left the others there, striking south at my best speed. I vowed to kill Nimrod at the cost of my own life. I was on my way to Shinar to fulfill my vow." The others were looking at him, stunned.

He smiled grimly. "Once again, Jael came to the rescue. As fast as I ran, Jael ran faster, and she caught me here this morning. She stopped me, and quite effectively too. My life is now precious in my sight because she will be part of it."

Mariel turned to Jael, wide-eyed. She smiled and let her eyes ask the question. Jael just blushed and nodded. Mariel clapped her hands. "You are happy, little one?"

"More than I can say," she answered. "I've found my man. He was in front of me for years, but I let hate and bitterness blind me. But now he is mine and I'm his. We'll face the future together."

"What will Father say?" asked Mariel. "Does he know?"

"Not yet," admitted Jael, "but I have the blessing of Shem and Madrazi. I'm sure Father will respect that."

Ham interrupted. "I want to hear much more of these stories, particularly how my little sister became such a ruthless warrior." He stared at Jael, who dropped her head.

"Be careful," grinned Heth. "She's perilous when pushed. Why I remember the time…."

Jael planted a solid elbow in his chest, interrupting the story.

"See what I mean," said Heth plaintively.

Ham laughed. It was a full, rich laugh. "You have amazing news, but I think ours beats yours."

"Then tell us," Heth choked, getting his breath back.

Anam interrupted with a nod to Ham. "The Creator has taken care of the problems in Shinar. You no longer need your vengeance." He glanced up. Mariel was already drifting off, but he had the full attention of Heth and Jael.

"Nimrod is dead?" breathed Heth.

"No," replied Anam, "At least, we don't think so. But there are rumors that Debseda was slain in the aftermath."

Ham grunted. "I'll believe that when I see the body." His eyes were dark.

Heth and Jael looked at each other and then back at the others. "Well, don't just sit there!" insisted Heth. "Tell us everything!"

Leaving nothing out, Anam told the story of the angelic visitor, of how men's tongues had been confused, leaving small groups unable to talk to each other. How the last act of cooperation had been a great mob that had besieged Nimrod's tower, braying for the life of Debseda. How the men inside—desperate to escape their wrath—had thrown her down from the very top. How he returned to free Ham and Mariel and take them to safety, along with his own wife. How he had taken Graemea to Mizraim.

"I heard you were married," replied Heth. "Graemea is a good woman. I hope you are happy together."

Anam blushed. "Our child will be born in a few months."

Heth looked at him and shook his head. "You amaze me, Anam. The heart of a lion in the body of a gazelle." He shook his massive head. "So you are going with your father?"

Anam nodded. "I married Graemea. She changed as we fell in love. She is not only a good woman… she is the woman for me, and even now she and my unborn son are heading south with Father. We intend to settle the river that flows up to the south coast of the Great Sea. We will build our own kingdom there, and by the time Nimrod recovers from this disaster, we'll be too far away and too strong for him."

He sighed as he looked up at Heth. "You will always be my great friend, Heth. I've always wanted to be like you…."

Heth shook his head. "You have surpassed me in every way, Anam. And beyond my beloved Jael, I will value nothing as much as your friendship and regard."

"Then you understand… about my love for Graemea?"

"I'll tell the others that they have nothing to fear on your account. Perhaps when things settle down, Jael and I can come to your magic land and spend some pleasant days with you two."

"Three," grinned Anam. "Maybe four or five by the time you get there."

Heth laughed. "You hear that, love. We have some catching up to do."

Jael snorted. "Only after you gather your courage and ask Father for my hand." Heth winced. "And then you'll have to ask Mother. Then Ashiel, Zeriah, Bethsalom, and Sherzala… and Japheth, of course."

Heth threw up his hands and turned to Anam. "It seems safe to say that you will stay well ahead of me."

Anam laughed and glanced at Ham, who nodded imperceptibly. "We have more news. Grandfather will join us there. His gifts will be most appreciated, as will his company."

Ham nodded. "I'm escorting Mariel to safety. Then Anam and I will return south, and catch up with Mizraim and Lud."

Heth shook his head. "I thought we had the best story, but I was wrong again. So the Creator proved His power to mankind once more. It mattered little that He had promised to refrain from another flood. He still destroyed the growing evil."

Ham frowned. "Destroyed? No. Weakened and delayed? Yes. But other than Debseda… if she really is dead… not destroyed. It still lives within each of us… always making us less than we were made to be." He looked at the sleeping Mariel. "And always marring the most beautiful."

Heth nodded. "Yes. Your brother's wife is fond of waxing eloquent about the mystery of lawlessness." He glanced down at the sleeping Mariel. "What will she do?" He held Jael's hand. "We'll care for her, if you want to start back." Jael nodded firmly.

"Thank you," returned the big man. "But Mariel and I have become fast friends. We shared too much to be otherwise. I promised her that I would see her safely home…." He drew in a deep breath and pursed his lips. "I just don't know where 'home' might be for her."

Jael put a hand on his forearm. "Perhaps it would be best to take her to Shem and Madrazi. They healed me… perhaps they could help, even if our parents…." She couldn't finish. She wondered what Noah and Wen-Tehrom would say… would do. How would they react if they saw Mariel and Ham? Especially coming hard on the heels of news that Canaan's son would be a son-in-law.

"Perhaps you're right," admitted Ham. "And there's Ashkenaz…."

"He's smitten with her," laughed Heth. "It was all he could speak of… for months. I didn't understand… until this morning." He glanced slyly over at Jael.

"Where is he now?" asked Ham.

"I left him with Shem and Madrazi. I expect they're back at the mountain."

Ham looked at Anam and shrugged. "Then that's where we need to go."

Chapter 67
FINAL REUNION

5-30-1762

Madrazi sighed as she sat up straight in the saddle, stretched her arms and rolled her shoulders. After walking halfway around the world, she relished the luxury of the back of a horse. The animal turned its head and rolled its eye at her. "Better your legs than mine," she growled implacably.

She continued to stretch her tired muscles and look around. They were now well out onto the plain; the foothills receded into the haze behind them and the mountains dominated the horizon to the east, across the green valley of the Tigris River.

"Have you no mercy for that poor beast?" teased Shem.

"Not a bit! Every time some little bit starts seeping into my heart, my feet interrupt and tell my feelings to try carrying my weight for two years! I'm afraid the poor dear is condemned to haul me down the river and over the plain and all the way back home. She'll be worn out then, and I still won't feel sorry for her."

Shem laughed out loud. Together, they looked south out over the endless plain. Shem sighed and then frowned. "I hope Jael was faster."

"If I had been chasing you, I would have been."

Shem smiled in spite of himself. He was about to respond when he suddenly snapped around, looking south. A couple of minutes later, Madrazi saw a faint smudge of dust in the distance.

"Let's stop and water the horses," suggested Shem, a little too casually.

He signaled a stop. The men all dismounted and handed Madrazi their reins. They had seen the dust too. "Dismount and keep them still," ordered Shem. She obeyed; he looked worried and she knew better than to add to it. He waved Jobaath over to a low swale, a few dozen cubits off to their right. He would be a nasty surprise if someone tried to attack the main party. Madrazi snorted to herself as she held the horses still. Who would be foolish enough to attack this group?

After Heth and Jael had left them at Arkaz, Shem had led the rest of the party to the Lake of the Islands at a more sedate pace. There they had received news of the race—Heth with Uz' two horses and Jael with Eber's finest. But the sudden appearance of Shem and the boys (that everyone presumed lost in the uninhabitable north), and Madrazi (who everyone had given up for dead long ago) brought the scattered villages together in a great celebration.

Eber held the feast, and Madrazi had been touched at the welcoming smiles and hearty congratulations. Little children had wanted to touch her—one of the mysterious elders who could not die. The people had mourned her after Togarmah had carried the news of her flight over the sea. Few had been optimistic that two mere women could survive Korac and his killers, even if they managed to survive the restless sea. Madrazi made sure that the credit was given to Jael, who had never been well received by the people of the lake after she had run away from home.

To their joy, they also had learned that their servants had not been idle. After Korac's men had left the farm, the people came down from the hills and began to repair the damage. The dead had been buried, the house restored, the barn rebuilt, and the fields plowed, sown, and reaped each season. Almost all of them stayed on, vowing to hold the farm ready for the return of their master. Arpachshad and Asshur had related their faithful work. "They refused to give up on either of you, and it seems they were wiser than the rest of us," he had said with a rueful face.

But not all the news was good. They learned of the solemn burials of Enoch, Zeb, and the women who had been inside the house. "They all rest together now in a place of honor," said Asshur. "The women have planted flowers around the graves, and their courage has been told from one end of the wilds to the other."

Despite the weight of those losses, their time at the lake had been joyful, with many happy reunions. The exception was Korac. It had taken all of Shem's authority to keep the men from attacking him on sight. Zeb and Enoch had been popular— good friends of many, and while the men obeyed Shem, it was clear that most would have stabbed Korac in his sleep, given the chance. Even Madrazi's best efforts could only blunt the animosity. But he had proven phlegmatic. "I deserve far worse," he had said lightly. "I don't blame them for their anger; I would feel the same."

But she knew otherwise; no normal person could just shrug off so much animosity. Perhaps that was why he had left unexpectedly the next day with Ashkenaz. Their mission was as curious as the two former enemies going together. "Just a little job that needs to be done," assured Ashkenaz. "Korac will help me take care of any problems on the way. We'll meet up with you somewhere along the upper reaches of the Tigris." That was all she could get from him, and the two had galloped away on two of Shem's best horses.

After the feast, Shem had told Madrazi that he was going south, first to find Heth and Jael, and then to see what he could do for Ham and Mariel. He would take Shelah and Jobaath. At that, her eyes flared. She crossed her arms, daring him to disagree with her when she had told him flatly, "You're not leaving me again. I suffered more in the wilderness from the fear of losing you than I did from any discomfort. I can't live through that again… not now, anyway."

Surprisingly, Shem had smiled. "I hoped you would come," he had said. "You weren't the only one who regretted that separation, but I didn't want to push you into another trek unless you wanted to go."

"Try and keep me away," she had replied. Shem had pulled her to him and she had clung to him for some time, savoring the feel of his hard body against hers. They had left that very afternoon, and though Shem did not set a hard pace, they covered the ground quickly. He knew the easiest routes, and they had left the hills behind, following unknowingly in the footsteps of Heth and Jael, hoping to meet them out here on the plains.

Now someone was coming. Was it Heth? Jael? Both? Or maybe some of Nimrod's men patrolling their northern frontier? Or was it traders that could give them news? Madrazi held the horses steady and impatiently watched the men.

Shelah remained a short distance south of the horses, bow out, ready to take shelter behind a small hill. But Shem was not content to let the strangers come to them. He began running towards them, an arrow set to his bow. Since she couldn't do anything else, Madrazi gave herself over to the pure pleasure of watching him run; his fluid motion made all other men look awkward and stiff.

She worried but was not afraid; Shem knew what he was doing and could flee just as quickly if needed, with Shelah to cover him. Engaged in the scene before her, she barely dodged a hoof from an unruly horse. She turned back to them. They smelled water and were not yet tired. They couldn't be thirsty—they had only been riding for an hour this morning—but the animals seemed inclined to be fractious. A few judicious tugs on the reins and curt words to the restless ones showed the rest who was in control, so they settled down to wait, swishing their tails at flies and waiting the will of their masters.

As Madrazi looked back south, a cool breeze blew out of the northeast, stirring dust devils that sprang up southwest of Jobaath's position and careened across the sand, obscuring sight of Shem. She could only see Shelah, ready to spring out to help his grandfather or to cover his retreat. Her impatience mounted. She was invisible among the horses. He had done it on purpose, of course. Someone would have to get close just to see her, and if she needed to flee, all she had to do was jump on a horse and ride away. As if she would!

Suddenly Jobaath was at her side, relieving her of the reins. "He's waving us forward, my lady," he explained. "Keep his horse with you." He sprang up, and handed her the reins to Shem's mount as soon as she scrambled back into the saddle. Trotting down to Shelah, they paused for a moment while he smoothly swung up on his horse. Madrazi kicked her horse into a canter and the men, grumbling under their breath, galloped to catch up.

The wind settled and the dust devils died. In the distance she could now see a party approaching. Shem and five others—two mounted. As she drew closer, she saw the riders were women, but it was the men who caught her eye. One—thickly muscled and lacking a beard was surely Heth, and the man beside him was even bigger. Who…?

It took her memory a moment to engage, but when it did, she gave a cry and kicked her horse, galloping past the others.

"Ham," she cried wildly, waving and shouting. "Ham!"

The wind brought tears to her eyes and blurred her vision. Within moments she had pulled her horse up hard and leapt down, running to the big man. She wanted to laugh, to cry, to shout, and sing, but she pulled up short when she saw his features. She barely kept the shock from her face. In just a few decades, he had aged a century. She noticed the few gray strands among his black curls and lines around his eyes and mouth. For a moment she thought she was seeing Lamech back from the grave.

So many years ago! Pictures of the town named for him flashed across her memory.

But those were fleeting impressions; in a moment she was in his arms. He lifted her off her feet and swung her around… at least he had lost none of his strength.

As he put her down, she saw Heth and Jael—his arm draped across her shoulder—facing the stern gaze of Shem. But as she caught her breath and cleared her eyes, she saw another surprise. In the background stood Anam, smiling broadly, and Mariel, looking at the ground. Ham smiled at her and stepped back. Questions rushed through her mind but seemed to find no ready outlet; she just stood and stared, mouth open, but no sound coming out.

Shem embraced his brother. "You always did leave her speechless," he chuckled, and Madrazi flashed him a dirty look. But his prod served its purpose; she was back on balance. As she looked around once more, her heart sensed the greatest need; she stepped around the others to Mariel and took her in her arms. Echoes of pain and shame filled her gray eyes, and Madrazi winced at all she saw there. But she kept her voice low and steady all the same. "Welcome back, Mariel," she said quietly. "I'm so very glad to see you."

"Are you?" she asked softly. "I thought you would hate me. I thought everyone would, but Jael has been wonderful."

"We were all disappointed when you left, and you hurt Mother and Father terribly." Madrazi kept her voice even. Mariel was looking down again, nodding. "I know," she whispered. "I was such a fool!" She looked up again. "I'm so afraid, Madrazi. Please help me."

"I will, my dear," the older woman assured her. "We're all fools… some of us more than others… but God remains gracious to those who repent and return to Him. And if God can love you, so can your family."

Mariel's eyes showed a shadow of hope. "Do you think that Mother and Father…" she began weeping softly.

"Maybe later," Madrazi replied. "Give them some time. They lost more than you can know."

"I understand now," Mariel whispered hesitantly. "I lost everything but my soul, and without Ham, I would have lost that too." She clung to Madrazi, weeping anew. "They even took my son from me. He's such a lovely boy, but for all I know, he's dead." Her eyes hardened for a moment. "I was going to kill Nimrod, but Ham stopped me. I wanted to so badly… I would have lost it all…"

"God has restored you to us," interrupted Madrazi, crushing the horror at the girl's words. "If He wishes to restore your son, is it too great a task for His arm?" She led the woman back to the others. Shelah leapt down and Ham helped her onto his horse.

Everyone began to talk at once. Shem interrupted with an upraised hand. "We left a good spring an hour back," he said. "Let's pitch camp for the day and let these women start talking. I suspect," he said smugly, "that the ladies will talk the sun down, even at this hour."

"Not just the ladies," rumbled Ham. "Anam and I have much to say too. Lead on!"

Mariel and Jael climbed back on their horses. Shem led off on foot, back along the river to their previous camp. It took two hours with Shem and Shelah on foot, but before midday, the horses were standing content in the shade, picking at the grass they had enjoyed the night before, while the men unpacked. The site was a small pond, a few hundred paces west of the river and shaded on the north side by a line of trees. Green grass grew thickly around the water, and the horses were happy to be tethered there after their roll.

Shem soon had a small fire going, and Shelah lashed together three spears for a tripod. Madrazi waved him away. "Heat some water," she instructed Jael. After we've cleaned up, we can start on a meal." She led Mariel to a seat in the shade. "Sit here, my dear, and let us help you. I assume you two…." She looked at both the women.

"Aye, aye, Captain," drawled Jael, standing up straight. Madrazi marveled at the light tone and peaceful face.

Jael grinned as if reading her thoughts. "She knows our tale and I've heard part of hers." She glanced innocently at Madrazi. "Did you know she's coming to live with you for a while?" she asked casually.

Madrazi shook her head. "Where will we put everyone?" she sighed. "After all, I was counting on Heth staying with us for a while too."

Jael stuck out her tongue and laughed. "We have our own plans, thank you!"

"I'm sure you do," murmured Madrazi, watching Jael blush.

"A year together in caves and I can't hide anything from you anymore," she complained.

Madrazi turned to Mariel. "You are welcome in my home," she said gently. "Forgive your sister; her manners have yet to be perfected."

Mariel nodded. "What about Mother and Father?" She asked, looking at the ground.

"You will need to talk to them eventually," Madrazi replied. "But give it some time. Let them hear your story from my lips first, and then go to them."

"I will," Mariel was close to tears again. "I know some of what they felt. God gave me that pain of loss and disappointment—maybe so I could understand."

Madrazi nodded. "Come here. Let's clean you up and brush your hair." Jael poured warm water on a clean rag and began to wash her sister's face while Madrazi worked on her hair.

"When will you have a meal ready?" Shem asked, walking over. Then, seeing what the women were doing, he crouched down behind them with a smile. "That's a big improvement, little sister. You look much better." His warmth brought a tentative smile to Mariel's face. Madrazi turned and winked her approval.

"Go along and talk with the men. We'll cook after we've cleaned up a little," she said.

Shem was about to say something else, but a shout from Heth, brought him running back to the men. Jael stiffened and stood, shading her eyes to the south. "There are horses coming… only a few… I'll get my bow."

Madrazi put a hand on her arm. "I doubt if even you can help anyone foolish enough to attack Shem, Shelah, Ham, and Heth. Don't you?"

Jael nodded sheepishly and put her bow back down. "Sorry," she said to Mariel. "I can't help myself." She looked back south and then at her sister, shuffling her feet as she tried not to stare after the men. Madrazi sighed. "I suppose we can at least go and watch the fun. The water won't burn."

As the three women walked over behind the men, they saw a plume of dust in the distance. It slowly resolved into two horses on the horizon, moving towards them at a canter. But the wind swirled again and dust devils obscured the river bank. By the time they had blown past, the horses were much closer.

"That's Korac and Ash!" exclaimed Heth. "And Korac's carrying a bundle on the front of his saddle. Something wrapped in blankets."

Soon the two men reined up and Korac slid down as Ashkenaz held his reins. Madrazi saw a head of curly light hair under the blanket and felt Mariel freeze beside her. Korac strode up to her and bowed his head. "Your son, my lady," was all he said, and he unwrapped the blankets to reveal a young boy, who was immediately enfolded by Mariel. She sank to the ground. The boy woke up and wrapped himself around her.

"My son," she cried. "Oh thank you, thank you." She began sobbing out his name, clinging to him as only a mother can, and thanking Korac over and over.

He looked around, embarrassed. "Thank Ashkenaz," he mumbled. "It was his idea to rescue the child. I only helped him look."

Ashkenaz snorted, looking at Korac with none of his former animosity. "He led me to an outpost a few days ride south of here. Nimrod kept some of his herds up by that stream that flows down from the mountains into the river. It was full of angry men… a full half dozen. While I sat and waited outside the camp, he went in alone that night and took the boy out from under three guards without their ever knowing he was there. It was a job that you would have been proud of, Uncle Shem."

Ham stepped forward and gripped Korac's arm. "It seems that the years in the wild north have done good things for you, my boy."

"Yes sir," Korac replied humbly. "I had some good advice." He looked up at Madrazi. Ham followed his eyes. "Yes, you certainly did," he murmured. Madrazi blushed. "God seems to work best when the odds are most hopeless," she said, and her eyes burned back into Ham's. He lowered his eyes and coughed. "Of course," he replied.

Ashkenaz handed the reins of their horses to Anam. In a moment he was kneeling beside Mariel, enfolding mother and son with his strong arms. "He's safe, Mariel. We're all safe. We can start anew, the three of us, if you'll have it."

Mariel's lip trembled. "Do you really mean it? The three of us?"

Ashkenaz smiled. "Absolutely."

Suddenly she shook her head and uncontrolled tears began to flow. Madrazi stepped forward and pushed Ashkenaz away. Jael did the same with the other men. Catching on, the others backed away, leaving the women alone with the child. Madrazi and Jael knelt beside their sister and held her as she sobbed into her son's hair. All the grief of the past years seemed to come out as her body shook.

The boy looked up. "Are you sad, momma?" he asked softly.

She shook her head. "No," she lied. "I'm just so happy to see you back. I missed you so much!"

"I missed you too, momma," he replied gravely. "Father's friends were mean. I didn't like them!"

"You'll never see them again, my son." Mariel hugged him to her again. "We'll stay together now."

Madrazi gently pulled the boy away. "I'm your aunt, Adan," she said gently, "and I need to talk to your mother for a moment. Can you say hello to Uncle Ham and meet your Uncle Shem?" The boy nodded gravely. Giving Mariel one more hug, he ran over to the men. Madrazi looked down.

"Ashkenaz?" she asked.

Mariel nodded, still looking down. "Look at me, dear," ordered Madrazi. "The time for shame is past. You have repented for your sins. You have been punished every day for the past eight years. You were lost and we have found you once more. It is time to put the past aside and rejoice in today and in the promise of tomorrow. Your days in the darkness are over. Do you understand?" A light seemed to well up around Madrazi as she spoke and it spread to cover Mariel.

Mariel looked up, a sheen of tears welling up. "I want to, Madrazi," she wailed, "but how can I give myself to Ashkenaz if I belong to Nimrod? Is it right?"

"I am not the law, Mariel," replied Madrazi. "If you truly wish to do right, then you should ask Father. Ashkenaz loves you very much. He will wait. But if Nimrod was unfaithful to you from the beginning, and has joined himself to another, then Father may well say that he is dead to you now. I'm glad that you are thinking about pleasing God before yourself. You have truly learned from your sin. Not everyone is so fortunate."

"Fortunate!" hissed Jael. "Do you know what her life has been like?"

Madrazi stared at Jael with narrowing eyes. "Don't let sentiment cloud good sense, Jael. 'Fortunate' is what I said and meant. We are made for God, not for ourselves. Anything that turns us to Him is a blessing. These few short years on Earth are nothing compared to the unending days of the true Eden. Don't measure the worth of your soul by what fills your years here."

Jael subsided. Mariel sighed. "She's right, Jael. I wouldn't wish these years on my worst enemy, yet God protected me from much evil. I never lost the truth of Father's teaching, even if I ignored it at times. And in the midst of my enemies, God gave me a brother I had never known. It was bad enough with Ham by my side. It would have been unbearable without him." She choked on her tears. "And out of the worst of it all, I gained a son. He carries Nimrod's blood, but he has Noah's heart."

She dashed away her tears and looked intently into Jael's eyes. "Before… at home… I proved my heart wicked in the midst of good. In Shinar, God proved good in the midst of evil. I understand my place in this world in ways I never would have known before. I am content. Share that with me."

That evening, they sat around a larger fire, still trading stories and jests. Jael sat beside Madrazi and gestured at the fire. "It's like all those nights alone, staring at the fire and wondering if we would be alive for the next night," she whispered, but Madrazi didn't answer.

Jael looked closely and saw that Madrazi's green eyes were lit with a curious light. Though she had only seen it this close a few times, she recognized it immediately. Madrazi was somewhere else, transported through the flickering flames to the world beyond sight. Jael smiled and shook her head. She would never understand, but she felt privileged to see... to feel the closeness of that touch radiating out from the older woman.

The others, distracted, hadn't yet noticed, until Shem glanced over and saw his wife's rigid form. He casually rose and came to sit on the other side of her, a wry smile softening his face. He traded glances with Jael, another bond that they shared was this amazing woman.

The others, still not seeing, kept talking. Anam was telling the men about Graemea and the songs they had made together. "Do you remember when we came to your shop for a flute, Grandfather?"

Ham nodded. "For more than a flute," he laughed. "But you were always a clever child, Anam. Do you still have it?"

"Graemea carries it with her. It's the only thing we took from Shinar, and we will treasure it all our lives."

"A song, Anam," cried Ashkenaz. "Sing us one that you wrote about your beautiful bride in the land to the south." The others echoed the call and Anam stood and sang, his clear voice unveiling a glimpse of his dreams, carrying them all away to the special places each treasured in their hearts.

Ham stood up as soon as he had finished—a look of puzzlement in his face. "I have a riddle for you all," he said. "The power of the angel confused men's tongues at Shinar, but we can all understand each other. Why? The others we met could not understand us, nor could Anam understand them."

Everyone stared at each other. Anam nodded. "It's true. I could understand none but my family after that hour, but I hear every word that all of you say. The others quickly grasped the import of Ham's question. They had not noticed before because all was as it had been for years. Looking around, they realized that every clan was represented, but still they could speak together. Eyes widened and mouths were stopped.

It was time. Shem shook Madrazi. "Why were we spared the judgment, my love?"

Startled, she blinked and looked up at him. She saw his eyes narrow against the residue of power in hers. She barely saw the others; the vision was strong upon her and her mind was caught between two worlds. But the words rolled off her tongue without thought.

"The judgment is real and lies on all mankind. But in His mercy, the Creator has granted this small band of friends one last day together... the last gathering of the clans of Noah in friendship and peace. The elders, except for Debseda, will retain knowledge of the language of the old world and they will also be able to speak and understand the tongues of their children and to teach them to others. The old tongue will be preserved in the line of Shelah and his descendents."

She stood and spread her arms. "As the years pass, the languages of Shinar will change and grow, creating an even greater barrier between the tribes of men. But all communication will not be lost. Though each man will have his native language, all are still made in God's image. Therefore the thoughts behind the words will remain the same for all, even if the sounds that convey them are not. Therefore any man can learn the words of another—it may be difficult, but it can be done."

Sadness came upon her. "In the morning, we will no longer enjoy this grace. Only Shem, Ham, and I will understand all that is said. I don't know who will be separated." She looked warily at Heth and Jael. Jael shrugged. "I too am a daughter of Noah. And if I cannot speak the words of Heth, I will learn. We belong together… we both know that now."

Madrazi looked at Ham. "Anam and I are going south," he sighed. "I'll send word when I can."

She nodded. "Ham," she said slowly, "you will be able to understand the tongues of all your sons. Help them to order themselves as they should. Teach them the stories of Adam, Enoch, and Noah, and all the other fathers. Tell them of the great flood and teach them to understand their Maker. Remind them of the evil at Shinar and encourage them to establish just laws and right worship."

She turned to the others. "Shelah," she said. "Your friendship with these men can continue, but it will be difficult to maintain. Your grandfather and I will help you learn the new tongues of Ashkenaz, Anam, Heth, and Jobaath, so that you will able to speak together as before. Remind your children that this burden was brought upon all by Nimrod and Debseda. Oppose them and their true children all of your days."

Heth stood and walked over to Shelah. "We do not need speech to know we are brothers," he said and embraced his friend. "We will overcome this…."

He choked as Shelah returned the embrace and replied. "I know, my friend. One day we will return to the great river north of the Qazvin Sea and our feet will walk those lands on the other side… together."

Heth nodded and gripped Shelah's arms. "I swear it."

Madrazi turned to Korac. "What of you, son of Gomer? Will you seek out your family in the western lands?"

Korac shook his head. "There is much to atone for," he said. "I know that I'm on the right side of the struggle now, even if I don't know how to fight." He glanced at Ashkenaz. "There are many debts…."

"You have repaid me many times over," interrupted Ashkenaz, gripping his arms. "Mariel's joy erases all the bad memories of Shinar."

"There are others," murmured Korac, looking at Madrazi. "I only know how to do only a few things well and I'm too old to change." He drew himself up and looked at Heth and Jael. "Your kingdom will protect the elders, will it not?"

Heth tightened his mouth. "It will. I swear it."

"Then accept me into your service."

Heth looked as stunned as the rest of the men, but Jael stared at him boldly. "And if you don't understand our words tomorrow?

"It is the Creator that gives us the power to speak and to hear," replied Korac. "Let the decision be His." He looked up to see Madrazi's smile. She knew, he saw, but shook her head slightly, telling him to wait until tomorrow.

Jael slid over to Heth and ran her hands up his arm. Smiling disarmingly up at him, she asked, "What say you, my lord?"

Heth crossed his arms and frowned down on her. "I say that I'll need every strong man I can find to rein in my queen!"

Turning to Korac, he shook his head and frowned, "And you're the only man I know who can outpace her in the wild."

Jael pulled herself close against Heth, her eyes alight with a fiery humor. "I'll miss you around the fire, my dear… since you'll obviously be on your knees all night, praying for your new general!"

Heth tried to frown, but failed. "I knew you were trouble the first time we met!"

Jael had the grace to blush, but the fierce light never left her eyes. "At least you know I'm a woman, now!"

Heth laughed long and loud before bending to silence her by the only effective means that he knew, and found himself equally uncaring for further speech.

EPILOGUE

6/10/2162

Lydia woke in a soft bed, warm and refreshed. For a moment, bad dreams lay at the edge of consciousness, but they fled before the need to rise and serve the Old One. She started to rise, but the weakness took her.

Gasping, it all came back. The Old One was dead and the nightmares were reality. But she felt much different. Her first sensation was of being clean. She reached up and brushed her hair from her face. Even that was clean and had been brushed free of dirt and tangles. A woman was dozing in a chair beside the bed. "What is this place?" Lydia wondered out loud.

The woman woke and shook herself. "You are the honored guest of the Queen of the Sea Peoples," she replied. "There is much to say and to hear, but for now, simply know that you are safe and under the protection of the King and the Lord Isaac. My name is Rohana, and I am the Queen's healer. You are my charge until I pronounce you fit to travel."

Her first thought was that the woman seemed young for such a position, but there was a gleam of intelligence in her eyes. A spark of humor too.

"Although you will receive the proper apologies from the King himself, let me assure you that we are all shamed by the treatment that you received during your captivity." Real anger was in her eyes. "I have personally requested that the Queen appoint Abigath to my staff. You may rest assured that she will spend the remainder of her days in suitably unpleasant labor!"

Lydia shrugged. For some reason, she no longer cared… which was odd. A few days ago she would gladly have killed the woman, had the opportunity presented itself. "And the others she mistreated?"

"A better woman has been given her position," Rohana replied soothingly. "The people who work in the King's kitchen will be proud servants of our lord, not terrorized slaves. After I explained at some length the many different ways that food can be poisoned, I found the King quite receptive to my recommendations."

She laughed dryly. Then she shook her head. "The question, my dear, is what we are going to do with you and your friend. The Phicol wants him to stay—in Asak's old command, if you can believe that—but having seen how he feels, I think that will be up to you."

"I don't think I could stay here," she replied. "It would be too much…."

The healer patted her head. "I understand, my dear." Then her face grew serious. "Most of us are not like Abigath and Asak. I hope that you will give us a chance to prove it. The King was livid when he learned the whole story. His father made a treaty of friendship with the Lord Abraham many years ago, and he feels honor bound to extend its provisions to the son, the Lord Isaac. Since you were sent to the Lord Abraham, your treatment and the destruction of his property is a great stain on his throne, and beyond that, he genuinely likes the Lord Isaac. Asak died that morning—the death of a rebellious slave. Likewise, the officers under his command. Yet the Lord Isaac has made it clear that the extent of reparations will depend on you."

Rohana laughed. "You could demand to be made a princess of the land, and King Abimelech would not blink an eye at adopting you and giving you a third of his wealth!"

Lydia began to weep softly. "I don't know who I am anymore. I began life as a daughter of Nineveh. That was stripped from me, and I became a servant of the Old One. Then I was the steward of her house, and after that, a messenger. For a year, I have been a slave of your people. I don't know how many more changes I can endure."

"Peace, young lady," soothed the healer. "Your body has been broken and your mind and heart were injured too. You must not think of such things until we have a chance to cure your hurts. Things will appear in a different light when you are well. Sleep now and let me do my work."

Over the following days, the healer was as good as her word. Life and strength returned, and although the dark shadows remained in her heart, they were at least relegated to the corners. Lydia was a strong woman, and with the proper care and food, she recovered quickly, much to Rohana's delight.

Despite the healer's admonition, Lydia found herself thinking long and hard about her future, primarily mourning the loss of Lud. Now that she could no longer have him, she found herself hopelessly wanting nothing else, remembering his courage and sacrifice. Love, like everything else in her life, had come at the wrong time and in the wrong place.

The day arrived when she was called into the presence of the king and the Lord Isaac. She knew she was a different woman on the outside. She had gained back the flesh that had been starved from her. The bruises had faded to dim marks, and her skin had regained its healthy olive glow. Her dark hair once again shone, and she had been given the finest clothes she had seen since her childhood in Nineveh. Oil, perfume, and expensive cosmetics—she suspected that they were the Queen's—completed her appearance.

She looked like a princess and knew she could carry off the charade but felt miserably out of place. The one thing she wanted now was a simple shepherd of the hills, and that was forever beyond her reach. When she remembered her years of coolness towards him, the pain of that guilt was even worse than her desire to be his. It would never be. She must find a new life, far away. Perhaps Egypt....

But there was one last task to perform... one last role. The nobles of the sea peoples would be gathered to hear the resolution of her case, but as she remembered and thought in the warm afternoons, she realized that neither she nor the King were on trial today. Her life had been given to the Old One, and the casual disbelief in even the existence of the elders raised her ire more than even her poor treatment. She would defend the truth today... that and the honor of the elders. In doing so, she would be piercing the hearts of these people in a way that nothing else could.

So when she strode confidently into the throne room, no inner turmoil showed. Walking slowly, she made sure to catch the eyes of every face; her own blue eyes as icy cold and hard as the stone beneath her feet. Not one of the assembled nobles could hold her gaze.

The King was sitting between the Queen and the Lord Isaac. The Phicol stood behind the throne and Lud was at his side. But she had expected his presence, and didn't falter at the sight of his rugged face, though her heart beat fast. She hardened herself to it and turned again to face the nobility of Philistia, watching their eyes drop again. Then she took the final few steps toward the throne, sweeping into the perfect bow she had learned in Nineveh years ago. There was silence; she let it linger. She would not be rushed into hasty words.

The King saw, nodding slightly before standing. "We are relieved that our healer could attend to your hurts, and happy that you come before us, now restored." He faltered for a moment, and she immediately understood. No healer could undo the vicious rape at the hands of Asak, and the King was wise enough to know it.

"We are faced with at least two problems," he continued seriously. "Both cut at the honor of my throne. Because insult has been committed against the Lord Isaac and his father, he will sit in judgment with me, both as my covenant partner and as my friend."

She nodded slightly, still not speaking, her face set like flint. A murmur of dismay filled the room behind her.

Abimelech's lip twisted in a wry smile. "I know not your story, young one, but I do know that you are noble. You betray it at every turn."

Still she kept her silence. She heard the discomfort of the others behind her, but kept her lips tightly together and her eyes on the King.

Abimelech sighed, acknowledging her right to silence. "Two crimes were committed by men under my command. The first was in laying hands on your person, compounded by nearly a year of abuse in my own house. That is a matter of great shame for me and my people, all the way down to the keeper of my kitchen. Therefore, as King, I have taken steps to secure justice. General Asak was executed for his actions. Upon further investigation, the woman Abigath was found guilty of many offenses. She has received seventy-seven lashes. Her thumbs have been cut off and she has been given over into slavery to the Lady Rohana for the remainder of her life. The Steward of my house has been relieved of his position and now sits at an oar in one of my galleys. Others bearing responsibility have received fitting punishments, measured to their actions in this heinous affair. Three of Asak's officers were executed, as they were deemed to have knowledge of his crimes. The other two who were not present on that patrol were reduced to the ranks." He sighed, and glanced sideways at Isaac.

"The second problem was the destruction of Lord Abraham's valuable property—from your account, an heirloom beyond price. That was also an affront against your honor, my lady, and so in both matters you hold the sword of justice to my throat. Know this, however. Every last man, down to the slaves who tended the horses—every last man who was present that sad night has been identified and punished in some way. In spite of their fear of their superiors, my soldiers must learn that my honor is of greater value than their skins."

He looked around the room, and she felt the chill that gripped the men present. Her esteem for the King rose somewhat; he was at least smart enough to use a great failure to strengthen his throne. She finally let a small smile cross her face to acknowledge his shrewdness, and he sighed as he saw it.

"Finally," he said, looking her squarely in the eye, "there is the matter of your future and that of your bodyguard. It is my wish that he remain as a lieutenant to the Phicol, though I pledge my word that he is free in every respect in this matter."

He turned to Isaac. "What have you to add, my lord? My gold is yours, as is my life."

Isaac paused and turned to Lydia. She shook her head slightly and he bowed his. She would speak for herself after he was done.

"My friend," Isaac began. "Our fathers made covenant together to live in peace in this land. Differences were settled and that friendship has endured to this day. Yet never has it faced such a threat."

He glanced keenly at Lydia, and for a moment, she thought he read her intent, nodding thoughtfully. He paused and continued, and suddenly Lydia knew he had discerned her purpose. Why else would he change his words?

She smiled to herself. This day would be remembered in Gerar for a long time.

Isaac continued. "I mourn the loss of the wisdom of the elders. Yet the Lord God has spoken to my father, and will speak again in ways we cannot predict, and often do not expect. We have His promises, and though my curiosity is aroused by the lost words of a lost world, I will one day hear the story from the lips of Noah in the halls of the Almighty. And we do have the short summary of the Lord Shem, provided by my new friend. I have offered one hundred shekels of silver to him for the privilege of copying those words for my family's treasure store. It is a measure of his character that he offered this service to me at no price, telling me that his old master would have wanted it so."

Lydia knew now. He was preparing the way for her, stripping away their armor of ignorance with a casual reference to Shem, and baring their breasts for her thrust. She resolved to sink it deep.

Isaac paused, letting the weight of his words strike fear into the nobles in the room. "Yet the true offense against me was not the destruction of the scrolls." His voice grew hard. "It was the kidnapping and abuse of this young woman, who served long and faithfully in the house of my ancestors. I appreciate the swift justice that has been done to those who perpetrated the crime, and yet no reparation has yet been offered to the victim. If just recompense is made, then I pronounce myself satisfied and willing to continue the covenant of our fathers. Yet I cannot name the payment for what she has suffered. That she must do herself."

The room was silent. Every eye turned to Lydia. She stood proud and tall, feeling their fear. First a king, and now a great lord, had given justice into her hands. She could ask for men's deaths, and the executions would happen before sunset. She could ask for their wealth, and the king would give it. She could become a princess and rule over them, repaying their cruelty for years.

All that she knew, but her mind was not on such petty things. She felt as if Madrazi were standing next to her. She remembered all of her wisdom—a gift far beyond the weight of all the gold and silver of this city. If she truly had become a daughter to the old woman, then she would show the quality of that kinship to a people who had never had the privilege of knowing the last survivor of the lost world.

"King Abimelech. Lord Isaac. Great lords and ladies of the Sea Peoples." Her voice was quiet, yet it echoed across the expectant silence in the room. "You have filled my hands at great cost to yourselves. In one you put a spear pointed at your own hearts, and in the other the keys to your storehouses."

She could feel the tension build as the duller people in the court finally grasped what was really happening. Her royal appearance, her haughty tones, and her iron face combined with the memory of what she had suffered at their hands, caused a chill to spread across the room. She could ask for anything, and the King was honor bound to grant her request... no matter what it cost the nobles assembled here. She let the silence build for a few moments, but then suddenly she laughed gently, breaking the spell.

Her voice rang out. "Know that I served a woman who lived to see more than five hundred and seventy years. Few of you will attain a fifth part of that. She taught me the true value of life and the false worth of wealth—gold means nothing when we return to the dust and face the Creator's justice. Our real treasures are measured by His opinion of our lives, not by these paltry days of passing pleasure."

She drew a deep breath. "And I know that He is jealous for His reputation. Yet even in our own days, we see honor given to gods that are not, and the truth of the past exchanged for lies that no sane child would believe." She felt the undercurrent. Anger was now present in the room, but fear was still greater. It was time to drive the lesson home.

"I lived in the presence of a daughter of Noah, heard her stories, learned her wisdom, and knew her love." Her voice finally quivered. "Your gold would be as brass compared to one hour in her presence. So I ask nothing from your possessions, for to do so would be to dishonor the memory of one who became my mother."

The room was as silent as a tomb. In these modern days of fast ships and stone temples, the story of Noah was often treated as a tale for children, doubtful and of little import. At best, it was an inconvenient part of the past that all wished to forget. She had struck at the heart of a nation's pride by shattering that comfortable ignorance with a few simple words. Truth rang in her voice—a power that they could feel but not understand. No one present could doubt that she had seen the elders, talked with people who had survived the great flood, and lived in their home.

It was no myth.

Lydia could sense the troubled faces. They knew exactly what she was saying—she had just pronounced judgment on their entire culture, exacting a cost far beyond gold. She turned back to Abimelech.

"As to justice, great king, I leave that in the hands of the Judge of the Earth. He has seen fit to accomplish a measure of justice through you. I rejoice in that, for that is why He ordains kings, and I pray that you might be an instrument of His righteousness all of your days. As to where I will go, I cannot tell you. In one night I lost everything. I failed in the greatest test of my life and lost the possibility of the only thing I wanted after my test was complete."

Looking at Lud, she could no longer restrain the tears that began flowing down her cheeks. Suddenly she was tired of the whole facade. What did it matter? Her voice became ragged. "You look at me as some noble lady, yet we all know the truth. I am degraded and stand today unfit for the only thing that my heart desires." With those words, she tore the dress she was wearing and sank to her knees, now weeping openly.

"No!" The hoarse shout tore through the room, and ignoring all protocol, Lud leaped down to her side, kneeling beside her. "You failed in nothing, my love!" His tears matched hers. "The failure was mine. I was charged with protecting you on your journey, and I failed in that from the very beginning. There is no shame on you; you have shown courage and wisdom and virtue under the worst of conditions. She would be proud of you! You passed every test!" He clung to her, trying to control her convulsive heaves.

"Clear the room!"

The sharp command came from the Queen, and the audience happily obeyed. "My lords," she continued, turning to the king and Isaac, "This is no longer a matter of state. By her own words she has absolved you and your kingdom of blame and freed you both to continue your covenant. The only thing left to be resolved is her future well-being, and that is of no concern of your court."

She rose and knelt opposite Lud and held the woman. Nodding to Lud, they lifted her up and helped her through the back door that led into the royal chambers. Abimelech, Isaac, and the Phicol followed at her imperious gesture.

When they were all seated, she leaned forward and gripped Lydia's hands, pulling them away from her face. "Tell me, my dear, of your days with the Old One." Her voice was gentle, yet commanding. The men sat silent, trusting a woman to know a woman.

Choking back her sobs, Lydia began to talk. Haltingly, she told of Nineveh, of her banishment, her journey north, her rescue by the old woman and the subsequent years—a strange cycle that took her from receiving care to giving it.

"I loved the nights the best, my lady," she sniffed finally. "I would sit in the corner where I could watch her. She seldom slept. She just gazed into the fire, seeing through it to the next world. I could feel the power, though I could never see as she did. The last months I spent reading her scrolls, night after night, trying to reconcile the woman in those stories with the withered body on the sofa. Sometimes I could almost see her as she had been... but perhaps it was a trick of the firelight."

"What was in the scrolls, my child?"

Lydia had been well educated even before coming to the Old One, and she knew the different modes of speaking to an audience—from debate to entertainment—and so she sat up straight and expertly summarized all three in less than an hour. The five others sat spellbound, amazed at the words and hungry for more. Finished, Lydia seemed to sag back down, all life draining from her eyes. The Queen would have none of it. She gripped the girl's hand.

"So the heart of all of these stories is forgiveness, is it not?"

Lydia nodded slowly, her face suddenly thoughtful. The Queen gave her a moment to gather her thoughts and then leaned in once more. "Then why can you not forgive yourself, and let the Creator determine your course?" There was gentleness in her voice, but an edge of command too. Lydia looked at her in amazement, her past flashing across her mind.

Suddenly, the Queen's eyes narrowed. Lydia dropped hers in sudden fear, but the Queen's question was as inevitable as it was gentle.

"What is your true name, child?"

Lydia went rigid. Her first thought was that this woman was truly fit to be a queen. She had glimpsed something Lydia thought safely locked away in the deepest recesses of her heart. But there was no unsaying the words or any possibility of halting the torrent of emotion that threatened to overwhelm her—like the very flood itself. All the days of her life suddenly came into focus, as she sat, looking at the Queen like a bird mesmerized by a snake. Guilt engulfed her and she could only shake her head as she clenched her fists.

"You bear no blame for your family," the Queen's voice was soft and the men had the good sense to remain silent. "Would the Old One have accepted you otherwise? Do you think she did not know... a woman who could see visions from the Creator?"

With those words, Lydia's carefully controlled world exploded. For years she had not seen, or perhaps had refused to acknowledge, something obvious to a complete stranger. How could she have been so blind? The Old One must have known all along and yet... oh, how much love had been hers!

The Queen gripped her hands, tears now pooling in her own eyes at the pain she was inflicting on Lydia. But like a lanced infection, it was the only way to health.

"Come, child. Unbind your heart."

Lydia felt her heart bursting as the blood roared in her ears. Yet the room was deathly quiet.

Finally her lips moved, almost against her will. "Nin-huri," she whispered, looking down.

"Daughter of Jursham?" The Queen's face had gone ashen, but kept her voice steady.

"Yes," she breathed.

Abimelech could not help blurting out. "But she died twelve years ago... something about falling from the tower of her home!"

Lydia hung her head. "I too have heard that lie. They created it to cover their shame. I dared to question the existence of the Queen of Heaven.

"Excuse me," interrupted Isaac. "I don't know the politics of the plain as well as the rest of you. You don't have to say any more, if it pains you," he added quickly.

Lydia lifted her head. She smiled through her tears. The Queen had been right. Her heart felt lighter... she was just now beginning to see something that had been in front of her face for years, but she had lacked the wit to see it. She remembered those knowing green eyes of her mistress. How could one person have so much wisdom... so much love?

She dried her tears and took a deep breath. Facing Isaac, she began. "I am the great-granddaughter of Nimrod and Semiramida," she said softly. "And Semiramida was once known as Debseda, the wife of Ham."

Isaac looked stunned. "Then you are a part of these stories, are you not?"

"Yes... I guess so," Lydia admitted. "After the confusion of tongues, a mob of Shinar sought Debseda's life. She and Nimrod threw down a servant whose appearance deceived the mob. She escaped and hid for many years, before rejoining Nimrod when she deemed it safe to emerge once more—during his conquest of the cities of the lower plain. She took the new name and identity, and had her servants spread fanciful tales of her origins and parentage."

She breathed in and looked Isaac in the eye, "The Old One welcomed into her home the direct descendent of her deadliest enemies—those who tried to slay her in the days before the confusion of tongues."

She broke down again. Choking through the tears, she wailed, "S...s...she loved me when she should have hated me and my family. Oh dear God, how I long to see her again!"

Isaac smiled suddenly. "You will, you know."

The tears subsided into a small smile and a sigh. "I know."

The Queen broke in again. "If the Old One could love you in spite of that burden, don't you think someone else might be able to love you now... in spite of... everything?"

Lydia understood immediately. She turned and looked up at Lud, who was staring at her with an open mouth."

"Please," was all he said.

"Are you sure?" she asked tentatively. "You know the evil that surrounds me now... all of it."

"God does not see you as evil," he said quietly. "That's what Shem told me just before he died. If I am to be His servant, then I must see with His eyes." He paused, looked away, and then back into her eyes. "And I do," he said quietly. She saw the love, shining there.

"I'm not worthy...."

"It's not about worth, is it?"

"If you'll have me...."

His hand covered hers, his rough fingers intertwining with her smaller ones. His smile was all the answer she needed.

"I suppose this means that I've lost a lieutenant," observed the Phicol dryly, breaking the moment.

"We'll find another," said the king. "But I must ask that nothing we have said in this room ever leave it. First, we do not want to bring further harm to this remarkable young woman by revealing her identify, and second, the news of the stench of Asak's wickedness might also reach the courts of Nineveh. That could prove a heavy burden for my people."

"They care nothing for me," replied Lydia, bitterly. "They proved that twelve years ago."

"Yet they might find you a convenient excuse for attacking my people," replied the King, clearly ill at ease in tainting a personal discussion with political issues.

Lydia smiled sadly. "You do not offend me by speaking the truth, Your Majesty. In fact, your concern for your people makes you worthier of your crown."

The Queen chuckled. "Our debts grow deeper every hour we know this young lady!"

"I would ask for two exceptions," said Isaac quietly. "If I am to have a new family in my service, I must tell my wife and we must all have a long talk with Father." The king nodded. "Beyond that, we will all say no more." Everyone nodded in agreement.

Lydia and Lud stared at Isaac. Before they could even ask the first question, he spoke. "Don't you see? It's the best solution. You were sent to my father. I am his heir, and that includes his obligations to you. It only seems proper that you come live with my family."

"But I lost your scrolls," she admitted, bowing her head.

"So you keep saying." He paused and looked at the floor. "Tell me, young lady, was the old woman wise?"

"Wiser than any I've ever known."

"Wise enough to perceive the hazards of your journey?"

"Well... yes. But she thought the risk worthwhile."

"Why?"

"Because she wanted her wisdom, her experience, her stories to be known to her descendents."

"Then why not send the scrolls by official courier? The Hittites would probably have done so if she asked them."

For the third time that hour, Lydia felt like a fool. It was true. Madrazi could have simply sent them to the Lake of the Islands. The old Hittite commander there had been healed by her many years before. He would have ridden south himself with a regiment, if asked. She shook her head as if trying to clear a fog that had blinded so much of her mind.

Isaac continued. "The scrolls were only a part of her gift," he said gently. "And I think all of us would now agree that they were the least part."

"I don't understand," she said in a small voice.

"*You* were the gift." It seemed Lydia's day for playing the fool. She shook her head.

Isaac persisted. "Even so, the scrolls are not truly lost. How well do you recall the stories?"

"I... I know them by heart," she replied, stunned now that the truth was burning away the fog.

"Then you can tell them to my children and grandchildren," he smiled. "Will you do that for me... for her?"

"Oh, yes," she breathed. She wanted to laugh and cry at the same time. "Oh, yes, my lord." Joy filled her heart. She knew her place now. Lud's hand tightened on hers in agreement.

"Before we leave," asked the Queen. "Please finish the tale, Nin-huri..."

"Please call me Lydia," she said shyly. "Nin-huri died twelve years ago."

The Queen nodded and smiled. "I'm from Erech originally, so I know some of these stories, but only small pieces as vague legends. I always wondered if the elders really existed. Please tell me what happened after the confusion of tongues."

Lydia composed herself and began to speak once again. Isaac winked at the Queen from behind her, and the Queen's lip quirked upward. Then they turned their attention to the words of the young woman.

"Shem and Madrazi returned to their home. With them went Ashkenaz and Mariel, who eventually married and settled to the east, between the mountain and the Qazvin Sea. They wandered together across the mountains and began a colony in the far western forests, where descendents are rumored to live to this day.

Of course, you all know of Nimrod's conquests and the diminished kingdom he established. It is said that he was one of the first to understand the decreasing span of man—something that even his Nephil blood could not change. It is also said that this added desperation to his days that often overcame prudence, and that the extent of his conquests was lessened by a driving need to accomplish nine centuries of work in the two hundred and thirty-three years allotted to him. Of my great-grandmother...." Anger rushed back into her voice. Lud's hand found Lydia's and its warmth restored her.

Taking a deep breath, she continued. "My apologies," she murmured. The others nodded, eager for her to continue. Her lips tightened, but she kept her voice even. "Semiramida ruled for a time after his death, but in her attempt to deify her son, he eventually rose against her, and most say that he slew her." The Queen was nodding; the stories of Semiramida were well known in Erech.

But Lydia pressed on. "There is a rumor in my family that she escaped once more down the river to the Sea of Ur. From there, she took a ship east, across the ocean to the city of Harappa, seeking, as always, to rule those she thought less than herself."

Abimelech shook his head in astonishment. "I have never heard of this... we all thought she was long dead."

Lydia shrugged. "It was a rumor kept by the women of my family. I do not know if it is true or false. At any rate, I was banished before reaching the age to have heard the full story from my mother." She clenched Lud's hand. "It only matters now that she is dead, and can now begin to earn payment for the full measure of her evil here on Earth."

Seeing her distress, the Queen intervened once more. "What of Anam, and the others?"

Lydia nodded and straightened her back, sadness in her eyes. "Anam returned south, caught up with Graemea and Mizraim, and helped his father create the kingdom of Egypt. Their fame is sufficient without me adding words to their achievements. Their enmity with Nimrod is carried down to this day; all of you know of the animosity between Egypt and Babylon."

She sighed. "Anam's story drifts into darkness. It seems he followed his family as the Egyptians gradually adopted the gods of the plains for their own mysterious religion. There was some communication between the Nile and the mountain in the early years, but it soon ceased, though Ashkenaz called Anam his brother to the end of his days.

As we know, Heth and Jael founded the kingdom of the Hatti, and their descendents protected the land of the elders for as long as they lived. Early on, Heth and Shelah explored the eastern lands beyond the Qazvin Sea together, finding grasslands and forests stretching far beyond the horizon. Some of the Hittites settled the high grasslands a few hundred years ago, but not much has come from their efforts. The Hittites are still friends to Shelah's descendents, the wise Bianili, honoring the bond between Heth and Shelah."

Isaac interrupted. "Some of the Bianili migrated to Ur. My father counts his ancestors back to Shelah, through Eber and Peleg."

Lydia nodded. "The Old One saw him travel from Ur into this wilderness, and instructed me to search the hill country to the east."

"Have many men followed the trails blazed by Shem and Shelah?" asked the Phicol.

"Not as many as they first envisioned," replied Lydia, "but the danger from the plains was not what it was under Shinar. Ironically, it was Jobaath who led most of the expeditions back to the far country the five explored, and he established settlements as far as the western sea. The Old One told me that he lived out his last years on the great island that they had seen at the far end of the western lands.

Japheth and his sons have spread farthest across the earth, some to the east and south, some north of the Black Sea, and some west along the Great Sea, as you well know, great king. I saw the pottery of Knossos... or should I say 'Keftiu' in these rooms."

The King nodded. "Either will do. The Pharaohs would insist on Keftiu, but we of the sea are more flexible in our speech. As are the Island Peoples. They are great explorers and traders."

"And fierce warriors," chuckled the Phicol.

Isaac interrupted. "What of Ham," he asked? "Did he go to Egypt?"

Lydia nodded. "He traveled with Anam and Mizraim to the south. Though he renounced his right to rule, his wisdom and skill were valued by his children, and he was revered by the House of Mizraim. Do you not wonder why the builders of Egypt are so advanced compared to those of the plain?"

She smiled briefly, but then sighed. "But Egypt was never his home. He returned north to the mountain three times. The first was to weep over the tomb of his mother, the second to mourn over Noah's, and the third came many years later. He returned one last time, near the end of his days, some years before I took service with the Old One. He lays there now, with the others... seven graves under the shadow of the mountain offering rest to the company of the ark until the world is remade."

"So he returned," breathed Isaac. "Really returned...."

Lydia nodded. "The Old One said that though his sons strayed, Ham was finally granted the hope which he had sought so long. He finally came to know the deepest meaning of the great mystery of lawlessness."

Other Books from Reasonable Hope Ministry

Visit our library at
www.reasonablehope.com.

Books by Dr. Gordon K. Reed

Plain Talk about Christian Doctrine
A pastor's perspective on the Westminster Shorter Catechism, with the systematic teaching of that great document interwoven with practical lessons from decades of Christian ministry (Published by Fortress Books).

Living Life by God's Law
Dr. Reed explains how the unchanging wisdom of God's Ten Commandments can enrich the life of the most modern Christian.

The Ministry: Career or Calling?
Is Christian ministry just another white-collar profession, or is it a unique calling from God? This modern parable illustrates the modern errors of the "professional" approach.

Christmas: Triumph over Tragedy
Developed from a series of Christmas sermons, this short book takes an in-depth look at the central characters of the incarnation, showing modern believers how they, too, can become a part of God's great kingdom.

Books by Dr. John K. Reed

Rock Solid Answers (edited with M.J. Oard)
Modern geology poses difficult questions for biblical history. Christian earth scientists come together to answer those questions, and to demonstrate that biblical history can hold its own with secular critics and can confound them in return (Published by Master Books for the Creation Research Society).

Mabbul
The second book of the Lost Worlds trilogy continues the story of Madrazi from her entrance into the great ark, through the terrible year of the Flood, and up to her final exit from the ship that preserved life from God's judgment. In an intensely personal spiritual journey, Madrazi finds that where good glows, evil also grows, and lines are drawn for the coming confrontations in the new world.

The Geological Column: Perspectives within Diluvial Geology (edited with M.J. Oard)
How does modern creationism deal with the geological column? At present, in a variety of ways. This book presents different points of view and summarizes the questions that must be answered by creationist geologists (Published by the Creation Research Society).

The Coming Wrath
The first book of the Lost Worlds trilogy begins the story of Madrazi, daughter of the world's foremost explorer, mariner, and trader. Everything changes when she agrees to a marriage to the oldest son of Noah—a marriage arranged by her favorite relative, Methuselah. How can a worldly intelligent woman possibly live with people who think the world will end in two decades? Even worse, what if they are right….

Crucial Questions about Creation
Laymen interested in origins issues will find a refreshing theological examination of creation, with an emphasis on knowing *why* God created the cosmos.

Plain Talk about Genesis
Using the Presbyterian Church in America as an example, Dr. Reed explains for Christian laymen the origins debate and what is at stake in those discussions.

Natural History in the Christian Worldview
Interpretations about natural history rest on worldviews. Any Christian thinker can discern truth from falsehood in this area by comparing those worldviews (Published by the Creation Research Society).

Plate Tectonics: A Different View (editor)
Technical critique of the dominant paradigm of modern geology from a biblical perspective (Published by the Creation Research Society).

The North American Midcontinent Rift System
Technical description and interpretation of one of the largest geological features in North America (Published by the Creation Research Society).